The Naked Diaries

Legends of Bare Entertainment

"I never had so much fun reading a book. The Naked Diaries is 100% pure Heterosexual entertainment!"

-J.D. Cohanick
Deerfield Weekly

"A bare-naked romp through a cinematic history not all us guys got to see back-in-the-day, with an exclusive sex-filled story to top it off....The Naked Diaries is one wild ride!"

Lighthouse Review

The Naked Diaries

Legends of Bare Entertainment

Ken Knight

authorHOUSE®

AuthorHouse™
1663 Liberty Drive
Bloomington, IN 47403
www.authorhouse.com
Phone: 1-800-839-8640

"Places, Names, Times, have NOT been changed. This is a true tell all story of actual events and time lines. Discretion is advised..!!"

First published by AuthorHouse 12/4/2009

ISBN: 978-1-4490-3605-8 (e)
ISBN: 978-1-4490-3604-1 (sc)

Library of Congress Control Number: 2009912960

All persons and events portrayed in the novella is fiction, and any/all similarities thereof are purely coincidental and unintentional. Photos and images included with the Interviews and Movie-Reviews are intended as fair-use for review and description thereof and no copyright infringement is intended whatsoever in this context of review and commentary. (Certain Commentary by the Author is from personal experiences). This Book is intended for Adult Readers Only.

Front Cover Photography by Dennis Berry (Front Cover Model~Kristie Walker)
Back Cover Photo of the Author being "frisk-searched" by one of his female readers.

Printed in the United States of America
Bloomington, Indiana

This book is printed on acid-free paper.

Dedicated to Gene Simmons and Shannon Tweed, Crown Jewels of American Entertainment!

Also to Hugh Hefner and Larry Flynt whom fought on the front lines against the censors all those years ago to help give consenting American Adults the freedom-of-entertainment we enjoy to this day.

For Andy and Arlene Sidaris, whose R-rated “Guy-Flicks” of the 80’s and 90’s set-the-tone for similar on-screen entertainment in the years following!

Not-to-mention Rob Zombie, Quentin Tarentino, Robert Rodriguez and Frank Miller who keep “Guy-Flicks” alive in the 21st Century!

A huge THANKS to my Fraternity Brothers Mike Long, Ken Crampton, Chris Decker, John Sweton, Dennis Berry, and Jason Morris for stoking the fires of my dirtball-imagination with conversations found nowhere else!

Also a Big Shout-Out to my buddies Jim Balent and Holly Golightly of Broadsword® Comics. Your Art is in a league all by itself!

And MAJOR PROPS to my friend and fellow fiction-author Hope Tarr. No one (not even me) can write a sex-scene in a novel quite like she does!

Sex …America's #1 of Brand of Late Night Entertainment!

THE NAKED DIARIES is a distinctly American history lesson of sexual urban-legends, reviews of some of the most titillating "late night" movies ever filmed and uncut commentary surely to amuse anyone who remembers back in the day when adult entertainment was for adults only……all of it jammed between a passionate-yet-deadly story never before told!

Chronology

Introduction

Guys, do you remember the first time you saw a Cable TV movie or Video Rental with what some call "gratuitous nudity" displayed somewhere throughout the course of the movie? Perhaps you might remember your first glimpse at the inviting pages of an "adults only" magazine to see what you weren't supposed to see so easily? Do you recall ever finding yourself smitten with an image on the newsstand or book-rack of a store and you just had to buy it, not for its content, but for the alluringly-sexy image on the cover? Did your attention-span suddenly switch gears when a beautiful, well-shaped female of the species entered the room wearing all-too-revealing attire and thus garnishing your full concentration no matter what you were doing seconds prior?

If the answer to any of the above questions was "yes" then it's cool....you're normal!

Of course, we've come a long way from the violent (and short life) years of our forebears whom roamed the countryside looking for food, shelter, and a female of the species to impregnate so that the human race might sally-forth into centuries more....least I think we've stepped out of that animalism to a degree, but don't quote me on it just yet!

From staring at a "cave woman" with the carnal urge to procreate or die trying, to gawking at a much less scary female in the pages of a magazine or on a theater screen with less thought on procreation and more on just having inconsequential "sport sex", men have come to view sex as not just the need to make babies so that one's race doesn't die out, but as a fairly new and delightfully-appealing form of ENTERTAINMENT!

Is it safe to say that a majority of the "sex-sells" appeal out there from the 20th Century to our present time is aimed mostly at men and for men's entertainment? Absolutely, and thus the premise of this book was realized once it became clear to me how sex does really sell half of the world's goods from chewing gum to imported beer (the cheesiest ads!) not to mention clothes, shoes, cars, cologne and body-washes, as well as even furniture.

The other half of the world's goods? Sold by the promise of more money in re-sale value!

Thus we conclude that there are two things which truly "Rule The World" and they are:

1) **Money**
2) **Sex**

Afterall, what is power, wealth, influence, fame, fortune, property, and ownership without one or both of these?! Unless he's a eunuch or too damn old to care, a man is going to march head-long toward success in order to **get naked** with a woman of his choice some point in time....whether he's filthy-rich or just barely able to afford a new sports-car, he's going to be motivated by sex or at least the promise/possibility of it!

And from this reality, springs the method of entertainment where a viewer/reader sees naked glory and alluring sexual congress keeping his (and her) full, undivided attention.

Was there an encyclopedia or reference-based book of research from which I drew this conclusion? Hell no, I'm speaking from experience as a grinning, willing "victim" of the allure of the naked female form in all it's billboard, front page, flaunting seduction! ☺

Adult Entertainment is not just "porno flicks" by any means, it is a media <u>not suitable for children</u> including TV programs, video games, magazine and novel content as well as feature films which display/discuss/focus upon adult-related themes such as nudity, sex, violence, profanity, and otherwise mature situations. In short, it's anything you wouldn't dare show to your 10-year old! (It isn't just X-rated films delegated as "Adults Only")

o then what is your favorite form of entertainment which one is supposed to be of age 18 to view, read, or gawk at?? Well yes, it is "entertainment" by the way it is packaged, "rated" and marketed for adult viewing....the display of nudity (partial or otherwise) in a fictional scenario or suggestive pose and/or the choreographed acting-out of sexual congress (romantic or otherwise) done to entertain the viewing audience, leaving absolutely no doubt that nudity and sex are attractive ENTERTAINMENT!

I originally began this project as a sort of "sequel" to my last book which was entitled

"*The Midnight Show~Late Night Cable TV Guy-Flicks of the 80's*"

but decided to focus here on the overall "Men's Entertainment Genre" which peaked between the late 1980's and early 1990's **before** the advent of the Internet! The early-to-mid 1990's were also the banner years for Hollywood's "Erotic-Thriller" genre of films, the most prevalent example being 1992's **Basic Instinct** starring Sharon Stone, but most of the others were shipped straight-to-video and to late night Cable TV airings all through the 1990's.

I also wanted to write about some of the finest females to ever pose nude in a magazine (and even interview one or two) and the effect it has had once their gloriously-nude physique was published for adults to see all over the world, even moreso (for better or worse) with the Internet taking hold in over a billion households across the planet! Plus I wanted to focus attention on how Exotic Dancers (especially the famous ones) were restricted to Night Clubs and not very easily found or heard of **prior to the Internet**!

I have also included here at the beginning and at the end a never-before-told "erotic-thriller" fiction tale of my own, which I feel adds to the "climate" I wish to provide as you read this book throughout, so enjoy my exclusive novella **THE STRANGERS**.

For any ladies reading this Intro, I can only say that I write from a man's point of view here, which I am sure you'll quickly notice, but you are certainly most welcome to read on so that you, ADULTS.... may have some ADULTS-ONLY FUN!

I wanted to fully address the arousing mediums that "appeal" to a guy making his way in the world such as men's magazines, men's products sold via a sexy female image, and of course the "gratuitous nudity" found on Late Night TV and in Feature Films in the good ol' USA scripted and filmed for the viewing pleasure of an adult male audience, a form of entertaining late night endeavor I myself enjoy to this very day.....

But this manuscript sorts of took on a life of it's very own as I began, the premise of how sex is entertainment (not "smut") as well as a naturally-wonderful human activity, "sold" not just in the brothels of the past, but now on TV, magazines, X-rated videos, Cable TV, and countless other media for the most trivial of reasons, the most simple of sales-pitches (and more importantly) becoming a major entertainment venue the likes of which our American history will never forget. Even if "political correctness" puts a damper on it in the next few years, the glorious and well-crafted female shape is still undeniably the most appreciated "entertainer" among men...and this book becomes one more way to prove my point about something many good folks may still deny, but I will always believe:

Sex is America's #1 brand of late-night entertainment!

The Strangers

What you don't know about other people……

The beautiful "Trophy-Wife" whom her husband uses to coerce, seduce, and manipulate other men to do his bidding…

The "Lesbian" Lawyer who has the goods on everyone around her, keeping secrets that cost lives and fortunes, all for her own nefarious benefit…

The Federal Agent tasked with uncovering ghosts of the past in order to stop a conspiracy of domestic terrorism reaching back over a decade, with a missing $2,000,000 and an X-rated Film Company's cast list as clues...

….is enough to fill a Funeral Home's guest-book!

THE STRANGERS

Stafford County, Virginia.
October 1, 2007:

It was dusk by 7:00 and the sky kept threatening rain, though Jamal Marx didn't care about the weather, he was going to party tonight one way or the other, the only downside being his lack of cash, though that would soon be taken care of once he finds the right "donor" in this shopping center that could help him out with party-funds! Finding the right one was easy enough in a dark parking lot like the one he now wandered through, and the 19-year old focused on an elderly woman walking alone toward him in the parking lot, a big black leather purse dangling from her right hand. She was old too, probably in her 70's and in no condition to chase him or get help with any quickness, a walking cane in her other hand! Jamal moved with a snake-like determination toward his target, noticing her gaze not on him yet, so he sped up his approach and easily reached out to snatch her big leather purse from her weak right hand, running past her like a bolt of lightning, sprinting in the opposite direction with the purse in hand, laughing as he ran out of the old lady's sight into the darkness behind the grocery store from where she had come from. Jamal had the old lady's purse and she just stood there looking around as if she hadn't realized what just happened to her, the one glance he threw back in her direction told him the old bitch must not have gotten a good look at him at all since she was facing the other direction, just standing there!

"Huh-huhh-haaah....gotcha...thanks a lot, ya old bitch!" Jamal quipped outloud in amazement as to how easy it was to snatch a purse from an elderly woman and take off without her getting a good look at him. Running to his parked car behind the video store, Jamal threw the big purse into the backseat and jumped behind the wheel to take off, gunning the used Honda to life and screeching tires out of there for Garrisonville Road, heading for home not far from the shopping center there. He had stolen from the elderly before of course, and they always seemed to have lots of cash on them, which is why he hadn't searched the purse just yet, assuming that there'd be enough cash for him to go to a club up in Fairfax tonight at least. His father would probably be home he mused, all happy and arrogant about being on the President's "short list" of nominees for the US Supreme Court, as if Jamal gave two shits about that, his old man a lawyer who always tried to get his only son to "tow the line" and kiss-ass along the way to make it in the world…yeah, the world run by whitey! Jamal would take what he wants and his father can stick it up his ass!

Driving along Rt. 610 toward his home, Jamal laughed at his theft of that old lady's purse a few minutes ago, it was so damn easy to do and the old bitch never saw what hit her!!

He hit the gas to pass a couple of slower cars, his music turned up and window down as Jamal laughed and voiced his pleasure to the night air, part of him wanting to go home and tell his father what he'd done, dare him to say anything about it or threaten to call the cops on him again. Jamal was 19-years old, he was a man…so what if he stole from weaker people, that's the way it is and he wasn't gonna let his lawyer father or the police get in his way of living life the way he wanted to, HELL NO…….

Robert Marx was pleased with himself, the day's news about him being put on the current President's "short list" of hopefuls for nomination to the US Supreme Court the icing on his cake this week, after his richest client was exonerated and he was able to pay off the note on this half-a-million dollar house he'd been living in for the past ten years, now he'd be able to afford better digs and a new wife to boot! Civil Rights Attorney Robert Marx was also pleased with the fact he'd just gotten laid by a beautiful, well-endowed white woman here in his own bedroom, someone he had met earlier while having a "power lunch" in D.C.

Her name was "Tiffany" and did she have a body on her….he almost worried it was a dream but once she put it on him he knew it was real, those big boobs of her nearly suffocated him when she was riding on him earlier! Relaxing in his bed with hands behind his head, he looked down the hallway from his master bedroom to see the well-shaped white woman leaving the bathroom fully-dressed now and heading for the front door.

"You leaving now baby?" Robert Marx called to the woman he'd just enjoyed all afternoon, watching her retreat to the front of the house as she had told him she had to get home to her husband before 8pm! Robert loved the fact he was "creeping" as they call it, with a gorgeous white chick who is married to some boring white man, and here he was snaking that pussy under the man's nose! Robert absolutely loved it….

"Yeah, hey…I'll call you sometime soon okay lover?" the brown-haired woman called back to the 45-year old black lawyer she had come home with after lunch today, having been paid to do such a thing, and paid well. The lawyer didn't know she was a high-priced Call-Girl and he didn't need to know either, for someone else had a reason for her to screw him….

"You do that baby…you do that….I'll be on the Supreme Court soon and you can divorce that geek you're married to and be all mine," Robert said to himself after he heard the front door click-shut behind the retreating female, hoping the neighbors see that fine specimen of womanhood leaving his house right now. Eat your hearts out you suburbanites!

Just as the woman was gone in the rental car she drove down here from D.C., another car pulled up onto the hillside driveway, stopping at the open indoor-garage of the Marx residence, Hip-Hop music still blaring until the key was turned off and Jamal Max jumped out from the driver's seat with the stolen leather purse in hand, slamming his car door shut.

Rain began to fall now so he stepped under the shelter of the open, indoor-garage and looked around for anyone else who might see him beginning to rummage through the thick purse's jam-packed interior. This was why he didn't just reach in and pull out the coin-purse like before and discard the purse, this one had everything in it up the goddamn kitchen sink, so he had to dig through it's crammed contents, pulling out tissue paper, a small radio, make-up kit, some empty prescription medicine bottles, even a small (empty) booze flask, his greedy fingers searching for the coin purse or money-clip a lot of old people carry, then he found something that didn't want to leave the interior of the big purse. He pulled on it hard but it wouldn't come out and it felt heavy too which made sense because the purse itself was heavier than usual. Standing at the front of the open garage struggling with the stuffed purse, Jamal failed to see a late model Trans Am roll by slowly on the street below, in its driver seat an elderly lady with something in her left hand out the open car window. She pushed the button on the small remote-detonator and within the next split-second the house on the hill owned by one Robert Marx erupted into a loud, fiery explosion from the garage all the way through the structure to it's other end in one cataclysmic melee. Jamal had discovered too late that the purse he had stolen from an old lady tonight carried no money but 4lbs of C-4 plastic explosive that was remote-detonated once he returned home to where the real target lay : Attorney Robert Marx. Young Jamal had inadvertently delivered a bomb to his father's house and the assassination was successful!

Stafford County, Virginia. 10:30pm: The incident scene was a mess after the Firefighters used water and dry-chemical to douse the raging flames that burned the three-level domicile straight to the ground. Not much was left except for a burnt husk of chest and pelvis belonging to a teenage black male whose wallet survived only because it was in the damaged car parked in front of what was the indoor-garage. Then there was a flattened remnant of skeletal embers burning in what was a porcelain bathtub, the adult male victim determined to be one Robert Marx, eyewitness-neighbors declaring the man was in the house when the blast hit. Not much left for forensics and fire investigators, but it was a welcome sight of the Bureau of Alcohol, Tobacco, Firearms and Explosives (ATF) Agents arriving now to check the scene for foul play. Since the victim of the explosion was a personal friend of the President of the United States and unofficially one of the big man's "picks" for a Supreme Court seat, the Feds were going to stick their nose in it deep, and so they begin.....

"So far, traces of cee-four plastique from the rim of the garage and through what was the ceiling above it, burn marks indicating synthetic ignition.....," ATF Agent Bob Parsons said to the senior Agent Clifford Stevens as he walked up to him in the blackened front yard of the residence, eyes on the older Agent in the blue "ATF" jacket. Clifford Stevens was a career Agent with 18 years under his belt, a 40-year old testament to Federal service by a single white male dedicated to hunting bad guys....least that was what his mother says!

"Blew the friggin' top off didn't they?" Agent Stevens quipped, looking around the scene.

Agent Parsons smirked at the man and nodded, handing him a sealed evidence bag with residue inside of it denoting military-grade C-4 plastique.

"One eyewitness had the teenage son...Jamal Marx...standing in the garage doing something then the whole place blew to smithereens in an instant, cee-four igniting the gas line behind the house and a five-gallon can of fuel in the garage to top it off," Parsons explained frankly, noticing Stevens absorbing the info as he looked around the yard.

"Does teenage son have a record for doing stupid shit like playing with explosives?" Agent Stevens asked his fellow Agent casually as he rubbed his head of short brown hair, thinking.

"Yes and no....mostly petty theft and drug possession as a minor, was under investigation for selling stolen guns but wasn't arrested for such just yet....nothing about explosives," Parsons added as Agent Stevens looked over at the flattened, burned-out household still smoldering in the night air, Fire Department lights shining over the perimeter.

"Of course not....but cee-four has to be ignited by a detonator and unless the kid got hold of a wired and fixed brick of cee-four then inadvertently tripped it's trigger here in his daddy's garage...we have a dilemma," Stevens added with a nod to his fellow Agent.

"Yes we do, how the hell does a kid find several pounds of the shit and why would he blow himself and his daddy straight to hell with it….suicide-patricide?" Parsons wondered aloud.

"No, don't think so my friend, this is a hit….a hit," Stevens said in a lowered voice so the Sheriff's Deputies nearby wouldn't overhear. Parsons' face practically went ashen white as soon as Stevens said the word. He knew Stevens well enough to know he is one of the Bureau's best known "conspiracy-chasers" and that is not necessarily a good thing!

"We'll have to do a lab test on the whole perimeter here over the weekend and check to see if the explosion matches a few past incidents I've worked…I'm willing to bet since this guy was a politician's buddy, we'll have similar traits at this crime scene as well," Stevens said.

"Meaning it could be a serial-bomber…like the one you've been chasing for years?" Parsons replied, not meaning to sound cynical in suggesting such, but didn't press the assumption.

"Yes…but we'll wait for the Lab guys to complete their canvass, might not be the same type of device used, and if it is, it's been awhile," Stevens said as he walked away from Agent Parsons to enter the crime scene for a better look at the end-result of a mysterious blast.

ATF Agent Clifford Stevens had seen sites such as this one before, in the all-too-recent-past and they all had minor and "circumstantial" similarities like the use of C-4 and the "overkill" implied when it came to the victim of the explosion. Would have been easier and simpler to shoot the victim as opposed to delivering an expensive device such as a brick of C-4 with an untraceable wireless detonator as suspected in six different cases spanning back seven years. None of the victims of what he personally calls the "C-4 bomber" over the past seven years or so were related to one another, all from different backgrounds, only one had a criminal record, and they were all located along the US east coast except one in Nevada.

The one small common denominator was that the victims were all individually linked in one way or another to politicians in office or were about to run for public office, be appointed to a Judicial Bench, or were politically-active in some way on the Federal Level. Just one victim of C-4 explosion seven years ago was not only the daughter of a Federal Judge but an actual eyewitness to a crime committed in 2002 and was about to testify. Of course, Clifford Stevens had Superiors to answer to and none of them believed his theory that a serial-killer was at work using C-4 plastic explosive as the murder weapon of choice. Agent Stevens was told then and he guessed he'd be told now that this politico got his ass blown to pieces, that the numbers don't add-up, that this case is not related to the stretched-out other bombings, no correlation except for the fact they all were "political" in some way. It was too circumstantial to declare it the work of a "serial bomber" and besides, the FBI and BATFE profiles done on serial-bombers clearly state that a serial-bomber attacks a particular kind of target and though patient, doesn't usually deliver the devices to target personally as Agent Stevens claims this one does! He could hear it now….

Just then his pager buzzed and a familiar number read on it's screen, which meant he had to call his superior for an update, so he figured he'd hear the usual crap about this case not being "linked" to any others, which he firmly believes otherwise. Walking around the burnt-out household and yard, he could smell the tell-tale aroma of seared human flesh, which was no surprise since there were two victims here tonight, a father and a son. Arrows point to the son as the possible perpetrator of the explosion and that is no doubt how the media will spin this story since the piece of shit kid was into bad shit anyway and likely could have come across a bomb which he intentionally or unintentionally triggered. He walked to the edge of what was the rear of the house, smoke in his nostrils as he bent down to find something of interest: a necklace of some kind which was made of a gold chain with burned emeralds on it, a piece of rather cheap jewelry that pretty much survived the explosion.

He didn't know what kind of wife or girlfriend this high-flutin' lawyer had here in his crib, but this kind of jewelry was the kind a stripper would wear not an upper-class lawyer's wife.

He pocketed the burned jewelry for later discernment, then stood up and looked around in pensive thought, reflecting on how the past explosions like this were eerily-similar.

One such explosion nearly cost him his life back in late 2003 when he participated in a joint-

FBI and ATF raid on a Mobster's mansion near Nashville, Tennessee, a booby-trapped device exploded inside the Mobster's private library and blew Stevens down a flight of stairs, saving his life in the process but killing the Mobster and two FBI Agents in the blast. Of course the Feds declared that incident "intentional" and blamed the Mafia Boss they were charging in to arrest for setting off the device in a suicide bid. Another bullshit "ending" as far as Agent Stevens was concerned and he nearly lost his career voicing his opinion on it.

It was the higher-ups who swept that particular "bomb" case under the rug afterwards, declaring the Marcano Mob case "suspended" as of 2004, and it just so happened that Mob "family" imploded by summer of 2005 anyway. Still, Agent Stevens saw a subtle "pattern" here with explosions like this one, it's done by the same perpetrator….a methodical one!

Arlington Virginia 11:35pm: The warmth of the indoor Jacuzzi room was inviting enough for 29-year old Michelle "Shelly" Jamison to remove her bathrobe and step up to the in-floor Jacuzzi tub where her friend, lover, and benefactor awaited her simmering in the hot, languid liquid, glass of red wine between her fingers as she gazed up at the blonde bombshell entering now, smiling at the younger woman she'd known for some time now, all too well.

"Mmmhh….that's it Shelly, water's perfect," Attorney Amber Duffek cooed to the shapely blonde vixen sliding down into the water in slow descent, her blue eyes lit up with glee.

"Amber, you called me over tonight just for a Jacuzzi sit?" the well-developed blonde asked impishly of her lawyer and occasional lover, moving closer for a kiss on the rosy lips.

"Yes, and I'm celebrating my victory in Court this morning," Amber answered softly.

"Oh, so you won the lawsuit against the State of Virginia about denying benefits to a gay man getting his deceased partner's retirement benefit?" Shelly asked in surprise, sitting down in the hot water beside the well-shaped, perky-boobed Amber Duffek in the Jacuzzi.

"Yes, it'll go to Appeals court but I think it'll survive and set legal precedent, hunh-hah," Amber said as she handed her "girlfriend" a filled glass of her favorite red wine, then touching her glass to Shelly's in a toasting gesture, kissing the sexy blonde once again.

"Heenh, you're a credit to 'civil rights' Counselor," Shelly cooed in the 35-year old woman's right ear, then sipped her glass of Amber's expensively imported red wine from France.

"Yes indeed Shelly my dear….and I make money for my friends don't I?" Amber chimed in less-than-subtle reference to the "deal" she brokered for Michelle Jamison just five years ago when the blonde cupcake was known as "Shelly James"~Adult Film Starlet! Shelly had been a young Catholic Nun in a rather loosely-cloistered Abbey in New York and for three years she had carefully, secretly "moonlighted" as an Adult Film Actress for the now-defunct

"Faster Productions" in New York City, having starred as "Shelly James" in 88 feature X-rated films legally produced and marketed in the US. Amber Duffek had been the lawyer for the owner of that Film Company and had seen to Shelly's easy "slip away" from the scandal and subsequent murder-investigation that shut it all down in the summer of 2005. Of course, a million-dollar book deal helped Shelly recover from being excommunicated from the Catholic Church, jettisoned from the Nuns Order by a decree issued from the Vatican itself!

Amber Duffek had helped her rise from a potentially-devastating "fall" and so Shelly owed her and it was times like this when Amber liked to politely "remind" Shelly of that fact.

"Mmmmhh…you are quite the accomplished-lesbian-lawyer," Shelly sighed to the naked woman in the tub beside her, then their lips kissed again and then an embrace, followed by a prolonged kiss of passion, Amber having indeed summoned Shelly over tonight for sex….

The only thing that would interrupt Amber Duffek from a piece of ass was her private cellphone buzzing….as it did right now on the outer deck of the Jacuzzi, "whirring" to life and making Amber break kiss with her female lover to reach for it.

"You have got to be shitting me?!" Amber quipped just seconds after answering the late nigh caller and knowing full-well who it was on the other end of the line, not pleased with it at all.

"Dammit….alright…alright….I'll meet you at the front door, gimme a minute!" Amber quipped in angry reaction to the caller's evidently-inconveniencing request of her right now.

Amber tossed the tiny cellphone across the tub room, it landing on her pile of clothes on the beanbag chair in one corner, Amber rising from the Jacuzzi with a sneering gesture of anger.

Shelly watched the lithe, well-crafted bare body of Amber Duffek rise from the tub water and onto the floor above, reaching for her yellow cotton bathrobe to pull on quickly.

"I'll be right back Shel, stay here, just be a few minutes," Amber said back to the stunned woman in the Jacuzzi who just nodded and relaxed back in the hot water to wait for her lover's return, guessing it to be "emergency business", a term Amber has used before.

Amber shut the tub room's door tight behind her and then hurried into her own bedroom throw something else on besides her bathrobe, considering who was approaching her front door right about now. She pulled on a black mini-dress over her still-damp bare body and then hurried down the stairwell to reluctantly greet her inconvenient guests driving up her horseshoe driveway as she walked toward her front door, reaching to remove the chain.

Attorney Amber Duffek had a laundry-list of clients, debtors, useful "friends", and even a shady business associate or two….. Steven and Shane Pillage fit in the latter category!

Twin brothers of the annoyingly-identical kind, the Pillage brothers were Real Estate brokers in three States, working close together in their hustling "business" and cleaning up with whatever they've done so far, despite being slightly less-than-legal in some of their transactions with clients. Amber had made the mistake of holding $50,000 cash for them in order to make a "straw investment" for them next week, but now the twin hustlers wanted their money back immediately and were coming to her place right now to get it pronto!

As soon as she opened the front door, Amber saw the familiar Mercedes roll to a stop alongside her parked BMW, so she just stood there in the doorway impatiently waiting.

Steven and Shane were identical twins of the annoying variety, both of them not only black but muscular, charmingly handsome, and everything from head-to-toe were the same, from their clothing, haircut, shoes, to even the Masonic rings on their fingers….. identical!

"What tha fuck guys…..really?!" Amber quipped outloud as the two thirty-six year old black men exited the Mercedes, both clad in khaki pants and long-sleeved black shirts.

"Amber….baaa-beee…..you're happy to see us and you know it, we just need the package we gave you to hold for us, that' all," Steven Pillage spoke in retort, gesturing with arms open wide as he walked toward the front porch of the million-dollar house here.

"Tha hell I am, you know what time it is?" she fired back in contempt.

"Change of plans Amber, we're sorry for the intrusion this late baby but we need the capital back tonight because we're going to need it to get out of a bind tomorrow," Shane Pillage spoke next as he approached the fort door behind his twin brother. The only way to tell the difference between the twin brothers is that Steven has a jagged scar on his forehead and Shane speaks with a slightly-different voice and tone than his twin does.

"Well how does that become my problem all of a sudden goddammit?" she sneered as the twin black men let themselves into her home, walking by her at the door with hands touching her at the arms and abdomen in greeting as they passed, pissing her off even more.

"Amber, we're sorry for the late intrusion but we need that investment capital back and we need it back tonight, it's urgent and we'll owe you a big favor," Steven Pillage said as he walked into her swank living room, looking around in interest as she closed the front door.

"You're killing me you know that?" she quipped with hands on her hips as she faced Steven and Shane in her living room, noticing they both had their hair cropped shorter since the last time she saw them, their style almost a "flat top" now, their cologne filling the air of course.

"We're out of here as soon as you get the money baby," Shane Pillage said next, grinning.

"How old are you Shane....you think I'd keep fifty-grand in cash here in my house?" Amber retorted with a scowl crossing her pretty, moon-shaped face right now, her damp hair hanging down to her shoulders telling the twin brothers she had either been in the shower or her Jacuzzi when they called her earlier, both of them guessing she might not be alone either.

"I'm going to have to go to the storage locker where I stashed it....about five miles from here, damn both of you," she sneered in contempt, hands made into fists as she stood there.

"We'll wait here for you Amber, and like I said...we'll owe you a big favor," Steven added as he sat down on her leather sofa, eyeing the shapely lawyer in the mini-dress a she walked over to her coat rack, grabbing a parka to go outside in the cool night air.

"Alright, alright....the two of you wait right here....do not leave this room, I will be right back with the quickness....and I'll have your investment money for you, just stay here and be cool, okay?" Amber chimed in sour tone, pointing a finger at the twin brothers now seated in her living room. She didn't go back upstairs to tell Shelly what was going on, not wanting to alert these two skirt-chasers to her girlfriend's presence here in the house, instead pulling on the parka and heading out the door with her set of keys, hoping Shelly stays in the tub room while she is gone to her storage locker just a few miles away. When Amber made it to her BMW, she realized she didn't have her cellphone with her so she couldn't call Shelly's cellphone to warn her about the two "intruders" sitting in the living room right now. She just hoped she stayed up in the Jacuzzi because she didn't think she'd be gone long at all....

Steven Pillage looked at his brother Shane and grinned knowingly, the two of them looking around the swank, artistically-decorated interior of the living room in humored observation.

"Brother, I bet Amber has other company here tonight," Shane said matter-of-factly.

Steven smirked at his twin and nodded in agreement, standing up from the sofa to wander around the plush living room, not too eager to go exploring the lesbian lawyer's domicile.

"No doubt in my mind…don't wanna scare whoever it may be so let's see if she comes out to see where Amber went," Steven suggested with a smirking gesture at Shane. Their last name was legally "Pillage" a name the family had for two generations and for them it was a fitting surname for their mutual world-view and outlook on life: "victory over other people".

"Another dyke like Amber," Shane sneered with a chuckle, relaxing in the reclining chair.

"Hunh-huh, don't count the beautiful Amber Duffek out just yet brother, she may claim she's a lesbian, but deep down she's a beef-eater," Steven laughed again in rebuttal.

"Hunh, miss-banana-titties sure keeps appearances as a lesbo," Shane chuckled back.

"Trust me, Amber likes men and she'll give in to the hunger for a man soon enough," Steven said matter-of-factly to his seated twin brother, both of them feeling the heating kick on inside the house now, relaxing in wait for the lawyer to return with the $50,000 they gave her to "hold" on their behalf. Amber was reliable in that way, and they trusted her 100%.

"You know…..Amber once sued some old guy for sexual harassment because he whistled at her client walking by….she won half the guy's pension in court and the old bastard had to go back to work at age sixty-five," Steven explained in humorous but true detail.

"Shit, I heard Amber once won a judgment on a defendant years ago where she got her Client a portion of the defendant's child-support check!" Shane snickered boyishly in turn.

"That's why they call her the "She-Wolf" in Legal circles," Steven added with a grin.

"I sure do like that body of hers though, man…we need to get her between us!" Shane snapped in excited assumption, making Steven laugh again, shaking his head in response.

"Dude, Amber Duffek may be the one white woman we don't get naked-on-all-fours between us my brother, I think she'll quietly hate us after tonight," Steven giggled next.

"Amber Duffek is the ultimate white chick I'd like to fuck, bar-none," Shane snickered.

"I thought you said Marilyn Monroe was the 'ultimate white chick' for you?" Steven laughed.

"Yeah, dead white chick….can't have her now, but you're right…. what straight Black man on Planet Earth would not like to fuck Marilyn Monroe if they could go back in time?" Shane quipped in humor, making his brother laughingly agree with his choice of fantasy.

"But Amber's got that perfect apple of an ass, those perky banana-titties and tight abs, mmmnnhhh!" Shane sighed in earnest, leaning back in the reclining chair as Steven walked around the living room looking with interest at the paintings Amber had on one wall.

"Just be patient my horny brother…like I said, Amber is really a beef-eater, so it's just a matter of time before she gives in, maybe we'll be there when she does?" Steven chuckled.

Michelle "Shelly" Jamison was getting impatient with Amber's absence, wondering if the woman got engrossed in another of her lengthy phone calls downstairs since she didn't hear anyone talking out in the hallway outside the tub room. She stood up from the hot water and stepped out of the Jacuzzi herself now, reaching for a towel to dry herself off then she slipped into the spare bathrobe hanging on the door and decided to go looking for Amber since the bitch had called her over here tonight just for sex….now she was wasting her time!

"Things we do out of bullshit obligation," Shelly sighed to herself as she left the tub room with cotton bathrobe around her otherwise nude physique, going to the stairwell and descending, not knowing there were two men in Amber's living room right now.

"Amber.....where are you babe?!" Shelly called out as she came down to the bottom of the stairs, sauntering on to the living room on bare feet. Finding two black men sitting in Amber's living room staring back at her was startling for Shelly at first, then she semi-recognized them as a pair of twin brothers Amber has introduced her to in-passing awhile back at an upscale D.C. restaurant. She didn't see Amber with them in the living room but she forced a gracious smile anyway as they both stood up to greet her....rather hawkishly.

"Hey girl....Amber will be right back, she told us to wait for her, I'm Shane....hey, you're Amber's friend Shelly, right?" Shane Pillage spoke first as he stood up, hands in pockets staring at her like a hungry man eyeing a juicy steak on his plate. The other twin brother was a bit more formal in manners, actually extending a hand to shake hers in hello.

"I'm Steven...good to see you again Shelly....sorry for the late night interruption but we had to come see Amber about something she's holding for us and she just left to go get it, won't be long I suppose," Steven said as he held her right hand in his for a bit longer than most handshakes go. Shelly smiled sheepishly, slightly unsettled by their presence but she just smiled and walked between them to go toward the dark kitchen for something to drink.

"I see, well...may I fix you guys a drink?" she chimed as she went to the kitchen, sensing the twin black brothers were focused on the obvious about her, the fact she was in only a bathrobe and that she was one of "Amber's girls" as some people call Amber's "dates".

"Yes ma'am, I'll take iced tea if there is any," Steven answered her, Shane staring at Shelly's ass jiggling under the bathrobe tail as she walked into the darkened kitchen of the house.

Steven turned to his brother and grinned knowingly as he leaned in closer to whisper.

"You remember who she is don't you....Shelly James, the former porn star?" he sighed.

"Oh yeah, Shelly James....Amber's squeeze....wow, what...a... piece," Shane sighed through gritted teeth in shushed response to what his brother just said, interested all the more now.

"Work with me bro," Steven whispered with a tap on Shane's arm just as Shelly re-emerged from the dark kitchen with two glasses of fresh iced tea in her hands, slowly walking back to the living room as Steven and Shane took seats across from one another, all eyes on her.

"I remember Amber introducing us awhile back at Rally's Restaurant in D.C.," Shelly spoke gingerly as she stepped between the identical-twin brothers, handing them their drinks.

"Yes, how could we forget?" Shane chimed from behind her, sliding forward on the sofa.

"Hey, we're all friends of Amber's....," Shelly sighed nervously with a shrug, then began to turn around to step over away from their reach instinctively, only to have the one named Steven with a scar on his forehead stop her motion by gently grabbing the hem of her robe.

"Yes indeed, and any friend of Amber's is a friend of ours," Steven spoke softly as she turned back to face the man tugging at the hem of her robe, a second more and his free hand found the tie at the front of her robe and pulled it loose. Before she knew it, he robe was open in front, and being pulled down off her bare body from behind, the twin brothers having "ambushed" her between them, disrobing her in no time flat....

"Guys....please...don't...," Shelly cooed in response, actually feeling aroused just standing between them naked like this, feeling Shane's left hand on her ass while Steven took her by the left hand, standing up slowly with a sly grin on his face as he stared into her blue eyes.

"Shelly-baby, Amber might be awhile in the traffic jam we came though while ago, so why don't we have some late night ice cream while we wait...vanilla is our favorite," Steven said next then with hardly any effort at all, he foisted the naked blonde up over his right shoulder, holding her at the bottom of her ass with only his right hand, and Shelly was aroused suddenly to the point of no return, giving in to their impromptu sexual gesture.

"Ooaah…heenh….ice cream hunh….heenh-heh, isn't this what they really mean by 'affirmative action'?" Shelly chimed from atop Steven's shoulder, seeing his twin brother Shane pulling off his own clothes behind his brother, eyes on her eagerly as he stripped off his pants. Steven started walking across the living room with the naked prize held high.

"You know it baby…you 'bout to learn all about the 'civil rights' movement," Shane laughed as he followed his brother and their new blonde conquest to a spare bedroom down the first floor hallway, neither of them thinking about Amber right now nor how she might feel about them seducing her ex-porn-star "squeeze" right here in her own household!

Amber's watch read 12:01 am and she was sitting in slow traffic along Arlington Road enroute to the storage facility where she had a rented locker to keep the cash stashed securely, cursing her luck tonight as she anxiously waited for the accident up ahead to be settled so that the flow of traffic may return to normal, especially since she was just about a mile away from her destination right now! She didn't even want to imagine Shelly back there in the house with the Pillage brothers lounging in the living room, hoping she stays upstairs and unseen by her "uninvited guests". If Steven and Shane find a naked white woman of Shelly's caliber there, they'd act on it, and Amber knew Shelly well enough to know she was no stranger to being seduced-on-the-spot….afterall, she was a former Porn Starlet (as well as a "recovering" nymphomaniac). Cursing the creeping traffic ahead of her, Amber kept thinking of how she has considered cutting the Pillage brothers' from her list of business-associates altogether, telling them to fuck off and die, once and for all. They had been more of a hindrance to her than a blessing business-wise and one of their goddamn parties last year was the reason she can't run for Congress as she had previously wanted to. Someone there took a photo of her naked with two men dressed up as cops at the Pillage brother's 2007 "Spring Costume Fling" party last April. Then there was the rumor about she being one of Steven and Shane's mistresses circulating the

D.C. "Swinger's" scene nowadays, a rumor she guessed they started of course! Those two sons-of-bitches, she really hated them.

Her Rolex watch read 12:20am when she finally made it to the parking lot of the rental storage facility, where she entered her password on the keypad to enter the facility's back lot of 4'x6' lockers, driving straight up to Locker #311 along the third row. Amber hopped out and quickly unlocked the secured sliding-door, yanking the heavy metal door up and open.

"Shit on me," she sneered to herself as she found the briefcase she had the money in wasn't sitting atop the pile of boxes she already had in her storage locker here, so she began to look around using the lightbulb in the ceiling to look behind her stored boxes, seeing the black briefcase had fallen down behind everything. She lurched forward and over the stacked boxes, bending over them to reach for the briefcase, feeling a "draft" as her mini-dress hiked up so that her bare ass underneath was exposed to the nightfall outside the storage locker.

A homeless man sitting inside one of the empty lockers along the next row saw what he couldn't believe at first, a well-formed woman's bare ass bent over in the locker space across from the empty one he was squatting in for tonight. Wonders never cease.......

Time was 12:42am when Amber was hurrying along the road leading back to her house without a traffic jam in the westbound lane of course, happy to at least be returning home without interference, and with the locked briefcase holding $50,000 in cash which belonged to those two hustlers waiting for her to return soon. That better be all they're doing in my house, she told herself, they better be just "waiting"!

"I swear, one of these days I'm gonna kill guys like Shane and Steven, and probably get away with it because they're such fukkin' pests....noone's gonna truly miss'em," Amber said to herself as she quickly pulled into her own driveway, parking alongside the black Mercedes.

Jumping up out of her car with the briefcase in tow, Amber hurried to the front door, letting out a sigh of relief as she pushed the heavy wooden door inward to cross the threshold into her own warm domicile. Stepping into her living room with the briefcase in both hands, she found it devoid of human beings, namely the twin black men she had left here an hour ago!

"Steven....Shane?" she quipped in worried wonder as she tossed the briefcase onto the sofa and walked around the living room, looking in the kitchen, not hearing or seeing sign of her male visitors anywhere nearby, surely not both of them would be in the bathroom at once?!

She then noticed two full glasses of tea sitting on the surface of her glass coffeetable, and it dawned on her as if she had a psychic vision as to what most likely happened to them.

"Shit......shit on me.....I don't believe this....," Amber sighed in realization as she turned toward the first floor's hallway where the stairwell was located, walking toward the stairs in nervous speculation that Steven and Shane had gone "exploring" in her house tonight.

As soon as she started up the stairs, she heard something distinctive which made her stop in stride, something she considered to be a "worse case scenario" considering the Pillage Bros.

The sound was of a familiar female voice groaning in sensual ecstasy, and it was coming from the spare bedroom on the first floor, so Amber walked toward the room, seeing it's door left ajar and something of a carnal nature going on inside right now, something that garnished her full-attention. Peering inside the spare bedroom she found three naked human beings atop the queen-sized bed, one of them Shelly on all-fours between Steven and Shane Pillage servicing her at both ends in a "threesome" sexual congress. Amber wasn't surprised the Pillage brothers would do something like this, but she had liked the idea of Shelly not falling for their charms within the 55 minutes she was gone from the house tonight!

Watching Shelly James getting hammered by two black men was kinda funny for her, so she stood there at the door silently viewing Shane drilling Shelly doggie-style from behind while she slurped on Steven's torpedo in front with that awesome mouth of hers.... what a sight!

They were really giving it to her at both ends now, hands gripping at her bare body greedily between them as they continued their fleshy indulgence in Amber's spare bedroom.

She turned from the door and quietly walked back into the living room, taking off the jacket she wore out tonight and tossing it aside. Amber was not pleased and this was one more reason to kick the Pillage brothers out of her life for good, although she thought about how she might "use" this disrespectful incident against Steven and Shane, even against Shelly, or somehow to her own advantage otherwise! Amber always thought to see things through to the point of a silver-lining, and so she paused for a moment to think of a way how the Pillage brothers interrupting her tonight (and subsequently taking her piece-of-ass) could be spun to work in her favor?? She would use it against them in some way and use Shelly some way in lieu of this transgression of disrespect shown her lawyer/lover tonight! Some people just don't see how easily they can be set up for "use" when they do recklessly foolish stunts such as this "threesome" in the home of someone more powerful and influential than they!

"Hell……is other people," she sighed to herself as she went to her kitchen for a shot of whiskey, intent on confronting the Pillage brothers once they finish-off Shelly.

1:25am: Amber Duffek walked back out from her dark kitchen with a refilled glass of her expensive Chardonnay when one of her uninvited guests finally walked out from the spare bedroom, naked and grinning with a condom still on his dick.

"Shane Pillage goddammit…..," Amber sneered in contempt as she faced the naked black man in her living room as he was going to gather up his clothing on the floor by her sofa.

"Amber…uhhm…Amber…I uhh…well…..shit," Shane stammered in surprise, facing the gorgeous but pissed off Lawyer standing there with a glass of wine in one hand and a stainless steel butcher knife in the other, having grabbed it from the kitchen to make a point.

"I oughta cut your balls off you back-stabbin' poonhound son-of-a-bitch, how dare you?!" she quipped with the knife raised in her left hand, scowling at her business associate as she stepped within four feet of the naked man in her living room, eyeing his genitals of course.

"Amber…please…it just happened…I got no excuse, really… please forgive us," Shane answered her meekly, eyes on her face then the knife she held in her left hand, not really suspecting she'd use it on him, but then again she had caught he and Steven fucking her girlfriend right here in her own home while she was doing them a big favor…

"I got your goddamn money asshole, there it is, and I see you at least had the goddamn common courtesy to wear a rubber when you screwed my girlfriend," she sneered as she pointed toward the man's semi-erect sex organ with the butcher knife, still scowling.

"Yeah…Amber, please don't hate us for this," Shane replied with gesture of hands, hoping the woman would not totally "disown" he and his brother regarding any future business.

"You go tell your brother to take his dick out of Shelly and the two of you get out of my house within the next five minutes or I will come back downstairs and kill both of you," Amber sneered in conclusion, walking across the living room toward the hallway and the stairwell to go upstairs now; Shane watching her, wanting to apologize in some kind of way.

"Okay Amber, we're going….we're going," Shane said in agreement as he started to head toward the spare bedroom where Steven was still nailing that bucking blonde Shelly James.

"And Shane…..call my office next week, because you and your brother owe me big time," she said flatly for a moment's pause on the stairwell then she vanished on up into the upper floors of her million dollar home here in northern Arlington County, near the Potomac..

Shane nodded in agreement with her remark, then walked on into the spare bedroom to find Shelly riding on top of Steven, vibrantly moving on his manhood like a human piston.

"We're busted brother, time to split," Shane said outloud in coitus-interruptus, Shelly turning her head to look at Shane with sweaty hair in her eyes, realizing what he was saying now, that Amber was home and she knew what was going on in her downstairs spare bedroom.

"Onnnh....shit, I'm dead," Shelly sighed as she rolled off Steven who thought it was slightly funny, himself still holding on to her while Shane was quickly pulling clothes back on.

"Gotta go Steven, she's given us five minutes or all bets are off with her," Shane added as he pulled his pants and shoes on, eyes on the naked and well-serviced former porn star on the bed with his brother, Steven not taking it as seriously of course but he reached for his clothes to get back into them.

"Hmmph...you guys like barbeque?" Shelly chimed with a heavy breath from the sex moments ago, lying on her side as Steven got up from the bed, pulling his pants on now.

"Hope so, because next time you come over to see Amber, she'll have my ass cooked up on a platter and served with cole slaw....," Shelly sighed in sardonic humor, knowing she was going to catch hell from her lawyer/lover after finding her with two black men here in her own house while she was gone for less than an hour to do the two black guys a favor.

"Awh, that's okay baby, as long as she's got some hot sauce to go on it, I'll fill my plate," Steven snickered as he and Shane headed out the bedroom door to leave with their money.

2:00am: Shelly hadn't screwed up the nerve to go back upstairs and see Amber just yet, though her clothes and purse were up there so she couldn't just leave without seeing the righteously pissed off Amber Duffek like she would have preferred. She instead jumped in the downstairs-bathroom shower and washed herself in the hot spray, thinking what to say to Amber and expecting her to "disavow" her after tonight, something she could survive of course but Amber has been beneficial to Shelly since 2005 and she didn't want to break off the relationship in a bad, irrevocable manner. The "rapport" between Shelly and Amber had been a tenuous one since 2005 and though Shelly was indebted to the crafty female lawyer for keeping her bacon out of the fire that was a major murder investigation following the collapse of Faster Productions in the last week of July 2005 and in getting her the book deal which netted her over a million dollars to pen her autobiography which was of course titled:

I AM SHELLY JAMES, released in July 2006. Mystery Writer K.R. Knight did most of the work and she just relayed her story to him, her story being that of a young Catholic Nun who carefully, secretly "moonlights" as an Adult Film Star. Once she was exposed by a nosy tabloid reporter in 2005, she was defrocked as a Nun and a Papal Decree from the Vatican censured her individually denying her the sacraments of the Catholic Church forever and in a statement that has not been issued by The Vatican against anyone in over 100 years, Michelle Jamison was "condemned to hell" by the Pope himself in the decree. Nothing like being "condemned" by The Vatican itself, Shelly had thought about the rejection from her Church in Rome. Regardless, life for her was never the same after July of 2005, and Amber Duffek kept reminding her of the fact that she owes her for getting her what she has right now....

Amber came back down the stairs to make sure the Pillage brothers had left and to see Shelly Jamison, having calmed down from earlier fury over the sex in her spare bedroom that of course did not involve Amber! Payback on the Pillage brothers will come soon enough she told herself. She figured she was taking a shower in the downstairs bathroom and walked to it, finding the blonde cupcake in the steamy bathroom taking a hot shower alone and quietly. Having inched the door open in silence, Amber stood there for a moment and watched the nude form of her "girlfriend" behind the shower stall's glass door.

"Shel...," Amber spoke up, getting the younger woman's attention in a slightly fearful reaction, turning toward the glass-door of the shower stall to slide it open and see her.

"Amber...I...I have no words to say...," Shelly sighed meekly as she slid the shower door open a few inches to find Amber Duffek standing in the bathroom wearing one of her cotton bathrobes now, the look on her pretty face a poker expression of smooth calm.

"Nor should you have Shelly...I'm not as mad about you being so easily seduced by those two womanizers as I am about you getting-it-on in my house with two men," Amber spoke eloquently as if conducting a job interview with the frightened blonde bombshell.

Amber then peeled open her bathrobe to reveal her own gloriously-naked physique Shelly was all too familiar with, letting the garment fall to the bathroom's rug at her bare feet.

She stepped on into the shower stall with Shelly now, her right hand going to the vixen's face in a gentle touch at the cheekbone, their eyes staring into one another's intently as the glass door was pushed closed again. Amber's silky brown hair was drenched wet as she stepped through the cascading shower spray, making Shelly step back in silent response.

"Ya know Shelly James…I'm surprised you can still eat with that mouth," Amber cooed as she touched two fingers to Shelly's lips, smiling in sarcastic remark, slowly embracing her.

Quantico, Virginia. 8:30 the following morning: Special Agent Clifford Stevens of the ATF wasn't used to reporting to an FBI Office here in the FBI Academy at Quantico, least of all the famous Behavioral Analysis Unit. He figured he was either in serious trouble or one of his cases crossed the line into FBI territory and he didn't have to wait long to be called into a subterranean office cubicle deep within the main building on the Academy grounds, deep within the "Threat Analysis Wing" of the Behavioral Analysis Unit.

Didn't take long to discover he was not in trouble and he had not crossed into another Investigator's territory, but still something he never thought he'd ever be briefed on….

Ushered into a sound-proof briefing room where only three other men were sitting in wait for his arrival, Stevens decided he didn't like the "cloak and dagger" theme of this meeting.

He recognized one man, one of his Superiors at ATF named Driscoll and the other two older men were obviously big-shots at the US Department of Homeland Security, and they introduced themselves as such, one being Deputy US Attorney Tyler Clark and the shorter, balding man an Assistant Director of Domestic Intelligence at DHS by the name of Bannon.

"Agent Stevens, take a seat please…we have a lot to discuss, and of course this briefing is not to be discussed outside these walls with anyone not possessing a DHS White-Clearance, undertood?" US

Deputy Attorney Tyler Clark informed the slightly-nervous ATF Agent.

"Understood sir," Cliff said in agreement, wondering what the hell this was about since it involves the highest clearance in DHS and Justice Department for dissemination. If it is a "White" Clearance then he is now involved in the shady realm of Homeland Security at it's highest levels as well as it's extremely-limited information dissemination level......not good!

"What we are about to show you is not an official investigation per se, meaning it is not open to public scrutiny," the DHS Intelligence man spoke next, readying a closed-circuit video on a plasma TV screen on the wall in front of the row of seats in this big "office".

"No public scrutiny" translates into "noone outside of this office knows about it" kind of shit and Stevens didn't like that either, more of the cloak-n-dagger bullshit he didn't trust.

"Agent Stevens, your name came across our desks because you headed up an investigation into the Marcano Crime Family years ago, investigating that Mob organization for selling illegal automatic weapons," DepAttyGen Tyler Clark spoke next, sitting in a chair facing Agent Stevens just five feet away, the expression on his face a sternly stoical one for now.

"Yessir, it nearly ended my career," Cliff said with a hint of contempt for the topic, since the botched raid on the Mafia Don's mansion in Nashville Tennessee resulted in a bomb exploding and deaths of two FBI Agents as well as injury himself in the unexpected blast.

"Well son, the chickens are coming home to roost and we're bringing you in on this matter because you were the one Federal Agent who got close in surveillance of the Marcano Mob eight years ago, and we believe to a certainty that illegal weapons sold by the Marcanos during the time period you were casing them....might be the one link to finally uncovering the most efficiently methodical domestic-terrorist plot on US Soil in all of American History,"Tyler Clark explained without cutting corners, the ATF Agent before him sitting there in stunned surprise. The Marcano case was the last thing he expected to be briefed about after the past six years of that damn case labeled as "closed"! Stevens was all-ears now as he sat there and watched the TV screen and it's DHS File-Footage. The first scene was of the Oklahoma City Federal Building bombing in April 1995 and the carnage there, some shots never released to the public of mangled bodies, then the FBI sketches of the wanted perpetrators: "John Doe #1" and "John Doe #2" side-by-side on the TV screen.

Oklahoma City Bombing in 1995....Olympic Park in Atlanta 1996....Abortion Clinic shootings and bombings between 1996 and 1998 across the US....Columbine High School massacre 1999... Abortion-Doctor murders in 2000 and 2001..... alleged "suicides" of three US Congressmen in 2001 and 2002....bombing-murder of Civil Rights Activist Randy Weston in 2003....the "race riots" in Atlanta Georgia that same year resulting in over 60 deaths and 12 Police Officers slain by rioters.....the "fire" at a DC Gay Nightclub that killed hundreds that same year...the bomb that went off during the joint- FBI/ATF raid on the Marcano Mafia compound in Nashville, TN in 2004.....the shootings of interracial couples in New York City in 2005 ....the mysterious deaths of two more US Congressmen in 2006....the "accidental" poisoning of a US Attorney that same year.....

So far, Agent Cliff Stevens was at a loss as to what route the three "higher ups" were leading him down right now, what possible "connection" his past case against the Marcano Mob could there be with an assortment of past domestic acts of terror/murder committed over the course of 12 years?! The briefing seemed to point in that direction though, and the Deputy Attorney General Tyler Clark seemed most adamant about the "tie in" not being successfully linked between 1995 and 2006 as these seemingly-unrelated crimes occurred without a hitch. Cliff had found the time now to interrupt his very own personal briefing.

"Sirs...a lot of the terror acts and murders your video just highlighted were either solved, the perpetrators either jailed or slain, no correlation between any of them or the Investigators and certainly the damn media would have jumped on it by now....," Cliff pointed out as he shifted in his chair, unnerved by the premise these men were delivering to him right now.

"Yes, some of the perps were patsies.....or 'lone-wolves', if you know what I mean?" Clark answered frankly with arms folded over his pin-striped suit, eyes on Agent Stevens intently.

"Lone-wolves....yessir, I know what that means...lone individuals carrying out violence in the name of a cause or organization without direct-involvement by anyone else," Cliff added.

"You're saying there is a broader picture to all this....a mastermind behind it all?" Cliff asked before the other two big shots could speak up next, stirring in his seat as he faced them.

"We believe so, yes...and unofficially we want you to re-investigate the Marcano Mob starting from where you left off years ago, try and find any and all links between Marcano gun sales and/or money-laundering between two-thousand-two and two-thousand-four, which we believe is one possible link to a domestic terror conspiracy behind most if not entirely all of these acts of violence in the past ten years....your investigation into the Marcano Mafia was the closest the ATF came to sticking their feet in that underworld syndicate which broke off into various shapes once the Marcano Family split into factions after the death of the Don....you could establish a foothold for us to bring down a much more dangerous perpetrator if you can find and establish a link," Clark continued frankly.

"Sir, if I may...any Cop on the street knows an 'unofficial;' investigation goes nowhere because cooperation with an 'unofficial' investigator is often non-existent," Cliff added.

"You'll be answering directly to Deputy Attorney General Clark here Agent Stevens, and mutual cooperation with local authorities shouldn't be a problem for a seasoned Field-Agent like yourself," the other DHS big shot spoke up matter-of-factly.

"Indeed, and the link between the Marcano Mobsters you investigated years ago for gun-running and the domestic terror conspiracy we at Homeland Security believe has been going on since nineteen-ninety-five is the one crack in the armor," the bald guy said next, handing Cliff a thick file-folder marked "Classified-D11 Eyes Only" which he promptly opened.

Detailed in the file were the FBI, ATF, USM, and even US Army Military Intelligence documents and briefs regarding the incidents and killings profiled in the video footage he was just shown, and more importantly, the similarities between those past crimes!

C-4 plastic explosive was the primary bomb ingredient in nearly all the aforementioned incidents, and military-grade at that. Bombs in all these incidents were remote-detonated.

Shootings were done with .223 caliber military-type rifles and three with a .45 Automatic.

Money trails from weapons procurement unknown but considering the "quality" of the weapons and explosive materials used in these incidents over the past 11 years, confidence is high that the perpetrators are not exactly "poor" when it comes to financing their violence.

Someone (or some organization) financed shit like this and no confirmed sources were highlighted in the file or mentioned by the three big-shots as they continued talking about what they wanted Agent Stevens to do in an "unofficial" investigation. The fact these three Federal "wise men" were tasking him with what amounted to a bone-chilling "cold case" far enough in the past to be as cold as the corpses killed in those attacks and other killings between 1995 and 2006. Though none of the three "higher-ups" were saying it, Cliff wanted to mention the inconvenient observation that the "terror incidents" hadn't continued in the same vein or increased in ferocity since last year except for the C-4 explosion that killed

Robert Marx and his idiot son Jamal just last night. Was it starting up all over again?

He wanted to ask them a ton of questions but he picked his battles, so just the facts necessary for him to make his decision whether or not he would accept or tell them to take their shady "unofficial" investigation and shove the whole damn thing up their fat asses!

The one other "similarity" found in three of the incidents where lone perpetrators were captured alive, namely the shootings in Atlanta and a bombing in North Carolina intrigued Agent Stevens as he sat there reading it while listening to the three big shots talk at him.

Three unrelated perpetrators who didn't know one another at all stated during Police and FBI interviews that someone else whom they knew only as "Horse Hair" had talked them into doing what they did, provided them with the weapon(s) and/or explosive and showed them a way to escape the crime scene, although those three didn't succeed in the latter.

"Horse Hair" sounded more like some geek's computer screen-name or maybe a CB-handle, but three of the "lone wolves" as the DHS calls them, all spoke of someone who went by that name conning them into committing a violent act and offering them whatever suited their fancy: money or something else such as getting one's gambling-junkie wife out of debt with a local loan-shark (according to one of the perpetrators interviewed).

Agent Stevens sat there for a minute absorbing what the three big-shots were still telling him, and for a moment of clarity beyond their grinding voices briefing him in a steady flurry of information, he recalled something from his own past field-work that was yet another strange similarity all of it's own……

"Shit….I've heard that goddamn name before…or something like it…..Horse…Hair," Cliff spoke outloud as he concentrated on his own memories for a moment, the three big-shots silent for the time he took to concentrate, hoping he might remember something of weight.

"You see Agent Stevens, you're a link yourself," Tyler Clark said in response, grinning.

"Hunh, alright then….I'll go for what I can find sir, report directly to you," Cliff said in a sigh, not remembering just where or when he heard or saw that "name" before today.

"Excellent Agent Stevens, you may begin immediately and your current caseload will be handed to someone else as this one takes priority," spoke the bald DHS man again.

"We believe the perpetrator is still out there and we'd like to establish a connection between the Marcano Mob as it was prior to two-thousand-five, and money that was likely siphoned from their illegal coffers to fund a domestic terrorist operation which we believe still exists," the bald DHS man said next, staring at the seasoned

ATF Agent intently as Cliff tried to absorb what was being asked of him. He was being asked to chase "ghosts" and he knew it!

"I'll start with my notes and surveillance findings on the Marcano Mob eight years ago, since you're convinced there's a weapons-deal between those goombahs and your terrorist," Cliff said with a straight face, though he didn't know how he was going to get anything from that!

"This investigation is to remain close-to-the-chest Agent Stevens, in other words we don't wish to see or hear of your work on this matter on any News Reports," the DHS man said again, eyeing the career Agent intently as he had been doing for the past hour.

"I know what you mean sir, and don't worry, it'll stay out of the news as best as I can keep it out of the news," Cliff told him with a smirk, silently musing that he probably won't ever make the news with a "ghost" case such as this unless he uncovers the suspected "terrorist" face-to-face and shoots the shadowy dog down, something he already seriously doubts!

"You're alone on this investigation because it cannot bear media scrutiny and because we all feel one Agent would best uncover a perpetrator such as this more efficiently than a task force," Clark spoke up again, nodding to Agent Stevens sitting before him.

Cliff realized that meant he was "on his own" in the sense that if he screws up, he can be easily dropped like a hot potato or conveniently blamed for whatever bad happens in the course of an "unofficial" investigation like this on was. He knew one good cop could be as expendable as any soldier in a war, though being this close to retirement made him worry.

"You have two years before you retire Agent Stevens," Clark spoke up suddenly, making Cliff feel as if he was reading his mind just then, slightly fearful of what he was going to say.

"Complete this investigation for us and you may retire immediately afterward with a full-pension and benefits, I can see to that," Clark said conclusively, as if Stevens had a choice!

Past cases like the one yesterday he had worked because they had an explosives element (namely C-4) and the incidents since 1995 weren't all tied to explosives-use, which meant in the broader scope of things, he could be on a wild goose chase for a shadowy terrorist who doesn't in fact exist…though it sure sounds like he does….and since nothing similar has occurred since 2006 except for the Marx explosion last night in Stafford County Virginia, he again doubted the validity of what he was being asked to do by his superiors. If the last half-dozen explosives-killings he's worked on in the past decade here on the east coast are "linked" but untraceable, perhaps by looking back into the past Marcano Investigation to find some sort of "tie-in" may be worth the stretch, as well as early retirement!

"I agree sir, I'll begin right where I left off on the Marcano residence in Fredericksburg as well as elsewhere, try to find a link to your shadow-terrorist," Cliff said in breaking silence.

"We've also discovered a bridge between the Marcano Mob prior to two-thousand-five and the now-defunct Adult Film Company in New York, Faster Productions," Clark added next.

"That legit Porn Company that shut down back in Oh-Five due to tabloid exposure of the actors who led secret double-lives as porn stars, a few bloody murders, arson, disappearances,?" Cliff chimed in knowingly, smirking at the bald DHS man again.

"Yes, and in the file there you'll also find a few names of past employees of that company who might recall a tidbit or two regarding Mafia investing, money-laundering, whatever…," Clark answered him with a smirk, then stood up from his seat in conclusive stance.

"Sounds like fun," Cliff said as he stood up along with the DHS big-shot, smiling at Clark despite the fact he still thought this "assignment" was for the goddamn birds. He would have to watch his back the entire time he was investigating this "unofficial" case, but he shook hands with the three higher-ups anyway, saving Tyler Clark for last.

"Sir, I think I'll take you up on early-retirement after this is over," Cliff chuckled as he shook hands with the Deputy-Attorney-General who seemed confident Stevens would agree to it.

"After this case son, you might need it," Clark said with a grin back at the ATF Agent.

Washington D.C., Georgetown. 9:30 that night: The upstairs "den" was her husband's personal little retreat here inside their cozy but ancient Georgetown home just off M Street and Canal St. within a block from the Key Bridge and the famous "Exorcist" steps where the finale of the famous 1973 horror movie was filmed. Having lived with him in this old but comfortable home on the Potomac River here in Washington DC since last year, 40-year old Shaya Kelsh was happy enough to put up with her 59-year old Husband's strange traits such as him eating dinner in front of the TV screens up in his private den on the top floor, where she was slowly approaching via the stairs now, clad in her blue silk bathrobe which barely covered her well-shaped physique underneath. He'd been done eating an hour ago but she wanted to look in on him anyway, because his strange "friend" was in the den with him talking privately this evening, talking about things a wife was not to be privy to of course.

Stopping at the closed door, she paused for a moment in thought. Her husband in there was US Senator Rupert Kelsh (D.NJ) who she married just one year ago after their mutual lawyer Amber Duffek introduced them. The visitor was named Duncan, a darkly-mysterious man Shaya found strangely-appealing, a man her husband let her "play" with a couple times already, since she and Rupert have an "open" marriage. Tonight would be one of those nights she hoped, and the muscular stallion named Duncan would adjourn with her to one of the spare bedrooms for a quick sexual tryst compliments of her husband who she thought "controls" Duncan somehow, for some reason....

She opened the door slowly and peered inside, finding her husband over in his favorite recliner with his back to the door, eyes on the three TV sets perched on one wall, viewing three different TV News channels at once, his male visitor over at the window of the den looking out with a glass of something alcoholic in one hand, his all-black attire formed over his taut, linebacker-sized body snug, but not too much to restrict movement. He was a handsome man the same age as she, built strong and tough as if he'd been in training for years on end, something she always liked about a man like Duncan....he was not a pussy!

"Shaya my dear, come in," Rupert spoke up from the recliner, not turning to look at her, her gaze fixed on the stocky guy in black standing over by the room's lone window, eyes on her.

"Duncan, so good to see you again," Shaya said softly, smiling at the dark-haired man she hoped would stay long enough to romp with her for awhile this evening, his "business" with her husband shady and secretive but she never asked about it, preferring the man in bed!

"Shaya....," Duncan said softly in his gravel voice, his deep-set dark eyes staring through her as she entered the room slowly, glancing over at Rupert over in the recliner, the TV screens of more interest to him right now than his sexy wife in the nicely-snug silk bathrobe!

Shaya was an unusual beauty who looked not a day over thirty even though she had recently turned forty, her looks and physique attractively-filled-out and smooth to a point she would make Jayne Mansfield blanch with envy! Shaya was an ethnic mixture of Turkish, Brazilian, and Italian, making for a lightly-bronzed complexion and exotic appeal about her.

Before Rupert had met her last year, she'd been employed in the Adult Film Industry under the moniker "Shaya Gold" from 1991 to 2005 mostly as an X-rated Actress with 400 films under her belt. Marrying a US Senator during his re-election campaign had been a media-circus for awhile last year but Rupert won re-election in New Jersey for his Senate seat by two percentage points against the Republican challenger. Seemed having a former Porn Star as his newlywed wife appealed to Independent and Libertarian voters in his district? Being a former porn star with the body she has and stunning good looks overall, Shaya is widely-whispered around D.C. as Senator Kelsh's "Trophy Wife" and the Senator encourages her to maintain that image for the most part, for he realized what kind of "hold" a sexually-alluring woman like Shaya has over most straight men, and that quality can be most useful.....

"Well Duncan, I approve of what you're doing naturally.....keep up the good work, and I'll see you next time my friend," Rupert spoke up suddenly from his chair, looking at the other man in the den as Shaya stepped toward the window where he stood like a human statue.

"Thank you sir," the dark-haired man said in his gravel voice, eyeing Shaya beside him now.

"You kids can go play now," Rupert said with a slight smirk at his buxom wife then returned his gaze to the three TV sets perched on the wall ahead of him, giving his "permission" for Shaya and Duncan to go get naked together in one of the spare bedrooms in the house here.

Duncan said no more as he walked toward the den's door in silence, Shaya following close behind, peeling off the silk robe she wore, tossing it toward the recliner where her husband sat, the garment landing on the top cushion of the recliner, just over his head. Rupert pulled the garment down off his head and let it lay across his lap as he watched the TV screens news reports on the "explosion" in Stafford, Va. resulting in the untimely death of one Robert Marx, Civil Rights Attorney and possible future Supreme Court appointee.

"Only reason it's untimely is because I didn't get to kill the bastard sooner," Rupert sighed to himself, smelling his wife's perfume from the bathrobe in his lap, imagining Shaya and Duncan getting-it-on right now down the hall in one of the spare bedrooms. He allowed her to take a lover now and then, as long as she was discreet and safe. Duncan being one of them, he let them romp in the house while he was there, a "reward" of sorts to the lonely warrior named Duncan Horsehair who does his bidding out there…case in point being that sanctimonious pro-minority asshole Robert Marx who had conned Republican Legislators and the current President into accepting him as a likely Supreme Court nominee when one of the Justices supposedly retires soon. Duncan Horsehair has done a lot for him in their mutual "war" since 1995 in a slow, methodical manner and it has turned out quite well according to Rupert's game-plan. Shaya was pretty much oblivious to his scheme, owing a lot to her husband as far as her own security and comfort was concerned. Rupert was rich, powerful, and protective of what is his, which kept her from having to work or get some kind of meaningless job to support herself. Of course, after 14 years working in the Porn Industry, it's not like she could put it on a job resume! He took another sip of his beer then once commercials were on the TV screens all at once, he got up from the recliner and wandered out to the dark hallway, deciding to take a quick peek in on his wife who actually liked him to peek in on her when she's with someone else! He knew she'd have the door ajar as always, so he silently walked down the hallway to the spare bedroom nearest the master, peering inside the lamp-lit room to find his shapely wife getting "hammered" by Duncan.

The two lovers were gripped in a fervent "missionary" position, with the muscled man driving into the voluptuous woman in steady, piston-like motion. Shaya wailed aloud in delight of the intercourse, her pretty face grimacing in orgasmic reaction, mouth wide open, eyes closed as the powerful male between her legs continued his onslaught, drilling her steadily. Rupert stood there at the cracked-open door for a moment, watching the two lovers in the spare bedroom, wishing it could be him screwing his wife like that, making love to her with such energetic tenacity as he would have in his younger years. Sex for Rupert Kelsh was now a rare occasion and only when he was in a certain "celebratory" mood, though not quite like Duncan Horsehair who laid-pipe to Shaya with a ferocious fervor Kelsh actually envied.

Stepping away from the doorway now, Rupert sauntered back to his private den, musing about how that bed-wetting liberal shithead Robert Marx got his tonight, thanks to Duncan and one of his "lone wolves" out there, killing in the name of his silent but deadly cause.

Duncan was a valuable "asset" in his grand plan, as was his "trophy wife" Shaya, which made him grin to himself…why not let his two prized assets fuck their brains loose?!

Fredericksburg Virginia. (same night): The address was one Agent Clifford Stevens remembered all too well, for he had conducted surveillance on this place a few years ago.

1705 Beverly Lane was the location of a "safe house" owned and maintained by the marcano Crime Family between 1990 and 2005 though it was one of the few Mafia "properties" which never got raided by Authorities because noone seemed to do anything 100% illegal here at this location, it served primarily as a "place to crash" for Marcano Mobsters and associated family, associates, even a lawyer or two.

Pulling his ATF-issued vehicle up in front of the brick house on the inclined cul-de-sac street, he shifted into park and got out, looking up at the brick house which had just a single light on inside it appeared. Cliff looked around and found the neighborhood quiet and noone else outside right now, so he walked on up along the brick walkway to the front of the Marcano Mob "safe house", memories of his past surveillance coming to mind now.

He remembered a couple of good-looking women frequenting this place back in 2002 and 2003, one being the Marcano Boss' niece Isabel Marcano, and what a piece of work she was!

Gorgeous, raven-haired, built like a brick shithouse, but afflicted with some kind of rare disorder barring her from direct sunlight, which meant the poor young woman slept during the day and "lived" primarily after dark, sort of like a Vampire would have to. She had a gorgeous tits-n-ass blonde friend named Danielle Kenyon who came here often with Isabel and used the in-ground swimming pool on the hill here while Isabel slept indoors. Danielle Kenyon as it turned out was a high-priced "Escort" girl who'd go out on a "date" with any man(or woman) who could pay her $400 per hour cash. Then there was Attorney Diego Tanner, one of the Marcano Boss' personal lawyers who frequented this place between 2002 and 2003 along with Isabel and Danielle, actually helping Isabel with a "discrimination" lawsuit she had filed against a former employer of hers and winning her a settlement. Cliff guessed Diego Tanner, a thirty-something shyster of a lawyer and self-professed "ladies man" was probably sticking it to Isabel back then as well as her friend Danielle. FBI and ATF sources estimate that Attorney Diego Tanner was likely dead considering the Marcano way of handling any "liability" and if he was sleeping with the Boss' favored niece Isabel, then he probably ended up with his balls pickled in a jar somewhere and the rest of him served up as dog food in a kennel… considering how the Marcano Mob handles a "liability".

He walked to the front of the house, guessing noone was occupying the house right now, though seeing in through the door's window-portal on the right he saw furniture but only an indoor security-light lit to ward off burglars. It was empty, though someone still owned it!

Walking around the front of the house in the dew-wet grass, Agent Stevens reflected on his surveillance of this place and it's visitors back in 2002 and 2003. He remembered seeing that chesty Isabel Marcano walking along the front yard like he was now doing, only she wore a bikini that barely fit her, walking up to the hillside swimming pool 25 yards from the house for a late night swim, that body of hers a sight for sore eyes! Isabel was a bit of a "shut in" though she didn't look like it judging by her beauty and bod....she only came out at night, usually alone, and when Cliff did tail her into downtown Fredericksburg once, he found her meeting not with Mobsters of her "Family" but a couple of young guys at a local Bar whom she showed her big boobs to in exchange for a marijuana joint she wanted to smoke outside.

Isabel Marcano had appeared to be a "good girl" up to a point, and though she was a suspect in Marcano Mob dealings after the death of her Uncle in early 2004, she seemed to hold a place in Cliff Stevens' memory....and not just because he would have loved to fuck her!

Cliff walked around to the rear of the house here on Beverly Lane, finding the grass not as well-trimmed back there, and the hottub cabana closed up tight.

He recalled Attorney Diego Tanner entertaining some lady-friends here years ago, using the place more than Isabel whose legal address was in Fairfax County, about an hour or so north of Fredericksburg. Walking down through a vine-covered archway into the rear "courtyard" of the place concealed by a high row of holly bushes, Cliff found rod-iron patio furniture and a barbeque pit as he stepped down toward the basement sliding-glass door entrance.

Looking in through the sliding-glass door, he could make out what appeared to be a "sitting room" complete with an old fashioned arcade-style pinball machine in one corner and a vintage-looking

TV set in one corner with a faux-fireplace on the far wall inside there.

He pulled on the sliding-glass door instinctively and it slid open! Looking around, Cliff was stunned to hear no burglar-alarm going off, the sliding door unlocked by chance. If the place had a "silent alarm" he would just have to identify himself to the responding local cops and tell them why he was snooping around an old Mafia "safe house" at this time of evening.

He crossed the threshold, which was technically wrong considering he didn't have a warrant but Cliff wanted to get a peek inside the place after all this time. Leaving the sliding door open behind him, he went on into the dark basement "den" of the house on Beverly Lane.

He could make out the slight smell of perfume on the warm air inside, the heating system still working, though he could also smell dust on the air which meant noone had been actually living in the place for awhile evidently, though it had been kept-up enough. A Pool table, shelves with books and sports memorabilia, a big framed "James Bond~Moonraker" movie poster on the wall nearest the Pinball Machine, and there was a pair of doors in the far corner of the huge room opposite the pool table, making him pull his pen-light out to investigate further...what the hell, this was an "unofficial" investigation anyway, right?

The one door was to a basement bedroom, one with no windows and one that looked like it had been intentionally left the way it was left many-moons-ago, the sheets on the bed ruffled as if someone failed to make it up years ago, dust being the order of the things in this basement bedroom. He shined his penlight on the nightstand and found a dust-covered 4x6 photo frame holding a photo of some kind, so he took a closer look and recognized the two women in the photo, both wearing string-bikinis and laughing for the camera.... It was Isabel Marcano on the left and her best friend Danielle "Dani" Kenyon on the right. This windowless bedroom was where Isabel Marcano had slept apparently! Made sense since this basement bedroom had no windows and was well-hidden from the outside of the house.

Cliff pocketed the 4x6 framed photo and stepped around carefully, finding clothes still in the slide-open closet, some trinkets and even a watch on the dresser, as if Isabel had left here years ago in quite a hurry?! Possible…even though he figured her deceased by now, considering how the Marcano Mob got rid of "liabilities" big and small. He walked back out into the basement "sitting room" and wanted to go upstairs but didn't, fearing lack of an easy escape-route in the event someone did show up here tonight and found him here. Standing at the pool table, he shined his penlight around the interior and took notice of little things there that might help him develop a "mental picture". Something he did notice was on one shelf across from the pool table, making him step up closer to find out what it was.

"Porn", Cliff sighed to himself as he slid a cover-boxed VHS tape from others on the shelf, looking at it with his penlight, reading the title and it's cast list, plot, etc. on the back of it.

The title was "Driving Nowhere Faster" rated XXX, starring Jonny Faster, Chrissa Bo, Leesa Teasa, Ebony Cane, and Ray Fury. It was a porn film about sex while "on the road".

There was that New York Porn Company name again, Cliff thought, Faster Productions.

Isabel had a small collection of Faster Productions films on VHS here, which steered Cliff toward the alleged "link" between the Marcano Mob and Faster Productions Porn in NY.

"You had these because you were a fan and/or you had an investment in that Porn Company Isabel?" Cliff spoke outloud in a question, then looked at another Porn Video tape in the collection on the one shelf, this was called "UnderStudy" starring Jonny Faster, Ray Fury, Shelly James, Chrissa Bo, Ebony Cane, and Woodrow Grande. The front of the box had an image of a shapely blonde "teacher" standing before two male "students" seated at old fashioned schoolroom-desks ogling her in the short-short skirt she wore.

"Hmmph, yeah…porn-filmmaking is an easy avenue to launder money through isn't it?" Cliff asked the videotape in his right hand now, smiling at the idea that what those "higher-ups" suggested to be true, may be valid afterall and perhaps he wasn't on the wild-goose chase he thought at first. Putting the videotapes back on the shelf, he then spun on his heels and headed back out the rear sliding-glass door, taking with him only the framed 4x6 photo of Isabel Marcano and Dani Kenyon in bikinis, a photograph taken indoors and at night.

Walking back around the house near the hillside pool area, Cliff spotted an older man wearing a yellow bathrobe and walking a small dog out near the cul-de-sac street right now.

It was the neighbor from the house that overlooked the pool area, someone Cliff knew hadn't seen him yet but he decided to approach him anyway and identify himself so that he could ask a question or two. Most "suburbanites" are more than willing to help cops with questions, he just hoped this one may have been living here back when the Marcanos still frequented 1705 Beverly Lane. Walking toward him slow and casual, Cliff quickly waved at the man in the bathrobe and smiled as the civilian nodded in acknowledgement, then Cliff pulled out his badge and ID as he addressed the man walking his tiny dog.

Georgetown, 10:30pm: Shaya was taking a shower now in the hallway bathroom she preferred over the one in the master bedroom, her lover gone as quick and silent as he had arrived hours earlier. Senator Kelsh stepped down the hallway to the bathroom and poked his head inside the steamy interior, finding his shapely younger wife showering, seeing her through the clear-plastic shower curtain. Shaya liked her long hot showers that was for sure, and he admired her in some ways, tolerated her in others, but mostly liked Shaya for the "difference" she made in his most recent year of life, meaning the end to the silent boredom and loneliness that had plagued Rupert for years before he ever met the likes of her. Strangely enough, he didn't "own" her like some men would think he does, Shaya is her own person with free-reign to do what she wishes, even have sex with whomever she wishes as long as doing so does not harm him in any way, shape, or form.......or cause a media blitz!

"Hey honey!" Shaya called out to him when she noticed the door was cracked-open and felt a slightly-cooler draft of air waft through from the hallway into the steamy bathroom there.

"Have fun?" Rupert replied with a chuckle as he stared at her appealing nude form through the clear-plastic shower curtain between them, until she peeled it open to look at him again.

"Oh yes...thanks, I appreciate you letting us fool around tonight," Shaya chimed with a girlish grin at the 59-year old Rupert Kelsh backing out the doorway now to leave her alone.

Rupert didn't feel jealousy with his "trophy wife" because they weren't the conventional married couple by far. His only daughter had died a suicide in 1995 and Shaya had no children because she had her tubes-tied back in the 1990's when she was at the height of her Porn Film career. He didn't feel jealousy over Shaya because he recognized her for what she was, a beautiful woman still in her sexual prime, libido as hot as a tamale and he could not be the "stud" she needed, not at his age and level of sex-drive. Rupert was also not amiss to the fact a woman such as Shaya could easily be used as a "carrot" to dangle in front of other men when necessary! Perhaps the main reason he treated her different than he did his first wife decades ago was that Shaya was still a Stranger to him in a way....he hadn't really gotten to know her 100% and didn't plan on it either.....

Beverly Lane, Fredericksburg Va. 10:45pm: Letting a Federal Agent into his home late at night for such a reason was not something Mr. John Hessman would have imagined doing up to now, but here he was, standing in the bedroom where his only son Michael had slept since childhood, the one room in the house next door to 1705 which directly over-looked the in-ground pool on the Marcano side of the fence below. Striking up a conversation with the ATF Agent on the street while walking his little dog Rusty earlier had ended up with Mr. Hessman telling the Agent about his son Michael (who was now attending College at Virginia Tech) and his penchant for videotaping others without their consent years ago, specifically the time period between May and October of 2002. Agent Stevens had been interested enough to ask for the VHS tape Mr. Hessman took from his peeping-tom son Michael back then, the old man having stashed the tape in a drawer and nearly forgot about it, forgetting to throw it away like he had originally planned! Agent Stevens stood in the bedroom looking out the window down at the closed-off swimming pool area where the Marcano "safe house" visitors often partook of when "crashing" at 1705 Beverly Lane.

It was a perfect snoop's nest to film or photograph persons at that swimming pool back then, and Cliff could not wait to view the old VHS tape now in his hands.

"I can't thank you enough Mister Hessman, really…your son's snooping might just net me a real criminal or two if he happened to film the right people at this pool deck back then," Cliff told the old man in the yellow robe amicably, shaking his hand in approval.

"Michael got his first video-camera for Christmas five years ago and he used it to spy on our neighbors, shit…you say they were Mobsters….lucky they didn't catch him filming them!" Mr. Hessman snickered back as he looked out the window along with Agent Stevens at the dark and closed-off pool area next to the Marcano Property of 1705 Beverly Lane.

"Hmmm…yes, they were Mobsters…but they behaved themselves here at the time…when did you say you last saw someone in that house?" Cliff replied, thinking of his next steps.

"I saw a rather good-looking young lady visit there about a month ago, dressed fit-to-kill with light brown hair and a set of legs on her….mmmhh…but she didn't stay long, like she just checked on the place and left," Mr. Hessman said matter-of-factly with a shrug.

"I think someone still owns it, just noone living there currently," Cliff said with a smirk.

"I did see a light-skinned black gentleman over there quite a bit back in two-thousand-two and two-thousand-three….seemed he was a bit of a 'ladies man' because he always had female company with him, one way or another….used to screw'em in the pool late at night which is why my son had an interest in videotaping back then, haanh-hunh," Hessman chuckled, walking around his college-student son's bedroom, arms folded as he reflected.

"I see," Cliff chimed, looking at the aged VHS videotape and wondered what he would see captured on it, curious as hell but not wanting to get too involved with Mr. Hessman now.

"One dark-haired young woman stayed over there on weekends back then too, though I think she hated the light-skinned black man....overheard them bickering late some nights outside either in front of the house or at the pool....Isabel I think her name was, and she had a healthy set of 'lungs' on her if you know what I mean?" Mr. Hessman added with his hands over his chest to express the fact the woman he was speaking about had big breasts.

"Pizza Delivery boys used to stop by that place a lot back then too, and I don't think they were deliverin' pizzas every time....they were looking-in on the young woman with the big cans, peeking through the windows...that kind of stuff...but one night something scared the hell out of three of them and they took off like bats out of hell...never came back again," Hessman explained as he and the ATF Agent walked back down the stairs.

"Something or Someone......?" Cliff chimed as he shook the old man's hand in conclusion.

Arlington Va. October 11th, 6:15pm: Amber Duffek was no stranger to men, though her male lovers since College and Law School she could count on one hand. Known in most east coast Legal circles as the "She-Wolf" who proudly calls herself an "Accomplished Lesbian", Attorney Amber Duffek has carved a reputation for herself in the Courtroom as well as in Business. Technically every bit a millionaire with Real Estate in four states, and a client-list that grows with each passing retainer, she is a vixenish white woman who almost always wears stiletto-heels and form-fitting attire even in Courtrooms attracting attention wherever she goes, whoever's side she takes in a Court case. She also excels in "information" on nearly everyone and everything she works with, around, or against. Amber Duffek operates on the well-oiled premise that everyone has a secret or two he or she tries to keep buried, and she almost always finds out what the secrets are and then "owns" the person she has uncovered, for future "use". Everyone uses everyone, that's the goddamn gospel truth!

"Yes Senator, trust me...it's a good road to take when you don't want the public to know who bought the place, I've known these guys for quite awhile now and do business with them myself regularly, they're shysters....but my kind of shysters, and they'll deal straight with you or I'll have their balls in a jar," Amber said into her tiny cell-phone pressed against her face as she drove through Rosslyn past the Pentagon and onto the Beltway for home, speeding in her BMW and not giving a shit if some cop catches her speeding either!

"Yessir, no problem....I can set it up for this month sometime and let you know when and where, I won't steer you wrong Senator, these guys are going to put that deed in your hand," she concluded then heard the other line go dead, and she dropped her cell-phone into her purse on the seat beside her, speeding onto the Interstate highway with the flow of traffic this evening, the sun setting in the west already reminding her of how long her day has been.

"Fucking Politicians...," she sighed to herself as she wrapped both hands around the steering wheel and relaxed as she headed for her residence just ten minutes from D.C. and five minutes from her Law Office in Rosslyn, Va. right on the Potomac River. She smiled at the thought of setting Senator Rupert Kelsh up for an "under the table" Real Estate deal with the Pillage brothers who hold the deed to some piece of property Kelsh wants. She could further slip both parties deeper into her own debt and use them later on when she needs to. Amber Duffek used everyone around her, even her "friends" and colleagues, though she often admitted that she has no real friends, according to the definition of the term, she has assets and liabilities.....allies and enemies.....gems and lumps of coal......

She pulled into her own driveway minutes later, getting out of her BMW without bothering to lock it, hurrying up to the front door of her house as dusk covered more and more in darkness of the encroaching nightfall. As soon as she slipped her key into the lock, something got her immediate attention....a man stepping into view off to her left side, from out of nowhere, a man flashing an official-looking Federal badge and ID, having been waiting for her to come home this evening no less! Amber turned and tried not to appear frightened by his unannounced (and therefore unwelcome) visitation here at her home.

"Attorney Amber Duffek....Agent Clifford Stevens ATF.... may we speak for a minute in private ma'am?" Special Agent Cliff Stevens spoke up with a calm disposition toward her.

"Oh, alright Agent Stevens....come on in," Amber replied in a cordial tone with a smile, opening her front door and escorting the well-dressed and handsome Fed inside her domicile, against her better judgment, though she sensed it wasn't she who he was after!

"Nice place ya got here Counselor," Cliff said as soon as he entered, looking around.

"Thanks...but you're not a Realtor, so tell me what you wish to discuss Special Agent?" Amber chimed amicably but with a request to get-to-the-point, so Cliff proceeded.

"The Marcano Mob and Faster Productions, both of whom you were retained by in the recent past, both of which you settled cases for and escaped unscathed once those two entities went into the shitter," Cliff spoke in calm honesty, taking into account a lawyer like Amber Duffek, considering her reputation, he could not bullshit for one moment or she'd shut him down. Being "direct" with a woman like this is the best avenue to travel!

"Now even a Federal Agent knows that little thing called attorney-client privilege, even if the client is in the graveyard or a missing person," Amber chimed knowingly as she slowly walked across her luxurious living room toward her kitchen for something alcoholic.

"Yes ma'am...but I am looking for nothing the Marcano Mobsters or those Porn Stars at Faster Productions did specifically, what I need is information on missing money to the tune of about two million dollars, because there are other criminal entities who escaped detection years ago, unrelated to the Marcanos and that porn company," Stevens added frankly as he looked around the swank living room at the woman's décor.

"Ah, you're chasing shadows aren't you?" she giggled from inside the kitchen back at him.

"Hunh, in a way, yes ma'am...which is why I thought I'd come chat with you, off-the-record, for a bit of knowledge you may have regarding other players in that ball game between two-thousand-two and two-thousand-five," Cliff said as he sat down on her sofa.

"I see, well you really should have called my office first, as opposed to stalking me here at my private home Agent Stevens....but that's okay, I do have friends at the Justice Department who'd not take too kindly to you harassing me over ghosts," Amber continued.

Cliff had expected her to threaten him some point in time tonight, so she got that out of the way and he almost laughed at how smooth she did so. Attorney Duffek was a beautiful woman to say the least, and real "looker" from head to toe, but he kept his composure.

"All I want is a shadow who latched onto the Marcanos and Faster Productions to launder money, dirty money as it turns out, nothing to do with the work you did at the time for those two entities," Cliff said matter-of-factly with a smile at her as she walked back out of the kitchen, a glass of white wine in her right hand, not offering him anything of course.

"And you assume I have information about peripheral persons lurking somewhere between the Marcano Family and Faster Productions years ago?" Amber responded girlishly this time.

"Yes, I was hoping you would Counselor," Cliff said frankly, getting straight to the point.

"Heenh, those idiots at the FBI have nothing.....they interviewed me after the fall of Faster Productions that summer, and I had nothing to tell them in regards to shadows," Amber answered in sarcasm, walking around her luxurious living room sipping her drink more.

"I have the FBI file on the matter, but it's got holes in it," Cliff told her frankly, smirking.

"Naturally, the FBI couldn't find a hooker in a whorehouse," Amber sneered in contempt.

"Money-laundering is a Federal crime Miss Duffek, you know that....how about helping me out and I promise the Faster Productions case will never be re-opened to mention your name in any negative way, just point me in the right direction and I'll owe you a favor," Cliff continued, offering her the carrot-and-stick as he had hoped he wouldn't have to do!

"Really…hmmm…a favor….well I happen to like a juicy bribe when I see it," Amber chimed with a sinister smile back at the handsome 40-year old Agent on her sofa now.

"Whatever you want to call it Counselor, we can work this out like adults," Cliff added.

"Oh of course my friend, we can work this out, sure thing," Amber snickered as she walked back to the kitchen and vanished for another minute, making him curious about her reply.

Amber then stepped back into the living room, this time totally-naked except for a string of white pearls around her neck and an apple in her left hand, a carving-knife in the other, slicing off thin layers of the apple to pop into her mouth as she faced her cop visitor with the intention of unsettling him a bit by this nude display.

"If I were you, I'd check out some of the Faster Productions cast-list, some of whom are still alive and living not far from here….like Shaya Gold, she lives in D.C., married to a US Senator actually…. she was a big-shot in that Porn Company up until June of that year, and then there's Shelly James, the Catholic Nun who secretly moon-lighted as a Porn Star for three years, she lives in Loudon County, not far from here…. and, if you're willing to dig deeper, you may want to check out the female Mafia heiress Isabel Marcano, if you can find what's left of her," Amber spoke casually, slicing her apple and popping the bits into her mouth, the mix of her standing there gloriously-naked with a body fit for a cheerleader eating an apple by way of a shiny stainless-steel kitchen knife quite "erotic" to Cliff Stevens.

"Isabel Marcano is a missing person, you know that….," Cliff added for effect.

"I know, and she's likely dead as a doornail….but she had a thing for Jonny Faster the man himself, and I do believe she made contact with him, maybe to 'invest' or somehow cloak herself with legal endeavors since the FBI and the other Mafia Families wanted her pretty head on a plate," Amber continued in brazen retort, smiling at her male guest intently.

"Was she fuckin' Jonny Faster?" Cliff had to ask, sounding blunt as ever of course.

"I think maybe....maybe so, I didn't keep track even though they both were my clients for a short period of time that year, and Jonny Faster was sticking his big dick in so many foolish ladies for sure, if he used that thing on Isabel....I didn't know," Amber said softly.

"Maybe Isabel was just a fan of Porn Flicks," Amber said with a shrug, then walked across her living room in a casual stride as if she still had clothes on, not caring about being nude in front of a Federal Agent who came here to politely grill her over past criminals.

"Funny isn't it...how Isabel Marcano, the female 'boss' of the Marcano Mob during the final year of that syndicate's existence and Jonny Faster, owner and operator of Faster Productions, the single biggest east coast Porn Film Production Company which unceremoniously shut-down around the same time that summer..... both Jonny and Isabel going 'missing' within the same time-frame?" Cliff spoke boldly, studying Amber's reaction.

"Yes it is funny Agent Stevens, very funny but tragic....," Amber sighed as she walked slow.

"Tragic because they were your clients?" Cliff chimed in his own brand of sarcasm now.

"Nope, tragic because I would have preferred to have had Isabel safe in my own bed, and I'd liked to have had Jonny Faster's unholy schlong cut off then stuffed-n-mounted and placed in a Feminist Museum somewhere, his balls pickled in a jar.....the rest of him barbecued and served to the homeless," Amber replied with a sly smirk crossing her moon-shaped face as she turned to look back at Agent Stevens standing up from her sofa now.

"Wow, they were fortunate to have a Lawyer such as you," Cliff added in added sarcasm, watching her lovely-shaped bare body walk toward a flight of stairs in a long hallway now, that ass of hers like the ass of a college cheerleader with a slight "jiggle" in the left cheek.

"Yes they were...and you're fortunate too Agent Stevens," Amber said with her back to him as she stepped to the stairwell to go upstairs and take a long, hot shower after a day's work.

"How's that Counselor?" Cliff chuckled as he turned to leave out the way he came in.

"Heenh, all you have to do now is keep on this path Agent man, and you'll find what and whom you're looking for, only catch is, your perpetrator may be someone you'd least suspect all along....trust me big guy, you're on the right track if you want to catch a ghost," Amber concluded as she vanished up the stairs and out of his sight, Agent Stevens shaking his head.

He left the house of Attorney Duffek with about as much as he expected to get from someone like her, though he still "interviewed" her just to shake things up. Perhaps now someone will target him for getting too close, least that's why he just ruined Miss Duffek's evening with a surprise visit. Getting back in his car he reminded himself to keep a loose tab on Attorney Amber Duffek as a "peripheral" suspect.

Greensboro, North Carolina. October 12th: The dusk had finally settled in and one man who could not walk in daylight was able to leave his motel room under another name and venture forth into his current mission. The target was a low-profile Congressman who was about to become a high-profile Vice Presidential Nominee in the upcoming 2008 election!

Duncan Horsehair was alone but not alone, his "lone wolf" backup just a mile away and ready to blow some shit up upon getting his cell-phone indication. The Congressman was in a Hotel here in downtown Greensboro with his mistress, and no security, which made this hit all the more easy but not as much "fun" for the man who has killed scores of people since 1995, all for a singular purpose.....

Clayton J. Musselman was relaxing inside the hotel suite on the top floor of the Regency, near to falling asleep after making love to Marina, his younger mistress from Mexico who he was helping get a green-card to remain in the US legally, leas that is what he told her he was doing for her in exchange for sexual liasions from time to time. The 50-year old senior Congressman from Raleigh had no worries in the world right now, the only thing he could hear right now as he closed his eyes was the sound of the shower going as Marina bathed in the suite's bathroom. He didn't even hear the room's door softly "click" open, and his senses fell into the first level of slumber as an intruder silently stepped into the darkened hotel room, letting the door close but not all the way to produce another "click" sound.

Duncan Horsehair wanted a stealthy kill this time when he carried out the hit personally, stepping up to the target on the bed, once again marveled by the sight of how out-of-shape this politician was, how easy he'd be to choke the life from. This was an easy kill, and he made it that way, using the same carving knife from the room service tray here in the room, a knife that would still have the mistress' fingerprints on it most likely, an easy weapon to cleave straight through the old man's heart in one swift swing! Old man Musselman didn't know what hit him as the kitchen knife plunged through his ribs to slice through his beating heart without fail. Death was appallingly quick, the man thrashing on the bed for a moment's reaction then all stopped and he lay there with eyes open, a dead man's gaze upon the darkly-clad individual standing over him. Duncan Horsehair missed not having someone to fight, an opponent who would actually fight back, someone who like him, would have easily heard an intruder and responded accordingly. No, "sheep" don't fight back.....they just die!

He was out of the room by the time the mistress finished her shower, and well before the screams following the Hispanic mistress discovering a knife buried in her dead lover's chest.

The blame for the murder would fall on the mistress whose fingerprints would be on the knife from earlier use eating dinner, and of course the Authorities would naturally assume it was the mistress who may have motive to stage her lover's murder......

Once he was street-side, Duncan Horsehair moved on foot down a dark back alleyway toward his parked vehicle two blocks west of the Hotel, having avoided the cameras in the Hotel lobby by raising his jacket's hood over his head and walking the left side perimeter of the lobby out of immediate range of the clerk-side security cam. He knew his "job" well, having done this sort of thing for over ten years now, with much success...despite the sometimes mind-numbing boredom "between" missions. Answering to Senator Kelsh was often frustrating his own thirst for vengeance upon the society he was once sworn to protect and defend. The dark alleyway was not without it's denizens, a male vagrant stepping into his path to beg for money, the bum dispatched to death by Duncan's kick and follow-up of chokehold-twist to break the man's neck. The bum's corpse flopped to the pavement in the dark alleyway as Duncan Horsehair walked on to the other end, slipping away in shadows as if he were merely a shadow himself.

BATFE Alexandria Va. Field Office. 9:20 that night: Agent Stevens was happy to have the VHS videotape despite it's often shaky footage from time to time making him feel a bit dizzy as he watched. First fifteen minutes was entertaining as it showed a man and a woman screwing their brains loose on a deck chair by the swimming pool one evening back in 2002. Cliff remembered this because he was across the street peering at the lovers through binoculars at the same time back then, and he knew who they were: Attorney Diego Tanner and "Professional Escort" Danielle Kenyon, both of whom are MISSING PERSONS to this very day! Danielle was a hot blonde cupcake of a woman age 25 at the time, and Diego Tanner was a light-skinned black man around 30 years of age and Marcano Attorney, both of them going-at-it at dusk up by the pool for about fifteen minutes that night. The neighbor kid's birds-eye view of them got closer than his binoculars did at the time, showing Danielle's pretty face in grimacing passion while riding up and down on Diego Tanner's manhood, "sitting" facing him in his lap on the pool's deck chair near the pool's ledge.

"What a freak," Cliff sighed to himself as he watched the entire footage, wondering what happened to both that hot blonde Danielle Kenyon and Diego Tanner, both of whom vanished right about the same time-frame in late 2003. The home-video then switched to another night at the swimming pool, thanks to the pool-lights the viewer was able to see pretty well, this time another young woman stepped into view, another woman Cliff recognized as a "regular" at the Marcano house at 1705 Beverly Lane in Fredericksburg.

"Isabel Marcano," he said outloud as he watched the footage here in the ATF Office's screening room on a 27-inch TV set, alone with his research into ghosts of the past.

The statuesque, olive-skinned Italian-American Bella stepped to the deep end of the pool and peeled off her bathrobe, making Cliff smiled as he watched her dive into the water naked, skinny-dipping as he had seen her do several times back then while casing the place from across the street. Back then it helped the big brick house directly across from the Marcano property was empty of it's deceased owner and ATF got the estate's permission to use it for "police surveillance" during the 60-day period prior to a brand new owner taking possession of it. Sixty days and nights was enough to determine the Marcanos were using the place as a "crash pad" but nothing worth watching except the Mob Boss' niece Isabel and her blonde friend Danielle. The video footage continued showing Isabel's nude swim that night in the summer of 2002, a leisurely exercise of over 20 laps from one end of the pool to another, then Isabel stopped at the deep-end, hanging onto the ledge and still all by herself.

"What, no boyfriends coming to join you skinny-dipping?" Cliff chuckled to the TV screen.

Cliff watched Isabel then go underwater, swimming all the way to the bottom of the pool's 8-foot deep end, staying under for about a full minute he guessed, then she re-surfaced in the shallow end and stood up, wiping her face and hair with both hands. The video camera then zoomed in on her standing there in the shallow end, those big tits of hers glistening wet on that hot night. Cliff wanted to thank the horny teenage "peeping-tom" who filmed this spy-video of his neighbor.....not bad for an idiot armed with a cheap video-camera!

Isabel then crawled up out of the pool at the shallow end, not bothering to grab her bathrobe, standing there on the cement pool deck totally nude and dripping wet, her hands wiping her face, eyes, and soaked dark hair which came down to her collarbones. She was a beautiful woman despite her affliction of "Helios-Porpheria" a genetic flaw which keeps the skin from direct contact with sunlight unless the person with the condition wants one hell of a painful suntan! Cliff watched as the kid's video-camera panned left, following the well-built Isabel Marcano's naked physique as she walked the length of the pool deck to the chain-link fence between the hillside pool area and the brick house. She had a great ass too, the kind jiggles ever-so-slightly as she walked.....then the video went black once more.

The next footage was of the pool area once again at night, the pool lights once again illuminating the footage captured by the cheap video-camera back in Summer of '02.

This time Attorney Diego Tanner stepped into view fully-clothed and holding a rather large suitcase with his left hand, walking across the pool deck along the ledge, stopping once another figure stepped into view over at the pool's deep end. A man clad in a black duster coat with dark hair and a ballcap on his head, hands in his coat pockets as Diego Tanner placed the big suitcase down about four feet from the man in black.

"Ah...exchange!" Cliff snapped in realization, moving closer to the TV screen to try and make out the second man in the video footage, not one he could recognize because the image was of the man's right side, a profile. The video then went black again.

"Shit....you sawed-off little bastard, dammit!" Cliff barked at the TV screen in frustration, certain the teenager stopped filming that meeting back then because no naked women were around for him to gawk at and film! Cliff fast-forwarded the tape which had a lot of dead space on it, then another ream of footage popped up, this time not of the pool deck but aimed toward the front yard of the Marcano "safe house" from the neighbor's front yard, this time right about at dusk on a clear evening that same summer. It was shaky of course since the peeping teenager was holding his video-camera on his own shoulder as he filmed the front yard of the place, zooming slowly directly up to the front door.

"Alright damn you....what are you waiting to see?" Cliff asked the TV screen, wondering what and why the kid was filming toward the front of the house for back then. Then he could see someone exiting the front door suddenly, and he saw that person to be Isabel Marcano once again, this time leaving the house alone and dressed-to-kill in one of those sleek mini-dresses some women (built like her) were born to wear! She vanished into the lower carport and driveway on the other side of the house, out of range of the camera.

The film then went black again and no more footage was left, as if the kid had perhaps switched to another tape or didn't record anymore of the Marcanos. Cliff ejected the tape and decided to have it analyzed by the video-forensics lab at Quantico, try and sharpen the image of that man in black with Attorney Diego Tanner by the pool that night in 2002.

Cliff reached over to the chair next to him here in the office space he had all to himself since the Alexandria ATF team were now all participating in an illegal-weapons raid over in Fairfax County. There he had three DVDs with colorful and provocative covers, all three of the DVD films being Rated XXX and purchased by him online for the purpose of this "unauthorized" investigation. Afterall, he did have to check out a now-defunct Porn Film Company's final months where it's believed two million dollars of Mafia money was secretly laundered! He waited until he had the office pretty much all to himself tonight so that some bed-wetting liberal civilian staffer or female Agent wouldn't be "offended" by him watching pornographic material and complain to the higher-ups. The former Porn Film Company

Faster Productions had a small but dedicated "cast list" over the last five years of it's existence and Cliff had obtained the names and locations of the former porn stars he felt might be able to shed some light on whether or not Jonny Faster and crew were complicit in laundering $2 million in cash for the Marcano Mob during it's final days with Isabel Marcano at the helm! Shaya Gold, Shelly James, Leesa Teasa, Woodrow Grande were some of the "aliases" he found real-identities on and located in the here-and-now. Some were easy to interview, like "Woodrow Grande" who was serving time for attempted-murder in Attica Prison up in New York, but a few of the others were not so easily-approachable such as the voluptuous "Shaya Gold" who was now Mrs. Shaya Kelsh, wife of US Senator Rupert Kelsh!

Cliff would take interviewing carefully and only the ones he feels his "case" necessarily requires, no sense in stirring up a hornet's nest when one of the directives given him from Deputy Attorney General Tyler Clark last week was "keep away from the news media" so he didn't want to spark a news report about a Federal Agent investigating Porn Stars….though he realized he was taking a risk confronting Attorney Amber Duffek the other night. Somehow though, he didn't think she would drop the Press on his tail when she is not exactly "clean" of dirt from the "Faster Murders" case of 2005 and those questions one newspaper threw out years ago about her being a "Lawyer in bed with the Mob".

He looked at the three X-rated DVD movies in his hands, one of them being a 1998 feature entitled: Big Bustin' Loose starring Shaya Gold, Carla Ferrari, Christy Cannons, Dick Maestro, and F.M. Dexter. Cliff found Shaya Gold on the cover with a bandana around her head and a slinky grin on her pretty face while a black man hugged her from behind with hands on her bikini-covered breasts while a white male actor stuck his head up between her thighs grinning for the camera. Cliff had to laugh at the X-rated film's box cover, typical of the type of "flick" actually. It did not star Jonny Faster in it but Jonny Faster directed it!

The second DVD was called Jonny's Girls and was a compilation of various sex-scenes between the legendary male Porn Star Jonny Faster and the female Starlets he'd screwed on film of course. It had all of the female starlet names on Cliff's list in it, all of them paired up with the horse-hung Jonny Faster.

The third DVD he bought online was a fairly new release (2006) which was a "collection" of short sex-scenes done by various Directors and was titled: Swedish ErotiXXX #19 and it featured one 12-minute "short" starring Shelly James and Ray Fury called "Job Interview" which was noted on the back of the box-cover to be "Faster's Final", denoting it had been the last pornographic sex-scene filmed by the now-defunct Faster Productions.

Part of many an investigation owed it's mettle to the Investigator looking back into the past at certain points within the scope of the case, and since he was technically researching a Porn syndicate, he had to see what these people did on film, see what they look like, as well as get a thrill watching a type of "film" most people don't watch on a regular basis, some not ever in their entire lives. Cliff had seen some porno flicks back when he was in College almost 20 years ago, but wasn't one (up until now) to ever actually buy and view X-rated!

"Alright ladies and gentlemen…and I say that lightly…..here we go," Cliff snickered to himself as he put in the first DVD into the TV's player and picked up the remote, glancing around the offices around this one to make sure once again, noone else was nearby to see.

He chose to watch the "Swedish Erotixxx" ensemble first, which had what was reputed to be the "final" Faster Productions sex-scene in it entitled: "Job Interview".

The opening credits rolled then the screen lit up with the interior of some "office" much like the one he was sitting and watching this in, then a gorgeous blonde vixen dressed in a pin-striped ladies' pantsuit and tie stepped into view, "Shelly James" in-character with her blonde hair pinned up in a tight bun at the back of her head, pair of big-framed eyeglasses on. She walked around a big wooden desk and sat down behind it as if she were a Corp. hot-shot.

Then a well-dressed athletic-built black man steps into view and calmly introduces himself to the blonde "boss" across the desk from him, beginning the "job interview". He sits down and prattles on about himself and his qualifications for the job in business management with the company that he applied for. The camera zooms in slowly on Shelly James' face as she quietly listens to the "applicant" telling about himself and his qualifications, her pensive expression one denoting her starting to "daydream" and the film began to "flurry"…..

The next sight appearing on the screen in clear focus was of Shelly James with her blonde hair down and all of her clothes off, kneeling before an equally-naked black male co-star

("Ray Fury") eagerly taking his schlong in her mouth for fervent fellatio as he stood there in what looked like a spare bedroom of some house, no longer an office-setting of course.

"Oh yeeaah...baby...yeeahh...that's it," Ray spoke softly to the bobbing blonde head orally servicing his rock solid manhood, her right hand gripping the base of his big dick as she slurped on him without fail. The camera zoomed in on the oral sex to show Shelly's mouth absorbing the manhood almost half it's length, back and forth in steady, convincing fellatio.

She sucked co-star's dick fiendishly for the camera, the scene lasting about a minute or more, then suddenly switched to Shelly James lying on the bed with legs spread wide for Ray to eat between them in a quick oral reciprocation, gearing up for the obvious intercourse to come.

"Oooohh.....oooonnnh....yesss!" Shelly quipped in delighted tone, looking down at her lover, pawing at his head in ecstasy of the act, then the man rose up to begin intercourse.

Next scene was of Ray ramming his spear inside Shelly missionary-style, steadily pumping into her flesh without reservation, which made Cliff chuckle at the sight...porno flicks like this one don't mess around with foreplay, they just go-to-it! The camera zoomed in on Ray kissing Shelly's face as he drilled her like that, her face a mask of raw ecstasy, eyes closed and mouth wide open....the scene then changed to Shelly on top of Ray, sliding his meat up inside of her as she straddled his hips, moving up and down on his pole in continuity, moaning in delight of the penetration as Ray reached his hands up to paw her jiggling boobs.

Cliff guessed Shelly to have about a 36D chest at the least, great perky tits too and nice ass!

Watching the film as it continued, with Shelly James bouncing up and down on Ray Fury's manhood in an easy motion, Cliff guessed this scene was probably filmed quickly and on a low-budget for the compilation DVD it ended up on, perhaps filmed days before the collapse of the Company up in New York?! Watching the interracial sex scene on the TV screen, seeing how the camera zoomed in and out to show the penetrating portions for a minute or so then settled approximately four feet from the bed and just filmed Shelly "riding" on Ray in passionate intercourse, her hands on his muscled chest as he reached hands up to caress her bouncy boobs every few seconds.....

and that's what was seen for the next five minutes or so, then as Shelly became more vocal in orgasmic relish and Ray groaned in delight from under her, the camera panned to her backside showing his spear impaling her steadily, then after a couple more seconds he pulled out of her and climaxed.

"The money-shot", Cliff laughed as he remembered the porn-slang for a man's climax.

Then Shelly and Ray rolled over in the bed together kissing, settling to a halt sprawled out on the bed together, their nude bodies lying entwined, her blonde head on his upper chest.

The scene then reverted back to the "job interview" with the clothed and bespectacled Shelly James looking up at the clothed black man Ray Fury who just finished his schpeel for a job.

"Well sir, it appears you're qualified....and I do happen to have an opening right here in my department....so you're hired!" Shelly spoke up gingerly as she stood to shake his hand now.

"Thank you ma'am, you won't regret it...I'll work hard for you," Ray said graciously as she led him back to the door of the office. "Oh I know you will," Shelly said in a slinky tone as she ushered him out the door, turning her pretty head toward the camera and winked.

Cliff stopped the DVD, not caring to see the other film "shorts" by other porn companies and directors. This X-rated "short" entitled Job Interview had been directed by Shaya Gold according to the back cover credits of the DVD case. That scene was one that played to the "taboo" of interracial sex, especially since Shelly James was a knockout blonde! he thought. Cliff ejected it from the DVD player and put in another one: Jonny's Girls.

Kelsh Residence, Georgetown. 10:05 that night: Harold McCassler was impressed to say the least, finding the Georgetown residence of US Senator Rupert Kelsh luxurious but sort of "bachelor" in décor he thought as he was led into the warm domicile by the Senator who invited him here tonight for a late dinner.....a very late dinner actually, considering the two of them had been working for the past six hours at his office on Capitol Hill drafting text for his final draft of the Crime Bill he wishes to pass by end of the year. For a Senate Page, 18-year old Harold McCassler was at the end of his tenure in the Senate Page program, hoping to attend Georgetown University.....though "affirmative-action" was stopping that!

"Wow, Senator, you got a nice place here sir," the young brown-haired man spoke as he walked on in to the swank living room, looking around as he smelled something good cooking over in the kitchen already. Senator Kelsh had mentioned his wife Shaya would have a light meal waiting for them, and Harold looked forward to finally meeting the Senator's wife in-person after seeing her in the 2006 photo on the wall in the Senator's office for the past year. Harold had heard the rumors about Senator Kelsh's wife being an ex-porno star and all that stuff, but he wondered what she'd be like to meet in real-life?

"Thanks...I'll introduce you to Shaya," Rupert said as he removed his grey blazer and stepped into the kitchen only to find a pot roast in the steamy crockpot and a pitcher of iced tea on the counter, but no sign of Shaya. He had to guess she might be using the bathroom or upstairs doing something, maybe working-out down in their basement "rec. room".

"I'll show you the upstairs Harold, come with me," Rupert Kelsh said with a laugh as he walked out from the kitchen and over toward the stairwell leading up to the upper floor.

The young Caucasian student-to-be followed him eagerly, marveled by the ancient splendor of the old Georgetown home right off the Key Bridge and just atop of the famous "Exorcist" steps, those long cement steps leading from M Street to Prospect and Canal featured in the violent climax of the 1973 horror classic "The Exorcist".

The upper floor was just as simple but luxurious as Kelsh led his young guest through it, even showing him his private "den" where he spends many nights alone, the kid noticing the well-stocked liquor cabinet and three TV screens perched on another wall. Rupert could hear the faint sound of a shower in use just down the hallway, and rightly assumed it was his wife.

"Come and I'll introduce you to my lovely wife," he said suddenly, his Page following him close in the darkened hallway until he stopped at the door of a bathroom, opening it to reveal steam from a recurring hot shower and the lovely shape of his naked wife in the shower stall through it's clear-plastic curtain! Harold McCassler froze in realization of what he was now invited to look at, stunned even further as the well-shaped woman behind the shower-curtain pulled it open to see the two men looking at her through the open doorway.

"Hey honey," Shaya said to her husband standing in the doorway with a much younger man standing nervously beside him not wanting to look but did anyway!

"Shaya…meet my loyal Page Harold McCassler…..Harold, this is my wife Shaya," Rupert spoke casually in introduction, pointing to the voluptuous bare body of a woman in the shower as she faced the two intruders naked and dripping-wet with hot water and suds.

"Oooooh…I heard of you Harold….nice to meet'cha big guy," Shaya crooned sleazily at the nervous young man in the doorway, his eyes glued to her big, glistening boobs as she spoke.

"Uhhhmmm….hello Mrs. Kelsh, nice to….meet …you as well… ma'am," Harold slowly stammered in response, licking his dry lips as the Senator held him still with hand on arm.

"I got dinner heating up down in the kitchen guys, gimme a minute and I'll be down," Shaya said impishly then closed the clear-plastic curtain to complete her hot shower quickly, her husband closing the door back and escorting their guest back downstairs. Harold was at a loss for words over such an unconventional "introduction".

Alexandria, Va. (same time): Agent Clifford Stevens relaxed in the swivel-chair watching the X-rated feature "Jonny's Girls" focusing on scenes showing the women on his short list of "approachable" former porn stars who worked for Faster Productions up until the end.

This one was a scene from a past film with Jonny Faster and Shaya Gold going-at-it inside of what appeared to be a restaurant's kitchen (after-hours).

"Hunh-hunh-haah…..now that's what I call….'stove-top-stuffing!" Cliff laughed to himself as he watched Jonny Faster engaging Shaya Gold in an inclined intercourse while she sat on the ledge of a big restaurant-sized grill-stove, her bare legs dangling behind his pumping backside, the two naked bodies grinding together in passion's grip atop the stove as the camera panned around them for the best angles. Jonny Faster was a muscular White man with Nordic good-looks and chiseled physique not to mention a foot-long torpedo he was launching inside the buxom and exotic Shaya Gold on the stove as she sat up there in what had to be a less-than-comfortable leaning-position Cliff imagined. The man was really "driving it home" as Shaya quaked under his onslaught, their bodies grinding together in an attractive union of fit, well-formed physicality...... which always makes for a great porn flick.

"Onnnhh....oooaaaannhh....yeeeaaaaahh......oaaannnnhh.... doahhnn't-sssss-top!" Shaya cried out in obvious orgasm as Jonny Faster continued drilling her like a champ, the camera then focusing on his pumping hind-quarters muscling his meat into her then zoomed in on the actual penetration between their thumping bodies, the prodigious man-meat sliding into warm, delicious womanhood. Kinda made Cliff wish he hadn't broken up with his last girlfriend... the slightly-overweight Molly Deacon who worked as a Law Clerk here in town.

Molly was no Shaya Gold, but female companionship was preferable over nothing at all!

"Give it to her Jonny....hunh-hunh, give'er what she deserves.... hunh-haanh, wherever your ass ended up after August of Oh-Five, least you got to hammer all kinds of ladies during your career..... shit, my job chases women away," Cliff said to the TV screen as he watched Jonny Faster and Shaya Gold fucking on the restaurant stove top for minutes more.

Something about Jonny Faster, a man whose real name was not "confirmed" during the NCIC check he ran on the man last week, just his aliases and the fact he was "missing" and wanted by the New York State Police BCI for questioning regarding the death of a former New York State Trooper Raymond J. Flintlock who had been secretly employed as one of Faster Productions' male "performers" from Sept. 2004 to his murder in late July 2005.

Cliff had just watched what was reputed to be the "last film" produced by Faster in 2005, the "short" flick with Ray sticking it to the blonde porn starlet Shelly James. Which reminded him again to pick himself up a copy of the autobiography written by her, a book aptly entitled "I am Shelly James" by Shelly James with K.R. Knight. Cliff hated to read but there may be something in the book worth reading, perhaps something mentioning shit he needs to know about the end of that goddamn porn film company and Mafia money that could uncover who the goddamn domestic terrorist is he's been assigned to track down!

Next scene on the X-rated DVD was of Jonny Faster and a huge-chested strawberry-blonde "Leesa Teasa" in a sauna....well-crafted bodies glistening with sweat and gorging in sexual congress made for a great porn flick, Cliff mused as he watched the well-endowed man thrusting into the overly-busty female "doggie-style" while on a wooden bench inside a sauna room. How they kept the camera lens from steaming-over was a mystery but it had worked, the camera zooming in on Jonny sliding his kielbasa inside Leesa's sweet spot from behind, his hands gripping her well-filled-out ass while he pumped into her. The woman had big titties Cliff imagined must have been well over 50DD or EE! Something uniquely entertaining about watching well-shaped men and women screwing their brains loose......

Georgetown, 11:00pm: Despite the fact the pot roast was "leftovers" Harold McCassler couldn't remember the last time he had enjoyed such a fabulous meal like this one in the recent past. His parents were both decent cooks but this late dinner was all the better perhaps not only because the food was good....but the woman who cooked it was such alluring company, seated across from the 18-year old male guest at her dinner table tonight.

Mrs. Shaya Kelsh served her husband and his Senate Page at the dinner table wearing just one of her tight-fitting silk bathrobes that barely covered her more appealing regions, her plump breasts bulging against the fabric as if to pop out at any time. Eating the hot and delicious meal nervously, the young man couldn't help but to envy Senator Kelsh for having such a smoking-hot and delicious-looking wife!

"So Harold, you plan on attending Georgetown University hunh?" she asked him to restart an earlier conversation about his plans for the future, making Harold smile in agreement.

"Yes ma'am…hopefully, my letter of intent goes in next month," Harold told her politely, again glancing at those big breasts of hers barely covered by the blue silk robe, trying not to look at her big tits but failing. She smiled at him knowingly, enjoying the fact she made him nervous and the fact her husband "showed her off" again by introducing her to a male friend while she was in the shower. Shaya enjoyed how Rupert enjoyed showing off his "Trophy"!

"Well Harold, don't place all of your faith in what they call 'higher learning' because you learn more about what life is all about by experiencing it…out there in the real world," Shaya explained frankly, noticing her husband sitting at the head of the big dining table forming a slight smile on his ruggedly-handsome face upon hearing her say that to Harold.

"Still, a Degree is better than nothing," Rupert said with a slight chuckle, eyes down at his plate which still had food on it, deciding whether to finish his meal or not. Shaya glanced at him knowing that remark was aimed at her own lack of education, something her husband had often chided her about, having only her GED when he had a Masters Degree.

"I just want to study Medicine at Georgetown University, hopefully become a Doctor eventually….and my father went there…. same Graduating Class as Bill Clinton," Harold said in his still-nervous tone, glancing over at Senator Kelsh then back at his wife Shaya.

"Hmmph, I wouldn't tell too many people that," Kelsh chuckled with a quick scowl.

"Rupert hated Clinton as President," Shaya whispered impishly across the table at him, smiling slinky at her husband then taking another swig of her wineglass.

"He was a Leftist in Moderate disguise…..a real weasel," Rupert snickered in response.

"I never even registered to vote, so I could care less who is President as long as there's food on my table and a roof over my head," Shaya said frankly, staring across at Harold there.

"I voted for the first time this year," Harold told them with a shrug, then took another sip of the delicious, tangy red wine he was not legally old enough to be drinking.

"Good, but I might add that voting by itself is not enough to really change anything, because Republicans and Democrats are all on the same team especially at the higher levels," Rupert said to his Senate Page seated on his right still nervous as they conversed. A nervous and insecure man is a useful one, easier to manipulate Rupert reminded himself silently.

"They're all screwing each other, sleeping with each other's wives, and snorting cocaine together in the private bathrooms on Capitol Hill," Shaya whispered impishly in a hurry.

Harold looked at the Senator for his response to that and he was in agreement with her.

"Most of the career-politicians are exactly like that and the ones who are queer....pederasts, and wife-beaters often get blackmailed by their colleagues and thus vote a certain way when called upon to do so," Rupert said matter-of-factly. Harold knew quite a few Senators in office right now have "issues" but he never heard of any of them being blackmailed. None of them ever propositioned him, unlike some of the other Senate Pages experienced!

"Ya know Harold....the Senator here is a veteran of the Grenada Invasion back in nineteen-eighty-three, back when he was a Captain in the US Army," Shaya said next.

"Really....Grenada....I read about it sir," Harold responded hesitantly with a smile.

Rupert shot his chesty wife a mild scowl, reacting to her payback for the veiled remark earlier aimed at the fact she never graduated high school. She had teased him about his combat role in the Invasion of Grenada almost 25 years ago, since it was just a few days of fighting and the enemy was crushed almost immediately.

"The Military got me where I am today," he told his young guest with a smirk at Shaya.

"A Senior Senator from New Jersey and married to me," Shaya quipped girlishly.

"Ah, my dear....your lovely form and superior wit is what got me married to you," Rupert added jokingly, making her laugh in response, then she swilled more of her red wine.

"You're a great cook Mrs. Kelsh," Harold spoke up suddenly in uncomfortable speech.

"Thanks Harold, and please call me Shaya," she chimed with a smile and a wink at him.

"You haven't had my wife's dessert yet Harold, so don't thank her yet," Rupert Kelsh spoke in his slightly-yankee-accented voice, standing up from the dining table and leaving it slowly.

"You're a good worker Harold, a real nose-to-the-grindstone kind of guy, and I like that but I still wonder how you are as far as loyalty goes.....bear in mind that you might not make it into Georgetown University to study Medicine....or any other major University for that matter, even with your Micro-Biologist Father's alumni status," The Senator spoke gentlemanly as he walked away from the table toward the liquor cabinet against one wall.

Shaya sat there across the dining table from the nervous young man just staring at him.

"You're a sharp and talented white male in the prime of his youth Harold....in this Country, in this day and age, that alone can put you behind the eight-ball....affirmative-action programs and minority-entry quotas will trip you up in University applications....deny you the benefits of all your hard work just so that some inferior-intellect who happens to be black, hispanic, asian, or some kind of mixed mutt can have your place at the table in the name of bullshit fairness and 'equality'....," Rupert continued as he poured himself a drink.

Shaya smiled at the stunned young man as he sat there absorbing what the Senator just said.

"For decades now America had denied the best of it's youth the fruits of their own labor and instituted a quasi-socialist system of give-aways that rob the nation of it's best and most productive and replace them with the have-nots and the stupid....my young friend, skin-color is just that, a color....but what you don't learn about from

Marxist Professors in those Universities is that INTELLIGENCE matters most, and with the most intelligent and productive class of American society being shoved aside and 'dummed down' by these liberal laws and softened standards, the future looks more and more....like hell," Rupert continued frankly, turning back to walk toward the dining room again, noticing Harold sitting there stunned by what he was hearing, trying to decide whether what the Senator just spoke was either "racist" or something he himself secretly agreed with!

"Honey...Harold here is cool with that, he's going to get into Georgetown University regardless aren't you Harry?" Shaya chimed as she leaned forward on the dining table a bit, accenting her big boobs bulging in the silk robe she wore by pressing them against the table.

"Uhhmm....yes ma'am, sure....," Harold said as he scooted back from the table now.

Shaya then stood up and stepped to the head of the table where Rupert had been sitting, eyeing her husband as he approached her slowly, his gaze on their young male guest.

The Senator then pulled the silk draw-string of his wife's robe in front, opening the garment to reveal her awesome assets underneath a she stood at the dining table looking at Harold, expecting her husband to do this, further stunning the nervous young man sitting there.

The robe fell from her shapely body to the rug at her bare feet, the voluptuous Mrs. Kelsh standing there at the head of the table completely naked with a ginger smile denoting she had no problem with her older husband showing her off like this, Harold awestruck as he stared at those big boobs of hers, the washboard tummy and inviting dark-haired muff between her smooth, athletic legs. For a woman of 40, she was intensely young-looking and like Harold recalled a friend of his saying once: "built like a brick-shithouse!"

"Work hard, play your cards right, stay loyal to those who help you....and one day you can have a wife like this Harold.....now please excuse me while I take my lovely wife upstairs and fuck her.... good night," Senator Rupert Kelsh spoke calmly as he hugged Shaya with his right arm into him, ushering her around to the other side of the dining table leading out of their dining room toward the dark hallway and the stairwell leading to the upper rooms.

Shaya was surprised, pleasantly, because she had been expecting Rupert to offer her to his young Page tonight, something he'd done before to men he wanted loyalty from, but this was a twist of plans, and she liked it....arm around him as they walked away from the stunned young man still seated at their dining table, pretty much speechless in reaction.

"Lock the door behind you on the way out Harry...nice meeting you finally....heenh-heeh, take it easy and don't be a stranger!" Shaya called back to their guest as Rupert gripped a hand on her bare ass, walking with her to the dark hallway for the stairs, the 18-year old Senate Page still sitting there at the dining table staring at the couple now vanishing into the upper ramparts of their old Georgetown home here in D.C.

"Wow...," Harold sighed to himself as he stood up from the table finally, still looking in the direction where Senator Kelsh and his big-boobed, way-too-hot wife Shaya disappeared, the image of her well-filled-out bare body still lingering in his mind, arousing him greatly.

He had yet to be with a girl himself, still a male-virgin at age 18 and hating that fact! Why the Senator would show him his wife like that was a wonder, but then again, just like his older sister Jill told him once: "politicians and men in positions of power often have sexual issues they have to deal with". That might explain why there are numerous homosexual Senators and Congressmen on Capitol Hill, as well as one who likes to flaunt his "trophy wife" in front of other guys, even someone like me, Harold thought as he picked up the silk robe Mrs. Kelsh had been wearing moments ago. It smelled really nice, one of those super-expensive perfumes no doubt, along with her natural musk scent, holding it to his face.

"To have a wife like that.....yeah, no kidding....something to work hard for," Harold said to himself as he walked from the dining room toward the front door, still holding the silk robe Shaya Kelsh had been worn during dinner earlier. It was late now and time for him to get back to the Page quarters a mile or so from here before he gets in trouble or gets mugged! This may be Georgetown but it was still the "People's Republic of D.C." as he has heard Senator Kelsh call it before. He opened the front door slowly so as to not make any sound, looking over at the stairs imagining Senator Kelsh enjoying the fruits of his beautiful (and much younger) wife up there in their bedroom now. As soon as he took the first step out the front door onto the cement steps, Harold almost didn't want to leave just yet, thinking about getting a look-see upstairs at Shaya with the Senator. It was then he was stunned by the fact someone else was on the front stoop behind him, someone with greater strength and the audacity to usher him right back into the Kelsh residence by force, followed by two other dark-clad men he didn't recognize, three male intruders letting themselves into Senator Kelsh's home here in Georgetown and Harold just opened the front door for them!

"Jeezus.....who are you....?" Harold stammered in reaction to the push-in intrusion, eyes on the three older men muscling him back inside, two white males and one a bald black man.

"Shut up kid...where's Kelsh and his bitch?" the older "leader" of the trio spoke.

"Rupert....," Shaya sighed in her kittenish voice of sensual demeanor, crossing the threshold of their master bedroom on his arm, eyeballing him in wonder of he was serious about what he told their guest downstairs or just pretending for the "looks" of it. He didn't let go of her arm as they entered the bedroom, smiling ever-so-slightly at her pretty face while his free hand unfastened his pants in front. He was serious! she decided happily.

"Oh baby, yes!" she hissed at him as she knelt before him to eagerly worship the manhood about to be loosed from his dress-slacks as he stood there two feet from their marital bed.

It was not often her husband wants sex with her, so she jumped at the chance when it came.

Taking his man-meat in hand as soon as he opened his pants, Shaya indulged him greedily as she had done countless times with her lovers, fellatio being a well-received talent of hers.

"Yesssss....Shaaayyaaahh....you're soooo....good at that," Rupert sighed in agreement as he stood there while his naked wife orally-serviced him, taking nearly his entire length in her mouth as she slurped on his rock-solid erection. Of course she realized it was the young man downstairs earlier who inspired this....her 60-year old husband suddenly "vexed" by the idea of her seducing Harold tonight, which was his original plan, becoming aroused enough to take her himself after telling the young man to split.

"Oooohh...my husband....you know...I love it when you want me," Shaya cooed up to him for the moment she freed her mouth from the tip of his spear, then gleefully resumed fellatio on her husband's boner as he stood there, running a hand through her long, silky dark hair.

Rupert looked around the bedroom with a smile crossing his face now, the type of smile rarely appearing on his visage, but there was nothing better than having a beautiful woman "worship" one's manhood like this....so he smiled like he rarely does anymore these days.

Shaya ran her hands up his chest, unbuttoning his shirt and tie now in suggestion they go to the bed and make this a formal lovemaking, not just a quickie blowjob like she'd done for him a few times before. She could tell he wanted her for more as well, especially after he pulled her to her feet and then gently ushered her onto their marital bed, quickly stripping off the rest of his clothes and tossing them all over the bedroom in excited melee.

"Ooaaah...Ruuu-pert!!" Shaya exclaimed in delight as he leapt onto the bed naked toward her, rapidly engaging her in missionary-intercourse, instantly sailing into his shapely wife lying there inviting him, the way he took her the same as before but with more energy this time, as if seeing her put forth for the younger man really got to him, a surge of silent jealousy perhaps fueling his ardor....and Shaya loved it!

Married lovers thrust together on the bed as it should be, the lean older man pumping into the soft, warm flesh of his younger wife, head buried at her neck, one hand on her left breast as he continued intercourse, arching his back each time he propelled forward, the sounds of her voice in moaning delight egging him on, thrilling him to continue. Rupert was a good, strong lover when he did make love to her, so she relaxed and enjoyed him now.

Rupert focused on the act itself, wanting to satisfy his wife, his younger "trophy wife" now grinding beneath him, his hands pulling her legs up behind his backside, thrusting into her vigorously as she groaned in reception of him. He wanted to make her come, his ex-porn star wife who'd been with so many other men in her past, younger men….bigger men!

Thrusting into her eagerly, he spread his knees out to better relax his back and continue missionary sex without halting for a second. Shaya squirmed under his onslaught, her face a mask of sweaty reaction to her husband's sexual energy, having already come and wanting more. Rupert pumped into her harder, his hands exploring her tight abs and big boobs greedily as he continued in search of his own climax, the feel of her so soft and wet as she moved beneath his energetic body, then Rupert let out a "yelp" of reaction to his own exploding climax inside of his wife…..

12:10am: Shaya pulled on her yellow cotton bathrobe as she stepped to the bedroom door, looking back at her husband now sprawled-out on their ruffled bed on his front, head buried between two pillows asleep. He always fell asleep after lovemaking, the rare times he does so with her. She enjoyed their twenty-minute romp though, tying the cotton robe in front and stepping out of the bedroom into the dark hallway thinking of how she inadvertently made her husband "jealous" by flirting with his Page at dinner earlier, something she had not seen in him before during their year-long marriage thus far. Something she would remember and later use to her advantage, for she was getting to know her older husband more and more.

Walking down the stairwell toward the living room and the liquor cabinet there, Shaya sought a nightcap of Vodka and juice, but what she found was Rupert's Senate Page Harold McCassler lying unconscious on the dining room floor, then two strong and unyielding male strangers stepping out of the darkness to grab her by the arms…

"Scream and you lose that pretty head," spoke a mild-sounding male voice from out of nowhere, not coming from the two men now holding her firmly by her biceps. Shaya didn't scream, deciding to take notice on what exactly was happening, and who had in fact broken into the house tonight. She kept her cool and stood still as the two unmasked goons held her by the arms flanking her, then the man who just threatened her walked into view, the living room not lit by the single tiny lap over on the liquor cabinet across the room from her.

She recognized the rather diminutive man stepping into view toward her, a balding fifty-something D.C. Political "Lobbyist" she'd been introduced to at a Democratic Fundraiser a few months ago by Rupert himself. She recalled Rupert remarking to her that Mortimer Green was a "rabid leftist" who wanted to purge the Democratic Party of Moderates and

"Blue-Dog-Conservatives"(like him) and will do plenty of under-handed crap to get it done.

Unlawful Entry and Kidnapping was a bit more than Shaya imagined a wealthy lobbyist and super-politico doing here in Georgetown at 12:20in the morning.....

"Mrs. Shaya Kelsh.....," the diminutive Mortimer Green spoke to her knowingly, standing about half-a head shorter than her as he stepped closer to the woman held by his two paid goons, none of them masked which surprised Shaya a bit. This was no ordinary "home invasion" as it turned out and she was about to find out the whys and where-fors of it now.

"Green....Mortimer Green....what tha hell are you....?" She quipped in a low voice, hoping that her husband was still asleep and that perhaps she could persuade these guys to leave.

"Oh, I just wanted to drop by and give your husband a tip.... since I know he's into paying people off and calling in favors from other simple-minded freaks like himself....but I'd rather talk with his trophy-wife....perhaps he'll get the message better if he hears it from her?" the weasel-faced, middle-aged political radical spoke to her with a subtle lisp, his eyes staring through hers as he spoke with a glance down at her boobs in the bathrobe she wore.

"He's going to kill you for this Green," Shaya sneered as the two men holding her tightened their grips, the one on her right snickering as he eyed her chest in the bathrobe.

"Oh no he won't, though I know he'd love to....Fascist that he is....but no, this is simple politics my dear Shaya Gold.....uh, excuse me...Shaya Kelsh, ex-porn star and now wife of a US Senator who needs to retire or be exposed as the secret fascist pig that he is," the man named Mortimer Green sneered toward her with his right forefinger pointing at her bust.

"Expose him?" she chuckled with indignant attitude now, hoping her husband if awake, might have already dialed the Police, though she doubted it since he sleeps like a log and it would take a nuclear detonation on the nearby Potomac River to wake him up prematurely!

"Awh, you think a fascist pig like Rupert Kelsh can keep his real intentions hidden from those around him for very long.....or that his hidden financial endeavors wouldn't point to something more than just a Senator's political funds?" the weasel-faced man continued.

Shaya looked over at the young man lying on his back in the dining room, obviously knocked unconscious, wondering if he would be alright after this caper ends. She hoped it could end without things getting worse, and the way the two men holding her by the arms were snickering and whispering to one another their approval of her breasts tucked in the robe, avoiding a gang-rape was fairly high on her agenda right now. Of course, being that she and Rupert reside in the confines of Washington D.C., owning firearms was a bit on the illegal side, so even if her husband awoke and came running down the stairs to confront the intruders, he'd be over-powered by these two goons unless he had a weapon. If her husband actually owned a handgun somewhere in the house here, she didn't know about it!

"Of course he probably keeps things from you Shaya, considering you're not lily-white Caucasian and just window-dressing for his appearance....but you can certainly convince him as wives of certifiable-assholes can occasionally succeed in doing, if they have the full story," Mortimer Green continued as he circled the restrained

Shaya Kelsh standing there in her own living room at the mercy of three unexpected intruders.

"Don't worry about the young idiot lying there....he was given a knock-out shot and won't remember much after he opened the door for us a few minutes ago," Green continued, stepping close to the busty brunette, the goon on her left raising his left hand for her to see a inoculation "gun" which they evidently used to administer a "knock out" to poor Harold McCassler as soon as he opened the door to leave. Funny how the silk robe she wore to the dinner table earlier this evening was now draped over him like a shroud of some kind.

"Your husband...your 'sugar-daddy' is a closet-fascist who should not be in public office, and I have proof from a recorded White Nationalist meeting he attended two years ago where he speaks his mind rather freely and...above that....I have a financial record detailing two million dollars laundered and wired to a Bank in Antigua two years ago this month in a bullshit-name I personally linked to your dear hubby," the weasel-faced Mortimer Green explained to her as he stood in front eyeing her boobs in the bathrobe. Shaya was surprised by what he was accusing Rupert of, but also by the fact she hadn't yet been bent over the sofa and screwed against her will like most male intruders would do with a woman such as she. Afterall, these three assholes were already committing at least three major felonies by being here so why not add rape to the list? She was glad that they aren't rapists, least not yet!

She was also surprised that these male intruders hadn't pulled off her bathrobe, least not yet!

"Why tell me?" she chimed calmly to her captor, eyeballing mister weasel in bold reaction.

"Because you are part of it all whether you like it or not and if your hubby doesn't want to be exposed as a racist and a money-launderer, then he'll quietly leave office this spring, citing 'health reasons' shall we say.....is he upstairs asleep?" Green chimed in fiendishly with a grin showing his little teeth as he spoke, yet another thing she hated about the man right now.

"Yes, and he may be calling the cops ya know?" Shaya snickered with a shrug, the two men holding her by the arms laughing at her response, which only made Green scowl in return.

"Oh no, he won't call the Police....because if I am arrested....the information I have on him will be released to the Press by six o'clock this morning, which is why I didn't bother wearing a mask to walk on in to the prick's traditionalist bullshit Georgetown house on the Potomac, and it's the reason why you...his big-titted, ex-porn-slut wife won't call the Police either because you don't want to see your sugar-daddy go to jail for money-laundering, which I assure you can be proven to a Federal Grand Jury," Moritmer Green said with another grin of bad teeth and rodent-like disposition. Shaya just stared back at the little man, no longer straining against the stronger male hands holding her at the biceps. Green laughed then walked around her as if thinking of what else to tell the well-developed and young-looking woman of forty standing there quietly held by the arms in a tight-fitting bathrobe.

"All your hubby has to do is announce his retirement from the Senate by March of next year, which will give a far more progressive candidate the chance to run for his Senate seat in the two-thousand-eight election, or face humiliation in the media and indictment by the Feds for two million dollars I have personally traced to an account that technically belongs to him, of which I don't give two shits about, he can keep his stolen money and the two of you can live happily-fucking-ever-after once he retires from the Senate," Green explained further.

"Wow, sounds like a deal," Shaya sneered back at weasel face in less than subtle sarcasm.

That pissed Green off and she knew it by the sudden change in his weasel eyes just now.

"Listen you....freak.....convince him to retire or when we come back again it won't be a friendly chit-chat like it is right now," Green sneered as he opened a shiny Buck Knife in his right hand, holding the blade toward her chest in a less-than-subtle threatening gesture.

He reached to her robe's tie in front with his other hand and pulled the garment loose, letting it fall open to reveal her bare front underneath, the two men holding her arms crooning in approval of her bare exposed physique until Green to them tc shut the fuck up.

"You got a beautiful body Mrs. Kelsh....be a damn shame for you to do something to ruin it in such a horrific way," Green said as he ogled her bare assets while holding the knife a foot or more from her chest, those plump n' perky 44EE boobs of hers nearly hypnotizing him!

"She sure does...mmmphh!" the black man on her left sighed in agreement then said no more because Mortimer Green was running the show here tonight 100% and she assumed he hadn't paid the "hired assholes" yet so they dutifully obeyed his commands and gestures.

"Or maybe if I have to come back to see your husband.....I'll just cut his balls off," he snickered with a wave of the sharp knife at hip-level, studying her reaction to his threats.

"What kind of husband would he be with his balls cut off, hunh?" Green chided her as he stepped closer, closing and pocketing the knife in his jeans, grinning at the silent and quietly-frightened Shaya Kelsh as she stood there at his disposal, still held by the arms, her robe lying on the floor at her bare feet now, totally-naked before the three intruders now.

"I'll talk to him," Shaya sighed in a near-whisper, watching the weasel-faced "lobbyist" pull something else from a pocket, a small vial of a white powdery substance, popping it's lid with his left thumb, his right hand cupping under her right breast suddenly, Shaya remaining still out of wonder of what he was doing, then she leaned her head back as Green patted what she assumed to be powdered cocaine onto the surface of her right breast and then leaned in to effectively snort it off in one motion of his head. The two goons holding her still laughed in response to Mortimer Green snorting cocaine off the plump, bare breast of

Mrs. Shaya Kelsh, wife of US Senator Rupert Kelsh.

"You see gentlemen, negotiating this time of night is not as problematic as you may have thought, even a Senator's whore of a wife gets the big picture eventually," the weasel-faced Mortimer Green spoke boyishly to the two muscled men holding the naked woman still, making them laugh in agreement with him, Shaya's face now a grimace of angry contempt.

"I'd like to show her my BIG picture…," the goon on her left snickered to the other one.

"Are we done negotiating?" Shaya chimed as she stared directly at Mortimer Green again.

"Yes, so good luck convincing that fascist to step down from the Senate and take his goddamn un-constitutional 'crime bill' with him….or otherwise my two friends here get to sample your lovely body all for themselves and Rupert Kelsh goes to a Federal Pen," Green sneered back at her as he walked across the room toward the front door, gesturing for the two men to follow him, so damn sure that what he wants will get done. The two men with Shaya took the liberty of feeling her up as they let go of her, one squeezing her ass for a second, the other tweeking her breasts with an eager right hand as he left her standing there.

She watched the three men exit the house through the front door, closing it behind them.

"Mutha-fukkas…..how dare you," Shaya sneered to herself as she stood there staring at the front door with hands on her hips feeling a mix of fear, humiliation, and anger all rolled into one. She wanted to kill those three bastards right now, but she had to stay calm and try to remember what her husband had told her about those in "D.C.Politics" who do some heinous shit in pursuit of their goals, and that he was not immune from those types and their lofty (and often illegal) schemes. She turned to hear someone coming down the stairs in the dark hallway now, her husband Rupert wearing pajama-bottoms with a cigar on one hand.

"Rupert….," Shaya sighed as she faced him walking into the living room now, his gaze not one of surprise or even worry despite the fact he obviously knew what had just happened!

"That was Mortimer Green, a very ambitious left-wing lobbyist and committed 'progressive' who wants me out of office in order for his demented half-brother Cecil Weissbaum, to get elected in my place.....he's pretty harmless for the most part except when he pulls stupid stunts like this one," Rupert spoke softly as he approached his naked wife standing there in stunned realization that he knew what was going on and didn't come down the stairs to confront the intruders, stand up for his wife being felt-up by strangers, nor his Page Harold McCassler getting knocked out! She faced him with a grimace of anger at this moment.

"You mean to tell me you were listening in from upstairs?!" Shaya quipped in reaction.

"Yes, calm down....I was not about to let them go too far... I kinda figured that worm Mortimer Green might try something like this, though I wish my Page hadn't seen those three assholes....no worries though, I got enough on this kid to keep his mouth shut," Rupert told her in all too casual tone, walking over to where Harold McCassler still lay.

Shaya was incensed, her husband worried about his knocked-out Senate Page when it was she who was held against her will in their living room and felt-up by the intruders! She kept her mouth shut and turned on her heels to walk down the first floor hallway, deciding to crash in the guest-bedroom there rather than re-join her husband upstairs after this caper had transpired. Rupert checked the still-breathing Harold McCassler and then turned toward his wife as she headed for the hallway, knowing she was pissed off to say the least!

"Shaya, darling....nothing bad was going to happen to you, I would have seen to that, and I guarantee you will never see Mortimer Green in this life...ever again," he called to her as she retreated to the downstairs guest-room, her response being to slam it's door behind herself.

Rupert Kelsh turned back at the young man lying unconscious on his dining room floor, obviously knocked out by a sedative from what he could tell, so he didn't call 911 which would have resulted in a media inquiry as to why a Senate Page was treated for mystery-unconsciousness at the residence of a US Senator?! Harold would be alright, and Rupert stood there waiting for him to awake, then he'd "explain" what occurred to his own accord, letting the kid know he was to keep tight-lipped about tonight's events if he wants to remain in the Senator's favor. Afterall, Kelsh can get him into Georgetown University as long as he and his Micro-Biologist father~Dr. Howard J. McCassler, plays along!

"My poor wife Shaya....mmmhh, you'll only be mad for awhile dear lady, and as long as you remain loyal and keep that beautiful mouth of yours shut about such things as what just occurred, then I'll look after you as well," Rupert whispered to the room around him, looking down the hallway where his voluptuous wife vanished into their guest-bedroom.

"Maybe I'll let you go when the time comes, as long as you don't become a liability to me and my plans," Rupert whispered in the direction his younger wife went a minute ago.

That reminded him to inform her they would both be attending the annual "Halloween Bash" at the residence of Steven and Shane Victory in Fairfax County, not for the party alone, but because Rupert had business to settle with those twin real estate hustlers.

Myrtle Beach, South Carolina. October 15th: The dusk had darkened to nightfall by 6:30 tonight and being off-season, the traffic and pedestrian crowds were minimal right now.

Nydia Cohen was in the rented hotel room trying to summon her "lord and master" via encrypted cell-phone as she sat on the end of the room's bed. At age 70 she was rather fit and able, despite the fact she is still considered "missing" from the Nursing Home her ungrateful grown children placed her in back in early 2002. It was then the grandmother of three was "rescued" by the man she calls "lord and master", a man she knows as Duncan Horsehair, a man she has routinely murdered for over the past five years.....

He had entered the nursing home one night and strangled an elderly retired Judge in his bed and Nydia saw him do it, asking him if he was an "angel of death", wishing for him to end her miserable and lonely life as well as that senile old Judge. Duncan Horsehair decided Nydia Cohen would better serve the "war" he was methodically carrying out on society, so he took her out of that hellish nursing home and gave her reason to damn well live again!

That pig Robert Marx was just one of over a dozen kills, and the brick of C-4 plastic explosive she had in her purse stolen by the target's piece-of-shit-bastard-son Jamal that stormy night was successful in blowing yet another liberal asshole into the next dimension.

"He must be busy, heeeh-heeee....blowing shit up somewhere else!" the old lady cackled to herself as she put the cell-phone down on the made bed, standing up only to wince at the throbbing pain of her bursitis. Stepping over to the sliding-glass door at the balcony of her room, she looked down at the dark beach below, seeing a few younger pedestrians walking along the beachfront. She reflected on her own past when she was that age, back in the late 1950's...a far more different time and simpler life she recalled. Being a young woman in that decade meant she had respect and care from her male counterparts far more than in the decades following....with "Civil Rights", "Feminism", "Equal Opportunity", "Integration", and even the proliferation of Gays and Lesbians....her America was never the same once those movements were allowed to take root....as real evil always seeks to accomplish!

Peering down at the Hotel Pool area below through her thick eyeglasses, Nydia thought about doing another bombing on her own, like Horsehair had allowed her to do before.

Simple just like the Marx hit....walk around a "bad part of town" with one of her big leather purses loaded with a brick of C-4 and a detonator, wait for some petty thief to come along and snatch the purse from her, then detonate the purse-bomb once the thief is far enough away from her to avoid injury herself but close enough for her to see and hear the explosion!

"Heeeh-heeee......heeeekkhh......all you dirty baboon thieves out there, how about a one way trip to the netherworld courtesy of Nydia Cohen?" she cackled to herself as she glanced back to where she had a big leather purse already wired and ready-for-use sitting on a pillow on the bed now. She giggled to herself in relish of what she was capable of and the fact a "little old lady" who uses a cane to walk in public never being seen as any kind of "threat" by the subhuman primates she targets, and never considered a "suspect" by the arriving Police!

She liked detonating the bomb that killed Robert Marx and his worthless thief of a son back in Stafford, Virginia. Matter of fact, she thought that hit might be her favorite so far, with the US Attorney she blew into the stratosphere 2 years ago in Tennessee and the fast-food restaurant run entirely by Hispanic immigrants in Manassas Va. back in 2003 which she blew up via one of her "purse-bombs" left under one of the restaurant tables after she had a quick dinner that evening. Those were her favorites, and with the higher body-counts as well. She reflected on the bombing she did in Manassas Va. over four years ago, remembering that was when she ran into Duncan Horsehair's "one true love" Isabel Marcano, who just happened to stop by for a sandwich until Nydia ushered her outside and blew the place up!

Loudon County, Virginia. October 17th: Strangers dropping by, hanging out, or otherwise showing up unannounced was not something Michelle "Shelly James" Jamison was a stranger to herself, by any means! Ever since she was exposed by a Tabloid Reporter over 2 years ago living the double-life of a Catholic Nun and a Porn Star, numerous strangers have succeeded from time to time in looking her up, leaving graphic notes in her mailbox, getting her personal email address and filling up her inbox with lovelorn-sexual messages, even knocking on her door from time to time.....

This was the first time a stranger showed up to her door flashing an official-looking gold badge and ID indicating him to be a Federal Agent from the Dept. of the US Treasury!

She glanced up at the clock on her Condo's wall nearest the front door as she unlocked the outer door to let the casually-dressed cop in, hoping he was the real deal and not some psycho who bought a real-looking badge and ID for himself. It was now 3:15pm when Shelly James let Special Agent Clifford Stevens through her condo's door and into her life.

"Sorry if this is an inconvenient time Miss Jamison, but I just want to talk with you privately about some things in the recent past regarding your former employer, and I assure you this is off-the-record and for my information only if you agree to speak with me?" Cliff Stevens spoke gentlemanly to the drop-dead-gorgeous blonde letting him inside her small but regal domicile in a Condo development perched right next to the Northern Virginia Criminal Justice Academy here near Leesburg, easy to find for an ATF Agent of course.

"A bit inconvenient but I have time....hunh, and if this talk was for the record, I'd have my lawyer here with me and you would not be coming here all by yaself would you sir?" the gorgeous blonde said casually as she invited him into her Condo's kitchen area where a tiny two-seat table was located, offering him a drink of juice or soda, Cliff electing to accept a cold can of Pepsi since he was a bit thirsty. She was dressed in just a pair of faded jeans and a grey sweat-shirt but he could make out her infamous porn-physique in it's covering, having watched some of her feature X-rated films of the past making him feel a bit "unusual" sitting here in the present time with the 30-year old woman.

"You got me there, and I appreciate you letting me ask you a few questions Miss Jamison, I don't want to take up too much of your time but it's just a research project into another investigation that began years ago and ended with the fall of Faster Productions, your former employer," Cliff added in jovial tone, studying her as she poured him soda in a glass with ice.

"I actually got tipped off that a Federal Agent might come snooping around from a lawyer friend of mine who you must have already spoken with, and please call me Shelly," she said matter-of-factly as she handed him his glass of cold soda, watching him take a swig of it.

"Ah, Attorney Duffek, yes, but I assure you it's not aimed at you.... Shelly, I am just looking for a perspective into Faster Productions during it's last months in business, during Jonny Faster's final stretch as the Porn King of the East Coast," Cliff said amicably.

"Perspective....heenh...that's funny, perspective is what I've been trying to grab on my past few years as a Nun and a secret adult film actress, which is why I wrote a book," she added.

"I AM SHELLY JAMES….yes, I just finished reading it the other day, well-written and very candid….good job," Cliff answered her softly with a sly smile to humor her ego a bit more.

"Heenh, well…K.R. Knight wrote the book, I just dictated all my info and memories to him while living with him for a few months following the scandal and those awful murders, and it was Amber who introduced me to him," Shelly explained as she sat down at the tiny kitchen table across from her Federal Agent guest, noticing he was not taking any notes nor appear to be tape-recording her, and she felt a little better about this impromptu "interview".

"Yes, Knight is a fairly popular Writer…lives in McLean, not far from here….so the two of you are lovers?" Cliff continued in casual tone, relaxing in his chair with his drink now.

"Yes…well, not steady…..Kenny is a fun guy but he works a lot and he's what some girls call an 'absentee-boyfriend'….heenh-heenh, besides…Amber doesn't want me seeing him anymore, says I need to 'diversify' my accounts," Shelly spoke candidly for the cute Agent.

"When did you leave Faster Productions in two-thousand-five?" Cliff asked her next.

"Right after the problems, the exposure of us in the tabloid which ruined several lives actually, not really my own….end of July, that last week," Shelly replied casually, thinking.

"Did Amber Duffek shield you like a good lawyer should?" he asked with a shrug.

"Not entirely….I was given an offer by the former Production Assistant Dave Solomon to join him in his new Adult Film Company he was lining up Investors for that Summer, I even signed a contract with him to do a series of adventure-themed X-rated films along with the actor named 'Ray Fury'…who was also leaving Faster Productions, then the attack on the cabin happened after I left Ray there and he died in that fire set by what they say was a deranged fan, along with Dave Solomon who got shot in a police raid on his apartment shortly after," Shelly detailed to Cliff knowingly, but with only partial honesty, though Cliff wasn't getting the "vibe" of a liar from her, at least not yet anyway!

"Dominoes fell," Cliff added in agreement with what she was telling him, thinking on it all.

"Yeah, sure did....I miss Jonny Faster alot.....they've never found Jonny have they?" she sighed in form of a meek question back at the handsome but stern man in front of her now.

"No, he's still a Missing Person unfortunately, I'd really like to interview him," Cliff said.

"I bet....he's probably deceased by now....he had some enemies, mostly people he had fired or muscled out of the porn industry over the years, so one of them might have killed him," Shelly spoke with a sullen matter-of-factness in her voice, spiking Cliff's next question.

"Enemies, like Mafia enemies?" he asked her frankly, hands on the table's surface.

"Probably...there was talk toward the end that some Mobster was demanding Jonny pay some bogus debt owed the Mob by the previous owner of the Company, and if he didn't they were going to hurt him personally," Shelly said with a slight smirk on her face now.

"They threatened to kill him?" Cliff asked in natural succession of the unofficial interview.

"Not exactly...hmmmh...they threatened to castrate him," Shelly said softly in return.

"Was he holding money for them...I mean, did they invest something he was holding?" Cliff asked next, trying to get her to talk about something that might mean "money-laundering".

"Not that I know of, Jonny was pretty tight-lipped about money matters, did his own accounting books from what I could tell back then, never talked about money matters with me I assure you," Shelly answered softly as she walked around the kitchen with her drink.

"I understand you were his Number-One Star for the last couple of years at the Company?" Cliff asked her next, studying her physiological reactions as she answered him each time.

"Heenh, maybe towards the end, yeah...he liked casting me with him in the last year of filming when he was performing in sex-roles....actually made me a more 'in-demand' actress by casting me with him, fans liked watching me getting hammered by Jonny," she snickered.

"I watched a scene called 'Job Interview' on a compilation film recently, the box-cover stated it was the last sex-scene filmed by Faster Productions? he mentioned casually, still staring.

"Ah, hunh-hunh....that scene for the Swedish Erotixxx series.... yeah, Shaya Gold directed Ray Fury and I for that one, and it's true....it was shot on-location in the New York offices of Faster Productions in late June of Oh-Five, just before Shaya got fired and after the last of the 'Blonde Avenger' flicks was filmed, Jonny didn't know about it," she explained softly.

"Jonny Faster didn't know about you doing film-short directed by Shaya Gold?" Cliff asked.

"Nope, not unless he found out later because that film-short wasn't released to the Swedish Erotixxx Video Distributor until late July by Dave Solomon, without Jonny's approval," Shelly said with a shrug of indifference, turning around to stare back at the Federal Agent.

"Ya see....Jonny was cautious who he paired me with for films because he sort of treated me special, especially in that last year or so, but he was warming to the idea of casting me with unknown, new actors like Dave Solomon kept suggesting, and then Dave talked Shaya into directing that sex-role 'short film' of me and Ray for the compilation video you watched," Shelly continued in calm, forthright tone, almost smiling at Cliff as he watched her speak.

"I really liked Ray...he was a real gentleman, one man I considered a friend unlike some others, there was something about him I found trustworthy," she continued frankly.

"Ray Fury.....real name Raymond J. Flintlock, a New York State Trooper who was secretly moonlighting as a male porn actor, guess he thought he could get away with that unnoticed and he's considered a homicide victim now....the two of you were lovers outside the course of X-rated filmmaking?" Cliff continued as he made "mental notes" of what she was saying.

Shelly looked at him with a slight scowl as he said all that detail within the same sentence.

"Hmmm…Ray and I fooled around a couple of times, like when he was first hired and was staying in the Faster Mansion for a night… .I slept with him in the guest-bedroom," Shelly said impishly to see if Agent Stevens was vexed by such a story or not.

"Ray and I weren't really cast together though, and we didn't see one another as often as I saw Jonny or Shaya and the others…plus I was a Nun in the Order of Magdelene in Yonkers and often had to lie and fabricate where I was to the Mother Superior of the Convent when I was really getting-it-on for film….a delicate balancing act but for the most part she and the other Nuns thought I was out doing missionary-work like I was supposed to be doing, which is why The Vatican issued a declaration of ex-communication on me once I was exposed in the tabloid press," Shelly explained as she circled the kitchen.

"Did you ever hear Ray Flintlock…..Ray Fury…talk about money or threats made?" Cliff asked her next with a poker face, concentrating to absorb what she was telling him directly.

"No, he was still fairly new, not even a year in….when he was killed at Jonny's cabin by that deranged fan…he wouldn't have been privy to money matters like Dave Solomon and Shaya Gold were I'm sure….poor Ray, he didn't hurt anyone and I was going to continue my adult film career with him if all that shit hadn't happened," Shelly continued in a more sullen tone.

"From the New York State Police file on him he was a good cop… until he got accused of hiding a gun used in a murder somewhere else and then Internal Affairs discovered he was secretly moonlighting as a Porn Actor along with the others," Cliff added for effect.

"Yes, but he was a good man….real good performer too….I miss him sometimes, like I miss Jonny Faster who I actually thought I was in love with back then," she spoke candidly.

"Okay, but the New York Police BCI had him under investigation just before his death in the Catskills that summer, and they spotted him visiting a known Mafia heiress by the name of Isabel Marcano in Fredericksburg Virginia shortly before Faster Productions closed up," Cliff informed her, even though what he was telling her had not been released to the press back when Ray Flintlock/Ray Fury was murdered in a cabin up in the Catskills Mountains.

It was one more subtle "link" between Faster Productions and the Marcano Mafia Family.

"I don't know anything about such a thing, really....Ray was a good guy and he was being screwed over by the Police Department he served for ten years, and I never heard him mention any Mafia people....like I said, he was a good man, like it or not....and if he were alive today I'd probably be doing films with him," Shelly added on a bit of defensive.

"Ah, but your book deal was a lot more lucrative and besides, how many people really buy porn videos on a regular basis....how often are you recognized in public?" Cliff retorted but then decided to calm his attack a bit or she might clam up and ask him to leave.

"You'd be surprised....not just lonely men and the handicapped or perverts....it's gotten more mainstream than it was a decade ago, and I enjoyed it because I liked the others in the Company at the time...Jonny, Woody, Ray, Cody, Chrissa, Leesa, and Ebony," she added.

"No illicit money transactions, bundles of cash you may have seen....I ask you this because like I said a few minutes ago Shelly....I am looking into the final days of Faster Productions because I want to find who may have laundered funds through the company and that someone is far more of a criminal threat than any pornographer who may or may not have been in bed with the Italian Mafia," Cliff continued in a softer, calmer tone of voice now.

"No sir, I didn't see any bundles of cash exchanged or tucked under any mattresses, I have nothing to hide so I'd tell you if I did.... like I told you, Jonny treated me every well, but as I realized later on after he vanished and after the murder investigation into Ray and Chrissa's deaths...Jonny used me as a sex-performer and wanted me close to him for that purpose alone, he didn't love me.....he didn't love anyone....I was a prize-pedigree-sex-kitten to him and his business, so he didn't lend my advice to financial endeavors or laundering of illicit cash, he wouldn't..... would you?" Shelly chimed in thoughtful response, hands on her hips as she circled her condo's kitchen, sensing Agent Stevens had more questions even still.

"No, I suppose not," Cliff sighed then took another swig of his soda, the ice melted now.

He wanted to ask her about the fact she made a lot of money on the sales of her autobiography which she got another writer to pen for her, yet she is living in this rather bland two-level condominium in Loudon County Virginia with a Ford Mustang parked out in front? She didn't seem to be living the life of a millionaire with a book that was on the New York Times' Top-Ten Best-Seller-List last year for over a month!

"I don't get recognized as 'Shelly James' too often in public anymore, just get stared at or followed around by guys now and then, which is why I have learned the art of 'dressing down' to conceal my features....heenh, no sense in getting stalked or harassed without good reason, right?" she snickered back at him as she stepped to her kitchen counter, thinking.

Cliff glanced over into the small living room where only a futon, TV set with a shelf full of DVD movies and one other wing-backed chair were located, also noticing a framed, 11x17 photo of Jayne Mansfield on one wall by the stairs leading up into the bedroom etc. above.

That was fitting, a chesty portrait of Jayne Mansfield on the wall of Shelly James' home, a sexy b-movie actress of forty years ago, held in high regard by a former Porn Starlet of today. Again, this condo appeared very "Spartan" for a woman who made a lot of money from the sales of her book according to the "financial" query he ran on her without a warrant the other day, thanks to a friend of his in the IRS. He wondered if she might be either really bad with money or perhaps a gambling-junkie and pissed-away most of the 1.2 million Advance she got for her best-selling book and subsequent royalties? That sort of thing could be useful if he has to apply pressure to her later on. She turned back to him and smiled gingerly which instantly softened his mood because it was a grin of friendliness.

"Agent Stevens, I do have to get ready to go to a party soon... may we chat some other time about this?" she asked with a softened tone of voice, eyeballing the handsome man intently.

"Sure Shelly, I just wanted to ask you a few questions face-to-face and if I need to ask anymore about Faster Productions, I'll just call you," Cliff replied as he stood up slowly now.

"Cool, sorry I don't know more about the Faster finances, hope you get your man," she said.

"Me too....and it was nice meeting you Shelly," Cliff said conclusively as he extended a hand to shake hers in farewell. Shelly shook it gently and smiled impishly at the gentleman leaving.

"You remind me of Jonny a little...nice and warm on the outside but a cold interior," Shelly spoke gingerly as she turned to walk into her small living room away from him as he opened the door to leave, Cliff watching her walk away without saying another word.......

Duffek Residence in Arlington, Va. (Later that evening): Attorney Amber Duffek was always the life of her own parties, her annual "Halloween Party" no exception, though this year she scheduled it earlier than usual. It was always an invitation-only event held at her residence here, and the number of costumed guests usually didn't exceed 30 in number.

Shaya Kelsh arrived with her husband Rupert around 7pm, wearing a rather revealing

"Pocahontas" outfit complete with thin leather top tied in front which accented her big breasts it barely covered, along with a skimpy brown frilly mini-skirt with tassels and a long white and black feather pinned to her curly dark hair hanging down past her left ear.

Rupert was clad in his "Count Dracula" costume, though only in attire, not bothering to put any ghoulish make-up on his face or wear plastic "fangs" either, just the tuxedo and cape.

He greeted Amber Duffek at the door with a hug and kiss to her left cheek, then Amber greeted Dracula's wife Pocahontas with a closer embrace and a quick kiss to her neck.

There were about 20 other guests in the house tonight as Shaya looked around upon entering the living room, smiling instinctively as she looked over the other faces and costumes, a few of them masked so she couldn't see who they were. One face staring back at her was instantly recognizable of course, for she was a former porn starlet like Shaya was, and according to D.C. rumors, Amber Duffek's "girlfriend", Shelly James! Shelly nodded to Shaya as she walked across the other half of the living room into the dining room, wearing a "Harem Girl" outfit much like Amber's, only Shelly's was practically see-thru!

Rupert and Amber stepped off into the kitchen talking privately, which made Shaya laugh slightly in realization that her husband cannot put "business" away for just an hour or so to enjoy a damn costume party! Shaya greeted some of the other costumed guests in the house as she made her way to the dining room where the food and drinks were located, finding one man clad in white "Stormtrooper" plastic-armor complete with helmet, a young woman was well-dolled-up as Hillary Clinton, and another was wearing a tricked-out "super-hero" costume complete with her boobs sticking out in front covered just with pasties. Everyone was either already drunk or all-too-friendly which brightened Shaya's own mood, still kind of pissed at her husband for the other night when those three assholes broke in, knocked out poor Harold the Page, and felt her up to "threaten" Rupert who'd been upstairs listening to the scene in safety while she had her tits in a ringer! Shaya didn't hold a grudge, least not yet!

"Shelly James....well, blow me down," Shaya spoke up in humorous tone, getting the younger woman's attention, turning to look at Shaya as she lowered the "veil" from her face.

"Shaya...been awhile....how are you?" Shelly asked nervously, the last time they stood this close to one another Shaya slapped the hell out of her because it was Shelly who snitched to Jonny Faster about Shaya wanting him to "retire", getting her fired from the Porn Company they both worked for at the time. Shaya didn't hold a grudge, least not yet!

"Yes it has, good to see you actually....I read your book, liked it....I'm doing well, got married to Senator Kelsh....he's over there in the 'Dracula' costume....you still look as delicious as ever," Shaya spoke gingerly to the comely blonde "Harem Girl" before her.

"So do you, Shaya Kelsh....hmmm...good to see you again too, though I hope there's no more bad blood between us now?" Shelly chimed with a hint of insecurity facing Shaya.

"Oh no, bygones-be-bygones Shel, since we're both friends of Amber's and the past is just that, the past....hey, I did get a recent boob-job, went to a forty-four-double-e," Shaya replied with a slinky smile at the shapely blonde standing there eyeing her bigger tits now.

"I see, sweeeet.....I kept mine the same, workout more to keep my ass and abs in shape," Shelly admitted as she stared at the beautiful older woman's impressive cleavage in the leather costume top that barely covered the 44EE chest Shaya is so proud of.

"So tell me Senator...how's married life treating you these days?" Amber asked Rupert as they stood in the kitchen together sipping on wineglasses Amber filled with her rare 100-year old Cognac just between the two of them. Rupert glared back at the sexy lesbian lawyer and smiled slightly, knowing what she was fishing for, to see if he and Shaya were breaking up?!

"We're doing just fine Counselor, happily-married so far, but I'll be sure to let you know when we are no longer on good terms," Rupert sighed then took another sip of his drink.

"Hmmmh....don't suppose you could loan Shaya to me for a Cruise I'm taking next month, hate to go alone ya know?" Amber chimed girlishly at him, then sipped her drink again.

"Nope, I don't loan my wife out...regardless of what you may have heard," he chuckled.

"Mmmhh, no harm in asking Senator...I am happy you brought her with you tonight though, that outfit she is wearing is so well-suited for a woman of her......stature," Amber retorted sweetly, eyeing him as they stood close together in the dimly-lit kitchen area, the music playing in the background almost drowning their conversation a bit.

"If we are still on for tonight's little discourse.....I might let you sleep with Shaya," Rupert said in a hushed voice, eyeballing the gorgeous female lawyer rather sternly, bringing up the fact Amber wants to have Shaya in her bed to get her immediate undivided attention.

"The package arrived….no problem, it's a done deal as long as you get that other item you need from the source, and don't try to drop me into a meat-grinder along the way dammit," Amber spoke softly in his right ear as she stepped up closer to the Senator from New Jersey.

Rupert smiled handsomely at the last portion of her statement, which shows she's thinking!

"Don't worry that pretty head of yours Attorney Duffek….before long, you are going to be arguing before the US Supreme Court when they pass that liberal shit like the 'Slave-Reparations' Bill and the 'Universal Heath Care' bullshit in the near future," he told her.

Amber smiled knowingly, one of the promises Senator Kelsh had made her before, to get her to argue for the opposing team when it came to the US Supreme Court taking challenges against some of her favorite socialist political ideas signed into law when the Liberal- Democrats take over following the 2008 Election! He played both sides to get what he wants and she liked that about him, playing along with a Fascist like Rupert Kelsh as long as it was beneficial to her. She ran a hand up his left forearm and smiled up at him as he faced her.

"Now when may I have a night with that scrumptious wife of yours?" she crooned girlishly.

"Anytime she decides….just ask her," Rupert snickered back at the pretty Amber in the sexy costume as he stepped past her to rejoin the other guests in the party-filled house. She was not pleased with that answer, hoping he could "order" Shaya to bed with her since Shaya has before declined Amber's offer to "play around" even though Shaya has been with women before back during her Porn Film Career! So far, Shaya has refused Amber's advances…..

"Hmmm…things we do for money, love, and good companionship," Amber sighed to herself as she walked back into the throng of party guests herself now, laughing with an overweight Jewish friend of hers named Deborah who became a Rabbi last year and was now dressed as an overweight "Ballerina" at Attorney Amber Duffek's Halloween Bash.

Shaya was eating some crackers w/caviar standing at the dining table when she spotted two other costumed guests she recognized and would rather have not seen here tonight, though they immediately spotted her and made their way through to where she now stood, smiling in approval of what Shaya Kelsh wore to the party this evening…the Pillage Brothers!

"Shaya…mmmhh!" Shane chimed as he stepped up alongside her at the dining table.

"Mrs. Kelsh….how do you do?" Steven Pillage, the more "regal" of the twins said as he stepped to her other side, touching his right hand to her shoulder so she'd look at him.

"Shane…Steven….I'm just great, my husband is here somewhere if you're looking for him, and aren't you guys feeling a bit chilly in those uhhm…costumes?" Shaya responded slow and casual, eyeing the twin black brothers with a cocked eyebrow as she looked at their matching "costumes". Both men wore nothing but a leopard-skin "loincloth" covering the lower portion of their chiseled, well-worked-out bodies and nothing else! They were a pair of twin black "Tarzans" and showed off their bodies as only overly-proud hustlers would!

"That's cool, we'll chat with the Senator later," Steven said in return, looking around.

"Ya know Shaya, the three of us wore costumes…. that are extremely easy to take off," Shane answered her remark about their leopard-skin loincloths, making her softly laugh.

Shaya knew Steven and Shane Pillage through Amber of course, and her husband had recently entered into a shady Real Estate "agreement" with them, so they had been coming around since this past Summer talking with Rupert and of course, flirting with her.

"Ya know Shane, you're an asshole," she chuckled back at him for that suggestive remark.

She could tell the Pillage Brothers apart by the scar on Shane's lower left jawbone and Steven's more "weathered" face, as if he was the "worry-wart" of the twin brothers, but other than that they were identical twin brothers with the type of attitude she kind of disliked in many black men she'd met over the years, that "hustler-friendliness" which often snares people into giving them what they want because they're so damn (falsely) "nice"!

"So Steven, sell any Churches out from under the congregations lately?" she chimed to the more serious and pragmatic of the twin "Tarzans" flanking her at the dining table now.

She referred to last month when she heard they sold a Church building right out from under it's congregation and the new owner kicked the church-membership out as soon as the ink on the deed was dry, it was a legitimately done! Shane just laughed at her bringing it up now.

"No, but the year isn't over yet, you know of a good Church for sale Shaya?" Steven replied.

"Heenh, yeah…there's a Mormon Church over on Route One….go see if they want to sell their temple to you…and wear the loincloths when you go," Shaya chided him in humor.

"Mormons….yeah, good-looking white women in that cult," Shane laughed in response.

"Are you two guys here to party or just to piss me off?" Shaya sighed with a smirk at Shane then looked around the room for Rupert, who was over schmoozing with some stranger.

"Party with you Mrs. Kelsh…maybe we could have more fun upstairs?" Shane added as he moved in close behind her, touching a hand to her middle-back in a less-covert gesture.

Steven shot Shane a glance of disapproval of such a brazen suggestion of sexual intent, she was afterall, the wife of a man they were currently doing important business with!

"Not likely, party is down here Shane….hmmh, besides…I hear the two of you are sharing Shelly James with Amber, and Shelly's here tonight so go stick it in her," Shaya crooned back in coy response, hands on her hips after putting her unfinished drink down on the table, now turning to step away from the twin black brothers in the matching leopard loincloths.

"My brother has a sense of humor harder than most I'm afraid, we don't mean you any disrespect baby, you just look super-fine in that 'Pocahontas' costume," Steven Pillage chimed in with a more sensible approach to schmoozing with the busty brunette.

"It's cool, I've heard worse at the high-flutin' DC Gala events and fundraisers believe me, all of my husband's politico friends suggest far worse when they talk to me while drinking," she said dismissive, letting Steven slip an arm around her waist for the moment. It's just good party-manners to let a man she knows touch her like that as they speak one-on-one.

"You know we're fooling around with Shelly James?" Shane asked her from behind next.

"Heenh, yep, Amber told me you guys got her to take her clothes off and do both of you one evening when Amber left you-two alone with that twinkie-blonde-cupcake for just a half-hour, heenh-heeh... incorrigible, you guys are incorrigible," Shaya snickered in reply.

"Mrs. Kelsh...you of all people realize the appeal female porn stars have with their male fans out in the real world, and by the way....your films are better than Shelly's," Shane added with a stoical voice, looking around the party as the R+B music became a bit louder now.

"Yes indeed, which is why I retired and married a rich n' powerful US Senator," she chimed, reminding the two horny men the fact she was a married woman and her husband was here tonight to do business with the likes of them and they had better "behave" with her!

"Touche' my dear lady...the Senator is a very lucky man," Steven said with a softer grin.

"I do have a photo I'd love for you to autograph to me," Shane said with another touch of his right hand to her back, closer toward her ass this time of course, since she let him.

"Okay, I can do that Shane....you got it on you?" she replied in cordial manner.

"It's out in my car...come on, just take a minute," Shane said boyishly as he took her right hand to lead her across the living room to the front door with him, assuming she'd go.

"Alright Shane, just behave yourself, will ya?" Shaya sneered as she followed him outside.

Rupert noticed his wife going out the front door with Shane Pillage and he didn't object, instead taking it as a cue to approach the more "sensible" of the twin brothers, Steven Pillage who was at the bar counter getting himself a mixed drink of some variety.

"Steven…glad you made it here tonight," Rupert spoke to the loinclothed black man as he stepped up behind him with a gentler slap of a hand to the more muscled man's shoulder.

"Yessir Senator Kelsh…good to see you too," Steven replied graciously, shaking the older man's hand as he looked at the "Dracula" costume the man was wearing to Amber's party.

"I'd like to iron-out the real estate issue between us before I leave tonight," Rupert said next.

"Sure, we can straighten it out now that it's just you and me talking…I'm afraid my twin brother Shane is a bit immature when it comes to business matters and I swear, if he and I weren't related, I'd have to kill him," Steven said softly to the US Senator in cool reply.

"Understandable my friend….we all have our liabilities, and mine just walked out the door with yours, so now is a great time to talk business privately," Kelsh said in a jovial manner.

Steven grinned at the older man's reference to his smoking-hot younger wife Shaya, himself hoping his brother at least brings her back to the party before it shows up as "obvious"!

The two men walked across the living room toward a door in the wall to the left of the stairs, a narrow passageway of steps leading down into the basement "den" of Amber's home here in Arlington, where none of the other party-revelers had been allowed, where their conversation would not be overheard by the curious. In this town, it's better served to be discreet and even more discreet, especially when one's "business" was not entirely legal!

Shaya found Shane's vehicle to be a brand-new, black 2007 Bentley Continental GT with shiny custom rims, a real classy automobile, though she thought her own Audi R-8 was finer!

He opened the passenger side door and she reluctantly climbed in as he circled around to the other side and got in, starting the car's engine so she could sit in it with the heater on, it was a bit chilly out tonight afterall, especially in skimpy "costume" attire they both were wearing!

"Nice wheels Shane," she said to him as the car doors shut, the two of them sitting in the leather bucket seats looking at one another in the dark interior illuminated slightly by the dashboard lights right now as Shane pulled out a brown manila envelope to hand to her.

"Thanks, it's cherry…those are the photos I've been wanting to get you to sign," he said as she opened the envelope to pull out six color 8x10 photos, then he turned on the car's ceiling light for her to see better. Shaya smirked back at Shane as soon as she clearly saw the six 8x10 photos of her. Two were "boxcover" shots of her from films, and the rest were what they call "action stills" from several different of her past X-rated feature films.

"Shane….hmmph, you are one-of-a-kind…a real shithead," she chimed in humor as he then handed her a thin black marker to sign the rather graphic 8x10 photos from her porn past.

One 8x10 was from the cover of her popular 1997 Porn Film "Big Bustin' Loose" featuring her on the front in a bikini along with black porn actor "F.M. Dexter" hugging her from behind and the other actor whose moniker she didn't remember, hugging her legs lustfully.

She signed that one "To Shane Pillage, a real piece-of-work!" Love, Shaya Gold".

"I'm a collector ya know," Shane said as he watched her personalize/autograph the photos.

"I just bet you are," Shaya sighed in sarcastic tone, glancing up at him in the car's dim light.

One of the 8x10s was of Shaya and Jonny screwing in the scene from "Jonny's Girls" where she sat up on the ledge of a stove while he rammed up into her, and she signed it like so:

"Do me! –Shaya Gold" and handed it to him with a giggle, then looking at the next one.

Another 8x10 was of her lying naked on a rug while F.M. Dexter drilled her in intercourse missionary-style as he relaxed up on his knees and Shane said that was one of his favorite all-time favorite scenes of hers from the 90's X-rated films she starred in at the time.

She signed that graphic movie-still: "Shane, keep it up!" –Shaya Gold then handed it back to him and looked at the next one of her sitting on a rope-swing totally-naked in the backyard of what was once the Faster Mansion in New Rochelle, NY. That one brought back memories as she remembered often frolicking nude on Jonny Faster's property back then, the nearest neighbors never minding the sight of good-looking naked people next door. She just signed her name to that one and then the last one, a shot of her performing fellatio on Jonny Faster, she signed her name over Jonny's balls since the photo was a "close up" shot.

Shane shifted into gear and the car began to drive off down the asphalt driveway, Shaya looking at him in wonder of what the hell he was now doing as they headed for the road.

"Just wanted to show you my new Bentley Shaya, around the block," Shane snickered as he gunned the accelerator onto the road leading back toward Rt. 66, Shaya just sitting there looking at him as he drove her away from the costume party unexpectedly, unwelcomed….

"Great car Shane, moves like my Audi does," she sighed as he sped onto Rt. 66 heading west then got into the far right lane to turn around at the next junction, "around the block" a bit.

"And I don't wanna know where you got those photos from," she giggled as they drove on.

"Online sources galore baby, you'd be surprised what's out there for sale," he chuckled, gunning the Bentley to 90 mph before slowing for the off-ramp up ahead, glancing at the chesty former porn starlet in the seat next to him, obviously enjoying the ride with him.

"This also gives time for my husband to talk with your brother in private, seems he doesn't think I'm worthy of overhearing his bullshit real estate issue, and he thinks you're immature and irresponsible, unlike your twin brother," Shaya chimed to intentionally goad the man.

"Oh really, hunh…hunh-huh-huh, prick," Shane snickered as he turned off to swing back toward Amber Duffek's residence just off Rt. 66 a mile east of where they'd driven.

"Hmmm…don't sweat it Shane, he likes you guys…as long as you fuckin' behave yaselves if you know what I mean….Rupert is a generous man as long as ya don't cross him," she said softly, staring at the driver in the dimly-lit car, watching him get back on Rt. 66 east to head back toward Amber's house now, and she could tell Shane was thinking hard on something.

"Heeenh….why Shane Pillage…does this car have two gear-shifts or are you just happy to have me riding with you?" Shaya asked him girlishly, noticing his loincloth was now a

"Tee-Pee" between his legs, pushed up by a full-mast erection underneath as he drove.

He laughed in spite of himself, and she was right, having caught him getting aroused driving.

"Hunh-hah, don't mind me Mrs. Kelsh….I'm cool," Shane chuckled in reaction to her remark, not being able to help himself getting aroused as he drove her in his new Bentley.

Just then, Shaya felt the tiny cellphone clipped to the waist of her skirt vibrate, so she picked it up to see the lit screen showing a text-message from her husband: "Stall him~20 min."

Amber Duffek was a gracious party host, always the life of the party, until now. Now it was time for the other guests to leave, even if it wasn't even 10pm yet! She told most of them she had something business-oriented come up and she has to attend to it, the rest were mostly too drunk to care and just left with their designated-drivers, gay-boy-toys, or just themselves.

Amber threw parties all throughout the year so being asked to leave early at this one just had most of her "regulars" looking forward to the next party hosted by the lovely Miss Duffek!

Shelly James was slightly-intoxicated herself as she walked up behind Amber and giggled.

"Oh hey, Shel…heenh, Steven and Shane will be spending the night in the guest-room," Amber said sweetly to the shapely blonde in the matching "harem girl" outfit, noticing Shelly roll her eyes in disagreement then step away, knowing Amber was ordering her to entertain the twin brothers again tonight! Walking to the front door, she saw some cars already leaving the horseshoe-driveway, another costumed couple stepping past her with kisses to her face on the way out, Amber wanting to make sure all of her guests were going out of the house now except for Shelly, the Victory brothers, and the Kelsh's. She didn't see Shane Pillage or Shaya Kelsh anywhere as she walked through her domicile, checking bedrooms and other private spots to make sure none of her more "amorous" guests weren't getting-it-on when they should be leaving the party! Noone was upstairs, no sign of Shaya or Shane, just Shelly sitting in the kitchen and Senator Kelsh negotiating with Steven Pillage down in her basement "den" now. Amber walked into the living room and smirked at the sight of the spilled food and half-empty glasses on tables and chairs now, something she did not plan on cleaning up, because after tonight it was something she didn't have to worry about!

Shaya looked at Shane as he pulled onto the road leading to Amber's address, and decided to "stall" him for her husband to make the deal with the more favor-oriented of the twins, Steven. She touched her left hand to Shane's right shoulder, getting him to look back at her.

"Pull over in the lot up here....let's not go back to the party just yet," she said softly, well-concealing her reluctance. Shane saw the construction-lot on the right up ahead and dutifully pulled his new Bentley slowly into the dirt off the road, hoping for the obvious from Shaya.

Shane's radio station playing softly was all R+B and easy listening which improved her mood into a more sensual one now, once he shifted into park in the dark construction lot just off the road, she leaned left toward Shane, smiling in the sparkle of the car's dashboard lights.

Her left hand reached to his loincloth and pulled it up to reveal the man's huge boner.

"Ooooh....why Shane...that's a big weenie you have there," Shaya cooed in slinky voice, smiling sleazy as she looked him in the face, their mutual-agreement being there in spades.

Shane raised the steering wheel up toward the dash and eased the seat back some, giving the former porn starlet ample space to perform fellatio on him in his new car. Shaya leaned over into his lap and took his manhood eagerly, surrendering to the oral act as she had done countless times with other men both for film and for personal pleasure, now beginning her talented oration with the boyishly "immature one" of the identical twin black brothers.

"Unnnooaah....yeeeaaahh," he sighed in delight as he leaned his head back on his bucket-seat's headrest, letting Shaya gorge on his raging manhood between his legs, her mouth possessing a life of it's own and it felt damn good. Shane was surprised she elected to blow him here in his car not long after telling him to "behave" with her, but he chalked it up to good-old-fashioned-sexual-arousal on her part! He didn't care about parking illegally in some construction site right now, relishing the fact he had yet another "former porn starlet" between his legs now, this one the wife of a US Senator too! Shaya fellated him passionately, keeping his entire focus on her special talent rather than returning to Amber's house where his twin brother was negotiating with her husband, something Shane was against as it turned out. Shaya had her husband's back, even with a man she didn't really want to indulge......

"Alright Steven....the original deed to the Laboratory in Cockeysville, Maryland...for fifty-grand in cash," Rupert said as he laid his losing hand out on the basement bar counter, his impromptu Poker bet with Steven Pillage having cost him the $50,000 cash he had in a briefcase at his feet right now. $50,000 cash for an original deed to a property in Maryland he wanted full disclosure and Real Estate paperwork on since he technically bought the illicit property two years ago but under another name and land title....from someone else entirely!

The Pillage brothers acquired the original deed to the property and Shane Pillage wanted to hold it for more money than it's worth, but his brother Steven was more naturally pragmatic and saw this negotiation with the Senator as lucrative since just two acres of land with a secure "Laboratory" on it was not something that sells easily considering the zoning laws!

Paying $50,000 for just an original deed was a stretch but Rupert was willing to do it in order to secure the final "paperwork" regarding the property from the public eye. Playing a round of Poker with the hustler named Steven was a rouse in itself, gave the idiot a sense of fairness and of course Rupert let him win so that he can leave with the original deed tonight!

"I'll give you my one copy of it along with the original....plus the money-trail bank notes as well, so it'll be free-n-clear from my end completely....if you let your lovely wife accompany my brother and I on a week-long Cruise we're taking next week?" Steven offered as he sat on the barstool across from the older man in the "Dracula" costume, re-shuffling the cards.

"You guys want Shaya to go on a Cruise with you?" Rupert reacted in not-so-surprised reply.

"Yes....as a gesture of trust...and....so we can keep doing business like this for a long time Senator, you have my word, noone will ever know about this transaction or that I even know you, that's the way I do business," Steven explained with his disarm-n-hustle smile at Rupert.

"Hmmph...well as you obviously know already, my wife and I have an open-marriage, and she'll do whatever I ask of her as long as it benefits us....you want her as your 'date' for a week-long Cruise.... that's possible....two out of three," Rupert spoke casually as he shuffled the card deck and began to deal them out between he and Steven again. Two out of three hands to "win" was fair enough for both men, and cocky Steven felt very lucky tonight!

Shane Pillage slipped his right hand and arm around Shaya's back as she lay over between the bucket seats while sucking his dick, his fingers finding the tie-strings of her soft-leather "Pocahontas" top in front, gently pulling on it to loosen the tight-fitting costume garment.

His right hand pulled her top down her back a few inches and Shaya felt her top loosen in front, her big boobs popping out and pressing against the emergency brake handle now.

Shane ran his right hand under to feel her bare boobs as she lay there between the passenger seat and his lap, continuing her fellatio on him as he greedily felt her soft, warm breast-flesh.

"Yeah baby....you're awesome," Shane sighed in delight of her oral talent, his head resting back on the seat's headrest again, eyes closed in delight, failing to notice the glimmer of another vehicle slowly pulling into the lot behind his parked car via the rear-view mirror.

He wanted to go all the way with Shaya right here in the car, hell, even out in the dirt!

Shane ran his hand through her silky dark hair as she bobbed up and down on him steadily, feeling his climax slowly approaching the point of no return, not telling her as she continued.

Glancing right, he saw a man-sized shadow of someone in his driver-side mirror and he instinctively sat up straighter in the seat to react, but with Shaya's head still buried in fellatio.

A gloved hand knocked once on the window and Shane could see a parked Police vehicle behind his car in the rear view mirror now, so he hit the window knob on his car door and the window lowered slowly. Shaya raised her head up as the Police Patrolman shined his flashlight inside the 2007 Bentley, clearly seeing what was going on in the front seat!

"Awhhh-shit," Shane sighed to her as she slowly raised back into her own seat, her hands coming up to cover her big boobs popped out from her costume top, but to no avail.....

Rupert folded his last hand, not picking up one more card but deciding that he was sorely "beaten" by his opponent, and thus letting Steven Pillage assume he will be getting Shaya to go on a Cruise with him and his twin brother Shane next week.

"I thank you for your sportsmanship and good business Senator... I'm going to give you everything right here and now to that property in Maryland, something I am happy to be relieved of...to tell you the truth....it's been hard keeping that damn place under the table," Steven spoke matter-of-factly as he handed the older man a manila envelope across the bar.

"Thank you Steven, I appreciate the full-disclosure of documents on the property as I tend to get rid of it under-the-table as well..... and I trust you and your brother will show my wife a good time on the Cruise next week," Rupert said as he stood up, pocketing the envelope.

"Oh we'll have a good time Senator, I assure you....," Steven chuckled in response, watching the man pull his cape back on to leave up the stairs, finding it strange the man gave up his wife so easy for a week to two black men knowing full-well what would occur on the Cruise!

"Hmmph, just send her back to me when the Cruise is over," Rupert chuckled in return.

"Sure thing Senator, don't worry....we'll be gentle with her," Steven added with a smile as the older white man turned to walk back up the stairs now, his demeanor one of calmness.

Shane Victory did have his wallet in the car so he was able to show his driver's license to the lone Police Officer who pulled in behind them while Shaya was administering a blowjob to Shane in the car parked here on a construction site! All that was going through her mind right now as she sat slumped back in the passenger seat with her boobs barely covered by the untied leather top, was getting arrested for "lewd acts in public" or some shit like that, and making the midnight news details saying: "Wife of US Senator caught performing oral sex in a parked car near Washington D.C." Still she hoped for a break as this Cop didn't seem too pissed off or over-eager-to-arrest (so far) running the car tags and license to make sure it's not stolen and the driver doesn't have arrest-warrants out for him.

"You two realize, I hope....this sort of thing is illegal and you're also trespassing on a construction site here....I suggest you get a motel room, are we clear?" the Patrol Cop spoke as he returned to Shane's car window to hand him his license/registration back to him now.

"Yessir Officer....yessir, I wasn't thinking....never happen again," Shane replied to the uniformed Officer standing at the window looking in at the busty brunette in the passenger seat. Shaya smiled up at the black man in uniform, hoping that was all he'd do was give a warning, and since she wasn't in handcuffs by now, she assumed they were very fortunate!

"Okay, but if you weren't a Brother Mason, I'd haul you both to jail," the Officer said with a slight chuckle in his voice as he eyeballed

Shane intently. Shane recalled he had a Masonic auto-emblem on the rear bumper of his Bentley and the Cop was evidently another Prince Hall Mason like he was! Shane extended his right hand for a shake but the Cop declined.

"Now get the hell out of here," the Cop said in a sigh, smiling in at the buxom lady in the passenger seat, then turned to walk back to his Police Cruiser as the couple in the Bentley quickly pulled out from the construction lot onto the road again.

"Hunh, some brothas get all the pussy," the Officer said to himself as he climbed back into his car and then marked back on with Dispatch, calling this stop a "broken down vehicle".

Shaya pulled her top back on and tied it snug to her chest, eyeing Shane in slight contempt.

"That could have gone way-wrong," she said in heated tone, but realized it was her idea to pull over in that "empty lot" and give him a blowjob there on the spot!

"I wouldn't have let you go to jail baby, I would have taken the heat," Shane said frankly.

"Really….hmmhh….well, we were lucky back there, getting caught by the one cool policeman in all of Northern Virginia," Shaya snickered, making him laugh as he drove.

Shaya's Rolex watch read 10:48pm when Shane pulled into Amber's driveway, both of them instantly noticing the lack of other cars parked along the way as there had been less than an hour ago! They saw just Shaya's Audi R-8, Amber's BMW and a Ford Mustang!

"Looks like the party ended all of a sudden, hunh?" Shaya chimed as Shane slowed his Bentley alongside the black Audi R8 she owned, himself curious about what happened.

"Funny, Amber never ends her parties before midnight," he said matter-of-factly to her.

"Oh well…park here and I'll go in first, linger a bit then come in, no sense in making it obvious we were up to no good," Shaya snickered in humor as she opened her car door.

"Right…hey Shaya, thanks form the signatures," Shane spoke up as she got out the car.

"Heenh-heh, I always take care of my fans," she giggled back at him then shut the door to walk back up to Amber's front door, adjusting her costume, night air chilling her a bit.

"I hope this was worth it Rupert," she sighed to herself as she walked to the front door, arms folded in the chill of the night air. She opened the door and went right on in, looking around to see the party had indeed ended, the place empty except for Amber walking toward her now with a forced smile, and her husband waving at her then vanished into the hallway in the direction of the main first floor bathroom.

"What's up Amber?" Shaya chimed with hands on her hips as the pretty lawyer approached.

"Party's over….I got business to attend to by midnight and I have to leave as soon as I get dressed….your husband got what he wanted from Steven by the way," Amber responded.

"Oh, so he got that damn deed he's been wanting from him?" Shaya chimed with a grin.

"Yes, but there's a catch honey….he'll tell you about it," Amber added, touching her arm.

"Catch?" Shaya quipped in wonder, feeling as if she was going to be unpleasantly-surprised.

"Yes…your husband and Steven played a round of Poker for the deed and Rupert won the paperwork he wanted….but he lost you in a bet, so you get to go on a week-long Cruise with the Pillage brothers….next week," Amber told her with a hint of "glee" in her voice.

"You gotta be shittin' me," Shaya sneered in reaction to the news, Amber grinning now.

"Nope, your husband folded his hand and so you're going on a Cruise with those two next week…have fun and take plenty of lubricant," Amber snickered as she walked to the stairwell across the living room to go downstairs where Steven Victory was still lounging.

"That son-of-a-bitch….put me up in a poker game," Shaya sighed to herself as she turned to see Shelly James coming down the hallway now, dressed no longer in her "harem girl" costume but in jeans and a sweat-shirt with purse around one shoulder and hair down.

"Don't feel bad Shaya....could be worse," Shelly said softly to the older woman standing there in the living room as if she had just been informed about something torturous.

"Yeah…..where you going Shelly James?" Shaya retorted with a chuckle as the blonde cupcake strolled past her toward the front door without missing a step along the way.

"Away….time for me to re-vamp my life….so tell Steven and Shane they can go fuck themselves tonight because I'm out of here," Shelly said softly as she stopped at the door.

Shaya smiled at the petite blonde she used to work with in Porn years ago, finding it funny but righteous the younger woman finally grew some nerve to stand up to Amber Duffek.

"You-go-girl….I'll deal with the Pillage brothers….take care Shel," Shaya said with a smile at Shelly, making her smile and wink in return then she was out the front door, saying no more as she retreated quickly to her Mustang, quickly before she changed her mind. Shane Pillage saw the blonde vixen hop into the Mustang and gun it's engine to life. She pulled her car out almost directly in front of him not caring that she only missed Shane by two feet, speeding down the other end of Amber's driveway to the road leading out to RT. 66.

Shane walked into the house and found Shaya standing over in the dining room with her husband Senator Kelsh right now, and she looked like she was quietly chewing him out!

"You wagered my ass and lost?!" Shaya quipped in hushed but heated voice as she faced her husband at the dining table, the expression on his face one of pensive visage, which pissed her off a little more considering how pathologically "calm" he always seemed.

"Don't worry my dear, you won't have to go on that Cruise with them….trust me," Rupert said softly to his wife, noticing her lower lip and the lipstick smear there, denoting she had done something with her mouth recently beyond sipping on Amber's high-dollar wine!

"Really....you gonna welch on your bet?" she snickered hopefully, folding her arms.

"That, or you spend a week on the ocean sandwiched between those two apes," Rupert chuckled back at her as he turned to look for Amber Duffek who was checking the rest of the house for stragglers, now pretty much certain her home was clear of other party-guests.

"Hey man, I did keep the one 'Ape' occupied while you hustled the other one out of that property deed, ya know?" Shaya chimed in soft defiance as he looked back at her calmly.

"I know, and thanks babe...what would I do without you?" Rupert sighed in reply, smiling slightly as he touched her chin with his right hand, forefinger touching her lower lip at the lipstick-smear, knowing full-well how she would have "occupied" a man like that.

Amber came rushing into the dining room looking like she'd lost something and was in a hurry to find it, then she stopped to look at Rupert as if to wait for some kind of "cue".

"We're leaving....see you soon Amber," Rupert said to the frazzled lawyer then hugged her casually and then turned to walk to the front door. Shaya looked at Amber in wonder of why she looked so "stressed" all of a sudden, as if she was expecting something to happen? Shaya tugged on her husband's costume cape, Rupert turning a head to glance back at his wife.

"I'll be right out honey, warm up the car....be just a few minutes," Shaya said as she turned to walk down the hallway to the nearest bathroom in Amber's house. Rupert didn't say anything on his way out the door, which was nothing new for him, and Amber just stood there looking around her living room and at her watch as if to be on a timed schedule or something. Shaya just walked to the bathroom and went on in, the door closing quickly behind her to reveal the bathroom's other occupant! Shane leaned against the closed door as he faced Shaya now grinning ear-to-ear at her, like a hungry lion eyeing his prey.

"We got interrupted baby, no sense in letting a good thing go to waste," he whispered to her as he dropped his costume-loincloth to the tiled floor at his feet, standing before her naked and at full-mast once more. Shaya had to chuckle and grin in response, surprised by his appearance and semi-flattered he was pursuing her like this, even though the party is over…

"Shane, honey….my husband just walked out the door, I have to leave now too….who knows, maybe we can party again some other time….?" Shaya spoke gingerly with her right hand to the man's smiling face, his erection nearly stabbing her in the lower abdomen as he stepped closer in the small bathroom, his right hand reaching to gently touch her breasts in the skimpy leather top tightly covering those "twin peaks" of hers.

"Promise me?" he asked in a hot whisper then hugged her into him in lustful motion, and his lips met hers in a kiss. She gave in to the kiss, feeling his "third leg" pressing against her abdomen, her left hand touching his shaft instinctively, then their lips parted after a moment.

"Yes, I promise….mmmmhhh….another time big guy, just you and me," she whispered to his grinning face and pulled back from him a step, looking down at his bare body there.

"I'm giving up white women altogether….I am gonna be down-with-brown from now on, and a woman like you, so smooth and bronze….you're one I would treat so gooood….," Shane spoke convincingly as he touched one hand to her face, the other at the hem of her leather skirt, biting his lower lip in resistance to his aroused sexual fury wanting satisfaction.

"Commendable, I'm sure Shelly James will be heartbroken….now take it easy and I'll see you soon," Shaya said soft and conclusively, opening the door to step back out.

11:05pm: Amber Duffek watched Shaya and Rupert leave the driveway in their Audi R-8, the car's taillights slipping into the night as she stood there on the front stoop nervously anticipating the next of tonight's events. The fact Shelly's Mustang was no longer in the driveway pissed her off, but then again perhaps it was for the best, especially for Shelly!

She turned back inside her home, realizing she had best get dressed in something more appropriate to the situation, as this see-thru "harem girl" costume was not conducive to what she had to do in the next few minutes. Shane had gone downstairs to bicker at his brother for the real estate deal Steven made with the Senator behind his back, and so both of them were down there right now, and she reluctantly hurried to the enclosed stairwell, descending to her small basement "den". Steven and Shane were sitting at the small "bar" as if waiting for her to arrive, and Amber knew she was pressed for time before the next of tonight's unorthodox "activities" occurred.

"Hey…Amber-baby…why did you kick everyone out….even Shelly James…who is gonna entertain us tonight…after all we've done for you?" Steven Pillage spoke first as he stood up from a barstool, slightly smirking at the lovely lady in the see-thru costume entering.

"My brother got you fifty-grand in cash for the Senator's original deed, and you end the party an hour before midnight?" Shane chuckled as he pawed a big envelope on the bar.

"Steven…..Shane…..I sent them all home because I wanted you two gentlemen all to myself, as I knew you'd get me fifty big-ones for that goddamn original deed Kelsh wanted so badly, and…you're both getting his wife Shaya away from him like I wanted….so, I'm gonna reward you both tonight, down here," Amber spoke soft and methodical, peeling off the see-thru outfit covering her well-crafted physique as she approached the twin brothers at the bar.

"It's about fucking time Counselor," Steven responded approvingly as he met her half way across the room, embracing her soft, bare body in cordial agreement, his twin brother Shane standing behind the bar a bit skeptical, surprised by Amber's sudden "change of heart" even now when they've done her just another favor that wasn't too damn hard as it was!

"Mmmmh…tell you what guys, stay right here while I go upstairs for a sec….I'll be right back and I'll be all yours…. it is about time I had two-for-one," Amber chimed as she gently stepped from Steven's amorous arms, walking back to the stairs totally naked except for her pearl necklace and dangling earrings. Shane watched the gloriously-well-shaped lawyer ascend the stairs in a rush, leaving he and Steven alone in her basement den once again.

"I told you I'd come though for us my brother....we're gonna get to bone Amber tonight, I got the Senator on a chain with that illegal property title...and....I won Shaya for the Cruise next week!" Steven quipped to Shane as he faced him across the bar counter now. They slapped hand in a "high-five" and Steven spun on his heels to circle the room excitedly.

"You got the Senator to let his wife go with us on the Cruise?" Shane asked in wonder, hoping his brother was not pulling his dick because he badly wanted Shaya for real.......

"Yep, he bet her when we were playing cards here earlier and he folded his hand, so she's ours for the Cruise, plus with that deed in his hand he'll do more good business with us considering we're the only ones who know he's got that laboratory property illegally!" Steven quipped in self-assumed triumph, slapping a hand on the bar counter's surface twice.

"Wow...I've been wanting to fuck Shaya since I first saw her.... she's a doll," Shane said softly, suddenly realizing he'd have to share her with Steven on the Cruise and for once he didn't like the feeling of that as he stared at his brother Steven across the room from him.

"Hey, didn't Amber say this old house had a storm-cellar behind the bar there?" Steven asked in change of subject, so content right now he was almost drunk with happiness.

"Yeah, somewhere behind the bar here," Shane said as his mind spun in circles of realization...what Steven just said about them being the only ones who know......

11:29pm: Amber Duffek had time enough to grab her purse and slip into a black jumpsuit she had draped over a dining chair earlier, then race out the back door toward the woods behind her home. The device she had delivered in the form of a large potted plant earlier this evening detonated from where she had placed it, inside the dining room! Five pounds of C-4 plastic explosive inside the ceramic "pot" exploded on cue at 11:30, consuming the entire household in an upwards fireball seen and heard for miles......

The force of the blast blew the female lawyer further into the wooded area in a violent tumble that knocked her out when the back of her head landed on a stump, her body rolling down into a small crevasse between her house and the next row of homes 30 yards away, which saved her from the thermal of the blast that caught the first row of trees behind her destroyed domicile ablaze. Knocked unconscious, Amber lay in the crevasse 15 yards from the burning remains of her million-dollar home here in Arlington, debris and burning material falling all around her as she lay unconscious but alive and relatively unharmed.

The blast was meant to kill whoever was in the house when the bomb went off, detonated by a man sitting in a van two blocks away, now driving off to get back on Rt. 66 east.

Duncan Horsehair had done it again, though this time at a prescribed time by Senator Kelsh, who had agreed to let Amber survive the blast because he had other uses for her anyway.

11:45pm: Shaya looked at Rupert in wonder as he drove across the Key Bridge into Georgetown now, heading for home. They had driven mostly in silence and he knew she had words for him but Shaya didn't bother to say them since she never seemed to be able to get a rise out of him when it came to lovers' quarrels, something they rarely had.....among other things! When Rupert pulled the Audi into the small parking space behind their home, Shaya got out without saying a word, walking up to the rear door of their home and unlocking it to go on in as if she were by herself, Rupert not far behind and not caring whether his "trophy wife" was pissed at him or not. When he walked into the heated household, Rupert saw his wife tearing off the "Indian chick" costume he had bought for her for this occasion as she was going up the stairs, tossing it's pieces everywhere as she headed for the shower no less.

"Hmmph...you really should thank me Shaya, after tonight you'll never see those twin apes Steven and Shane alive again and Moritmer Green no longer walks the earth either," he chuckled to himself as he walked into the kitchen, removing his costume cape and blazer.

"After tonight, it all kicks into overdrive," Rupert said to himself as he left the kitchen, walking through to the stairwell, slowly walking up them and thinking if Amber Duffek made it out of that explosion alive tonight. If she did, then she'd continue to be useful to him, but if she did not survive the explosion, then que sera sera….. she was a dyke anyway.

When Rupert came to the top of the stairs, he stopped as soon as he heard something he'd heard before, coming not from one of the guest-rooms but from the master bedroom! He walked to it and found the door ajar, peering inside to see his wife engrossed in missionary-intercourse on their marital bed, with another man…. Duncan Horsehair!

Senator Rupert Kelsh had let Shaya take other lovers, one of them being the one man who knows everything about Rupert and their mutual "war" of what most will call domestic terrorism, but even an open-marriage like theirs had it's "ground rules", one being that Shaya was to not make love with another man in the master bedroom, in their shared bed. Here she was violating that rule with Duncan Horsehair, who just blew up Amber Duffek's house back in Arlington and personally strangled the slimy Jew lobbyist named Mortimer Green hours before Amber's costume party. Rupert stood there and watched Duncan ravaging his wife in vigorous intercourse on his bed, the shadow-warrior having slipped into the house unseen as before, to slip it to the Senator's wife….

Stafford, Virginia. 12:30 that morning: Agent Clifford Stevens was no stranger to late night spent mulling over evidence, clues, and paperwork on a given case he investigated, nor was he a stranger to lack of sleep because of bullshit and "dead-ends" of a given case!

The FBI Video-forensics report on the old VHS tape he submitted for analysis was not something he wanted to read. Yes, after five straight days of a detailed computer-search of archived photo-files stretching from Felon databases to Military Veteran Medical files, the videotaped image of "Stranger #1" in the videotape footage taken by the horny teenage neighbor of the Marcano property on Beverly Lane in Fredericksburg. Sitting in his two-level apartment at FoxChase just off Rt. 1 in Stafford County not far from the historic City of Fredericksburg, he had the papers and print-outs spread out on his biege living room rug, coffeetable, and chairs. He preferred the peace of home than the office in Alexandria where he was assigned, concentrating on the "clues" found thus far, which was not yielding much to go on. The FBI Video Analysts came up with a good image of the man in black greeting Attorney Diego Tanner that night at the Marcano pool back in 2002, and the image run through all those databases at the behest of Deputy-Attorney-General Clark came back with the identity of a dead man! Cliff wanted to get drunk and pass out after reading the report.

"Second Lieutenant Duncan Hardesteadt….First Infantry Division US Army, Veteran of Operation Desert Storm….combat medal awarded….diagnosed with previously-unknown 'disease' upon his return home from active-duty in Nineteen-Ninety-Three….died at Walter Reed Army Hospital March Nineteen-Ninety-Four…. remains cremated," Cliff read to himself outloud as he looked over the report one more time, having also been sent a mugshot photo of the man from his Army Service Record, and it looked like him in the video footage! Only the candid videotape footage at the Marcano pool was filmed in the Summer of 2002, well beyond this soldier's death date of March 19, 1994.

"Dammit..all this trouble to get an ID and they tell me it's some wet-behind-the-ears Army Lieutenant from the first Gulf War fifteen years ago who died at Walter Reed Hospital," Cliff sneered to himself as he stood up from the futon he sat upon and walked around his Spartan living room, thinking on the matter closely. All he could do is re-confirm that soldier's death with the Dept. of the Army but why bother when the FBI and ATF both ran the face against every face they have in the system, coming up with a dead, forgotten soldier!

He walked around the living room of his apartment in simmering frustration. As it turns out, the "ghost" those assholes in the DHS wanted him to pursue is actually a "dead end" like he suspected but made it this far anyway! Two million dollars "missing" from Marcano Mob assets recovered, a now-defunct Porn Film Company with ties to the underworld, and the face of a dead man taken from a 2002 videotape, only the dead man was walking on two feet and meeting with Marcano Mob Lawyer Diego Tanner in Fredericksburg Virginia approximately 8 years after his death at Walter Reed Army Hospital and alleged "cremation"!

"I'm working in the goddamn 'twilight zone', I don't believe this…shit," Cliff said to himself then grabbed his leather jacket and keys, stepping to the door of his apartment to leave, grabbing his paddle-holstered Glock pistol and the small box of items he's accumulated as clues up to this point. Out the door and to his car, Cliff Stevens wanted to drive into Fredericksburg right now and to the old Marcano "safe house" again, hoping to "jog" his memory a bit more and recall in intricate detail his pat surveillance of the place and those who stayed there between 2002 and 2004. His pager was buzzing on his left hip, but he didn't want to answer it because the number on the tiny pager's screen was the Alexandria Field Office, probably his Supervisor paging him and since he was now working directly for Deputy Attorney General Tyler Clark, his regular Supervisors were a lower priority….

Georgetown, 12 Midnight: Rupert Kelsh watched his three TV screens in his upstairs den while also holding his laptop PC in front of him as he sat in his favorite recliner, eyes on the three TV screens as news reports came in about two points of interest for him: One, the murder of controversial Democratic Lobbyist Mortimer Green in his own home at 6:00pm, the other being the explosion and fire destroying the home of Attorney Amber Duffek just 30 minutes ago. The first story was being reported primarily then as more information came in, the unexplainable explosion that occurred at the residence of Feminist Attorney Amber Duffek at approximately 11:30pm. Duncan Horsehair had accomplished both "errands" for him as he had successfully done numerous time before, and was now helping himself to Shaya in his bedroom. The master bedroom came up on the laptop PC screen quite clearly from the hidden security-cam Rupert had installed in the wall over the bedroom door, seeing his wife getting hammered by Duncan on his bed right now, the two of them fucking like there is no tomorrow….perhaps they realize the precarious situation they are both in now and that neither of them had a place in Rupert's life for very much longer? He doubted his wife suspected anything, though she will once she learns of what happened to Green and Amber's house this evening as soon as she left with him almost 45 minutes ago!

"Say good-bye to the Pillage brothers…hunh-huh, talking-monkeys thought I treated them as 'equals' when I was setting them up to exit the stage all too easily," Rupert said to himself as the news about Amber's "house fire" came on three separate TV News channels now.

"Talking….hustling….monkeys," Rupert snickered in contempt for the twin brothers he rightly assumed were vaporized in the explosion, wondering if any news about Amber would be reported tonight? If she did get out of the house in time before Duncan set it off, she will need to be "covered" by his friend in the Justice Department, spin the "investigation" as something like a gas line breech causing the explosion, or some bullshit like that. Amber Duffek was still a bit "useful" so keeping her pretty ass alive for now was his decision.

Rupert saved five minutes of footage from the two lovers in his bedroom right now to a file, he then emailed the video-wave file to an encrypted email address to be accessed later if needed. He always hedged his bets, and Shaya was expendable, just like Duncan Horsehair.

"Give it to her Duncan….yeah brother, give it to her good n' hard…never know, might be the last time you two get together like that," Rupert snickered as he watched the muscular, long-haired man screwing his wife in a vibrant missionary-position, Shaya rocking to and fro with his pounding body, yelping out in reaction to his pelvic thrusts, her face a grimace of sexual surrender to the man gorging into her flesh. Rupert had to grin at the sight, silently wishing he could take her on like that, to really make her wail out in delight like Duncan did.

He hadn't told her of his diagnosis several years ago, Multiple Sclerosis is often something one of his age group can "hide" symptoms from family members. Legs going to sleep often, and his often-erectile-disfunction easily chalked up as "getting old", Senator Kelsh kept the fact he had MS from his constituents, staff, and more especially from his younger wife.

"If I had a younger body my dear Shaya....I would fuck you all night," he said to himself as he then lowered the laptop PC screen and turned his attention back to the three TV screens.

"But, as it turns out...my plan is full-steam-ahead....and I will soon achieve what I set out to get accomplished over ten years ago.... the 'change' the American People deserve, 'change' within the very government those idiots vote for....stemming from an 'emergency' situation that'll be like the Reichstag Fire, only far less overt," he said to himself as he watched the news about the home of Attorney Amber Duffek being destroyed in a mysterious explosion just an hour ago and the murder of Lobbyist Mortimer Green earlier the same night at 6pm.

"Hmm...maybe doing both on the same night was a bit hasty, but then again getting rid of those targets was necessary right-away," Rupert said to himself.

1705 Beverly Lane, Fredericksburg Va. 1:05am: Agent Clifford Stevens was not really trespassing, it was more like investigative-follow-up with a twist of "unlawful entry" plus the fact there was no active alarm system alerting the local Police to him opening the basement sliding-glass door again, made the excursion here a walk in the park. He came here to jog his own memory from years ago when he had this place under surveillance, back when the things occurred he is just now uncovering in an "unofficial" investigation into someone who may just be a dead man come back to life or.... someone who looks like the man carrying out clandestine terror operations over the course of a decade. The house here smelled dusty and of cedar like it did the last time he was here. Walking on into the basement interior and shining his flashlight in front of him, Cliff wanted to get drunk and just fall asleep here, it's "coziness" calling to him, or maybe it was just the fact he hasn't gotten much sleep lately.

He placed his "clue box" on the dusty pool table, then checked to make sure the power was still on in the house, the ceiling-fan light coming on with a single yank of it's chain. He then stepped into the sitting room area of the basement here and turned on the 27" TV set on the wooden stand by the fake-fireplace, wiping dust from it's screen with his windbreaker sleeve as he took the jacket off to stay here awhile. The TV was on and he recognized a Cable TV channel, which also proved the house here was paid up on it's cable bill as well as light bill!

"Interesting," he sighed as he stepped back to see the TV news report as it explained the details of an explosion that just occurred in Arlington over an hour ago. Cliff had to sit down when the TV News Reporter mentioned the name of the homeowner whose house just got blown up somehow following a "costume party" earlier in the evening.

"Amber Duffek....you gotta be shittin' me," Cliff said to himself as he heard the name.

"Someone got to her," he told himself then was surprised to hear the TV news report say that the Attorney is being treated at an undisclosed hospital for superficial injuries.

"Wow, now I know my next stop in the morning," Cliff said to himself, guessing that was why his Supervisor in Alexandria was paging him over and over again earlier. He then stood up and took a disk to the DVD player on top of the TV set, putting it in and hoping the DVD player will work after sitting here for a long time without use. The screen came to life and since he had no remote control, he engaged the "movie" on the DVD Player itself, seeing the title and credits come alive on the TV's 27" screen, making him smile in reaction.

Big Bustin'Loose starring Shaya Gold, Christy Cannons, F.M. Dexter, and Horny Jack.

It was Directed by Scott Metzenbaum and Produced by Midnight Video.

"Here we go," Cliff said to himself as he fingered the DVD player's buttons to select the first scene showing Shaya Gold in action, then he sat back in the bean-bag chair with his recently-purchased stainless flask which had Jack Daniels in it, feeling like a drink right now.

"Now show me something I don't know yet....give me a reason why there's some kind of link between the Marcano Mob, Faster Porn Films, and a domestic terrorist?" Cliff spoke to the screen as it came to life with X-rated theme. 'Shaya Gold" was a "kidnapee" tied up and kept by two male "kidnappers"(both of who are the male actors in the cast credits of course) and she was now getting loose from her binds as the camera zoomed in on her pretty face.

"Hey....guys...untie me and we can work something out....I don't know where I am so I'm not going anywhere....some on, let's play nice for a change," Shaya Gold spoke in a calm voice that wasn't "accented" at all (as Cliff expected by the lightly-bronzed skin and "foreign" looking features of the Starlet) bust sounded like an average American!

"We can untie you but we'll uhhm...have to take your clothes too...so you won't be able to run away," the black male actor (F.M. Dexter) said to her as he began to untie her binds.

Shaya Gold agreed to the condition and the next scene was of the black man and wispy-blond-haired white actor pulling off her clothes as she stood up, the camera focusing on

F.M. Dexter slowing pulling down the gym-shorts she was wearing and the lace panties, then he leaned in and kissed her right ass cheek lightly for the camera and then he bit down into her buttock, making her giggle in reaction. Cliff had to laugh, all porn films are grossly unrealistic like this, almost comical in their premise and themes of sexual play.

Next had Shaya Gold on her knees with the bandana-gag now loose around her neck, both men standing to flank her, hard-ons out for her to take. Typical porn film "double-suck" Cliff thought as he watched Shaya Gold slurp from one actor's big dick to the other's.

Shaya performed a double-fellatio on the two actors without fail, going from one to the other, keeping both men's erections in her hands, gently stroking one as she fellated the other. Cliff took a swig of his booze from the flask, thinking about the woman on the screen right now, this X-rated film having been made back in 1997 and not by Jonny Faster.

Shaya Gold (now Shaya Kelsh) was a "career" porn actress and spent most of her adult life up to 2005 in the adult entertainment spectrum. Having left it suddenly in 2005 and married a US Senator, she had jumped from one life to a whole new and different one far quicker and easier than it would take most people to accomplish similar....maybe it was just luck?

Cliff Stevens knew better than to assume "luck" had anything to do with strangers like this leading extraordinary lifestyles forged out of "thin air"....something BAD was brewing in the lives of strangers like this because nothing just happens by accident!

He watched as Shaya Gold straddled the black actor FM Dexter on a big wicker chair, facing the camera as the man sat beneath her, shoving his lengthy spear up into her sweet spot, and she began to "ride" him at an odd angle for the camera as the other actor sat down across from them watching and waiting his turn. Shaya moved on the actor like a champ, taking his manhood up in her nearly all of it's length, moaning in delight of the penetration, her big boobs jiggling as she moved up and down on her male co-star, moaning aloud in delight of the act. Cliff wondered if women like "Shaya Gold" actually enjoyed the sex as they were being filmed or was it all an act? Shaya sure looked "worked up" in this scene, he thought.

"Now a Senator's wife....wonder how you managed that, considering the very conservative voting record of Senator Rupert Kelsh, hunh-haanh," Cliff said to the screen then took another sip of the booze in his tiny flask, enjoying the numbing sensation of alcohol now.

"Does Senator Kelsh know about you getting boned by a black dude in this film Shaya?" Cliff laughed as he watched the X-rated sex scene continue, eventually becoming a

"threesome" with Shaya on all-fours between the two male actors, the black one drilling her doggie-style from behind, the white one in front with Shaya eagerly tasting his big pickle.

Cliff pulled out a thick magazine from the box he brought here with him tonight, one dedicated to the X-rated Film Industry called "XVN Periodical". Thumbing to the profile page of "Shaya Gold", he re-read the lengthy bio and profile on the veteran Pornstress:

Shaya Gold hails from Brazilian and Turkish stock, an exotic and well-developed beauty to come into the "Jizz Bizz" in the early 90's. Won XVN Awards for "Best Blowjob Scene" and "Best Orgy Scene" in the 90's and became a fan-favorite for her good looks, big tits, and uncompromising sexual talent which always seemed to light up the screen no matter who her partner was. Known best for her group-sex scenes (as in 1995's "Devil In The DD-Tails") and her willingness to be cast with men of color such as F.M. Dexter and Mered Alladin, she was cast with Porn Super-Stud Jonny Faster almost exclusively during the late 1990s up until her retirement from Porn altogether in 2005. Shaya Gold was also one of the rare Adult Film Starlets who never danced in men's clubs on the side, but making her living solely in X-rated filmmaking.

Georgetown, 1:55am: Shaya rolled over on the bed, realizing the covers had been pushed off to the floor during her energetic romp with Duncan earlier, and she felt a slight chill as she lay naked on the uncovered bed now, drowsy enough to fall asleep and was close to it.

She looked up as she heard the bedroom door creak open, expecting Duncan but it was her husband, reminding her that Duncan has pulled yet another one of his vanishing acts after screwing her brains loose once more. She rolled right to face her husband in the doorway as he stood there like a steamed parent about to scold a child for wrongdoing, and she knew exactly what he was about to "scold" her for!

"I know....we did it in our bedroom....our bed....one of the rules, I know....and I apologize Rupert, it's just we got groovy really fast and....ended up right here," Shaya spoke up before he could say anything, eyeing him as he stood there with his arms folded tightly.

"It's a rule-breaker Shaya...you know how serious it is....even if it was my friend Duncan," Rupert spoke in a calm but stern tone of voice, eyeballing her fiercely to the point of anger.

"Yes, a rule-breaker....hmmmh....I don't have anything to say but I'm sorry," she sighed with a shrug acknowledging her guilt, eyes down in the slight sting of realization now.

"This is an eventful night for us my dear....Amber Duffek's house just blew up, killing the Pillage brothers and almost killing her.... and Mortimer Green was found strangled to death in his mansion over in Arlington as well," Rupert said as he closed the bedroom door behind him and walked around the room, arms still folded as he went, not looking at her right now.

"What…Amber's house…..blew up…is she okay…..the Pillage brothers?" Shaya quipped in surprise of the news, sitting up on the bed in fearful reaction to what he was telling her.

"Amber is in a hospital recovering from minor damage….the Pillage brothers were in the house when it blew up, so they're gone," Rupert answered her matter-of-factly.

"You said I wouldn't have to go on that Cruise with Steven and Shane….that I would never see that bastard Mortimer Green ever again…did you have it done?" she replied fearfully.

"Maybe, or maybe someone linked to me, regardless…it's done and for good reason my dear, and you will be wise to never mention what you know to anyone outside this room, because it would be a shame if something negative happens to you," he continued flatly.

Shaya licked her dry lips, nervous and scared as she sat there naked on their marital bed, but part of her was aroused by the "power" she was being told about now, the power to kill people and get away with it, the power to take whatever a man wants and go unnoticed by authorities, it made her gush! Maybe that was her real feelings defined when it came to her husband, the power he wields….only now did he share with her the extent of his power, and she was silently in awe of him for the moment, wishing she hadn't broken one of the few "rules" of their open marriage tonight! She knew some form of punishment was coming from him, and she could only guess what it will be….what, is she going to resist it…how could she when her husband is the powerful man he is, having just reminded her of the fact?

"Whatever you want to do to me, I deserve it for breaking the rule tonight," she spoke up.

"Of course…hmmmh….I want you to go to the hair-stylist in the morning and get your hair cut the way I suggested to you awhile back, then I'd like for you to pay a visit to my friend in the Justice Department….you know the address…give him my regards and inform him that the ball is rolling," Rupert explained to her softly as he walked around the room with arms still folded denoting his displeasure with her tonight. Shaya nodded in reluctant acceptance of her husband's "punishment" for her. She had this length of silky dark hair since her Porn Film days and he now wanted her to cut it short and he wanted her to go fuck one of his political buddies, least this one was one she enjoyed screwing around with once before!

"Whatever you say honey, and once again.....I'm sorry," Shaya said in conclusion as he left the bedroom to go sleep in one of the guest rooms, leaving her there to think about it.

Fredericksburg, 2:14am: Cliff put another DVD into the player, this one being entitled:

Tha Bone Shack and it starred Jonny Faster, Christy Cannons, Shaya Gold, FM Dexter, Woodrow Grande and Carla Ferrari. This one opened with Jonny Faster whipping out his tube-monster for Shaya Gold to feast upon in a lengthy oral-sex scene on an old-looking sofa. The Flick's "storyline" was on wife-swappers who fool around in a little pool-house.

"Looks like love to me, Shaya," Cliff said outloud as he watched the scene from the beanbag chair in the dark basement of the old Marcano "safe house", sipping on his flask of booze and relaxing a bit more than he should have. Trying to see the rapport his suspects had with one another back then, he was beginning to come up with a profile of "motive" and he was beginning to "see" it in the Porno Queen of over 400 feature-films: SHAYA GOLD!

"Looks like you really loved Jonny Faster....judging by the way you performed with him in these porn flicks....hunh-hunh.... man-oh-man, does it look obvious!" Cliff quipped to the TV screen then took another swig of his liquor flask, watching as Shaya Gold performed ardent fellatio on the incredibly-well-endowed Jonny Faster. That bastard had to have been a foot long! Some guys have all the goddamn fun these days, Cliff mused to himself, watching.

"Now tell me you two lovebirds....where's the two million dollars laundered through your company in two-thousand-five, hunh.... couldn't have hid it all between those big tits?" Cliff spoke to the TV screen as Jonny and Shaya switched to intercourse on the sofa now, the blond-haired German-looking Jonny Faster plunging into the bronze-skinned, big-breasted Shaya Gold in a vibrant missionary position, and she wailed out in delight of him impaling her like that, her shapely bare body shaking on the sofa beneath her lover as he plowed inside of her in steady motion, pumping his manhood into her sweet flesh vigorously.

The tryst between Jonny and Shaya lasted a few more minutes then ended with Jonny giving Shaya a "white pearl necklace" and the scene faded to black. Next up was Carla Ferrari in a lesbo scene with Christy Cannons in the "pool house" but with Christy seated on a wooden chair while the blonde cupcake Carla feasted between her smooth legs below.....

Cliff sat up in his beanbag seat and managed to reach the TV's DVD player with one finger, forwarding the X-rated movie to the next scene with Shaya Gold in it, this one showing her walking into the pool house with black actor "FM Dexter" and getting eaten-out by him on the sofa then she fellates him while he gets undressed and then Shaya lay on the white rug on the floor and her black male co-star engaged her in a vaunted missionary-position as she squirmed on the floor on her back, taking it from the man on his spread-out knees as she lay there with legs open and big boobs bouncing to and from as her body moved with his mounting thrusts. Shaya moaned outloud accordingly, her face turned aside as the porn actor drilled her continuously for the camera, that sex-scene lasting like that for another minute then it switched to Shaya up on all-fours getting hammered "doggie-style" by her male co-star, his hands squeezing her bare asscheeks as he pumped into her steadily, making her yelp in reception of him, or maybe that was just her "acting", Cliff couldn't tell. Shaya Gold seemed to take on a more "passionate" personage during sex-roles with Jonny Faster he noticed so far......something she did no seem to have with the other actors!

He pressed the stop button on the DVD player and fished another X-rated DVD movie from his "clue box" he had here with him, this one called Take My Wife and it starred Jonny Faster, Shelly James, Chrissa Bo, Cody Abs, and Lacey Lovitt. Feeling the effects of the alcohol, Cliff put the flask away and stood up for fear of falling asleep now. He wanted to see a film with Jonny Faster and Shelly James, since he just interviewed Shelly recently, a woman he didn't think would be a murderer, but she could be holding some vital info, so he wanted to see if she had that telling "passion" like Shaya had with Jonny Faster!

Georgetown, 2:45am: Rupert Kelsh relaxed in his plush living room with a glass of juice and the big screen TV on, remote in his left hand. He now found it humorous that Duncan and Shaya ended up in the master bedroom earlier, engrossed in passion's grip they failed to consider one of his "house rules" about noone but he and Shaya romp in that bedroom. He knew Duncan had stopped by to pick up the original deed to the Laboratory property purchased in Maryland a year ago, for he would take care of the necessary "placement" of that deed. Duncan of course then helped himself to the Senator's wife, which he was allowed to do whenever he "dropped by" unannounced like he has in the past.

Rupert chuckled to himself as he engaged the remote to play a DVD he had in the machine already, one of his wife Shaya's early X-rated features entitled: Cake! (and Eat Her Too).

He watched the opening credits, seeing the names of the cast such as Shaya Gold, Fanny Hotts, Dina Bell, Rafael Mendes, FM Dexter, and Chesty More. It was a 1992 film made by "Vick Flick Productions" re-released on DVD in 2003. Rupert liked watching his wife's past porn films from time to time, mostly when he was irritated with her or to remind himself why he married her and her "purpose" in his grand scheme of things. As the X-rated film began on his 57" TV screen, he sipped his drink and watched in solitary silence.

It began with an older man seated in a wheel chair at a dining table as eating dinner served by his scantily-clad "Maid" who happened to be none-other-than Shaya Gold! She wore a skimpy "French Maid" outfit that barely covered her tits and ass naturally, and she brought the old man a dinner plate and big glass of red wine to the table as the credits ended.

Rupert had to laugh as the scene unfolded with an "intrusion" by three other actors, one being a sexy female starlet (Dina Bell) holding a very plastic-looking handgun with two male actors coming in behind her as "goons", one being FM Dexter and the other Rafael

Mendes, he surmised from the names on the DVD box. The chick with the gun dialogued with the old man at the table about a "deal" he broke with her while the black actor FM Dexter and the other guy grabbed the maid, (Shaya) bringing her into view of her boss at the table, holding her by the arms and back of the neck in a definitely gentle manner for the camera.

The chick with the gun then said the three of them were going to "make ourselves at home" here until the old man gives her what he "owes" her, which the old man quietly refused.

Rupert didn't recall watching this particular film before now, so he sat there taking it in.

The "maid" was then ushered into the living room set by the black actor FM Dexter, where he casually bent her over the armrest of the big sofa there, lifting up her frilly skirt to reveal her sexual region for the camera then the actor casually pulled out his erect member and without any resistance or words to the contrary, shoved it up inside of the willing "maid", Shaya Gold, as she bent over the armrest of the sofa. Anywhere else (but in a porno flick) that would be considered a rape, but for X-rated film....it's a fantasy-sex-scene where the black male intruder takes liberties with the passive (and willing) female "maid"!

The first sex-scene was underway: Shaya bent over a sofa getting long-dicked by FM Dexter doggie-style for the viewing audience. Rupert had to laugh at the sight of his younger wife in this scene from 1992, she was in her mid-twenties at the time and had even longer dark hair, cooing in delight of her co-star's penetration of her, performing as she always did for the cameras, making it look awfully enticing as the man pumped into her in steady intercourse.

The female with the toy "gun" kept talking to the old man at the dinner table, demanding he "repay" his debt, the camera rotating from her back to Shaya the maid getting reamed, and back again. The old man kept glancing into the next room as his maid was getting-it-on with the both men now, Rafael Mendes kneeling on the sofa in front of Shaya to get his lance waxed by her while FM Dexter continued on her from behind, Shaya's boobs conveniently popped out from her maid outfit now for the camera to focus on for a moment's "jiggle".

Rupert smiled at the sight of his wife's "performance" on the screen, once again finding himself amused at the sight of her with other men. Though Rupert disliked Blacks and Latinos privately, he dealt with them when it was necessary to get something done that suited him. Seeing a Black man fuck Shaya on film was not threatening to him at all really, considering his wife is a non-white woman herself, Turkish and Brazilian heritage mixed with Italian was not exactly the "Aryan Ideal" as far as his personal, deep-core beliefs went!

Shaya could never bear his children, so he was not violating his ideal in the manner of flesh.

Still, he wished he could sexually ravage Shaya like those men in her past porn films did....

"After tonight, the ball is in play....it's gonna be a whole new game," Rupert Kelsh said to himself as he watched the X-rated movie continue, thinking on his overall plan.

Fredericksburg Va. (same time): Cliff was starting to nod-off as he sat back in the beanbag seat watching the porn film on the old TV set here in the Marcano Mob "safe house" on Beverly Lane. Time was getting away from him and he did not want to fall asleep here, that was for sure. The TV screen was now displaying the famously blonde cupcake "Shelly James" getting screwed by the overly-endowed Jonny Faster in a semi-vertical sexual intercourse resulting in her pretty face pressed against a cabinet door inside of a kitchen while Jonny drove his big torpedo up inside of her for the camera. The camera zoomed in on the penetration itself again for a moment, showing the man's mammoth boner sliding up inside of his female co-star's sweet spot gently, making her wail aloud in delight, face against the cabinet as she bent over the kitchen counter, only an apron around her waist as her lover hammered her into obvious orgasm. Cliff laughed then forced himself to stand up, realizing he had too much whiskey awhile ago and the effects of the alcohol was apparent now.

He killed the TV set and ejected the DVD, tossing it back into his "clue box", stretching his arms upward and yawning, the weariness of lack of sleep and the booze making sitting down for him an all-too-inviting prospect, so he sat back down, this time on the dusty sofa there in the dark sitting room of 1705 Beverly Lane. He kept thinking of the "links" he was told to look for by those higher-ups in DHS and Justice, the "links" between the Marcano Mob, a now-defunct Porn Company, and a shadowy domestic terrorist whose facial-ID registers as that of a deceased Gulf War soldier. An impossible investigation to say the least, but he was on the trail tonight, reflecting back into the past when he had one of the players under surveillance here at this very house. Now his alcohol-consumption was impairing her vision as he sat there on the sofa.... he could "see" someone appear over by the dust-covered pool table, a young woman clad in a string-bikini....and judging by the shape of her, he knew he had to be hallucinating. When he concentrated on the apparition, he even recognized her!

"I drank too damn much....Isabel....Isabel Marcano?" Cliff chimed in stunned realization as the ghostly mirage moved to the front of the pool table in his direction, then his ears played tricks on him as well. "Like my new peach bikini?" came the soft female voice to his ears.

"Hmmh, too bad I can't walk on a beach during the daytime and show it off," the voice answered her own question as the well-developed dark-haired woman faced the intoxicated Federal Agent sitting on the dusty sofa in a silent stupor. He couldn't believe it, it was her!

What a lucid hallucination too, almost as if the real Isabel Marcano stood six feet in front of him wearing nothing but a tight and skimpy peach-colored string-bikini, the top of which bulging and barely covering the more alluring centers of her plump and perky breasts.

"Isabel...I thought you're dead....I mean....what's up?" Cliff spoke wearily to the "ghost".

"Diego Tanner is dead…I'm really all alone…..damn, wish I had someone….he might have been the one for me and he's gone…. his balls in a jar," the ghostly image spoke to herself.

It was as if he was listening to someone talking from in another room, the sound of her voice meeting his ears as if he were listening to her on a wire-tap or something like that.

Cliff was sleepy as hell but it felt as if he was witnessing a very lucid and clear "ghost" walking and talking but not specifically to him, almost as if he were not there in the room!

He slowly stood up from the sofa, hoping the image would not vanish as "ghosts" tend to do when one approaches them, seeing the bikini-clad woman by the pool table looking back in his direction though as if she were staring right through him, as if he were not there!

"Diego….I regret what happened to you….you never did anything to harm me and now you're gone….damn it," Isabel sighed gingerly with her pretty head bowed as she spoke.

It was as if Cliff was witnessing a very "clear" ghost of some kind from the recent past, and it was Isabel Marcano! The 25-year old Niece of the Marcano Crime Boss who inherited the "Family Business" after her Uncle's death in the botched FBI/ATF raid back in 2004, the young woman who was also afflicted with a rare genetic disorder barring her from walking out into broad daylight. It was her, he determined as he cautiously stepped closer, feeling unbalanced in his steps due to his alcohol intake this evening.

"Isabel?" Cliff chimed softly as he moved closer toward where her image now stood by the pool table, hands on her hips, not seeing him or acknowledging him at all even now. He recalled reading somewhere that "ghosts" may be apparitional "imprints" in a given dwelling, like a photographic "memory" in an old house like this one, so he considered that.

"Duncan…another man I could have loved…..Duncan Horsehair…..left me," the apparition spoke, again sounding like he was hearing it from outside of the room in surveillance, once more reminding him this had to be a dream, a very lucid hallucination!

"Wait.....Horsehair?" Cliff chimed in realization of what he was hearing, struggling with the reality of the spoken words he was hearing from a "ghost" and the fact he was intoxicated.

"I'm alone.....I'll always be alone unless I do something about it...Jonny Faster, that son-of-a-bitch owes my Family over two-hundred-grand.....I gotta get to him and convince him myself, make a deal with him, heenh-heeh...I've been watching his fuck-movies for years now, and I am a fan of his....why not?" Isabel chimed, talking to herself as she circled the pool table away from the staggering ATF Agent trying to move closer to his ghostly visitor.

There, she just mentioned Jonny Faster, the "missing" Porn Mogul! Cliff told himself.

"Isabel......Isabel.....?" Cliff spoke after her as he leaned on the pool table, the light of the small lamp in the sitting room barely illuminating the basement beyond the pool table. He could still see here now, walking gracefully for the wooden stairwell leading up into the house above. Again, he thought this had to be an "imprint" left here like the ghost stories of old, and he imagined he was witnessing something which occurred some time ago, back when Isabel Marcano resided here at 1705 Beverly Lane, a visual "recording" imprinted for an intoxicated ATF Agent to witness at 3:00 in the morning while trespassing here!

The shapely female apparition stopped at the first few steps and turned to look back at the basement "pool hall" of the household, that bikini she wore bulging tightly against her better physical portions, Cliff staring at those big breasts of hers as she stood there all too clearly.

"Is there someone there?" Isabel asked in a casual tone, this time a bit clearer than before.

"Heenh-heh...if some guy is stalking me, show yourself now and I'll take you up on it!" she chimed girlishly with both hands pushing against her big bikini-clad boobs to "shake" them in lewd gesture toward the basement pool hall and sitting room. Cliff spoke up again as he stepped within two feet of the apparition, but she didn't appear to have heard him for real.

The lovely image of the bikini-clad Isabel Marcano then vanished up the stairs, and Cliff knelt at the base of the stairwell, vision spinning due to his intoxication.

Duncan Horsehair glanced at his watch and saw 3:25am, walking from his parked car on Beverly Drive down to the woods behind the address he'd frequented quite a few times in the recent past. He was re-visiting the empty residence this early morning before sunrise for two valid reasons: 1) to get a couple of bricks of C-4 plastic explosive he has stashed on the property. 2) to reflect on the one true love of his life, who used to stay here a few years ago.

Walking quietly through dead leaves and shrubbery leading up to the rear portions of the house at 1705 Beverly Lane, Duncan Horsehair went unseen and unheard by the sleeping community around him, moving with a cat's stealth up to the dark rear courtyard.

Clad in black duster coat over black BDU pants and t-shirt with black leather boots, the man fit the darkness well, cloaked in the night as he had survived in for over 12 years now. He knew there was no alarm here so he walked on up to the rear sliding-glass door to make an entry, finding it slightly ajar, which was unusual....thus setting off his own "alarm"!

Agent Clifford Stevens had been a Field Agent for most of his 17-year career, and in that time his reflexes had been honed to a sharp 96% infallibility, a trait that served him well right now, even while intoxicated here in a dark house he knew little about. Hearing and seeing the man in black enter the house via the sliding-glass door in a tactical movement done by virtually any good cop or soldier, letting off a thin profile, with a weapon in front to scan the interior of the room he was carefully entering, Cliff knew the intruder was not a cop or he'd hear police sirens and radios outside and there was no announcement or identifying marker, so this guy was fair game.... even though he was an intoxicated Federal Agent "trespassing".

"ATF Agent.....freeze!" Cliff shouted toward the shadow-man side-stepping the sliding door entrance, Cliff now using the pool table as cover as he brandished his weapon out at the ready, seeing only a thick shadow ahead, the lamp light not enough to give a better look.

The shadow moved with inhuman speed, shooting out the lamplight in one shot while capping off three more shots in Cliff's direction, directly over his head into the wall beyond the pool table, the roar of the handgun inside of a domicile deafening, and Cliff guessed the weapon to be a higher-caliber automatic such as a .45 Auto. The man in black was back out the door in retreat after firing, Cliff's return-volley of three shots from his little Glock .45 striking the wood panel around the sliding door, his ears sore and hearing gone for the time being due to the loudness of the gunfire. He instinctively moved around the pool table toward the sliding door, making it there to shove his weapon out the open doorway to see if he could get a glimpse of the intruder in black who just committed a Federal Crime by shooting at a Federal Agent! If this man-in-black was a Marcano Mobster coming here at this time of night, he was arriving expecting trouble and was ready to fire at a moment's notice, Cliff kept thinking as he tactically assessed the outside patio area to venture out there now.

This was no ordinary cat-burglar though, he told himself as he swallowed hard and leapt out to the dark patio area, expecting an ambush but knew the other guy could not see in the dark either unless he had a night-vision scope! A burglar would not have reacted like that, almost taking an Agent's head off with a handgun fired in a darkened room, this was something else

entirely and he was going to try and bag this shooter himself, though getting on his cell-phone to call the local Police for back-up did cross his mind. Sure enough, the neighbors will be calling the PD after hearing gunfire, so Cliff pursued in hopes the perp doesn't slip into the night unseen. He slipped around the BBQ pit and into the dark courtyard, glimpsing a darker shadow move up where the hottub cabana was, so Cliff point-shot at the shadow, the muzzle-flash of his weapon illuminating the terrain ahead of him for just a second, a second he gained by continuing to move as he fired. Duncan Horsehair had no idea how this could have happened, but whoever this "ATF Agent" was, he would never take **him** alive……

Cliff hurried up the brick steps to the closed hottub cabana and tactically maneuvered as best he could under his own intoxication, his weapon in both hands in front and weary eyesight focusing as best he could on the dark terrain leading up to the closed off pool area.

The shadow moved fast and sleek up the incline to the pool area, Cliff barely able to make him out in the darkness but he pointed his Glock .45 and squeezed off two more rounds in the direction of the darting shadow, getting one round fired back at him, striking the dirt at his feet just six inches from his left ankle as he crouched to fire again. Cliff ducked and dodged, rolling right though moving like that did wonders for ruining what coordination he had right now, dizzier than before as he climbed the hillside leading up to the pool deck.

If the shooter gets to the neighboring property, he might take a hostage or kill eyewitnesses!

Once he made it to the chain-link fence surrounding the pool area, Cliff circled around to the pool house as he thought the shooter in black headed to the other side of the pool, and that was the one intoxicated mistake which quickly cost him.

He crouched by the cement pool house to reload his weapon with a fresh magazine, and he suddenly found himself pushed off-balance by what felt like a sledge hammer striking his left side, but turned out to be the man in black's two hands shoving him to the chain-link fence with the force feeling like he'd bee struck by a car! Landing against the old chain-link fence, Cliff Stevens nearly went through it to the other side, the wind knocked out of him and his spine in pain from the blow, he didn't feel those same pair of hands picking him up by the shirt and foisting his entire body up and over the fence to drop him into the pool itself.

Landing on the tarp covering the closed-off swimming pool, Cliff felt it collapse downward into what felt like a liquid mass.... the pool was not empty of water under the tarp, which was better than landing 8 feet further down on solid cement.......

Duncan Horsehair did not pursue eliminating the ATF Agent or whoever he was further, leaving the scene as soon as he tossed the man into the closed swimming pool, already hearing police sirens in the distance. He was gone from the property there and back to his parked car ¼ mile away, driving off safely in the other direction by the time the first police vehicle turned onto Beverly Lane. Inside the closed pool, Cliff struggled to regain his full breathing and to recover from sinking into the cold tepid water under the tarp which threatened to drown him if he could not get a hold on something that would keep him from descending. He kept thinking of what he saw in the house earlier before the attack, that ghostly image of Isabel Marcano talking to herself, mentioning Diego Tanner, "Horsehair", and even Jonny Faster! This was no coincidence, it was FATE with his name written all over it, damned if he was intoxicated or not.... he struggled to survive the enveloping water and tarp swallowing him up as he descended like an animal caught in quicksand......

Managing to find something metal in the pool shaped like a rod to hold on to and keep from sinking, he relaxed and waited for help to arrive. He kept thinking of who would shoot at him like that, who would toss him into this closed swimming pool like a rag doll then vanish into the night, who would have come here to this address (like he did) at three o'clock in the morning armed and looking for something? Not some random burglar or even a mobster...

"Holy shit....I think I just met the man himself..... that slippery, invisible motherfucker named Horsehair, and he sure as hell ain't dead n' cremated!" Cliff quipped up at the starry night sky over the closed off swimming pool he now lay in. This morning's unimaginable events were not coincidental, it was FATE and Clifford Stevens was written all over it....

When Police alley-lights shined across the pool area and he could hear Police Radio-traffic from radios in the near vicinity, Cliff fished out his badge and ID with his free hand to hold up as soon as the local cops shined their lights down into the closed off swimming pool.

Fairfax Hospital, Fairfax Va. 1:15pm the following day: Whether it was the "tests" conducted on her or the food, staying just for "observation" at a Hospital was the worst and Attorney Amber

Duffek was not in the mood to speak with the Doctor who just walked back out after being referred to as "Doctor Prick" again by his attractive (but mean) patient.

Amber climbed back onto the hospital bed wondering if the bruise on her neck would fade away soon and the soreness in he legs and back would continue any longer, being "tossed" by an exploding house was worse than she had anticipated. Of course, she managed to convince the Police Detectives and even the FBI Agent who came by to interview her over the course of the past 8 hours so far. Amber knew the Law and she knew most kinds of Police Investigations all too well to be tricked into "implicating" herself in the explosion which cost her a house and the lives of two party guests who hadn't left when told to!

She imagined what Steven and Shane Pillage must have felt during the final seconds of their lives downstairs in her basement "parlor", just before the explosion brought the household down onto them below! She wanted them dead almost as much as Senator Kelsh did, but for a different reason altogether. She owed the Pillage brothers a lot of money over a "sports bet" a year ago and she did not want to pay them, even though sleeping with them both would have solved the debt altogether, far be it for Amber Duffek to surrender to those two!

"Bye-Bye Steven....Bye-Bye Shane.....heenh-heeh, see you in hell, if there is an afterlife," Amber whispered to herself in triumph as she lay there staring up at the TV perched on the wall overhead in the small Hospital room, also lamenting the fact she was stuck wearing a thin hospital-gown, her jumpsuit from her "escape" last night taken by the Fire Marshal as part of the fire-investigation. At least the Police Officer guarding her outside the room's door was gone, relieved of his post after the FBI declared she was "safe" considering the initial report of a "gas line" being the likely culprit of the explosion(not a "hit" on her) pending further investigation. She had Senator Kelsh to thank for that, as well as the "potted plant" which held not five pounds of dirt but five pounds of C-4 plastic explosive, something when mixed with the natural-gas heating of the house, would be burned away as tell-tale "evidence" except for an

ATF analysis of the explosion-scene, something Kelsh could silence easily-enough. Her agenda worked in tandem to his, so she was happy for now.

Amber looked to her right to see the hospital room's door opening slowly, expecting the visitor to be another Nurse, but it was someone she had hoped would not come calling on her again, but of course after last night….no such luck!

"Counselor, how are you doing after being blown up?" ATF Special Agent Clifford Stevens asked her in a soft tone of voice, wearing a fresh set of typically-Federal blazer/shirt/slacks but this time he wore a white bandage tape to the right side of his neck and his left eye was slightly bluish from a blow of some kind, Amber staring at him in wonder as he walked in smiling like a goddamn Chesire Cat of the fascist-white-man variety she always feared.

"Agent….Stevens," she chimed hesitantly, remembering his last name and how handsome he was for a cop troubling her at her residence not long ago, wishing she had lodged a formal complaint against him at the time so it wouldn't be him walking in right now….

She noticed he held a small blue gym-bag which had a white Masonic symbol on it's side, wondering if that was something he brought to show her, use against her, or what?

"Yes ma'am, good to see you again Amber, really….and I'm glad I didn't have to pick pieces of you from the burnt-out carcass of what used to be your residence before last night," Cliff spoke gentlemanly, stepping to the foot of the hospital bed, placing the blue gym-bag near her feet at the end of the mattress. Again, that handsome smile of his disarmed her a bit, and she hated when a man could do that to her…..

"How may I help you?" Amber asked him nervously, noticing the obvious "fatigue" on the Agent's face denoting sleep-deprivation, which told her he was not at full-strength right now.

"Well you are certainly welcome to speak freely with me Amber, though I doubt you're going to inform me of anything else beyond the bullshit story you've told the Arlington police and Fire Marshall's

Office up to this point....so I'll let you know what I have discovered on my own, though it is not...yet....official," Cliff spoke uniformly, eyeballing the pretty thirty-something woman lying curled up on the hospital bed in front of him now.

"The house suffered a detonation....not the accidental fireball a gas-leak would cause, and without even combing the burnt-out scene personally I would wager my career it was caused by a professional explosive charge.....the two male victims being Steven and Shane Pillage of Fairfax City Virginia both pretty much vaporized in the blast and collapse of the structure, scant-few body parts found.... though the brand new Bentley owned by the late Shane Pillage parked outside in your driveway was un-harmed by the blast, and was ordered impounded by me......," Cliff explained in a soft, lowered voice as he faced Amber Duffek.

"I see, and you see that as some kind of implication that it was foul-play....by me?" she asked in return, licking her lips in slight nervousness right now, not sure this Agent being here all by himself would be going about his duty 100% professionally considering how tired he looks right now. The thought of a "bad cop" interrogation came to her mind just now!

"Remains to be seen Counselor....remains to be seen....but there is no such thing as coincidence when it comes to this sort of crime, and if you're totally innocent of what I might be implying here....then the flip side of the coin has the most successful domestic-terrorist in US History with you in his sights, and that dear lady... means the man gunning for you will not make the same mistake twice, so the next time I see you will be when they find you barbecued on a spit somewhere," Cliff continued in coy frankness.

"Oooh....barbecued on a spit...," Amber cooed in genteel sarcasm as her response.

"I brought you something to wear on your way out of here," he said, opening the gym-bag.

"Doctor just told me he won't discharge me 'till tomorrow morning," she said as she looked at the attire falling out of the Masonic gym-bag now: a set of O.R. Scrubs and new sneakers.

"You gotta be shittin' me?!" she quipped as she realized what the Agent was offering her.

"You and I waltz on out of here unnoticed….consider it my way of covering your ass since it might be in very immediate danger," Cliff said as Amber took up the OR scrubs now.

"Heenh, or your way of getting my confession?" Amber chimed in humor as she swung her legs over the side of the hospital bed, deciding to take the man up on a most unusual offer.

Cliff looked back at the room's closed door as Amber Duffek slipped out of the hospital-gown to stand there totally-nude and not caring if the man looked at her bare body either.

She slowly pulled on the OR Scrubs to cover her physique, slipping into the sneakers he bought new for her, the Converse brand sneakers fitting her size 6 feet actually very well!

"That's spooky…you knew my shoe-size," Amber giggled as she stood up from lacing them and smirked at the unorthodox ATF Agent standing there at the end of the hospital bed.

"Lucky guess, and I take it a woman like you didn't lose your entire wardrobe in the so-called 'accidental explosion' last night?" Cliff responded in a more jovial tone, exhausted.

"You are correct Agent Stevens….I also own a house in Manassas, not far from here actually, if you don't mind driving me there?" Amber answered as she stepped to the foot of the bed alongside him with a gingerly expression crossing her pretty face. The two of them walked out of the room together, appearing as a plainclothes cop with a hospital staffer strolling along beside him, heading for the elevators.

Cockeysville, Maryland. 2:30 that afternoon: It was clear to Senator Rupert Kelsh that his plan was coming along as he had expected, though slower than originally laid out, but he was just one man who had to "depend" on other less-intelligent and less-motivated than he.

Entering the secure but secretive "laboratory" he had bought a year ago and paid to have set up for one man to work inside of it undisturbed, Rupert found that one man diligently working in the "clean room" with respirator-mask on his face complete with a blaze-orange protective suit over the rest of his body. Dr. Peter McCassler, Micro-Biologist and a man with a shady past to escape from, as well as his only son Harold who he wanted to get into Georgetown University no matter what....a man who was easily bought!

Rupert did not have to wait long for the Scientist to come out from the static-free room after decontamination procedures and the shedding of the protective equipment of course.

"Doctor McCassler....good afternoon my old friend, how's your work coming along?" Rupert asked the fifty-something white man now looking back at him pensively.

"Good, Rupert....good, it's done....for the most part, contained in an airtight lock-vial like you requested....two locked vials as a matter of fact," Dr. McCassler said frankly in his robot-like tone, staring at the seated US Senator in the "lobby" of the Laboratory and not saying what he'd like to say to the man who had him over a barrel and kept him there!

"Outstanding...slightly behind schedule, but outstanding Peter....and it is as viable as I want it to be for the demonstration?" Rupert replied in a calm demeanor with a sly smile at him.

"Yes, yes....it's viable alright....deadly....and if this sort of virus was to fall into the wrong hands Senator, it could kill millions," Dr. McCassler said matter-of-factly with a scowl.

"Especially if released in a major population-center, yes....I know, which is why I wanted you to weaponize the virus for me so that I could have it delivered to the Defense Department as a shining example of what the terrorists overseas could concoct easy-enough with limited resources....I will not stand idly by and allow the liberal bed-wetters in Congress wring their hands aimlessly while America's enemies gain a weapon like this virus to use against us," Rupert explained as he had before to the nervous but compliant Scientist.

"And you're going to show them what could be manufactured into a virus," Dr. McCassler said in repetition of what the Senator has told him before.

"Precisely, and I cannot thank you enough Doctor McCassler, you're a patriot," Kelsh said as he stood up to shake the "less-motivated" man's right hand in agreement.

"Yessir, and the terms we talked about before I began this project for you?" McCassler asked in return, shaking hands with the US Senator he did not entirely trust 100% of course.

"Ah yes…it's taken care of….you will not be indicted by the Justice Department for embezzling that Federal Grant money a year ago, it's not going to ever be brought up, and your son Harold will get into Georgetown University like the both of you want so much, it's a done deal," Kelsh explained in cordial voice, almost smiling again but he could tell the Scientist was still unnerved by the fact he had just finished creating a virus that rivals all other strains of the Avian Flu to date and "weaponized" it into two locked vials for the man who wants to "show it off" to the US Department of Defense soon as an example of what an overseas enemy could do in short order with a meager "lab" like this one. Something was bugging Dr. McCassler though, something about the US Senator who agreed to get him out of trouble with the Justice Department and get his son Harold into the University.

"Good luck convincing the liberals Senator," Dr. McCassler said meekly as he walked across the lobby of the closed-off laboratory building here near Baltimore, wanting to take a hot shower and spend the next two months with his mistress in the Virgin Islands to try and forget what he just created for a US Senator alone, violating every safety protocol in the books and going against what he would never do in any other life….but this one.

3:35pm: Agent Clifford Stevens was not operating under SOP or ATF Protocol now or for the rest of this goddamn investigation, he was sure of that and hoped it didn't bite him.

After dropping Attorney Amber Duffek off at her Manassas residence, he continued north on Rt. 28 into Fairfax County, thinking about his duel-dilemma regarding the gorgeous but dangerous lawyer Amber Duffek. She could be a legitimate "victim" of a legitimate "hit" considering her house in Arlington blew up with the same force of plastic explosive as Civil Rights Attorney Robert Marx in

Stafford County two weeks ago and the myriad of other mysterious "explosions" over the past 12 years mostly along the eastern half of the USA!

She could also be complicit in something bordering on major conspiracy, and that was what Cliff was banking on right now, that the bitch knows something and he cannot find out what she knows if she is kept in a hospital or secreted away by other investigators.

Driving north, he decided to pop-in on the man himself, the man he has been solely answering to since he began this "unoffical" case two weeks ago: Deputy Attorney General Tyler Clark who resided in Centerville north of Manassas across the Fairfax County Line.

Finding the place easily-enough, Cliff pulled into the short paved driveway behind the parked Cadillac Escalade SUV in front of the house's garage, paying no mind to the shiny black Audi R-8 parked at the street in front of the two-story brick house belonging to

Deputy Attorney General Tyler Clark. Walking right up into the open garage port, Cliff walked to the door leading into the house and knocked twice. Not hearing anyone coming to the door on the other side and impatient enough as it was, he didn't bother knocking again.

Cliff turned the doorknob and pushed the door inward to step on inside. Walking on in and gently closing the door behind him, Cliff looked around the "bachelor's pad" the house clearly was, not a feminine touch showing throughout the joint as he walked on into the kitchen and looking across the dining room and living room areas. Clark was an avid Hunter and outdoorsman, that was for certain. Framed photos of Clark and buddies with slain deer, huge fish caught, and posed pictures of Clark on a shooting range. He almost called out for his superior but something told him not to, then he heard something from down the first floor hallway, a female voice! Cliff knew Tyler Clark was divorced but if he had a girlfriend over, maybe this was not the time to come calling on the man? Cliff asked himself silently.

No, this is the time to talk with him about what he has found so far and the ramifications, and this is the place to talk about what he has found so far and the implications, safe from prying eyes and ears in any US Govt. building, safe from interruption!

Cliff walked across the living room toward the short hallway, curious now despite the fact he has just inappropriately entered the home of a Justice Department Official without being invited and considering the homeowner is an avid shooter, Cliff regretted not wearing body armor right now. He hoped he would not surprise DATG Tyler Clark too much once he runs into him here in his cozy but sparsely-furnished Fairfax domicile.

The bedroom door was ajar and Cliff told himself he had come too far now, peeking through to the bedroom's interior and glimpsing something he shouldn't have, namely a rather well-built woman riding up and down on a man laying on the bed on his back now in sexual congress! Cliff froze where he stood in the hallway, the rug keeping his footsteps from being heard as he stepped closer for a more candid view of the lovers on the bed.

The woman was physically-appealing with big knockers up front, her back to the door as she "rode" on Tyler Clark laying beneath her on the bed, though he did not recognize the short-haired woman with the big cans sliding up and down on his boss' pole and verbally stating how good it felt. Cliff stepped away from the bedroom door and walked back into the living room to sit down and wait. He thought about the situation like he always did, using a detective's angle for even something like this. A man doesn't generally romp with a girlfriend in the afternoon inside of his own home unless they are "new" to each other and are still in the "new car" phase of the relationship. Or, the woman could be someone else's wife, which would be the reason why Clark is screwing her at 3:30 in the afternoon…because it is a "window of opportunity". Or, they are co-workers who are on their "lunch-break"!

Cliff smiled to himself in a slightly vexed feeling as he sat on the sofa in silent musing.

The "supervisors" always get the best piece of ass in any department, agency, company, etc.!

That was the sort of thing Cliff often regretted about his own career with the ATF, the fact that as in most other Law Enforcement

Agencies, "screwing around" was epidemic between members of the opposite sex employed together! He had always been "straight-laced" when it came to that and never participated in dalliances with female Agents the entire 17 years he carried a badge and gun. Nowadays, toward the end of his career, Cliff wished he had done some of the extra-curricular activities with his female counterparts over the years, like what Clark was doing in the bedroom down the hall right now…so Clifford Stevens would have more than just five women in his past whom he was intimate with! Every man was a "loser" in something during his life….some men "lose" in military service, others "lose" at sports, some men "lose" at making money, but Cliff Stevens was a "loser" with women! Being single at age 40 was something he could never be proud of or brag about, something other people view him with contempt, even his own parents before they passed away.

When he used to attend Church, the other parishoners saw him sitting in the pews each Sunday alone and wrongfully assumed he must be "recovering" from something and Church was part of his "program"! Sitting here in the living room of his "boss" while the man was busy laying-pipe to some well-shaped honey-bun down the hallway, Cliff felt that familiar "vexation" again, the cold reality that he was not getting any and hadn't for quite some time.

Nothing worse than to "serve" for the protection of society like a Federal Agent does, and not enjoy what the people he helps protect enjoy….not even the basic things a man gets in this country, (i.e. a woman) just a paycheck and a lonely apartment with the promise of a retirement by age 50 so that a human "sheepdog" like him can be ushered out to pasture where he is expected to live quietly wearing a gold watch and play golf until he dies!

"What the hell am I doing?" Cliff chuckled to himself again as he sat there listening to the moans and yelps down the hallway as the two lovers wrapped up their lovemaking.

"Chasing ghosts and corrupt lawyers around the block, coming here to report to the one ranking official I was told to answer to and I'm waiting in his living room because he's down the hall playing hide-the-salami with one fine piece of tail…..," Cliff sighed to himself out of both self-pity and frustration. That's what happened when one gets too goddamn lonely!

He heard the creak of a door opening and looked up to see a bathrobe-clad Tyler Clark walking toward him now, a look of surprise on his middle-aged face but not too surprised.

"Stevens....you ever hear of knocking on a door before entering, or at least a phone call before you show up?" Clark chuckled in greeting, walking on into the living room with arms folded, sensing the ATF Agent would not intrude here at his residence unless it was crucial.

"Sorry sir, it's not something I want to discuss or even mention over a cell-phone and I knew you were off today, so I dropped by....I did knock, then let myself in," Cliff said amicably to the man, his gaze going right when he glimpsed something fleshy in his peripheral, the well-developed bare form of a woman coming out of the bedroom and walking down the opposite direction in the hallway, seeing only her bare back, ass, and meaty legs that belonged on a Tennis Pro. What an ass too.....appealing in "jiggle" as she walked to the bathroom at the other end of the hallway, again not seeing her face.

Clark noticed him watching his "date" go to the bathroom to use the shower, and he chuckled again, though proud to have another man see what he just sexually-indulged.

"Horsehair sir....I've identified his captured image and he's a dead man, least according to his Walter Reed Army Hospital Record and the DOD mortuary report....if this guy is the one you're having me uncover, he's a corpse and unless he rose from the dead over ten years ago or someone is wearing his face, it is a ghost I'm chasing," Cliff spoke up in explanation.

Just then the older man's face changed from poker to pensive, as if Cliff just opened a can of worms, then he handed the Deputy Attorney General a copied 8x10 image on photo-paper.

"That image I got from a video-camera footage taken in Oh-Two at the Marcano-owned property in Fredericksburg Virginia... that guy was meeting Mob Attorney Diego Tanner at the time and I believe strongly it was the pay-off for those weapons used in Atlanta almost one year later, and that image corresponds directly to the face-ID of a dead American soldier at Walter Reed Army Hospital in nineteen-ninety-four.....no mistake about it according to the FBI Lab," Cliff explained as Tyler Clark stared at the print-off image of "Horsehair".

"So, he made a mistake afterall and got his mug on camera," Clark said flatly, looking at him.

"Sir, that image is of a dead Gulf War Veteran, can't be a domestic terrorist," Cliff added.

"This is a living and breathing man Agent Stevens, I just wanted to see proof, and it appears you have found it, even if it won't hold up in a Court," Clark said matter-of-factly, handing the photo back to Stevens then sat down on his favorite recliner, thinking.

"You're telling me this guy in the video footage is the terrorist you're talking about, the ten year pain-in-the-ass the FBI couldn't catch or identify after the Oklahoma City Bombing?" Cliff retorted in surprise, trying to absorb what the man was now telling him.

"Yes, you've uncovered him and now I want him eliminated, period," Clark replied flatly.

"Do what?" Cliff asked in stunned reaction, not even telling Clark he had come face to face with the super-strong "shadow man" at the Fredericksburg property just last night and got his ass kicked but survived....no need to share that at this point because Tyler Clark had apparently been waiting for him to bring him something "confirming" the existence of this man known only by the monicker "Horsehair"! Now he was telling a Federal Agent to actually KILL the suspect....to eliminate the threat wholesale.

"Uh sir, I'm not a Navy Seal, I don't assassinate suspects," Cliff said as he stood up now.

"Agent Stevens, what part of this unofficial investigation did you not comprehend, what part of my original orders did you not read between the lines of?" Clark spoke in softer tone.

"You're saying I should eliminate this man who is by official accounts, already legally 'dead' and obviously one of those 'black bag' jobs we read about in conspiracy novels, a killer who has been running around free and killing people on US Soil since nineteen-ninety-five," Cliff said next, more of a talk-around-speech to try and digest what was being asked of him now.

"A man who is already legally DEAD," Clark sneered to the Agent in exclamation.

"Sir, respectfully, I am not an assassin, and I may not find him again if he knows someone is already getting close to his backdoor," Cliff said as he walked closer to Tyler Clark.

"Agent Stevens, this sort of thing will never see the inside of a Courtroom....never be brought before the American people by any means, cannot be....you must complete this assignment by making sure 'Horsehair' doesn't continue his activities," Clark added.

Cliff turned on his heels and walked back to the garage door to leave without saying another word to his superior, for now he had a lot to consider, a decision had to be made that would affect his career and his life from this point forward. As Clark stood there watching him leave, the short-haired woman fresh from her hot shower walked out from the hallway up behind him, touching a hand to his arm as she stopped alongside her extra-marital lover.

Shaya Kelsh stood beside Tyler Clark naked with a sly smile on her pretty face as she watched the door slam, the ATF Agent never seeing her there before he left in a hurry.

"My fall-guy is on the march.....hunh-huh....and I do like your hair," Clark said to her.

5:25pm: Shaya left Clark's house twenty minutes after the ATF Agent left without knowing she was even there, the man's attention-to-detail not good enough to catch her with the man who was his ranking superior in G-Man World! She was fortunate for that, for she had been told by Amber Duffek about an ATF Agent "re-investigating" the Faster Productions last days looking for "laundered Mafia money" and she expected the prick to drop in on her as well to ask awkward questions. She didn't like the fact there was a lone Federal Agent snooping around the past which involved her because she had been there in the middle of a Porn Film Company that no longer exists....it was only right that the Fed looking into it would come knocking on her door anytime he felt like it! She of course assumed her husband being a senior US Senator may have caused the Agent to "pause" before walking in on her like he had Amber Duffek and Shelly James so far! The idea of the Agent interrogating that idiot blonde bimbo Shelly James made her laugh when she imagined it, because that little bitch didn't know jack-shit about Jonny Faster's financial matters for lack of intelligence as well as the fact she was Jonny's own personal sex-puppet during the final year of Faster Productions. Shaya on the other hand knew enough, and for that reason alone she now walked along the interior of Fair Oaks Mall here in Fairfax County to do some shopping, get her mind off the idea of a Federal Agent snooping around pieces of the past she had a hand in. Maybe he'll fall into a meat-grinder, she mused…bad things happen to cops all the damn time, right?! Shaya strolled along in the Mall's pedestrian throng of customers, thinking about buying herself a new pearl necklace with Rupert's debit card!

Shaya Kelsh tried not to "worry" about things she really didn't have any true control over, plus the fact that she has been through a lot in her life so far, though being in the crosshairs of a Federal Agent hadn't been one of them until that fateful Summer of 2005. Walking along the Mall looking at the variety of shops and stores, some of them her favorite, others ones she has never set foot in, Shaya glimpsed the stares and hawkish glances from men passing by her, something she had been used to all of her adult life of course, no matter what she was wearing in public, a body like hers doesn't ever go "unnoticed" by straight men and the amount of lesbian women out there. Right now she wore a dark blue mini-skirt topped by a floppy red blouse and leather belly-belt in front with a shiny buckle, her shorter hair slightly curled so that it parts at the left side of her head, her face made-up good as always.

Shaya Kelsh was a striking woman even if she wore sweats, sneakers, and a ball-cap!

She slowed walking in front of a Gaming store where a pack of teenage guy were inside trying out a console video game, the interior of the place wall-to-wall video games, something Shaya never had an inkling to even try ever since the "arcade" days of her youth back in the 1980's. Men are far more inclined to that sort of entertainment she mused as she continued on along the mall thoroughfare, eyes on her as always as she strolled along, failing to notice one man in particular who had been lingering about 15 feet behind Shaya now, following her ever since she walked past the Mexican restaurant about a hundred feet back.

Walking to the center of the bristling Mall, Shaya stopped for a moment to decide where she would eat dinner since she was alone tonight, and then walked onward toward the other end of the Mall where an Italian-Cuisine place was located. She reflected in daydream as she walked along with the throng of October shoppers, going back to what her husband calls her "porn past", since she'd been worrying about what the ATF was "re-investigating". Shaya recalled one stormy night she spent with Jonny at the mansion in New Rochelle in the Fall of 2004, not realizing it was to be her last year with the man and his Company. After a nice dinner made by the black actress "Ebony Cane" before she had to leave for the Air Force Base she worked at during the week, Shaya and Jonny made love on the big circular sofa in the living room, as they often done before because he liked doing it on sofas.

The two of them were interrupted by Dave Solomon that night, who had come all the way from Manhattan during a violent rain storm just to tell Jonny about a dip in quarterly video sales in the western half of the US. It seemed the curly-haired little man lived for intruding upon Jonny Faster while he was "rehearsing" as he called it. Shaya had it happen to her a couple times before, the little man came barging in while she and Jonny were getting it on.

Trouble was, Jonny rarely resumed his tryst with whoever the Starlet was he had been "rehearsing" with once he was interrupted. Maybe the late Dave Solomon did that shit intentionally Shaya had considered, because the Production Assistant secretly hated Jonny Faster and wanted him out of the picture, to "take over" the Company from within!

Once Dave had left, she remembered the storm raging wildly outside, making the power flicker on and off as she sat naked at the in-house Bar with a glass of cold beer. Jonny had walked back across the huge living room and over to the sliding-glass door to the outside patio, looking out at the raging storm outside. Shaya remembered sitting there watching him just stand there at the glass door with hands on his hips, a naked and mighty sculpture rivaling those of the Greek gods....she liked just looking at Jonny Faster's chiseled physique.

"Looks like it's gonna storm all night,"Jonny spoke in his slightly-Euro tone of voice, the Nordic-American man in this mid-thirties speaking to her but not looking back at Shaya.

"Yes, and it's just the two of us here tonight...," Shaya responded gingerly toward him.

"Hmmmh...you and I have come quite a way since we first met in nineteen-ninety-one," Jonny spoke softly in slight change of subject, his cut and well-muscled back to her still.

"Yes we have Jonny....I still remember when I first met you back then, it was on the set of that film 'Thunderballs'....the one that made you famous at the time and it's still on our marketing list, since you bought the rights to it n' all....heenh, I remember being a bit apprehensive when you walked onto the set naked and at full-mast," Shaya answered him as she left the barstool and walked toward him, lights flickering on and off steadily, giving the living room a surrealistic "disco" setting for a minute or two.

"I remember Jonny...mmmhh....I remember," Shaya cooed as she stepped up behind him and ran her right hand around his taut buttocks to his washboard abs and down to his famous genitals as she stopped close behind the Male Porn Legend.

"Thirteen years ago baby, seems like yesterday...," Jonny whispered over a shoulder to her as he just stood there letting her run her exploring hands over his bare physique like she did.

"Mmmhh...let's go upstairs to bed Jonny, finish me off....," Shaya cooed in his left ear then bit the earlobe in carnal suggestion, the statue-like man just standing there staring outside.

"Shaya Doll....where will we be in the next thirteen years?" he asked her softly as he turned to look her square in the eyes as lightning flashed outside and the mansion's power went out.

Only Jonny Faster called her "Shaya Doll" and quite often she fondly recalled, remembering.

Shaya Doll had been one of her early "aliases" in Porn Films until she took the moniker of

"Shaya Gold" in 1992. She had wanted to be "retired" from the X-rated Industry in the next 13 years she wanted to tell him, and preferably married to him! Shaya never shared that pipe-dream with the Adult Film "Legend" Jonny Faster, a man she had loved since 1991....

Coming back to reality as she walked along the center thoroughfare in the Mall, Shaya Kelsh saw a young couple walking hand-in-hand past her, something her husband didn't like to do whenever they were in public, the man never being one for "public displays of affection".

She attracted male attention along most of her route in the Shopping Mall, a couple of black teenage guys looked her up and down while saying something racy about her physique as they strolled past her in the other direction. She didn't mind strangers saying shit like that, as long as they left her alone otherwise! The stop-talk-flirt guys she found annoying, but admirers eyeballing her from afar never harmed a damn thing.

ATF Field Office Manassas, Virginia. 6:48pm: Cliff Stevens didn't care to share his Intel with fellow ATF Agents here at the Manassas Field Office next door to the Regional Jail and Courthouse just off Rt. 28. After meeting with Deputy Attorney General Clark earlier, he was at a loss for a "next step" since the man insisted that "Horsehair"be killed instead of arrested next time he runs into him... not exactly the sworn duty of a Federal Agent and not something he would ever expect a DATG to order him to do.

He had the Facial-ID, the US Army Personnel File, and of course the numerous FBI/ATF "eyewitness" reports between 1995 and 2005 regarding "John Doe #2" dismissed-sightings and "Horsehair" stories about a shadow who uses other people to carry out violent ends.

Sitting at another Agent's desk while he went over it all on his personal laptop PC, Cliff had one hard-copy file on the desk as well, in it 8x10 color photos freshly-autographed by the well-built female

"Celebrity" in the pictures, namely one Porn Star known as Shaya Gold.

The photos had fresh-ink on them, signed to Shane Pillage, having found them in the backseat of the late Shane Pillage's 2007 Bentley parked in front of Amber Duffek's house when it blew up into a fireball the Fire Chief is calling "accidental" as of this morning.

"Son-of-a-bitch….it only gets better," Cliff sighed to himself as he read the fine print in the US Army Records on his PC screen now, the page that detailed the "late" soldier Duncan Hardesteadt's entry-level West Point Information. As it turned out, the Infantry Lieutenant who died at Walter Reed Army Hospital in 1994 of "mysterious illness" had attended West Point and graduated 88th in his Class! The fine-print also indicated who the Politician was who got the young man into West Point in 1986……

"Senator Rupert Kelsh," Cliff sighed matter-of-factly to himself as he read the text regarding a certain dead soldier's sponsored entry into West Point over 20 years ago.

"Fukkin' circumstantial," Cliff reminded himself as he looked down at the signed color 8x10 photos on the desk now, graphic X-rated photos signed by Shaya Gold who also happened to now be the wife of US Senator Rupert Kelsh who happened to be the one who got the "dead" soldier appointed to West Point in 1986 and here the face of the "dead" soldier shows up many years later as part of a domestic terror investigation where one lone Federal Agent is unofficially assigned to check things out……and the "leads" are two million dollars in missing Mafia/Porn money, grainy videotape footage of a "dead" soldier showing up 8 years after he was "cremated", a shady female lawyer with a taste for "sushi" over "beef" getting her house blown up while she was conveniently outside after kicking all of her party guests out….one of whom was Shaya Kelsh, wife of US Senator Rupert Kelsh, who signed these pornographic photos to Shane Pillage….whose remains had barely been discovered in the basement of the burnt-out Duffek house on that same night…. great…just great!

"Hunh, they're not strangers….they all know each other," Cliff said to himself in circumspect, trying to concoct an angle in which he could possible tie these players together, and it couldn't be by "gut instinct" either, not well-connected folks like these. Then there was the dead man factor, his primary "Horsehair" suspect being identified as a deceased Gulf War Army Lieutenant and West Point Graduate who was then allegedly cremated!

"They all know each other...and coincidences like this only come along once in a lifetime, meaning it's too goddamn rare to think it's just coincidence....Amber Duffek knows more than she's letting on....I'm gonna have to squeeze that grapefruit 'till it squeals," Cliff said to himself as he held up one of the graphic 8x10 signed photos, staring at the image of a gloriously naked Shaya Gold getting reamed by the mule-hung Porn Actor Jonny Faster.

"Not strangers at all....they all know each other," he said to himself as he stood up abruptly.

6:55pm: Shaya walked out from the restaurant immediately after eating dinner, deciding to finally go ahead and buy something expensive to ease her mind, heading straight for the jewelry store on the one corner here in the Mall not far from the entrance where she came in an hour ago. This time she noticed a semi-familiar-looking man following her for sure, someone she had spotted trailing her before she went to eat dinner, and here he was again just about 20 paces behind her and pretending not to be watching her. Was he just an "admirer" like the guys who tend to follow her around a public place just enjoying the view, or was he a Cop tracking her? He was an average-looking white male about age 35 or so with casual attire but no jacket to conceal a gun and badge, which meant he was unlikely a Cop!

"Heenh-heeh....buy one of my films, you'll see more...you idiot," Shaya chimed to herself as she walked into the jewelry shop near the Mall entrance/exit, not too stressed about him.

She looked at the pearl necklaces in the showcase and focused on what she might buy this time, and seeing the pearl necklaces made her reflect on a time in her past when someone else gave her a pearl necklace for her birthday, though not as expensive and pretty as these.

Back in 1998 at Christmas time, her fellow porn actor and frequent male co-star "F.M. Dexter" approached her at an Xmas party the then-Director was hosting at his house in Buffalo NY, and gave her a wrapped present. She opened it to find a string of pearls intended for her and she was pleasantly surprised! She remembered hugging the actor who gave it to her, even kissing him in gratitude over it, though she wondered why the often curmudgeon Frankie Drisler (FM Dexter) would give her such a pricy gift? She had been cast with him numerous times, more especially times when White actresses refused to work a sex-role with Frankie either because he was Black or because he was oftentimes….a Jerk !

Shaya never minded working with the easily-angered F.M. Dexter, he performed well with her for the cameras and knew how to make her feel good during the act. She still had that pearl necklace given her by FM Dexter, somewhere at home in her dresser drawers. She had the Sales Lady pull the most expensive pearl necklace on lay-away for her and left the store to walk out of the Mall, not thinking to look around for the guy following her earlier, but she soon found him waiting for her outside the exit doors, sitting on a bench out in the mild air.

Shaya looked at him with a slight smile as their eyes met for the first time, and she didn't break her stride walking in the direction of the bench because the parking lot was beyond it.

"It's real good to see you in-person after all those years of watching your movies," the man spoke up in a rather calm, disarming tone of voice, sitting up straight on the outside bench.

"Excuse me?" Shaya chimed as she kept walking with intent on passing the seated stranger.

"Shaya Gold, it's good to see you ma'am," the handsome but ordinary man said next.

"Oh really….hmmph….heenh-heeh….my fan-club," Shaya snickered in reaction, relaxing her guard a bit as she stopped to face the smiling white guy who kept his seat on the bench.

Maybe it was the way he spoke to her that made her feel less-threatened by the interruption.

"Nice to meet you too," she said as she extended a hand, the man shaking it gently in reply.

"I'm Sammy, and I've been a fan of your films since I was in the Army," he told her softly.

"Oh, that's really nice Sammy….hmmh, I rarely get recognized anymore these days," she said matter-of-factly to the nice-enough male fan sitting on the bench smiling up at her.

"I wasn't sure at first, you've cut your hair…but you look the same otherwise," he said next.

"Heenh, with my hair cut and clothes on, you pegged me as Shaya Gold, hunh?" she chimed as he stood up to walk alongside her into the Mall parking lot. Most women would be spooked by a stranger walking them into a parking lot at night, but this one didn't give her the "creep vibe" so she let him walk with her. She gave him a kiss on the cheek and a hug before they parted ways, the guy happy with that instead of an autograph. She didn't mind fans like Sammy, because they were respectful instead of creepy…..

Driving along Rt. 66 west, Shaya kept thinking how funny it was to be recognized by a fan of hers after a couple of years being out of the Jizz-Bizz and with her hair cut short like this and in Virginia of all places! Shows there are men out there who have not forgotten her as

Shaya Gold and she had to appreciate that. Driving onto Rt. 28 South from I-66, she headed toward the Manassas residence of Attorney Amber Duffek, someone she needed to see after the calamity the other night, talk with her now that she was afraid of approaching the topic with Rupert. Shaya thought of her husband and wondered what he was doing up on Capitol Hill today, when the Senate was "adjourned" for the week? Probably making some poor sap do his bidding….someone he is "blackmailing" for something she guessed.

Shaya drove listening to satellite-radio in her Audi R8, getting gawks from other drivers as they passed her in the left lane, a beautiful woman driving a $100,000 sports car gets stares.

Driving into the historic little City of Manassas, she kept in the right lane, trying to recall exactly how to get to Stonewall Drive because she had been there only once before. Shaya passed the Courthouse and Regional Jail on her right, and found Stonewall Drive at the next light, turning there past the Catholic Church and driving a quarter-mile up the street to find the well-lit "second home" of Attorney Amber Duffek on the corner hill to her right just before the street dipped into an incline. Parking to the right of Amber's BMW, she noticed a familiar-looking Ford Mustang parked on the street near Amber's mail box. Getting out of her car, Shaya left her purse in the Audi and walked up to the side-door of the brick house.

She was met by Amber clad in one of those silk robes the lawyer liked to wear, as well as the more-intimate-than-not hug and kiss from the lesbian lawyer.

"So glad you could make it Shaya, really....been wanting to talk with you honey," Amber said as she ushered the buxom woman into the living room of her "second home" here and put a mixed drink in her hand right away, having been expecting Shaya any minute now.

"And I'd like to talk with you too Amber....good to see you're still alive after what happened to your main residence shortly after Rupert and I left your party the other night," Shaya said as she sat down on the sofa with the amorously-appearing Amber Duffek now.

"Mmmh...I wasn't worried, even if someone wants to kill me, I'm safe enough....though too bad about the Pillage brothers, hunh?" Amber chimed in a rather cordial tone this time.

"Yeah, Steven and Shane....too bad....guess you don't owe'em anymore," Shaya mused with a slinky smirk of sarcasm at the pretty Amber Duffek sitting close enough to her on the sofa.

"Mmmh...funny how things work out, and besides....they were a pair of womanizing sharks whom didn't deserve all the money they won hustling real estate," Amber sneered in reply.

"I kinda liked Shane," Shaya said then took a sip of the Apple-Martini Amber poured her.

"Heeh, if the house hadn't blown up, you would be on a Cruise with both of them this coming week...your husband lost you in a round of Poker with Steven," Amber reminded.

"Yeah, I know....hmmh....I'm glad you survived Amber, no better Shark in the Courtroom when I need one, which brings me to the second reason I wanted to speak with you privately Amber, that Federal Agent you told me about....snooping around in Faster Productions' final days and the cast list leading up to the collapse two years ago," Shaya spoke gingerly.

"Agent Clifford Stevens ATF....yes, he's interviewed me, Shelly James, and one or two others under Jonny Faster's employ at the time...glad I was just the lawyer," Amber chimed.

"He hasn't contacted me yet, maybe because of Rupert," Shaya spoke in a lowered voice, eyeballing the comely lawyer sliding closer to her on the sofa more and more.

"I got you covered Shaya....trust me," Amber said softly as she touched her right hand to Shaya's alluring face, then her hand fell to Shaya's blouse, unbuttoning it slowly.

"Amber.....please," Shaya sighed in weak resistance to the woman's amorous advance.

Amber discussed her visit by the ATF Agent with Shaya while the two of them walked upstairs to the master bedroom, Amber pulling off Shaya Kelsh's clothes along the way.

The Agent was interested in what Amber knew about Faster Productions' finances while she was retained as Jonny Faster's lawyer prior to July 2005, not much of which she admitted to.

Right now, Amber was interested in getting Shaya's clothes off as well as her own as the two of them walked up the stairs talking about whether or not they'll end up arrested....

"Shaya, you are amazing," Amber cooed as she pulled off the woman's lace bra, hands going to those big breasts eagerly, almost tripping on the top step then they stepped into the big bedroom where Amber shed her panties and bra and aggressively cornered her nude friend.

"Amazing body, beautiful mouth, eyes.....I want you to consider becoming my girlfriend after your husband drops you," Amber spoke in a sinister voice, stepping up to the ripe and voluptuous beauty named Shaya Kelsh, pawing her 44EE bust like a hungry kitten.

"Amber, just because I did lesbo-scenes in adult films back in the day doesn't make me a lesbian, you know?" Shaya chimed impishly in response, surrendering to the lawyer's desire to ravage her like Amber had been wanting to do since they first met back in 2005.

"No, but it makes you open to suggestion, and besides....Shelly James is going to leave me soon enough, and I just love former porn stars," Amber said as she moved in for a kiss, Shaya giving in for a long gentle kiss, their well-crafted bodies pressing together standing at the foot of the bed now. Shaya had been with beautiful women before of course for X-rated filmmaking, but she preferred to make love with a man....things she has to do for a "fan"!

The two female lovers fell to the bed and enveloped under the covers in passion's embrace, kissing strong as hands explored and legs entwined. Shaya went into the same mode she put herself in back when she did lesbo-scenes for films years ago, showing Amber Duffek her "routine" as if it were second nature to her, and Amber was thrilled to pieces....

With soft R+B music playing in the background of the bedroom as Amber and Shaya made love, the other female visitor in the house right now rose from her hot bath in the bathroom down the dark hallway, guessing who had finally arrived as Amber told her she would!

Shelly James stood up and rinsed herself off in the shower, knowing the sound of R+B music was her "cue" to come join Amber and Shaya in the bedroom, something she had promised Amber Duffek she would agree to do awhile back if Amber ever got Shaya in bed!

Drying herself off with two towels, Shelly stared at her nude reflection in the vanity mirror and picked up something unusual from the vanity sink.....a foam-rubber dildo sculpted precisely in likeness (the erect penis) of Adult Film Star Jonny Faster! It also had a screw at it's base to attach to a leather strap-harness allowing the user to wear it as a sex-toy also.

It was an exact flesh-colored foam rubber replica of Jonny Faster's nearly-foot-long-schlong!

"Heeeh, the things we do as a last favor," Shelly snickered to herself as she teased her blonde hair in front, then brushed her mane a few strokes with a brush and opened the bathroom door and stepped out into the carpeted hallway on bare feet. She slowly walked toward the other end of the hall where the master bedroom and two women she knew very well copulated in another casual affair all three of them were adept at. Carrying the strap-on "Jonny Faster" dildo in her right hand, Shelly approached the cracked open door and stopped to peer inside. There they were….Amber on her back in cheerful glee while Shaya gorged her sweet spot, lying stretched out between Amber's smooth legs, covers askew.

Shelly watched them for a moment then pushed the door inward and entered the room.

"Ooooh-baaabbee…..I gotta yummy-yummy treat for you….," Amber cooed to Shaya as both of them looked up to see the naked Shelly James stroll on in while strapping on the big dildo of the brand Shaya instantly recognized, grinning at the sight of Shelly James with a foam rubber version of Jonny Faster strapped to her groin as she approached the bed…..

Georgetown, 8:15pm: Senator Rupert Kelsh liked entertaining important guests in his home, especially ones he can coerce or manipulate easy enough. One has to deal strategic with one's inferiors in order to get done what has to be done before dispensing with them.

Harold McCassler, only son of Dr. Peter McCassler, was sitting on the sofa in the living room while Kelsh walked the perimeter of the downstairs interior explaining what he wanted the young man to do for him in the next couple of days. So far, the favor sounded like fun to Harold whose father begrudgingly drove his son here tonight, something his father said about Senator Kelsh he had not heard before and he warned his only son to "be careful".

Regardless, Harold thought the world of the Senator and dutifully heard him out tonight.

"I will have the package for you to take all the way to California for me where someone else will meet you at the Airport to take possession of it, and I will pay all of your expenses to fly out there, stay a few days to relax and see the sights, then fly back," Kelsh explained in simpler terms than he had been talking about, and he could tell Harold was game.

"You leave the day after tomorrow at Dulles Airport, ticket will be in your hand by then, and fly first-class to Los Angeles International Airport....deliver the package and you're done," Kelsh repeated with a gesture of hands to the young Senate Page seated on the sofa now.

"Okay Senator, okay, sounds easy enough," Harold said in verbal agreement with the man.

"Make this important delivery for me Harold and I will guarantee your acceptance into Georgetown University," Rupert spoke matter-of-factly, seeing the young man's eyes light up in surprise and even more solid agreement, a young man who was easily "bought"!

"Great sir, no problem, consider it done....and the package is uhhm....totally legal right?" Harold replied with hesitation in his voice on the last part.

"Harold, it's nothing for you to worry about son....tell you what, when you return from California, I'll let you sleep with my wife Shaya," Rupert retorted with a chuckle this time.

Harold's eyes lit up when he heard that one of course, sitting up straighter with his imagination running rampant with images of what he saw the last time he was here, not the home invasion the Senator told him to "forget about" but the bodacious beauty in the shower he introduced Harold to, the lovely and incomparable Shaya Kelsh!

"Like I told you son, stay loyal to those who matter in life and you'll go far," Kelsh said next as he stepped up to the sofa and extended a hand for the young man to shake in agreement.

"Yessir, I'll fly out to Los Angeles and deliver the package for you, no problem," Harold said as he stood up now, walking alongside the Armani-clad US Senator crossing the living room toward his liquor cabinet, asking the 18-year old Senate Page if he wanted a drink, which he was happy to accept. Harold had stepped fully into the Adult World and he was loving it....

"And I think you'll do well at Georgetown University Harold, just keep in mind what I've told you before about how a College Degree is no guarantee of intelligence nor success, you'll make your own success as you go along, like you're doing now," Kelsh continued as he poured them both a glass of Cognac, the younger man wide-eyed in acknowledgement.

"Yessir, I plan on it and I can't thank you enough," Harold said as he took up his glass.

" Like I said Harold, stay loyal to those who help you," Rupert said with his glass up in toasting gesture as the two men faced each other in the living room now, plans in order.

"Trust in this business is a rare commodity so use it well when it favors you," Kelsh added.

"Yessir, I understand, and I'd like to uhhm....yes....uhmm, with Shaya," Harold stammered.

Kelsh chuckled at the young man's eager agreement with the additional "bonus" he offered.

"As soon as you return from California, you'll get my wife for a night," Kelsh said softly, once again noticing how the promise of sex coerces a man into doing almost anything.

Manassas, 8:46pm: Amber Duffek was having way too much fun with her two female visitors this evening, and as she now rolled to the left side of her King-sized bed, she giggled while watching Shaya (now wearing the strap-on dildo) engage Shelly in a vaunted missionary position, pumping into the blonde cupcake like a man would!

"Oaannnh.....onnnnhh......ohhh-yeeeaahh!" Shelly bellowed in reaction, Shaya thrusting between her legs like a man would in intercourse, hovering above the writhing blonde below her like a bird throttling it's prey. Amber lay on her right side just watching in amusement after Shaya had finished her off a minute ago, then before that, Shelly had feverishly drilled Shaya with the "Jonny Faster" strap-on. Amber loved sex like this, it made her life worth living to indulge her fantasies like this. She found that she could have fun like this without the nuisance of a man and all the drama that comes with a man, though women can be worse in the "drama" category sometimes, especially fellow lesbians....which is why Amber preferred straight women like Shaya and Shelly who would agree to "play" with her in bed but not have a conventional "girlfriend" relationship with her, thus no pain-in-the-ass drama!

"Give it to her Shaya....give it to her.....give her what she deserves," Amber sneered playfully to the two grinding women on the bed beside her still going-at-it in fervent sex.

"That's it baby," Amber giggled as Shelly bellowed outloud in orgasm while Shaya continued her onslaught with the strap-on, enjoying the act because she got to do it to Shelly James after all this time hating the bitch for getting her fired by Jonny Faster back in June 2005!

"Jonny.....oooohh-Jahnnneeeeee!" Shelly wailed as she squirmed violently beneath the pumping body of Shaya Kelsh, her eyes closed in remembrance of their shared Porn Star Lover, Jonny Faster whose "likeness" was marketed as a sex toy now being used on them!

Amber giggled as she slipped of the bed and stood up, stretching her arms skyward with a yawn, fatigued a bit from the sex but not worn-out enough to fall asleep just yet.

She sauntered over to the dresser against the wall by the door, picking up a pearl necklace she owned, putting it around her neck as she turned around to see Shaya and Shelly rolling in the bed together in conclusion of their romp, and Amber laughed at them again.

"Heenh-heeh, you two oughta do another porno flick together," Amber giggled in reaction.

"Never, hunh-haah....come over here you bitch and pay your respects," Shaya chimed back at Amber as she sat up on the end of the big bed holding the big dildo with both hands in lewd gesture, giggling herself as Shelly lay flat on her front beside her now. Shaya then popped the thing off it's screw-on harness and tossed the big sex toy at Amber who caught it in her left hand, laughing along with Shaya. Amber held it up like a sword and swung it around in lewd gesture again then she lay the likeness of Jonny Faster's manhood on the surface of her dresser there, taking a Buck Knife out from the top drawer, opening the blade to unceremoniously chop the foam-rubber dildo in half with just one swing of the knife.

"Awwwh....you shameless hussy, you didn't have to do that!" Shaya quipped in reaction.

"Oh yes I did Shaya baby, heenh.....end of an era," Amber sighed with a slinky smirk back at the big-busted former porn starlet sitting on the end of her bed staring back at her now.

"End of an era.....heenh, ain't it the truth," Shaya sighed with a hand to her sweaty face.

"Jonny Faster and his big mighty dick may rest....in pieces," Amber said coldly with a smirk, stepping back across the room toward the naked Shaya Kelsh who sighed in response, silently wishing she could see Jonny Faster for real just one more time, tell him she really did love him back then, tell him she was sorry for undermining him before the Company ended.

"Mmmmhh...Shelly's passed out," Amber cooed as she stepped up to Shaya, running a hand through Shaya's shorter hair, eyes on the bare body of Shelly James lying prone on the bed with head buried between pillows, asleep.

9:25pm: Cliff Stevens left the Manassas ATF Field Office without hurry since the address he was going to right now was just around the corner on Stonewall Drive, a mere two minute drive to Amber Duffek's house there on a hill overlooking Beauregard Avenue.

Walking out to his car in the parking lot adjacent to the Regional Jail here in town, Cliff looked over at a bunch of uniformed Jail Officers coming out of the Jail building during what he guessed to be Shift Change. He had to respect the Sworn Officers who do that kind of Law Enforcement duty, because he could never work inside of a Jail or Prison himself!

Jailers work(without a gun) inside locked facilities noone else wants to go near, and patrol the meanest beat imaginable with the most unruly and dangerous criminals imaginable.

Getting in his car and gunning it to life, Cliff thought about how he was going to approach Attorney Amber Duffek tonight, how he was going to present the fact he now has her by the short-hairs and unless she cooperates and agrees to help his investigation resulting in the arrest of someone goddamn it.....he is going to focus on her as the main suspect!

Driving onto Rt. 28 and turning right onto Stonewall, Cliff slowed down as he approached the location he was returning to tonight, where he dropped Amber off earlier. The explosion of her home in Arlington and deaths of Steven and Shane Victory may be in the "cover up" phase by the powers-that-be, but Cliff was not about to let the obvious fact Amber Duffek is being "protected" by someone ON-HIGH stop him from getting what he needs from her.

Slowing down to park on the street curb just left of the residence, he noticed Amber's BMW in the carport along with a Ford Mustang parked on the curb directly in front of the place, and he instantly recognized the Mustang to be the personally-owned-vehicle of a pretty lady he recently interviewed: Michelle "Shelly James" Jamison. Cliff thanked his lucky stars for this break, for he was going to have both Shelly James and Amber Duffek together denoting yet another "link" in this goddamn unofficial investigation!

Cliff got out of his car and walked up to the side-entrance to the house, knocking on the door as he looked around at the neighboring homes nearby, not seeing anyone else outside on this rather mild and dry night. He knocked again and waited, but noone was answering.

Though he knew the ramifications of unlawfully entering someone's residence unannounced under the color of authority, he gripped the front door handle and found it to be unlocked.

Slow and careful, Agent Stevens entered the Manassas residence of Attorney Amber Duffek, finding himself in the home's kitchen area which was lit only by the stove light, looking around the sweet-smelling interior to find it sparsely-furnished with nothing on the walls except for one painting of a nude female backside (not surprising considering Amber) so this was truly a "second home" she probably rented out on occasion, he told himself. Stepping into the living room toward the stairwell, he heard something and instinctively walked up the carpeted stairs toward the sound. He stopped at the top of the stairs and a female voice from out of nowhere startled the hell out of him for the immediate moment.

"She's not here dammit....but she'll be back," the soft and slightly-southern voice spoke in the dark hallway, seeing the male intruder before he saw her, recognizing him immediately so stepping into view at the bedroom's open doorway completely naked was of no real worry.

"Shelly James," Cliff said in realization as he stood frozen at the top step now looking across the wide hallway to see a gloriously-nude blonde vixen standing in the bedroom doorway staring back at him as if it were no big deal he was here uninvited.

"Agent Stevens, what brings you here this time of night?" Shelly asked him casually, not threatened at all by the man's intrusion into Amber's house as she stood facing him naked.

"I uhhm....came to see Amber Duffek, crucially-important," Cliff said softly, staring at the hot blonde's headlights as she leaned on the doorframe smiling slinky at the intruder.

"Oh, crucially-important hunh....bad enough to barge right on in?" Shelly giggled in reply.

"Yeah, something like that, sorry for the intrusion Shelly," he said as he turned to look back down the stairwell and walk back down them until she said something to stop him.

"Heeh-heh, isn't like you haven't seen me butterball-naked before is it....surely you've watched at least one of my X-rated films over the course of whatever you're now surely investigating?" she chimed girlishly at him, making him grin as he looked at his shoes.

"True, I saw your last film actually," he said with a shrug, thinking out his next move.

"Oh, the scene I did with Ray Fury in that 'Swedish Erotixxx' compilation," she chimed.

"Yeah, look...will Amber be back soon, maybe I can wait downstairs in the living room?" he spoke in response, eyeing her bare form as he asked the question.

"Yes and no....yes, she'll be back soon, and no...you can't wait for her in the living room, are you crazy...she'll cut your balls off if she finds out you walked in here uninvited like ya did, or maybe you want to get fired from the ATF?" Shelly retorted in humored tone.

"Well I could wait for her outside," he added as he stepped back down the stairs further.

"Agent Stevens….honey, it'll be a much more plausible story if she thinks I invited you here and brought you upstairs for sex…. so take your clothes off big guy," Shelly said softly with one finger gesturing for him to come with her into the bedroom now. He did not refuse, though his mind did consider the possibility of a "trap" and he followed her anyway.

It had a been a long time since he had last been with a woman (and never with one so well-put-together as Shelly James) so he followed his instinct and walked into Amber Duffek's bedroom with the gloriously-naked Shelly James, seduced by her suggestion alone.

Considering how this investigation was going, Cliff gave in to the woman's offer, stripping off his clothes, holstered weapon, handcuffs and all as the blonde vixen sat on the end of the ruffled bed. The "trouble" of doing something like having sex with an interviewed-suspect inside of a house one actually entered unlawfully just didn't worry Agent Stevens right now.

Shelly smiled slinky at the sight of the man's body after he shed his pants, wanting to romp with a live male of the species after her "threesome" with the ladies earlier this evening.

"Oooooh, I'm gonna call you 'Taco'….yummy taco with cheese," Shelly cooed as he stepped up to her, his hands reaching for her perky 36DD breasts eagerly, seeking immediate intercourse more than foreplay, so damn hard n' horny right now he could cut diamonds!

They were on the bed in a rush, Cliff going for her boobs with a hungry mouth first, moving between her legs to enter her moist canal, surrendering wholesale to the carnal desire he had been denied for so long, his stressed mind focusing on nothing else but the act of sex itself.

The feel and smell of her was intoxicating, their bare bodies entwined in pure carnality then he slipped into her and thrusted forward, hearing her moan in delight.

"Oooaah…Clifford……ooonnnnh-yeesss!" Shelly chimed in reaction to his increased ferocity in intercourse now, feeling his ardor for what it was, a man with a lot of pent-up energy and sexual frustration he was now gleefully taking out on her! She relaxed and let him plunge his manhood into her with every pelvic thrust in the vibrant missionary-style intercourse they landed in, both of them enjoying the sensation of the act with a stranger, both feeling nothing but carnal delight, and Cliff Stevens was ecstatic to "surrender" like this to something so fucking good, which rarely came his way since College.

"Don't stop stud…don't stop….keep it up!" Shelly cooed in his ear as he lay over her pumping into her steadily, not even wanting him to slow down at this point, enjoying the intercourse and the weight of his heavier male body encompassing her lighter female form.

"Unnnoooh….unnnngggh….oooaaaahhh!" Cliff groaned out in sheer sweet sensation of release, climaxing as he thrusted inside of her steadily, only 5 minutes after he had begun, the feel of her and her cooing vocals driving him to a long-lasting eruption of his own.

10:55pm: Cliff awoke in a shudder, his re-awakening senses alerting him to the fact he had fallen asleep after sex with Shelly James here inside Attorney Amber Duffek's very upscale Manassas Virginia home! Rolling left on the bed with no covers on it anymore, one hand rubbed his eyes and his mental alert went into overdrive the moment he could clearly see Attorney Amber Duffek walk into the bedroom alone and wearing a black jumpsuit.

"Good evening Agent Stevens, fancy meeting you here in my own bedroom sir," Amber spoke to the naked Federal Agent sitting up on her king-sized bed now, weary-eyed.

"Amber….Amber….I uhhm….I can explain….really," he stammered in freaked reaction.

"No need, I heard it all from Shelly before she left a few minutes ago….said she saw you waiting for me outside, invited you in, and the two of you had a quickie on my bed here, then you fell asleep and she couldn't wake you up," the pretty Amber Duffek spoke to him in casual explanation, a story he almost wanted to believe himself because the truth would surely end his career and lose him his retirement pension.

"Yeah....yeah...sorry," Cliff sighed as he scooted to the end of the bed, sitting at the corner with a hand on his head of short, mussed hair. He looked at the comely Amber as she walked around the room as if looking for something important.

"It's understandable Agent Stevens, I can't resist Shelly either.... she smiles at you with that delicious body of hers...and before ya know it, she's riding on your dick," Amber snickered.

"Yeah," he sighed as he fought to clear his vision completely from sleep-mode, wanting to get up, get dressed, and talk (nicely) to Amber Duffek now after she found him like this....

but he didn't see his clothes anywhere in the bedroom as he sat there, and where was his

Glock .45 auto he seemed to recall laying on the rug here at the foot of the bed??

"I wanted to speak with you about the past again....like when you were a Marcano lawyer and what happened to Attorney Diego Tanner who worked for the Marcano Mob same time you were," Cliff said as he sat there with hand on his head, looking at her.

"Diego Tanner, yes...nice enough guy if you didn't mind his bullshit cowboy charm and his penchant for sticking his dick into nearly every female client he had," Amber replied as she walked up to the big wooden dresser where the chopped-up foam rubber dildo still lay.

"I heard that about him, and he's likely deceased considering how the Marcanos dealt with liabilities, but you knew him well didn't you?" Cliff continued, wanting to know something he didn't already know about the man in that video footage with "Horsehair" in 2002.

"Yep, I knew Diego ever since Law School, son-of-a-bitch was the first man I ever slept with and subsequently the only real 'boyfriend' I've had in my life, since I am now an accomplished lesbian," Amber explained in soft detail, looking back at the naked cop.

"I see....well, hmmmh....okay, and you both went to work for the Marcano Mob," Cliff said matter-of-factly as he sat there still wondering where his clothes and weapons vanished to.

"Yes, lawyers don't all work for corporations and squeaky-clean people," she chuckled.

"Do you know anything Diego Tanner may have been involved in on the side, like other connections or side-deals?" Cliff asked her next, slowly rising to his feet, yawning.

"Heenh, why don't you ask him yourself Agent Stevens?" Amber chimed as she stood at the dresser, leaning on it as she stared back at the naked Federal Agent standing before her now.

"He's in the closet right there, see for yourself," Amber said impishly as she pointed to the wardrobe closet on the other side of the big bedroom, making him curious enough to go see.

Cliff gave the woman a smirk of disbelief as he sauntered toward the closet, hoping his clothes and firearm might be there actually, deciding to demand them back from her next.

He opened the sliding closet door and found a thick, padded footlocker on the floor of the closet, along with a bunch of clothes hanging from the rack above. On top of the footlocker was a sealed jar like one of those "pickling" jars one stores garden vegetables in, and something unseemly was floating in a thick liquid inside the sealed Mason Jar, his curiosity making him reach down to pick it up. He looked at the jar in wonder of what Amber said.

"Diego Tanner?" he chuckled as he held the jar's content up to see better in the light.

Amber stepped up behind the naked Clifford Stevens as he looked into the sealed jar containing a pair of biological pieces the shape of which he only realized one second later.

"His balls," Amber Duffek sneered in reply, then she quickly stabbed her Inoculation-gun into the man's neck, the injection instantly rendering him unconscious where he stood, a narcotic concoction she got from a Micro-Biologist she knows well. She caught the jar as the naked man fell to the floor like a dropped rag doll, totally unconscious but still alive.

"You got too close Agent Stevens.....hmmm, hope you enjoyed fucking Shelly James, 'cuz that was your last piece of ass," Amber spoke over the sacked-out naked man at her feet.

She walked back to the dresser and put the injector-gun down on it's surface, picking up her tiny cell-phone to dial a familiar number now, holding it to her right ear listening to it ring.

"Yes, it's me...the pig is now bacon," Amber said as soon as she heard the voice of Senator Rupert Kelsh on the other line, then she ended the call after leaving the cryptic message.

Keeping "nosy cops" away from the grande plan was part of her job as Kelsh's lawyer, but this Federal Agent had stepped beyond protocol, beyond legal investigation, so she has to deal with him this way and set up yet another "fall guy" like she's had to do before.

"Now for the hard part, shit..... if those two insufferable Pillage brothers were still alive right now goddammit....they'd do this for me," Amber sighed to herself as she pulled on a pair of leather gloves, zipping up her black jumpsuit all the way to her neck as she walked back over to where the unconscious Agent Stevens lay in a crescent-moon posture.

Georgetown, 11:00 that night: Shaya returned home after "visiting" with Amber Duffek who had asked her over not to really discuss the Federal Agent on their tails, though Amber did go for a drive with her after their "threesome" to discuss private matters, the Agent snooping around being one of them, then Shaya dropped Amber back at her place and took off for home around 10pm. She guessed Amber knew a lot more about what was going on than she did, even when it came to her husband Rupert. Amber advised her to leave the Senator soon, for she felt he might not need his "trophy wife" anymore and she had to look out for herself. Shaya chalked that up as Amber wanting her for herself and thus wanted to break she and Rupert up post-haste. People are like that, selfish even while "helping" others.

Walking into the living room and looking at the big screen TV set where the weather report was on display, she found her husband nestled comfortably on the loveseat watching it.

"Honey, I know you have a lot going on….I don't demand to know your business affairs, but I would like to help you whenever I can, I mean….well, we are husband and wife," she spoke as she crossed the room in front of him, getting his attention for the moment.

"Shaya my dear, you do help me….more ways than one," he said with a slight smirk.

"I am more than just a body to lure men into your sphere of influence," she admonished.

"Yes, you're my wife and companion, what more could I ask of you?" he chuckled.

"Rupert, seriously…why don't you and I take a long vacation together, go somewhere far away for a month or more, just the two of us….husband and wife?" she suggested softly.

"Maybe next year, I am too engrossed in work now to take a sabbatical," he said in return.

"Your work is the problem….what I do know about it, what you've shared with me, is that it's stressful on you and you need a break," she added but knew it was to no avail with him!

"I appreciate the concern Shaya, but maybe next winter," he said in conclusive tone of voice.

"Okay, I'm going to bed," Shaya said as she walked out of the living room to the hallway.

"See you in the morning baby……I do like your hair cut," Rupert said in a voice too low for her to hear him as she went on up the stairs to adjourn to the master bedroom.

Rosslyn, Va. 11:08pm: The lone young man was set on his course right now, having fixed his targets and called them out. Gang members they were: five black males who sold dope to white yuppies here near D.C. and Georgetown and claimed this area near the Pentagon as their "turf". White man with a Glock-17 9mm pistol in hand, dressed in all black walking alone here would normally get attention as he did tonight, only the five thugs meeting in front of their favorite little restaurant where they intimidated (and often robbed) customers found this to be a situation they were not prepared for. Five gang members who were all armed were still not fast enough for Trevor Scott and his 9mm pistol at a distance of 25 yards out in plain sight but cloaked by nightfall.

"You fukkin' apes aren't faster than me!" the 24-year old Trevor Scott barked to the five corpses lying on pavement in front of the tiny restaurant near the Key Bridge, feeling some satisfaction by standing there in triumph over his five victims, police sirens in the distance as the folks in the restaurant had surely phoned 911 as he expected, and he didn't care. He wasn't about to be taken alive anyway and he had "backup" in the form of the man who convinced him this was the right course of action for a man of his quality.

"Horsehair," Trevor Scott said to the night air around him as he walked up to the restaurant windows, looking in. It was a noise he wanted to hear anytime now....and there it was! A distinctive "boom" in the near-distance on the other side of the Pentagon row, a detonation he was told would "cover" his escape by sending Police and EMS personnel in the other direction. Trevor saw a Hispanic waitress inside the restaurant scurrying across the dining area, so he raised his pistol to take quick aim for two shots through the restaurant window glass, the woman falling for cover inside, not knowing if he hit her or not, not really caring.

Taking off in a run down the sidewalk, the "lone wolf" terrorist was about to make it to his getaway car when he stepped into view of three police vehicles responding to the shooting despite the explosion on the other street ¼ mile away, spotting the lone white male with weapon still in his hand....Trevor Scott who had practiced fast-draw techniques and his marksmanship for months just to prepare for tonight, was not faster than three Police Officers with guns drawn and cornering him. The "lone wolf" went down in a hail of Police gunfire there on the street leading up to the Key Bridge and Georgetown, and that was what the man who convinced him to carry out what later would be called a "vigilante shooting" had expected to happen to this particular "lone wolf". Trevor Scott was too impulsive and didn't think too clearly in high-stress environments, which is why he'd been kicked out of the US Marine Corps just last year. The bomb set off ¼ mile away was detonated by Duncan Horsehair's premier "lone wolf" Nydia Cohen, the "little old lady" who prefers to carry around big leather purses loaded with C-4 plastic explosive and blow shit up!

Tonight's violent endeavor so close to home of the Senator who'd supported him for all these years was no accident, nor had it been authorized by the Senator himself, but Duncan Horsehair, so that the man in the glass cathedral might feel the "heat" a little. Police and Fire Agencies will be cordoning of this area for miles to get to the bottom of the explosion and shooting that just occurred within a stone's throw of Washington D.C. and the Pentagon.

"That should get your attention Senator, remind you of why we do this," Duncan said to himself as he stood up against a street corner at a Bank on one street, surveying the shooting scene and explosion/ fire just four blocks over here in Rosslyn. Not the most he could do in one night but enough to wake up all of Georgetown and get the Feds hopping since it was a shooting and bombing at the same time in close proximity to Washington D.C.'s "elite" part of town. He had a mission to accomplish and it was far from over, the Senator was losing sight of their shared ideals with his "slow down, cease fire, and wait for orders" bullshit.

Manassas, Va. 12 Midnight: Agent Cliff Stevens awoke in a blurred stupor, realizing he was lying on his back, but with his arms forced back over his head, restrained at the wrists by something that felt like metal. His vision cleared enough to see that he was still inside the bedroom of Attorney Amber Duffek, but this was stretching way beyond kinky-sex, least that is what he initially hoped it might be! Cliff tried in vain to free his hands from what appeared to be one hell of a strong "bed post" behind him, seeing that he was laying there on the bed naked and helpless, his voice returning to speak out in protest.

"Shut up Agent Stevens, you'll just get hoarse calling for help, noone's going to hear you in here anyway, as this house has plenty of distance between it's neighbors so that even muffled shouts will not make it the fifty yards next door…and you're wasting your energy too, not much left for the duration I'm afraid," spoke Amber Duffek as she walked back into the bedroom wearing the same black jumpsuit and boots she'd been in earlier and one of those coy smirks on her pretty face denoting she had done this to him for a nefarious purpose.

"Duffek, you release me right now and I won't press Federal Charges against you for kidnapping a Federal Agent," Cliff sneered up at the woman with a hot scowl of anger.

"Ooooh…that's irrelevant Cliffy….it's you who has violated Federal Guidelines by coming into my home without a warrant… stalking me ever since the first of the month, even before that I could claim…..and it was you who blew up my friend and fellow attorney Robert Marx a couple of weeks ago, so don't point the dirty stick at me sir….besides, it is not going to be me who makes tomorrow's headlines as the 'Mad Bomber of the ATF'….something like that anyway," Amber cooed in explanation, circling the bedroom that appeared to be all cleared-out except for the bed he was now restrained upon. He squirmed despite the restraint on his wrists over his head, looking for any way to free himself despite the handcuffs locked tight.

"Yes, you've been set up….yes, you've been screwed over…..yes, you're going to die tonight and become the 'fall guy' in a scheme which is beyond your pay-grade, so relax Cliffy and let the poison take effect…..same shit they use in chemical warfare only less ghastly and more humane for cops like you…..I chose it because I like cops, always have," she continued.

"Damn you Amber….release me or….or you'll go to Prison…. they'll catch you for it, I have superiors to answer to and they know I came here goddamit….you'll get the death penalty for killing an Agent!" Cliff snapped at her loudly, straining against his arms-restraint again.

"Ooooh….sorry, wrong again honey, but your superiors are covered and they will see you as the 'perpetrator' easy to pin the last few terrorist incidents on….you're expendable, surely you knew that already, and as for me….I have a get-out-of-jail-free card compliments of a US Senator and my buddies in the Justice Department," she continued as she circled him.

"Don't tell me…Senator Rupert Kelsh….and Tyler Clark in the Justice Department," Cliff said in a sigh of realization now, eyeballing her intently as she stopped at the foot of the bed.

"Bingo….you win the booby-prize Agent Stevens…yes, Kelsh and Clark are part of a grand conspiracy the likes of which you began to realize just enough to get you dropped into a meat grinder tonight!" Amber Duffek laughed outloud in delight of his answer, clapping.

"Awh, sorry you didn't realize you were being set up to take the fall for the real 'terrorist mastermind' as Clark calls him….heenh-heeh, but that's life in modern America, it's hard and it's not fuckin' fair at all for a good civil-servant," she continued in calmer tone now.

"My god…..Clark, Kelsh…..the Marcano Mob…Faster Productions Porn….Horsehair?" Cliff sighed as his mind tried to comprehend the complexity of what he had fallen for.

"Yes, Clark and Kelsh have this thing going which will eventually transform the US Government at it's highest levels to something of a Fascist state, all under the banner of 'safety' of course….kinda racist if you ask me, but I'm in it for my own reasons and I have been instrumental in covering their asses…..from the Marcano Mob and it's underworld fortune siphoned through Faster Productions during the final months before that Company's downfall, laundering and secreting millions of dollars for the activities you yourself have been investigating over the past few years….not just the two million dollars your so-called 'superiors' in DC had you looking for…..and that 'Horsehair' guy….heenh, he's a ghost….and you're taking his place tonight as far as recent blame goes," Amber spoke gingerly, touching a hand to his bare feet as Cliff just lay there trying to absorb her words.

"You bitch…you're letting a governmental conspiracy take place and for what….what are they paying you?!" Cliff snapped back at her with a dry mouth, eyes red with angst.

"Oh it's not entirely for money baby, no…ya see, it's a lifestyle really, one I cherish…and key persons in positions of power allow me to continue as long as I help them out when necessary, secrets shared....secrets kept....the Senator from New Jersey has some really good blackmail on me which if he dropped, would mean my cute ass in prison for life, so I help him out when he calls, though that stops after tonight anyway....I'm going to be free of Rupert Kelsh and his fascist conspiracy as soon as I leave you here tonight and detonate one more explosive.....hmmmh, hate to lose another house but one has to keep your 'motis operandi' the same....it'll appear you tried to kill me with another of your bombs after the one in Arlington failed," Amber explained with casual aplumb.

"Murder...is that what you did to Diego Tanner....Isabel Marcano....Jonny Faster....all to get money laundered for a terror campaign on American soil...which sets up fascists in the government for future power?" Cliff spoke with dry mouth, trying to absorb it all now.

"Heenh, Diego Tanner was a man I loved once, but he was a fool who stuck his dick where it didn't belong and got his balls cut off.....I simply kept them pickled in a jar as a momento....Isabel Marcano had been a friend of mine since we were in grade-school, I helped her out when I could and saw in her a chance to make some money being a lawyer for her Mob Boss Uncle.....there I found an even more lucrative gentleman who wanted me to help slowly funnel illicit money made by the Marcano Mob through other resources allowing him to access it for his own use, one of those resources for money-laundering at the time was the biggest Porn Film Company on the east coast....Faster Productions," Amber explained in detail, walking around the room with an easy smile on her face, arms folded.

"More lucrative gentleman?" Cliff asked in a sneer, watching her in helpless realization.

"Senator Rupert Kelsh....yes, he came to me after personally halting a Justice Department investigation into my own insider-trading scheme that could have meant ten years in a Federal Pen for me if I was prosecuted.....I helped him get what he wanted, laundered criminal money for use in his secret 'war' against the very society he was sworn to protect," Amber continued frankly, telling the Agent the truth because he was dying anyway.

"Incredible," Cliff sighed in belief of what she was saying, for he had come close to uncovering something just like that in his "unofficial investigation", the sting of being set up and betrayed by his superiors almost mind-numbing to think about.

"I am going to get what I want more or less, and everyone else gets theirs...you're the sacrifice I'm afraid....then again, people have been dying so that others may live since the beginning of mankind, it's the natural order of things I guess," Amber said impishly.

"You have no wife, no kids, no parents.....perfect lone-wolf terrorist," she added for effect, studying his facial reactions to her words as she circled the bed again.

"Sacrifice...hunh....you're lucky they don't kill you along with me," Cliff sneered back.

"Mmmhh, not this time stud...I'm still a cog in their wheel, but if it's any consolation to you, at least you're not leaving behind a widow and kids....one man gets dropped into the meat grinder, this time it's gotta be you Cliffy....," she continued in softer tone.

"I never had a wife and kids dammit, is that why I was picked for this?" he asked next.

"Partly so,yes....makes for a neater cause-and-effect,no screaming widow to raise questions and no kids demanding reparation money for your death later on....plus the criminal profile for such 'lone wolf' domestic-terrorists you fit almost perfectly Cliffy......you're a lonely white male close to middle-age with no wife, no kids, questionable performance history with your job.....no close friends, no property, no prospects,"

Amber told him in a frankness that unnerved him as he listened to her in silence now.

"But hey...look at it this way honey, a wife often leaves you and takes half of everything you got, kids forget about you in time and go off to disappoint you, and there are plenty of other men out there reproducing like crazy, so it's no big deal you're not in the gene pool," she continued in a patronizing tone, though for Amber Duffek she was being "nice" right now!

"You said I was poisoned?" Cliff asked her, starting to feel a bit woozy as he lay there.

"Yes, it's called sodium-borezene, a new concoction of sorts taken from the same properties of nerve gas only slower and easily-injected, so I'm told....you'll simply fall asleep and die within say, the next ten minutes or so," Amber answered him matter-of-factly with a shrug.

"I don't believe this shit....hunh....I got picked by a Fascist asshole in the Justice Department to uncover a domestic-terrorist noone else seems to believe exists...my only clues are missing porn film money that was actually laundered Mafia cash, and videotape of a dead Gulf War Veteran who is very much still alive....to be murdered and set up as the

'scape goat' covering for the real terrorist mastermind on Capitol Hill...whom the fascist asshole I work for is in-cahoots with all along," Cliff sighed as he stared up at the ceiling.

"Pretty much, that's it," Amber chimed with a smirking grin down at the naked man.

"It's just like that hunh....I'm easily expendable," Cliff sighed again, looking at her intently.

"Yep, soldiers....cops....firemen.....men who are necessarily expendable for the greater good of the majority of others who live on....necessary sacrifices," Amber answered him.

Amber noticed the man lying there chained to the bed was now getting a hard-on, lying there like a human "sun dial" as she explained his predicament to him a bit further.

"At least you got to fuck a former porn actress.....Shelly James, before you die," Amber said with a giggle, then stepped to the foot of the bed and unzipped her jumpsuit in front.

"I like you Cliffy...tell you what, I'll treat you before you pass out and die, call it a 'professional courtesy'....," Amber said gingerly as she peeled off the black jumpsuit to reveal her totally-naked body underneath, shedding the garment as Cliff watched in awe.

"Why not....since I'm a dead man in the next few minutes," he sighed as he watched the lithe nude body of Attorney Amber Duffek snaked between his legs to come face-to-face with his rock-hard erection. She winked at him then took his member in sweet fellatio.

"Onnh-yeeaah!" Cliff sighed in a loud whisper, closing his eyes in delight of the oral act Amber Duffek was now performing on him as a "final" courtesy before the poison kills him.

This was not a bad way to go, he told himself as he lay there in her grip, not a bad way at all!

A slow-acting "humane" poison, a beautiful woman giving the best blowjob of his life, and the fact he doesn't have a wife and kids to miss and/or suffer because of his death.....yeah!

"Oaaahh-yeeaaahh.....Amber....thank you," Cliff sighed in delight of her slurping on his shaft in passionate fellatio, feeling woozy all the more now as the poison encroached.

"Mmmmhh....you're welcome," Amber cooed as she lifted off his member to look up at the man's weary face, seeing his eyes close as she gently stroked him, and he climaxed just as he faded to oblivion. She rose to her feet looking at the Federal Agent who just expired, almost a smile on his face in conclusion.

"And to think my Law School Professor said I was a heartless bitch with no compassion for others around me....," Amber Duffek said in conclusion as she pulled up her jumpsuit.

Georgetown, 5:30 the next evening: Rupert Kelsh relaxed in his recliner inside his private den, eyes glued to the three TV screens on one wall, watching the latest info on his "events" since yesterday. Only one that stuck in his craw was the shootings and explosion in Rosslyn just up the street from here as well as the Pentagon last night! Duncan did not run that "event" by him as he had always done before, though he knew it was something he had carried out just by it's "earmarks". The explosion that occurred in Manassas Va. right around the same time frame was a planned event, and one which went off without a hitch like the last one.....only this time Amber Duffek properly set up a lone Federal Agent to take the fall for the past few bombings, his body found by the Fire Department (though not yet identified). Nothing better than the blame for something being laid upon a "rogue agent", Rupert told himself as he watched the TV News.

ATF Agent Clifford Stevens will be blamed for the two bomb-attacks aimed at Attorney Amber Duffek and the bomb that killed Civil Rights Lawyer Robert Marx and his piece of shit son Jamal three weeks ago as well. Very neat and orderly, Rupert thought as he watched the footage of the burning house in Manassas on one TV screen, another part of his plan coming together like it righteously should!

"Hmmh…maybe next time you won't make it out of the house prior to explosion," he said to himself as he leaned back in his recliner, thinking about how she was still "useful". Rupert took another sip of his Cognac, wondering if the Feds and Police have lifted the blockade of the Pentagon and Rosslyn area searching for more bombs or other "terrorists". It made driving into Virginia from here a slow-moving venture, so he hoped it was over by tomorrow morning! With Harold McCassler flying out to Los Angeles on Monday unknowingly carrying a vial of the virus his father engineered in the lab Kelsh bought from the Victory Brothers, the final stages of his decade-long plan was coming to fruition and Rupert Kelsh was happy about it.

Pawley's Bar n' Grill, Fairfax Va. (same time): Shaya Kelsh just wanted to relax in a common restaurant like this while dressed common and around common folks, no "DC Elite" telling her what to do, no strangers dropping by the house to fuck her because Rupert has them on his "use list", no lesbian lawyer wanting her to spend the night again, no goddamn Federal Agents stalking her (as she had been told one was). No, just a lonely excursion out tonight for seafood and a few drinks by herself without distractions or pitfalls, she had promised herself earlier this afternoon.

Sitting in a corner dining booth to the rear of the restaurant, Shaya had an order of shrimp and scampy in front of her along with a pitcher of beer, not wanting to be bothered at all really. As in any restaurants, if you sit there long enough, you tend to overhear the conversations of other patrons whether you like it or not. Shaya kept hearing the rather boisterous remarks of two men seated in the booth behind hers, and for some strange reason the voice sounded familiar! Wanting to sneak a peak around the corner of her booth at the two men out of curiosity, Shaya glimpsed around to glance at the two men seated in the booth behind hers without them noticing. She leaned back in her own booth and rolled her eyes in disbelief, though she was not in error.

The two familiar-sounding assholes seated in the booth behind hers right now, in all the cheap seafood bullshit-bar-and-grills on the east coast, were the two goons who barged into her home almost two weeks ago with Mortimer Green and threatened both she and Rupert, the skinny white guy and bald black dude who held her while that prick lobbyist Green made threats against she and Rupert in their own home!

No mistake about it, she told herself, it was them and they hadn't seen her sitting there.

"Just my luck.....hmmm....well, like Rupert always says....there are always ways to use other people, even simpletons and vagrants if you have a purpose," Shaya sighed to herself as she unzipped her leather jacket in front, reaching in to pull down the sports-bra she wore then zipping it back up. She slipped to the end of her booth's bench seat and slowly rose to her feet and glanced around the not-so-full restaurant.

"Guys....hey there....remember me?" Shaya spoke up as she stepped in front of their booth, unzipping her leather jacket in front for the two surprised men her bare boobs for about three seconds, guessing noone else would see her expose herself like this.

"Omigod," the black guy said as she re-zipped her jacket and smirked at them knowingly.

"You!" the white guy on the other half of the booth said in a stunned sigh of surprise.

Shaya took a seat next to the skinny white guy in his half of the dining booth, her jacket zipped up and a serious look crossing her pretty face glaring across at his black counterpart on the other side. She ran her left hand under the table and to the crotch of the man beside her, getting his full attention now, suddenly sitting up straight as the woman's hand gently gripped his genitals covered by his worn and faded jeans there.

She slipped her left foot out of her shoe to put her foot between the black guy's thighs, against his genitals as well, her gesture getting their complete and undivided attention.

"Guys…I know who you both are and I hope you realize what happened to your pervious employer not long ago…..remember Mortimer Green?" Shaya spoke softly to the two men as they sat there looking on her with stunned realization, not to mention a bit of fear.

"Uhh….yeah, he got killed," the white guy on her left spoke up first in response to her.

"Bingo, and I understand two assholes like you and you are likely just temporary-hires for a prick like Mortimer Green, a small-time crew willing to act like goons for money….which is why I stopped by here tonight to have us a little chat," Shaya spoke, lying about the premise this was an intentional "visit" on her part, better to let them think she knows all about them!

"I need two goombahs myself….for one night only, five-grand a piece….no questions and you leave the area after it's done….you in or out?" Shaya offered them in a whisper they barely heard but understood because all other sound around them was turned out.

"Five grand…..hell yeah," the white guy chuckled as he looked at his black buddy .

"Okay, what's the job?" the black guy asked with a nervous expression of doubt.

"Write ya cell-phone numbers on this napkin and I'll call you both really soon…I also assume the two of you don't want to end up like your last temporary-employer, so keep this under your hats and stay cool or it's a dirt nap for both of you," Shaya spoke in a sinister but alluring tome she was not used to performing.

"No problem….no problem…..," the white guys said in return, licking dry lips now.

"Just be cool and wait for my call and it's five-grand for each of you," Shaya said as she let go of them and slipped her shoe back on then stood up from the booth to leave the men sitting there in perplexed wonder of how a woman like that found them and why she's now hiring them all by herself like this…very damn unusual!

"I don't believe this shit, do you?" the white guy asked his black buddy with a nervous chuckle, slapping a hand on the table surface between them, nervous sweat on his brow.

"Oh I believe it, man….that chick is no joke," the black guy said in a huff as the smart-ass waitress sauntered up to their table looking at them with a slight scowl of suspicion.

"You getting the check man?" the black one asked the white one with a glance at the not-so-attractive and outwardly smart-ass waitress.

"Your food and beers just got paid for…..but tell your lady friend that the Manager says if she flashes her big tits again in this restaurant, she won't be welcome back," the waitress spoke as she chewed gum, then stepped away from the table, the two booth's checks and tips paid for in cash by the brunette woman with the big tits who just walked out the door.

Shaya walked to her car feeling food about herself, about what she had just done and how she did it so easily-convincing! She had their phone numbers now and would call on them to take care of something in the very near future because they were perfect for the part, and expendable if things go wrong. Driving off into the nightfall, Shaya listened to satellite radio in her Audi R8, thinking about her husband and the very real probability he will be "disposing" of her and pretty damn soon if her sixth-sense was serving her right.

He had used her from the beginning, she realized that, and he had been beneficial to her in many regards, such as keeping her money safe and keeping a nice roof over her head, but things were getting "hairy" nowadays and the illicit activities she assumed her husband may be involved in were coming home to roost, so to speak, and she knew it was just a matter of time before Rupert ends up indicted, arrested, murdered, or worse…..in the White House! She sped along Rt. 50 and turned onto a back-road route that would take her to Rosslyn and then Georgetown. With all the Police activity in Rosslyn after the shootings and bombing 24 hours earlier, she knew it would take some time to get across the Key Bridge and home, though "home" was not the same place of refuge as it was for her a year ago…. she figured she might have to move out anytime now!

Washington D.C. 7:25 that evening: Deputy Attorney General Tyler Clark sat at his desk inside the US Department of Justice and studied the "official" press release issued just 30 minutes ago to the mainstream press venues from the Dept. of Treasury and DHS regarding the premise of a "rogue agent" being responsible for three, possibly four bombings this month as well as multiple-murder. The press-release was fine, as it detailed the "problematic" career of Agent Clifford Stevens who as it appears, stalked and bombed his targets while "investigating" some shadowy "domestic terrorist" he wasn't authorized to be properly (and legally) investigating in the first place!

Yes, Agent Stevens was set-up to end up as the "fall guy" with reputation forever sullied but then again he was an expendable asset to the Government, a wifeless, childless career-cop with a penchant for breaking the rules.....and he could have declined Clark's "unofficial" offer three weeks ago if he had wanted to!

Looking at the ATF photos of the charred remains of Agent Stevens found in the remains of the Duffek residence in Manassas, he wondered if the man went quietly or painlessly? No matter, Agent Stevens served his purpose in this greater scheme, so it was all good. Makes for a great cover-story for the press despite egg being thrown on the face of the ATF, he thought as he looked at the photos of Agent Stevens' charred corpse again.

Sitting there alone at his desk, Tyler Clark thought about his grand plan alongside of Senator Rupert Kelsh and others in the US Government taking so long as it did.....it'll be worth it once the ball starts to roll in what he likes to call "covert dominion". What the American Public doesn't know.....makes them the American Public, and what ¾ of the US Congress and US Supreme Court doesn't know....might just save Western Civilization!

Tyler thought back to the other afternoon when he spent time with Senator Kelsh's lovely wife Shaya at his home in Centreville, the final time he saw Agent Stevens and told him to KILL the man known only as "Horsehair", which if the Agent had proceeded to carry out, the idiot might still be alive and useful! Shaya had been sent to him as a "gift" of sorts from her husband (and Clark's cosonspirator) Senator Rupert Kelsh, who considers Clark a "fellow traveler" on the same frequency of course.

Without Kelsh and his demonic super-soldier "Horsehair", the plan would not be where it is today, the public would not be willing to choose safety over a few personal freedoms by allowing their Government to stomp out "domestic terrorists" wholesale. The plan had come full circle and though Kelsh wanted to proceed with a faster regimen by introducing some kind of contagious disease into the illegal immigrant populations here in the US and thus alarming the public to the point even the most liberal politicians will vote in favor of rounding up immigrants all across the US to avert further spread of the disease. No, not quite yet! Clark kept thinking to himself in pragmatic relflection.

Kelsh wanted to be appointed as Attorney General or perhaps Vice President for his role in the plan over the course of the past 10 years, and he may well get it. Clark knew the man wanted to speed up the process they had begun in 1995 with the Oklahoma City Bombing, creating a climate ripe for tightening the reigns of centralized control in order to save America from a hostile outside world and muddy hordes of third-world races desperately clamoring to invade it's sacred shores....

Clark thought about the Senator's wife again, that busty brunette who was a former Porn Actress and would have been the next suspect Agent Stevens would have pursued if he had lived: Shaya Kelsh aka "Shaya Gold", a forty-year old woman of third-world extraction Rupert Kelsh married in 2006 in order to use her as "proof" he was not a racist as alleged during his last re-election campaign, and as a "trophy" which he often shared with other men he sought to befriend, coerce, and manipulate. Shaya was the perfect "trophy wife" and "hand-maiden" for a man like Kelsh.

Clark sat there wondering what happens to her once Kelsh is either where he wants to be in position of power, or....indicted and arrested? In this game of love and war, there always has to be one or two "scapegoats" ready for slaughter, just as Agent Clifford Stevens had to become! He considered taking Shaya for himself if something bad happens to Senator Kelsh, and she wouldn't refuse him since doing so would mean her own ass in jail or broke and on the streets. Then again, having an ex-porn star for a wife may have worked for Senator Kelsh, but she may not work for me, Clark told himself.

Still, the woman was a dynamo in the bedroom and so he would "look out for" her if and when the time comes. Something told him a man like Rupert Kelsh viewed most people around him as expendable, and in this business, rightly so….which means Kelsh might soon drop that lovely, smooth and well-filled-out trophy wife of his into a barbecue pit!

Glancing over to the corner of his desk here, Clark saw the sealed file folder containing the only evidence that he and those other department-heads had met with Agent Stevens three weeks ago to assign him to an "unofficial" investigation. It was to be shredded of course, and the shreddings burned by himself tonight. Stevens had to be seen as his own "lone wolf", a "renegade operator" with questionable mental stability, committing acts of terror while "investigating" them personally, sort of like the rogue Fireman who commits arson in order to "respond" to the fire himself….

Georgetown, October 22nd, 9:35pm: It was already storming outside like the weather report said it would, and a cold, hard rain was the order of the evening making traffic and even air travel difficult all along the eastern seaboard. Harold McCassler made the 6pm flight out of Dulles Airport and was now flying west toward Los Angeles as ordered to.

Rupert Kelsh was pleased with things so far, despite the "upset" shooting and bombing near here a few nights ago which turned Rosslyn and most of Georgetown into a "police barricade" for over 24 hours. Looking at himself in the vanity mirror of the bathroom, he almost smiled at his reflection, reminding himself that once the 2008 Election kicks off beyond the primaries now unfolding, he as a Democrat would have the advantage of being seen by the Democratic Nominee as a "Moderate" Running Mate material, despite the fact he has a former porn star as his wife, or should they say **had**.....past tense!

He had already mentioned to Shaya that she may want to scope out another "avenue" to travel once he gets to where he is expecting to go, something they had discussed when they agreed to marry over a year ago, the fact their union may become untenable and they would have to go their separate ways. One of his fellow conspirators recently suggested he get rid of Shaya as in an "accident" or by one of the various "acts of terror" like the two bombings that plagued Attorney Amber Duffek recently. After letting Duncan Horsehair have sex with Shaya numerous times, Rupert felt the man might be reluctant to put Shaya into the crosshairs for elimination not because a warrior like him **cares** for any one woman he's gone to bed with, no....because Shaya reminds Duncan Horsehair of the one "true love" he felt in his dark, violent lifetime: Mafia Princess Isabel Marcano!

He opened the bathroom door and stepped out into his master bedroom, looking over to the king-sized bed and found his wife lying on her right side on the bed now, totally nude and staring back at him with that kittenish expression of hers he always found enticing.

"Lover...where do we go from here....really?" she asked him soft but candidly, the start of a conversation he had been expecting to have with her, just not right now this evening.

"Hmmph.....Shaya my dear....I could not ask for a more loyal companion who would do nearly anything for me," Rupert said as he walked toward the foot of their marital bed.

"Mutually-beneficial my husband, isn't that what you told me when you asked me to marry you more than a year ago?" Shaya replied in a soft tone of voice, smiling sly.

"Yes, and it has been as far as I can tell, but we are coming up to a period of transition, and not just for the two of us, for the entire country and the government," he added next.

"Hmmm....yes, scare the hell out of everyone in the country and they let their elected government do what the men in government feel is 'necessary' to save everyone from future dangers," Shaya sighed matter-of-factly as she lay there on her side, staring at him.

"Something like that, yes…you are most perceptive my dear….. yes, many millions of spoiled Americans will give up certain liberties such as unrestricted travel, unhampered immigration, and other pleasantries if they think it will guarantee their safety from a dangerous entity such as terrorists…..or perhaps the plague," Rupert told her frankly.

"Hunh, politicians like you put Hitler in power," she sneered in a lowered voice this time.

"Touche'…..sticks and stones, but yes…it's always been the real face of power wielded from behind the scenes in history…behind the recognized leaders of centuries past, behind dictators like Hitler and Franco, Mussolini, even American Presidents," he added.

"And what does that make a woman like me?" she chimed with a slinky expression.

"My 'Mata Hari'…..," Rupert said with a smirk at his busty wife on the bed facing him.

"Heenh, that's real good….Mata Hari….well kiss my ass," Shaya snickered in contempt.

"Shaya, seriously….have you given some thought as to what avenue you might take if we end the marriage sometime soon?" he responded with a business-tone the same as if he were suggesting what she might prefer for dinner, and she wanted to curse him for it.

"Well actually now that you mention it Rupert, yes….I've been thinking hard about what I may do once we go our separate ways," she said in a more cheerful tone, studying his reaction as he stood there at the foot of their bed, arms folded in his pajamas now.

"You still have your money in the off-shore account as I promised," he added frankly.

"Yes, and it'll keep me afloat for quite awhile…..maybe I'll move to another country where two million dollars goes further than it would here in Washington D.C.," she chimed impishly as she pondered her options again, lying there naked before him.

Two million dollars of Marcano Mafia cash "laundered" through Faster Productions Porn Film Company in July of 2005 thanks to Rupert's contact in both of those shadowy realms of business: Attorney Amber Duffek! Amber had seen a loophole to funnel $2 million dollars of Marcano capital the cops hadn't seized by July 5th 2005 through the accounts of Faster Porn in New York and within one week's time wired to an off-shore account sitting on the island nation of Antigua earning 4% interest. Rupert would have already used the money to help fund Horsehair's activities as well as other things in their "war" if it were not for the $8 million he succeeded in embezzling from a Jewish Charity in 2002. The extra $2 million Amber Duffek secured for him was more than enough to secure Shaya's hand in marriage and agreement to help him in more "carnal" matters dealing with other men and other imaginations. The $2 million in the off-shore account was hers for the taking once they split-up, no questions asked and a fast divorce, since it was not like she could put "Porn Star" on any ordinary job resume and they both knew it.

"I might re-introduce myself to that deposed Sheik from Bahrain we met at the gala-dinner fundraiser a couple months ago in Alexandria, he liked me a lot," Shaya snickered.

"Yes he did, but I don't imagine you converting to Islam," Rupert chuckled back at her.

"True.....well, there's always Amber, she's already asked me to be her girl after you leave me behind on your climb to power and glory," Shaya chimed in next, grinning.

"I kinda figured she would, but you like men too much," Rupert reminded her in humor.

"True, besides...Amber is too damn sexy to remain lesbian for too long," Shaya giggled.

"What about returning to uhhm....adult films?" he asked her as he circled the bedroom.

"Heenh-heeh, not likely, though I have thought about it a few times, it's just that once a Starlet is over thirty-five years of age like I am, she loses roles more and more until she becomes a 'cameo' actress much like what Jonny Faster did with me in the last few years with his Company, even though I may still look good at age forty, my star has fallen and 'comebacks' are rare in the X-rated Industry," she explained casually as she rubbed a hand over her breasts lying there curled on the bed watching Rupert walk the bedroom.

"Even with you being the ex-wife of a US Senator?" he asked back at her in a chuckle.

The fact he just used the term "ex-wife" in the manner as if they were already divorced stung Shaya a bit as she lay conversing on the hurtful topic of ending their marriage.

"Well, maybe it might get me back to doing a few more films, but I'm not interested really unless I needed the money....never was into shaking my ass on stage in a nightclub either, like most of the porn girls do," she added with a shrug, staring at her husband.

"Perhaps you could hook back up with some of those other porn stars you worked with?" Rupert suggested amicably as he stopped at the window to stare out at the night sky now.

Shaya wanted to laugh at that suggestion, for he didn't know she had done just that the other evening with Shelly James and a strap-on dildo over at Amber's place in Manassas!

She had never really "kept in touch" with most of her former X-rated co-stars anyway.

"A lot of them are deceased actually," Shaya snickered in sarcasm at his suggestion.

"I know….what about those ones you starred with back in the Nineteen-Nineties, like the ones in the videos I have of yours here….. Dexter and Carla…..that guy called Mered Aladdin?" Rupert asked in curious wonder for the moment, looking back toward the gorgeously-nude woman on the bed he has called his wife for more than a year now.

"Heenh, Carla Ferrari became a Nurse somewhere in Ohio…. Mered Aladdin vanished shortly after I left the Company two years ago, and F.M. Dexter….his real name was Frankie….last I heard, he married some wealthy older white woman and moved to Delaware…I got a postcard from him about a month or so before you and I got married last year, but that was the last I ever heard from him or any of the others except Shelly James of course, considering Shelly is Amber's on-again-off-again squeeze," Shaya explained casually with a lingering smile.

"So the Porn Industry is not a close-knit family of performers hunh?" Rupert chided her.

"Nope, more like a dysfunctional family considering many of it's performers hail from broken homes, bad backgrounds, and lead secret double-lives, so I'm not gonna get an invitation to the Nineties X-Rated Films Reunion," Shaya chuckled in retort.

"I never asked you Shaya....what got you in that business in the first place back in what year was it...nineteen-ninety-one?" Rupert chimed in renewed interest on the subject.

"March of Ninety-One, yeah....I was waiting tables in a Pub up in New York City, when a high-ranking member of the Porn Film Circuit in New York walked in one night and asked for me to wait on him, threw a lot of money around and talked me into auditioning as a nude model at first.....within two weeks I was scheduled to perform in my very first X-rated feature film.....it was something I guess I was meant to do because I never did feel any regret over it, four-hundred films later.....," Shaya explained softly to him.

"Later that year I was cast with Jonny Faster for the first time in the now-classic film

'Thunderballs' which you like to watch....," Shaya chimed impishly as she watched Rupert circle the bedroom slowly, obviously thinking about something of weight.

"I liked that one, yes," Rupert said as he walked around the room not looking at her.

"They don't make'em like that anymore....nowadays porn flicks are all wall-banging compilations made by no-talent amateurs using webcams and digital," Shaya sneered.

"You could become a Porn Director," Rupert chuckled in a humored tone of voice.

"Ha-hah...no chance, not nowadays....though I did direct three films for Jonny and one scene he did not know about," she snickered in a more relaxed demeanor, lying flat on her back for a moment. Rupert considered asking Shaya to leave the Country with her

$2 million just so she'd be "free" of the coming storm and escape what might be her own demise considering how the others in his ongoing plan might consider her a liability! "Maybe that FM Dexter guys is divorced by now?" he snickered casually to her again.

"Rupert…you like watching Frankie and me on film!" Shaya quipped as she suddenly rose up on her haunches, mouth open in a "I caught you" girlish expression now.

"What….I just suggested him since you know where he's at," Rupert said uncomfortably.

"Hunh-haah….no, I've caught you watching a few of my past films here at night before, and it was those interracial scenes like the ones I did with FM Dexter back in the nineties!" Shaya spoke in a cheerful voice of realization, only now concluding that about him. Rupert often debased and denigrated black and Hispanic people when alone with her but he sort of **liked** watching her having sex with a black man in an X-rated film! It made Shaya view her husband as even more of a **Stranger** to her now……

She could tell her husband was about to clam-up and leave the room, for Rupert Kelsh was no gentleman who could take criticism of the embarrassing variety well at all and he would shut up and shut the door whenever she "called" him on something like that. Shaya decided to shut the valve off herself by changing the topic rather quickly.

"Honey….seriously, let's just you and me take off somewhere…. go overseas for awhile and enjoy a long vacation just the two of us, re-consider splitting up?" she spoke next.

"Sorry Shaya, no can do….things are rolling here and I am a cog in the wheel….if I was to leave the Country now, I'd never be able to return…..though I might suggest you take that long vacation yourself, and take your money just in case….I'll leave the pass-code on the refrigerator for you by morning if you'd like," Rupert said as he opened the bedroom door to exit, looking over a shoulder toward the naked vixen on the big bed.

"Damn you Rupert…..you make love to me right here, right now, and I'll be yours forever and a day….your wife for life, and never let another man touch me…..but if you walk out that door right now….then I am no longer your wife and you'll never see me again," Shaya spoke up as she rose up to her knees, making him look back at her again.

He stopped at the threshold of the open door to face his lovely wife and her ultimatum, then reached up to where his grey three-piece Armani suit hung on a hanger by the door, taking the attire in his right hand as he looked at her to give an answer.

"All good things eventually come to an end....thanks for being there Shaya," Rupert said conclusively as she stared doe-like back at him, only to watch her husband turn his back on her and leave the bedroom, door closing shut behind him as he descended the stairs.

She rolled over onto her right side on the bed and let out a sullen sigh of realization, though not too surprised to discover he did not love her afterall, not after a year of an "open marriage" nor after all she has done for him....she was just an "asset" he was now cashing in so that he may slip away into whatever "new life" he was crafting for himself.

"Heartless old man," Shaya growled to herself as she rolled onto her back on the bed now, reaching for the portable phone on the nightstand, and dialing a memorized number to leave a quick message then a second number to leave a quick message, as planned.

"Now it's look-out-for-Shaya time.....," she said to herself as she sat up and slipped to the end of the big bed, standing up and stretching arms upward. Shaya shouldn't have been shocked to finally learn how her husband was USING HER ALL ALONG, but it still "stung" her heart to see and hear him blow her off so casually just now as if she were a whore he dropped cab fare to and walked out the door.......

She walked over to the dresser against one wall and looked at the divorce decree he had lying there waiting for her to sign, surprised to see papers like that lying there for her with all the consideration as if it was a bill unpaid she had to put a signature on. She picked up a pen and quickly signed her name to the proper locations on the paperwork, signing away her marriage to Senator Rupert Kelsh tonight.

"There you have it old man.....done deal," she sneered to the paperwork and walked away from it, opening the wardrobe closet to begin packing some of her clothes and personal effects now, thinking about getting a Hotel Suite for the night instead of sleeping in one of the spare bedrooms, not knowing if he was going to stay here or go somewhere since he grabbed his new Armani suit on the way out the bedroom door.

"Thanks for being there....hunh....you motherfucker, I would have been yours for life if you loved me you ungrateful son-of-a-bitch," Shaya sighed to herself conclusively.

Rupert Kelsh was dressed minutes later and ready to go out to his clandestine, late night dinner-meeting with other "players" in the game, namely the two men in Department of Homeland Security whom are going along with the plan he and Tyler Clark have laid out!

Walking into the dining room to look at himself and his new Armani suit in the mirror there, he suddenly felt the obvious presence of another man in the room.

"What tha hell?" Rupert sighed in surprised reaction as a stranger stepped from the shadows, only he wasn't entirely a stranger to Senator Kelsh however he was supposed to be deceased but wasn't, walking calmly across the dining room toward him now.

"Good evening Senator....so glad you were home right now so we can talk," spoke a very much alive Shane Pillage who looked a little different, namely in the way of his head shaved bald and what appeared to be a burn mark on his right cheek from the jawbone up.

"Don't look so surprised sir, you did kill my twin brother Steven but I survived the blast and crawled out of the rubble with just minor injuries thanks in no small part to Amber's house there having an underground storm-cellar I jumped into just as the explosion hit," Shane Pillage explained to the stunned older white man facing him perplexed.

"Underground storm-cellar......no shit," Rupert sighed in realization he was now facing off with a "liability" he thought for sure he had vanquished forever last week. This was not good, actually never good to have a liability coming through your door 10:00 at night.

"No shit....hunh-huh, after I recovered from the shock and injury over the weekend and made plans for a new identity now that the media reported my death along with my brother, I came to the conclusion there could be only one son of a bitch who'd pull something like that to get rid of the two men who set up a bullshit property purchase for him not long ago, a Laboratory in Maryland noone else was buying....which told me and Steven you wanted it for illicit reasons, and that was cool....then you killed my brother and almost vaporized my black ass in that blast," Shane Pillage spoke in heated voice, facing the Senator wearing all black and with clenched fists down at his sides, no weapon appearing as of yet but Rupert was sort of expecting one as Shane walked the room.

"Yes, it was just business....nothing personal," Rupert said in apprehension to him.

"Business, yeah...hunh-huh, but the kind of business I didn't sign up for old man, and as for my twin brother Steven.....to hell with him, he was secretly planning to have me clipped later on anyway and take all of our fortune for himself," Shane continued next.

"What do you want then?" Rupert asked the visitor flatly, getting right to the point.

"Well old man, I did consider coming here to bust a cap in ya, which under the circumstances would very understandable to all parties involved, but then decided that killing a US Senator like that would bring way too much heat when what I really want is to slip away from all this white-man's-burden horseshit and start a new life with a new identity," Shane explained as he circled the Senator in the dimly-lit dining room there.

"You want money then," Rupert said in a rather brazen reply, staring at the black man.

"Oh, like the money you have stashed away in an off-shore account to the tune of over two million dollars.....which isn't yours?" Shane chimed matter-of-factly. Neither man knew there was another set of ears listening to what was being said between them right now,

Shaya Kelsh sitting at the middle of the stairwell listening intently in silence.

"Yeah, my brother and I dug deep into your past and present Senator Kelsh, since we were entering into business with a super-politician, it behooved us to know who, what, where, why, and what-for.......man like you gets around and screws a lot of other people over in the course of his daily routine, and though I did not see that fuckin' bomb at Amber Duffek's party last week coming, I survived it so I do want something in the way of recompense....or as they call it on Capitol Hill, 'Reparations'," Shane continued.

"What do you want Shane....the two million dollars I have off-shore?" Rupert retorted, and upon hearing that, Shaya stood up on the stairs almost shouting down to them in protest because that laundered $2 million dollars secreted off-shore was her money!

"I am already richer than that since my brother's death thanks to you....what I want is a cease-fire from whatever goon-squad you have at your disposal blowing shit up or a homeboy of mine will forward the info I have on you to the FBI upon my untimely death," Shane said frankly, leaning on the dining table with one hand pointing at Kelsh.

"Done, no need to try and kill you again since you're going to have a new identity, and I will be busy doing what I want to do elsewhere, so I guarantee you won't be assassinated on my orders ever again," Rupert spoke in hope of that request being the only one made.

Shane was not done making demands though, and the next one was yet another surprise.

"I also want your wife," Shane spoke up as if he'd rehearsed saying those words before.

Rupert looked at him with a cock-eyed expression, and Shaya sat back down on the stairs still unseen and unheard by the two men "negotiating" in the dimly-lit dining room. She was surprised by the "demand" as well, and wanted to hear more from the two shysters.

"Shaya?" Rupert replied hesitantly, wondering to what extent Shane Pillage was going.

"Yes Senator, I want your wife Shaya.....all for myself," Shane spoke in a cordial tone.

"She might have something to say about that ya know," Rupert added defensively.

"Just divorce her as soon as possible, leave the rest to me," Shane chuckled in return.

Rupert mulled it over in about 5 seconds and nodded in agreement, deciding that if this yard-ape wants a woman over the money he could throw at him to keep him quiet, then it was a bargain! Especially since he was now getting rid of his "trophy wife" anyway......

"Alright Shane, alright....I can do that, that's actually an easy divorce because Shaya and I have a pre-nuptual agreement, but you'll have to convince her to roll with you," Rupert spoke with a gesture of hands denoting he was in agreement with the demand.

"Just leave that to me Senator," Shane sighed in confident demeanor, staring at the older white man in both contempt and admiration, for the man was definitely one of a kind, to "ante up" his own sexy wife like that without even trying to weasel out of doing so!

Shaya stood on the stairs in her peach-colored silk robe now, listening and deciding as the two men talked, still shocked by the fact Shane survived the horrid explosion at Amber's Arlington residence last week and that her husband was in fact behind the bombing that did kill Steven Pillage and almost killed Amber.....maybe Amber was in on it as well?!

Shane was now asking Rupert for his wife, for her, not the $2 million or anything else!

"I've wanted Shaya since I first saw her and besides Senator....a white supremacist like yaself wouldn't abide a non-white woman for too long now would you?" Shane chimed as he walked around the dining room while Rupert poured himself a quick drink now.

"You have a point there Mister Pillage, my wife has been most useful to me over the past year and a half but she is like all of my minions, expendable," Rupert said in response.

Shaya shook her head in contempt for the man she had professed love to and wanted to keep, the man who made her wealthy enough to embark out on her own if she wanted.

"After tonight, I daresay much is going to change in this country, change for the better and to hell with the worst.....I'd recommend leaving the USA if I were you, take Shaya to Brazil like she's always wanted," Rupert added then wolfed down his shot of whiskey.

"I might, as long as you don't try to kill me again Senator...just remember that I have someone with all the info on you and your illegal money-laundering ready to spill the beans if anything beyond natural death happens to me," Shane told him casually. Again, Rupert was surprised the real estate hustler wasn't demanding money from him as well!

"Point taken Shane, I will not move against you again," Rupert said in a calmer mood.

"Cool.....cool....I'm going to take a long vacation from all the back-stabbers around here in the DC region, cement my new identity, and treat your ex-wife to the time of her life far away from the likes of you and other white motherfuckers out to use us," Shane added frankly as he looked around to make sure noone else was nearby to listen, see, or attack!

He still failed to see Shaya standing half way up the dark stairwell taking it all in, almost revealing her presence but didn't. Rupert was showing his true colors and it was kinda scary despite the fact she was leaving him....if Rupert had those bombings committed so easily to get rid of certain people, then he could easily have a device placed near her and Shaya Gold would join the long list of DEAD PORN STARS in the United States!

"Well I have to go to an important meeting right now, so unless there is anything else you wish to discuss, I will take off now," Rupert spoke gentlemanly as he headed out of the dining room, Shane still looking around to make sure there was no hidden "hit man" in this creepy old Georgetown house the old man and his sexy younger wife resided in.

"Nope, we've come to an agreement Senator, hope to never see you again," Shane said as he watched the Armani-clad Senator

Rupert Kelsh walk to the front door now. He wanted to slap the shit out of the man for what he did to him, though as it turns out, it was a good deal for Shane because his twin brother Steven was planning to kill him in the future anyway and therefore this was a far better consequence than what might have been! Shane knew better than to look a gift horse in the mouth and so he didn't demand more from the old man who seemed to have a far reaching "agenda" anyhow. Kelsh was out the door seconds later, leaving the "deceased" black man in his dining room and didn't give two shits about it either. Tonight was the night he will step into a grander part of the overall "plan" and all the things he had overseen and done in the past ten years will not be in vain….once Harold McCassler unknowingly delivers the virus his father mastered and weaponized in a vial to the Hispanic population of California, part 2 of the plan goes into effect and Senator Rupert Kelsh will be in a position of greater authority for the "National Emergency" to be declared…. and Western Civilization saved! Walking to his car, he told himself to get a hold of Duncan later and have him eliminate Shane Pillage and anyone the man knows or hangs out with, to make sure that asshole doesn't hold an axe over him for the duration, regardless! Leaving Shane back in the house was of no real concern to Rupert now, for he had bigger fish to fry and besides, maybe Shane will take Shaya with him when he does leave….one less "liability"!

Getting in his Mercedes, Rupert keyed the ignition and backed out of the tiny carport, onto the street below. He didn't have far to drive to meet Tyler Clark and two other men of like-agenda for a late dinner and a chat about the next step they are all going to take now that they have three of the Joint Chiefs on-board with their plan as well as the latest Supreme Court Nominee who is sure to be confirmed by the Senate after first of the year.

Shane walked around the first floor of the house, marveling at the antique furniture and the view the Kelsh's had of Georgetown and the River just outside, betting it was far prettier during a sunny day of course. He thought he was alone in the house right now until he glimpsed a light come on at the top of the stairs down the hall from the living room, making him realize either it was someone

Kelsh might have in here to kill him or it may be the Senator's lovely wife Shaya……soon to be ex-wife that is! He walked to the bottom of the long stairwell, looking up toward the light which appeared to be coming from a room just atop the stairs to the left, but he thought it could also just be a "night light" of sorts as he started up the stairs now out of curiosity. Shane Pillage had taken a grave chance coming here tonight like this, exposing himself just to get an ounce of satisfaction from the man who killed his twin brother and tried to kill him as well, but he had to do it, to bring dire "closure" to the mess he had been in recently as well as demand something from the Senator….something he was surprised to be "given" so goddamn friggin' easily!

Walking up the wooden stairs, Shane found the light to be from inside what appeared to be the master bedroom judging by the size of it, so he walked to it's open threshold to look inside and see if Shaya Kelsh might actually be in there of course.

"Looking for me Shane Pillage?" came the familiar female voice of Shaya Kelsh from off to his right, stepping toward him from the darkened hallway where he hadn't seen her approaching the bedroom with a gun in her right hand, leveling the weapon toward him.

"Shaya….oh damn," he said in surprise, eyes not on her body covered tightly by the peach-colored silk robe she wore but the little black automatic gripped in her right hand.

He stepped on into the master bedroom as she continued toward him, training the .380 caliber Walther PPK automatic at waist-level toward the intruder. Her husband did keep a handgun stashed here in the Georgetown home, and she inadvertently discovered it the other night when cleaning out the spare bedroom down the hall, inside a hollow book.

"You came to blackmail Rupert….you found out about the two million dollars he stashed in an off-shore bank account did you?" she chimed as she ushered him into the bedroom.

"Uhh…yes, I did but I uhh…..well, you got me," Shane stammered in retort, hands up.

"That's my money goddammit….all two million plus interest… yes, it was siphoned off Faster Productions and used to be Mafia cash.....but it's mine you arrogant hustler, my 'retirement account' as I like to call it, since ex-porn stars don't get a pension and have a bad tendency to not fit in too well in the regular, everyday job market," Shaya continued.

"Okay Shaya, okay, it's yours....I didn't come here to blackmail you out of it, I just.....well, brought it up to your husband so he'd listen to me and not shoot me dead on the spot like a racist bastard typically would," Shane responded in kind, hands still up.

"I see, and I heard.....all of it, your entire conversation including what my husband told you, heenh-henh....he is a racist bastard and more, believe me," she snickered then lowered the gun in her right hand, holding it down by her thigh now, her other hand gesturing for Shane to have a seat on the big bed behind him now, which he quickly did on the plush bedroll.

"I gotta hand it to ya Shane...surviving the explosion at Amber's place by ducking down inside the old storm cellar in the basement, then climbing out later when there was noone around to see you, quite a feat despite the burn on your face," Shaya said softly as she began to circle the bedroom, gun down by her side, talking to her captive guest here.

"Yeah, feels like a dream of some kind, a bad dream, but I survived," he added softly.

The burn on his cheek still appeared fresh enough for a bandage which he didn't wear.

"Does anyone else know you're alive....Amber....Shelly?" Shaya asked him next.

"Hell no, Amber would snitch me out and I believe she had a hand in the bombing of her own house that night, seems it happened again just the other night as well and the blame is being laid at the feet of a Federal Agent found dead in the remains of her house in Manassas, but even I know that's the kind of bullshit story a powerful politician like your husband could cook up and send to the media..... as for Shelly James, she was just a plaything to me, and I have since sworn off white women just like I'm swearing off alcohol for good," Shane told her in honest candor, making her smile in reaction.

"Mmmmhhh…sounds like you think things out afterall Shane, I like that," Shaya sighed.

"Hunh, I know who will benefit me and who will eventually stab me in the back, and I knew your husband was the latter so I and my late brother Steven checked into his whole damn background as far as money would pay for us to go….Rupert is a piece of work," Shane said to her with a smile, eyes more on her huge boobs snug in the silk robe and cleavage with it's "jiggle" as she walked around the room talking and listening to him.

"You're telling me?" she giggled, her right hand waving the Walther PPK as she laughed.

"Hey, uhh Shaya baby, could you maybe be careful with that damn thing?" Shane chortled as he pointed toward the gun in her right fist. Shaya held it up toward her own face, barrel toward the ceiling and a smirking grin crossing her beautiful face that did not appear anywhere close to forty years of age even without makeup.

"Oh, this….oh I don't even know if it's loaded, belongs to my husband," she said rather dismissively then reached over to the top of the dresser against the wall behind her and placed the handgun down on it's surface, letting go of the firearm and easing Shane a bit.

"You took an awful risk coming here tonight Shane, announcing your intentions to Rupert like you did, and dropping my name so freely…..you know, a man like Rupert might have this already figured out and have set a bomb to go off right here in this house tonight, with the both of us right here to die together with one press of a button," Shaya said with hands on her hips facing the muscular-lean black man sitting on the bed still.

"Shit," he sighed in realization, thinking about the two bomb-attacks on Amber Duffek within days of each other and the fact Senator Kelsh was behind those bombings and could easily have rigged this old Georgetown house to erupt into a fireball on command.

"Most guys would have asked for money ya know," she chimed in a girlish tone of voice, stepping back toward the open doorway of the bedroom, eyeballing Shane intently.

"I've got money, after my brother's death I accessed his accounts and mine for a grand total of four million and change.....besides, if I traced laundered cash to an off-shore bank account linked to the Senator, how easy will it be for the FBI to do the same once he crosses their radar....if I took money from your husband, I'd be in jail along with him, eventually," Shane answered her calmly, studying her facial expressions as he spoke.

"Wise man.....very wise," she sighed with her kittenish smile. Shane glanced down at her feet, seeing those 80's-style wrap-around stiletto heels worn like in her past X-rated films and he had to wonder why she was wearing them here at home tonight when she wore nothing else but a skimpy silk bathrobe that barely covered her more pleasant regions.

"I see you cut your hair," he said in momentary change of subjects, smiling again.

"Yes, Rupert made me trim it like this, I hate it....but he's history now so I'll grow it back out like I had it before," Shaya said with a giggle, looking over at the dresser where the handgun lay on top of the divorce papers she just signed about 30 minutes ago.

"So, Shane Pillage....you risked yourself to come here and confront Senator Kelsh over

him trying to kill you last week, and when he asked you what you wanted from him, you simply asked to have his wife?" Shaya spoke gingerly as she stood in the open doorway, hands on her hips as he stared back at her, eyes more on her cleavage than her face.

"Yes....I did, I asked for you....ever since Amber's party.....even before that, back when I first met you almost a year ago....I have wanted you," Shane spoke in almost a whisper.

"Of all the women you and your brother shared, all those young and gorgeous white women who throw themselves at wealthy black men like you nowadays, you're choosing me?" Shaya asked in retrospect, wondering if he was still on the "conquer" frequency other men like him tend to remain operating on, because he didn't have her 100% yet?

"Yes I am, if you want me in return that is....I've had it with the player's lifestyle and sharing women with my brother all that time was a waste, because I wanted a woman like you Shaya, a beautiful woman of color, a 'United Nations' of womanhood just like you are Shaya, not the blonde-blue-eyed-devil-girls my late brother was obsessed with," Shane told her truthfully, his gaze and his tone making her believe what he was saying right now.

Shaya stared at the handsome but scarred 30-year old Shane Pillage and made a decision of sorts. She hated being all alone without a man at all in her life, and now that Rupert was leaving her (to say the least) she now had another option besides becoming a lonely and paranoid ex-porn star with $2 million in the Bank. She didn't like Shane since last week, but she really liked the loyalty he showed toward her earlier with her husband and with her right now, risking his own hide to be with her here in the home of the man who tried to kill him a week ago……though even now she could easily say NO and tell Shane to go fuck himself! Shaya smiled slinky at him for a moment's contemplation as she stood in the doorway of what had up to now been the marital bedroom of the Kelsh's.

"Well my friend….I may be a former porn actress who many would consider a whore, considering the way my husband 'pimped' me out sometimes, and I may not have an ordinary employable 'skill' or college degree to my credit, but I am not easily bought by any man walking on three legs……know what I'm saying?" Shaya chimed in a slightly humored tone in order to get her point across without offending him in the process.

He had to smile slightly when he heard the "three legs" part of her statement just now.

"Yes I understand, and I believe you," Shane answered her dutifully with a slow nod.

"Good, and I might add that I admire loyalty in people, I really do, and I cannot tell you how it felt when I overheard you telling my husband that you wanted only me, not his money or his properties, that is loyalty like I have never known it," Shaya continued in a softer, more emotionally-backed voice, standing there with hands on her hips.

"I may not be your type Shaya…but I can't help it, I adore you," Shane added softly.

"Oh honey, unlike my soon-to-be-ex-husband.....there's not a racist bone in my body, speaking of which....needs tending to," Shaya cooed as she untied her robe in front and peeled the garment off her statuesque bare body with a motion of her arms, standing there in the open doorway gloriously-naked except for the black stiletto heels on her feet, eyes on the grinning Shane Pillage, already pulling his long-sleeved shirt off. She stepped toward him as he scooted to the foot of the bed to greet her, Shaya's well-crafted soft physique a warm thermos of refreshment to him, for he had risked his own survival by coming here on a cold tonight unarmed and alone like this. The embraced lovingly and Shaya was pulled onto the bed with him, their lips meeting for a kiss as her left hand tugged at the front of his pants now, wanting him now as much as he wanted her.

"Rupert.....he might kill us both tonight," Shaya whispered to her new lover in a word of final warning before they became so enamored together there would be no other options but to remain here to make love and suffer the consequences if there were to be any.

"Then I die a happy man.....again," Shane said to her in bold response, then kissed the nape of her neck ardently as his pants slipped off to the floor at the foot of the big bed, joining her bare body with his own body still sore from being "blown up" last week.

"Oooooh....this for me?" Shaya chimed as Shane's "third leg" arose to the occasion, suddenly in her right hand being stroked gently as she moved to take him like she had before, though this time in a cozy bedroom not the front seat of a brand new Bentley.

"That's the ticket......annnnh-yeeeaaah," Shane groaned in delight as he relaxed back on a pillow while Shaya fervently fellated him, slurping up and down on his spear without hesitation or reservation, surrendering to the glorious endeavor made best by her own unspeakably-ordained oral talent. Shaya relaxed as she lay between his legs now, head bobbing up and down as she performed eager fellatio on her new lover, despite the urge to get the hell out of this house before Rupert decides to kill her, something she knew he was very well capable of, considering what he did over the past week!

Shane lay there looking down his chest at the brunette ardently worshipping his manhood without fail, her mouth possessing a life of it's own as she continued fellatio on him.

"You're the best Shaya, the best....that's why I came back for you," he sighed in an unusually romantic voice, enthralled by her fleshy service he wished would never end.

"Ooooohh....you know it Shane.....mmmmhh.....I like you too," Shaya cooed as her head rose up from it's work for a moment to speak then resumed slurping along his shaft, consuming his flesh with hungry energy as he lay there letting her continue her fellatio.

Shaya then rose up for a moment and swung herself around to lay horizontal over his bare body in a "sixty-nine" position, the both of them gorging on one another in eager oral copulation, Shane's hands reaching around to squeeze her asscheeks as she lay over him.

Shane and Shaya were ensconced in their passion lit by the fire of both desire and danger, the two of them giving in to what they both wanted right now, neither of them worried about what might or might not happen to them here in the Georgetown house of a US Senator who was planning something of the "highly-unconstitutional" variety.

Downstairs, the front door swung open and in-walked Rupert Kelsh once again, having forgotten something he will need at the "dinner meeting" he is attending tonight, namely his "palm-pilot"(personal digital assistant). Grabbing the device from the kitchen counter, he walked back for the front door and looked toward the stairs, seeing the hallway light on at the top. He stopped to wonder if Shane Pillage was up there with Shaya right now?

Curious and with time to kill, he walked to the stairs and tried to ascend them quietly, afterall this was still his house and will soon be occupied by him alone once Shaya vacates it soon enough. Coming to the top of the stairs, he heard the familiar female voice of his wife as it sounded while engaged in sexual congress, not too surprisingly of course.

Rupert stepped close enough toward the open bedroom door and saw Shaya and Shane over on the bed going-at-it in a vibrant missionary-style intercourse with Shane on spread knees thrusting into Shaya who was on her back with legs spread dangling behind her lover's pumping backside, those big tits of hers jiggling wildly as she rocked to and fro under the man's onslaught, moaning outloud in giddy delight of the ongoing penetration.

"Be careful what you wish for," Rupert said to himself as he turned back down the stairs, not wanting to be seen by them now, leaving his wife behind with her new lover.

Rupert Kelsh opened the front door to leave again but was suddenly halted by the presence of yet another man who snuck inside the Georgetown domicile without difficulty, making the Senator turn around to face him with a decidedly grim visage.

"Duncan," the 59-year old US Senator said with a poker face at the dark-clad warrior now standing in the dark living room staring back at his mentor and benefactor.

"Senator, your house is not in order sir," Duncan Horsehair spoke flatly to the man.

"Duncan….jeezus you picked a good time….and my house is none of your business my old friend, trust me…it's going the way I want it to go," Kelsh replied in his forthright demeanor, walking slowly toward the darkened living room as he spoke.

"Are you at your end-game or should I turn up the heat out there?" Duncan asked next.

"I told you to stand down Duncan, chill out awhile 'till I call for you, that shooting and bombing near the Pentagon the other night had this area locked down for almost two days, and it had your markings all over it….what tha hell is going on?" Rupert spoke to the broad-shouldered, long-haired "domestic terrorist" standing in all black by the fireplace, eyeballing the Senator from where he stood, hands in pockets of the black duster coat he wore. Rupert couldn't guess what sort of weapons the man would have under that duster coat he wore, and would he ever use them on the one man who has covered for him.

"While your plan to put yourself in a position of power in the government-to-come and declare marital law in order to save western civilization from it's own liberal softness is coming to fruition Senator, your cohorts in the pipeline are plotting to count you out as soon as the virus you sent to California takes hold....you are the sacrificial lamb who can take the blame if need-be, much like the dead ATF Agent who is now taking the blame for the past few bombings you had me set up," Duncan Horsehair spoke in his gravel voice, not moving an inch as he spoke to the obviously nervous Senator.

"I will be the next Vice Presidential Candidate on the Democratic Party Ticket for two-thousand-eight Duncan....even if the candidate is that black bastard from Illinois, I will get placed on the ticket and from there I will take the Presidency after an emergency is declared and illegal immigrants are rounded up to prevent the spread of the virus, I and my 'cohorts' are going to save this country from itself and the American people will go along with it out of fear....the fires of fear which you have helped stoke since nineteen-ninety-five my friend," Rupert spoke abruptly to the seasoned warrior in black.

"Everybody uses everybody Duncan, you of all people know that....just as you set up and use those 'lone wolves' out there, the countless losers who kill and bomb under your orders, my direction, and noone but I know who you really are.....that goddamn Agent Stevens got close but as I have always done, I got it covered and he's now the fall-guy for the past few bombings I ordered," Rupert continued, speaking exactly what he had been wanting to say to the "dead" man in front of him right now, the terrorist who has been getting rather "independent" lately and wanting to do more without permission.

"I awoke on a morgue slab thirteen years ago and left the hospital unseen.....I was declared dead and cremated by the Military Hospital Staff in order to cover up the fact they lost a body since I had no real family left back then and I was 'expendable' in the eyes of the Government I once served," Duncan Horsehair spoke up in gravel voice.

"Yes, something of a miracle you waking up alive after being clinically-dead for fifteen minutes, and you had no family left, making it easy to write you off as a dead veteran, though you almost got caught after the Oklahoma City bombing", Kelsh added frankly.

"You covered for me and I continued killing ever since, both of us having a similar agenda, the same cause....to destroy American society a little bit in order to save it," Duncan said matter-of-factly, watching as Kelsh stepped toward the sofa now, thinking.

"Yes, and the fear you created in the wake of those shootings, bombings, 'accidents', and set-ups have done wonders preparing the public for an 'iron hand' leadership and the upcoming suspension of certain liberties in order to save the nation from sliding into the mud, not to mention the attacks on the World Trade Center on Nine-Eleven by those goddamn towel-heads helping to further push Americans toward accepting a leadership that guarantees their security and safety for the near future," Kelsh continued.

"It's all bigger than me Duncan, bigger than the both of us actually, this thing we are doing to save the USA from the deadly diseases of liberalism and multi-culturalism, whether it results in me being named Vice President next year or my death, whichever comes first…it's going to eventually happen or America collapses," Kelsh said flatly.

"Even when the ones you trust are using you to an end you may not see coming?" Duncan asked with a shrug, his right hand coming up out of his coat pocket now.

"Son, I've been using everyone around me for this cause ever since my daughter died in nineteen ninety four…..even a US Senator could not get her justice after that French Diplomat's son raped her and caused her to commit suicide soon afterwards, justice denied because of political-correctness and 'diplomatic immunity'," Kelsh added.

"Everybody uses everybody, and nothing in my area-of-operations goes unnoticed or without my allowance….I allow you to continue waging a war out there free from prosecution or discovery by Law Enforcement…..I allow other men whom I plan using to fuck the socks off my wife, like the idiot screwing her upstairs right now," Kelsh added.

Duncan scowled slightly at that remark since Kelsh had allowed him to romp with Shaya quite a few times in the past year or so, and now the not-so-deceased Shane Pillage who survived the bomb place at the Duffek residence last week, was upstairs now, with Shaya!

Duncan saw before him not a man who he could trust any longer, but a man who was getting "soft" in his plan, "soft" in the war they both have been waging for years now.

If he could not trust Senator Kelsh, then there was noone else at all, noone, and the war would soon be over because he will have lost his "combat support" system.

"You're slipping Senator, and it's gonna bite you," Duncan said frankly without regard.

"No Duncan, remember who covered you all these years, who kept you out of the news media and out of FBI hands all this time, my plan has come full-circle now and a great foot-soldier like you should just relax and relish the victory….now I don't need to see you again after tonight until I call you," Rupert said conclusively as he turned to walk toward the front door again, still not late for his dinner-meeting with Clark and others.

"What about your wife sir?" Duncan asked outloud before the Senator opened the door.

"Shaya…..hmmph, she's still a liability ….make it quick and painless if you don't mind, and be damn sure you kill that baboon she's in bed with," Kelsh answered him with a chuckle, opening the front door to leave for his dinner meeting in Virginia tonight.

Duncan Horsehair walked to the front door, looking out it's port window sill to see the Mercedes leaving the small driveway and onto the Key Bridge toward Virginia now.

"Quick and painless….yes sir," Duncan sighed to himself as he pulled out a remote detonator from the pocket of his duster coat, thumbing the three-digit code and pressing the kill-switch right about the time Senator Rupert Kelsh would have crossed into Virginia, the Mercedes exploding into a fireball, cremating Senator Kelsh instantly.

Duncan walked toward the stairwell slowly, his right hand reaching for the holstered handgun under his left armpit, his intention being to shoot Shane upstairs now and offer Shaya a "way out" if she'll leave with him, but if not then she'll have to die too.

She reminded him of Isabel Marcano almost to a fault and she was worth the risk of taking with him, that is if she'll go. Duncan started up the stairwell when he felt a sudden "pinch" at the center of his back, then a sharp pain as if he'd been stung by a bee. He spun around reflexively and then another sharp pinch-pain struck his abdomen, this time he could see a yellow-tailed "dart" sticking out of his abdomen just above his navel now.

He reached for the dart, realizing it to be of the "tranquilizer" kind, but his eyesight and physical balance was slipping away from him as he stumbled to the bottom of the steps.

It was then he sensed two male figures appearing from out of the dark dining room now, both with weapons in their hands trained on him…..tranquilizer guns!

"Man, there's enough of that shit in three darts to drop a Rhino and he's still standing!" one of them said as Duncan Horsehair heard his own weapon drop to the floor below, unable to hold it as his extremities failed him, tranquilizer taking hold of him completely.

He fell to his knees first then flat on his face as the two strangers walked up to him now, unable to see their faces nor determine why two strangers would be in the Kelsh house the same time as he was tonight, shooting him full of tranquilizer??

"Five-thousand dollars….no sweat man….wish she would've let us use real guns instead but what-tha-fuck, money's money," the skinny white guy chuckled as he and his black buddy stood over the downed man in the black duster coat. Shaya Kelsh called them earlier and told them to come here to "defend" her from intruders she suspected, only she had two tranquilizer guns for them to use instead of live ammo since real handguns were illegal in Washington D.C. and she wanted to them to keep her out of trouble it seemed.

"That's a big boy there, took three darts to drop his ass, wonder what he would've done if he made it upstairs to miss big tits in tha bedroom?" the black guy asked in a whisper.

"Hunh, probably would've killed her with this," the skinny white guy said as he picked up the loaded .45 automatic Duncan had dropped seconds ago when he passed out.

"What's she doing upstairs anyway?" the black guy asked his fellow "mercenary".

"Don't know, but she said we should stay out of sight and that sounds like police sirens approaching doesn't it?" the white goon retorted as he headed for the kitchen and back door where they had entered about 10 minutes ago. What they didn't know was there had been an explosion a few minutes ago across the river in Rosslyn Virginia and the sirens were in response to that, though the two men Shaya had "hired" the other night to protect her in the coming days were taking no chances of running into the Police unnecessarily so they took off out of there the route they came in. They left the man they shot with tranquilizer darts lying unconscious at the bottom of the stairwell while Shaya and Shane continued their lovemaking upstairs in the master bedroom, oblivious to what was going on around them right now as they continued their carnal tryst in joyful indulgence.

Shane now lay on his back as Shaya "rode" on him, nearly his entire length up inside of her as she moved up and down, up and down in intercourse on her new lover, both of them enjoying one another's flesh as if it were their last. She bounced on his dick in steady, piston-like motion, coming twice already and wanting him to climax now as well, the look on the man's face denoting anytime now, and when he did, Shaya kept going, allowing him to come inside of her, both of them crying out in sheer delight as their vigorous lovemaking ended. 12:01am: Deputy Attorney General Tyler Clark walked into the Kelsh residence using a key he had all along, followed by two Deputy US Marshals he trusted to bring with him as protection. Following the car bomb that killed Senator Rupert Kelsh an hour ago just over the Key Bridge in Virginia, he was taking no chances. Entering the darkened house with the two Marshals quietly following him, he found the unconscious body of a man he actually worried might try and kill him some point in time, lying dormant on the wooden floor at the bottom of the stairwell here in the Kelsh home!

The Marshals checked Duncan "Horsehair" and found him alive but severely sedated by three tranquilizer darts, and determined that he would be "out cold" for quite some time.

Clark made a quick call on his wireless and told the two Marshals with him to handcuff the unconscious individual and haul him to the back door for him to be "taken into custody" as he called it for effect. It was the last thing he would do to the man he knew to be Kelsh's "Horsehair" because how could he explain a "dead" Gulf War Veteran turning up alive more than a decade later killing people! That was what he used Agent Stevens for, and so this terrorist was going to be put "on ice" and he knew exactly how to do it.

Walking around the first floor of the Georgetown home owned by the now deceased Senator Rupert Kelsh, Tyler Clark wondered what would become of this magnificent "antique" domicile overlooking the Potomac River now that Senator Kelsh would become another domestic terrorism statistic and hopefully more fuel that'll drive the public to accept a tighter governmental "grip" on things and even types of people allowed in the Country. The bombing death of Kelsh could also be blamed on Agent Stevens because Clark could spin it that Stevens had been trailing Senator Kelsh and the device he planted in the good Senator's car did not go off until days after Stevens died in nearby Manassas trying to kill Feminist Attorney Amber Duffek "again"!

A "Rogue Federal Agent" went along with the grand plan quite well, as it creates a fear in the public about how their own Law Enforcement could be "infiltrated" by a domestic terrorist with a deadly agenda! Walking around the plush living room, the Deputy Attorney General mused about how Kelsh was no longer going to be a "Running Mate" prospect for the next Presidential Candidate, but a "martyr" example of how even an American serving his Country in the US Senate can be cut down by terrorists at home.

The Marshals waited with the unconscious body of "Horsehair" at the back door for the "pick up" (Clark's cohorts in the Department of Homeland Security) so Clark took the liberty of walking upstairs now, guessing someone else had to be here in the house tonight and he quickly discovered his assumption to be correct. Shaya and Shane had fallen asleep after over an hour of riotous sex on the king-sized bed, and both of them were oblivious to the events that had transpired downstairs minutes, even an hour, ago.

Clark stepped to the open doorway of the master bedroom, looking in to see two naked bodies lying like spoons on a tussled bed together, heads buried in pillows and clearly in a relaxed state he could walk out of here with "Horsehair" and these two would be none-the-wiser. Seeing Shaya lying there with a black man entwined with her, Clark had to wonder if she had been cheating on Rupert with this guy or was it "allowed" as Rupert had done with other men, he being one of them?! Clark stood there for a moment just watching the two lovers lying there embraced in the after-sexual moments following a "good time". Shaya was one hell of a good-looking woman for age 40 and he lamented the fact theirs had been just a strictly-casual rapport up to this point, for Clark would like to take her himself now that her husband was dead....but then again, no dice.

Shaya opened her eyes with instinct warning her sixth sense that she was being watched.

Seeing Tyler Clark standing in the open doorway of the bedroom staring back at her now almost made her fall right out of the bed in reaction. She didn't say a word though, slowly raising up to slip off the bed to her feet and letting Shane remain asleep on the bed now, the well-shaped former porn star stood up straight, stretched, and walked toward the Deputy Attorney General standing alone in the hallway now, hands on hips facing her.

"Tyler....jeeezzus," she sighed as she walked over to him, still wearing only her stiletto heels and nothing else (much like she wore in half of her X-rated films back in the day).

"Shaya, bad news....your husband is dead," he spoke casually, sensing she might not be too upset over the news since Rupert Kelsh made no bones about divorcing her as soon as he was elevated to "higher office" in 2008. The expression on her face was demure, but not outwardly sad, though it took a few seconds for his words to sink in. Rupert was dead and the Deputy Attorney General he had sent her to "socialize" with was here at midnight to inform her of her husband's untimely demise....or maybe not so untimely.

"How?" she asked next, a poker expression on her pretty face now as she stared at him.

"Car bomb, forty-five minutes ago across the bridge," Clark sighed as she stepped into the hallway with him, not bothering to cover up with a robe or anything, not yet.

"I see, hmmm.....well, I'm a widow now," Shaya sighed as she turned to look back in her bedroom, seeing Shane Pillage lying prone on her bed, head buried in pillows, asleep.

"Yes you are, and you may want to consider how the rest of your life is going to play out, remember what Rupert told us both.....no matter the situation, you can always make it work for you in some way," Clark said to her softly as he backed up to the stairs again.

"Yes, of course.....so why are you telling me this?" Shaya chimed, leaning on a wall.

"I came to see him for dinner tonight and his car blew up....the back door was unlocked so I came on in...you been here alone all evening?" Calrk replied with a question.

"No, well....Rupert was here earlier and then left about an hour or so ago, and my boyfriend Shane dropped by about the time Rupert left, that's it....why?" Shaya replied with a sleepy-eyed gaze at the man now, answering his question like he had hoped.

She did not know about the unconscious man at the bottom of the steps, though if she had shot the man with tranquilizers herself, wouldn't she have hidden the body or had it removed as Clark was doing now? If she had known about "Horsehair" lying out cold at the bottom of her stairwell, she would have instantly offered an explanation to Clark right now as to why he had to step over a human body at the bottom of the steps!

"I guess with your husband's lifestyle and all, you kinda expected this to happen?" he asked the voluptuous naked woman standing in the dark hallway with him right now.

"Yeah, I guess I kinda did....we were talking divorce anyway," she sighed with a shrug.

"I'll be in touch...don't say anything beyond what you just said to me when the FBI comes knocking on your door soon, okay Shaya?" Clark spoke conclusively then touched a hand to her shoulder in a kindly "don't worry about anything" gesture.

"Will do Tyler, and thanks....," she sighed in response as he started back down the stairs, not looking back as she watched him go. Clark had to wonder how "Horsehair" got to be tranquilized right here in the Kelsh house without Shaya and her new "boyfriend" hearing anything? He believed what she told him and began to guess that maybe Kelsh left the house after shooting his "errand boy" full of tranquilizers then ended up blown to smithereens by a C-4 detonation which Horsehair seemed to excel at using! Regardless, he now had "Horsehair" and knew precisely where to put him into "storage"!

Shaya stepped back inside the master bedroom in tense thought. Her husband is dead, victim of the same kind of terrorist bomb he had used against others, which made her wonder whether or not she may be implicated in a subsequent investigation into Rupert's past and present? No, she reminded herself, she was just his "trophy wife" as all of Washington D.C. viewed her, and trophy wives aren't going to exactly be considered "accomplices" to their husband's illegal activities, especially since it was fairly well-known that she and Rupert had an "open marriage" of convenience and therefore it will be easy for her to swear that they were not close, and that she knew nothing of his underhanded activities, deals, murders, etc. etc. etc. Clark had it right when he said any "situation" may be turned, spun, re-worked to one's advantage if one knows how to spin the bottle in the right direction! Shaya looked over at the slumbering Shane Pillage on her big bed, considering his loyalty to her and the fact he was a millionaire along with her, and like her, he was a human being living on the "fringe" since he was now operating under a false identity, his death "official" with the Coroner's Office but not in reality. Shane wanted her with him, but she didn't really know the man beyond the fact he was a good lay and was one of the few single black male millionaires on the planet who wasn't a stupid ball-player! She considered his offer earlier, to go away with him for a long vacation and re-vamp their lives with their money and their safety far away from the claws of white men and their agendas. She had already been a "trophy wife" to one man, be damned if she was going to be one for Shane or anyone else. Men often liked to fuck a former porn actress but they don't want one as a wife, Shaya reminded herself as she stood at the foot of the bed staring at the naked black man lying there, deciding right here and now how she was going to play this next hand dealt.

She turned and walked over to the wall-mirror on the bathroom door, looking at her nude reflection again, viewing her bare body down to her black stiletto-heels on her feet, this body, stiletto-heels, and loop-earrings were often the "attire" she wore as Shaya Gold

in half of the X-rated films she did back in the 1990's, funny she would come to this crossroad in her life wearing the same and lack thereof anything else!

"Shaya Kelsh......Shaya Gold......who am I....really?" she whispered to herself as she ran a hand over her 44EE boobs and down to her taut abs then her upper thighs, staring at her shapely, well-filled-out physique she had worked so hard to maintain over the years.

"Shaya Gold....Lives," spoke Shane Pillage as he sauntered up behind her weary-eyed from just waking up, oblivious to what had happened tonight, his hands sliding around her waist to gently hug her into him from behind as she pressed back against him, eyeballing one another via the wall-mirror on the bathroom door. Shaya almost wanted to laugh at his remark just now, for he didn't know how ironic that statement actually was!

"Mmmmmh...baby, we could go to Rio for a couple of months, maybe make a sex-video of the two of us and market it, make even more money," Shane suggested boyishly.

"Mmmh...just take me to Rio and I'll think about it," Shaya said gingerly as she turned around to embrace her new lover properly for another impassioned kiss.

"Shane and Shaya....has a sweet ring to it doesn't it baby?" Shane sighed in her ear as their lips parted for a moment, his hands sliding down her back to squeeze her ass cheeks.

"Heenh, you are a piece of work," she sighed with a slinky expression then kissed him again as he ushered her back to the bed for another round of sexual congress, now wanting to just forget all about her late husband, Senator Rupert Kelsh.

McLean, Virginia. 12:45am: The house was easy enough to find even in the dead of night, Amber Duffek being well-versed in navigating Northern Virginia all these years of working Courtrooms in this vicinity. Fiction Author K.R. Knight had bought this place just a few months ago, and she had thought a man of his good fortune and best-selling novels would have chosen a bigger and newer house than this one! Parking behind his black 2008 Dodge Challenger, Amber got out and walked on up to the front door of the house, ringing the doorbell twice as she expected him to be home. The fact another familiar-looking vehicle was parked across the street, the Ford Mustang owned by Shelly James, stuck in her craw as soon as she arrived here in the dead of night. Confronting the writer and his mistress after midnight like this was not her usual style, but things have changed in the past few hours and Amber was afraid, just a little....yeah, a little......

She tried the door and found it unlocked, so she walked on inside the place, finding lights on but noone was on the first floor it appeared. She closed the front door gently, wanting to shout out to the home's occupants but didn't, instead just looking around because she had not been inside Mr. Knight's new house here until now. A framed "Star Wars" poster mounted on one wall along with framed 8x10 autographed photos of celebrities and a statue of some half-naked female "super hero" atop a big-screen TV set in the cozy, well-furnished living room. K.R. Knight was one of those "fantasy-oriented" guys, which explains the kind of novels the jerk writes, not to mention the biography of former porn starlet Shelly James which had been a moderate-best seller as well. Amber walked around in interest, looking at the posters on his walls and in his kitchen where she found the gold Rolex watch she had given Shelly for her birthday last month, laying on the small kitchen table along with Shelly's small leather purse. She was here with her Biographer alright, getting-it-on somewhere else in this bullshit suburbanite stone house of his.....

Amber headed for the stairs, wanting to see for herself if Shelly was in fact here and confront her now that Amber herself was practically "homeless" and without her benefactor in the US Senate.

The news about Senator Rupert Kelsh being identified as the sole victim in a car explosion an hour ago had frightened her into a near-breakdown.

Without the Senator, Amber may very well be killed next and she damn well knew it!

"Shelly?" Amber spoke up as she crested the stairs to the top floor of Knight's house, going down a short hallway toward a lit room at the far end, a bedroom no doubt. She walked up to it and stopped to peer inside since the door wasn't actually closed all the way. What she found, illuminated by a single lamp over on the nightstand, was Shelly James in a very cozy-looking bed with Author K.R. Knight, making love. Amber froze where she stood for the moment, just silently watching as the Shelly straddled her male lover in steady, vertical intercourse. That tail of hers going up and down, taking Knight's manhood up inside of her sweet canal with each motion of intercourse, up and down in a bouncy ardor so good she was expressing her satisfaction verbally.

"OOOOAAAHH-KENNY......OOOOAANNH-YEEEAAAHH!" Shelly wailed outloud in orgasm as she rode on the man harder and faster for the sensation of it, getting her rocks off as Amber Duffek watched in vexed dismay. The Writer rolled her over and re-took her in a hastened missionary-style intercourse, Amber seeing his body pumping into her "girlfriend" in steady man-to-woman carnality she secretly missed and even moreso... secretly desired for herself. Shelly's face was a visage of raw carnal pleasure, eyes closed and mouth wide open as she yelped in delight, a display she had never shown while Amber was making love to her....making the observer feel even more vexed now.

"That bastard....," Amber sneered to herself as she stepped away from the wooden door momentarily, her mind flashing a variety of options to choose from in retaliation against what she was seeing and feeling just a second ago. The rack of kitchen knives down in the kitchen was one flashing image, and so she could go back down there and get one of those knives, come back up here to the bedroom and go to work on both of them. She'd slice Shelly's all-too-pretty cupcake face and slice up something else of Knight's! Amber just stood there in the hallway outside the bedroom door thinking and feeling that strange mix of vexation and arousal right now. The sight of Shelly and Kenny was arousing to her, she had to admit it though part of her was pissed off because she had tracked Shelly here and wanted to get her to stay with her, for she did not want to be alone during this dangerous time for her, she didn't want to die but dying alone at the mercy of some bomb or hit man was even worse a fate in her mind! Amber also wanted to relay her story to the writer K.R. Knight so that he could write a book about her, in case she is killed, she wanted her story told....though minus the implicating parts such as the fact she had let Rupert Kelsh's terrorist goon blow up two of her homes to frame a Federal Agent hot on his tail! She wanted to tell someone her story, all the way from Law School lesbianism to her stint as an Attorney for the Marcano Mob, Faster Productions Porn, and currently a lawyer in the crosshairs of a domestic terrorist. Yes, she had come here for those two reasons, only to find her ex-porn-starlet "girlfriend" fucking the famous writer here inside of his dimly-lit bullshit suburbanite stone house on Tusken Lane. Amber turned back to the door and peered inside again, seeing Kenny hammering Shelly in a vibrant missionary-position and really giving it to her, his lean fit body merging with her shapely physique very well in raw sexual intercourse, her legs and feet dangling behind his pumping backside as if riding on a bucking bronco. Amber was impressed by the sight, and Shelly was having a ball as her lover plunged into her in passionate ardor, his hands on her boobs as he arched his back for more thrusts of energetic, unyielding manhood from another arousing angle.....

"Oh I can't take it any longer....," Amber said to herself as she stepped back from the door again, this time pulling off her own clothes, dropping her car keys, purse, and shoes to the hallway floor below. Amber quickly disrobed right there in the hallway, not caring if she interrupts them, sure they won't mind another woman joining-in uninvited tonight.

Afterall, she did come here this late to see the both of them, so why not hop in the bed with Kenny Knight and Shelly James and "discuss" things right there in sexual comfort?!

The door swung inward, and a completely naked Amber Duffek walked right on into the bedroom, getting the full attention of the two lovers already in the bed, stopping them in "mid-stroke" as the saying goes. Shelly looked up at her with a grimace of surprise while K.R. Knight just lay there in silent observation, eyeing the lovely bare body of Attorney Amber Duffek now stepping to the foot of his bed, hands on her tight bare hips.

"Amber, what are you....what are you doin'.....here?" Shelly stammered as she rolled over to her lover's left side, looking at the naked, well-crafted Amber Duffek quizzically.

"I came to see both of you actually, and I see you're too busy fucking, so I thought I'd just come in here and join-in," Amber answered girlishly then she crawled onto the bed toward them, and they welcomed her despite apprehension at first, her lips going to kiss Shelly first as the one man in the bed welcomed her arrival with a hand caressing her 34DD breasts. Amber turned her head as she lay down between them and found herself kissing Kenny while Shelly hugged her ass into her, kissing and gently biting Amber's back in greeting. Before she knew it, Amber was "sandwiched" between a man and woman there in the all-too-comfortable bed, the man's raging erection sliding up between her legs for what Amber had wanted for quite some time now but didn't admit it, and that was a good man between her legs! She welcomed him as he slipped up inside of her, Shelly kissing her lips lovingly as the man engaged her from beneath, Amber settling on top of him now, moaning in delight of the sensational penetration, resting back to take all of him up inside of her. Shelly kissed Kenny long and hard as Amber arched back to "ride" on his pole in steady motion just as Shelly had been doing earlier, then Shelly slid to her right and stood up from the bed, reaching for her black garter belt and stockings.

"Where you....going.....ooonnh....Shel?" Amber asked in a huff as she rode on man-meat for the first time in over a year. Shelly winked at her as she pulled on her garter belt and fishnet-stockings then her black lace bra, and mouthed the word "Nowhere". Amber then faced Kenny and threw herself into the sweet fleshy act of heterosexual intercourse with a handsome, well-crafted man now servicing her. Shelly winked at Kenny as he looked past the bucking lady on his pole to see her going for the bedroom door. Shelly then looked at him again and mouthed the words "Good Bye" to him with a smile, then slowly turned to saunter half-naked out his bedroom door to the stairs, her clothes downstairs.

He knew that would be the last time he ever sees Shelly James, the sight of her perfect bare-ass-jiggle as she walked out of his bedroom door now, his final memory of her.

She had come here tonight to say goodbye to him for the final time, her plan being to go to Amsterdam where she has an offer to do a "Live Sex Show" with a famous (retired) NFL Football Player and it's going to pay very well according to the Danish "Promoter".

Amber continued her steady "ride" on her newfound lover, enjoying the sensation; his hands reaching up to gently caress her boobs as their bodies grind together righteously.

She cooed in relish of the act, her mind focused solely on sex now, nothing else as she and K.R. Knight continued in ardent intercourse. Shelly James got dressed downstairs and collected her purse and Rolex then headed for the front door to leave, looking around Kenny's place one more time, for the final time. She liked the guy a lot but she wanted to do more for herself other than be one man's girl, besides, it looked like "love" up there in bed between Amber and Kenny, so she guessed they'll write great books together.......

Kenny heard the sound of Shelly's Mustang roaring off into the night as the woman left him for good, their time being over now, leaving with a noted female lawyer straddling him in bed, best looking damn lawyer he ever knew!

Amber then rolled left and he rose up to take her into a vigorous missionary, pumping into her while arching his back, Amber crooning outloud in agreement, delighted by his lovemaking as he continued to play her body as if conducting a symphony orchestra....

"OONNHH-OOOONNHH-DOHHHN'T-SSSTTAAHHP!" Amber groaned in thrilling orgasm, her lover steady in thrust and rigor, servicing her without fail as their lean bodies fiendishly wrestled in the flesh. Amber hugged the man's torso as if for dear life, crying out in delight of the feeling of being taken by a man such as this, her mind awash with the passion fruit of sexual desire and satisfaction....impaled in the flesh, satiated in the scent, covered in the warmth, safe in the strength, and conquered in the mind as her new male lover consumed her like a ravenous beast she had gleefully jumped into bed with.......

Amber moved up onto all-fours with her man kneeling behind her for a continuation of their intercourse "doggie-style" now. It was something she rarely did before except with the one man she had secretly loved years ago, now relaxing with her head down in a pillow as K.R. Knight resumed intercourse from behind her, hands squeezing her soft asscheeks greedily as he pumped into her in thrusting continuity which she was enjoyed immensely. Amber wanted this to last for hours, and the man seemed up to the task, his energy not failing in the slightest despite the fact he had been giving it to Shelly James for who-knows-how-long before she showed up! He slapped her asscheeks gently as he sailed into her faster, harder, making her yelp in delight of the feelings overcoming her once again, the sweet sensation of orgasm swelling up inside of her once again as her lover continued driving her "doggie-style" on his bed, non-stop exactly the way Amber desired him to, as if he were reading her mind, her unspoken desires!

Her body moved along with his, sinking to the warm bedroll into another position of intercourse, Amber lying on her right side with Kenny alongside her in a sideways "spoon" maneuver, re-engaging her with his left hand pulling her left leg up, gaining better access to her sweet spot, and it was so good! Amber wailed out in gleeful agreement as her man slid up into her in curved sex at an angle she had yet to enjoy until tonight. Amber knew then and there she had finally found a man who was way more than just a "five-minute-mench", one who seemed to know her every want and need in bed after only meeting her once before tonight, he "knew" what she needed and was more than qualified to give it to her. She surrendered to him tonight and it felt good, her new lover overcoming her senses to the point she had almost forgotten Shelly James or the fact the Senator who she trusted to cover for her was now dead, even the possibility of criminal prosecution of her in the event anyone finds out she set up an ATF Agent to die along with the Pillage Brothers, was out of her mind as she made love with fiction writer K.R. Knight here in his bullshit suburbanite stone house in Fairfax County Virginia. They were back to an easy, steady missionary position after another 20 minutes and Amber had come again as Kenny sailed into her with piston-like regularity, his body an unyielding engine driving into hers.

"OOOAAAAHH.....OOOONNNHHH.....YESSSSS!" Amber cried out with tears of ecstatic joy streamed down her face looking up at her new lover steadily ravaging her, then hugging his handsome head to her breasts as he leaned into her to suck at her breasts while still drilling her like a champ. He was a champ in the bed, with the stamina she had not experienced in a male lover before now, as if the two of them were destined to be joined at the hips like this....literally! Kenny sighed in grinning satisfaction and thrusted himself forward into her as far as possible as he climaxed in flooding release, two bodies ground together in perfect sexual union. Amber hugged him tightly to her as he collapsed in conclusion over her, rolling over in the bed together in passionate adoration, Amber's tears of delight still sliding down her cheeks as his head rose to look her in the eyes now, their lips locking in a kiss as they held one another as if hanging on for dear life.

"Oooaahh....Kenny," Amber Duffek cooed as she touched a hand to his face, staring into his blue eyes as they relaxed, breathing heavy from their two hour lovemaking here.

"You came here to ask me something didn't you Miss Duffek?" he asked her softly.

"Oh yes....mmmhh...will you marry me Mister Knight?" Amber cooed gingerly.

Cockeysville, Maryland. October 25th: The laboratory illegally purchased by Senator Rupert Kelsh a year ago was still viable and "under the radar" as far as documentation was concerned. Deputy Attorney General Tyler Clark now stood in the inner-lab's clean-room wearing a static-free jumpsuit as he observed through the insulated glass viewport into the next sealed chamber here at the Lab. Standing alongside Dr. Peter McCassler and another man who was a Cryonics Technician, Clark looked through the thick glass to see a man laid out inside a "tube" of sorts, wearing only boxer shorts and unconscious ever since he had been found at the Kelsh residence three nights ago. Clark had ordered the man he knew to be "Horsehair" to be cryo-preserved in a sedated "coma" per current technology, and it just so happened the man could be safely kept here in this secret lab just an hour's drive from D.C. Clark did not want to "prosecute" Horsehair anymore than he wanted himself prosecuted, for one would lead to the other, and with Kelsh's death and funeral this coming weekend, the plan was still in effect, only with a slight change of "schedule". It seems the virus Kelsh sent to California with Dr. McCassler's son Harold on Monday evening perished when the plane crashed in the Rocky Mountains at approx. 11:50pm CST, taking Harold McCassler, 98 other passengers, and one customized virus!

The virus was still stored here at the Lab now secretly "confiscated" by the Justice Dept. under Deputy Attorney General Clark's auspices, along with "Duncan Horsehair" aka:

Lt. Duncan Hardesteadt of the US Army, now secretly "frozen" here at the Lab via the latest in Cryonics Preservation Technology, supervised by Dr. McCassler and the Cryonics Technician hired by Clark personally. Putting the domestic terrorist in "cold storage" like this was not only illegal and could put Clark in prison himself, it was necessary because Clark wanted "Horsehair" for possible future use! The man was legally deemed "deceased" since 1994, had no living relatives to ask questions, and had carried out a war of slow and methodical acts of terror over the course of 12 years without being caught, witnessed by reliable sources, or even properly identified by Law Enforcement beyond 1995's fabled "John Doe #2" conspiracy theories and the like.

"Doctor McCassler, I cannot thank you enough for taking care of this for me....and I am very sorry about your son dying in that tragic plane crash," Clark said to the Scientist.

"No problem Mister Clark, my son volunteered to help that bastard Kelsh and didn't listen to me, so he paid the price in a senseless goddamn plane crash," McCassler sighed.

"Well I appreciate you staying on to see this project through," Clark said with a gesture to the younger Cryonics technician to leave the room now and let them talk privately.

"I fathered that damn thing Kelsh wanted to infect California with and I want to be the one who safeguards it, as well as this man you've had cryo-frozen…work is all I have now that my son is gone," Dr. McCassler said in a sullen voice, staring through the glass.

"Yes, and I will look after you my friend, trust me," Clark said with a hand to the older Scientist's shoulder as they looked in at the cryo-frozen comatose "Horsehair" lying in a sealed "tube" bed inside the bio-hazard chamber converted to a cryonics storage room over the past two days, post haste. Clark thought about the engineered virus he was keeping here since the amount bound for California went down in that plane crash the other night. He would keep the virus stored here until the time is right for its use.

Kelsh had jumped-the-gun in sending a vial of it to California like he did, but fate stepped in and there was plenty of time to create an "epidemic" allowing men like Clark to declare a "national emergency" and save western civilization. Now all Clark had to do was decided whether he wants to be Vice President or Attorney General in 2009……

Rio De Janeiro, Brazil. October 31st (Copacabana Beach): This was almost like paradise as Shaya had imagined such a thing to be. Paradise as long as you've got money and an American Passport. Hard to believe she was here in Rio "vacationing" after what had all taken place back home in the USA and all so close to her…..from Rupert's death being called an "assassination by domestic terrorists" and "Rogue Agent" Cliff Stevens being blamed for the bombings that killed the Pillage Brothers as well as Robert and Jamal Marx, the media promptly calling the dead Agent a "racist assassin" since his victims were all black men, though the press hardly mentioned the fact the woman who lost two homes to the "rogue agent bomber", Attorney Amber Duffek, escaped unscathed both times! Shaya had been interviewed by the FBI and DHS twice since her husband's death but they were just asking for info on the last time she saw him, etc. and not really demanding anything from her which would denote viewing her as any kind of "suspect".

She left for Brazil here just two days ago with Shane Pillage, or "Charlie Rosco" as he is calling himself now, new "official" identity and all. Arriving yesterday evening, the two of them spent all night fucking their brains loose in the $800 per night luxury loft, then Shaya spent breakfast alone because "Charlie Rosco" had become enamored with the gambling scene here in Rio and went to play a game of poker with $5,000 cash, then she saw him again at 1:00 for lunch in the restaurant below their rented Loft, when she asked him to join her here on the famous Copacabana beachfront for the rest of the gloriously beautiful day. Again, Shane insisted on gambling in a game of poker at this "club" he found while walking around when they arrived here yesterday. One does not get to truly "know" someone else until one actually spends living time with that person, and Shaya was quickly discovering the black millionaire she had hooked up with after the untimely death of her bastard of a husband….was a goddamn degenerate gambling junkie!

Walking along the fairly crowded beach with her sandaled feet in the warm surf, Shaya wore a red cloth vest on this "topless" beachfront, her big boobs jutting out of the open garment of course, but easy to simply button-up when she wanted to walk up to a shop or place where she couldn't be so exposed like on the beach. She wore a bikini-bottom like half the female population did in this city, and carried a tiny purse around her shoulder with just enough cash to buy a few drinks, weary of purse-snatchers in a place like Rio.

Her hair was starting to go back down her neck and over her ears, and she could not wait for her shoulder-length dark hair to return like before, but she was learning to worry less and focus more on the future….the future of herself, one item on her "to do" list is to legally change her name from Shaya Kelsh, but not back to her maiden name of Mahrabar. She was seriously considering changing her last name legally to Gold, because the name of Shaya Gold is what she spent half of her adult life under anyway, and it sure rings better than the Arabic-sounding Mahrabar. She wondered if her new boyfriend would join her for dinner tonight at the upscale "Toney's" Portuguese

Bistro or remain gambling with his new poker buddies here in Rio? She was glad he didn't have access to the $2 million she had spread out in three separate bank accounts in Florida now, her "laundered" cash Rupert stole from Faster Productions two years ago safely in her control. Shane would gamble her money away if she let him, for he was already foolishly spending the $4 million and change he got from the Pillage estate after his "death" and the death of his twin brother. One does not truly know someone else until they live with them awhile, and the past week with Shane aka: "Charlie Rosco" was an eye-opener to say the least, getting to know him all too well.

Shaya already began to plot a course "away" from her new boyfriend once they get back to the US, and he won't be able to do a damn thing about it because she could so easily expose him as having "faked" his own death by surviving the bombing that killed his twin brother and not telling the authorities about that particular detail! Shane was a gambler, a trait she did not like in a man because it was a vice that easily destroys everything in it's path once it eventually gets out of hand. Considering Shane's immaturity when it comes to money, she didn't foresee him managing his newfound wealth with even the slightest conservative attitude. No way was she going to let him siphon any of her money once his own has run out, he'll wake up with his throat cut before that would happen, she promised herself. Walking along the beach passing countless other tourists and locals enjoying the hot and sunny beachfront, she noticed the "ease" of which she and most other women could stroll along topless without being gawked at or harassed by male passers-by. It was an everyday thing down here in Rio that's why, topless women galore so it was no big deal! She strolled along the surf and sand enjoying the day, no longer caring where Shane was, hoping "Charlie Rosco" and his bullshit plan to gamble for even more spending money here in Rio was having fun with the local poker hustlers instead of being with her right now! Shaya decided to hit the Italian restaurant tonight for dinner, with or without her new "boyfriend", and she reminded herself to keep working out at gyms whenever possible, keeping this figure as she just gets older was becoming more and more difficult, despite the fact she doesn't "look" like she's forty years of age! Eating well on "vacation" like this was the best excuse to wake up one day soon with some flab or more of a tummy and she knew it.

Still, "Shaya Gold" was in near-perfect shape physically and every straight man who gawked at her knew it! Walking along the surf and sand of Rio's Copacabana beach, the shapely brunette reflected on her more pleasant past, back when she was in the good graces of Jonny Faster and his Porn Film Company under the "Midnight Stars" label.

She had a lot of good times as one of Jonny's top female Cast after he took control of the Company in 1998 then as his "Talent Coordinator" from 2001-2005. Memories are what keeps life either worthwhile or bearable when bad times come, though Shaya was now thankful to be walking along a sun-lit beachfront in Rio De Janeiro rather than sitting in a jail cell like she imagined Duncan Horsehair was doing right now according to Tyler Clark when she saw him last, or lying in pieces inside a tomb like her late husband Senator Rupert Kelsh. Shaya was lucky she didn't get "implicated" in any of the bullshit her husband had done recently, and she knew Tyler Clark had something to do with her being "off radar" from the FBI, ATF, DHS, DC Police, etc. etc. Her two goons she employed to watch over her the night Rupert left her had taken their $5,000 cash each and she never heard from them since, as if something was scaring them off and she didn't know what it was. As far as Shaya was concerned, paying those two clowns $5,000 each to watch over her for 12 hours the night of the 22nd was a waste of time and money because Rupert was killed before he could do anything to her!. Turning to head back up the beach toward her rented Loft, she considered leaving Shane Pillage aka: "Charlie Rosco" here in Rio and fly back to the US alone. What's he going to do to her when he could so easily be turned into the authorities for "faking his own death"? Just because he was now a self-made millionaire with a big dick he thinks he's somehow invincible and untouchable! Funny how one does not see the foolishness and bad habits of a lover until one lives with them awhile, she mused as she walked back to the rental Loft she shared with a "dead man" with a new name and a gambling habit. Shaya began to seriously consider leaving Brazil without him! Shane Pillage was really just a "passer-by" in her life, a temporary lover whom she was in no way going to keep around for much longer.

3:50pm Brazilian Time: Be careful what you wish for, as the saying goes, because it may just come true! Shaya had returned (clothed) to the Rental Loft apartment to find three uniformed Brazilian National Police on the doorstep waiting for her, her first thought being that somehow she was in "trouble" afterall back home, but it was not her at all, it was her erstwhile "travel companion" as they called him, "Charlie Rosco"!

The Policemen let her ride to the hospital with them, not telling her much except that

"Charlie Rosco" was seriously injured in an attack approximately two hours ago and he mentioned her name and address of their rental loft before he passed out. She knew Shane had been gambling with some locals because he thought he was a better Poker player than the natives here, and she could only guess what kind of trouble he found himself in, until she walked into the crowded hospital and met with the Surgeon on duty, who lucky for her, spoke good English. Shane had been gambling alright, somewhere in a "bad" part of the City about a mile from here, and he had beat his opponents out of $3,000US cash before the other players caught him **cheating**! Shane had not factored in what "cheater's justice" is down here in Rio, nor the whispered fact that black men are not too well liked in this part of the world.....he got his balls cut off by a Portuguese Gambler armed with a Bowie knife, castrated for cheating in a street game of Poker and taking $3,000!

Shane was asleep when Shaya walked into the cubicle where they had him on a bed following emergency surgery to sew-up his gaping groin wound which almost caused him to bleed to death before the Medics got to him. He didn't know she was there in the hospital room staring down at him, thinking about what to do next. Shane's bag was on the table near the bed so she checked it out and found all of his cash gone of course, but his US Passport and "Charlie Rosco" ID was still in the bag, both of which she took and shoved into her own tiny purse as she stared at the sleeping black man in the hospital bed.

"You should've listened to me Shane, and went out on the beach with me you stupid ape....well this is good-bye, thanks for the good time....while it lasted," Shaya said to him even though he was asleep from the pain-killers right now. She turned and walked out the hospital room, passing a couple of nurses coming in, taking Shane's US Passport and ID with her so that he would be essentially "stranded" here with no ID and no cash because the cash he kept back at the Loft was leaving Brazil along with her in the morning. She had already reserved a standby-flight for tomorrow as a "Plan B" in case Shane pissed her off later tonight, and she thanked herself for thinking-ahead like that.

Shane was a degenerate gambler who cheated at poker and now lost his balls because of such a habit, so she was leaving him here, a broke and unidentifiable eunuch. Justice has a way of finding some people, and for some strange reason, Shaya just didn't give a shit about him all of a sudden. Afterall, he was a "mister-right-now" type of guy, what chicks in the X-rated world refer to as a "fun dick", a guy who provides a good time in the sack but was usually utterly worthless or later becomes a "liability" outside of the bedroom!

Despite the violence Shane had suffered at the hands of those gamblers, Shaya felt a strange sense of "relief" as she walked out of that Brazilian hospital into the setting sunlight, walking back out onto the beachfront so she could untie her top and let her boobs out for a stroll again. She was silently happy to be rid of Shane Victory even if it was a macabre way of getting rid of him. Tossing his ID and Passport into the ocean water, she laughed outloud in that renewed sensation of "relief", for she was truly "on her own" again, worth over $2 million dollars. Funny, she thought, how a woman like her actually ended up owing it all to the untimely interruptions of .....**Strangers**!

Fredericksburg, Virginia. June 1st, 2008: It was a wedding in a back yard amidst a freshly-trimmed lawn, trees, and shrubbery here at 1705 Beverly Lane, a property owned by Attorney Amber Duffek, though up until recently, still considered a Marcano Mafia "safe house". She wanted to get married here at this beautifully-adorned home she recently had fixed up from it's "unoccupied" status of the past 3 years, and so she did, exchanging vows with the Groom, famous Author K.R. Knight in the rear courtyard of 1705 Beverly Lane with a minimal audience of guests, his parents and a few of her friends which included Herb and Mimi Rosenfeld of the Rosenfeld Banking dynasty, Senator Thomas Young who took the seat of the late Senator Rupert Kelsh for New Jersey, and of course Shaya Gold, who has now formally and legally changed her name.

"Never thought I'd see the day...you, of all people, marrying a man," Shaya spoke soft and gingerly to Mrs. Amber Knight standing to greet her guests and friends lining up to see her and her new husband as they stood by the brick wall of the house in the shade.

"Wonders never cease....heenh, glad you could make it babe," Amber replied as she hugged Shaya lovingly then faced the voluptuous ex-porn star (and new millionaire) who wore a one-piece red dress that reached down past her ankles but accented her bust in front of course, once again showing up with the biggest boobs at the party, Amber mused.

"Oh, I wouldn't have missed this for the world Amber," Shaya cooed back as the two ladies stepped off toward the grass together for a more private conversation. Amber's white wedding-dress was a slippery white mini-dress with sleek stockings, a garter, and a see-thru veil down her head and back, a real "sexy" wedding dress some of the more conservative guests found inappropriate but wished the couple well all the same.

"I read about what happened to Shane Pillage in Brazil, though the Tabloid called him

'Charlie' I assumed it was him in the photo....man castrated in Rio for cheating in a Poker game," Amber spoke softly to Shaya whose silky dark hair had grown down her neck again, almost to the length she wore before she had cut it 8 months ago.

"Mmmmh...yes, he may have survived your inferno in Arlington but he lost his balls in a card game in Brazil," Shaya chimed impishly with a smirk at her newly-married friend.

"Serves him right, some guys never learn, and I take it you left his ball-less black ass down there in Rio De Janeiro, hunh Shaya?" Amber said next, looking around

"Oui, que sera sera….," Shaya said dismissive, taking another sip of her champagne.

"Mmmhh, I like that about you, sever the ties that bind, or the men who are more of a liability than a lover," Amber said softly, eyeballing Shaya this time.

"Shelly James isn't here for your wedding, thought she'd be here considering both the bride and groom were fucking her over the past two years," Shaya said with a smirk.

"Nope, the little blonde bitch skipped out on me while I was in bed with Kenny for the first time, she may have even left the country but considering how awful she is at managing money, she'll be back on US soil soon enough, taking her clothes off for cash and attention," Amber said with casual aplomb, looking over to see her husband posing for pictures with his parents by the vine-covered, flower-embedded, brick arch way.

"He's a handsome devil," Shaya remarked about the Groom, smiling slinky at Amber.

"Yes he is…you're welcome to join us in bed sometime Shaya darling," Amber replied.

"Heenh, maybe I will," Shaya said with a slinky smile at the now-married Lawyer in the all-too-sexy wedding dress. Amber touched a hand to Shaya's back as they stood there in the warm courtyard of the property, looking around at the wedding party as they spoke together in semi-privacy now, enjoying the fact they had both come out "on top".

"So tell me babe, where are you going from here now that Rupert's extended family lost the injunction against you for the Georgetown house?" Amber asked Shaya casually, not looking at the busty brunette as she spoke to her casually, referring to the fact Shaya had been "challenged" by her late husband's nephew for the ownership of the house since it was not in Rupert's last will and testament. Shaya won the argument in court last week.

"Hmmh, I think I'm going to sell the house in Georgetown, even though the housing market is going down the toilet nowadays," Shaya answered with a shrug and a smirk.

"Oh, and where you gonna settle next?" Amber asked her in curious tone of voice.

"Maybe back up to New York.....or maybe the Bahamas, don't know yet," Shaya replied in uncertainty on the matter, not having decided where she will "settle" now that her late husband's "Estate" has been settled, and in her favor no less!

"Hmmm…hate to think you'd leave the country Shaya, you're an American legend," Amber said softly with a poker face, eyeing the former porn star up and down with a slinky grin.

"Right, heenh-heenh….just to diehard adult-film-fans maybe, and they're not reason enough for me to stay here….I'd like to stay in the Georgetown house yes, but the place is becoming even more of a goddamn 'tourist attraction' nowadays from the horror film geeks who come to take pictures at the 'Exorcist Steps' around the corner, or the newly arisen 'conspiracy' buffs who think my husband was murdered by the government, then there's the ones who peek into the windows trying to get a look at me when I'm home, they're all becoming a pain in the ass, which is why I'm thinking about moving," Shaya explained softly to her newly-married friend and lawyer now facing her with a demure attitude of leisurely confidence.

"I see, but maybe it's time for you to return to your real talent Shaya my dear," Amber said with a straight face, referring to Shaya's considerable past in Adult Entertainment.

"Heenh, figured you'd say that, and don't think I haven't thought about it even though I'm a millionaire now that Rupert's estate is mine and I got my off-shore money safely in American Bank accounts, taxes paid," Shaya chuckled in confident-sounding response.

"You got your ball rolling, congratulations babe….I'm happy for you, even though I must admit I'd love to see you in a new adult film sometime, 'cuz I'm a fan too ya know," Amber said impishly with a hand to Shaya's back, looking around at her other guests.

"Yeah-yeah....who knows, if I get bored, I might step back into the jizz-bizz for a hot minute or two, it's a 'talent' of mine like you said," Shaya giggled in retrospect.

"Right on.... but it feels good to be rich and comfortable doesn't it?" Amber chimed softly then leaned into Shaya for another kiss on the lips which Shaya afforded her.

"Yes it does....so tell me Amber, you like the wedding gift I gave you?" Shaya replied in slight change of subjects as they walked more toward the wedding party in the back yard.

"Oh yes, a brand new set of tires and rims for Kenny's car and a big Grandfather Clock for me, which is something I've always wanted to put in my home just never got around to it, so yes...thank you so very much Shaya darling," Amber answered gingerly.

"Mmmmh, glad you like it," Shaya sighed as she looked over to the cash-bar where she wanted to walk for a refill of the expensive-tasting champagne served here this afternoon.

"I do, you were too generous honey, so I thank you," Amber said staring at her intently.

"Well it's still a shock....you, of all people, getting married to a good-looking man after a whirlwind courtship," Shaya added matter-of-factly, folding her arms for the moment.

"Mmmh-yesss, I found a man who made me feel in a way I hadn't felt for years, so I'm keeping him, and he's going to write a new book soon about the Faster Porn Murders back in two-thousand-Five," Amber replied softly with a wink at the chesty Shaya Gold.

"Really....," Shaya said gingerly with a smirk at the leaner but well-shaped Amber standing there with her as other guests strolled by wishing her luck, kissing her, etc.

"Yes, and I suggested he use you as a source," Amber said with a responsive giggle.

"I'll help him, sure.....I'm gonna be around D.C. for awhile anyway," Shaya said casually then got a re-fill on her champagne as they walked over to the cash-bar together, still talking even as Amber was greeted and congratulated by other guests.

"Good, so we can have some fun," Amber chimed in her ear, which meant she intended to have "threesome-fun" between herself,

Shaya, and Kenny, and that was cool. She had to marvel at how Amber picked a man who was not only superb in the sack as she claims, but also accepts the fact Amber still likes "sushi" every now and then!

"Shaya-babe, don't leave until you get your gift…..I didn't have bridesmaids, I know, but I got you something in the same tradition," Amber said as she leaned into her ear again.

"What's that?" Shaya chimed in humored wonder of what "gift" Amber has in store.

"Well I knew you were coming to my wedding alone, so I got you a date, only he didn't feel comfortable about attending a wedding where he didn't really know the bride and groom, so I told him to wait up in the house upstairs in the den behind the kitchen," Amber said gingerly to her busty brunette friend staring back at her in surprised gaze.

"Hunh….what are you talking about Amber…you joshin' me?" Shaya quipped in doubtful humor, then took a swig of her champagne glass, feeling better with alcohol.

"No bullshit, go up in the house and see for yourself, the den on the other side of the kitchen, go ahead….consider it a token of my thanks for showing up on my special day here my dear friend," Amber said softly then turned to schmooze with other guests and take photos with the Groom and his parents, leaving Shaya to wonder what Amber was talking about as far as a male "gift" up in the house right now, half of her expecting it to be a bullshit prank, considering Amber's shitty tendency to make situations she explains sound better than they actually are! Walking away from the wedding party, she stepped to the carport where her Audi R8 was parked, almost just getting into it and driving off, but she was still curious enough to turn right and walk up the brick steps and brick walkway toward the front door of the house here at 1705 Beverly Drive in Fredericksburg Va.

The door was unlocked so she went on inside, feeling the coolness of the air-conditioning and the smell of roast beef met her nose from the food cooked in the kitchen earlier. She looked into the swank living room and walked through the lavish dining room to the swing-door of the kitchen, entering to find a narrow hallway connected to it on the left, so and she continued even though she had never been in this house before today. The short, narrow hallway wasn't lit but Shaya saw a sealed card-sized envelope taped to the wooden frame of the open threshold leading into the next room, with her name on it!

Opening the card as she stood there wondering what kind of prank "gift" this might be, she found the card's message written in Amber's own loopy handwriting style, reading:

Shaya, Thanx 4 being here today for my Wedding! (U R A Dear Friend)

I found a former "Co-Star" of yours and he agreed to be your date for tonight.

Love and Kisses, ~AMBER. Shaya walked on into the secluded den and found herself looking at a familiar-looking man seated over on a sofa against the far wall, staring back at her with a poker expression as a basketball game played on the TV set in the den there.

"Mered……Mered….Aladdin?!" Shaya quipped in surprise, recognizing the Turkish man she had performed with in numerous Adult Films back in the 1990's and during her final film for Faster Productions in 2005. She didn't recall his real last name but she damn sure remembered his face on sight. She walked toward him as he stood up, still staring back at her with a straight poker face as they stepped closer. Shaya threw her arms around his neck in a greeting embrace, his going around her back hugging her into him in warm welcome. She had been slightly "fearful" of the man in the past, but welcomed the familiarity now.

"Shaya Gold, as I live and breathe…you have not changed a single bit since I last saw you," the 40-year old Turkish National said in his accented voice, smiling through his thick bushy moustache at the beautiful Turkish-Brazilian-American woman he had performed with in about twenty or so X-rated films in the past.

"Why Mered, you look like you've been working-out a lot and you still dress damn good, Shaya chimed girlishly as she stepped back to check out his expensive-looking suit and shined shoes, the man always was a "dapper" dresser even if he often had what many would refer to as "mean" manners and a "hostile" disposition.

"Yes, life's been busy for me after I left Faster Productions shortly after you did, hmmph, all of the shit that happened almost made me leave the country for good, goddamn cops crawling all over the place looking for whoever had been employed by Jonny Faster that Summer," Mered the Turk said in a huff, shaking his head as he stared at her lovely visage in remembrance of how Shaya Gold looks without clothes on and in the heat of carnal activity!

"Tell me about it....it's over though....I'm glad to see you're still out and around my friend, so many of our former co-stars are dead, in prison, or listed as 'missing' somehow," Shaya said matter-of-factly as they walked around the well-furnished den in casual conversation.

"Yes, I read where 'Leesa Teasa' died in that plane crash this past Fall," he said casually.

"Yeah, the one in the Rockies, I knew someone else who died in that one too, hmmh....I was sorry to hear Leesa was one of the passengers on that doomed flight as well, she was a nice girl for the most part, good actress in the films," Shaya added with momentary grimace.

"Only the best survive," Mered said with a poker face, eyeballing her with that stony gaze that always seemed to unnerve Shaya before and he was doing it again right now, though she was genuinely happy to see the man from her porn past, still wondering how Amber "found" the reclusive and stand-offish Mered to invite him here today? Wonders never cease and Amber had done some mysterious shot yet again which was unexplainable to most.

"Mered, how did Amber find you?" Shaya just had to ask, nervous as she asked the question.

"I found her actually," he said softly with a sly smile at her through his thick, dark and bushy moustache, his olive-skinned Turkish features slightly darker than hers and his deep-set dark eyes staring right through hers as they faced one another at the bay window here in the den.

"Oh, I see....hmmh," Shaya said softly, still curious as to why he had come all the way down here to Virginia to a wedding of two people he didn't know just to see one of his former female X-rated co-stars? Mered Aladdin was not a man who struck her as one who'd have a years-long "crush" on anyone to come see them out of the blue, three years later! She was beginning to wonder about what the rumors about this man years ago and if those rumors were true: that Mered was some kind of "contract-killer", an assassin-for-hire who kills people for money, working for the Mafia and/or anyone else who could afford his retainer!

"So where are you living now?" she asked as Mered looked out the bay window toward the driveway where the convertible BMW with the Bride and Groom in it was now slowly backing out to the street, the newlyweds waving at the wedding party guests as they set out on their honeymoon. Mered glanced back at Shaya as she looked out the bay window to see Amber and Kenny leaving in the BMW for their honeymoon trip to Hawaii.

"I'm staying in D.C. now, I have a house in Georgetown," he said to her softly as she waved toward the leaving BMW, smiling as she watched Amber and her new husband leave.

"I didn't know they were going to leave so soon, gosh....who is gonna lock up the house once everyone else leaves?" Shaya mused in small-talk, eyeing Mered in study of him now.

"She may have left that to you," Mered said in his baritone voice, dark eyes piercing hers.

"Mmmmhh...yeah, maybe...this is a nice house here and it's so damn hot outside this evening ya know?" Shaya chimed with an impish grin at the mysterious Turk.

"Amber is a very giving person I take it, trusting her friends with her home like this, this place which used to be a Mafia 'safe house' years ago....hunh-huh, the Marcano Mob to be exact, and yes it is nice....wonder what the rest of the place looks like?" Mered spoke on as he began to walk around the well-furnished den, hands behind his back as he walked.

"Heenh, well I take it it's okay to wander around since Amber's taken off with her new husband for the honeymoon and the other guests are leaving," Shaya said as she watched out the bay window as other cars left down the driveway and others walked to their own parked cars out on the cul-de-sac street. The wedding event was over now and it appeared only she and Mered were inside the house right now, not hearing anyone else coming indoors out of the June heat. Shaya glanced back at her former X-rated "co-star" as he walked around the room as if thinking about whether or not to do something. Her mind began to wonder if the old story about Mered the Turk being an "assassin-for-hire" was true and if he was here to see her again because someone had hired him to kill her?? If that were true, then Amber would have to be in on it or else she'd be a "witness" and a professional hit man, if that was what Mered really is nowadays, he would not have allowed her to know he was ever here!

Still, this was strange because the man she had not seen in three years suddenly appears thanks to Amber, from out of nowhere. Was Mered somehow responsible for what happened to the others in the Company three years ago, did he do something to Jonny and burn down the Catskills cabin? She seriously doubted it, wondering still why he was here to see her alone like this on Amber's wedding day? Wonders never cease, especially when it came to strangers like this man, yes....he was a "stranger" to her even though she had done about 2 dozen films with him as his female partner for sex-scenes in the past. Mered was one of those men who didn't chat about his own life very much at all and was usually blunt and "mean" when it came to most of the Porn Starlets he dealt with at the time, though he did warm-up to Shaya some in the late 90's before he left the business the first time and then returned to perform in two of the final Faster Films of 2005. She still found him mysterious, someone who is "hiding" something deep down, and that was a male trait that both aroused and terrified Shaya when she thought about it. Maybe he "liked" her because she was of Turkish extraction like he was, and Turks are kinda rare here in the US for the most part?

She remembered numerous female starlets would refuse to work with Mered Aladdin back in the day because he was rough with them, whether it was his tendency to spank, slap, or squeeze a bit harshly. If he was here to kill her, surely he would have done so by now, with no witnesses around he could strangle her to death or shoot her through the heart right here and walk way, least that was what Shaya told herself as she re-engaged him in conversation.

"So what have you been up to since you left the Porn Industry three years ago?" she asked with a smile at the man, turning to face him as he walked back in her immediate direction.

"Busy traveling the world actually, doing jobs here and there, keeping myself in shape and out of the crosshairs of other people," Mered answered her in his usual cryptic manner.

That answer is what an assassin-for-hire might give when asked, Shaya thought to herself.

"Wow, a well-traveled man....you married, any kids now?" she chimed girlishly to him.

"What do you think...hunh-hah, I'm not the marrying kind and I don't practice Islam," Mered said with a slight smile though that bushy dark moustache of his, eyeing her fiercely.

"Heenh, thought so....mmmhh, so what's your plans for tonight, Amber did say you were my date for the evening ya know?" Shaya asked next with a slinky smile back at him.

Mered Aladdin walked closer, his right hand reaching up to her red dress at her right shoulder, peeling it downward off her shoulder there in a disrobing gesture, Shaya grinning up at her fellow Turk knowingly and in agreement with what he was recommending.

Washington D.C. (same date and time): Deputy Attorney General Tyler Clark drove his Justice Dept.-issued vehicle from the Hoover Building to dinner at one of his favorite upscale Chinese restaurants in the DC area: "Great Wall of Golden China". Though alone as he often is this time of afternoon, he had cause to celebrate! The powers-that-be, part of which he is a participant, have informed him that he will most certainly be nominated to fill the Attorney General position for the new President to be elected this November!

That was how it worked here in Washington D.C. in reality, positions of power were clandestinely granted not confirmed or elected, in the same way the next President was to be **selected** not elected! That was a done deal, the Democrats were to take the White House while the Republicans take the back seat for a couple of years and by 2012 the Democrats are to take a loss of power so their Republican counterparts come back in, continuing the shell-game of American Politics with those holding real power in the "appointed" positions calling the shots from out of the public eye. That was exactly where Tyler Clark wanted to be, and he had so far managed to get what he wanted.

Driving his car into the parking lot behind the Restaurant, he parked and locked it up before heading for the side-entrance of the upscale "reservation-preferred" restaurant not far from the Hoover Building. He was a regular customer here, and the Chinese staff knew him at first glance, cheerfully greeting the "Government Big Shot" as they call him.

Clark asked for his favorite secluded booth over in a far corner away from most other customers, nice and quiet for meal time. He now wished he had a girlfriend or even the late Senator Kelsh's widow Shaya to "celebrate" with when he gets home. Nothing better than a glass of wine and a piece of ass to enjoy one's triumph, he mused to himself as he sat in the cozy leather booth, removing his tie to relax as the Asian waitress asked what he'd like to drink first, handing him the menu. He elected to get a draft beer then the waitress left him to relax there alone. Again, he kind of wished he would have kept touch with Shaya, even though hooking up with the "ex-porn star" would not have benefited his political career like it (strangely enough) benefited Senator Kelsh's, least for awhile. Shaya in his bed tonight would be icing on the cake, and he had to wonder where the lovely big-boobed Turkish-American honeybuns disappeared to? The brick house in Georgetown was still in her name as Rupert Kelsh's next-of-kin, but that old home had been vacant for three months according to a friend of his in the FBI and was on the Real Estate market now going for just under a million dollars. Clark sat there for a few silent minutes reflecting on how most women in his life so far had "come and gone", often leaving him because of his slavish devotion to his work and his secretive planning they often found to be strange and unforgivable. Shaya hadn't contacted him since her husband was killed back in October of last year, and that was fine because it meant she was not going to become a "liability" to him like she almost had to her husband at the time, so Clark let her go on with whatever life she chose. His right foot kept hitting something bulky under the table which did not feel like normal restaurant furniture, so he reached a hand underneath to pull it up onto the table. It was a black leather purse, one of those old-fashioned "granny" purses that locked at the top and he assumed the previous customer had left it behind after her meal here in the booth. "Well, someone's going to be happy I'm not a purse-snatcher," he chuckled to himself as he popped it open to look down into the big purse for identification or phone number.

The contents of the purse were not ordinary contents for any purse, but before he could react in realization of it, the C-4 plastic explosive device inside the purse **detonated**.

Nydia Cohen cackled madly at the sight of the entire Chinese restaurant erupting into a fireball as she gleefully watched through the glass of her car's windshield, sitting there about 100 yards away from the target area in her late model Trans Am alone and in triumph. She had targeted an enemy all by herself and got his ass with a brick of C-4 that vaporized the prick as well as deep-fried the Chinese restaurant staff along with him!

Deputy Attorney General Tyler Clark had betrayed her "lord and master" Horsehair by sealing him in some kind of frozen stasis in a secure laboratory in Maryland, a place she alone could not free him from, but she could at least slay the asshole who is responsible!

Satisfied with her "operation" here this afternoon, she shifted into drive and drove off onto Pennsylvania Avenue to head back to Virginia, cackling in humor about how easy it was to "track" the Deputy Attorney General who liked to dine at the same restaurant in the same booth, around the same time and day once a week, with no protection around him at all. It was an easy kill for her, her only regret being that her source of C-4 and detonators dried up with the loss of "Horsehair" to the cryonics chamber in Maryland!

She wasn't going back to the Nursing home, no matter how bad her health was getting, she decided to just pick a new target and strike all by herself without the "back-up" of her lord and master to support her like he had done for five years. Nydia decided to track down another "target" who happened to really piss her off, though at this current time she had not one damn clue as to how to locate that one. Driving onto the 14th Street Bridge and heading back into Virginia, the 80-year old Nydia Cohen turned on the country music station she often enjoyed listening to and rode in happy contentment, sure of one thing being that the man who rescued her from the nursing home five years ago would be proud of her "cooking" the Deputy Attorney General at that gook restaurant back there!

"Muthhhrrr-fukkkrrrs….I'll git yuuuuhh….myyyh….. prettieeee!" Nydia spoke in a long sentence of humored invective, driving along the Beltway southbound as the sun was going down, which heralded her favorite time, the nightfall! So much better to operate after nightfall, after most of the human herd turn to slumber or lethargy, so much easier to operate as a "lone wolf" during the nighttime! She sped up to 70mph, listening to her country music and her car's 350 engine rocketing her southbound, relaxed but feeling melancholy over the loss of her lord and master Horsehair, shivering at the thought of him asleep in cryo-freeze, wondering if in that condition he may be "brought back" easy enough? That was why she didn't plant her last brick of C-4 in that goddamn laboratory and blow it sky-high, because Horsehair was in there and may survive to fight another night in the future, and maybe that's what the "powers that be" wanted afterall?!

Horsehair was unlike most human men, he had survived his own clinical death back in 1994 to rise and wage war on the streets of America, a war against the weak and the stupid, against the corrupt and the mongrelized, against those who'd drain America's greatest assets and darken it's future. Nydia carried the banner as much as she could, but she was old and nearly handicapped, limited but willing to kill for the greater good, as well as for a pound or two of revenge…. revenge on the kind of people who'd stick her in a "retirement" home because of her age and "worthlessness" even to the grown but spoiled children she raised to adulthood decades ago. She was by no means a warrior like Horsehair was, but she did what she could, from the "hate whitey" church she blew up to the tour bus of spear-chuckers she tossed a grenade at, that asshole Robert Marx and his piece of shit son Jamal……they were all strangers to her, and she was a stranger to them, ending their lives when none of them even noticed a stranger beside them.

1705 Beverly Lane, Fredericksburg. 6:30 that same evening: The bartender and photographer had just left the backyard when one of Amber's old friends from Law School Paul Marsden (and his wife Janet) helped put the tablecloth and chairs inside the in-house garage as the sky was darkening and threatening a storm now. They were the last ones there of the wedding party but lived in nearby Spotsylvania County so it was no rush to get home.

Paul had known Amber since their Freshman year at the University and his wife Janet knew Amber through him of course, so they were happy to come see Amber get married off, something they and the rest of the guests had never thought they would ever see!

The 35-year old Paul Marsden walked into the house through the garage's inner door past the laundry room and into the dark basement "rec. room" that had been cleaned and fixed up for the occasion, guests using it's bathroom before and after the outdoor ceremony.

His wife Janet walked in behind him bitching about how hot it was and how she'd have to take her dress to the dry-cleaners because she was sweating so much in it, then she remarked how cool the place felt and why someone would leave the AC running full-blast like that when they had left for the airport and a flight to Hawaii? Paul disliked the fact his less-than-lean wife had become way too "bitchy" and uninteresting over the past couple of years, and he began thinking how much he would like to leave her if they had not had a daughter together whom they both loved more than anything! He calmly agreed with her as he started up the wooden stairwell, his wife coming up behind him griping about how they shouldn't go upstairs into Amber's house here uninvited. He just wanted to make sure it was secure since he was assuming everyone of the wedding invites had left by now.

"It's okay, I don't wanna leave the house here unlocked and all the lights on, Amber wouldn't mind us checking before we leave, trust me," Paul said to his wife coming up behind him as he stepped up into the upstairs dining room. He stopped in the dining room to turn off the chandelier light, seeing his reflection in the crystal-glass of the Wine Cabinet to his left, seeing the balding white man with thick glasses on his face he'd always known as Paul Marsden, Attorney at Law, and then he saw Janet Marsden Elementary School Teacher stepping alongside him with a scowl of impatience on her scowling, 36-year old face.

"Place is as clean as a museum," he remarked as they crossed the dining room together.

"Yeah, let this show you how cleaning our own home better would pay off, hunh?" Janet fired back at him, yet another recent trait he hates about his wife besides the weight-gain: her penchant to "dump on" just about anything he says, no matter what it was!

Paul walked across to the front foyer then looked down the long dark hallway as he closed and locked the front door. He saw the glint of light through the cracked-open door of the master bedroom at the far end of the hallway, wondering if that was just a light left on or perhaps someone was down the hall in that bedroom? He turned and headed down the hallway quietly out of curiosity, Janet not far behind him, quiet (for once) herself. Both of them felt a strange and eerie "presence" right now, as if someone else was in the house....

Paul stopped short of pushing the door open, peering into the lamp-lit master bedroom via the 2-inch opening since the door was not closed all the way. What he saw froze him in his spot, staring into the bedroom in awestruck silence as his wife tugged at his shirt from behind. Paul found himself peeking in at a pair of naked bodies over on a canopied bed having very vibrant **sex.** The very-well-built female straddled the man's hips as he lay on his back and she was moving up-and-down on the man's erection in steady, wet intercourse like a human piston! He couldn't look away, fixated at the carnal sight of a man and woman making love on the bed fully-exposed and in a manner he had not experienced for so long.

Paul felt his wife Janet push her way alongside him on the left, getting a look-see for herself.

"Oh my….," she sighed in his ear as she saw the two dusky-hued lovers on the bed in there grinding together in relentless intercourse, the shiny apple of an ass on the well-shaped female bouncing up and down absorbing the man's obviously well-endowed organ capturing her gaze as well, the long-married couple finding what they were seeing very interesting…..

They remembered seeing the dark-haired woman with the big breasts at the wedding earlier, another of Amber's "wealthy friends", though they did not recall her name, but the dark-haired man with bushy moustache they did not see at the wedding. Curious and entranced by the sight, Paul and Janet watched the couple go-at-it through the cracked-open door, marveling at how the woman was "riding" on a man's sex organ of that size so easily, her backside moving up and down like the piston of an engine, the woman moaning in ecstasy of the act, her big tits jiggling wildly over the man she was "riding", his face a tense grimace of enjoyment as he lay there letting the big-breasted woman continue on him.

Paul turned to glance at his wife, noticing she was now blushing as she stared into the room through the opening in the doorway, watching the other couple, complete strangers, fucking!

Her eyes met his and he could tell by the glow of her round face she was aroused by the unusually bawdy and energetic sexual display in there, and it was a look Paul had not seen on his wife's face for quite some time. She then spun around and started walking back down the hallway without saying anything else, her left hand waving over her head in gesture for him to follow her out of there. Paul looked back at the two lovers in there on the bed once more then reluctantly followed his wife down the hallway to the dining room and stairwell.

"Can you believe that….?" Paul Marsden asked his portly wife as she stopped at the stairs.

"Two strangers doing it turn you on Paul?" Janet asked him in curt reply, hands on her hips.

"Yeah," he sighed as he faced her with arms folded, aroused and wanting to "do it" himself.

"Okay then, Jenna is staying at my Mom's for the night anyway, what do ya say we get a motel room around here and see if we can out-do those two?" Janet suggested to her surprised husband standing there, smirking up at him for a moment then spun around and headed down the stairs to the garage where they came in at. Paul grinned ear-to-ear as he followed his wife back out of the house to go and have some sexual fun like they hadn't had for quite some time as a married couple. He saw that look on her face earlier, a look of arousal he hadn't seen for a long time, and he wished he could send a thank-you card to the couple they just peeked in on for setting a fire back in his wife's libido. On the way out the garage door, Paul kept thinking about those lovers in the master bedroom, assuming they were allowed to stay here now that Amber and Kenny were off to Hawaii, wondering who they were……no, they were just a pair of unknown **strangers** who showed he and his wife what they'd been missing for so long in their marriage!

Shaya relished the sexual congress with her former co-star, enjoying the sensation of penetration, the fleshy union of their bodies at the most intimate level, not for filmmaking this time, but for the sake of it, the pure pleasure of the act and because they knew each other from years ago, having made love before just not privately like this. Mered was enthralled by the feel of her, enjoying her flesh in near-silence, grinning up at Shaya Gold through the thick bushy moustache covering most of his mouth as she rode on his pole in steady pumping motion, "bouncing" on his dick like she had done for films in the past, only now it was better because they were alone, no Director, no cameras, no filming……

"Ooooaaannnh…..unnnoooaaah, Merrrrr…ed!" Shaya groaned in orgasm as she slowed on him now, head up toward the mirrored canopy over them, groaning in quaking delight of the carnal act she was engrossed in. Before she knew it he was rolling her over to re-engage her in a missionary-position, sailing into her with vigorous ardor.

Shaya relaxed on her back now, though Mered pulled her backside up off the bed with his greedy hands as he thrusted into her, making her yelp out in reaction but enjoying it just the same, her head and shoulders lying on pillows as Mered the Turk serviced her ardently.

"Ooooh-unnoooaaah….yeeeaaahh……ooonnnnh….feeels…. gooood!" Shaya quipped outloud in delight of the sex, his lean but muscled body thrusting into hers with all the intensity of a man possessed, much like he was known to do back during their porn career, only this time it was real and un-coreographed, which made it better. She let Mered pump into her fiendishly now, her moans and wails of reaction egging him on, making him fuck her harder. Arching his back with each thrust in to her, Mered's face made that same grimace of passion, what "passion" the mean Turk could show anyway, his entire body, like hers, devoted to the sexual intercourse 100% without the slightest distraction or hesitation.

"Unnnoooaah….unnnoooaah!" Shaya yelped in escstatic rancor of the sensations he caused her as he continued, pumping his manhood into her sweet canal without fail, thrilled by the sweet feeling of Shaya Gold, a woman he had enjoyed before, now even moreso!

His hands slipped down from her shoulders to her big boobs, squeezing as he continued sailing into her love canal, tweeking those big nipples as she squirmed beneath him in orgasmic delight, eyes closed and mouth wide open, sweat lines streaming down her face.

Nothing else existed at this moment, just the two of them in the flesh, gorging on one another madly in sexual hunger consuming their minds and bodies so that nothing and noone else around them mattered whatsoever in the slightest…….

The late model Trans Am driven by an unseemly elderly white lady pulled up onto the inclined Beverly Lane and slowed to a parking halt directly in front of the house at 1705, right in front of a rental sedan parked facing the opposite direction. Nydia Cohen looked around the darkening area as she got out of her car carrying a black leather purse and heading up toward the house via it's long brick walkway, noone else nearby to even see her.

This was the location she knew very well for she had met Horsehair here several times in the past to be briefed on "hits" he assigned her, and this was where the lovely Miss Isabel Marcano had resided for about a year or more at one time, Horsehair's "one true love" though the bitch didn't know it! This house was now owned by Attorney Amber Duffek, one woman who pissed Nydia off because she was a noted Feminist and avowed lesbian, though before tonight she could not kill the dyke because Amber was a "protected asset" as Duncan Horsehair had once said, but now with Horsehair "on ice" like he was, surely her "lord and master" won't mind if she uses her last C-4 device wisely and blows that prissy cupcake Amber Duffek into a million lesbian pieces?!! Nydia feebly walked to the front door, her right hand sliding down into the big purse she had slung over her right shoulder to touch the brick of C-4 and it's detonator inside, trying to think of how she was to do this in the same "discreet" but efficient manner as all of her other hits. Walking straight through the front door seemed easy enough as long as it wasn't locked, and she found the front door to be actually be unlocked! A "little old lady" walking up unannounced into a stranger's home was unusual yes, but something Nydia could quite easily act out as an "old woman with dementia/alzheimers" wandering into a house she "thinks is her own" if caught by the house's occupants. Nydia pushed the big door inward and stepped inside the house looking around hesitantly as she heard thunder overhead behind her, a storm forecasted for tonight.

Place smelled of expensive perfume and potpourri she thought as she walked on into the large living room, finding it lit only by a solitary lamp over at one end of the big sofa there.

Crossing the living room toward one corner upon seeing an antique piece of furniture that caught her attention, Nydia inadvertently stepped out of sight just as a stark-naked woman exited the kitchen with glasses of wine in her hands, walking toward the hallway.

Nydia froze where she stood, glimpsing the big-breasted brunette strolling along totally-nude with full wine-glasses in her hands, heading past the living room (not spotting the elderly intruder) into the dimly-lit hallway. Shaya was oblivious to the elderly woman in the living room but Nydia watched her in stunned realization and doubt. The woman was nude, filled out in a way she had never seen before, and looked like Isabel Marcano! Nydia stepped to the threshold at the front foyer to watch the naked harlot waltz on down the hallway, wondering if what Horsehair said about Isabel being "lost" was perhaps a bad assumption or was this woman just favoring her with the same kind of dark hair, olive skin, and similar shape? Nydia had to find out as well as why such a woman was here where Amber Duffek lives, was she a lesbian-lover of Amber's and was Amber down the hall in the bedroom?

The naked harlot with the wine-glasses entered the bedroom at the far end of the hallway, letting the door close most of the way but not clicking-closed so Nydia walked down the hallway against her own better judgment to see for herself, to visually confirm if her target was in the house tonight or perhaps someone else was living here at 1705 Beverly Lane now?

Nydia closed in on the door, finding it ajar about an inch or so, pausing to quietly lean forward and peer inside the bedroom. She saw the well-filled-out naked brunette walking up to a naked man sitting on the end of the big canopied bed in there, handing him a glass as she stopped at his legs, the man's one hand taking the glass of wine, the other sliding around her his to squeeze her buttocks gently, pulling the woman closer into him as he sat there.

"Mmmhh....Mered....I'd like you to consider coming to work for me baby...I'm thinking of starting up a new Adult Film Company in New York....I'd have you as the top male actor, I mean what the hell...it's something we're both talented in, performing sex for film?" Shaya cooed to the Turkish man sitting on the end of the bed running his free hand down her ass.

"Hmmph, why that is a crazy idea Shaya....it would put us both on the same chopping block that Jonny Faster ended up on....," Mered sighed as he looked up into her eyes intently with a slight scowl of contemplation, his erection still at full-mast as he sat there with wine-glass in his other hand. Shaya took a sip of her wine and ran her right hand through his thick dark hair, gently down his face as she stared back into his deep-set dark eyes again.

"It'll be different this time Mered, I assure you….I have a few good connections in the government now and I might be better protected at running that kind of business than Jonny Faster was, and I know how to reach some of the veteran performers from the past such as F.M. Dexter, Jamie Autumn, Lacey Lovitt….I'll even return to star in some features myself since I still look good at age forty," Shaya explained to her new lover whose attention suddenly shifted past her toward the bedroom door. Shaya looked over her left shoulder and saw the bedroom door open-inward suddenly, the two of them seeing an elderly white lady standing there at the threshold looking perplexed and confused as she stared back at them.

Nydia had accidentally stepped forward and pushed the door inward to reveal herself to the naked couple in the bedroom now, standing there stunned and mortified.

"Heenh, hey there….the wedding is over honey, Amber and Kenny took off for their honeymoon and left me to watch over the house with my friend here," Shaya spoke gingerly to the old lady standing quivering in the doorway, guessing she must be a "late arrival" to Amber's wedding earlier and got confused like old people tend to get. Nydia forced a smile at the naked lovers at the bed and raised a hand in a pardon-seeking gesture.

"Oh dear, I'm so sorry to…disrupt you folks….I missed Amber's wedding," Nydia spoke meekly in response, wondering why the "lesbian" Amber Duffek got married to a man named Kenny?! Wonders never cease. Shaya smiled sweetly at the old lady as she stood there close to the seated Mered Aladdin whose hand was still on her bare asscheeks, both of them looking at the elderly intruder at the bedroom door as if it were no big deal.

"It's okay sweetheart…..Amber should return in two weeks, have a nice evening and be careful out there…a storm's coming," Shaya said in polite conclusion with a wave of her free hand as Nydia started to back out of the door into the hallway in retreat, Mered chuckling.

"Sorry for the intrusion dear, you two lovebirds have fun," Nydia cackled back at them as she turned to walk back down the hallway, pulling the door behind herself as she went.

Shaya looked at Mered with a sleazy smirk then they both laughed for a moment and Mered dropped both of their wine-glasses to the rug below and stood up with Shaya, embracing.

"Time for Round-Two....Shaya Gold," he said through his thick bushy moustache, forcing the naked Shaya against the nearest wall where she giggled in anticipation of him re-engaging her while standing vertical against the it. Mered considered the strange circumstance where an elderly lady like that would walk in on them, something about that old woman made him feel uneasy, as if the old woman was giving off some kind of subtle "threat" vibe.

"Would you prefer she stay and watch?" Mered sneered to Shaya as he caught her looking at the bedroom door again, leaning back against the wall to take him on as he plunged into her.

"Unnnoaaah.....ooonnh...Merrrrr-ed!" Shaya groaned in reception of him, her bare feet leaving the floor below as he thrusted up into her in vertical intercourse, pinning her to the wall and taking her off her feet. Shaya wailed outloud in reaction to how damn good it felt.

Nydia had stopped in the middle of the hallway, listening to the pair inside the bedroom.

No, that was not Isabel Marcano (but the woman favored her) and she was obviously no lesbian considering the Middle-Eastern-looking man with the huge penis in there with her!

If what the chesty brunette said was true and Amber Duffek was not to return for two weeks, having married a man named Kenny.... then why blow the bitch up afterall? Nydia asked herself, knowing she couldn't wait patiently for two weeks to kill that uppity bitch Amber Duffek like she had wanted to. Nydia wanted to use her last bomb though, looking back at the closed door of the bedroom where those two younger people are fucking their brains loose as the saying goes....made her wish she was forty years younger herself so she could enjoy sex like the dusky-hued pair in the bedroom were indulging right now!

"Heeh-heh, why not….," Nydia snickered to herself as she pulled the C-4 plastique and it's digital detonator out of her purse, holding it in both hands as she stood in the center of the hallway. She had killed complete strangers before without reservation, and those two naked lovebirds were strangers to her, so what if these two hadn't actually done anything really "treasonous" as she called it when she blew up gay bars, abortion clinics, and liberal lawyers.

She engaged the detonator's timer on the brick of C-4 and decided to set it for 30 minutes, giving those two fuckers in the bedroom another half-hour of fun before "bingo" time!

Nydia opened the linen closet in the hallway next to a bathroom a few paces from the bedroom and shoved the timed device in there on a shelf of clean sheets, closing the door gently and softly giggling to herself as she headed down the hallway to the front entrance.

"Good-bye lovebirds….enjoy yourselves in there 'cuz it's your last," Nydia sneered softly as she looked back down the hallway one final time, hearing the woman wail out in carnal delight again in almost a scream of delight. "My-my, what a harlot," Nydia said as she exited the house back onto the brick walkway toward her Trans Am parked out front, hurrying as rain began to fall. Her vision became suddenly "two-dimensional" and her legs felt like noodles as she neared the end of the brick walkway toward the street and her car, then she went dizzy and spun around, the rainfall increasing in it's heavy downpour while she stopped and stood there at the top step facing the street for a moment's realization. Nydia then let out a sigh as the feeling in her upper chest and face vanished, her extremities failing to hold her up and she collapsed down onto the street at the bottom of the brick steps, landing in a curled posture in front of her late model Trans Am, victim of a major stroke…….

Shaya was bent over kneeling on the floor now with her face on the plush carpet as Mered drilled her from behind in a faster intercourse, hands roughly squeezing her ass while he pumped into her fervently. Surrendering to this man was easy for her, for she was always a sexual-submissive at heart! Shaya groaned in approval as

Mered continued "round two", his hands exploring her soft, sweaty body as they continued their feverish percolation.

"Unnnooaannh.....oooaaaahh.....come with me Mered...join me in films again!" she bellowed in orgasmic delight once more, the man not ceasing in stride the least bit, drilling into her core as if it were his last, soaking up every moment of hot fleshy rhythm greedily.

"Nnnnhhh....shut up.......you talk too much....unnnngghh!!" Mered moaned with his back arched in violent thrusting, finally reaching his own climax, enjoying it's rushing feeling.

Shaya didn't mind him calling her names during sex, she liked it actually, and Mered was known for talking trash during his "performance" though she sensed he meant it this time!

Next thing she knew he had her up against the foot of the bed and then flopped over the end for a "cradle-doggie-style" motion with him holding her legs as she lay prone over the corner of the bed, drilling into her as he held her at the thighs with both hands down by his thrusting sides. Shaya grabbed onto the bed's comforter so she wouldn't slide of the bed and land face-first on the floor below, Mered pumping into her relentlessly that way and despite it's roughness, she was ecstatic, enjoying the "tubing" as he gave it to her, feeling like she was being "wish-boned" by her lover, and it brought her to orgasm yet again. The man was a machine, corresponding with a female dynamo of sexual energy threatening to break both of them as they continued their ardent campaign. Mered pulled her legs behind him as he pumped into her sweet spot quick and steady, her groans and yelps of passion egging him on to continue like this, almost pulling her outstretched body off the bed as he hammered forth.

"Oonnnh....ooohhhhnnnnnnh-oooaaahh......that's it.... ooohhh....Merrrr-rrred!!" Shaya wailed in fiendish delight, not wanting it to end, coming to an entirely new plane of pleasure in sexual intercourse as her former X-rated co-star pumped in and out like an engine. He then pushed her further up onto the bed by her legs and jumped onto the bed with her, re-engaging Shaya in a spoon-motion from behind, hoisting her left leg up at the thigh and re-entering her for more, their sweaty bodies sliding around the bed together in continuing intercourse, the thrilling sensation keeping them both happy to continue on. Shaya lay there nearly numb from the sheer pleasure of the act as he lover continued in that spoon position, his end coming soon enough from exhaustion, and when it did a couple of minutes more, Mered slowed in his motion curled like that and still attached to her, Shaya leaned in for a kiss as he came for the final time, his mouth stretching wide open in reaction to the final explosive sensation, and both bodies fell limp in that spooning curl, groaning together in spasmic collapse. Shaya closed her eyes as she lay her head back on the pillows behind her, Mered rolling from her after biting at her left breast for a moment, letting out a loud sigh of relief and exhaustion now. Her eyes opened to gaze on the man who just serviced her in a way she hadn't experienced in years, not since Jonny Faster shared her bed! Mered was just as talented and energetic as Jonny, but more ferocious with how he handled her, which at times she really liked a man to be! Shaya rolled over, nearly passing out from the sensation.

"Oh Mered....omigod, that was awesome....you're better than when we did films together, mmmhh...please say yes to my...offer... ...I want you with me," Shaya cooed as she raised her sweat-streaked head back up to see him rising to a sitting position at the foot of the bed.

"Shaya....you are too much," he said as he stood up slowly and stretched his arms upward.

"We'd make a great team you and I," she sighed as she rolled over onto her front again while Mered walked to the bedroom door to go use the bathroom in the hallway, glancing back at the naked woman lying on the bed and realizing how much he just enjoyed her.

In the hallway, Mered found a door he suspected was to a closet and he pulled it open, seeking a fresh towel and washcloth, but upon opening the door he found something else besides a towel and washcloth, something that froze his blood for a moment. A brick of C-4 plastic explosive coupled with a digital detonator and the timer screen read two minutes thirty-nine seconds....thirty-eight.... thirty-seven....thirty-six........

"What is this doing…here?" Mered sneered to himself as he carefully reached in and picked up the device, finding it was not a gravity-sensitive bomb, just one on a timer and there was now just two minutes remaining before five pounds of C-4 detonates and with it this entire house would go up into a fireball of pure incineration, that much he was certain of because he had long ago been trained in military explosives. He reached a thumb to the left side of the detonator attached to the C-4 and pressed down on the small key-pad there, disarming the device and stopping the digital countdown at two minutes-one second.

Mered was a "contract" killer, an assassin-for-hire, and his mind immediately focused on this type of threat being aimed at him as a retaliation, but noone except Amber Duffek even knew he'd be here tonight and she didn't give a shit to see him dead or otherwise. However Amber Duffek had been the target of that "rogue agent" reported in the newspapers recently, some bad cop tried to kill her by blowing up two of her homes with her in them but she managed to escape both times! If this bomb was meant for Amber Duffek, the asshole who left it is incompetent because Amber had left for Hawaii and wouldn't return for two weeks. Mered held the device in his right hand as he stepped back to the bedroom door, inching it open to look in on Shaya Gold, the former "Porn Queen" he just had ravenous sex with. She was still lying flat on her front on the bed, legs spread and clearly oblivious to the fact a timed bomb had been ticking-away outside the bedroom door.

The bomb would have killed them both instantly if it had gone off two minutes later, and that realization straightened Mered Aladdin's mind into survival-mode now.

"What are you getting me into….hunh Shaya?" he whispered to himself as he looked in on the naked woman sprawled on the bed, probably having fallen asleep by now after sex.

"What am I doing….hmmph, time for me to bail and take the job in Spain," Mered said to himself in a huff, walking down the hallway to where he had jettisoned his clothes earlier, forgetting about a shower now, just wanting to get dressed and leave without further trouble.

He placed the disarmed bomb down on the coffee-table of the living room and quickly pulled his clothes on, hearing the thunderstorm outside and silently cursing the fact he had let his guard down enough while boning Shaya (for old times sake) that someone had planted a goddamn bomb in the house during a thunderstorm without him knowing.......

"The old lady.....holy shit," he sneered to himself in wonder, for something about her unnerved him when she opened the door on he and Shaya about a half hour ago, something strange about that elderly female stranger, and he should have acted on his suspicion, at least escorted her out the door so she could not have planted a bomb, if she was the one who did.

But no, he was too busy up to his ears in pussy at the time and it would have cost him his life if he had not opened that linen closet door when he did.....two minutes later and the local cops would be picking tiny pieces of he and Shaya out of the yard for weeks!

Once he was dressed, Mered picked up the disarmed device again, deciding to take it with him considering it was a very professional device he could use himself later on if need-be.

Looking back down the hallway thinking of Shaya again, he shook his head in dismissal.

Sure, he would have liked to get back into the porn business with her, with many more sexual delights to be had with her and other "Starlets" but Mered had another "profession" which paid far more for his time. He was a killer afterall, not a lover, so he walked out the front door quietly into the rainfall, heading for the parked rental car he came here in.

Shaya rolled over, head still buried between pillows as her bare body lay stretched out on the ruffled bed now, still asleep as the thunderstorm raged outside and Mered Aladdin quietly left the house, leaving her alone after their two hour sex-fest tonight. Her mind's subconscious slipped into lucid dreaming as she lay there prone, uncovered and spread out in slumber. Oblivious to what was going on around her right now, she lay there in peaceful sleep dreaming of things she quite often dreamt of........

"Hey there Shaya Doll," spoke the hauntingly familiar voice of Jonny Faster, making her look over to the bedroom doorway to find the Adonis-like man standing naked there smiling back at her handsomely as he leaned on the door frame, muscular arms folded, those blue eyes of his staring her down as she sat there on the end of the bed sleazily smiling in return.

"Jonny….my man," she said in response, standing up from the bed to find herself in the master bedroom of the Faster Mansion in New Rochelle, NY not Fredericksburg Virginia anymore! It was surreal but lucid, and she felt like she had just woke up from a long dream and was back where she "belonged", back at the Faster Mansion in New York and back with Jonny Faster who was now standing nude in the bedroom's doorway, that cut n' chiseled body of his a welcome sight, not to mention the famously well-endowed "kielbasa" hanging between his muscular thighs, waiting for her!

"To thine own self….be true," Jonny Faster said with his handsome smile then he stepped back into the dark hallway and vanished, Shaya suddenly finding herself in the downstairs living room of the Faster Mansion, clothed in one of her silk robes like she often wore back then. She saw the huge circular sofa, the custom bar and huge entertainment center all there as if the place was still there, still the "Faster Mansion" and she had returned to it! Over at the bar was Ebony Cane, the one full-time black actress employed by the Company and veteran of over 100 X-rated features since 1999. Ebony was in a pink string-bikini, filling it out all too well as she poured drinks on the bar counter. Over by the big "theater" TV screen was Shelly James, fiddling with the remote control and wearing only a towel around her torso, hair damp from an earlier shower. Coming out of the kitchen now was Cody Abs, the porn actor who'd hung himself after the company went under in late 2005…still alive! He smiled at Shaya as he walked over to the bar, himself also wearing just a pair of boxer shorts. Down the stairs came the black actor Ray Fury, clad in a yellow bathrobe, eyes on Shaya as he strolled into the huge living room where Shelly James met him half-way for a hug and a kiss. Ray pulled off her towel and slapped Shelly's bare ass as they walked together to the bar where Ebony Cane had drinks poured for everyone. Shaya walked over to the bar where the others had congregated, smiling as they all smiled at her as if they all knew something she didn't just then. Shaya picked up the glass of champagne poured for her and stood there looking at the others, the two of whom were "dead" last she knew, and the other two gone on with their lives elsewhere. Shaya looked around again but didn't see Jonny.....

"A toast.....to fond memories!" Ebony Cane announced with a giggle, the others raising their glasses in toast, waiting a few moments for Shaya to finally raise hers in agreement, then they all wolfed down their drinks at the same time, Shaya finding it odd they were toasting such a thing, not fully getting the reason behind Ebony's toast. Ray and Shelly left the bar to walk across the living room naked together, hands on one another's buttocks as they walked toward the stairs together, heading up to one of the bedrooms no doubt, Shaya watching them go. She turned to see Cody Abs walk to the sliding-glass door and vanish out into the darkness of the back yard, then the shapely, long-haired Ebony Cane walked around to the front of the bar in her tight-fitting, pink string-bikini. Shaya looked at the comely black woman who still had a drink in her left hand as she stopped in front with a smile.

"Where are you going now Shaya?" Ebony asked the voluptuous raven-haired woman as she reached her right hand to the front of Shaya's silk robe, tugging on it right there between her big breasts. Shaya stared at the black woman's pretty face in wonder, not having an instant answer for the simple question, though the smirk on Ebony's face was a knowing one, as if the porn starlet had an answer for her but wanted to hear Shaya say it first.

"I don't know," Shaya sighed finally with a shrug as she faced her former co-star and friend.

"Of course you do, babydoll....to-thine-own-self-be-true," the gorgeous, well-endowed black woman said impishly with that trademark smirking-grin of hers, handing Shaya Gold the re-filled glass of champagne as she pivoted on one heel and began to slowly walk away from the still-surprised Shaya Gold who realized those were the same words spoken by Jonny Faster to her minutes ago: TO THINE OWN SELF BE TRUE.

"Ebony....where's Jonny...where's everyone gone?" Shaya asked next in a near-whisper.

"Everyone leaves eventually, didn't ya know?" Ebony Cane replied with a giggle as she sauntered across the living room of the Faster Mansion, that well-filled-out physique of hers jiggling in the bikini that barely covered it's better portions, walking toward the kitchen door where she stopped to look back at Shaya once more. Ebony winked at her then turned and vanished into the kitchen, leaving Shaya Gold alone in the suddenly darkening living room.

Shaya walked to the big sofa and sat down as the room became darker and darker as if the light was being slowly and purposely dimmed now. Taking a sip of the champagne glass in her hand, Shaya relaxed back on the sofa behind her and laid out on her right side.

"Good-bye my old friends...I'll never forget you," Shaya whispered as she closed her eyes.

3:01am: Shaya opened her eyes and raised her head wearily from the pillows, finding herself in the dimly-lit master bedroom of Amber's house on Beverly Lane in Fredericksburg where she had fallen asleep after sex with Mered. It was a dream, but one not easily forgotten as she rose to a seated position, looking around as she yawned and stretched her arms upward.

She was alone in the house, she knew it already, sensing that Mered had left her hours ago.

Still hearing rainfall on the roof above, she rolled over on her back and stared up at her bare reflection in the canopied bed's overhead-mirror, smiling in sardonic humor as she thought about her options for the immediate future. Comfortable, independently-wealthy, and still damn sexy at age forty....she silently cursed the fact she had been left all alone, though a woman like her never has to be "lonely" for too long unless she wishes to be! Shaya stared at the reflected naked image of a human female who'd spent most of her adult life making money (making-a-living) by using her body and exotic good-looks to **entertain** other human beings. Her body teased, seduced, entertained countless men (and women) over the past 20 years, and it was still good if she wanted to continue in her chosen "career field" (though she was now considering other options) funny how a sudden influx of money and renewed personal freedom can offer one such things that were never available before! She had been with a hundred different men, most of them **strangers**, even the few she had loved like Jonny and Rupert. Staring up at her famous bare body in reflection, Shaya silently wondered how she had never had a family of her own, having always been an orphan of some kind, living her unique life for the benefit, adoration, and entertainment of complete **strangers**.

To be continued immediately following the Commentary and Reviews!

SEX IN URBAN LEGEND

According to the corresponding definitions of "urban legend", such is a form of folklore crafted of stories thought to be real or factual by those circulating them despite the propensity for such folklore to be distortions of the truth, exaggerated, and even embellished upon as time goes by and the story is re-told over and over again.

One of the most infamous of "urban legends" is the one told of a lone, college-age female getting her car gassed up during a storm and when she goes to pay for her it, the gas station clerk tries to warn her (but she doesn't get the message) that a man just snuck into the rear seat of her car! Another favorite of mine is the one where a soldier (or sailor) on weekend-pass gets himself a Hooker and lets her tie him up, only to have the Hooker rip him off of all his cash and clothes, to leave him tied up naked at the motel (which is in a bad neighborhood of course). Then there are the truly sexual urban-legends of note.....

Stories about other guys getting laid in nefarious (often-impossible) situations, tales of women either being implausibly-willing or happily a nymphomaniac, and "sure fire" methods, techniques, or intoxicants of getting a woman to desire the man in question....

Stories and legends told in locker-rooms, gymnasiums, Bars and Nightclubs as well as at Poker parties and on "guy's night out" have always been extremely entertaining, even if the storyteller is not the best source of reality!

Wherever there are men gathered together with no women (or their mothers) to overhear them, stories are crafted and told in an oral tradition handed down from one generation of American men to another, without fail! Wherever there are poker-parties, strip-club outings, and guys-night-out events where the men are men, one of them will tell a tale of dramatic-erotic "success" with a woman (or two) and naturally the storyteller is always the "hero" who scored the "smokin' hot babe with big tits" in a quick and easy manner. Now the storyteller is likely telling the truth or at least a portion of the real story as not everyone has the flair for telling fiction convincingly, and thus if they were lying, their buddies would see right through. The storyteller may at the very worst tell a fantasy of his to his buddies but in the first-person as if the fantasy had really occurred, though this takes some convincingly-thorough detailing. For those "fantasy-storytellers", I'd strongly suggest "rehearsing" your tale of sexual conquest well-before you initially tell it to your buddies, as no greater lie-detector there is than a group of friends who know you!

What fantasies would there be without fabulously-titillating stories even if some are embellished or fabricated? Some of the most entertaining man-to-man tales deal with pleasures of the flesh (or wishful thinking thereof) and thus sex in "urban legends" is enticing enough for both storyteller as well as the doubtful listener!

I recall one of the earliest "legends" I heard spoken about between young guys like myself was when I was a teenager in the early-to-mid 1980's, one about a young guy delivering flowers to the address of a lonely middle-aged (38-45 years) widow who subsequently invites the delivery guy inside her domicile and instead of paying cash for the flowers/delivery she seduces him for a no-strings-attached romp in her bedroom.....

I call this the Older Woman Wants Young Stud legend and I remember hearing stories of such a scenario when I was in high school, though I'm sorry to admit it had never happened to me... maybe because I didn't deliver flowers or food to lonely widows as my job back then, I was stocking the shelves of a Department Store from 3:30 to 11:00pm!

I've seen this similar scenario played out in a few well-done R-rated films such as

The Last American Virgin (A Golan-Globus Film directed by Boaz Davidson 1982)

where three Senior High buddies deliver pizzas to a voluptuous (and older) Spanish woman named "Carmella" who seduces two of them into screwing her brains loose in her bedroom...then her sailor hubby comes home unexpectedly and just imagine the rest!

Reality of this sexual urban legend is that it often rings true as far as older women hooking up with younger men goes, and in the recent year or so of this book being written, several high-profile cases of hot female school teachers having carnal relations with their male students has been all over the media. However, it's a CRIME guys, if you are under the age of consent! So don't get the hot teacher arrested just for playing strip-poker with the likes of you….yes, it's a great "conquest" to lay an older woman but wait until you're 18 so the hot older woman doesn't get locked up, she'll do no good in Jail!!

There is also the Sexy Female Hitchhiker who may be hitchhiking alone in attractive attire with a proclivity for seducing whoever picks her up….unh-hunh, this legend is more apt to be seen in an X-rated movie than in reality but it is something that has made the rounds in urban legend! Trouble is, the sexy female hitchhiker is usually one of the following: an undercover cop looking to bust truckers for solicitation, or she is a serial killer who "rides" the horny, unsuspecting guy then brutally murders him.

Most women wouldn't hitchhike alone, mainly out of modern women's collective fear of men and even if they do, they're generally not standing on the roadside for very long as a woman hitcher is not seen as the possible lunatic a male hitchhiker might be. Still, a sexy female hitchhiker is a sexual urban legend mixed with whatever the subtext may become such as the driver getting "repaid" for giving her a ride via oral sex or a "quickie" romp in the backseat or sleeper-cab. In reality it's possible, but you'd have better luck knocking on doors to try and find a horny widow somewhere than a horny female hitchhiker!

Then there is the Couple in the Crosshairs as I call it, something Hollywood has portrayed in horror/suspense films quite often. A (usually young) couple go off to a secluded area in a vehicle to make out or have sex and someone sees them (or has followed them) then that someone watching the lovers gets pissed off and murders them both right where they are doing it. Couples making out late at night in cars were often targets of the serial killer David Berkowitz (Son of Sam) in NYC of the late 1970's, FBI Profilers denoting the killer had been sexually-frustrated when he killed them.

One of the best Hollywood films on this "theme" is one of my favorite Charles Bronson movies, 10 To Midnight (A Golan-Globus film, Directed by J. Lee Thompson 1983) where a seasoned cop has to hunt down a serial killer who targets gorgeous women and their boyfriends just because he is unpopular with the ladies! Great movie and it's readily available on DVD, I recommend you checking it out if you haven't seen it already.

How many of us normal guys have seen a beautiful woman paired up with some other dude we felt was less of a man than we are, to be with such a hot chick?! It's only natural to feel that angst, especially if the guy is a fat-ass troll or some disheveled loser, but we don't follow the couple to their car and shoot them, of course. A couple making out in a parked car out in the middle of nowhere where they're approached by a darkly-clad individual who may or may not have a weapon and is pissed off because he doesn't have such a tasty love affair in his own life, a shot rings out and a scream, then a second shot.

Yeah, it's typically the male lovebird that gets clipped first, followed by his girlfriend's scream and then a second shot to finish her off. So why does the legend have it always a sexually-frustrated male dispatching the loving couple to oblivion, why not a frustrated female armed with a pistol or machete who gets so incensed about the man she wants sticking it to her female rival (that bitch on the cheerleading squad, etc.) and she goes out to clip both of them at "the point" where they're making out???!! Sounds reasonable

Let's not forget the famous "Honey, it's not what it looks like!" legend of a husband coming home from work (early) to walk into his beloved home and find his lovely wife engrossed in a torrid sex act right on their marital bed....with another man!

What happens next is open to suggestion, as most married guys reading this might conclude with the "I'd kick his ass" statement or the "I'd kill'em both" response, but real-life scenarios usually end up somewhere in-between. I've heard stories of this where the extramarital lover bails out the bedroom window (regardless of how high up it is) upon hearing the husband entering the house, or the wife's "boyfriend" narrowly escapes her jilted hubby's wrath by being lightning-fast on the way out the door, window, etc.

Of course the cheating wife will, in usual fashion, have an "explanation" of some sorts, which is where the popular "Honey, it's not what it looks like" remark comes from!

This is yet another urban legend that's been played out in X-rated films and a lot of Hollywood features over the years, usually as comic relief. Now there are documented murder investigations where the husband came home to find his wife cheating, grabs a weapon and commits a double-murder or a double-murder-suicide, but those cases are few and far between. Still, it behooves a cheating spouse to make sure their significant other is indeed staying at work for the duration of the time they'll be playing hide-the-salami with their newfound lover. So much for having one's cake and eating hers too!

Yes my friends, there are real "Swingers" out there…couples (married or otherwise) who "swing" with other couples at exclusive parties or sleep-overs and it's where the term

"wife-swapper" comes from. Some Swingers magazines in the 80's and early 90's before the Internet, advertised couples who swapped with strangers and even some married men who liked to watch while other men pump-the-daisies out of their wives. This is that

Take My Wife urban legend where a married man lets another man (usually younger and more physically-endowed) to fuck his wife, oftentimes while watching up close, through the keyhole of a door, or video-monitor.*The 1991 Erotic-Thriller film Animal Instincts is about this very sort of legend! Outside of adult-themed movies and the dreams of every normal guy who has ever eaten his heart out over a buddy's smoking-hot wife, this sexual urban legend is a rare oddity, though not an impossible one! Despite what may be a rare couple's sexual proclivities into cuckolding and voyeurism, the green-eyed monster of jealousy will more than likely raise its ugly head to take a big wet bite out of someone's bare ass at some point in time. Actually, that's about the time you might see a shotgun barrel leveled at your head as you rise up from the bed to leave. Hell, it might even be a set-up for the old man to kill his wife and blame it on the "intruder" (THAT'S YOU!!!)

Murder mysteries and swinging couples aside, getting "permission" is extremely rare.

Show me a husband who lets other men pump their fuel into his wife and I'll show you a divorce settlement that comes quicker than the wife does!

It's within every normal, horny young man's fantasy-catalog to wish indulgence with more than one sexy female at a time. The ever-elusive Threesome where one man is cool, attractive, and built well enough for two women to want his bod at the same time can be viewed in porno flicks and drunken frat parties but is rarely accessible in the average working-class venue. If one wants a threesome with a pair of lovely ladies at the same time, I recommend traveling to a Nevada brothel and paying for two women to screw your brains loose together! It's safer that way, trust me. Imagine being told that you're gonna be a daddy by both of the women you hammered on that special night?!

Generally speaking, if any of you guys are lucky enough to score two women at the same time (in real life!) don't be surprised when those two lovely ladies unleash their petty insecurities and fits of jealousy upon you after your pleasurable threesome ~

"Hey, why did you come with her and not me?!" "What, I wasn't good enough for you?" "You're in love with that bitch aren't you?!" "I'm gonna kick her ass….and yours!!"

Now when it comes to one woman getting-it-on with two men at the same time, better watch one of Amber Lynn's Porn Flicks to see what it looks like because in reality, it just doesn't happen! Okay, two men….getting naked and going horizontal with one woman in the same room, on the same bed or sofa….yeah right!! That would run about as smoothly as a gerbil in the washing machine. No friggin' way, unless the two men were identical twin brothers and had everything the same physically, no man would get anywhere near another naked man to "share" a woman between them at the same time because of the obvious "homo" concerns and the "what if he's better than me?" worry. In reality, I've seen where a woman took on two guys in the same night (because I was one of them) but we took turns with her in the bedroom individually, not at the same time! That was an older-woman-wants-two-younger-men party I had the luck of attending back in 1991 and it's a fond memory now but that's how I once "shared" a woman with a buddy!

Then there is what I call the Ghost Romp where a man (sometimes a woman) claims to have had a sexual dalliance with a stranger whom they never see again once the sex is over. Sounds like someone might have been drinking too much or they may have been experiencing what is commonly called lucid-dreaming. A man finds himself in bed with a woman and she "rides" him all the way to Phoenix, then he wakes up to find her gone but in a place where he couldn't have possibly met a woman so quickly, no one else saw her leave, he can't recall her name, etc. etc. Another "legend" spoken of this scenario has the woman unseen in a mirror she walks by and another had a woman appearing totally nude in a public place to escort the man to a motel room....again, this one has lucid-dreaming written all over it since no one else seemed to witness a naked woman in public! Perhaps a bit too much alcohol included in the storytellers spreading this legend, but this one is a fairly old story beginning with the ancient "Hag" tales of men being "raped" by a female spirit (Succubus) draining their life-energy while having sex with the men, and these such ancient stories actually led to "witch hunts" in Europe and America over 200 years ago!

Yes, there is the female version of this legend in the form of "ghost lovers" often written about in Romance novels penned by female writers of note. Seems women's fantasies regarding a male ghost-lover of their "ideal" guy driving home his manhood between her thighs in the dead of night are quite prolific, and that's cool.... though in reality a ghost can't open the door for her or pay her way when it comes time to eat dinner and go shopping for new shoes!

Not to mention the UFO Abduction-Seduction, where a man is "abducted" by an Alien Spacecraft (not witnessed by anyone else of course) where the man is taken up into the ship and introduced to a naked humanoid female alone in some kind of chamber, either lying on a sofa or bed of some kind asking the abducted man to "make love" to her, which of course he promptly does, having sex with a Alien Woman who resembles a human female for the most part. Soon afterward, the hot alien chick informs her kidnapped mate that she will have his offspring up-up-and-away in her own galaxy!(talk about no worries with child support payments!). This "legend" has actually made the "UFO Hunters" circuit in the USA for some years since the 1970's and I remember one tabloid newspaper when I was a kid, telling one version being some Brazilian Farmer abducted by a UFO while he was tending his crops on a hot afternoon, and he was summarily seduced by a curvaceous female alien who resembled a human female in most ways except that she was bald and had a pointed chin. After their lovemaking occurred (that would be where I'd wonder if the other Aliens on the UFO were watching and/or filming me and the hot alien-chick as we go-at-it) the shapely, pointy-chinned alien chick tells the lucky farmer in sign-language that she will give birth to their intergalactic-interbred child somewhere far off in outer space where she hails from. The human farmer is then unceremoniously "dropped off" back in his own farm field and noticed that the time-elapsed had been just 2 minutes! (that's what I call a "quickie" even if time-travel equipment is used). He tells his story to the Tabloid newspaper of course and remarks how he often wonders about his "child" being up there in space somewhere. Yeah Bub, you got to dump your probably-toxic genes into some alien chick from another galaxy....AS IF some superior species of inter-galactic-traveling beings would fly millions of light years to this soaking-wet dirtball of a planet just for the privilege of mixing it up with some peasant human miscreant? COME ON!!

Anyway, it's another sex legend that bears mentioning, and one I've read about consistently in UFO Lore (I am a Science-Fiction fan though). The idea of space aliens capturing humans for DNA-swaps would probably be of the needle-prick-extraction or cut-a-chunk-out-of-your-ass variety, not humanoid sexual congress as suggested by the outlandish stories told of such in tabloid newspaper history. Hey, since "inter-racial" relationships seem to be so in-vogue nowadays, how about "inter-species" relationships? Yeah, hot, well-shaped, bald, pointy-chinned alien chicks come down to hook-up with human men and instantly become popular in the United States…Why??? Because the alien chicks don't hate your parents, they don't take all your hard-earned money and they never-say-no to sex with their human guy….

Then to be fair, alien males come to earth and mix it up with human women and that becomes "hip" as well….docile, smiling-all-the-time, filthy-rich, clean-shaven, and "sensitive" Alien guys with detachable sex organs, in demand by women everywhere!

(Yes, "detachable" so that the woman can take it from him before he goes anywhere without her!). Then there would be the "jealous" human men who'd shoot a woman with her space alien lover in their parked car or complain about their wives leaving them to go get "alien dick"….and a human woman suing a pointy-chinned alien chick in court over stealing her prom date! Yes, inter-galactic sex would be so much fun, wouldn't it?

There is also what we all know as Peeping Tom, a crime in most jurisdictions nowadays because it is synonymous with an individual(usually a man) sneaking a look-see through the window, glass-door, or otherwise clandestine view of a domicile wherein another individual(usually a female) is conducting private endeavors such as showering, sleeping, having sex, or just being naked. Basically a "peeping tom" is looking (literally) for a cheap thrill by going for a glimpse through some woman's window in the dark of night, hoping to see some bare booty without getting caught and rightly arrested!

The term "Peeping Tom" is about 1,000 years old from a time in Medieval England where an English Lord raised taxes on his Serfs to the point his beautiful young wife, Lady Godiva, begged and pleaded with him to lift the taxation, stating his higher taxes were "stripping the shirts off the backs of peasants". Well the Lord told his Lady that if she were to ride naked on horseback through the town, he'd relax the taxes on the Serfs.

A woman of her word, Lady Godiva set out to carry out her soon-to-be-infamous ride, informing the town so noone would really see her naked, something the local peasants of that time evidently took seriously (fearful of her husband) and everyone took shelter at the exact time Lady Godiva took off nude on horseback to ride through the town. Everyone left the streets, locked their doors, shut their window shudders and cowed upon hearing the hoof-beats of Lady Godiva's horse approaching….everyone that is…except a local Tailor named Thomas! He bore a hole through his shudders to sneak a peek at the gloriously naked Lady Godiva riding along the front of his shop, and he was as the legend has it, the only man in the countryside that day who saw the ride of Lady Godiva!

1892 Oil Painting "Lady Godiva"(at her moment of decision) by Edmund Blair Leighton

ADVENTURES IN EXOTIC NIGHTLIFE

So be honest…how many of us guys have crossed the threshold into a Night Club which happened to feature Exotic Dancers as the main attraction? If there could be a realistic count done, I'd wager there would be about an 85% ratio of American men whom have attended a Strip-Club during some point in their lives! Yes, I can speak only for American guys because I haven't lived anywhere else on this muddy planet (nor would I want to)."Gentleman's Clubs" as they're often called, are not as common as one may think on the American landscape, but one can find Strip-Clubs (as I call them) in most major US Cities, Resort Towns, and popular "Vacation-destinations" on shore or off and nowadays the gentlemen seeking entry into any of these places need to be at least the age of 21. **Before** there were theaters, Cable-TV, VCRs, Home Computers and DVD players where a man could view the naked female form, there were only the Burlesque Halls/Strip-Clubs! American Strip-Clubs are like most "restaurant" establishments: lower-tier, middle-class or upper-class depending on the local clientele and patronage. Having patronized all three types in the past myself, I can say the old adage of "your get what you pay for" applies with Strip-Clubs as it does most other things and if you are seeking a fun evening with some of the finest-looking female beauties undressing and dancing in front of you while you drink a beer and eat hot wings, then you have to factor this in! It is a strong indicator that once you walk into a Strip-Club and you instantly have to dodge a thrown bottle of beer and see a Bowie Knife held up by the guy in front of you (yes, this happened to me once) then it's a good idea to turn your ass around and drive off to an "upscale" Strip-Club where you're less likely to need stitches by closing time! A Strip-Club you have to "fight your way out of" is also the type of establishment I'd strongly advise avoiding (unless of course you like going to jail or the emergency room on a Friday night). Now if you are a man seeking the kind of late night entertainment involving scantily-clad women taking it off on stage to the sound of popular music while you drink your favorite late night beverage, there are a few choice "Rules" I hereby recommend you follow in order to have a good time at such:

1. A Strip-Club is not a Brothel (they're not hookers, so don't treat them as such)
2. The Dancers do not love you and generally never will (so don't fall for them!)
3. Keep your damn hands to yourself (most Clubs will throw you out for touching)
4. Use cash, not credit cards! (credit card use in strip-clubs will bankrupt you!)

In any given Strip-Club there are those ladies who are "House Dancers", the regular fare of exotic dancers~usually local gals~who frequently, if not weekly, dance at that particular Club and are on the payroll there. House Dancers are the most common at any Gentlemen's Club whether the place be lower-level or upper-crust. House Dancers are the bread-n-butter of the Strip-Club, bringing in the "regular" male patrons from the Local Guys to the Golfers, Vacationers, Bachelor-Partiers, or occasional customers who pop-in once a month or so. The House Dancers often become "popular" with some male patrons and keep the guys coming back again and again to get a lap-dance from them, thus keeping a regular patronage for the Strip-Clubs they work for and thus the happy guys tell other strip-club seekers about the dancers they like and thus more guys pay the $10-to-$20 entry fee to go inside the Strip Clubs to see the regular House Dancers they've heard other men talk about. House Dancers can be some of the best-looking and best-shaped young ladies you may have ever laid eyes on (minus their clothes) and they are the ones who are dancing at Clubs almost every night of the week and on Saturdays, some of them taking on "personas" and funny names such as "Desiree", "Diabla", "Betty Big Boobs" and even "Asslee". Yes, they can be a lot of fun....when they're dancing for you! But woe unto those fellas whom allow some of the lovely ladies to sit at their tables for too long a time…sitting there telling you all about their worries, hopes, fears, and wretched boyfriends, while sipping drinks you pay for and making you listen to all of their personal "drama" is enough to #1 Bankrupt you for all the money you end of spending on that one chatty dancer sitting with you #2 Drive you crazy with all the insane chatter about boyfriends ruining their lives and how much they hate the other dancers in the Club! So never let one dancer hog all your time by planting herself at your table for the duration, no matter how delicious she appears to be! The other ladies whom appear exquisitely nude on stage in Gentlemen's Clubs are known as "Feature Dancers" and they are the "special guests" to say the least, often showing up for one or two nights at the Strip-Club for usually a higher price than the House Dancers ever see and at the behest of the Club Owners. Feature dancers are the commodities of the Dance Circuit and are in-demand because they are often huge-breasted "Stars" of the dance circuit by having made a fabulous name for themselves and posing nude in men's magazines in the past, or they're X-rated Film Starlets whom take it off in Strip-Clubs for extra cash (which they get a lot of) and to broaden their Adult Entertainment Career. It is usually a rare treat to walk into a Strip-Club on a night when a Feature Dancer is strutting her stuff on stage, for Feature Dancers are truly the professionals of the Exotic Dance Circuit and travel the Continent on "tours" of the upper-class Clubs from coast to coast.

House Dancers hate the Feature Dancers, but both can be very entertaining as long as you don't show your ass in the process and tip'em good! Strip-Clubs are one medium of "late night entertainment" you can't find in the comfort of your own living room, unless you rent a stripper video, which many of the famous "Feature Dancers" have made available these days. Sitting inside a Strip-Club watching the ladies dance as they take it off for tips and your applause (mostly for your tips and never forget Strippers do not love you!). Still one of the few places where adult entertainment is restricted and guarded against viewing by those under the age of 18, Strip-Clubs are a man's nighttime entertainment of the vicarious-but-expensive variety and definitely fit into "adult entertainment" where it is relatively safe and accessible by ADULTS ONLY! Though I could fill a volume about all the "House Dancers" I've met over the years at Strip-Clubs, I have to focus on giving honorable mention to the few "Feature Dancers" I have met and enjoyed a drink with back in the 1990's when I traveled up and down the eastern USA hitting the Clubs during my gambling days. Whether or not a Feature Dancer was a full-time Stripper, Porn Star, or one of those uniquely-endowed femmes famous for their layouts in men's magazines, I met a select few whom are best remembered as the most talented in their entertaining craft, ladies with stunning beauty and incredible bodies that I'm sure are remembered to this day by a million men who cheered them on from the floors of Gentlemen's Clubs.

The one thing special about Adult Entertainment of the Strip-Club variety, besides the fact it is safely away from kids and those who don't wish to see it (unlike what pops up on the Internet nowadays) is that Strip-Clubs and other similar places such as "topless" restaurants give a gentleman the opportunity to appreciate live-and-in-person, the God-given human female physique in all of it's natural splendor, some of whom have "famous" bodies like the shapely Exotic Dancers profiled on the preceding pages. True, it's not everyone's cup of tea but one usually has a good time in a Strip-Club as long as it's an upper-class joint with a fairly high cover-charge to keep the real riff-raff scumbags outside. The ones where you can have a meal while watching the dancers on stage are a premium, because there is something about having a topless waitress bring you a steak dinner that just seems so "righteous"! ☒ Strip-Clubs are often a punch-line for most people who'll laugh upon hearing one even being mentioned, or just an excursion with an excuse attached to it such as the "Bachelor Party" or the "Golf Trip". Yes, every avid Golfer I know goes to the Strip-Clubs during their trips to Golf Resorts such as in Myrtle Beach SC and Orlando, FL. (though I personally never understood the appeal of Golf!) If you are the "Bachelor" at a Strip-Club with your buddies, don't be shocked if they tell the DJ about you and you find yourself foisted up on stage to be fondled by a dancer or two then ridiculed by the DJ along with the jeering male audience! Exotic Dancers tend to treat either "birthday boys" or "last night bachelors" really special with close up lap-dances and maybe even a special treat such as a couch-dance in one of the back rooms where she'll dance all over you while you lay down on a sofa, or maybe put her boobs in your face without you having to tip her. Feature Dancer Tawny Peaks was once sued by a Club customer for allegedly hitting him with her big boobs during his bachelor party in 1998 but the Judge ruled in her favor! I remember walking into one Club up in New York and seeing Feature Dancer Tiffany Towers dancing totally-nude on stage except for a blue head-band around her head and a fake hunting-Knife strapped to her right thigh along with her garter....she was a huge-busted blonde vixen (55FFF I was told) and she danced along the edge of the stage trying to keep up with the beat of the heavy metal rock music playing, those monster titties of hers nearly causing Tiffany to topple off the stage a few times as she leaned over to kiss her male admirers! Tiffany Towers was a sweet gal whom I had the off-chance to meet at one of that Club's Bar counters after her show, she was getting a drink before retiring to the locker room...what other Bar could I walk up to and find a well-stacked, totally-naked blonde standing there smiling at me? I also met Feature-Dancer Sarenna Lee at the "Crazy Horse" Strip Club in Myrtle Beach back in 1995 and her dance-routine was uniquely-sexy, not to mention the fact she looked like a Marilyn Monroe with humungous boobs! The Crazy Horse in Myrtle Beach (now out of business) didn't allow it's dancers to go bottomless so Sarenna Lee pulled down her red bikini-bottom at the end of her routine for the audience, only she had a skin-colored g-string beneath it anyway and pointed at me standing there to say "You looked!".

I'll never forget seeing Sarenna Lee do one routine on stage involving the center pole, the way her huge boobs squeezed around the brass pole as she climbed it was a sight to be seen, every man in that audience was eating his heart out over that performance!

The "Crazy Horse" of Myrtle Beach back in the mid-1990's also had incredible House-Dancers such as Robin Thomas and Alice Gordon, two of the best-shaped females I ever laid eyes on. Robin and Alice were the best "House-Dancers" to ever wear a g-string in all of Myrtle Beach, South Carolina!

One night back in 1996 after spending the better part of a rainy evening at the Crazy Horse Strip-Club in Myrtle Beach, I walked out to the parking lot to find two of the regular "House Dancers" standing under the awning, waiting for a ride from someone who was not coming afterall. They asked if they could hitch a ride with me and since I had already gotten to "know" them in the Club, I agreed so two barely-dressed blonde strippers jumped into my Chevy Blazer and we ended up back at my Hotel room. I never got the real names of the two twenty-something bleach-blonde strippers just their stage-names: "Sunny" and "Stormy". Needless to say the giggling conversation between me and the two sexy strippers turned to doing shots of Goldschlager off the top of the Hotel suite's TV set with me getting more intoxicated than the two strippers were! Before I knew it the room was spinning and I was flat on my back on the bed, with one of the ladies pulling my shorts off as I lay flat on my back laughing at the two blondes who were already naked and smoking one of my cigars! Long story short…both Sunny and Stormy took turns riding on my "pogo-stick" as I lay there drunk on my back wearing just a t-shirt and a grin. I remember looking up to see each stripper take turns riding on my rod while smoking one of my cigars and talking shit back and forth to one another.

I pretended to stay "passed out" on the bed while Sunny and Stormy had their fun swinging on my pole, enjoying the sensation myself even with the room spinning and my head about to explode from the alcohol consumption. Just as one of the blondes finished me off, I passed out for real and didn't wake up until about 5am to find myself half naked with one hell of a hang-over, my money-clip missing (but they left the traveler's checks) a black lace bra hanging off the doorknob, and of course both Sunny and Stormy were GONE! I couldn't complain too much, I had a good time and didn't care about the cash in the money-clip, as it was my "stripper money" anyway! Being taken advantage of by two hot blondes is a good thing, though I must admit it would have been much more memorable for me had I not been roaring-drunk! That's what can happen to a man who takes two silly strippers back to his room and drinks a bottle of Jack Daniels with them

Many Exotic Dancers tend to view their male patrons as "money-clips" and therefore you'll be disappointed once you figure out the dancers do not love you and only want to tease the cash out of your pants, nothing else! Still, it's a good time if you've got your head screwed on tight and use your money wisely, though not impossible as I discovered, it is unlikely you'd get most Exotic Dancers to go back to your Hotel Room with you.

Like I mentioned previously, only use CASH at a Strip-Club because once you begin using credit or debit cards, I assure you that you might regret it later on because those expenditures in such an establishment will show up on bank statements and/or credit card bills in greater amounts than you had imagined they would be at the time. If you wish to imbibe alcohol at a Strip-Club, by all means take a Taxi Cab to and from the Strip-Club because the local cops often sit outside waiting for drunk patrons to get in their cars and drive off. Cab fare is far less expensive than a DWI Conviction I assure you!

There is an undeniable aspect of "entertainment" for men when it comes to watching pleasantly-built women in various stages of undress, whether it is dancing on a stage right in front of them or on a videotape. Naked women dancing, teasing, bouncing and posing provocative have a fantasy quality that exceeds interest in virtually all other forms of entertainment with few exceptions! From the early burlesque halls of the 1940s to the advent of adult-rated filmmaking in the 1970's, to the Strip-Clubs and major men's magazines of the 80's and 90's, naked women have entertained men with a vengeance!

Exotic Dancer

NIKI KNOCKERS

"I just love a Cop with a big gun!"

Of all the Professional Exotic Dancers I have met over the past 20 years, there is one who sticks out as the best dancer to ever set foot on a stage with the most well-shaped female physique and prettiest head atop of it all, and her name was "Niki Knockers"! I first saw Niki in a men's magazine back in the early 90's posing nude in a classy, less-than-hardcore manner, because as I found out later, Niki was a Class Act! When I saw her perform on stage in an upscale New York Strip-Club in the late 1990's, I and my buddy Terry were lucky enough to find stage-front seats where we'd be right there in front of her when she danced along the horse-shoe stage. Sitting there watching intently as the DJ announced the arrival of NIKI KNOCKERS on stage, I found myself transfixed, almost hypnotized by the voluptuous blonde dancer coming out of nowhere in an outfit that seemed like a second layer of skin she would soon shed for her male audience. Niki moved with the music in a snake-like fashion, grinning ear-to-ear like a hungry lioness. I let out a howl of approval, then low-and-behold Miss Niki danced her way over to the section of the stage where I and my buddy Terry (both of us were Law Enforcement Officers from Va. at the time, on vacation) sat staring up at her. She decided to begin peeling off her attire over us as we watched in awe of how she did so in such a short circle (only the best ones can dance and strip in the same spot!). Her big boobs spilled out in bouncy melee as the music played, shaking those righteously huge ta-tas of hers over my buddy and I as we stared up at her like helpless puppy dogs. Niki danced across the stage to the howls and applause of every man in the joint, shedding the rest of her skin-tight outfit seconds later, everyone on their feet in glee of the naked vixen. She then gyrated back toward me, that incredible body of hers keeping up with the music in a way I didn't think would be possible!

It is well-proven that Exotic-Dancers "pick" men in the Club they'd feel most comfortable with giving a lap-dance to or talking with after their routine is over, so Miss Niki chose me and my buddy Terry as guys she felt comfortable flirting with. She spoke to us as she danced at our end of the stage again and I put a $20 bill in her g-string as she knelt down, then when she turned to face us again, Niki Knockers let Terry shove his hand (and $20) right up between her big boobs, making an "OH!" face as she sandwiched his hand between her huge "knockers".

*Note~ About a month later, I looked in a men's magazine that was featuring photos of Niki Knockers on stage at that same Strip-Club we met her at, and one photo was of a black man's hand shoved between her big boobs with that look on her face! That was my buddy Terry's hand tipping her $20 between her tits!

Niki's dance routine was absolutely stunning that night, and she had the guys on their feet clapping, whistling, and howling in approval of her on-stage talent. Shortly after she exited the stage and just before Terry and I got up to leave (since it was 2am!) out came Niki Knockers walking over to us at our seats wearing only a tube-top over her boobs and a skimpy mini-skirt over her g-string, her shoulder-length blonde hair down and wavy as it had been earlier, a humored expression on her face as she greeted us. We talked and talked, Niki sitting down at the stage between Terry and I. As it turned out, Niki really liked guys who worked in the Law Enforcement Field and she wrapped her arms around my neck to whisper in my ear: "I just love a cop with a big gun!" Niki was way too cool, chatting away between Terry and I like she'd known us for years. We had a round of drinks, then she had to leave because the Club was closing soon. She got up, gave us both a hug and a kiss, then walked back to where she had come from to leave, waving back at us as she left . No longer an Exotic Dancer, Niki is now a legend all her own!

Exotic Dancer Niki Knockers (signed photo to Ken Knight circa 1993)

Exotic Dancer

BUNNY JO TYLER

"Hop this way please…"

Exotic Dancer "Bunny Jo Tyler" was a staple in major men's clubs throughout the American South from the very late 1980's to the early 90's, known for her outrageous outfits (never worn for very long of course) and wigs of platinum/bleach-blonde/redhead etc. accenting her marvelous physique and adding to her gyrating dance routines. Never to pose nude except for her own personal mail-order-fan-club photos, Bunny Jo Tyler was sweet to her fans as long as they behaved themselves. I caught her dancing at a South Carolina Strip-Club in 1990 and remember her taking a wad of money from my mouth by squeezing her big boobs across my face as I stood there at the stage (some Clubs allow that). A memorable dancer and gorgeous woman of the busty variety who retired from the scene sometime in the early 1990's, Bunny Jo Tyler is one of the "Ultimates"

Bunny Jo Tyler (autographed photo to Ken Knight circa 1990)

Exotic Dancer

LOVETTE

"Want me to tattoo you?"

One of the most popular American Feature Dancers from the late 1990's up until about 2006 was a gorgeously-endowed little lady who went by the stage name of "Lovette" and toured the USA coast-to-coast exotic dancing in the finest Gentlemen's Clubs to include on in Richmond Virginia where I first met Lovette face-to-boobs and got to hang out.

To tell the truth, I had been a member of her mail-order fan club for two years beforehand because as it turned out Lovette was also a top-name Adult Film Starlet during the mid-to-late 1990's and she had picked up one of my earlier novels and read it, so she already knew who I was before I ran into her at that Richmond Strip-Club in August of 2002.

Lovette was a lady whose short size made her a very appealing big-breasted dancer whose overall shape was gloriously rare to behold, that body of hers dancing on stage an awesome sight to say the least. She was a Feature dancer who was very friendly to her fans (if she knew you) and if you weren't a creep. I remember Lovette once told me she carried a Glock 9mm pistol that she kept just for "creeps"! Her stage show was extravagant in costumes, my favorite being the "devil" costume she wore often during her dance routines. Lovette liked to pick a man out of the audience to pour baby-oil all over her nude body on the stage and that night in August of 2002 I was the man she picked for that duty. In the Club's "couch room" (where the photo of Lovette and I was taken) she told me about her side-work as a tattoo-artist and that most of her own tattoos were done by herself. She then offered to tattoo me as long as I got naked with her! I would have taken her up on it but alas, I had already spent all of my cash by that time so I couldn't get a naked tattooing from the gorgeous and incredibly-well-shaped Lovette ☹

If you ever get the opportunity to view any of her X-rated films such as Flip of a Coin,

I wager you will find Lovette a very unique specimen of female you won't ever forget! She also may be found in many soft-core DVD features by Napali Video as well as in other straight-to DVD and/or CD-ROM videos available online and online-auction sites as well. She told me she was a "Closet Goth" and loved horror films, particularly Vampire flicks and she did pose nude for a comic book series by Kirk Lindo in the late 1990's, her petite, well-stacked body lending a whole new delicious appeal to "sexy vampires" in comic books! Lovette and I kept in touch for a couple of years later though her mail-order fan club and email exchanges, and by 2006 she had gone back to College for a Degree in Nursing, thus leaving Exotic Dance and X-rated films behind to pursue a career in Medicine. I cannot think of a better-looking woman I'd want standing by my hospital bed, checking my vitals and giving me a shot of morphine!

If any of you guys happen to wake up in a hospital in the near future and a beautiful petite blonde nurse with huge "headlights" walks in, she might just be this gorgeous former Exotic Dancer who will save your life but break your heart.......

LOVETTE (with Ken Knight) in Richmond Va. August 2, 2002.

Exotic Dancer and Film Review

EBONY AYES

Arguably the sexiest Black Female Starlet to take her clothes off between 1985 and 1995, Ebony Ayes is a legend of erotic entertainment from Adult Films' memorable "Silver Age" and one of the most talented Exotic Dancers I have ever laid eyes on! Having seen her dance routine in an Atlanta Strip-Club in the 1990's, I had to mention her here because woman had a body shaped like no other (36JJ bust) bouncing on stage in jiggling sync to Motown music. Ebony Ayes starred in numerous X-rated feature films such as THE GODMOTHER where her uniquely-crafted physique was used ever so abundantly with her co-stars! If my memory serves me right, in the 1987 X-rated spoof Flesh For Frankenstein Ebony Ayes "rides" black porn actor Ray Victory on top of a bar counter, which was actually funny to watch because the two performers were a bit over-lubricated (if you know what I mean!). Ebony Ayes left Adult Films in 1995 but continued Exotic Dance in her home town of Atlanta GA. Without a doubt, the finest quality X-rated film starring Ebony Ayes is THE GODMOTHER.

Ebony Ayes in THE GODMOTHER (1988)
X-rated film Directed by John Stagliano

Yes, many Feature-Dancers on the Strip Club Circuit have done X-rated films, though certainly not all of them! X-rated films are, well, what they are…depictions of actual sexual congress between consenting actors and actresses for a limited (and legal) adult audience. Back before the advent of the Internet and computer-downloads, films that were rated "X" were truly restricted and pretty much inaccessible by minors under the age of 18 as far as marketing was concerned. Confined to the back rooms of Video Stores and Theaters mostly in or around major cities and mail-order catalogs (i.e. one had to search!) X-rated videotapes of the "Silver Age" (1984-1995) were performed by and directed by paid "professionals", and oftentimes filmed as scripted erotic stories, not just "wall-bangers". Even the video box-covers of the time had class, often appearing sexy and alluring but leaving more to the imagination (instead of hardcore images). The "Silver Age" of American X-Rated was the peak of the "soap opera" theatrics seen in such features, not to mention the "time travel" scenarios which had the sexy starlets dressed up in Medieval, Renaissance, or Colonial costume attire while "getting it on" for the cameras all the while acting out some humorous plots around the sex scenes.

There were also X-rated "spoofs" of popular Hollywood films, pop-culture themes, and even some classic literature stories such as one 1990's VIVID® video about "Sinderella" starring the late great porn starlet Savannah. I even remember one porn film spoofing a certain popular science-fiction TV show about "boldly going" somewhere (ha-ha).

Christy Canyon's "Canyon Video" series in the early 90's also had "detective thriller" themes to them which were some of the best films Christy ever got naked in. Though XXX-rated films are not known for their trained Thespians, many of the "Silver Age" performers such as Christy Canyon, Lynn Lemay, Victoria Paris, and Sabrina Dawn did know how to ACT and their films were all the better for it, not to mention the outstanding Directors of the time such as Paul Thomas, John Leslie, John Stagliano, as well as Henri Pachard obviously knowing how to direct dialogue and human interaction as well as all those sex-scenes, not to mention having an eye for choosing the best-shaped and "sized" performers for their films. Unlike the "amateur" porn videos that flooded the market after the advent of the Internet, the professionally-made adult films of the 80's and early 90's had very attractive "cast lists" and gave it's limited adult audience the big tits, bigger dicks and overly-vibrant carnal relations expected in an X-rated feature film of the time.

Yes, "excess" was always welcome in the 80's/90's porn films which is why some of the best-shaped female starlets such as Christy Canyon, Sabrina Dawn, Tami Monroe, Aja, Britt Morgan and Tori Welles were usually paired with some chiseled "big guy" like Randy Spears, Peter North or Steve Drake for their sex scenes back in the day. Adult Video-buyers wanted to see only the best bodies "hammering-away" at one another on their TV screens, so those X-rated films of yesteryear gave their adult audience exactly that! Despite the fact that X-rated films are about SEX (and the entertainment derived from watching other people do it) it still was neat to watch the "in-between" scenes while one's favorite nude-performers are clothed and interacting with one other. The Films of the late 80's/early 90's also played more on certain elements of entertainment value such as "anticipation" and "leaving more to the imagination" for the adult viewer. Leaving more to one's imagination is oftentimes entertaining in itself, a sort of "tease" that leaves you wanting to see a sequel or just IMAGINE in your own mind what might have really happened next between the actors and actresses on screen. This is one element of exotic filmmaking not found very often in X-rated films after the mid 1990's.....

One example of how "Silver Age" X-rated films were filmed (in the way of "leaving more to the imagination") is the ending-scene of Paul Thomas' classic Beauty and the Beast Part 2 with the shapely blonde actress Sabrina Dawn kissing black actor Ray Victory as they sneak off together, then the credits roll, with what actually happened next left up to the viewer's imagination! (And that was the only inter-racial scene ever done by porn actress Sabrina Dawn: just kissing a black dude). There never was a "Part 3" to that film series, but if there was...I wonder if Sabrina Dawn would have reprised her "Princess" role and picked up where she left off with the Black "Pope" Ray Victory???

Adult Film Starlets often got to choose who they work with in a film, which is probably why there has been only a small cadre of adult male performers in that particular Industry up to now, especially back in the years before those "amateurs" flooded the adult film market! My research into that Industry as it was back in the 80's (and early 90's) found X-rated films to be scripted, professionally-cast, and oftentimes filmed with "soap opera" style theatrics whereas most films of the type today are just "wall-bangers" without storylines and with "amateurs" rather than professional performers. This time period in the X-rated film business also proved "conservative" compared to nowadays, though it was during this time that interracial sex in X-rated films became less "taboo". During the 95% Caucasian "Silver Age" of X-rated films, there were few Black Actors and Actresses, namely just Ebony Ayes, Ray Victory and Sean Michaels, but these three performers pretty much single-handedly "integrated" the small American Adult Film Industry from the late 80's-on. Anyone who was a fan of Adult Films back in the late 80's might have seen one with the "token black guy" Ray Victory fucking the socks off gorgeous white starlets like Tami Monroe, Cheri Taylor, Britt Morgan, Lynn Lemay and Aja in "interracial" X-rated films such as I Found My Thrill on Cheri Hill, The Bod Squad, and Hustler's Mystery of the Golden Lotus. One very popular X-rated Film from 1990 entitled Kiss My Grits was an X-rated spoof of the old "Alice" TV shows of the late 70's filmed in an after-hours Diner where "Mel" (Ray Victory) is working hard at "servicing" **both** of the shapely blonde waitresses (Tami Monroe and Cheri Taylor) at the same time! Fans of the legal Adult Films of this genre got to see their favorite sex-film performers paired with other performers in scenes and scenarios that were either funny, shamelessly-inventive or comically-impossible to ever experience in reality, such as getting-it-on in the back seat of a moving police car or having one's "horn blown" while under water in a public swimming pool. I even recall seeing one such scene where the male actor is dressed up as a cop and pulls the female starlet over, walks over to her car window and drops his pants to lift himself forward and get a blowjob from her there at the open car window saying it was her "breath-a-lizer"! Another of my favorites is one where a hot blonde starlet takes on three guys while standing up inside of a restaurant. Seeing sexual congress played out on a TV screen whether on VHS or DVD or even on one's PC is safely "vicarious" as it stokes one's imagination (among other things). **Sexual fantasy can be very safely indulged**, even if it is just secretly stashed inside one's mind…since not everyone is as well-built as a porn star or as rich as some of the characters are made out to be, nor may they have the guts to have sex in strange places with strange people, under stranger circumstances! That sort of thing was part of the "appeal" that X-rated films offered it's limited viewing public...a chance to see other people have torrid, kinky, and "taboo" sexual relations which the real-life (adult) viewers either cannot (or will not) ever really engage in themselves.

In March of 1999, I got the opportunity to meet and hang out with a former Adult Film Starlet of the late 80's/early 90's era of X-rated films, the one who originally held the nom-de-plume of "Tabitha Stevens" (not to be confused with the later-90's X-film Starlet using the same name). The **original** Tabitha Stevens had posed nude in numerous men's magazines such as "Hustler Busty Beauties" between 1988 and 1993 along with about 20 X-rated feature films between 1988 and 1992 such as **Camera Shy, Under the Law, Buns and Roses, In Loving Color**, and **Stairway to Heaven** as well as an R-rated "Stripper Video" entitled **No Body like Tabitha**. She was occasionally billed under another tantalizing moniker: "Lisa Lamborghini". A beautifully well-built Blonde with a long and frizzy 80's hairstyle and "Prom Queen" good-looks, the original Tabitha Stevens was a sweet-natured gal who agreed to meet me in Atlanta back in '99 where we spent a weekend together and had a blast! Among some of the many things we talked about was the Adult Film Industry of that time period which having been a fan of, I was naturally curious as to what it was like working in that field. She told me she had done feature dancing for awhile but didn't like it and only regretted not having saved more money from her X-rated film days. Posing nude for men's magazines was her preference in the

Adult Entertainment Field, and her return to the pages of **Hustler Busty Beauties** throughout the decade of the 1990's was a good time for the original "Tabitha Stevens".

Between eating dinner at a Steakhouse in downtown Atlanta and going to see the Nicholas Cage film "8MM" (in theaters at the time) Tabitha told me stories from her X-rated film days, tales about the men and women she performed with and how she felt about the ill-fated ones (i.e. the suicides of porn stars Savannah and Cal Jammer).

I teased her about how she facially resembled a certain Hollywood actress and how she had been cast along with certain other porn stars in her films but didn't have sex with all of them! For nearly all of her X-rated films, she was paired with male performers Randy West, Tom Byron, and Buck Adams (The late Buck Adams was the brother of Porn Super-Starlet Amber Lynn) and Buck Adams was the one who "discovered" the original Tabitha Stevens for X-rated film work. I remember her telling me that it was normal for a Porn Starlet to request being paired with a male actor she felt comfortable with (and knew ahead of time) not to mention one she actually found attractive!

She had the wickedest "giggle" of any woman I have ever met and all the hours we spent talking over the phone both before and after our weekend of fun in Atlanta Georgia, I have to say that listening to a woman talk has never been more pleasant for me than listening to Lindsey (her real name). In her years after leaving the Adult Film Industry behind, the original Tabitha Stevens/Lisa Lamborghini returned to College and became a Chiropractor with her own Practice in Alabama, a State she later told me she grew to dislike because there wasn't much there to entertain her. After a fond farewell at the Atlanta Airport and after another few years of chatting over the phone, I no longer heard from Lindsey after 2002. Life goes on for her and I certainly hope it goes along well!

Long gone from the Adult Entertainment genre, her porn name taken by another Starlet, and her films from the late 80's/early 90's never being marketed onto DVD, the **original**

"Tabitha Stevens" aka: "Lisa Lamborghini" is but a memory for us fans of the American Porn Industry's VHS-only late 80's/early 90's time period…….a fond memory!

Ken Knight with the original "Tabitha Stevens" in Atlanta Georgia, March 1999.

The 80's and early 90's VHS videotape versions of X-rated films usually had box-cover images that were "conservative" in comparison to the more explicitly hardcore covers of today. Those X-rated Video box covers of the 1980's and early 1990's often "left-more-to-the-imagination" and here are some of the BEST adult films produced back in the late 80's and early 1990's>>

It takes a special kind of person to take off their clothes for a camera and agree to have their naked image broadcast across infinity, but the person agreeing to take off their clothes and perform a very real sexual act for cameras knowing their torrid sex act will be duplicated and then marketed to a worldwide viewing audience is unique indeed. Adult Film Stars all know the catch: SEX CAN BE ENTERTAINMENT. Unfortunately, most of the Adult Films of the late 80's/early 90's are now out-of-print, although many of these X-rated films were "edited" for late night Cable TV release and could have been seen on Cable TV at the time shown alongside the "Erotic-Thrillers" of the early 90's (just no penetration shown). Christy Canyon, Victoria Paris, Lynn LeMay, Cheri Taylor, Tori Welles, Aja and Sabrina Dawn of X-rated's "Silver Age"……we miss you!

I Found My Thrill On Cheri Hill starring Britt Morgan and Ray Victory (Pleasure Productions 1988).

Sabrina Dawn (left) and Victoria Paris starring in The New Barbarians 2 (VCA 1990)

So how long has the naked human body been "entertainment" you ask? I daresay ever since men first picked up a stick to draw or paint with, creating those classic images of well-formed nude females on stone, papyrus, and canvas…giving the world "Art" which served as a glorious form of still-life imagery thus "entertaining" the viewers in one way or another. It also harkens back to Western Civilization's Pagan Ancestry in Europe and even far away as Ancient Persia where our ancestors delighted in the strong, well-fit, **naked** human form female and male, where public nudity was no "sin" and sex was a procreative must delighted upon by those who saw something they liked in a mate of the opposite sex, the uncovered human shape almost solely responsible for the birth of generations that preceded us all! The Greeks and Spartans gave us the immortal statues and images of well-developed human bodies many consider to just be "Art" today, few seeing the correlation between erotic art and the inner desire for stimulation through appreciating (being entertained by!) the human body. You, I, and every single one of the six billion lives inhabiting this planet all possess a physical body. Who are the Priests, Nuns, Missionaries, Pastors and Mullahs of the "Clergy" to tell you that looking favorably upon the bare body of an adult member of the opposite sex is sinful when it is **naturally-imbedded** inside you to do so? If our Ancestors had all obeyed-to-the-letter those celibate Judaic-Christian Priests and Monks of two thousand years ago, none of us would be here right now because none of them would have procreated! (Well, maybe just the Chinese would have inherited the Earth instead). You yourself would never have children nor ever been born, if a man and a woman didn't find one another physically-attractive enough to get naked together and make love! Personally, I never understood the concept of young Catholic Couples consulting a celibate Priest before their wedding day.

How could a celibate Priest who has never known a woman's intimate caress, possibly advise about a couple's marriage?? That's like asking a mechanic about your taxes.

Despite our "Puritan" origins with the original English Colonists, Quakers, etc. America has become a bastion of freedom (compared to most of the world's nations) on a personal level never imagined by generations past, setting the tone for many Western nations on our level to aspire to. Where else can an ordinary citizen enjoy all forms of legal pursuits and entertainment without governmental objection (As of the 2008 Elections~ at least for the time being!) including the viewing of legal adult entertainment in the privacy of one's own home without fear of police arresting you for it?! BTW: *Perverts who talk shit to minors on the Internet deserve to be not only arrested but also beaten within an inch of their worthless lives*. The "entertaining" bare human female form is enticing for the sexual reason naturally, and for centuries has been codified as "verboten" by politicians, clergy, and red-faced-busy-bodies whom cannot stand the fact someone else may be admiring (or even indulging) a lovely naked physique out there somewhere, so many Americans in the 20th Century went to jail for publishing the naked images of beautiful women (i.e. "obscenity" charges). I will admit that the sexual impulse in human beings is rather strong and can, yes, get-out-of-hand in regards to immature or perverted men and women whom cannot think beyond their genital appeasement. Men and women who prey upon weaker (and underage) people for sexual gratification should be punished! But this is no reason to codify and enforce a new "Puritanism" outlawing entertainment enjoyed by an adult fan base, the majority of whom are not perverts! I think Hugh Hefner said it best when he remarked how certain people cannot stand the fact that somewhere out there, someone else is having a good time!

There are two major annual "Conventions" devoted to adult entertainment: Glamourcon (often hosted in the American mid-west such as in Chicago) and the

Consumer Electronics Show (known to most as just CES) hosted in Las Vegas.

These are the major events where a fan of the genre can meet their favorite adult entertainers, nude models, and erotic-thriller actresses for autographs and schmoozing.

One other Convention known as DragonCon in Atlanta Georgia each summer also tends to have a few Playboy Playmates from the past and other famous models and actresses signing autographs there as well. It was there I ran into Nude Model Aria Giovanni and I met Actress and Playboy model Sandra Taylor at DragonCon back in 2004 as well as actress Sybil Danning, famous for her nude roles back in 1980's Hollywood films like "Malibu Express" and "They're Playing with Fire". At DragonCon in Atlanta each Labor Day Weekend, if you're willing to wade through the mob of geeks costumed in weird outfits, you'll surely find some of the finest ladies to have ever taken their clothes off for men's magazines as well as Hollywood itself!

Now there are a few places a man should never go…two of which I feel are well-worth mentioning here in Adventures of Exotic Nightlife because they usually occur in the evening to nighttime hours but primarily because I have subsequently learned of what happened when an idiot (associate of mine) didn't heed my warning about attending these places where a straight male of the species (in his right mind) should never tread……

1) **A Bridal/Baby Shower** ~ Only a completely hen-pecked clown would go to his bride-to-be's "shower" surrounded by all of her friends or to a Baby Shower, and for the same reason! You're gonna feel like a shithead sitting there while the girls giggle and make fun of you as the only dude queer-enough to attend such a traditionally-all-female "party". And take a guess who will be taking out the trash afterwards as well as hauling all your lover-girl's gifts and crap to the car?
2) **A "Sex-Toy Party"** ~ Kind of like a "tupperware party", only for you-know- what! Ever notice how most "sex toys" are engineered for the female of the species??? Well you should have by now, and if you're a straight guy who is confident in his ability to please his lady in the bedroom then you don't need to go with her to a "sex toy party" or whatever the sellers of such wares (usually horny, middle-aged-women) call it these days. Then again, maybe you won't mind seeing the "love of your life" buy one of those huge monster dildos??

Legendary Porn Actress Christy Canyon with Ken Knight (May 1997)

RECKLESS EYEBALLING

I remember first hearing the term "reckless eyeballing" many years ago while attending an EEOC "sensitivity" class required for the job I had at the time. Of course it referred to an employee gawking at the physique of another employee and the official message was

"Don't do it!" Well, those prudish game hens that came up with that EEOC bullshit obviously weren't worth gawking at or they were frustrated lesbians looking to "bash" straight men in the workplace by getting "sexual harassment" laws to become more and more draconian. Ever notice the only ones who ever really get reprimanded for "sexual harassment" are straight men? (George Orwell had a point about how some people are "more equal" than others!) Well my friends, all workplace prudes, Methodist pastors, Muslim Imams, and fat-ass socialist weasels aside, Reckless Eyeballin' is what the straight, red-blooded American man does best in his extremely-well-deserved free time!

The fundamental **Right** to look upon the glorious shape and curvature of an attractive female of the human species is paramount in any normal man's life, unless of course he plans on spending his earthly days cloistered inside of a Catholic Monastery.

Hell, if everyone 2,000 years ago followed Priests 100%, none of us would be here today because of none of our forebears would have ever procreated (i.e. the sin of "lust").

Whether it be a religious zealot or the liberal "politically correctness" crowd, the threat of having Men's Entertainment such as Playboy® Magazine (and others) as well as adult video games, theatrical films and even strip-clubs taken away from us.....is very real.

Don't believe it can happen here in the USA? Well, for starters, an associate of mine almost got himself arrested next door in Canada for selling a science-fiction fantasy patch at a Sci-Fi Convention in Toronto which depicted a female Alien hottie in a sexually-suggestive pose. The Canadian cops told him he had to take that "offensive to women" patch down from his display or they'd arrest him under a "hate crimes" law! Do you think that form of direct censorship couldn't ooze across the border into our country's culture in some way, shape, or form? Well if it does, I predict it would have full support and backing of <u>all three</u> of the modern Censorship-lovers on both right and left wings:

1) Religious Fundamentalists
2) Muslim fanatics
3) Liberals and Feminists (political-correctness crowd)

Yes, all three of these modern Inquisitors would be united in getting rid of "pornography" and "offensive material" you and I find entertaining and would lick their chops at the idea of putting guys like us in jail for being "immoral". I have **personally** crossed swords with two specific types of censorship-loving individual archetypes so far:

1) The "Loser" who never had a date in his or her life while hating any and all lovers he/she sees around them, all grown up and in a position of authority to write rules and regulations regarding "codes of conduct" in the workplace.
2) The "Recovering" former sex-addict/alcoholic/smoker/gambler who once he/she has "recovered" they absolutely despise anything that reminds them of their former "behavior" and therefore advocate strongly for the abolition of their former vice which is being enjoyed by others.

It stands to wonder why I even mention censorship here, but I think it's important for those whom enjoy men's entertainment (the likes of which I've profiled in this book) keep an extra look-out from time to time for the "censors" who want nothing more than to ruin your fun and punish you for liking it too damn much. There are always folks out there who fancy themselves "moral crusaders" when in reality they are just insecure guys and gals who relish the sadistic pleasure of being an operative "Kill-Joy" to those around them who are actually enjoying this thing called Life! In this day and age, it seems the Straight American Male (S.A.M.) is at odds with the "politically-correct" crowd (as well as the Religious Fundamentalists) where his tax dollars, his privately-owned firearms, his right to freedom of speech and his adult-entertainment, are all targeted for termination!

I mean, when a governmental EEOC "Sensitivity" training class actually points out to the employees that by just having a Playboy magazine inside of one's personally-owned vehicle parked at the workplace is a "violation"…..guess who they're targeting? (You).

Those same "sensitivity-training" jackasses also want to make it a "violation" to speak ill about against fat, gelatinous, unattractive people who are walking-heart-attacks anyway.

Most female plaintiffs in "sexual harassment" claims are reacting against being pursued by males they personally find unattractive, and the government provides an axe to swing.

Reckless Eyeballing is a straight man's prerogative, gazing upon the natural endowments of beautiful women walking by and appreciating them all the more. Nothing obtains a normal man's attention quicker than for a beautiful woman to walk through the door wearing attractive attire covering an attractive physique. Some women even master this reality and use their feminine wiles to get what they want from their male admirers, sometimes without having to make physical contact at all, just by their sexy appearance!

I've known a few gals whose sultry appearance got them off of a traffic ticket because the cop stopping them was smitten! Then again, I wouldn't suggest this as a usual tactic to use ladies, because a lot of street cops nowadays are those "Losers" (see preceding page) who got their lunch-money taken from them and had no girlfriends back in high school, so they'd write you a ticket whether you showed them cleavage or not!

I used to date this lady who was very busty and I encouraged her to wear alluring tops and dresses, etc. which accented her big boobs whenever we went out. Why? Because a woman like that has "power" over men, for example: We ate for free at one restaurant because she flirted with the Manager who couldn't take his eyes off her big tits, and in another instance she got movie tickets on the house for saying something nice to the security guard at the movie theater. Having an attractive woman on your arm is a symbol of your manhood's potency as well; let no one tell you otherwise! Other men and women look at you as a success if your girlfriend or wife is smoking-hot. Horseshit "equality" aside, if you were the Owner of a Restaurant or Night-Club, and you had to hire a dozen waitresses, wouldn't you choose the physically-attractive female applicants over the homely and frumpy ones? Wouldn't you want an attractive female secretary at the front desk to represent your business? Doesn't a Congressman (a straight one) often hire a pretty, well-shaped female secretary for his office on Capitol Hill? Of course, because attractive females make for a more relaxed and amenable environment, and to hell with those frustrated chumps who'll say they're being used as just "sexist window-dressing"!

What (straight) bachelor's pad doesn't have some form of alluring female poster, picture, or some other kind of femme-image posted in his "man-cave"? It's that simple, and once again proves my point that images of the opposite sex **entertains**! ☺

Looking at an attractively-figured woman from afar or up closely can be done with little effort and without anyone else noticing the direction of your gaze, if you are slick about it and don't spend an awfully long period of time staring….just a glance is worth an hour's viewing if you lock it into your memory and be on your merry way! I've met women who bask in their own feminine attraction, enjoying men taking glances at them (and far outnumber those hussies who'll show cleavage in the workplace just to trap some guy in a "sexual harassment" complaint).One time when I was walking through a shopping mall many years ago, I saw this well-packaged young woman in a tight black mini-skirt and fishnet stockings who caught me looking at her caboose, and started talking up a storm with me, not offended at all. After lunch and plenty of chit-chat, the two of us ended up doing it in one of the dressing-room stalls in a Department Store where she worked there at the Mall. So never think that instant-sexual-attraction is not a good "ice-breaker"!

Now I'll never advise against being a "Gentleman" with the ladies, though I must admit my own good fortune with "keeping it real" (as they call it nowadays) whereas my own adult honesty got me in the good graces of a female or two in my past. Yes, telling one 38-year old woman in a Night Club that she had "great set of lungs" (big tits) got me invited to her apartment soon after for a two hour "meeting" with her big boobs minus bra, panties, and any other forms of attire! Yes, telling one lady in the gym she had the body to rival any Porn Star got me an instant date with her, but casual remarks of this sort don't always get the woman's juices flowing, saying such things to the wrong lady might get you slapped upside the head instead of laid as any man of experience already knows.

Having a "friendship with benefits" has its rewarding side as well>one female chum of mine years ago bet me I couldn't catch her running along a beach (since she jogged every morning) and if I caught her, then I could HAVE HER! Needless to say, I never ran so hard in my life and I finally caught her. She was a good sport, so we did it in the shower once we got back to the Motel room. Even married women like to be seen as attractive to other men, which is why billions are spent in gyms and health clubs by women every year (not to mention boob-jobs!). Though I don't recommend having affairs with married women, I have to acknowledge how easy it is nowadays. I couldn't tell you how many times I have had a married woman proposition me all because I was NICE to her. Every married woman I've known who got her boobs pleasantly enlarged, did so because she likes other men looking at her chest the way they do, (all of that "reckless eyeballing").

For every man who doesn't fire up enough nerve to go up to an attractive female stranger and say SOMETHING, there is at least two guys who will, and those are the studs seen with the sexy vixen later on by the weakling who didn't think he could score with her!

For the eligible Bachelor out there looking for a girlfriend (or wife) you are reading a "menu" my friend, and you don't order the first thing you see, no....you LOOK over the entire "menu" before eventually deciding what you want! So in this regard, "reckless eyeballing" is a necessary part of life for men in the free world despite those prudish hens and faggots in the EEOC trying to cut everybody's balls off.

Author's Note> With many "Generation Y" guys (clowns about 15-20 years younger than me) there's a tendency to take offense at another man eyeballing his girlfriend even in the slightest. My only advice to those insecure "rapper-wannabes" is this: be careful who you task about such a common thing, for the man eyeing your girlfriend is likely more of a man than you are, and may subsequently knock your dome off ☺

Now which would you prefer....a hot totally-naked female dancing in front of you, or a totally-hot female wearing alluring attire or a hiked-up skirt? Both are attractive of course, but each one attracts differently! One gets full-on attention right away and it's a good thing seeing well-shaped naked women, but then there is not too much more to imagine once you've seen the bare goodies. Now a woman whose mini-skirt may be showing more than expected as she sits on a stool or bends over to pick up her keys in a restaurant thus affording the normal man a quick glance at her, appeals to the "more to the imagination" side of things and is the "cheap thrill" as they call it.

There are also certain forms of attire worn by certain types of women which men find attractive, and most of them are pretty simple. For example, I myself just love to see a well-shaped female wearing bib-overalls or a really busty femme wearing a tube-top.

Others will say it's a mini-skirt or just tight jeans that get a man to "recklessly-eyeball" a woman in public as he's walking along. I admit its cleavage which gets me looking every time but a nicely filled out ass and athletic legs on a woman that'll have me staring also.

Nowadays, under-age girls wear sexy attire they shouldn't and are being gawked at by older men but they are just kids trying to act like they're adults... I just have to say:

"Leave the sexy attire to real **women** and go back to your cheerleading squad, girls!"

In some countries "reckless eyeballing" will get you locked up (so stay the hell out of the Middle East and other Muslim territories) and the aforementioned "trio" of censors will surely like to have men locked up for being "offensive" here in the USA if they could!

Believe me, there are those who'd have every woman on the planet wearing Burquas if it were up to them (the same type of asshole who sends suicide-bombers out to kill in the name of a fictitious deity). Islamic Censors have even come up with a "Burkini" which covers a woman from the neck-down with only the face, hands, and feet exposed, allowing Muslim chicks to swim with "modesty" because Western-style swimwear is too "revealing". So do those radical Meccan rock-worshippers have the slightest chance of ever adversely affecting free western peoples' fun in the sun? Just ask the Australian chicks sunbathing on a beach in the land down under in 2006, whom were publicly accosted by Muslim immigrants who found their bikini attire "morally-offensive" and a subsequent race-riot ensued shortly after!

Belly-dancing originated in the Middle East and North Africa, alleged to have begun with the ever-traveling Gypsies. Definitely an ancient reason for "reckless eyeballing", Belly-dancing has survived the centuries (and influenced exotic dance) to this very day, it's original meaning and purpose speculated to have been either an "exercise to ease childbirth" or used to entertain Sultans and/or visiting dignitaries, etc. Stamped out by radical Islamic Governments, belly-dancing can still be had here in the Free West in certain Moroccan-themed restaurants, certain dinner-theaters, and of course on DVD.

Costumes can be as sexy as they want to be without showing the obvious portions of the female physique, leaving more to the imagination and with more male eyes glued to the lovely female shapes wearing such alluring, enticing attire which reminds me of another great excuse to go "reckless eyeballing": **Halloween**!

Nothing like a Halloween party where ladies are dressed up in sexy costumes such as "Belly Dancer", "Vampiress", "Hooker", and my personal favorite~ the "Sexy Nun"☺.

"Reckless Eyeballing" is without a doubt, the all-time-favorite American past-time!

Nowhere else does a straight American male feel more "entertained" than when he is within close proximity with an alluring female presence, no matter if the lady is intimate with him or not, the entertaining aspect of her sexy visage keeps the man's eyes on her!

Some people use this undeniable fact to their advantage....I've seen where a criminal confession was obtained from a suspect because of the attraction the suspect had for the sexy female Detective interviewing him (he just couldn't lie to her). I've also known some women whom use their "feminine wiles" to get men's attention and favoritism when they are in public, thus making their travels a bit easier as far as cooperation goes.

Even if a man is happily-married, he has the right to "look" at other women, which does not mean he will cheat on his wife; he just likes to look at the "menu" out there and enjoy the sights walking along the thoroughfare of life. Plenty of married women keep in shape, get a boob-job, and keep themselves well-groomed in order to remain "sexy" for their husbands and therefore have no reason to worry about his wandering eyes. Those who do I applaud you (because I look at you too, haha) and because you recognize the fact that keeping a pleasing shape and appearance keeps your man interested!

LEAVING MORE TO THE IMAGINATION

A few years back when after I wrote my first novel CRYPTX, I learned from my research into the suspense-thriller genre I was writing for, that many readers tend to prefer sex scenes between characters that lean toward "leaving more to the imagination" rather than hard-core depictions of carnality. Hell, it's easy (and fun) to write in sexual detail about a character in the story but doing so may turn some readers off and/or sour the storyline by switching gears between the actual plot and gratuitous erotica thrown in. So I learned to leave some sex scene details "to the imagination" of the reader as I write. Mainstream Motion Pictures depicting scenes of lovemaking tend to do precisely this, but in different ways, not to mention the fact they answer to a Motion Picture Rating System and rarely ever wish to garnish beyond an R-rating. (NC-17 and X-Rated films are never widely-distributed to Theaters). Often called "soft-core" for not showing overly explicit sexual congress but "softer" sexual motions and alluring choreography eluding to the obvious, films such as 1992's BASIC INSTINCT and 1994's COLOR OF NIGHT are two "Erotic-Thriller" films which became mainstream Hollywood Hits of their time.

It was back in the 1980's when the term "gratuitous nudity" was coined, and defined primarily from films shown on late night Cable-TV back in the mid-to-late 1980's showing in millions of American households via Cable or personally-owned VCRs.

"Gratuitous Nudity" refers to the naked element in a film where (usually female) Stars disrobe for a comical or "unnecessary" scene and more often than expected! Gratuitous refers to a "gift or favor" and certainly in 80's films such as MALIBU EXPRESS; the Director gave us viewers the gift of seeing Playboy Playmates Kimberly

McArthur, Barbara Edwards, and Lynda Wiesmeier....**naked**! ☺ From my own fondest memories back in the mid-80's there were "B-movies" such as MALIBU EXPRESS, directed and written by Andy Sidaris, which was the epitome of campy action, adult innuendo, and gratuitous nudity from start to finish entertaining the viewer with a fun "escapist" atmosphere and bare busty babes. There was also 1985's R-rated YOUNG LADY CHATTERLEY 2 directed by Alan Roberts (loosely based on a DH Lawrence novel) and starred the awesome blonde bombshell of the 1980's, Sybil Danning! It was campy and gratuitous, mixed with plenty of sexual activity between the characters all in unlikely scenarios which entertain us because we never seem to have it that good....I mean, how often do you have a gorgeous female boss drop by your cabin for an afternoon "boink", a sexy female co-worker who curses you out just before you screw-her-silly seconds later, and how often do you get to seduce the drop-dead-gorgeous blonde maid by simply pulling your pants down? YOUNG LADY CHATTERLEY 2 is another of the finest examples of the "gratuitous" 1980's filmmaking that launched the "Erotic-Thriller" genre of the upcoming 1990's. "Leaving more to the Imagination" in the way of say... a super- hot blonde "riding" atop of the male actor simulating sexual intercourse but not actually doing so, more especially not showing actual penetration or even the genitals of the actors/actresses as they go-at-it and rarely showing an "ending" to the carnal escapade, leaving the viewer to "assume" the rest! Or say....oral sex without showing the actual act, just eluded to and the camera turns away just as the lovers are about to begin. That is leaving more to the imagination and a lot can be done with these tactics of entertainment!

From the early 1980's came the hey-day of "Sex Comedies" such as 1981's PORKY'S followed by gratuitous-nudity titans THE LAST AMERICAN VIRGIN and BACHELOR PARTY, not to mention MY TUTOR, R-rated films with good budgets and "teen" themes acted out by adult actors and actresses of course. Maybe it is the "adults are very boring" thing that kept the 80's sex comedies stuck in the land of "teenage angst" where horny High School Seniors or College Freshmen seek out the always-elusive "easy lay" and sex without consequence! Most of the 80's sex-comedies such as PORKY'S operated on the "leave more to the imagination" sex portrayal, but with more-than-obvious stunts such as the scene where the guy shoves his dick through a peep-hole in the girls' shower room at school, only to have the fat-ass female gym teacher grab it on the other side!

Yes, those films are entertaining and usually had some smoking-hot actresses playing the female roles with tight well-filled-out bodies to strip clothes from! Gems like Phoebe Cates's famous "swimming pool" scene in FAST TIMES AT RIDGEMONT HIGH and

Kimberly McArthur's "topless sunbathing" scene in EASY MONEY made the sex-comedy genre all the better viewable for the straight American male audience back then.

From the early 80's between 1981 and 1985, I noticed a subtle evolution of filmmaking from the nude Frat romps depicting College-Age shenanigans to a campy and vibrant adult genre of films depicting both humor but adult situations and intrigue far beyond the easy on-campus lifestyle. It was then films such as Andy Sidaris' MALIBU EXPRESS came to Cable TV bringing a fun theme but with older adult characters and R-rated sex scenes that were both tasteful and humorous for the viewer, leaving much to the viewer's imagination but still making you laugh and enjoy the shoot'em up, tail-chasing hi-jinks of a Private Detective as opposed to a Fraternity Prankster or High School Senior!

MALIBU EXPRESS and YOUNG LADY CHATTERLEY II are prime examples of this mid-1980's evolution from the sex-comedy film to what I call the "Sex-Satire" which depicts entertaining adult situations with an often-humorous outcome and sort of pokes fun at sexual situations and innuendos the adult viewer sees and maybe identifies with!

Nothing like a way of life being depicted on screen where the hero and heroine get-it-on but have a funny mishap or conclusion as a result, and these two films give you that.

MALIBU EXPRESS and YOUNG LADY CHATTERLEY II are both available on DVD today and both co-star the incomparable

Actress Sybil Danning whose **bare assets** improved both of these films (and prove my point on how female nudity can entertain).

You may find Sybil Danning today at www.sybildanning.net and in some upcoming feature films as well as signing autographs at Fan Conventions which is how I met her.

Once I saw Sybil Danning's performance in MALIBU EXPRESS back in the 80's, I wanted to join the CIA just to meet a sexy Agent such as her "Contessa Luciana"!

I first saw MALIBU EXPRESS quite by accident one Halloween Night back in the mid-1980's (I was about 17 years old) when I stayed up on Friday past midnight to watch the then-annual "Creature Feature" double-hitter of classic Frankenstein starring Boris Karloff and Dracula starring Bela Lugosi which concluded at 1:00am. Before switching off my parents' TV set in our basement den, I sat there channel-surfing in the dark for awhile and stumbled across a movie on a Cable-TV Movie Channel I hadn't ever seen before. It grabbed my horny attention quickly in its opening scene showing the shapely blonde vixen Lynda Wiesmeier as "June Knhockers" peeling off her white jumpsuit to seduce the male character Cody Abilene, a scene which ended in just a loving embrace (teasing the hell out of me to want to see more of the movie!). I sat there in the dark room watching MALIBU EXPRESS all the way to it's sunny ending, enthralled by the unique blend of beautiful babes such as Kimberly McArthur and Barbara Edwards (whom I already knew from sneaking peeks at my Uncle's Playboy Magazine collection) and the "action" of guns blazing, scumbags getting bumped off, and a helicopter-vs-car chase which the main character survives with the help of "June Knhockers" big boobs!

I was awestruck by this form of movie and kept note when it was to come on Cable TV again and again in the near future, so I saw MALIBU EXPRESS several times over back between 1986 and 1988, and I thankfully had two great parents who let their only son stay up late on weekend nights to watch Cable TV and whatever was on after 11pm!

I think the fact that I wasn't a troublemaker, didn't get any girls pregnant, and had decided to enlist in the US Army (delayed-entry program) at age 17 made my parents see me as mature enough to handle R-rated movies on Cable TV! Yes, I did sneak peeks at my Uncle Harry's Playboy Magazine collection when I visited his house on Beverly Lane in Fredericksburg to use the swimming pool there (the same house I write about in my "The Strangers" novella in this book) back in those days. It was in my Uncle's collection of early-1980's Playboy Magazines where I first saw what **beautiful women** really looked like! Roberta Vasquez, Patty Duffek, Kimberly McArthur, Barbara Edwards, Lorraine Michaels, Penny Baker, and Liz Stewart **epitomized** what feminine beauty was for this young man starting off in life, their Playboy® pictorials outstanding testimony to the female of the species. Playboy Magazine and the Sidaris' MALIBU EXPRESS were this young man's introduction to adult (yet conservative) well-proportioned female nudity back when I was age-appropriate and just before I left to join the US Army. Between late night Cable TV flicks like MALIBU EXPRESS and YOUNG LADY CHATTERLEY II as well as Playboy Magazine, I enjoyed the men's entertainment genre without becoming a "pornography-seeker" and developed a healthy attitude toward beautifully-crafted women and adult entertainment depicting their lovely shapes and sizes. Some people say that such entertainment is "addictive", but I tend to use that description only for those who over-indulge their tastes, much like an alcoholic, and subsequently suffer for it! (which I never have because I maintain a day-job and a life beyond the TV set). Without a doubt, I enjoyed watching those films late at night back in the 80's and looking at my Uncle's collection of Playboy Magazines whenever I'd visit 1705 Beverly Lane in Fredericksburg Virginia back in the day. Matter of fact, my family held a crab-feast and BBQ cook-out for me during my last weekend before going into the Army back then, there at my Uncle's house on Beverly Lane. I enjoyed one last "family reunion" before getting on a plane bound for Fort Benning, Georgia as well as saying farewell to the freedom of watching my favorite R-rated movies on Cable TV and of course, my Uncle Harry's closet-bound Playboy Magazine collection! ☺

One can enjoy Playboy Magazine and R-rated movies such as MALIBU EXPRESS "vicariously" in the way that you imagine yourself in that action or lifestyle, knowing that you could have a life similar to that shown on film because life does often "imitate" art, I'm here to tell ya! So what became of the young dude named Kenny after his 2-year enlistment in the Army was over? He pinned on a badge and served a local community in uniform, later writing fiction novels. What of his favorite Playboy Playmates and R-rated actresses of the 1980's? He ended up meeting and /or corresponding with many of them! The only sad thing about all of those 80's "guy-flicks" is that those bare naked ladies portrayed in them such as Lynda Wiesmeier, Lori Sutton, Kitten Natividad, Kimberly McArthur, and Harlee McBride were not in more movies during the years to come!

From 1985 to about 1987 the "Sex-Satire" type of film was welcomed mostly on late night Cable TV and usually (at the time) only on well after midnight, and I remember 1987's HARD TICKET TO HAWAII (also directed by Andy Sidaris) to be the pentacle of this type of film, possessing the entertaining "flavor" I found in MALIBU EXPRESS.

Leaving more to the imagination of the viewer can, and often does, leave the viewer truly wanting to see more.....and more....and more! That is why these films were put on to DVD 20+ years later because they are in demand by us "nostalgic" fans from the 1980s.

In 1988, Andy and Arlene Sidaris gave the world PICASSO TRIGGER which became a staple of late night Cable TV and Video rental stores across the USA. The Sidaris Family had inadvertently created a genre of their own with PICASSO TRIGGER.

PICASSO TRIGGER (1988) Rated R. Directed by Andy Sidaris/Produced by Arlene Sidaris

Director Andy Sidaris and his wife Arlene conjured stories to be acted out on screen which gave the audience action, adventure, exotic locales, beautiful well-shaped women, and sex scenes that were enticing, alluring, (but not smutty romps) filmed in a way that left plenty to the imagination of the viewer, and that my friends.... is entertaining in it's own way. A sex scene leaving more to the imagination is one where, for example, the lead female undresses with her male counterpart and they begin their foreplay then get into the motions of lovemaking for the camera with soft mood-music playing in the background, then the two lovers either finish their copulation in another minute or so, or the camera cuts to another scene just as the two lovers are getting close to the end, and without showing "everything" as far as body parts go, just enough to wet the appetite!

A testament to this style of filmmaking, the Sidaris Family's stunningly well-made film PICASSO TRIGGER blends the elements of humor, action (plenty of gun-play and explosions) nudity and romantic frolic with a pleasant background-climate (such as Hawaii) that relaxes and amuses the audience as the story's action unfolds. I daresay the sunny disposition of the Sidaris films such as PICASSO TRIGGER makes me want to quickly book a plane trip to one of those exotic sun-drenched locales where the sexiest women walk around town in bikinis all day long!

One extended love scene in PICASSO TRIGGER between the characters of "Pantera" and "Travis" (Roberta Vasquez and Steve Bond) goes from romantic kissing and petting fully-clothed with a passionate embrace with the male character's hands gripping the woman's asscheeks through her ripped jeans, to her top peeled off as they stand together in the living room, and the lovers step out of view together for what is left to the viewer's imagination! Actress (and former Playboy Playmate) Roberta Vasquez did an excellent job in-character for this film I thought, carrying herself well as the curvy femme fatale "Pantera" whose real motive the audience doesn't discover until the very end of the film.

Roberta Vasquez is one woman who can look at you with those beautiful brown eyes of hers and have you "smitten"....just watch PICASSO TRIGGER and you'll find out!

The late 1980's and early 1990's Sidaris Films such as PICASSO TRIGGER, HARD TICKET TO HAWAII, SAVAGE BEACH, DO OR DIE, HARD HUNTED, and KIT TO KILL, all possess the unique form of adult entertainment that breaches the R-rated sex scene level but in their own alluring manner of nudity mixed with "you know what's going on" assumption which entertains the viewer and leaves them wanting more, a subtle "tease" which makes for great adults-only entertainment without being X-rated!

Andy and Arlene Sidaris cast many former Playboy® Playmates in their films such as

Dona Speir, Roberta Vasquez, Hope Marie Carlton, Kim Malin, Patty Duffek, Cynthia Brimhall, Devin Devasquez, and even renown Sex-Therapist Ava Cadell!

My personal favorites are Patty Duffek and Roberta Vasquez, the best of the Playmates from the Year 1984 (as well as Penny Baker but she was not in any of the Sidaris films unfortunately). Patty Duffek played the shapely character of "Agent Pattycakes" in PICASSO TRIGGER, HARD TICKET TO HAWAII and SAVAGE BEACH, her most lengthy presence found in PICASSO TRIGGER where she does a slinky "cowgirl" dance for the bad guys, slips naked into a hot-tub for a very alluring scene, then gets into a gun fight with the villains and takes a bullet for the team, carried off by a big black dude.

Check out Playboy magazine's May 1984 issue and you'll see (Miss May) Patty Duffek at her best, arguably one of the finer Centerfold layouts of the 1980's with Patty posed in outstanding locations, showing us how she looked so much better...without clothes on! ☺

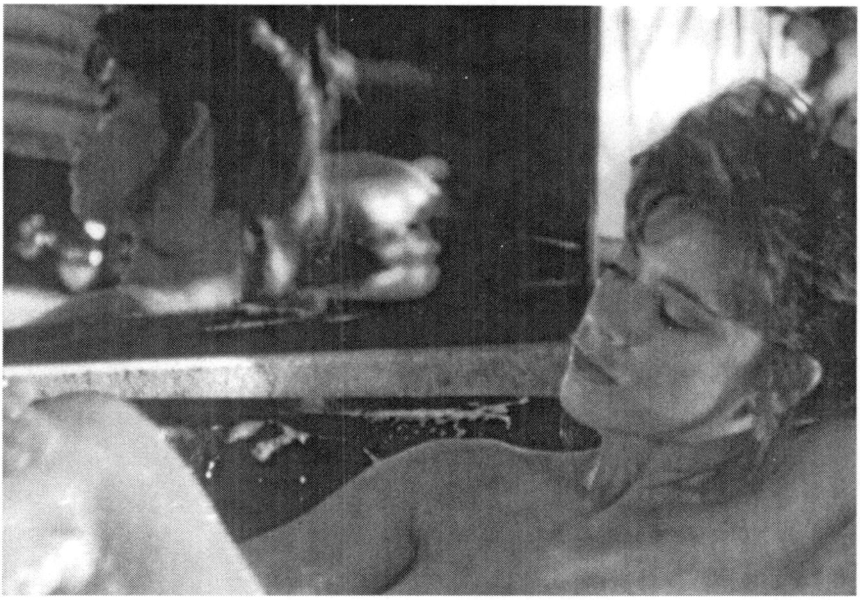

Patty Duffek in PICASSO TRIGGER Malibu Bay Films® 1988 (photo courtesy of Arlene Sidaris)

PICASSO TRIGGER shines as a "guy-flick" because of the superior directing and cast such as Patty, Roberta, Dona, and Cynthia. It's action-erotic theme and pleasing aesthetic was uniquely an 80's gambit which pretty much set-the-tone for the upcoming American "Erotic Thriller" genre of the late 80's and early 90's. Andy and Arlene Sidaris wrote the book on how beautifully sexy women coupled with action/adventure can make a film entertaining to watch **without** being labeled as Rated X. The Sidaris family also coined the saying "Bullets, Bombs, and Babes" and righteously so because that is precisely what their films are about. I'd also add in the word FUN because the Sidaris films such as PICASSO TRIGGER are savagely fun to watch......over and over again! Andy Sidaris left this world in March of 2007 but his work lives on and he will always be remembered as one of the Greatest Writers/Directors of "Guy Flicks" the Free World has ever known.

Andy and Arlene crafted a fictional "world" in their "Triple B" Series of films that is still on the DVD market to this day, therefore making their shapely and often-nude characters "Pattycakes", "Pantera", "Dona", "Nicole", and "Edy" **Legends of Bare Entertainment**!

Bullets, Bombs, and Bare Entertainment……

An Exclusive Interview with Erotic-Action Film Producer Arlene Sidaris

Producer of the uniquely-entertaining Sidaris Films, also know as the "Triple B" Series

(Bullets, Bombs, and Babes) Arlene Sidaris worked for two decades along with her husband Andy to give us guys a form of entertainment throughout the late 1980's and 1990's which stands firmly in a class of its very own. Arlene graciously agreed to an exclusive interview for "The Naked Diaries" in 2009.

Ken: Arlene, of all the movies you and Andy worked on, which one is your favorite?

Arlene: It's hard to say….the movies become like children; you don't love one more than the other, it's just different. However, if I had to choose I think FIT TO KILL would be the one. I think it's the sleekest and sexiest with great action and humor and it's the one where we introduce Julie Strain!

Ken: Was 1985's MALIBU EXPRESS difficult or easy to shoot?

Arlene: Malibu Express is the one film in the "Bullets, Bombs and Babes" Collection which I did not Produce.

Ken: Whatever happened to some of your films' cast such as Darby Hinton, Lori Sutton, Roberta Vasquez, etc. and do you keep in touch with any of them?

Arlene: I hear from several people on a regular basis. Julie Strain is a part of my extended family. Ronn Moss and Devin Devasquez just became engaged! Devin just introduced her "Devin's Kick-Ass Cajun Seasoning" at a terrific party in Hollywood.

You can find it online at www.devronn.com and I highly recommend it! Part of the proceeds will go toward rebuilding New Orleans as a gesture from Devin who is from Louisiana. Lynda Weismeier (Malibu Express's "June Knockers") moved back to Los Angeles a year or so ago and keeps in touch.

Ken: In the Sidaris films, the name "Abilene" is mentioned in nearly all of them. Was there a reason behind it?

Arlene: It was a reference to the first "Abilene" in MAILBU EXPRESS, portrayed by Darby Hinton. Just a bit of info for ardent Sidaris fans to relate to!

Ken: Have you ever found actors and actresses whom film love-scenes together ever becoming romantically-involved after filming?

Arlene: I'm taking the 5th on that one!!!

Ken: Did you and Andy have any trouble finding and hiring former Playboy® Playmates such as Kimberly McArthur, Shae Marks, and Roberta Vasquez for your films?

Arlene: The Playboy® folks were always very cooperative with us. We always treated the Playmates very well and appreciated their talents as well as the fine trademark they represented!

Ken: Did you And Andy hold auditions for each role you cast and did you have any trouble getting actresses to agree to nudity in the films

Arlene: We never had trouble with nudity because we were always very straightforward about the necessity for us to have nudity in our films. If the women or men were opposed to doing some nudity for the film, we did not interview them.

Ken: The Sidaris Films are uniquely-entertaining. Would you consider letting someone write a "novelization" (book-version) of one of your films such as "Malibu Express" or "Enemy Gold"?

Arlene: We are very interested in such an enterprise, especially since we have hundreds of unpublished photos from each of the films!

The sexy actresses of the early-90's Sidaris Films (left-to-right) Carolyn Liu, Dona Speir, Roberta Vasquez, Cynthia Brimhall, and Ava Cadell. (Photo Courtesy of Arlene Sidaris).

THOSE AMERICAN "EROTIC-THRILLER" FILMS...

The early 1990's was the peak time period that defined an evolving genre of filmmaking, and became the focal point from which the "Erotic-Thriller" film became a whole new brand of adult entertainment. Mostly released straight-to-video, the "Erotic-Thriller" was a feature film with an R or NC-17 rating and a suspense-thriller-action storyline coupled with plenty of sexual congress (fully-nude sex scenes) all throughout though not explicit enough to garnish an X-rating. Simply put, the "Erotic-Thriller" is a suspenseful film filled with choreographed sex that clearly shows the nudity of the actors and actresses.

If I asked most adults over age 35 to give their best example of a 90s "Erotic-Thriller" they'd probably choose 1992's **Basic Instinct** starring Sharon Stone. Of course, that hit film was the peak of it's genre because it was a major theatrical release with a large budget, a well-known cast-list, and a very good overall plot, not to mention steamy sex scenes between Sharon Stone and Michael Douglas. The second Mainstream-Hollywood Erotic-Thriller hit was 1994's **Color of Night** (starring Bruce Willis) an alluring climate, sexy female antagonist, plenty of nudity, and great soundtrack making it easy to watch.

Despite the success of these two films, the "Erotic-Thriller" genre is mostly confined to lower-budgets and straight-to-video release. Some of the straight-to-video Erotic-Thriller films of the early-to-mid-1990s were cast with some well-known actors and actresses of the 1980's like Marc Singer in **Body Chemistry** and Tanya Roberts in **Sins of Desire.**

I personally suspect the 1989 film **Fatal Attraction** (starring Glen Close) actually kicked-off the early 90's load of Erotic-Thriller films because in many of them the "woman scorned" theme plays out in a variety of ways, often mimicking the premise of that earlier suspense film in the strong but vengeful and deceptive (damn sexy) female characters.

With Basic Instinct and Color of Night as major Hollywood erotic ventures, 1984's They're Playing with Fire (starring Sybil Danning) being the best example of an "Erotic Thriller" of the decade before, it was films such as 1990's Night Eyes (starring Tanya Roberts) and 1991's Animal Instincts (starring Shannon Whirry) that capped the stone of what we now know as the "Erotic Thriller genre" **parallel** to the equally-sexy "Erotic-Action-Thrillers" of the early 90's like Andy Sidaris' feature films Fit to Kill and Hard Hunted. Now the Erotic-Thriller and Erotic-Action films went alongside hand-in-hand all through the early to mid 1990's showing up on late night Cable TV as well as onto VHS and later DVD at the Video Rental stores all through the decade of the 1990's.

It's clearly shown that the early-1990's was the "peak" of this genre which sort of rounded third base by 1995 and finished off with re-runs seen on late night Cable TV throughout the rest of that decade. Former Playboy Playmate of the Year Shannon Tweed is arguably the most-recognized acting veteran of the Erotic-Thriller film genre from 1990 through 1996, her roles in Night Eyes II, Hard Vice, Illicit Dreams, and numerous others making her a Star on countless television sets across the USA during the 1990's.

Reviewing some of the best of the 90's "Erotic-Thriller" films here is my salute to all of them really, a hats-off to some of the "un-sung" films of yesteryear that could not be seen by all but have a quiet legion of adult fans just the same........

HARD HUNTED Malibu Bay Films (1992). Directed by Andy Sidaris/Produced by Arlene Sidaris.

One of the best of the "Erotic-Action" films of its genre, Andy and Arlene Sidaris gave us guys yet another R-rated romp with plenty of gun-play, bomb-play, and foreplay!

Roberta Vasquez (right) in HARD HUNTED ©Malibu Bay Films (photo courtesy of Arlene Sidaris)

Director Andy Sidaris crafted an intricate tale of espionage, corruption, and sexual frolic within an easy two hours of footage that to this day entertains with it's lavish and sunny locations, guns-a-blazing, bombs made to look like anything, and bad guys mixing it with the good n' sexy gals like James Bond never did! HARD HUNTED takes an evil Mobster named Kane and pits him against the never-clothed-for-long American female Secret Agents Nicole Justin (played by Roberta Vasquez) and Donna Hamilton (Played by Dona Speir). Both Roberta and Dona came onto the entertainment scene after their mutual 1984 appearances as Centerfolds in Playboy Magazine and the late 80's/early 90's "guy-flick" genre is all that much better because of them! Federal Agents Donna and Nicole have to figure out how best to stop a criminal overlord (Kane) from getting the best of his unique criminality (as well as a priceless Jade artifact) Actress Roberta Vasquez really excels as "Nicole" in this film, reprising the role she had in DO or DIE alongside Dona character where they both continue the cat-and-mouse game with their arch-nemesis "Kane".

Yes, Hard Hunted is one of my favorites because of its enticing "climate" displayed throughout the film, a really seductive atmosphere captured by the Sidaris team which makes it uniquely appealing. From Picasso Trigger in 1988 to Do Or Die in 1990 then Hard Hunted in 1992 and Fit to Kill in 1993, the name **Sidaris** stands above all the rest as making late night entertainment worth staying up for! WWW.ANDYSIDARIS.COM

Steve Bond as "Travis Abilene" and Roberta Vasquez as "Agent Pantera" in the Sidaris film PICASSO TRIGGER. The passionate love-scene between these two in the film is arguably one of the most alluring of the genre, not to mention the fact there is a betrayal somewhere between the two characters later in the film's plot! Andy and Arlene Sidaris had a way of bringing characters "from out of nowhere" to make us adult movie-goers genuinely-interested in them as well their fates. Casting well-known Playboy® Playmates such as Roberta Vasquez (Miss November 1984) in films such as PICASSO TRIGGER gave us fans an additional treat as well as a cinematic salute to the Playboy mystique.☺(Photo courtesy of Arlene Sidaris)

Andy and Arlene Sidaris (photo courtesy of Arlene Sidaris)

Movie Review

SINS OF DESIRE 1993. Starring Tanya Roberts and Nick Cassavetes. Directed by Jim Wynorski. Written by Peter Liapis and Mark McGee. Rated R.

A sinister Doctor and wife use drugs and sex therapy on others, using the "clinic" to their personal advantage! An insurance investigator and a nurse investigating the death of her sister join forces to get the evidence against them. Nudity, gun-play, twisting drama, and a good plotline overall, SINS OF DESIRE was one of the best of the early-to-mid 1990's "Erotic-Thriller" genre and once again showed how a sexy actress (Tanya Roberts) along with brooding nighttime climate set-the-tone as the quintessential R-rated "Erotic" film.

One of the most enticing sex-scenes ever filmed in an R-rated movie where the shapely Tanya Roberts and Nick Cassavetes indulge one another (in-character) at a motel room punctuates this highly-entertaining Erotic-Thriller and helped make it one of the best of its kind. That lengthy sex-scene between Tanya Roberts and Nick Cassavetes was very well-choreographed to say the least, and also one of the longest of R-rated love scenes I can recall in a film back then. This film is also a great-great-great example of those 90's "Erotic-Thriller" films' penchant for detailing sinister plots hatched by evil-but-sexy women and conniving, screw-everything-that-moves men with murder and casual sex throughout! Though many of the Erotic-Thriller films of the time period were marketed straight to VHS video release and found primarily in video rental stores, for those of us fortunate enough to find these R-rated gems of adult entertainment it was well-worth the $3 rental fee at the Video Store back in those days.

One more aspect of the early 90's Erotic-Thriller films such as SINS OF DESIRE that I noticed was that even the most minor of characters gets listed in the credits! Now that is only fair of course, and afforded us film-history buffs info on who played some of the sexy but "blink and you'll miss'em" roles in these straight-to-video features. In the case of SINS OF DESIRE, the "Motel Girl" role was played by ultra-sexy actress Roberta Vasquez (Playboy's Miss November '84) and the part consisted only of her stepping in front of the soda machine and speaking to Nick Cassavetes' character briefly then taking off in a run when gunfire erupts seconds later! For me, it was cool to see one of my favorite 80's Playboy Playmates cast in this film even though it was a very brief role as the "Motel Girl" ☺ Films like this I predict, will one day be praised as a "time machine glimpse" back to a Hollywood era of adult entertainment before the advent of the Internet showing a fantasy world not shown by filmmakers since! If you can find yourself a copy of SINS OF DESIRE, grab it. You will not be disappointed....

Tanya Roberts with Ken Knight in Atlanta Ga. (August 2003)

The highly-talented Singer and Actress TANE MCCLURE, star of Erotic-Thriller films such as SCORNED 2, and SEXUAL ROULETTE which are among the finest of their kind ever produced. Tane McClure was also featured singing on the Soundtrack of the 1984 Sci-Fi action film THE TERMINATOR. (Photo courtesy of Tane McClure))

The Female STARS of the 1990's "Erotic Thriller" Film genre were the beautiful…. SHANNON TWEED JULIE STRAIN

TANYA ROBERTS

JULIE K. SMITH

TANE MCCLURE

DONA SPEIR

SHANNON WHIRRY

MARIA FORD

MONIQUE PARENT

LISA PESCIA

ROBERTA VASQUEZ

WENDY SCHUMACHER

These lovely ladies made the 1990's late-night Cable TV worth staying up to watch!

Movie Review

SCORNED 2 1996. Starring Tane McClure, Wendy Schumacher, and Andrew Stevens. Directed by Rodney McDonald. Written by Sean McGinly. Royal Oaks Entertainment Inc. Rated R.

The "sequel" to it's predecessor SCORNED starring Shannon Tweed (1994) this film picks up with a silently dangerous housewife Amanda (played by Tane McClure) married to a college professor who has tried to help her battle strange dreams from her shadowy past. Amanda is a sexy woman who likes to ravage her husband but the nightmares haunting her takes it's toll and her loyal hubby begins to stray.....right into the manipulative arms of one of his sexy college students (played by Wendy Schumacher) who wants the successful older man for herself even though she does have a boyfriend more her own age. You know what they say about college chicks "experimenting"?!!

Well the film flows along rather well with gratuitous nudity galore and classy sexual congress with the two female stars (McClure and Schumacher) working over their male counterparts rather convincingly, some of the best-choreographed sex scenes I have ever seen in an R-rated film are right here in SCORNED 2. The "jealous wife" Amanda slowly uncovers her hubby's dalliance with his hot College student and decides to do something about it. After watching this film the first time, I was wishing Tane McClure had been cast in 1987's FATAL ATTRACTION (instead of Actress Glenn Close) because Tane has this "fury" about her that is both alluring and frightening at the same time, her "woman scorned" personae in SCORNED 2 performed in such a manner the viewer doesn't know if she's just acting or perhaps she's really royally-pissed-off!

Convincingly, Tane McClure stalks her prey in-character, even seducing the young man who was the college slut's boyfriend, all for a chance at revenge and to bring her own ongoing nightmare to a close. Hands-down the sexiest woman in the entire film, Tane McClure's portrayal of "Amanda Foley" ranks up there with mainstream Hollywood's awarded performances of similar note. I have not seen any actress portray that peculiarly frightening "fury" in a film role since Tane McClure in SCORNED 2.

This film is also one of the best examples of "classy sex" found in the Erotic-Thriller movies of the early-to-mid-1990's where the scenes are often slow-paced "lovemaking" scenarios rather than quick porno-style romps in many R-rated films nowadays.

Well-directed and written as sort of a cautionary tale of lust and betrayal where the main female character who exacts vengeance is not really the "villain" for those who might empathize with her plight and genuinely **like** her (as I did while watching the film!)

SCORNED 2 is a masterpiece of the 90's "Erotic Thriller" genre and may still be found on VHS at some video rental stores that might still have a copy or two and online as well.

Arguably one of the most enticing movie posters/box covers of the genre with face of actress Tane McClure looming behind the female seducer of a married man suggesting that old warning about infidelity: "Hell hath no fury like a woman scorned!"

Movie Review

ILLICIT DREAMS 1994. Starring Shannon Tweed, Andrew Stevens, Michelle Johnson and Joe Cortese. Directed by Andrew Stevens. Written by Karen Kelly. Republic Entertainment. Rated R.

The uniquely sexy and talented Shannon Tweed at her finest along with veteran of the genre Andrew Stevens, directing and acting in this film that brings two "Icons" of the 90's Erotic-Thriller genre together for one wild ride of a movie. Anyone who checks out the filmography of Andrew Stevens and Shannon Tweed will see what I'm talking about!

The beautiful and neglected trophy-wife of an abusive husband who is screwing around on her with his female patients, keeps having erotic dreams of herself with a man she does not know personally but knows that he exists....one of those "soul mate" type of scenarios played out in erotic-thriller format and very nicely done!

Much like the early 90's NIGHT EYES Erotic-Thriller film series done by Stevens, this film takes the viewer for a soothing ride through great sexual congress acted out slow and easy between the two imaginary lovers who eventually do meet up.....contrasted by the quick and loveless way the cheating husband screws his mistresses!

This film is a testament to my view of how some of the most entertaining films to come along over the past 20 years often went "straight-to-video" rather than playing inside of a movie theater and the best movies made were not always "Academy Award" winners!

I first saw Andrew Stevens play an obsessed stalker in the 1982 suspense film THE SEDUCTION with Morgan Fairchild and his ability to both act and direct added fuel to the fires of the 1990's Erotic-Thriller genre that you are reading about here.

Shannon Tweed (former Playboy Playmate of the Year 1982) has been in more Erotic-Thriller films than most of the others cast throughout the 1990's and it was her beauty, her body, and acting talent that kept her showing up in role after role in such films now considered the "classics" of their kind, as in ILLICIT DREAMS. Shannon is a talented actress not afraid of the camera, also possessing a very alluring facial expression when portraying emotions such as rage and/or lust on screen. Stunningly gorgeous, Shannon was always on the box-covers of the Erotic-Thriller films she was cast in, the cover of ILLICIT DREAMS shows her and co-star Andrew Stevens in a bare embrace, proving once again how highly-sexualized-yet-classy covers sell videos!!

For any of you wishing to complete your collection of R-rated Erotic Thriller films of the 1990's, you just have to find a copy of ILLICIT DREAMS for it to be complete. This film is one of the best of its kind thanks to the Director and the incomparable Shannon Tweed who looks gorgeous to this day and who may be seen on the **only** "Reality Show" worth watching nowadays: Gene Simmons Family Jewels.

THE STRANGERS

~CONTINUED~

The "Best Laid" Plans of Intimate Cohorts…

Some past events are best off left alone and undisturbed.

Some people of the past are best left alone and isolated.

But there is just something about the lives of "strangers"

which occasionally become an obsession for those who should mind their own damn business….before it's too late!

Don't always come with a bullet-proof vest…

THE STRANGERS (continued)

New Rochelle, New York.
May 23rd, 2009:

It was an annual event "closed" to the general public for obvious reasons, and supported by a few wealthy benefactors who wish to keep the traditional MISS NUDE NORTHEAST Pageant alive well into the 21st Century. Booked here at the secluded and very exclusive

"Collins Country Club and Sail" located on the shores of New Rochelle and surrounded by tall fencing and pre-fab walls to keep out non-members and the curious, more especially on a day like today. This afternoon's crowning event will mark the latest in a proud 25-year tradition of "Miss Nude" Pageants here in New York going back to the early 1980's.

There were 39 naked female contestants this year, thirty-nine lovely ladies from all along the American Northeast, Maine down to New York and Jersey, as far south as Maryland and they all had one thing in common: each and every single one of them looked spectacular in the raw! The long stage perched five feet over the lush green lawn behind the huge Country Club "Clubhouse" building was now supporting the shapely, nude models as they slowly walked along its surface in front of the mostly-male audience and the five Judges seated at the forefront of the long stage. One of the first nude contestants was a 25-year old Black woman from Cleveland Ohio named Terri Clark, a lean and buxom African-American lady with straightened hair worn down, the number "11" on a frilly, black-n-white lace garter wrapped around her right thigh (where the other contestants wore their own numbers).

She strolled along the stage with hands on her bare hips, looking out at the crowd with a broad smile to the sounds of claps and whistles from her admirers, then she stepped in front of the panel of Judges and spun around for them to see her bare physique in its entirety.

"April Hunt from Louisville Kentucky…number eight," the announcer called out over the Club's outdoor PA system, the next nude contestant a well-filled-out redhead with perky boobs at 38DD and a muscular physique all around, cheers for her even louder as she walked her routine along the lengthy stage. One contestant was still nervous even as she stood at the stage's entry-way from the changing tent, next in line to be announced and stroll out into the sunlight to have 300 men stare at her totally-nude body which was being judged for prize money and a trophy as well as a title of "Miss Nude Northeast". Justine Cheeks was not normally one to take her clothes off in public like this, even if it was a legal place to do so, so she was still apprehensive, nervous, shy, and unsure of herself. When the name she used was called, Justine stepped out onto the runway wearing only sandals and her garter that bore the contestant number of 19. This sort of thing could get her fired from her job, but she thought this was the best way to get close to information she wanted to hear, one of the Judges sitting there waiting to gaze upon her bare assets and decide whether or not her body was well-honed and sexy enough for a prize. Detective Justine Cheeks of the New York State Police Bureau of Criminal Investigations (BCI) Division, working a "case" which she was not officially assigned to, nor should she be since it was bordering on personal obsession for her. Entering a "Miss Nude" pageant in her home state of New York was the craziest damn thing she had ever imagined herself doing, just to reach a source of Intel…..

Despite the fact she was using a phony name, Detective Cheeks assumed the risk of being recognized by one of the 300+ male attendees at this unusual, adults-only event. All it takes is for a co-worker, fellow Officer, or even some scumbag she's arrested in the past to notice its Detective Justine Cheeks totally-naked on stage in a "Miss Nude" pageant and her career would be in jeopardy. Shit, her career was already in dire jeopardy as it was! Here she was, carrying out an unauthorized investigation into a cold-case murder that was all but officially considered "closed" for lack of any further evidence to open its lid once again. She was looking into a case that resulted in the death of a New York State Trooper four years ago, one of her own and one she knew at the time, a man named Raymond J. Flintlock.

How in the hell does a cop uncover new clues while participating in a Nude Beauty pageant?

One of the Judges of this year's Miss Nude Northeast Pageant is a woman who also knew Raymond J. Flintlock back in 2005 before he was murdered, "Miss Nude Northeast 2006" herself: Ellen Conyers.....formerly known as "Ebony Cane" of the Adult Film Industry.

Ray Flintlock had moonlighted as a part-time Pornographic Film Actor for the infamous New York Porn Film Company "Faster Productions" and kept it a secret until he lost his job with the NY State Police just prior to being killed and burned at a cabin up in the Catskills in July of 2005. Trooper Flintlock was known as "Ray Fury" in the X-rated film world and was often cast with "Ebony Cane" who was no longer a Porn Star herself, having obtained a role on a TV Soap Opera....but today she had returned as a Judge for the Miss Nude Northeast pageant and was now looking up at Justine as she walked along the elevated runway to the sounds of male cheers and clapping. Admitting that she was nervous would be understated and Justine silently thanked herself for all those sessions in the Gym for the lean but filled-out body she was now strutting totally-naked in front of total strangers....

3:00 that afternoon: The winner was a busty blonde named "Amy Wine" whose melon-sized boobs bounced as she walked along with the ass of a cheerleader. Justine was happy to not have been the winner or one of the two "runner-ups" so the attention was not focused on her as she made her way from the sun-drenched stage area here in the rear property of the Country Club on the shore, still naked except for her garter with it's #19, toward where she noticed the shapely black woman named Ellen Conyers walking with two other Judges to congratulate the beaming blonde winner of "Miss Nude Northeast 2009".

Justine Cheeks stepped off the stage surrounded by male attendees of today's event, their comments and remarks flattering but she wasn't really paying attention to them but she was glad they all seemed top be "Gentlemen" for the most part, none of them getting frisky with their hands as she stepped down among the 300+ crowd of on-lookers.

Being totally-naked in a crowd of strangers is not a natural act, least of all for a female cop who was not really supposed to be at an event like this, least of all participating in it! Justine walked along the grassy property opposite the runway stage, greeted cheerfully by more admirers of her physique, and she just smiled and spoke cheerfully in return, looking over to where Ellen Conyers was still visible, wanting to speak with her privately. Some guy wearing a "Rob Zombie" T-shirt stepped in front of her requesting a photo with her, so Justine agreed but kept her eye on where Ellen Conyers was while the guy slipped an arm around her and his girlfriend readied his digital camera to take the shot. Justine didn't mind his hand slipping down to her bare ass just as the photo was taken, and the "fan" gently tapped her ass as he thanked her and walked away with his camera and accompanying girlfriend. Justine found it funny actually, for some women allow their husbands/boyfriends to patronize adult-entertainment like this "Miss Nude" pageant here in New York, either out of trust and or enjoyment for themselves or because the wife/girlfriend just doesn't mind her man gawking at other women in the buff like this!

Justine turned and walked toward the Country Club's on-site building where the festivities were adjourning out of the heat now that there is a winner of "Miss Nude Northeast 2009".

It was just as she got closer toward the pretty black woman named Ellen Conyers, she felt a male hand touch her between her shoulders…more of a get-her-attention poke, so she turned to see who was behind her and came face-to-face with someone she recognized as well as someone she had not wanted to run into at an event such as this!

"Jeezus," she sneered in realization, turning to look the man in the eyes, quickly feeling that distinctive "oh shit" sensation overriding her usual senses at this moment, hands on hips.

"Detective Cheeks....if it's any consolation for you, I would have voted for you to win if I was on the Judging panel," spoke Lieutenant Rory Jameson of the Bureau of Criminal Investigations/New York State Police, standing there in Hawaiian-shirt, shorts, and sandals.

"Uhhhaaahh....yeeeeah," Justine sighed as she stood there, her Lieutenant looking her up and down approvingly, knowing full-well that while it may not be an "ethics violation" for him to attend a Miss Nude Pageant as a viewing member of the audience, it was a violation for her to participate in a Miss Nude pageant and they both knew it.

"Consider yourself suspended pending investigation by Internal Affairs....turn in your badge and duty-weapon no later than tomorrow morning," the older man said frankly, looking around as he spoke to his subordinate standing there a little embarrassed now.

"Sir, I was here to get a sit-down chat with one of the former porn stars from the 'Faster Productions' crew....her name is Ellen Conyers and she's one of the Judges here today," Justine spoke up in explanation to him, knowing it would not make any difference anyhow.

"Justine, that case is closed, you know that....and re-opening a murder investigation without my authorization is one more violation to add to the list, I recommend you not tell me any more Detective.....see you when it comes time for your Internal Affairs interview," replied Lt. Jameson as he stared into her brown eyes, then glanced down at her perky 36C boobs and dark-haired patch between her thighs for a moment and turned to leave. Justine just stood there in awe of what had just occurred.....that asshole must have been following her unless he was truly an invited "audience member" here at the Pageant. Either way, she realized that she was screwed. Sneering a few words of profanity under her breath, Justine spun around on her heels and headed toward the Country Club "Club house" where the pageant crowd was now slowly spilling into, including the shapely black woman she came here to speak with in the first place! "Officialdom" be damned, she mused as she walked to the rear entry doors of the Country Club building, she was going to speak with that former female porn star who might be able to shed more light on the demise of one of her fellow State Troopers almost four years ago. She had worked alongside Trooper Raymond Flintlock a few times between 2002 and 2005 that last year of the man's life being the time he had been secretly "moonlighting" as an adult film actor, using his big dick on sexy women of the X-rated Film Industry up until his untimely homicide in July of 2005.

The inner Country Club was fabulous in its interior, though enjoying the surroundings and the continuing flattery of men walking in with the naked Contestant #19 was hampered by the bad news she just received. Suspension meant no duty until resolution by Internal Affairs, so she decided she may as well stick around here for the after-party and get to talk with Ellen Conyers. Having watched an X-rated video of the late "Ray Fury" (aka Raymond Flintlock of the New York State Police) fucking the socks off "Ebony Cane" (aka Ellen Conyers) Justine promised herself that she'd keep a straight face when talking to Ellen here, despite the fact she was naked and she was now a Cop on-suspension! She wondered how people like that could get naked for a filmmaker and do the nasty for other perverts to watch on their DVD players. Well, Justine told herself, look where I am right now, of all places.....

Fredericksburg Virginia.

1705 Beverly Lane (same day and time): Dr. Peter McCassler did not like leaving his comfort-zone much less driving all the way here to historic Fredericksburg just to meet a female lawyer face-to-face about a topic that was slowly burning his ass day after day.

Walking up the brick steps from the carport to the front of the big brick house, the Scientist was alone with thoughts of what he was going to say to such a woman. The bitch was not very conducive to someone making ultimatums; he already knew that from the one other time he's had to deal with her. When Attorney Amber Duffek can get away with telling Senator Rupert Kelsh to "go fuck himself" after the late Senator ordered her to cover the paper-trail regarding the secret Lab in Maryland, it meant Miss Duffek wielded "power".

Dr. McCassler recently found out Amber got married last year to some fiction author and was cleared by the FBI and ATF from any wrongdoings regarding the mysterious bombing death of a Federal Agent at her former ultra-luxury-domicile in Manassas, Va.

Before he could reach the front stoop, out came the lady he came to see this afternoon, wearing a black, two-piece string bikini and mirrored sunglasses, I-Pod hugging her left bicep with earpiece in her left ear as music played. She noticed the older man approaching but didn't break her stride, fully-expecting his arrival and for him to follow her up to the in-ground swimming pool on the hill beside the house here on Beverly Lane.

"Good afternoon Doctor McCassler, let's chat out here since it's such a nice day," Attorney Amber Duffek spoke first, breaking the uncomfortable silence between them as he followed.

"Counselor, yes…we have to talk in private," Peter said to the shapely thirty-something woman in the tight-fitting string bikini, her well-filled out but athletic body making him suddenly think of something else besides the pressing matter-at-hand.

"I am a patient woman Doctor McCassler, and you should be a patient older gentleman if you know what's best for you in the long run, patience is what gets you to your twilight years in one piece, not to mention keeping you off a radar screen monitored by other far more nefarious gentlemen with the power to have us both drop into a meat-grinder somewhere,"

Amber explained smoothly as she casually walked up the stone path to the swimming pool, the older man sweating in a three-piece business suit following her like a puppy dog.

"Oh, congratulations on your wedding last summer, sorry I missed it," McCassler added to try and relax himself a bit, though such a remark didn't amuse Amber Duffek of course.

"Hmmh, thanks….most people I know never suspected I'd marry a man …..but that is yet another exercise of my patience, my husband is good for me so far and is an asset….ya see, all of us use other people in our lives mostly for selfish purposes and mutual interests, which is why I agreed to see you today McCassler," Amber answered him soft and casual, walking up onto the cement pool deck, looking around the pool area as the sunshine baked it.

"Yes, so you're well-aware of the situation I am in and how untenable it is soon going to become....the goddamn GAO is going to audit the Laboratory's books any day now and they'll find it's not 'decommissioned' like it's supposed to be, which means they'll find Senator Kelsh's two 'packages' being secreted there," Peter spoke in a hushed tone now.

"The General Accounting Office is not to be feared my friend, trust me....I can get an injunction on such an 'audit' no later than tomorrow if you can secure the paperwork to justify it, maybe make the place a 'contaminated' Lab for awhile?" Amber offered as she stepped over to her favorite deck chair, feeling the sun tan lotion on her skin beginning to get slippery in the heat now. McCassler stopped at the ledge of the pool's shallow end, hands on his hips as he stared over at the sexy lawyer in the thin black bikini.

"Right, just nuke the whole lab, turn it into a big fucking Bio-Hazard, that's your answer?

McCassler snipped in sudden change of tone, making Amber take off her sunglasses to look over at him pensively. She knew he had a point but there were fewer other options since the two of them were the scant-few players remaining in this conspiracy of subterfuge.

"Yes, it'll keep the Feds.....the ones who don't know about Clark's grand plan and our involvement anyway....away from the site for a few months at least, you can have a private

'clean-up' team working there as a front then clean the place out of incriminating evidence,"

Amber told him in her all-too-cool demeanor, her over-confidence infuriating him already.

"Part of the so-called 'incriminating evidence' is a man being kept in cryo-suspension," Peter reminded her frankly, folding his arms as he stood his ground by her big swimming pool.

"Cryonics is a bullshit pseudo-science, surely the man can't live through the freezing processs?" Amber remarked as soon as he finished speaking, sitting back up in her chair.

"He's suspended in milder temperatures, alive but in an induced coma," Peter told her.

"I see, and that frozen stud is the asshole Kelsh used to commit virtually every domestic terror operation on American soil since Nineteen-Ninety-Five?" she had to ask him next.

McCassler nodded his head in the affirmative and then turned to step closer toward her.

"Hmmm....I thought that monster was as dead as Kelsh is," Amber sneered in retort.

"Maybe you should have checked out the Laboratory for yourself since you were Kelsh's lawyer and you knew a Federal grant built the goddamn place years ago so naturally the Feds are gonna check it out now that Senator Kelsh is pushing up daisies," Peter added for effect.

"Point taken," Amber sighed as she stood back up from her deck chair and slipped her sunglasses back over her pretty green eyes, then starting to walk back toward the house.

""I don't suppose I could ask you to properly dispose of the bastard's body without anyone else ever finding out?" Amber asked McCassler over one shoulder as she walked back down the stone path toward the front yard now, the Scientist in the suit following her once again.

"I am not experienced in such things as proper corpse-disposal," he answered her frankly.

"No, you're the expert on creating a virus which can make millions of corpses in a matter of just days," Amber said back to him with a hint of a smile on her pretty face.

"Touche'," Peter remarked in retort to her musings, following that delicious-looking body all the way to the front door of the big brick household here on Beverly Lane.

"Hmmm....I'm glad you stopped by Doctor McCassler, because you have just pointed out something pertinent to me and I appreciate it," Amber said as she walked to her front door.

McCassler was not feeling the same way, wishing he could sever the ties to people such as this wealthy and corrupt lawyer and the others hiding in the shadows of a conspiracy to end all conspiracies! McCassler had lost his wife in a divorce because he worked for years on the virus strain Kelsh wanted to use in order to save western civilization....McCassler lost his only son in a plane crash last year while he was on a trip for the now-deceased Rupert Kelsh.

All he had left now was the virus itself safely frozen along with that terrorist he had "on ice" at the Lab Kelsh had owned in Maryland. Amber here was his only original "link" to the high-level conspiracy he had once volunteered for....the "cleansing" of western society in order to save it from the hordes of an over-populated Third World as well as the sickness of liberalism and egalitarian policies that prop up the weak at the expense of the strong!

He followed her into the air-conditioned house, marveling at its plush interior with the antique furnishings and luxury settings. Amber stepped to the end of the marble foyer near the front door, facing down a long dark hallway, hands on her hips as she thought on it.

"I have a few phone calls to make....hmmph, shouldn't be a problem if you can get rid of that terrorist's body you've got frozen in the Lab," she said back to him gingerly.

"Okay, okay, I think I know a way to do that without problems," McCassler replied softly.

"Good, ya see....you're still an asset after all Doctor McCassler," Amber cooed sweetly to the nervous-looking older man sweating in his suit, her over-confidence downright appalling.

"Right," he sighed and swallowed hard, eyes on the lovely female in the black string-bikini.

"Heenh, you seem un-convinced," she said as she turned to face him eye-to-eye once more.

"Are you certain this won't bite us....I mean, the goddamn Feds snooping around?" Peter responded with his eyes to the marble foyer beneath his shoes now, unsure of himself.

"I'm sure....I'd bet my husband's balls on it....now go take out your trash and leave the wheeling n' dealing to me," Amber said softly as she untied her bikini top in back, letting

the garment come off her perky boobs as she stood there facing him, then casually turned and untied her bikini-bottom to slip out of it as she started down the hallway from there.

McCassler could say no more as he watched the naked woman stroll on down the darkened hallway totally nude and care-free, figuring she did that just to further "goad" him. How any man could marry a woman like that was beyond him! McCassler left as quickly as he had arrived and was glad to get on the Interstate back toward Maryland.

"Hmmph, Kelsh should have clipped that weakling before he bought the farm himself," Amber said to herself as she entered her master bedroom, stepping up to the wall-mirror on the bathroom door, ogling herself in the mirror as she thought about who to call now.

McCassler was already a "liability" she'll have to dispose of personally if he screws up what she wants him to do, only this time she can't just ask Kelsh to have him discreetly murdered.

Her husband Kenny was downstairs writing in his private den, where he spent hours-on-end working on his next manuscript(s) so he was predictably "out of her hair" most of the time and that was one more thing she liked about the man along with his agreeable knack of not asking awkward questions of her! She picked up her cordless phone from the nightstand and dialed a familiar Washington D.C. number she had memorized a long time ago.

"Yes, put me through to his personal cell-phone," she spoke to the voice that answered on the other end, standing there in her master bedroom naked with the phone to her left ear.

"Hi, this is Amber....I need a small favor, and trust me...it benefits us both this time," she said into the phone when a familiar male voice spoke on the other end of the secure line.

"Yes, yes, I can do that for you, just see to it that fuckin' Lab isn't compromised by the goddamn GAO," Amber was saying over the secure line as her husband suddenly entered their bedroom, winking at her first then crossing to where the walk-in closet was located.

"Thought you were going up to the pool babe," her husband said from the closet, picking out something to wear because he had a book-signing to attend in Richmond this evening.

"Duty calls," Amber answered him casually, calling another number on the cordless phone.

She turned to look out the window nearest the bed and stared out at the hillside pool area, thinking that she needed some leisure time all to herself sometime soon because she's been working too much lately. Relaxation was the key to stress-reduction and she needed it now.

"Amber, why don't we take off to Bermuda next week, soak up some sun?" he asked as he stepped up behind his shapely, fit wife standing naked at the window. She felt him snake two fingers down along her right asscheek, gently squeezing as he slipped fingers down between her thighs and to the sweet spot, making her flinch slightly in agreeable reaction to his touch.

"Mmmmh…I'd like that, keep it in mind and if I'm not called away, I'll take you up on it," she cooed over her shoulder to her husband, his left hand sliding up her back to gently caress her neck under her long and wavy brown hair. Amber closed her eyes as sexual arousal began welling up inside her now, her husband's exploring, expert hands nearly driving her to orgasm right where she stood. She turned to face Kenny and they kissed, then he ushered her over to the bed for a quick lovemaking, since she was already naked and all…

New Rochelle, NY. 4:35 that afternoon: Meeting someone like this wasn't exactly the usual manner a woman meets another, then again it was at a "Miss Nude" Pageant after all!

Ellen Conyers aka: "Ebony Cane" was an attractive, mocha-skinned Black woman with big breasts and a thick-but-athletic physique overall, looking about the same as she did in the men's magazine Justine saw her in no long ago.

"I take it you've lost your goddamn mind Miss Cheeks….delving into a cold case murder even the friggin' FBI won't touch anymore…. lucky for me baby, I was on the outside when all that shit went down with Jonny, Shelly, Chrissa, Ray, and Dave Solomon….tragic," Ellen Conyers spoke to the still-nude Justine Cheeks as they both stepped into a hallway away from the "after-party" still going on here at the Collins Country Club.

"I'm extremely interested because I knew Ray Flintlock…..aka 'Ray Fury'…..," Justine repeated from her earlier introduction and questioning, glad the woman was talking to her.

"You said that already, and if you're a cop then you're certainly an unusual one because most female cops wouldn't enlist in a 'Miss Nude' Pageant just to speak to an old witness," Ellen said softly to her naked "fan" standing in the dimly-lit, carpeted hallway with her now.

"Tell me about it…but I want to get a better picture of what could have happened to Ray, he was a State Trooper ya know and the State Police have pretty much closed the case, blaming it all on the Porn Kingpin Jonny Faster and his ties to the Italian Mafia," Justine spoke eloquently as if rehearsed. Ellen sensed she was either an undercover cop or some kind of "tabloid reporter" much like the one who exposed her as a secret porn actress four years ago and ruined her daytime career in the Air Force!

"Heenh, girl….Jonny Faster wouldn't have murdered a single soul, he was too much of a gentleman, and the Mafia wanted Jonny's balls in a jar over some bullshit 'debt' his company owed them from the previous owner….Ray Flintlock was the new black guy on the cast-list of Faster Productions that year and he stepped into a pitfall not of his own making I'm afraid, you know…wrong-place, wrong-time, tough-luck?" Ellen continued frankly.

"Just like in the Hollywood movies baby…the black dude always gets killed some point in time," Ellen snickered as she started down the hallway slowly, feeling better walking with this curious contestant while talking as opposed to standing still. Justine shook her head at that crass remark, but listened to Ellen's dissertation without interruption, absorbing it all.

"Jonny was rumored to have been 'retiring' soon and Ray Fury was the Talent Coordinator's choice to 'replace' Jonny as far as a 'male leading man' in upcoming X-rated features that year, and Dave Solomon the Production Assistant, wanted to replace Jonny Faster in the Director's chair, so there was a lot of speculation and back-stabbing going on in the months leading up to July of two-thousand-five when the shit hit the fan," Ellen added politely.

"Jonny fired the Talent Coordinator Shaya Gold....but he didn't get rid of Dave Solomon, and he seemed willing to allow Ray Fury to take his place in upcoming feature films Jonny had cast himself in, which also meant Ray would have been paired with Jonny's favorite little blonde cupcake Shelly James....if Ray had survived the murder and arson at Jonny's private mountain retreat that summer," Ellen spoke gingerly, not upset by re-hashing the memory.

"I liked Jonny a lot, he was truly color-blind.....and poor Ray just wanted to have sex for the cameras and get paid for it because his personal love-life was non-existent, too bad they both had to end up victims of foul-play it seems," Ellen said next in a conclusive tone of voice.

"I'd recommend you go and see Shaya Gold....she recently bought the old 'Faster Mansion' here in New Rochelle from the Church that had it after Jonny....she might shed some light on the matter more than I can....hope you find what you're looking for Officer," Ellen Conyers said with a smile and wink at the naked Justine Cheeks, walking away abruptly.

"Yeah," Justine sighed as she watched "Ebony Cane" vanish on down the hallway.

Justine strolled back toward the "after-party" where she was now only one of two naked female contestants left, the remaining others in robes and bikinis by now, but Detective Justine Cheeks didn't care at this point. She was suspended from duty pending a breech of "ethics" a la willful-participation in this year's "Miss Nude Northeast 2009" Pageant and unofficially conducting an unauthorized investigation into the "Faster Murders" of 2005.

Walking up to one of the cash-bars, she ordered a Rum-n-Coke and got it quickly from the ogling bartender whose eyes didn't leave her bare frontal assets even as he poured her drink.

"I didn't expect today to end up like this...actually, and on top of it all, I found my witness to be rather uncooperative and I'm gonna have to dust off my resume' for a new line of work after Internal Affairs gets done with me, shit....," Justine spoke to herself in a sigh, then took a swig of her mixed drink. More male guests of the Pageant wanted to take pictures with the naked "#19" chick, and at this point she didn't care so Justine posed for photos with a whole bunch of strangers there in the Country Club hosting the event today.

One thing she did not know until Ellen Conyers spoke with her minutes ago, was that Shaya Gold had purchased the "Faster Mansion" here in new Rochelle recently and that was something Justine did not see in any of the online news sources, guessing that big-titted bitch must have done it under false-pretenses or used another "under the table" method of buying such an infamous location in this area without the major media picking up on it!

Shaya Gold had been married to the late Senator Rupert Kelsh before his untimely death at the hands of "domestic terrorists" (according to the ATF) and before that, Shaya Gold was a famous Porn Starlet who usually worked for east coast Porn Mogul Jonny Faster in the years leading up to the summer of 2005. Fuck it, Justine told herself as she stood there nursing her drink without a stitch on except for her garter and the #19 on her right thigh. She had to find out what really happened to Trooper Raymond J. Flintlock aka "Ray Fury" because she knew the man, having worked with him in the NY State Police for five years. She didn't owe the late Ray Flintlock anything, but he "owed" her and that was why Justine Cheeks risked her own career with the State Police to dig deeper into the mystery after four years. Four years she kept her mouth shut and played the game, hoping the official investigation would not go "cold" like it has as of last year. Juggling her real job with her "hobby" was coming to a boil now and she felt the heat....despite being totally-naked in a stranger's Country Club!

"Why Detective Cheeks…fitting you'd be a contestant here today," spoke an eerily-familiar male voice from behind her, the man's left hand tapping her on her bare ass before she could turn around and confront him defensively, knowing to whom the voice belonged.

It was one Decker Matheson, an Irish prick whom she owes money to, and his appearance here marked the peak of a day's bad strokes of luck…..the first being her Police Supervisor showing up to see her butterball-naked and suspending her from duty on the spot, then the mostly-uncooperative former porn starlet Ellen Conyers, and now this!

"Motherfucker," Justine sneered to the lean and well-dressed-like-a-pimp Decker Matheson.

"Justine, don't blame me baby doll, I would have voted for you so that you could win the prize money and pay off your gambling debt," the handsome but sinister man softly spoke.

"Right, so what did Bruno say about me putting double on the World Series game?" she asked him in a lowered tone of voice, looking around to make sure no one else heard her.

"Hunh, you kiddin'….Bruno's not gonna hold you over until the World Series when you can't even pay half of what you already owe him for the last two games," the man chided.

"I'm good for it, and he's chicken-shit,"Justine sneered in sarcasm, looking away from him.

"Justine baby, Bruno's a nice guy, but he's gonna collect one way or the other, and it's not gonna matter that you're a cop…..but hey, maybe sports-gambling isn't your thing?" the "Bookie" said frankly to her with another tap of a hand to her bare ass.

Upstate New York, 7:05pm: The Kawasaki Ninja was her newest "toy" and the woman straddling the powerful crotch-rocket loved it. Flying around the sharp turns like she did, the former Mrs. Shaya Kelsh relished the sensation of the ride she was enjoying today, well up into the Catskills and back toward New Rochelle now. Learning to pilot a motorcycle was not as difficult as Shaya first imagined, though she had already two speeding tickets to prove how much fun she was having on her new motorcycle! Well, at least up to this point....

A grey Van was following her and had been for some time now, making her wonder who was driving and why they were lagging behind her about 200 yards or so steadily, even taking the detour she took out of the Catskills awhile back? Shaya's paranoia was returning but she had long realized that if her late husband's shadowy pals in the US Government had wanted to eliminate her, they would have done it already! No, this "stalker" was something else....

Inside the grey Chevy van, the driver and his buddy in the passenger seat were laughing between themselves as they followed the female on the Kawasaki Ninja at what they thought to be a "discreet" distance, and they were following her because they had seen her at the diner she stopped at back in the Catskills two hours ago and took her helmet and leather jacket off at the lunch-counter. Barry and Sal had been smitten with the raven-haired, forty-something woman and decided to follow her as she drove off along on her crotch-rocket.

Barry and Sal were just two contractors off work this afternoon and looking for a bit of fun, finding it in trailing a hot chick on a motorcycle. Barry and Sal weren't stalking rapists, just a pair of middle-aged horny guys having a steady laugh as they followed their female "target".

"Hunh-haanh...lookit that ass straddlin' that Bike......mmmhh!" Sal said from the van's passenger seat to Barry behind the wheel, both men laughing as Barry sped up behind the woman on the Motorcycle, getting closer, no longer caring if she knows they're following.

Shaya hit the gas, speeding far up ahead of the slower, late-model work van, and taking the next curve a bit too shallow, almost wiping out but recovered well enough to easily shoot up a narrow two-lane road leading up a hill from the main highway she'd been on, knowing where she was at actually. The van was too far behind to have seen her divert, and Barry the driver slowed down at the long curve to make sure he and his buddy didn't miss her eluding them, taking for granted that sexy female Biker had shot up way ahead of them on the highway here. Coming up on a bridge overpass, Barry and Sal noticed someone stopping at the bridge, facing down at the highway toward the oncoming van. It was her!!

Shaya saw only that damn grey van coming down the highway toward he this moment, so she did what she'd hoped to do in response to those assholes following her like they were.

She opened her leather jacket and pulled up her pullover shirt beneath, popping her big boobs out of her lace bra and leaned forward over the bridge's rail to flash her admirers.

"Holeeee-sssshhhit!" Barry snapped in gleeful surprise as he and Sal watched the helmeted female Biker expose her big boobs to them up at the bridge as they drove toward it to go under. Barry stomped the brakes to slow down but overcompensated and lost control of the van as they drove under the bridge, tires screeching on the pavement as the van's driver tried to regain control. Shaya covered back up and broke out into laughter as she heard the van crash just on the other side of the bridge, a sickening "slap" of metal into tree trunks, denoting that the vehicle had careened off the roadway into the trees on the road side. She laughed as she zipped up and climbed back onto her Kawasaki Ninja, gunning the accelerator and speeding off along the two-lane road which she knew will take her back to the Highway below, only several miles south of the accident she had just caused.

"Serves you guys right for following me around like a pair of creeps," Shaya said to herself as she drove away, heading south to New Rochelle and her recently-purchased mansion.

The "Faster Mansion" New Rochelle, NY.
9:50 that night:

Shaya was happy to be home in the mansion she had spent far too much time in years ago when she was what most of her fans call a "Porn Queen". She felt peaceful here despite the tragedy of it's past occupants and the stigma hanging on this exclusive New Rochelle address even to this day. Shaya Gold stripped and headed for the shower on the second floor of the luxury mansion, just wanting to relax in the piping-hot water alone and perhaps order-out some dinner when she was done. Reflecting on how difficult it was to convince the former owner of this infamous house to come off it and sell it to her despite the dropping market value, she had poured a considerable amount of money into re-furnishing the place. The former owner from 2005-on was a Church congregation that was using it to house it's AA, NA, GA, sex-addicts, and other 7-day-a-week "addict" programs. Needless to say, the mansion was not as well-kept as it was when Jonny Faster owned it but Shaya had been gradually returning it to its former glory the time she's been here so far.

Funny it was being used as a classroom-setting for "sex addicts" being that the mansion was once the home and primary filming-location for the east coast's top Adult Film Mogul and famous Porn Star, "Jonny Faster"! Shaya relaxed in her hot shower, standing there idle for minutes on end just enjoying the hot spray on her skin, reflecting on her past and what she plans to do in the near future. Now that she was worth a little over $4 million total in net assets, she lived alone and even legally changed her name to her former porn film moniker "Shaya Gold" soon after her husband's death. Depending on men or a "career" to sustain her was a relic of her past and being independently wealthy felt extremely liberating....

It was now almost 10:00 and she had almost forgotten about the pizza delivery she ordered when she first walked in the door earlier! Killing the shower, Shaya quickly dried herself off, wondering if she might have already missed the delivery since she might not have heard the doorbell ringing while in the shower. Dry enough to wrap one of her red silk bathrobes around her voluptuous body, Shaya hurried downstairs to the huge living room area, going to the front foyer and door in wonder if she may have missed her late dinner delivery.

It was at the moment before she could grab the brass doorknob of the heavy front door that the doorbell "rang" loud and clear from the other side, her pizza order has now arrived!

When she pulled the door open, she came face-to-face with a staring young man about age 18 or 19, his gaze on her impressive cleavage in the tight and skimpy silk robe she wore, not looking her in the eyes at all until she spoke to him: "Good, I thought I had missed you".

"Uhhhmm…yesss-ma'am, here's your uhh…pepperoni and mushroom pizza," the nervous young man said as he handed her the boxed pizza pie, eyes on her big breasts bulging in the tight-fitting silk robe that barely covered those plump, perky melons of hers.

"Thanks big guy, come on in and I'll get your money for ya," Shaya chimed girlishly as she let him cross the threshold, herself turning to walk back into her living room with her pizza.

The dark-haired kid looked Italian-American, Shaya mused as she led him inside, noticing how nervous he was in her presence, that "power" she held over most men coming into play once more and she always loved it. She had some cash in her leather jacket lying on the big circular sofa, so she walked over to the sofa she recently purchased and grabbed a $20 bill.

"What's your name sweetheart?" she had to ask the teenager ogling her cleavage again as he took the money for the pizza he just delivered, nodding his head in thanks, stepping back.

"Paul….Paul Verducci," he answered her hesitantly with a slight smile, backing up more.

"Ah-hah, I knew you were Italian, only fitting you'd be bringing me a pizza," Shaya chided him with an impish smirk as she watched him retreat toward the front door.

Cockeysville, Maryland. 10:20 that night: Dr. Peter McCassler had one of two key-cards granting access to the clandestine laboratory here in what was supposed to be a "vacant" Lab building just outside Baltimore. The other one was presumably blown to smithereens along with U.S. Senator Rupert Kelsh over a year ago. A lot has not happened in over a year's time, he mused as he entered the secure Lab where he maintained two dark secrets that if revealed could bring down his hidden co-conspirators and get himself the Death Penalty.

As soon as he buzzed himself into the "containment" portion of the laboratory, he sensed something was wrong as he looked over at the hermetically-sealed "cryo-stasis" container which held one domestic terrorist no one was to know existed....well, it did...past-tense!

"What in god's name....?" the Scientist quipped in stunned realization that the man he cryo-suspended in a coma over a year ago for Tyler Clarke was no longer inside the container.

It was then he felt a sharp sensation in his back and chest centered between his spine and sternum, and then he felt nothing as his sight left him, blacking out. The thin and sharp rod stabbing through Dr. McCassler's chest right now killed the man before he flopped to the cement floor below. Duncan Horsehair stood over his victim on feeble legs; weary and weakened from the lengthy "coma" he'd been in, barely able to walk and in searing pain from the chest-down. He could see what they had done to him, and now he just killed the one responsible for keeping him in such an unholy condition. He had awoken from that chamber and his coma just like he had awoken from his own clinical death at Walter Reed Army Hospital all those years ago. He had cheated final death yet again, his last memory being inside the Kelsh residence in Georgetown, going up a flight of stairs to see Shaya Kelsh when everything got blurry and then he hit the deck at the bottom of her stairs.

Senator Kelsh was dead in a car explosion of his making, the old man a victim of his own arrogance really, Duncan just supplied the means to end his life right on time.

"Shaya.....Shhhhaaaayyyaaaa.....," Duncan Horsehair sneered as he stumbled across the laboratory floor, his legs still numb and difficult to move in a normal walking manner, just thankful that he could at least move like this, that he wasn't paralyzed for lack of use over the course of what he suspects has been quite awhile in a forced "coma". He kept thinking of the Senator's wife and if she was still alive herself, and if she might have had a hand in doing this to him? Questions filled his mind right now but Duncan was trying to focus more on his next step now that he was a free man once more, free and "clear" as far as anyone actually knowing about him, surprised that he was kept in a coma like this, and not just killed and disposed of like he had expected might happen one day. To every damn thing under the sun, there is a fucking reason! Right now he just had to find some clothes to fit him and get out of this place without being compromised or caught. Being unarmed was not something he was used to, so weapons were next on his priority list as well as food and water a close third because he was starved to say the least. This was a laboratory alright; a very strange place for him to find himself, and the fact just dawned on him as to why he would have been kept in such a "comatose/frozen" state within the confines of a secure laboratory.

"The virus," he said to himself out loud, stopping at a counter to better balance his body.

That was the reason for it and for his own survival....Kelsh and his fellow Neo-Nazis wanted him to deliver the virus sometime in the future...maybe be it's "host" and carry it somewhere to effectively wipe-out inferior humanity like it should be wiped-out. That goddamn virus was a "pesticide" of apocalyptic proportions, its antidote a rare serum held by a few in Washington D.C.'s inner-circle of Social-Darwinists like the late Senator Kelsh.

"So we're right here....two deadly weapons stored together for future use," Horsehair said to himself as he looked around the laboratory with a slight smirk crossing his chiseled face.

Faster Mansion, 11:05pm: Paul wasn't one to goof-off on the job nor did he have any sort of "life" that would get in the way of his routine pizza-deliveries in New Rochelle NY, nor even anything that would interrupt or distract the simple guy waiting until August when he is slated to go off to US Army Boot camp at Fort Benning, Georgia. Sonny and Manny had dropped by the last known delivery address of their friend's route tonight since their boss was threatening to fire Paul for not returning to "Pizza Shack" for the duration of his shift (which ended fifteen minutes ago). Getting out of Sonny's Mustang parked behind Paul's vehicle, the two 18-year old high school seniors approached the dimly-lit mansion here at a rather infamous address known all over New Rochelle as the location of those media-hyped "Porn Murders" four years ago. Manny was beginning to regret teasing Paul earlier about getting a delivery-call to this place, hoping nothing bad happened to the guy just before he was to graduate and go into the Army at age 18. Sonny, the bolder of the three friends who deliver pizzas for their asshole of a boss on weeknights like this, walked up to the front door and knocked twice, then knocked again after no answer.

"There's lights on inside man, and his car's still here....shit," whispered Manny, a skinny Puerto Rican teen who was barely graduating due to his poor grades, standing on the walkway leading up to the big house as Sonny stepped back toward him shaking his head.

"Not answering his cellphone, no answer to the door....damn, the place done swallowed him up," the red-headed Sonny snickered in crass humor that was his personal trademark.

"Let's check it out!" Manny quipped nervously, then followed Sonny around the dark exterior of the mansion here, around to the back yard in search of their wayward friend who was about to lose his pizza-delivery job for goofing-off while on the clock. The back yard was lit by a single flood light over the wooden patio deck, not much to go on vision-wise but the two teenagers made it to the patio deck and found a sliding-glass door showing a well-lit interior and what had to be the largest, fully-furnished "living room" they had ever seen!

"Jeezus....look at this place....dammmmmn!" Sonny chimed as they stood at the sliding-glass door peering inside, Manny trying the door but it was locked-shut of course. Sonny then noticed another source of light coming from one of the ground-level windows at the other far end of the rear patio deck, and started walking toward it with the nervous Manny not far behind, both of them knowing full-well they could get arrested for "trespassing".

That window at the far end of the long patio deck with a light on inside was that of a bedroom, which the two snoopers quickly discovered as they cautiously peered inside.

Along with the well-lit spare bedroom lit by a few lamps inside, Sonny and Manny found a naked couple on a bed in the center of the room, going-at-it....and they both recognized the naked young man now plunging into the big-breasted dark haired female in a very vibrant missionary-style intercourse! There he was, their "missing" friend Paul Verducci, screwing the socks off the lady customer he had brought a pizza to earlier....

"Awesome.....man, he's fuckin' her.....dude....," the one named Manny exclaimed in delight of what they were looking in on right now, both of them surprised at the sight of their friend Paul dipping his wick into a very well-built older woman tonight. The two of them always thought Paul was too "shy" around girls and teased him about being a virgin, but there he was...plowing-a-row into the flesh of a well-developed woman here inside the infamous "Porno House" as the locals called it in the past.

"I don't believe this....holeeee-sheeeetth.....Paulie's tappin' dat ass good!" Sonny quipped as he watched through the window along with Manny on the outside, seeing their skinny friend steadily missionary-pumping into the dark haired chick like a champ! They couldn't hear the sex going on from the outside here but it looked enticing enough.

"Hey.....you...peepin' toms!" came a female voice from out of nowhere, startling the two teens peeking through the window at the lovers inside. Sonny and Manny spun around to find a lone figure standing on the deck in the form of a feminine shadow, hands on her hips as she faced them about 10 feet away on the wooden patio deck.

"Whoah...we're just ahhh....looking for a friend of ours..... uhhmmm," Manny spoke first with his hands up, seeing the glint of a metal badge dangling down from around the short-haired woman's neck, knowing that usually denoted a Cop in plain-clothes...... BUSTED!

"Police Officer.....you've got five seconds to get your asses out of here or you're gonna be peeking through Jail bars by midnight tonight," Detective Justine Cheeks spoke next in a calm but serious tone of voice, standing there with hands on her hips as the two "peepers" retreated from the window and back toward the direction from whence they came.

"Okay, okay Officer...sorry, we were just looking for a friend... he's inside the house right now, honestly....we're out of here," the one named Sonny remarked as they passed her, eyeing the fact she was a good-looking female cop and badge on a chain around her neck.

"Four.....three....two....," Justine spoke calmly and slowly in response, watching the two young guys break into a run back around the corner of the mansion to return to their car.

"Pervs," Justine sighed to herself as she strolled over to the window herself now, looking in to see their young friend nailing Shaya Gold doggie-style now on the bed in there. That had to be Shaya Gold the former Porno Star, Justine mused as she watched the action a bit, at least it looked like the same dusky-hued slut on all those X-rated film box covers!

"And Bingo was his name....oooohh!" Justine chimed to herself as she walked to the sliding glass door, deciding to make her entry there since sliding-doors are the easiest to jimmy-open, something she learned as a Police Detective, a job she had been suspended from but still had an old badge to "look the part" when needed, like tonight.

"What a joint," Justine snickered as she freed the sliding door lock and quietly opened it enough to slip inside the air-conditioned living room area, looking around the well-furnished interior that rivaled most basketball courts in square footage. The woman she wanted to speak with tonight was getting hammered by a guy young enough to be her son just down the hallway there, so she waited patiently there at the custom, in-home Bar, close enough to the sliding door to rush out if she had to flee all of a sudden.

She didn't have to wait too long after pouring herself a small glass of Chartreuse and water, seeing a naked young man coming rushing out down the hallway, grabbing his clothes he had deposited there earlier, heading to the huge living room. As soon as he spotted the women wearing a badge on her chest and holding a handgun in her right hand, drink in the other, instincts made him freeze in reaction, stopping just eight feet from her, naked with a hard-on, clothes around one forearm, eyes like a deer's fixed in the headlights of a car.

"Hey there stud….you'd better run-along now that you got your dick wet, and do it quickly while I count to ten….one…two…..," Justine spoke gingerly to the stunned young man.

He didn't waste any time after she raised her handgun and began counting, he even ran out the front door naked with just his jeans, dropping shoes and shirt along the frightened path.

"Hunh-hunh…all balls and no courage…. make a good husband to some bitch one day," Justine remarked as soon as the front door slammed shut. She wolfed her drink then put the glass down on the bar, turning toward that dark hallway, having decided to go confront "Shaya Gold" exactly where she was. Shaya was still lying on the bed of the spare bedroom where she had seduced her pizza-delivery guy tonight, feeling wickedly great because of it, not to mention having enjoyed the sex with the virginal Paul Verducci.

"Oh shit….hey…he said he was eighteen!" Shaya quipped as she sat up on the bed, watching a stranger step into the room with badge and gun, instinctively putting her hands up.

Chicago, Illinois (same night and time): Being a Fan of an Actress wasn't strange at all, but one exception to which sort of stands out enough for most fans of this "genre" to keep their enthusiasm close to their hearts and away from family/friends. When his mother found out he liked to watch "Adult Films" a few years ago, she chastised him for it and remarked how her only son would never have a girlfriend if he keeps watching "pornos" all the time!

Of course Rufus Seastone didn't mind hearing shit like that even from his parents, because he enjoyed watching adult films, and as far as friends went, they often wanted to watch them as well when they came over for beers to his one-bedroom apartment here in downtown.

Chicago was a city with plenty of sources to buy legal DVDs of X-rated films and Rufus had quite a collection for the most part, a floor-to-ceiling shelf full of adult films in his closet, and his favorite ones overall were the "Faster" films produced between 1999 and 2005.

At age 32, Rufus was a single black man with a good job as a mechanic who worked long hours but made up for it by enjoying precisely what he wants during his spare time, and one piece of that was his vicarious enjoyment of adult films. Walking into his bedroom while R+B music played on his stereo system, Rufus stopped a moment to look up at the framed poster of X-rated Film Starlet SHAYA GOLD next to his computer and desk. It was a life-size poster of the raven-haired Shaya barely covered in camo-tatters with a Rambo-style tied-off headband, a plastic-looking machine gun in her hands staring slinky-faced. It was the cover of her 1999 X-rated feature film "Boobs of War" starring Shaya Gold, Lacey Lovitt, Ebony Cane, FM Dexter, and Woodrow Grande. He had ordered the poster from Shaya Gold's Fan Club back then and she autographed the poster to him personally, having written in black marker : "To my Number #1 Fan Rufus Seastone…Love and Tickles, Shaya Gold".

"Shaaayyaah….what a piece of work," Rufus sighed up at the framed and signed poster of his favorite Porn Star, the sight of her always making him smile even if it was just a poster.

Rufus raised his glass of protein drink to his lips and swilled it down as he stood there staring at the poster of Shaya Gold, trying to decide if he should go out to a Club tonight or just chill here at home and watch some flicks, get drunk right here as he watched his favorite porn films. His Mother derided him for not getting married and not "dating" like he should, even though he has told her over and over again how most of the women in his age bracket are already hooked-up/married, have kids by other guys, not to mention the fact his own taste in women kept him from fooling around with fat chicks and the habitually ugly ones!

"Ghetto-Fabulous" just didn't cut it for Rufus Seastone, no…he wanted a woman that looks like Shaya Gold, for the most part. Why not, everyone other nigger seems to get the type of honey they want so why should he be any different? Shaya had that lightly-bronzed skin tone he preferred as opposed to the lily-white pale complexion of white women, and Rufus liked corresponding with her via her mail-order fan club address in New York. Though he had never met Shaya face-to-face, he relished the idea of her, his ultimate woman, even if she is getting older and doesn't do porn films any longer. He was thankful Shaya wasn't caught up in that "murder conspiracy" thing back in 2005 that brought down Faster Productions and resulted in Jonny Faster himself considered a "missing person", two other porn stars murdered and one Staffer shot dead by Police. Rufus wrote her a letter at least once a month and she often wrote a quick not back to him, or just sent an autographed 8x10 photo to her "Number One Fan" here in Chicago. Rufus Seastone always felt better whenever staring at a photo of Shaya Gold, and watching her films over and over again always cheered him up, no matter what was going on in his reality....he could always relax into fantasy....the fantasy where he's not just another American "Black Dude" but sharing an evening with the lovely Shaya as her chosen consort....yeah man, that fantasy kept him from melancholy.

New Rochelle, NY. (Midnight): Shaya wrapped a silk robe around her body and walked out into the mansion's huge living room with the female cop close behind her, gun still in one hand down by her thigh. The Cop was alone, which was strange because if this was a "raid" there would be a dozen of the pigs in the house by now.

"I don't suppose I can consider this to be some kind of joke, hunh?" Shaya had to ask.

"Nope, it's no joke Shaya Gold, considering your penchant for slipping out of every goddamn tragedy you help bring on.....from the so-called 'Faster Murders' to the untimely demise of your husband Senator Rupert Kelsh a year ago....I'd call this a reckoning," Justine Cheeks spoke to the shapely former porn star now walking over to the in-house Bar.

"I had nothing to do with either one of those, and the Police... FBI, even the ATF questioned me extensively after both, why are you here Detective?" Shaya chimed defensively, glancing around to see the gold badge dangling from the female cop's neck, seeing it to be a New York State Police BCI Detective's Badge.

"Ah yes, but the case isn't over....primarily the case involving the death of one Raymond J. Flintlock of the New York State Police, a victim who also 'moon-lighted' as a male porn actor for the now-defunct Adult Film Company known as 'Faster Productions', a company you were high-up on the Totem-Pole with at the time," Justine explained as she raised her handgun in gesture, keeping her eyes of the ravishing Shaya Gold as the woman sat down on a barstool and stared fearful back at her. Justine stepped behind the bar, looking at the bottles of booze aligned there, considering fixing herself a stiff drink for the hell of it.

"Ray Fury….he died at the Catskills Cabin four years ago, I was fired by Jonny himself a month before that happened," Shaya said softly, knowing it would not placate the visitor.

"Right, and the BCI as well as the FBI cleared you of any wrongdoing back then even though you had just as much cause to exact revenge on the Company that fired you as any of the other 'enemies' Jonny Faster and crew made over the years prior," Justine added next.

"What is this about Detective…..really, you come into my home without a warrant and wave a gun in my face all by yourself, surely you don't expect me to believe you are acting according to Departmental protocol?" Shaya responded calmly but curt.

"Hunh-haah, you're right bitch…I'm here on my own and so are you….the teenager you were balling ran out of here so scared, he won't tell anyone about me….he thinks I'm a cop who was coming to arrest you and I let him go," Justine told her with a reassuring smile.

"So let's get down to it then Detective….what is it you want from me?" Shaya chimed.

"Aaaahhh….what I want from you….well that's a tad bit complicated but I'm sure you'll understand my situation if you value your own," Justine said as she picked up a bottle of Tequila from behind the bar counter, placing it on the bar counter between them.

"Ray Flintlock…aka 'Ray Fury'…..I worked with him back in Oh-Five when he was a very-much-alive State Trooper, and he owed me some money…money he was set to pay me in-full in exchange for me not telling our Departmental Superiors about his extra-curricular activities as a Porn Actor with your company," Justine explained slow and smooth.

"You were blackmailing Ray," Shaya spoke up in surprised realization of the situation.

"In a word, yes…he was so stupid…he let his face get put on a porn flick's box cover that spring and I saw it at a video store where I was looking for a porno to play at a bachlorette party I was invited to," Justine continued as she popped the top off the tequila bottle.

"I discreetly approached him about it and he agreed to pay me ten-thousand dollars cash if I would keep my mouth shut about it….then he turned up dead on the evening news as you well know, shot and burned to death at Jonny Faster's cabin in the Catskills," Justine spoke.

"What….you want me to pay you the ten-grand now…after four years?" Shaya quipped.

"Unh-hunh, I do….and with interest, or I will ruin you Shaya Gold….whatever your name is, I'll ruin you….ya know, Police Officers have incredible lee-way when it comes to belief in the Courts, say if I planted evidence here some point in time, you'd go down for it because you've already been on Police and FBI radar twice in the past few years, they'd arrest you," Justine told her in a lower voice of malice, eyes denoting how serious she now was.

"I don't have ten-grand cash on me tonight Detective….even if I did, I'd still tell you to go fuck yourself….I'm not gonna be treated like this," Shaya replied back in firmer reaction.

"I see, figured you'd say that….how about the others around you, say…that young stud you were entertaining in the bedroom earlier… .I could simply find him and castrate him, blame it on you since his DNA is somewhere in this house after tonight for sure, or…I could just shoot you right here and now…..it'll be blamed on the two young guys I caught outside awhile ago peeking through the bedroom window at their friend the pizza-boy getting laid," Justine explained in casual aplomb, convincingly enough so Shaya believed her.

"Then again maybe you don't give two-shits about anyone but yaself Shaya Gold, and I could do anything to anyone else because none of them are worth ten-thousand dollars?" Justine continued in her frank, spooky tone of voice, then poured Shaya a shot of tequila.

"I will see you put in prison one way or the other, cops can do that....I'll definitely set you up for a felony charge and not lose a wink's sleep over it," Justine added with a scowl.

"Or, I can have a local street gang I know of come in here one night to take all kinds of liberties with the interior here as well as your beautiful body," Justine added coldly.

"I believe you Detective...I believe you....," Shaya sighed then wolfed down the tequila.

"Hmmmm.....well I'm certain you have something inside this friggin' mansion worth ten-grand or more, something I could carry with me?" Justine chimed with a smirking grin.

"Yes, but how do I know this isn't just a one-time shakedown?" Shaya asked flatly.

"You don't know, you'll just have to assume I'm good-natured and won't come calling on you again, which I don't plan on doing as long as I can get ten-grand plus five-percent interest from you within the next twelve hours," Justine answered in kind, pouring herself a shot of tequila this time and quickly wolfing it down, slapping the shotglass to the counter.

"Doesn't leave us much time," Shaya sighed matter-of-factly as she sat there staring.

"There's an ATM just a mile down the road," Justine responded with a sinister grin, waving her Glock pistol in her left hand now as she faced the homeowner across the bar counter.

Shaya stood up from the barstool and nodded reluctantly, turning around to walk across the living room slowly, knowing that this rogue cop might shoot her in the back if she tried to flee or escape the mansion, call for help, etc. She was trapped and she knew it, for any bullet fired from firearm can out-run any human being alive!

"Why me?" Shaya asked next, curious and furious at the same time. This cop came out of nowhere and was demanding money for a debt "owed" her by a man who used to work for her Porn Company four years ago. Shaya was no Investigator herself, but she gathered enough intel from what the comely female cop was telling her to believe that the cop herself was in a bind of some sort and needed money right away, why else would she pursue this angle four years after the death of the man she was originally blackmailing??!!

"Why you.....hunh...because you're a 'Fringe Element' Shaya Gold....a fukkin' fringe element no one of weight is going to take seriously when you make accusations against ordinary, upstanding citizens like myself for instance....who tha hell is gonna believe a former porno-star who has been questioned in more than one homicide case in the recent past and who doesn't have anyone to stick up for her?" Justine explained rather coldly.

Shaya couldn't respond to that remark because in a very real way, the bitch was right.

"So, you were blackmailing Ray because he was secretly moonlighting as an Adult Film Actor and now you want me to pay the amount or you'll 'ruin' me in some way, shape or form...so may I ask why did you blackmail Ray in the first place, just out of meanness?" Shaya spoke softly as she walked over to the sofa, turning to face her unwelcome visitor.

"Not meanness Shaya Gold....out of necessity.....I saw an opportunity and I took it from a man who was too goddamn shy to go out with women like every other normal man does, but he can get paid to fuck white chicks for X-rated films, hunh...he was weak and stupid for his type, and I took advantage of his situation, hell... women take advantage of men all the time, every single day of the week!" Justine quipped in retort, almost laughing.

"True," Shaya sighed as she turned from her intruder , thinking of what best to do now.

"Heenh, even in these more 'enlightened' times....guys have to open the door for us, pay our way, and kiss our asses like they did in the Fifties....and the Courts back us up on it all, so taking a man's money via blackmail is not that different from those fat bitches suing their ex-husbands for half of everything they own," Justine Cheeks continued on a rant.

"I see, you're quite the Feminist Icon Detective....which reminds me, since you're on a blackmail kick...there's someone else you should pay a visit sometime soon in your spare time, I'll even give you a little something to leverage her with," Shaya spoke up as she stepped over to the entertainment center of the living room, taking up a DVD disk covered by a plastic sleeve, turning to hand it over to the armed intruder following her closely.

"This is the sole copy of an in-home surveillance video taken from the Faster Cabin up in the Catskills, just days before Ray Fury was murdered there…it's some hot footage taken in the bedroom there of Ray getting-it-on with a certain female Attorney who was working for Jonny Faster at the time….I'll give you this and her current address, she's worth more than I am blackmail-wise," Shaya explained as Justine took the DVD disk out of curiosity.

"Gee, thanks…but we're still going to the ATM and I want something of value from your domicile here, all these nice things around this place, surely a rich slut like you has jewelry you could part with since you don't keep much money in ready-accounts?" Justine chimed.

"Sure, just don't point that goddamn gun at me okay?" Shaya snipped back as she walked toward the stairwell now, Justine following closely behind as Shaya led her up to the second floor where the master bedroom was located. Justine wasn't particularly worried about Shaya over-powering her anytime, because the big-boobed porn queen didn't seem like the female "fighting" type at all. Shaya had just given the intruder a disk containing security-cam footage of Attorney Amber Duffek and the late Porn actor Ray Flintlock ("Ray Fury") doing it on a bed at that mountain cabin four years ago, something never seen by the Cops and FBI investigating at the time because all of the security-cam videos filtered back to the mansion here and the hard-drive taken by Amber Duffek the day Jonny Faster vanished, and now Shaya had it unbeknowing-to Amber of course! Shaya had sensed she might "need" that footage one day and this was it….once this rogue cop confronts Amber Duffek with this, it'll be the end of one of them, and Shaya didn't worry about Amber Duffek getting the shit end of that stick! Shaya found the solid-gold Masonic ring which belonged to Jonny Faster worth over $5,000 and handed it over to the intruder as Justine stopped over by the bed, rubbing a hand over the silk sheets covering its King-Sized mattress and down pillows.

"I bet a whole lotta fukkin' went on right here," Justine snickered in her Yankee accent.

"You don't know the half of it babe," Shaya sighed with a leisurely smile at the intruder.

"This belonged to Jonny Faster hunh....solid gold?" Justine snickered as they left the room.

"Yep, it's worth about five grand.....I don't want it anymore," Shaya answered casually.

"Still I want some cash, so let's drive to the nearest ATM," Justine chimed as she touched the barrel of her weapon to the raven-haired vixen's left shoulder-blade.

Speeding out of the driveway in her black Audi R8 with a rogue cop sitting in the passenger seat was not something Shaya imagined doing tonight after midnight, or any other time! She headed for the convenience store lot about a mile south of the mansion's cul-de-sac where she knew a 24-hour ATM was located. The bitch with the gun and badge didn't even let her get dressed into some real clothes before their little trip out tonight, guessing that her captor judged her less of an "escape" risk wearing only flip-flops and a too-tight silk bathrobe!

"So you worked with Ray at the State Police?" Shaya asked to break the uncouth silence.

"Yep, for two years....before he was murdered, yes....I liked him until I found out what he was doing on the side in secret....son-of-a-bitch was accused of being gay or just plain weird by his fellow Officers because no one ever saw him date a woman, but I found out he was just what they call 'love-shy'," Justine explained in calm, actually-interested tone of voice.

"Love-shy," Shaya sighed in wonder, glancing right to the woman in the dark car with her.

"Unh-hunh...Ray Flintlock was a nervous wreck around attractive women but he sure got his freak-on when it came to performing sex for X-rated films," Justine added girlishly.

"He was bound to have become the top male performer in the Company once Jonny Faster retired and if he hadn't been killed," Shaya spoke up in a more cheerful voice this time.

"No shit….and he would have paid me ten thousand dollars to keep my mouth shut too," Justine added for effect, her pistol in her lap now but still at-the-ready.

"Were the two of you lovers?" Shaya had to ask the short-haired woman beside her.

"What do you think….no, like I said he was love-shy….and he was even more nervous around white women back when I worked with him, heenh-heenh… but I'll bet he put his meat in you Shaya Gold, didn't he?" Justine answered in a crass manner, almost laughing.

"You could say that, yes….quite a few times," Shaya said with a snicker at her female captor.

"I saw his final film, the one he did with Shelly James, which was directed by you wasn't it?" Justine chimed in humored tone, sitting back in her seat as Shaya slowed the car down.

"Yep, a short scene for a compilation video….if he had lived and Jonny Faster retired like he was supposed to, Ray would have been the next top male performer in the Company," Shaya said matter-of-factly as she turned right at the next stop light to enter a dark parking lot where an ATM booth was located. Of course, this time of late night made the lit ATM booth appear downright foreboding; then again she has an armed police officer with her!

"Pull up close to it, but out of camera-range then I want you to get out and make a withdrawal, try anything cute and I will shoot you, do you get me?" Justine spoke softly as she raised her weapon up in her right hand as Shaya parked her car in front of the ATM.

Shaya was glad to get out of the car without a gun at her head at least, but she wasn't going anywhere fast wearing flip-flops on her feet and only a tight-fitting silk robe over the rest of her body, and she realized the bullets in that cop's gun can all run faster than she!

She put in her Pin # and extracted $4,400.00 cash for the rogue cop, a pittance of what she was really worth but worth giving away to the bitch just to get her out of her life, least for now! Sending the blackmailing chick to Amber Duffek will likely be the last thing this cop ever does while above-ground, so Shaya silently hoped Amber will make short work of her and either gets her bumped off or thrown into prison! Walking back to the car, Shaya saw the female cop now standing at the front of the idling Audi, facing her with stern expression.

"Gimme the money……thank you…..now get in your car and drive home, forget you ever saw me or they'll find you floating tits-up in the Hudson River," Justine sneered as she took the bundle of cash, not bothering to count it, gesturing for Shaya to return to her car.

"No problem, hope you choke on it you thieving bitch," Shaya sneered in response as she got back behind the wheel of her Audi R8 and turned the ignition key again. Justine had a Taxi Cab coming for her a block away, as planned.

Fredericksburg, Virginia.
May 25th:

Justine Cheeks relaxed inside the motel room just off Jefferson Davis Highway, not having really desired travel this far south, but Miss Amber Duffek was her next "mark" as far as siphoning-some-funds goes. With another $10,000 cash Justine will be totally free of her gambling debt to the Jersey Mob Boss named Bruno and then she realized she may have to look for another line of work because the NY State Police is fixing to terminate her employment for "conduct unbecoming an Officer" thanks to the Miss Nude Northeast pageant she infiltrated without permission. Using her laptop PC she accessed the DVD given her by Shaya Gold and sat there on the motel room's bed with eyes glued to the laptop computer screen as the security-cam-video began to play.

"Yeah, there she is, that liberal lawyer twat herself," Justine sighed with a grin as she watched the 2005 footage of a naked Amber Duffek approach a bed where a familiar-looking black man lay waiting for her, joining "Ray Fury" on that bed in Jonny Faster's Catskills cabin.

"Oh of course, first-things-first," Justine snickered to herself as she watched the naked Amber Duffek crawl between Ray's legs to eagerly suck his dick as he laid back on pillows.

The hidden security-cam didn't zoom-in of course but it held a good position approximately six feet from the bed on its right side, a great angle Justine thought as she mused about how that sex fiend Jonny Faster must have liked filming his personal bedroom endeavors while staying at that Catskills Cabin. Amber Duffek was going-to-town on Ray's big black dick, that pretty head of hers bobbing up and down, devouring his meat-sicle quite feverishly.

Before she knew it Justine was watching Attorney Amber Duffek engage Ray in "cowgirl" intercourse, riding up and down on his manhood as he lay beneath her with hands reaching up to paw her jiggling boobs. Justine recalled the infamous Attorney Duffek being hailed as an "accomplished lesbian and feminist" in the media before....and now here she is on a 2005 home-video getting long-dicked by a male porn star who is now deceased via homicide!

"This is perfect material for use as leverage," Justine said to herself as she watched more of the torrid affair on her laptop PC, guessing that Ms. Duffek the controversial millionaire lawyer, would **not** wish for this sort of home-video to be released to the press, or sold over the open market like some of those "celebrity sex tapes" have been in the recent past!

"Even a lesbian dog needs a good hard BONE now and then hunh?" Justine laughed at the computer screen as the recorded sex changed to doggie-style intercourse on that bed, the camera showing more of Ray drilling into Amber from behind, hands gripping her bare ass-cheeks as he drilled-it-home inside of her sweet canal. Too bad it didn't have an audio recording as well, but this was the best damn blackmail material Justine could ask for and she wagered Miss Duffek would pay handsomely for the CD footage!

"Well Bruno, you're gonna be laying another bet for me coming up, 'cuz I'm gonna have the money I owe you plus a down-payment on the World Series game," Justine said outloud. Sports-gambling was one of her few passions in life, it had made her more money than her job with the New York State Police, and got her a nice house and sports car, though the past few "losses" with her Bookie and his Jersey Mob handlers.

"Haanh....poor Ray....afraid of women in his personal life but screwed all kinds of hot chicks in his secret porn life....hmmmph, I usually don't go for black guys myself, but I would have done it with you if I had seen this video back before your murder....rest in peace big guy," Justine sighed as she closed the laptop PC and ended the video. Justine giggled to herself as she began to strip off her clothes for a hot shower.

Chicago, Illinois. 6:30 that evening: Rufus Seastone had a few friends that he tolerated and a few whom tolerated him for the most part! J.J. Mallz was one of them, and he had expected tonight's "beer and movies" guys-night-out with Rufus was going to be pretty much the same as last time: stay in his apartment with a couple of six-packs watching movies on his 57" Plasma-screen TV. J.J. was one for going out to a Club for a few hours but knew his old buddy from College Rufus was more inclined to stay here in his "bachelor's crib"!

When it comes to a single man, most people can sort of "tell" when a single guy does not have a woman in his life....it's like a "vibe" or something like that, one can just determine that the guy is single and alone by the way he carries himself and the fact he's hardly ever seen with a female of the species in public or at parties, after work, etc. etc. Single-guys-without-girlfriends are also easy to spot due to their innate penchant for boisterous, often self-defeating and/or dangerous behavior in public as well as in private!

With a single woman it's easier to tell she's man-less by her physicality (i.e. overweight) or by the similar social scene where she grows older and older, never seen with a man in public.

J.J. saw his old College buddy Rufus as one of those guys who never seem to have a real-live girlfriend available and when he does, she doesn't stick around for very long! Maybe it was because Rufus stuck his black head into fantasy too often and it had essentially kept him from taking chances in live situations where meeting real women was fairly easy. By sticking to fantasy-entertainment like he tends to do, Rufus was shutting himself out of the pleasures of the reality of a major American City within which he lives and works.

"Homie, you gotta see this one.....maaan-it's awesome!" Rufus spoke up as he hurried back into the apartment's living room with a flashy-covered DVD in hand, making his friend chuckle in knowing reaction. Another porno-flick as the entertainment tonight! J.J. thought with a smirk then took another swig of his cold bottle of beer.

"Shaya Gold again....c'mon man!" J.J. snapped back to the other black man putting the DVD into its player atop his TV set, grinning ear-to-ear as he turned to face J.J. again.

"You haven't seen this one brotha," Rufus laughed at his slightly-frowning friend.

"Doesn't really matter Rufus, ya seen one porno-flick, ya pretty much seen them all," J.J. remarked back at Rufus with a facial expression denoting personal boredom, something Rufus Seastone managed to never take notice of nor really give two shits about!

"It's called 'Thunder Balls'.....a retro-classic from the early nineties, and they don't make films quite like this these days," Rufus continued as he took his seat in the living room.

J.J. glanced over at his buddy and stared for a moment, seeing the "happiness" in the man's eyes as the video began on the 27" TV screen. It was something the man truly enjoyed, just sitting and watching porn films starring his favorite porn starlets, even with a friend in the house who offered to take him Clubbing tonight and be his designated driver!

"Trust me, this one is tha best," the excited Rufus Seastone snickered as he took his seat, pressing 'play' on his remote to begin Thunder Balls starring Jonny Faster, Shaya Gold, Christy Cannons, and Jack Hammer. It was all he could muster to stay cool and not get up and walk out the door right now, because J.J. wasn't particularly keen on spending time watching (mostly) white people fuck on his buddy's TV set again!

"Homeboy, you should just go out and find you a honey like that Shaya Gold chick, man this city is full of hot ass," J.J. quipped in a humored tone of voice as he eyed his friend.

"Yeah-yeah-yeah....it's all good, plenty of time for dat....check this out, Shaya is about to get reamed by that Jonny Faster dude," Rufus chuckled in response, pointing to the TV.

"Man, you're unbelievable," J.J. had to laugh as he relaxed back on the small sofa now.

Fredericksburg, Virginia. 8:00 that night: Quiet as a church-mouse....as the saying goes, and Amber liked it that way, although sometimes the sounds of Rt. 1 highway do creep up onto Beverly Lane from time to time, she enjoys living here at this infamous address despite the warnings not to. Stepping from the warm hottub cabana with only a towel around her shoulders, the nude Amber Duffek stepped not back to the master bedroom's rear door, but around to the rear courtyard of the house, casually walking in the flood light-lit rear property toward the basement patio area, deciding to go down to the basement pool-room and get a bottle of Scotch from the cabinet there. She failed to notice the fact that the sliding-glass door was unlocked and went on in, failing as well to see the intruders before it was too late.

"Counselor.....Counselor.....don't scream and we won't gut you like a fish," came a stern male voice about the same time a pair of strong male paws reached for her forearms to restrain them behind her back upon entry. Amber didn't scream or even resist the man yanking her arms behind her back, stopping face-to-face with a semi-familiar male figure stepping into view from the shadows of the downstairs parlor.

"You...what is this shit?" she sneered in response, rather calm in spite of the situation.

"Amber Duffek, the 'She-Wolf' herself....what a piece of meat.... hang her up Vince," the familiar-looking Jersey Mobster spoke with a toothy grin as he approached her, the goon holding her from behind pushing her under where a ceiling fan had previously been, taken off to reveal a "hook" in the ceiling where the intruders had clipped a chain to...for her!

Before she knew it, her wrists were cuffed to the chain hanging over her head up to the ceiling and she was not strong enough to rip it free, hanging there totally naked facing two male intruders with her toes barely touching the floor below, strung up like a piece of meat.

"What is it you assholes want from me?" Amber sighed in calm repose, not panicking despite the fact she was helpless right now, her husband Kenny gone to Myrtle Beach South Carolina this weekend on a book-signing tour, no one else in the house tonight nor any chance of someone coming to the rescue either, it was just Amber and her wits against two Jersey Mob goons whom didn't come here for a consultation.

"Baby-baby-baby....we're here to see to it you get what's been comin' to ya...a long time coming actually, ever since you skated out from under the Marcano Mob and screwed over enough people to a point we have to take it out of your ass," the lead goon spoke as he circled the captive woman, running a hand along her bare body, squeezing her ass cheeks as he finished speaking, then he slapped her ass once and stepped around to face her in the dimly-lit basement parlor. Amber recognized the lead goon from her many dealings with the Jersey Mob in the past and knew why they were here, exactly that...take it out of her ass!

"Seems like a waste of a good piece of ass," the other goon behind her remarked as he ran his right hand around her bare backside, giving it a slap as well as she hung there helpless.

"Shit Vincey....this broad's a lipstick-lesbian who collects the balls of guys who cross her, literally....hunh-huh, you still got Attorney Tanner's nuts in a jar Counselor?" the lead goon chimed in as he tweaked her perky boobs with his hands as he faced her there.

"Yeah....Diego Tanner was a pussy just like you and I took his balls," Amber sneered back.

The goon behind her laughed slightly in reaction then she felt the pain of the lead goonbah's right hook in a hard slap across her face. Amber forced a smile after being hit like that, for it had been many years since a man had struck her in anger.

"Beautiful body ya got there Amber…too bad we gotta fuck it up," the lead goon snickered as he pulled a 6-inch straight-razor from a pocket, opening it to reveal its thing, shiny blade.

Just as Amber closed her eyes in defeat, the roar of gunfire cancelled all expectations.

The deafening "pops" made her ears ring painfully and her head hurt as she hung there on the chain from the ceiling with eyes shut in stunned realization that someone had fired a gun inside the basement parlor all of a sudden yet she was not experiencing the pain of being wounded by such gunfire. Amber risked opening her eyes slowly, the ringing in her ears and smell of gunpowder met her senses as he eyes fought to focus and make sense of it all.

Two Jersey Mafia goons lay sprawled on the floor in front of her, dead from the gunshots, and someone was slowly approaching from out of the shadows of the area around the big pool table toward her now. It was a hulkish male figure she didn't recognize at first but with his immediate appearance, she took a guess who and what the third intruder might be!

"Thanks," she spoke up to break the eerie silence as the darkly-clad stranger approached her.

"Don't thank me…I didn't want those clowns to kill you because that's my job," Duncan Horsehair sneered in return as he walked up to face the strung-up Amber Duffek face-to-face, staring into her fearful eyes as she stared back in mortal terror. She had heard rumors of the sort of man the late Senator Rupert Kelsh employed to do his "wet work", the names people like Shaya called him…..names like "Horsehair".

"Great, come to finish the job a hundred-percent hunh….even with Kelsh dead and his plans put on the back-burner?" she spoke in a stunned voice of defeat, staring back.

"It's called cleaning-house Counselor….but look at it this way sweets, least it's not these two wop shitheads slicing you into ribbons while you're still alive……my method is quicker," Horsehair said through his teeth at her. Something about the way he spoke denoted that the man was walking around in pain, and Amber knew that meant he was not in the mood for any last minute negotiating. Guys like this are ruthless killers and with all she has survived, it comes down to a man like this being the one to assassinate her, not the Marcano Mob, not the Jersey Mob, not the laundry-list of pissed off defendants she beat in Court over the years, not even those fascist conspirators in the US Government she secretly helped.

Horsehair held up something which resembled a brick of some kind with a control-panel on its face. It was a bomb and she knew it, just like the kind supplied her by Senator Kelsh when she blew up two of her other homes to cover the Senator's grand scheme (as well as her own). Fitting end, she thought as she watched "Horsehair" trigger the device on its tiny control panel, beginning its electronic countdown to detonation.

"You now have ten minutes Amber Duffek, enjoy...," Duncan Horsehair sneered to her then stepped behind her and out of her sight, vanishing out the sliding glass door after laying the C-4 device on the sofa off to her right, it's electronic timer counting down.

"Dammit!" Amber quipped as she struggled against the chain holding her arms over her head, a struggle that was in vain and she knew it. She was about to be blown sky-high to smithereens right here in her own home thanks to the fact Senator Kelsh failed to kill that son-of-a-bitch called "Horsehair" before he was eliminated himself. She lowered her head in defeat as she hung limp on the chain, waiting for the bomb to go off, resigning to the fact she was about to die naked and strung-up like a side of beef at market in the basement den of her own home along with the bodies of two dead Mafia hit men. Being blown up in a consuming blast wasn't too different than the funeral plans she already had: cremation.

Closing her eyes, Attorney Amber Duffek waited for death, and failed once more to hear or sense the intrusion of yet another stranger into her home here tonight, not even feeling the cooler outside air on her bare skin as the sliding door opened slowly, a darkly-clothed female entering the downstairs parlor to find a fit and well-shaped naked woman hanging on a chain along with a time-bomb counting down over on the sofa. Justine Cheeks hadn't expected to walk in on something quite this "dramatic" but it wasn't something she couldn't handle......

10:15pm: Amber was thankful she was still alive and free of that damned chain, not to mention the added bonus of the two Jersey Mob goons dead on the basement floor thanks to the shadow-that-talks "Horsehair" who tried to kill her as well with a hand-held bomb which this cute but serious chick named Justine switched off when she entered the house ten minutes ago. Amber was thankful but she knew why this female cop from New York was here to see her, she had just not known when the bitch would make her appearance, but right now she was...thankful. Shaya Gold had called her yesterday and warned her about a weird female Detective who was coming to see her about a "video" she had of Amber with the late Ray Flintlock aka: Ray Fury. Amber knew it must be security-cam footage from the Catskills cabin four years ago when she had a little private "party" with Ray at Jonny Faster's cabin shortly before the shit hit the fan. Amber wasn't surprised really, but WHY a female cop who used to work with Ray on the NY State Patrol was now standing in the living room with her after saving her ass from being blown into tiny pieces ten minutes ago.....that was still a damn curious wonder! Amber pulled on a bathrobe and fixed them both a stiff drink, then made a phone call for someone she could trust to properly dispose of the two bodies down in her basement parlor tonight. No sense in calling the local police and turning this "slight distraction" into a cluster-fuck, right?

"I admire your calm, cool, collected disposition Miss Duffek," Justine remarked as she walked around the swank living room, looking around at furnishings and walls in interest.

"No sense in being a basket-case even when one is nearly murdered twice in one night and has two dead assholes in her basement, and I'm married by the way, my husband is doing a book-signing tour this weekend," Amber answered with a casual shrug, handing Justine a glass of bourbon-and-cola as requested.

"You married a man?" Justine had to ask, knowing Amber Duffek had the reputation for being a "radical lesbian and feminist" up to now, so she was a bit surprised at the truth.

"Mmmhh-yes, a good one….and one who doesn't ask awkward questions of me or stick his nose into my private affairs like tonight's debacle, and he serves a purpose for me," Amber answered honestly as she walked around the living room of her Fredericksburg Virginia home, eyes on the stranger who both saved her and put her into a bind all in the same night.

"I'll get right down to it Counselor…considering tonight's events and the fact I have some incriminating home-video footage of you doing the nasty with a male porn actor four years ago, I'm gonna need some capital-investment from you if you wish to be totally-clear of what you call a 'slight-distraction', do ya feel me?" Justine spoke up, getting down to it.

"Be frank, by all means….," Amber sneered with a "jacking off" hand gesture response.

"I didn't come here to rescue you from whoever left that bomb and killed your first two intruders, I could really give two shits….I am in need of a financial settlement from you which I know you'll agree to because this is not something you want to be released to the police or the public…you have a reputation to uphold," Justine explained as she put the DVD into Amber's player on top of the 62" TV there in one corner of the living room.

Amber sat down on the sofa in relative silence as the blackmailer played a disk from a security cam showing Attorney Amber Duffek in a "compromising" situation 4 years ago.

It was footage of she and Ray back in 2005 at Jonny Faster's Catskills cabin after all, Amber smiling as she watched the video footage begin on the big-screen TV now, seeing herself worshipping the "third leg" of porn actor Ray Fury on a big bed at the time, the hidden camera about six feet away and stationary so Amber surmised it had to have been inside the "book case" she recalled being to the right of that bed.

"Surely you don't want this video releases to the press, what would your good husband say?"

Justine snickered as she looked over at Amber who was staring at the TV in silent study.

"He wouldn't care, and that was four years ago....," Amber responded to Justine curtly.

"Really, no one would care you were fuckin' a black dude who happened to have been brutally murdered soon afterwards?" Justine snapped back in arrogant retort, scowling.

"Nope, maybe the police but that case is pretty much cold anyway and I am a damn good lawyer who can get my own ass out of just about any legal difficulty," Amber continued.

"Twenty-thousand dollars gets you this disk, no copies were made.....and it gets me out of trouble where I wouldn't have to tell the cops about the two dead mobsters downstairs," Justine offered up in calmer tone, hands on her hips as she faced her prey in the sweaty jeans and sweatshirt she wore tonight. Amber's pretty face just portrayed pensive consideration.

"Is that all....twenty-grand and you go away?" Amber quipped with a sly smirk back at her.

"I didn't say I was greedy," Justine snickered in coy sarcasm as she stood there letting the security-cam footage continue playing on the big-screen TV for Amber to see.

"You're a gambler, I can tell....just enough to pay off a debt hunh?" Amber added girlishly.

"In a way, but I also realize that the higher the financial amount, the easier it is to trace and account for, plus anything over twenty grand the Feds would get in on if you go to the Authorities, which I seriously doubt you'll do," Justine explained calm and casual.

"I'll give you twenty-grand for the disk and your promise to never contact me again, only I'll have to wait until nine in the morning for my Bank to open," Amber replied with a smile.

Justine nodded in agreement, knowing one cannot get $20,000 cash from any damn ATM.

"Do you mind if I stay here until you do?" Justine asked next, studying Amber's reactions.

"Oh please do, mi casa su casa and all that...I'm considering this a legit business transaction and you did save my bacon downstairs earlier," Amber retorted with a giggle, glancing over to where the brick-sized bomb was now sitting disarmed thanks to Justine's intervention.

Justine felt more at-ease with Amber Duffek than she did with that porn-slut Shaya Gold the other night, at least this famous lawyer was grateful and appeared to be harmless for the most part. She appreciated the "you scratch my back and I'll scratch yours" mentality which the noted feminist lawyer seemed to possess. Amber walked back to her kitchen and thought about the call she got from Shaya Gold yesterday about this bitch from the NY State Police and how she will likely come calling on her, which she did tonight and to Amber's benefit!

She decided to placate the rogue cop on a blackmailing binge and set her up for something else that will be beneficial for the one lawyer in the house tonight.

"Welcome to my parlor....mmmhh...said the spider to the fly," Amber whispered to herself fiendishly as she entered the kitchen, thinking about how to effectively "use" this woman.

When she walked back out into the living room, Amber found Justine still watching the security-cam video from that Catskills Cabin four years ago with her and Ray screwing their brains loose. Amber got Justine's attention as she strolled in with drink in hand, smirking.

"You see something you like?" Amber chimed with a sinister expression at the short-haired brunette now sitting on her sofa facing the big-screen TV and the sexual congress displayed.

Ray was drilling Amber doggie-style on the video now, almost the end of that recording.

"Heenh-heh, it's kinda funky how a shy guy like Ray Flintlock got involved in boning chicks for film when he was too shy to ask any women in his life out for a date, but he seemed to take a liking to you Counselor...you weren't a porn star and there he was nailing you at Jonny Faster's retreat in the Catskills," Justine spoke as she pointed toward the TV.

"People are often not what they seem to be…everyone's got hidden fetishes and desires, and I have to admit I liked Ray Flintlock, he was quite…useful," Amber chimed with slinky grin.

"He was going to pay me to keep my mouth shut once I discovered he was doing porn films," Justine admitted freely, studying Amber's facial reaction to that bit of news.

"So you were blackmailing him back then hunh?" Amber chuckled in non-surprise.

Shaya had informed her of this conniving little bitch blackmailing Ray before his death four years ago and that she was doing the same to the two of them now, all due to gambling debt.

"Yeah, and he was going to pay me too, then he bought-the-farm shortly after he screwed you in that cabin in the Catskills…. according to the timeline," Justine added for effect.

"Shame….Ray was a nice guy, but nice guys like him get the shaft more often than not and so his black ass got roasted along with the other idiot who burned up in that cabin four years ago," Amber continued in her cold tone of voice as she circled the living room again.

"Wow, you're as cold-blooded as they come Counselor," Justine snickered as she stretched out on the long sofa to relax now, her handgun still holstered at the small of her back.

"I call it like I see it babe, so do you trust me enough for both of us to catch some shut-eye between now and nine o'clock in the morning?" Amber asked, stepping to the hallway now.

"Sure, I'll just crash here on your sofa if you don't mind?" Justine replied with a chuckle.

"Suit yaself….unless you wanna share a bed?" Amber replied in sarcasm, opening her robe to shed it there at the hallway's threshold, turning around to walk down the hall totally nude.

"No thanks…..hunh-hah…..by the way Counselor, what about those two dead bodies downstairs in ya basement den?" Justine called after her as Amber went down the hallway.

"I've called in someone to come and get them, clean up the mess and make it look like it never happened, they'll be here within the hour and they'll come in downstairs, shouldn't disturb us any up here," Amber answered out loud as she sauntered on down the hall.

"Great," Justine sighed to herself as she sat back on the sofa, knowing that she wasn't about to get any shut-eye tonight hardly at all. Just then, she saw the nude Amber Duffek reappear at the dark hallway's threshold facing the living room, eyeing her with a kittenish gaze.

"And by the way Justine....I have an appointment with my queer masseuse in the morning around eight-o'clock, so you might want to wake up before then," Amber said softly with a slinky expression toward the younger, armed woman sitting on her sofa now.

"No problem at all, thanks for the warning," Justine snickered back at the shapely lawyer.

"Sure you don't wanna fool around a bit?" Amber chimed impishly as she ran a hand over her perky 36D boobs, down to her dark patch of hair between her smooth-as-porcelain legs.

"No thanks, I'm straight," Justine said with a poker face, not taking kindly to the proposal.

"Hmmmph....suit yaself Detective, see ya after sunrise," Amber quipped in retort, spinning around to retreat back down the long dark hallway to her master bedroom at the other end.

Justine sat up abruptly in stunned realization, for she had never told Amber Duffek she was a Detective! Amber knew about her ahead-of-time, likely from Shaya Gold after Justine left that big-boobed bitch back in New York the other night. No sense in confronting Amber about it now, but it made Justine put her guard back up like before and curse the fact there was no realistic way she was going to get any real sleep tonight, not here with a woman like that with two dead Mobsters in the basement! She then looked over at the professionally-made bomb sitting on the end table across the sofa from her, the device she disarmed by flipping a switch on it's control panel, something she assumed whoever shot the Mobsters had left to blow up and incinerate the evidence, taking Amber Duffek along with the blast!

Justine's cop-mind took over, assuming the lawyer was so damn calm, cool, and collected after almost being slaughtered in her own basement tonight because she had faced similar danger before and was used to such "attention" given her by thugs and terrorists?

"What did I get myself in to?" Justine asked herself in a whisper, stretching out on the sofa with eyes over at the TV screen, deciding to play the video of the late Ray Flintlock boning Attorney Amber Duffek before he died four years ago.....wanting to watch it again.

New Rochelle, NY. 12:01am that same night: Shaya Gold had wanted to spend the night sleeping soundly, but to no avail she was dreaming lucid once again, images from her past filling her sleeping hours and waking her up on-the-hour it seemed, no rest for the wicked...

She kept seeing Jonny Faster, the strapping white man in his thirties, well-built and hung like an Ox, handsome to a fault and capable of making her do just about anything for him. She had loved him back then, even though he was incapable of returning love to anyone around him, something she discovered when it was too late. Shaya had wanted him to "retire" from Porn Filmmaking primarily so that she could have him all to herself. Selfish she knew, and a pipe-dream, because men like Jonny were almost destined to never spend the rest of their lives bound to one woman, and she knew it.... deep down.....she had known it to be true.

Walking out of the master bedroom and down the hallway wearing only her watch and pearl necklace, Shaya stopped at the stairs, looking over toward the second floor's "den" with its light on and something going on in there, so she walked over to it, but it was her mind playing tricks on her again of course, no one was there.... except her vivid memories of a more simpler time in her life..... she could see Shelly James posing nude with Ray Fury while Dave Solomon took photos for "Faster" Magazine, the monthly periodical fans of the Faster Films subscribed to (along with limited newsstand distribution). Dave liked showing an "interracial" theme despite Jonny's reservations, but since Dave Solomon had been the Assistant Manager of Productions and in charge of the softcore Magazine "Faster" he took the liberty of showcasing Jonny's favorite blonde porn actress Shelly James posed with the few non-white male actors for the magazine layouts. Shaya remembered Shelly James posing with Ray Fury for the last issue of "Faster" magazine prior to the end of the company and the photos were tantalizing! One had the naked Shelly lying on top of Ray on a sofa, face-to-face with him while his erection was sticking up between her thighs just below her bare ass.

Jonny approved that one grudgingly but it skirted "softcore" limitations and once again proved Dave Solomon's penchant for interracial themes. She remembered the front cover of that final issue of "Faster" magazine had a shot of Shelly's bare ass with Ray's hand on it, the caption saying: "Faster's upcoming new breed of adult films". Shaya smiled as she stood in the open doorway of the second floor's den, reflecting on the final days of a life she had led for over a decade and one she enjoyed and never would see again. She then remembered Jonny Faster getting pissed off when she ordered Shelly James to "rehearse" with the new guy Ray Fury shortly after the man was hired, but he seemed even more offended when Shaya casually referred to Ray Fury as a "good replacement" for Jonny on-screen, saying such because she had assumed he was going to retire within another year or so anyway!

Jonny did not like the idea of being "replaced" or maybe he didn't like a black actor replacing him and becoming Shelly James' "leading man" in adult films? Shaya mused.

He and Shelly had a slightly-more-than-professional rapport with one another, something Shaya had felt threatened by and so she was not exactly "innocent" of trying to pair Shelly up with other male performers more and more during that final year, wanting Shelly to ask to be paired with new actors like Ray Fury and Paco Schwartz. Jonny fired her for being "disloyal" and partially because he knew Shaya had more in mind for him than just being her Boss, so he got rid of her a few weeks prior to the shit hitting the fan at Faster Productions.

Shaya turned and walked down the stairwell, into the dark living room of the mansion where she lived alone for now, the place she had many memories of, so her desire to remember and commemorate those past years spent here got her to buy the mansion from the Church that owned it after Jonny Faster became a "missing person".

Yes, it cost her an even $1 million dollars but for her it was worth the price. Memories are what kept her from despair and she needed to live here for awhile longer even if she can't sleep some nights.

All she had been through, from her years as a Porn Starlet to her time as a Senator's wife and now a widow over the age of 40, Shaya felt like a "pariah" of sorts now, a woman without family or real friends, a woman who is wealthy but alone and stalked by dirtbags like that female cop who took money and jewelry from her under threats, plus there was the fact she was sort of "answering" to a woman like Amber Duffek for two undeniable reasons:

Amber was a damn good Attorney who has helped her out for several years now

Amber was juiced-in with the Govt. and knows too much anyway.

Shaya wanted to be totally free of her late husband's shadowy cabal and schemes and be free of the "Faster Murders" that are still biting at her ankles to this day, the latest bite coming from that cop who admitted to blackmailing the late Ray Flintlock while he secretly worked as a porn film actor between 2004 and the summer of 2005. She didn't know how to do that unless it meant leaving the Country, something she did not want to do. Thinking of Ray Flintlock (aka "Ray Fury") Shaya felt sorry for him once again, sorry he had to get murdered like he did because he was a good man.....a New York State Trooper who "moonlighted" as an Adult Film Performer not just for the money but for female contact. It seemed he was "shy" around women otherwise which she noticed the first time she met him as Talent Coordinator for Faster Productions in the Spring of 2004. Ray was one male performer she actually enjoyed "rehearsing" with from time to time whenever Jonny wasn't available!

Shaya returned for one final X-rated performance herself in 2005's "Turkish Poker" where she had sex-roles with Mered Aladdin and Ray Fury. Out of all of them she had dreams of Jonny Faster the most, some good, others terrifying, one dream had her marrying Jonny yet another had her castrating him while the other Performers watched! Shaya stepped to the bar and poured herself a shot of bourbon then wolfed it down, thinking about the letter she got in the mail today, yet another "nostalgia" from her past....a former male performer of Faster Productions was being given "conditional parole" from his prison sentence for attempted murder and he wanted to see her, even went as far as to ask her to pick him up at the Bus Terminal tomorrow. "Woody" was who she knew him by, his porn screen-name having been "Woodrow Grande" before the collapse of the Company in 2005 and his divorce from the rich Doctor Wife he had forcing him into homeless bankruptcy. Seems Woody had demanded a loan from an old friend, the friend refused, then Woody tried to kill him and got sentenced to 20 year in Attica Penitentiary for his trouble! He had been in for the past

3 ½ years and was being paroled now. Shaya mused to herself as she wolfed down another shot of bourbon, deciding to pick Woody up at the Bus Terminal at 4pm and at least chat with him over a meal about old times....her penchant for "nostalgia" striking her again!

"Hmmmph.....men...gotta love'em!" Shaya sighed with an exclamation, turning to look out over her huge living room as she raised another shotglass of bourbon to her lips.

"My past is either gonna haunt me forever or kill me tomorrow," she laughed to no one as she sauntered on across the living room, feeling the effects of the straight alcohol now and enjoying it since she couldn't sleep tonight. She thought about going out even a this late hour and finding a suitable man then seducing him for casual, unattached sex. That was easy though, because most men married or otherwise will fuck even a half-ugly woman if she offers him pussy for free and no strings attached! Shaya giggled to herself as she reflected on the countless times she used her feminine charm and physical assets to woo, seduce, and manipulate men to do her bidding. Even Jonny Faster caved in to her once in awhile, and she still "had it" as far as looks and slinky charm goes, despite being age 41. No straight man could easily refuse her and she knew it, and with her olive complexion she is still often mistaken for Hispanic and therefore attracts Latino and Black men just about anywhere she goes, sometimes garnishing more male attention than those countless sexy White chicks!

Fredericksburg Virginia. 7:45 the next morning: The Masseuse arrived early and went straight for the room down the hallway where Amber awaited her weekly rub-down and massage. Justine had been awake since seven o'clock and let the man in when the doorbell rang. He was a damn handsome devil and very fit-looking, making Justine again wonder why some of the prettiest men she meets just gotta be homosexuals?! Actually, Amber told her before he arrived how she insisted on a gay masseuse because she didn't trust straight men to give her a full-body nude massage and though this guy looked more like the "Marlboro Man" than a gay queen, Amber seemed convinced the man was queer as a three-dollar bill and was now getting a massage from him in the spare bedroom down the hall.

That sure-to-be-an-hour-or-so offered Justine time to "look around" the house here out of Amber's view, so she proceeded to do just that, her neck-length brown hair in a muss from sleeping two hours on the sofa but she would grab a quick shower when Amber leaves for the Bank at Nine. Justine quietly scoured the master bedroom, searching it but not making it appear like it's been rifled-through of course. What she did find was surprising though nothing of real monetary value she could steal. There was a huge foam-rubber dildo in the top dresser-drawer that had to be almost a foot-long, and then there was a box of Magnum condoms (the ones for men with extra-lengthy penises) and then she found a sealed mason-jar in the wardrobe closet and took it into the light to see what was being kept in a jar by the lawyer she was blackmailing. Justine was no medical professional but she determined the fluid-filled jar to contain what surely appeared to be a pair of human male testicles still wrapped in scrotum and floating in what she guessed to be formaldehyde and sealed shut.

"Wow...she collected some poor guy's balls," Justine whispered to herself as she studied the jar of anatomical proportions. Justine put the macabre jar back where she found it and then pried into Amber's wardrobe, finding the bitch to have expensive tastes in that department.

"Versace.....Dior.....no shit," Justine said as she looked over the lawyer's clothes, also finding some male attire there as well, no doubt belonging to her new husband Kenny who was gone on book-tours and business more than he spent close to Amber, she surmised.

Before she knew it, Justine was in the hallway just as the naked Amber Duffek was coming out of the spare room fresh from her hour-long massage, smiling in satisfaction.

"Justine....I'm going to get dressed and go on down to my Bank... it'll take awhile so why don't you get a massage from Tyrone...you won't regret it, he's the best....and it's on me," Amber said gingerly to her uninvited guest with a hand on Justine's left shoulder. Looking into the room, Justine saw the handsome Tyrone and a professional massage-table in the center, an entire room of the house devoted to getting rub-downs, massages, and backrubs!

"Oh, okay....why not?" Justine replied with a shrug, going on into the room where a smiling blond Masseuse named Tyrone stood at the table smiling back at the comely brunette.

Amber winked at Tyrone before she left to go get dressed, shutting the door behind herself.

"So, you're a friend of Amber's....she is a fine lady," Tyrone spoke as soon as the door shut, Justine beginning to get undressed right there in front of the gay masseuse, wanting the same type of massage a rich bitch like Amber Duffek gets on a weekly basis.

"You could say that, yeah...she's special," Justine said with a chuckle of humor, stripping down to her panties and bra then casually losing those as well, climbing up onto the table and stretching out in the prone. Tyrone ran a warm hand down her back to her bare butt, then when his hands touched her legs, she shivered slightly in agreement, lying her head off to her left on the padded table, fixing to enjoy the massage the professional was to give her.

As soon as Justine felt his hands touch her, she sensed something about the man, something which told her he might not be as "queer" as Amber claimed he was....

9:38am: Getting $20,000 cash from one of her accounts didn't take as long as she had expected, namely because the male Clerk at the counter was enamored with her and so the process went a bit faster than usual. Amber was never short of male admirers and she was not afraid to use the fact she was an attractive woman to her advantage, naturally.

Driving back onto Rt. 3 in her Mercedes, Amber took her time as one of her favorite songs played on the car's radio, taking the scenic detour through Oak Hill Cemetery which was just on top of the hill from her home on Beverly Lane. It was here in this Cemetery where her "friends in dark places" occasionally stashed bodies, like the ones she called for disposal of from last night's "near death experience". She only wished she could have them bury that shadowy bastard "Horsehair" here in this graveyard as well! Something told her that monster may come back to finish the job if he thinks she may still be alive…considering his C-4 bomb did not detonate her ass into the atmosphere last night like he had planned!

Taking the return-trip through the big cemetery was also done so as to give someone a little more time before she walks back through the door. Amber had $20,000 cash from her bank account for someone else other than the blackmailing bitch who arrived last night just in time to prevent her untimely demise. For that reason alone, Amber wasn't going to have Justine killed outright like she would have done any other blackmailer with no back-up.

Driving out of the cemetery and across Westmont Drive onto Beverly, then down a hill and around to Beverly Lane's cul-de-sac, Amber slowed her Mercedes to a halt on the incline directly in front of her brick home on the right. She got out with the leather satchel under one arm, walking casually up to the front door of 1705 Beverly Lane knowing the door would be unlocked, going right on in. There was "Tyrone" in the hallway rubbing his hands and smiling as soon as he saw Amber re-appear from her jaunt to the Bank.

"So, do we have an arrangement?" the man asked her casually, then she tossed him the satchel full of crisp $100 bills totaling $20,000 cash neatly packed in the leather satchel.

"What do you think?" she chimed as she walked past the Jersey Mafia "Fixer" there in her hallway, opening the door to her massage room to find Justine Cheeks lying prone on the padded table totally-nude and restrained by plastic "flex-cuffs" around her ankles as well as flex-cuffs tying her wrists behind her back, a red ball-gag strapped in her mouth and a sour facial expression as Amber walked into the room to see her "blackmailer" tied up now.

"Thought you could shit on me so easily, hunh?" Amber quipped to the restrained woman on the massage table, then slapped a hand to Justine's bare ass cheeks for further cruelty.

"I withdrew twenty-grand alright, but it's gonna pay for your disposal you thieving bitch, how dare you try to pull one over on me….I don't give two shits if you are a cop….or should I say soon-to-be-ex-cop who is on-suspension for immoral behavior…..Shaya told me all about it over the phone the other night and then I checked into you Justine, seems you're quite the gambling-junkie who happens to be into the Jersey Mob for a lot of money, which is why my friend 'Tyrone' here tied you up like this….after he took care of the mess downstairs, which I am going to be forgiven for because I am handing you over to Bruno's boys in exchange for them leaving me the fuck alone," Amber explained intimately to her quarry stretched out on the massage table, unable to voice her opposition nor fight back.

"Hope you like beef stew Detective Cheeks….heenh...cuz you're gonna be a soup-bone in the pot once Bruno gets done with you…. you really shouldn't have been late in paying him your gambling debt stupid....," Amber continued as she circled the table, running a hand over Justine's smooth skin and curvy bare body, slapping the woman's bare ass once again.

"Take this bitch outta here….and ask Bruno to give me a call later," Amber said to the Mafia Fixer she called "Tyrone" as he stepped back into the room again.

New Rochelle, NY. 12 noon that day: Nothing like nostalgia to brighten the mood, especially when one had been locked up for almost four years and all he had to reflect on was memories of the past, memories of places like this and the people he once knew.

"Woody" Ganderson was once an employee of Faster Productions for almost six years and using the pseudonym "Woodrow Grande" as he performed legal sex acts for film. Woody had been a Porn Star from 1999 to 2005 (albeit secretly) until fate played a cruel hand and his secret double-life was exposed in July of 2005, ending his marriage of ten years and putting him onto the streets. One conviction for Attempted Murder later that year got him a 20-year prison sentence from which he was now on "conditional parole" from. Of course he never imagined that he'd be standing inside the "Faster Mansion" ever again, yet here he was, standing at the in-home Bar of the huge living room now, a guest of the mansion's newest owner, a woman he'd worked with all those years ago: Shaya Gold. She had treated him to a delicious lunch at his favorite Seafood restaurant after picking him up at the Bus Terminal, then brought him back here for chit-chat and to just show him the place again.

"So tell me Woody, if ya don't mind…is Prison as bad as they say?" Shaya asked him as she stepped around behind the Bar to face him across it's broad counter, smiling as she spoke.

"Yep, and Attica is a first-rate shithole, the ninth circle of hell, hunh…worst part is being around the other prisoners, and the racial problems….blacks hate the whites, latinos hate everyone, and you either joined a gang while inside or took your chances," he replied softly.

Shaya's pretty face lost its smile as she listened to her former "co-worker" talk about it.

"They gave me twenty years for nearly killing my old friend Barney when I didn't mean to kick his ass that badly….having been a porn actor didn't help with the Jury, they saw me as a 'dengenerate' according to my Public Defender….hmmph, but I kept up with the news while in Prison, saw that the investigation into the Faster Murders didn't net any arrests and it's now a cold-case I guess since they never found Jonny?" Woody spoke in change of topic.

"Mmmmh….no, Jonny is still listed as a missing person but I have a feeling he's dead, and you're right…it's a cold case now, no more suspects….and I bought this place from the Church that bought it after Jonny vanished….really because it felt more like 'home' for me than anywhere else, so here I am," Shaya explained with gesture of hands at Woody.

“I see, and you’ve restored it pretty much to the way it was four years ago, similar furniture like before, the Bar here,” Woody added matter-of-factly as he looked around from his stool.

“Haah, the Bar here was covered over and used to store boxes and stuff when that Church had the place, but I had a home-improvement company come in and restore it,” Shaya said.

Shaya had already asked him about the conditions of his early-parole and what he had going for him now that he was out, of which he was not saying too much. Seems he had won a conditional-parole from out of the blue, maybe because he had been a first-time felon?

“I really like what you’ve done with the place Shaya, really…you figure on re-starting the Company and produce more films?” Woody finally got up the nerve to ask, grinning.

“Oh hell no, my porn flick days are over, heenh-heenh….like I said earlier, the California companies have taken the market higher not to mention the swarm of amateur porno-makers out there on the Internet…..X-rated video is nearly a thing of the past thanks to cheap downloads and pirating,” Shaya answered him with a slinky smirk.

“You’re still young enough yourself Woody, why not take off for California and get back into performing in films?” she had to ask, studying his reaction to the question.

“No, my parole keeps me here in New York for at least another ten years,” Woody responded with a shrug of avarice, then took another swig of the iced tea she served him.

“Well we both have fond memories here don’t we Woody?” Shaya asked him as she stepped out from behind the Bar and walked on into the huge living room of the mansion, seeing the sun vanishing outside behind overcast clouds, a storm being forecast for this afternoon.

“Yeah, don’t know how many of my films were shot here in the mansion or outside in the pool, on the patio deck….hmmph, I remember that scene you and I did out back in a hammock hanging between two trees, Jonny wanted me to drill you in the hammock even though we kept flipping over and falling out and Dave Solomon was worried we'd all get arrested if the neighbors called the cops on us for indecent exposure," Woody told her.

"Yep, I remember....we did the scene for the film called 'The Takers' and I remember having to do it doggie-style with Jonny immediately after the hammock scene upstairs in one of the bathrooms, you guys really gave-it-to-me that day," Shaya replied humorously.

Woody chuckled at her remark, the fondest memories in his head were of those times spent filming X-rated movies and partying here at the Faster Mansion in New Rochelle along with some unique people such as Shaya Gold, Shelly James, and even the boss Jonny Faster who let him do pretty much whatever he wanted while he was here back then as long as filming went as planned! Woody remembered Shaya "rehearsing" (as they called it) with him a few times back then in-between films, just screwing for the hell of it up in one of the rooms or in the Jacuzzi! That was why he risked losing everything he had back then (which eventually happened) to have sex-without-consequence with the female cast list of Faster Productions when his own fat wife at home wasn't interested in making love with him anymore after the birth of their two kids back in the late 90's. Woody watched the shapely Shaya Gold walk over to the sofa with her drink in hand, sipping on it as she obviously thought on something.

He couldn't believe how GOOD she still looked at age 41, and if he didn't already know he would have guessed her age to be about 34 or 35 instead! She still had a tight but well-filled-out physique like before, that ass of hers still had a little "jiggle" in the mini-dress she wore like it had before whenever he saw her fully-clothed, but those tits of hers were a little bigger than he remembered, even covered up he could tell she had some cosmetic enhancement done on her awesome boobs since the last time he'd seen her in-person.

"I have been seriously thinking of hosting a big party here this summer....a kind of reunion of the surviving cast members from Faster Productions and some other Industry hot-shots from our past, right here in the mansion.....maybe even some of the fans of our films as well, like the exclusive 'Fan Parties' Jonny and I used to throw here years ago?" Shaya spoke, turning to glance over one shoulder at "Woodrow Grande" still sitting at the custom Bar.

His short brown hair had a lot of grey in it and his physique was tight but he had lost weight since she had last seen him, prison life takes its toll on a guy she surmised.

"Wow, yeah…why not…like the parties Jonny used to throw back in the day," he chimed with a shrug of feigned interest, but clearly showing that he was not too enthused about it.

"Just one more, for old times' sake, one more Porn Bash here at the mansion," Shaya added.

That was what the Adult Video News writers called Jonny Faster's private parties whenever they would get wind of one, "Porn Bash" at the Faster Mansion…..

Shaya smiled as she turned her head from her guest, eyes across the room at the kitchen door as she circled the sofa. She had expected Woody to ask her for money since he knew that she was now very wealthy, like that rogue cop who was being taken care of by Amber!

He hadn't asked her yet or even broached the topic of money, but she expected him to and it wouldn't automatically be a "no" because she liked Woody, always did find something "good" about the man even though he had been cheating on his wife all those years ago when he was secretly working as a male adult film actor!

Shaya started walking toward the stairwell while looking to her right at Woody at the Bar as he kept talking about the past as if it were just yesterday, something she was not opposed to.

"I remember one time when it was just a few of us in the mansion here during a really heavy snowstorm one winter….you, me, Jonny, and Leesa Teasa?" Woody chimed boyishly.

"Unh-hunh…I remember, we played poker and ate chips 'n dip all day and then we played a few sex-games here in the living room," Shaya snickered in fond reflection of the past event.

"You and Leesa tied a rope around Jonny's big dick and led him around like a slave boy, then he got to hammer both of you while I cleaned up the mess down here," Woody said in laughter over the memory, making Shaya giggle in response as well.

"I loved that man ya know….and not just because he had the body of a Greek god….I really loved the bastard, which I later regretted of course," Shaya spoke up with indignant repose.

"I know you did Shaya, and all the other guys envied him…. including me, cuz not only was Jonny Faster hung like an Ox but he was damn good-looking, cut n' chisled, and filthy fukkin' rich!" Woody snickered in reply, grinning as she popped another laugh back at him.

"He was one of a kind…never another stud like him, though Dave Solomon and I tried to find another dude like Jonny year-after-year….we knew Jonny couldn't last as the 'King of Porno' forever," Shaya added with a sleazy expression, walking toward Woody at the Bar.

"Jonny was good to me though, kept me on the cast-list all that time, made good money behind my then-wife's back, still have fifteen-grand in one account," Woody continued as he stared at the beautiful and busty olive-skinned woman of Turkish-Brazilian extraction.

"You were a reliable male performer Woody, which was the reason Jonny liked you, because you could get-it-up on command for filming and you showed up on-time," Shaya answered.

"Yep, guess it always comes down to that, being reliable or not," Woody chuckled in return, smiling softly at the woman he used to perform sex acts for film with, her eyes staring back.

"Woody, it's been a long time since you've been with a woman, hasn't it?" she asked next.

"You kiddin'…almost four years now," he chuckled back, thinking she was joking with him.

Shaya then reached hands to the hem of her black mini-dress and without further adieu, pulled the garment up and off her bare body underneath, standing before him now naked except for her earrings, necklace, and Rolex watch, the look on her pretty face priceless!

"How about we go upstairs and 'rehearse'....for old times' sake?" Shaya chimed impishly as she spun around and started walking toward the stairwell naked and incredibly horny.

"Oh absolutely Shaya baby, you must've been reading my mind," Woody replied in earnest as he hopped off the barstool with drink in hand to follow her, marveling at how that body of hers didn't look too different than when he saw it last, her boobs bigger now!

"Mmmmhh...I'm gonna take you at your word everything is good n' clean Woody," she said casually as she started up the carpeted stairs, glancing back at her old friend following her.

"Prison Medic gave me a clean-bill-of-health before I was paroled....and I never took it up the ass while I was in the joint," Woody answered her boyishly, making her laugh again as they climbed the stairs together, his right hand sliding down to her bare ass as they reached the last step on the second floor of the mansion, pausing for a quick kiss on the lips.

"Well then, I guess you can fuck my brains loose for old times' sake 'Woodrow Grande', right here in the ol' Faster Mansion," Shaya whispered to him as they embraced there in the hallway of the second floor, slowly moving toward the infamous master bedroom where Jonny Faster himself once slept, among other things. Shaya led Woody inside and he began to disrobe quickly, eager to indulge womanhood after having been in prison for almost four years. Shaya sat back on the big canopied bed watching Woody undress, smiling at the man she had done about a dozen films with back in the day. She used to call him "Banana-dick" back then because of the "curve" his sex organ took when erect.

"Mucho...bueno, Senor Grande," Shaya cooed impishly at the man as he got naked and approached the delicious lady on the bed waiting for him, and like before, never a problem or "wait" for a hard-on, same ol' reliable Woody!

"Banana-dick has returned home," Woody said with hands on hips as he faced the former Porn Starlet brazenly, watching her lie back on the bed, inviting him to come play with her.

Four years he had been without the touch and feel of a woman, four years without sex and humanity, four years locked away from the pleasures of the physical world, but right now none of it mattered because he was where he "belonged" once before….this time it was not for the benefit of an X-rated film but just for the raw pleasure of healthy sex. Skipping foreplay and oral delights, Woody sailed right into intercourse with Shaya, gorging into her sweet flesh in an excited missionary-position, both of them moaning out in delight of the sensation they mutually caused. He was ecstatic in his thrusts, arching his back to plunge into her canal as far as his torpedo would slide, pumping into her with a vigor that had not been alive for years now, a desire that had been squelched by Prison walls. Woody relished the moment, the FEEL of a woman after all that time sending his mind and body into ecstasy as their bare bodies joined together in rapturous, locomotive indulgence.

Shaya surrendered to the act itself, in the way she did not during filming years ago, just with certain men while having sex in private, men like Jonny Faster and now Woody Ganderson.

She let herself be taken by him, ravaged without complaint as he thrusted into her in steady pumping rhythm, seemingly hell bent on spearing his manhood as far inside of her as he could, and it felt good. Hands reaching to paw her bog boobs roughly, Woody yelped out as if he had been suddenly accosted by something utterly enjoyable and she knew he was coming by the facial expression he made now, exploding inside of her with leering glee.

They had been going-at-it for just minutes so far, but Shaya realized he was a man who just got out of Prison and she was his first piece of ass for almost four years! Woody's entire body quivered in the eruptive sensation, still driving his spear inside of her as he climaxed.

"Ooooaaaaahhh…..Shhhhhaaaa….yaaaaahhh!" Woody exclaimed with mouth wide open as he arched his back, slowing down in reaction to the draining-feeling of a man's climax.

"Ooooh-yeah-baaaa…..beeee…..whoah," Shaya crooned under him, wrapping her legs around his backside as he descended over her torso, mouth seeking to suck on her breasts.

"Woody…..oooh, my Woody….poor guy been locked up so unfairly, you missed your Shaya didn't you baby?" she cooed in girlish voice to the man sucking at her tits now, making him smile as he went from one to the other, feasting on them like a hungry animal.

"Yes!" he bellowed in sheer enjoyment of the moment, mouth-worshipping her big cans continuously as they lay together on the ruffled bed. Shaya felt his hands and legs move to re-engage her and she relaxed to let the eager lover do his best with her body, Woody once again sailing into her in steady intercourse, resuming the warm, wet action with all the desire of a schoolboy's first time… not wanting to cease the sweet pleasures of the flesh anytime soon! In Woody's mind, this was his salvation….his "return" to the world of the living!

They rolled over and Shaya came to be on top of him suddenly, straddling his hips as she took his pole back inside of her, moving up-and-down on his erection in bouncy ardor.

"Ooonnh….yeah, oooaaah…..feeeeels……good," Shaya crooned as she rode on Woody, up and down, up and down on his stiff dick without fail. Seeing his manhood absorbed up inside of the soft, wet flesh of womanhood was the thrill he had almost given up hope of ever experiencing again back before he got his parole. She felt so good, and he felt blessed like he had never been blessed before, getting free of prison to come here and get laid by a woman who had been with bigger and better men than he, men like Jonny Faster….

Fredericksburg, Va. (same time): The wire from her Bank to Shaya Gold's account up in New York took a matter of minutes and Amber knew her friend would be pleased to get her $4,000 back from the thieving bitch cop named Justine Cheeks. Justine was surely regretting her choices by now, Amber mused to herself as she walked back outside in the afternoon sun here on Beverly Lane toward the hillside swimming pool she owned, clad in a blue two-piece string bikini with her tiny cell-phone clipped to the garment hugging her ass.

Right now, she guessed Miss Justine Cheeks was being taken down I-95 in a truck to meet Bruno, the Mafia Capo she owed money to over an ill-advised gambling bet. Sports Betting nails a lot of people each year, but this time the loser was going to pay with more than just all of her money! Bruno owed Amber a favor for getting him out of a bind a few years back, so he was going to forget the money Justine was close to paying back, and take it out on the woman's ass after all, like Amber suggested! Bruno didn't give two shits whether Justine was a cop or not, she had gotten herself mixed up in the rackets, resorted to blackmailing for the money and time ran out, so she was going to pay the fiddler like any other scumbag with a gambling problem who made the mistake of making bets with the Italian Mafia.

Amber relaxed up at her pool and made a few quick calls, one to her husband Kenny to find out when to expect him home. Her husband rarely ever called her for anything, she usually calls him and Amber likes that, one more reason she adores her husband the Writer!

She had to worry over the fact that "Horsehair" guy was still out there, and surely he knew by now the bomb he left here did not go off and kill her like he had planned, so the bastard might come back to finish the job, she told herself in her usual pragmatic manner. No matter, because Amber lived her life on a razor's edge most of the time and getting cut (or cut up!) was a risk she took anyway and that was that....she had sacrificed other people before to avoid the Grim Reaper, but she knew that her fortunes might not always be in her favor and even she has to die some day. Men were the most "expendable" to her, and she occasionally gave the ones she's "sacrificed" a passing thought here and there. Her fellow Attorney Diego Tanner was her first male lover back in Law School and the first man to ever make her come.....his balls floated in a sealed jar of formaldehyde down in her bedroom. Then there was that donkey-dick Jonny Faster who she indulged shortly before he disappeared four years ago, the second man to ever make her come and the only one she ever let bend her over a barstool like he did that evening! There was Ray Flintlock, aka "Ray Fury" who moonlighted as an X-rated performer while being a NY State Trooper, also a lover of Amber's for a short while....and one she was going to use against Jonny Faster's Porn Empire (to her advantage) before the house of cards came crumbling down in 2005.

She smiled up at the hot afternoon Sun in the sky as she thought of those three men again.

Amber even had a recurring "nightmare" where she is being barbecued-alive on a spit by Jonny, Ray, and Diego as they sit around smoking cigars and laughing about her!

She chalked that recurring dream up to having the slightest amount of "guilt" because she has out-lived those three integral men in her life, but she was feeling less and less "guilty".

Amber was still alive and married to the next man who can satisfy her in bed, one who doesn't try to "own" her nor control her in the ways other suitors have tried and failed.

Bi-sexual, Amber was beginning to see that she cannot live without men like her husband, even though they are rare. Women in her life have been too much of a pain in the ass with other issues like what Shelly James put her through, so Amber was less inclined to become truly "involved" with another woman like she had invested in the past. Lessons learned…

"Hmmm…what was it that Sartre said…..Hell is other people?" she chuckled to herself as she rested back on the pool's deck chair, arms behind her head and eyes closed.

Sunnydale Nursing Home, Stafford County Virginia: Being an invalid was hell in itself, more especially for an elderly woman who had a "mission" in her sunset years, a mission unlike that ever taken by someone of her age and gender. Nydia Cohen lay in the bed inside her small room here in the "Direct Care" wing of the Nursing Home on Brooke Road in Stafford County just a ten minute drive north of Fredericksburg where she had a massive stroke one year ago. Lying here with half of her body fully-paralyzed and only her memories for company, the elderly Nydia kept her eyes closed most of the time since no one came to visit her and her "mission" had ended with her stroke one year ago.

She wanted to carry out more bombing runs for Horsehair, more eliminations of pinko- liberal traitors, faggots, and anyone else she hated with just cause. Horsehair had provided her with the means over the course of years and she had successfully killed scores of blacks, liberals, and race-mixers with her bombs between 2002 and 2008. Opening her eyes for once as a presence caught her senses just now, she saw one of the nurses entering her room now holding a flower pot bearing yellow Mums and the flowers were obviously for her!

"You have a friend out there after all Miss Nydia, what pretty flowers," the young Nurse spoke girlishly as she placed the potted plant down on Nydia's nightstand, off to her left.

Nydia forced a crooked smile as the pot of yellow Mums were placed on the table's surface, realizing full-well who was the only one to have sent her such a thing here, and it was good!

Within ten seconds of the pot being placed on the table, the gravity-switch detonator on a timer within the soil of the potted plant struck its limit and 12 ounces of hidden C-4 plastic explosive erupted to consume the contents of the room in a cataclysmic fireball that was too fast and far too lethal for anyone to survive. Nydia went with a smile…

New Rochelle, NY. 1:00pm: Doing it "doggie-style" was something Woody often got ordered to do back in his porn film days, only now he was enjoying it without a Director telling him to stop, change position, or go for the "money-shot" as they call it in Porn.

"OOOOAAANNH…..WOOOHH-DEEE……UNNNOOGH-YEEEAAH!" Shaya bellowed in orgasm as her lover drilled her from behind in thrusting intercourse as she remained on all-fours on the bed with Woody mounted behind her. He pumped into her as hard as he could, gently squeezing her buttocks as he drilled deep, enthralled by sensation.

Shaya reached a free hand over to her nightstand and picked up her buzzing wireless phone, seeing a text message on the tiny digital screen notifying her of a transfer of $4,200.00 to her account here in New Rochelle. She grinned impishly as she raised her head up to glance over one shoulder back at her lover still servicing her on all-fours. Amber Duffek had come through for her yet again…and she hoped that thieving bitch cop is getting her just desserts.

"OOOOHH...GIVE IT TO MEEE....OOOAAANNHH!!" Shaya groaned aloud in delight of the unyielding penetration, her sweat-soaked bare body still a vibrant engine on the bed with Woody, the pair still driving for more and more of the carnal pleasure, more and more.

Woody yelped out loud again as he came for the final time, slowing in sexual stride as this second sweet sensation of release exhausted his 4-years-denied libido, both of them collapsing to the bed together in finale after over an hour of steady lovemaking.

"Mmmmnnhh......dammmmn.....Woody....that was terrific," Shaya sighed as she relaxed on her back beside him, eyes up at one another reflecting in the mirror at the ceiling of the canopied bed they lay upon. Woody smiled and nodded in agreement with her conclusion.

"Shaya-baby, you're fine as wine....thank you," he sighed as he caught his breath, staring up at the mirror as he lay beside the incredible woman he had been re-united with here today.

Shaya looked up at herself as she lay there with wet hair in her eyes, feeling good and yet still wondering what Woody was going to ask of her....besides sex?

Woody got up from the bed all of a sudden, his back to Shaya as he stood up and stretched, her eyes on him in wonder if he was in a hurry to leave already, doubting it. Something told her she was about to learn what "Woodrow Grande" truly wanted from her now that he was out of Prison. He turned to look at her with arms folded over his lean chest, prick at half-mast, eyes appearing sad right now as if he was bearing something denoting "bad news".

"Shaya, I have to tell you the reason I was given conditional-parole," he spoke meekly.

"Reason....I thought it was good behavior?" she chimed with a sarcastic smirk as she rolled over to face in his direction, still smiling kittenish at her former X-rated film partner.

"The Feds, Shaya.....the fuckin' Feds.....they want me to set you up..., close the Faster Murders once and for all....they got a hard on for anyone involved in our Company back then and I am supposed to…..," Woody spoke hesitantly as he faced her at the bedside.

"Spy on me?" she sighed as she sat up at the side of her bed facing him now, poker-faced.

"Yeah, something like that…..but we can work something out Shaya, I mean….you and I can give'em something….if not, then I go back to Prison," Woody continued in nervous frankness, noticing Shaya's face slightly contort into the visage of a woman pissed-off.

Before he could react, Shaya's right hand shot out to quickly grab his genitals as he stood there, her grip one that immediately assaulted his senses, the pain of which doubled him over toward her as she stood up from her bed in motion opposing his, pushing him backward.

"BASTARD!!!" she screamed to his grimaced face as Shaya let pent-up rage spill forth into ever muscle of her being now pinning her naked lover to the far wall, gripping his genitals in a painful hold causing him to reel in reaction, unable to fight back at the painful moment as fingernails dug into his scrotum, hand of anger squeezing his testicles to paralyze him now.

Shaya felt like demon-possessed as she squeezed the man's sensitive genitals mercilessly, holing him to the wall in agony, Woody not even trying to fight back, crying like a child as she gripped him where it severely hurt! When she finally let go of him Woody collapsed to the floor balled-up in agonizing pain, curled into a wailing fetal-position holding his genitals as he fiendishly cried out in protest of the assault: "MY BALLS……MY BALLS!"

"I should tear them off of you…..you son-of-a-bitch….paroled to screw me over hunh, you're not a man, you're a piece of shit!!" Shaya proclaimed with fiery indignation as she stepped back to look down at the fallen man before her, the fact that he "fessed-up" not a consolation at all considering she trusted him enough to bring here into her home and bed!

"Who was it goddamn you….. the FBI……ATF?!" she quipped with shaking fists over him.

"FBI…..they…they…want you for Jonny Faster and for the other murders…..Ray Fury…and for your….Senator Husband….

unnnnggh!" Woody groaned in grinding pain, doubled-over in front of her bathroom there in the master suite as Shaya circled him slowly.

"I didn't murder anyone goddammit.....I didn't do anything wrong goddamn you Woody!" Shaya crooned as he crossed the room to her big dresser while Woody began to crawl into the bathroom, wanting to shut the door so that she could not attack him so easily again.

Shaya pulled open her dresser's top drawer and reached in for a heavy piece of metal she kept in there: a Walther PPK .380 caliber pistol, palming the weapon as she turned around.

Woody didn't see the gun as he slipped inside the bathroom and closed the door behind himself, locking it to prevent her from assaulting him again, hoping there would be a phone inside the bathroom so he could call for help but there was none.

"I'm going to commit my first murder tonight Woody, and it's gonna be you....you're a rat not a man, a stinkin' rat!" she bellowed out in anger, aiming the un-registered handgun at the bathroom door, chambering the first round but not touching the trigger just yet, thinking.

"Rats are vermin Woody, rats get exterminated!" she yelled at him through the locked door.

Shaya almost pulled the trigger as a vice-like hand from behind her reached over her right shoulder to grab her forearm, another hand at her waist, a man stepping up close behind her from out of nowhere, startling her to scream but she didn't, all of her vocal fury having been spent moments ago with Woody, who was now cowering inside her bathroom.

It was Duncan Horsehair, come from out of nowhere to walk on in like he had always done in the past, without notice or warning, like some kind of ghost....with 18-inch arms.

"Duncan!" Shaya quipped in surprise as she spun around in his arms, embracing him as he held her, their lips meeting in a feverish kiss. After their lips parted, he pulled her over to the bed where he spoke in a hushed tone, knowing there was someone else in the bathroom who Shaya just assaulted for betraying her trust and he would deal with him later.

"Where have you been.....jeezus.....Duncan, it's been over a year since...," Shaya spoke in lowered tone to match his, staring into his deep-set dark eyes in tense wonder, standing there naked with the man clad in black attire he always seemed to wear whenever she saw him. It was also still light outside, so he was risking exposure to sunlight by being here at this time!

"I've been in the house since this morning before sunrise....I will leave tonight at dusk.....I was detained by your late husband's friend and now I'm on my own," the darkly-clad man from nowhere spoke to her closely, his thick hands holding her at the hips facing him.

"How did you find me?" she had to ask, then kissed him again, emotions flipping from delight to fear and worry because she had realized what Duncan had done for her late husband and so she was righteously scared of him at the moment, this visit being either one out of affection considering their sexual liaisons of the past, or one of intended murder?!

"I have something for you Shaya," Duncan Horsehair spoke softly as he took something from his black jacket to lift over her head....a necklace. It had a gold chain with a strange-looking "tube" of sorts dangling at the end. She let him pull it down over her head and the tube came to rest just over her bare boobs on her upper chest.

"This is the virus your late husband was counting on to save the country from itself....this is the last sealed vial of the stuff.....it's safe as long as you don't smash the tube ...I want you to hold on to it for me as a memento of my trust," Duncan said softly to Shaya Gold.

"The virus....yes, he spoke of a virus that would wipe out millions," she sighed as she looked at the sealed resin-like tube at the end of her new necklace "memento" from her shadow lover, then they kissed again as Duncan pulled her close once more, the feel and smell of her intoxicating to him and for a moment he almost forgot himself. Across the master bedroom behind the door of her bathroom, she could still hear the fading wimpers and groans of Woody Ganderson holding himself like a wounded infant.

"What are we to do now Duncan?" Shaya asked him then stood there eyeing her deadly necklace as he turned to walk around the bedroom, thinking of his next answer for her.

"I came here for you….I want you to come with me Shaya," he said with back turned.

Shaya had put her gun down on the bed behind her, but she calmly reached her right hand behind her and took the weapon back into her right hand, leveling it toward its target.

"Sorry Duncan," she said flatly then squeezed the pistol's trigger as she aimed it at the man's back, the gun going off in a loud "pop" inside the bedroom, it's single 9mm bullet punching the target just above his left shoulder-blade "I'm not going anywhere lover….you are," Shaya sighed despite the louder gunfire, watching the big man fall forward into a slump on the rug below, motionless and appearing to die instantly, at least to the untrained eye of the shooter.

"I belong to no one….and you're too dangerous to be left alive," she spoke to the corpse.

The bathroom door flung open, a naked and stunned Woody standing weakly in the doorway, stunned by the incredibly loud "boom" he just heard through the door, equally stunned to find himself now facing Shaya Gold holding a smoking handgun as she stood over a stranger slumped on the floor by the bedroom's one window, clearly shot to death.

"Shaya…..what tha?!" was all Woody's voice could muster speaking, then Shaya tossed her handgun at him, his hands reaching out instinctively to catch it, and he did, the metal weapon now in his trembling hands, getting his fingerprints all over it as Woody stood there looking down at the hot pistol in his hands then up at Shaya Gold as she pulled on a robe.

"Thanks Woody….you just did me a huge favor….so I forgive you for trying to rat me out to the Feds….heenh-heh, don't feel bad….he was a far worse felon than you were," Shaya snickered as the ringing in her ears from the gunshot subsided, pulling on the silk robe now.

"I uhhh…whh-whhh….what?" he stuttered as he stood there holding the handgun in his nervous hands, looking at Shaya then at the dead man lying on her bedroom floor, shot dead by her while Woody was doubled-over in the bathroom from her grabbing his balls in a fit of rage earlier. Shaya winked at him with her kittenish smile then turned to head for the bedroom's door across the bedroom about seven feet away. Woody didn't know much about guns but by looking at this one, he could tell it was now empty, its slide locked open on an empty ammo-clip! It had been fired just once by Shaya and then she tossed it to him….

"Shaya…I uhhh….what tha fuck…is goin' on?" Woody stammered as he still felt the pain of his assaulted testicles, still fighting the urge to bend over as he stood there in shock.

"Take it easy Woodrow Grande, it was nice while it lasted baby… .I'll send you a postcard when you go back to Prison," Shaya spoke as she left the bedroom with one hand waving back at the bewildered, naked former-porn-actor standing there over the body of the late Duncan Horsehair with the smoking murder weapon in his hands. The scope of what she was telling him only now began to sink in, just as she made it downstairs into the huge living room. For Shaya Gold, this afternoon's fateful events could not have happened more to her own immediate favor. Much like her friend Amber Duffek, she had learned how to "read" a situation in a vain and selfish prism…. thus seeing the opportunity to rid herself of the threat of death by Duncan Horsehair by using the back-stabber Woody as the "set-up" whom would take the fall for killing Shaya Gold's lover in a fit of jealous rage, considering he just got paroled from Prison two days ago….the cops would believe her over him and such a case would force the FBI to spin it in such a way so that "Horsehair" and his real identity does not embarrass the US Government who had twice tried to bury him into obscurity.

The Feds would surely leave her alone after this "neat" little mess comes to light!

"I think the so-called 'Faster Murders' just got solved....heenh, thanks Woody," she snickered to herself as she slipped into her sandals by the Bar, picking up her tiny cell phone on the counter there and dialing 911. She had been a Porn Film Actress for most of her adult life, but an actress just the same...so whipping up tears and acting out the role of a crime victim was not going to be difficult at all for her. The fact that she had just killed a man in cold blood didn't feel as bad as she had expected it to, even when the man had been a lover of hers before. Murder didn't feel so bad, especially now she was getting away with it!

"I belong to no one, no one.....I'm Shaya Gold goddammit, and all of you back-stabbing fuckers can kiss my famous ass," she snickered out loud to herself in triumph as she waited for the dispatcher to answer on the other end of her 911 call, her right hand gently touching the hard resin-like tube on the necklace around her neck.

Fredericksburg, Virginia. July 4th: It had been over a month since the "slam dunk" Police Investigation into the murder at the infamous "Faster Mansion" on May 26th.

Recently-paroled Woody Ganderson had been arrested for the murder of 44-year old

"Duncan Hardison", a formerly homeless man Shaya Gold had "hired" there at the mansion and who Woody "murdered in cold blood" in a "fit of jealous rage" when he stalked Shaya after being paroled from Attica two days prior. Of course Woody denied it all but the evidence and Shaya's testimony not to mention the fact his fingerprints were all over the murder weapon which also happened to be an "untraceable" black-market handgun the Police believed he had access to once he got out of Prison. The story was playing well!

Rolling over, Shaya's lips met those of Amber's husband Kenny as he pulled her onto him again after Amber had taken a turn with her, the three of them in Amber's King-sized bed for a delicious threesome and still indulging one another. Shaya took on the man "cowgirl" style as she preferred, bouncing up and down on his manhood while Amber straddled her husband's head, facing Shaya and reaching hands out to tweek the tits of the woman now riding up and down on her husband's dick.

"Oooohh.....that's gooood....yeeeaaahh!" Shaya cooed in delight of the sex, Amber leaning forward to kiss her as she leaned in toward her. Kenny feasted between his wife's legs as a good husband should, relishing the moment both women were gorging on him now. Not every day a man gets to nail two ladies at once, one being his very willing wife!

"Heeenh.....ooooohh-yuuuuu-knooooowh....it....baaabeee!" Amber crooned aloud in near-orgasm, her boobs pressing against Shaya's now as they both straddled her husband in bed.

Amber and Shaya kissed lovingly over their male lover, hands on his chest and abs as they rode on him head and tool! Today was a day to celebrate the holiday and Shaya's "freedom" from her recent past, Amber having made certain that the Feds were no longer investigating Shaya as a suspect in the 2005 "Faster Murders" and that they had unofficially covered-up "Horsehair" as far as his real identity went....the media had him as just a "hired-handyman who was murdered by a jealous ex-con". The story spun well and both Amber and Shaya were pleased to say the least. Amber had taught Shaya pretty well in regards to recognizing "opportunities" when they arise and quickly take advantage, no matter how many other insignificant men or women get their asses roasted in the process!

"OOOOAAAANNH!!" Shaya wailed with glee as she moved faster and harder on the manmeat, up-and-down like a human piston as Amber rolled to Kenny's right to let her husband finish Shaya off. Kenny was all smiles as Shaya romped on him in carnal intercourse without fail, her shapely body appealing for Amber to just lay there and watch as it giggled and bounced atop of her husband like that. She adored Shaya Gold and the bitch knew it, which is why they had remained close friends through everything in the past four years.

Shaya and her husband rolled over for a vibrant missionary-style fuck and Amber just relaxed beside them watching as her husband did his job with her best friend, tubing the former porn starlet like a champ! Shaya's head turned right, eyes on Amber who grinned back at her as Kenny went-to-town on her, pumping into Shaya in a steady intercourse as he rested on his knees and hands, her legs dangling behind him as he thrusted into her.

"OOOOOAAAAHH……YEEEAAAAHH……OHH-MIIIII-GAAWHDD!!" Shaya bellowed in orgasm as Kenny drilled her vigorously now. Amber giggled at the sight of Shaya's sweaty face grimacing in raw pleasure, her body quivering under the man.

Amber then looked up at her husband's face and saw that tell-tale expression of his she knew all too well as he climaxed with Shaya himself now. Kenny and Shaya both rolled over together along with Amber for a threesome-embrace, all three delightfully pleased….

A few minutes later, Amber rose from the sheets and gently pulled Shaya's right arm to gesture her out of the bed with her. Sleepy but agreeable, Shaya followed the naked lawyer off the bed, leaving their male lover on the bed wondering what was going on.

"And where do you-two think you're going?" Kenny asked the two gloriously-naked ladies he just ravished as he slowly sat up in the middle of the bed, grinning at Amber as she looked back at her husband, smirking at him in coy response.

"Don't worry about it dear….you've had enough pussy for one day sir," Amber said girlishly at him, making both he and Shaya laugh at such rancor, partly because she had a good point!

Shaya waved a set of fingers back at Kenny as Amber ushered her out the bedroom into the hallway, closing the door behind them. Kenny just rested back on the pillows, hands behind his head and a smile on his face as he looked up at the mirror overhead, happy as a clam.

His wife just let him party with both she and Shaya Gold, and his latest book was completed and on it's way to the Publisher. "NAKED FURY: The Faster Murders" was the title and it was to be his first Non-Fiction title so far, the real-life account of the life and times of Jonny Faster and his secret porn stars leading up to the murders in 2005 which the Police now have Woody Ganderson (one of the former male porn actors) in custody for murder plus suspect in all the other killings that happened in 2005 in Jonny Faster's circle of friends. Of course he had the best "source" to tell him the tale in-depth! That source just walked out the bedroom door with his wife, and what a piece of work Shaya Gold is....

Shaya walked down the hallway arm-in-arm with Amber, into the sun-lit living room where they had drinks and seafood platters earlier celebrating the July 4th Holiday. Amber had decided that a threesome was the best way to celebrate she and Shaya surviving their latest brush with death and settling old accounts thanks to the idiot named Woody, plus the soon-to-be-published book NAKED FURY: The Faster Murders by K.R. Knight which they both contributed to immensely. The story had to be told, Shaya had insisted and what better way than to have Kenny write it and Amber cover all the bases like a good lawyer should?

"Mmmhh...now I know why you married that guy, wow," Shaya cooed as they came into the lit living room together, making a face at Amber denoting she enjoyed the sex.

"Glad you enjoyed him, but don't get used to it....I don't call for threesomes too often," Amber giggled in return, slapping Shaya on the bare ass playfully as they stopped in the center of the living room, both of them picking up champagne glasses to pour some.

"Well after all the shit that's happened in the past five years or so, here we are....," Amber said as she poured them both a glass of expensive champagne for a toast.

"Here we are Counselor, still alive and kickin' it," Shaya chimed with a beaming smile as she stood there naked alongside the naked lawyer, hands on the other's ass in kind, other hands holding up filled glasses of champagne for a toast.

"To all those others.....those strangers we had to step on, crush, or discard along the way in our unconventional...but successful.... lives," Amber spoke as she raised her glass in toast.

"To all the strangers....," Shaya sighed in toasting agreement as she touched her glass to Amber's and then they each drank their glasses dry as they stood there naked in the living room together. Amber smiled as their eyes met again, and had just one more question.

"Well did you dispose of that necklace the 'homeless' dude gave you?" Amber asked.

"I did, and let's just say it's in good hands where I sent it," Shaya snickered impishly which made Amber giggle girlishly in response, only caring that such a deadly virus was out of their vicinity. The two naked ladies hugged and kissed once again, not a worry in their minds now.

"We should take a Cruise together," Amber suggested with another slap to Shaya's bare ass.

"Yeah, but the ship would probably sink," Shaya chided back at her, then they kissed again.

Standing there at the living room's huge bay window naked and sipping their champagne, Shaya and Amber watched the growing thunderstorm outside now, not realizing they were within a neighboring home's viewpoint from one angle (nor would they give a shit either).

The three-story house just on the other side of the wooded ravine area separating the two streets was home to a family of three, the only son of the lawyer and wife living there now upstairs in his loft bedroom preparing to carry out his own suicide. The noose was perfect, rope thick enough to support his lean 160lbs and tied in the hangman's knot just right, today's culmination of his seemingly-worthless 18 years on the earth coming to a close now.

Damien Wolfson was now ready to hang himself inside of his own loft bedroom, recalling that old Italian poem about "let my own home be my gallows".

Stepping around the room one final time, thinking of what his parents would do once they find him, perhaps cry at first but would miss him more for the fact he wouldn't be around any longer for them to crow about to their wealthy friends: "If only my son Damien was like other boys his age and going to a prestigious University" then there was his father's lament:

"Damien…..I'm afraid he's going to be one of those young men who never get a date".

The noose was tied tight around a hot water pipe at the ceiling, secure enough to hold him once he slips off the wooden chair with the rope around his neck. Damien was prepared, still wondering why tears streamed down his face right now, he had been ready to kill himself for two years now! this was it, no more chickening out, this was it! he kept thinking as he walked to face his noose hanging from the pipe, looking up at it then just before he could step up onto the chair and begin the hanging, his vision caught something out the window to his immediate left, something visible despite the ongoing thunderstorm outside now, something across the trees and over on Beverly Lane's cul-de-sac.

"What tha....?" He asked himself in sudden wonder, turning to step up close to the window and peer across the small ravine separating his home here from the big brick domicile with the in-ground pool and fancy back yard, the house of that female lawyer whom his father knows! Damien couldn't believe what he was seeing despite the rainfall and the trees there, over there at the big bay-window of what he assumed to be the living room, stood **two naked women**...his eyes weren't playing tricks on him, no way! Damien stood there gawking through his bedroom window at the enticing sight of two totally-nude females of very attractive proportions, drinking from champagne glasses and talking to each other.

"Jeezus.....who is that.....wow," Damien said to himself as he ran a hand up through his thick blonde hair, staring through his bottle-thick eyeglasses in an feeling he had not felt for quite some time. The female attorney his Father knows, she had to be one of those two he guessed, though Damien had not seen her in-person before now, the other one a dark-haired fox with hug boobs, the two of them very fit and well-built he thought in angst of the sight.

Damien didn't even glance up at his hanging noose, almost forgetting his lethal intentions of just moments ago, his attention now focused on something he had never really seen in reality like this, which was one of his complaints in this life.....naked womanhood!

"Sheeeeze....I gotta see'em a little closer," he sighed to himself as he reluctantly left the window and hurried out of his room, going downstairs in a rush for the back door, hearing his parents arguing over what was to be for dinner in the kitchen. He slipped outside into the driving rainfall, not caring about the weather, hoping those two nude lovelies were still standing at that window over at 1705 Beverly

Lane! Running through the rainfall to the backyard his father hated mowing, he struggled to get a better view of the neighbor across the tiny ravine and woods between their properties. Damien's purpose had flown from suicide to getting a better view of two naked ladies like some "peeping tom"!

"I have spoken with my friend in the Justice Department and he told me the FBI and ATF are no longer interested in you now that strange man called 'Horsehair' is dead, your friend Woody taking the fall rather well for that and neatly closing the whole goddamn thing from your late husband's shadowy endeavors to the missing money to the 'incidents' caused by Mister Horsehair....it's all dismissed into a variety of crimes and terrorist incidents not related to one another now," Amber explained in a soft voice to her buxom companion.

"Hmmm....good, great to know all that shit could be spun that way among all those police agencies and of course, the news media," Shaya added then sipped her champagne again.

"Oh yes, it is a glorious fact that the American media can be manipulated to accept and announce such bullshit...and as for the cops, well....profiling and speculating is part of any murder investigation and without solid traceable evidence, it's all conjecture," Amber added.

"I owe you Amber, big time," Shaya whispered softly to the pretty Attorney next to her.

"Yes, but I'm calling us even....you owe me nothing now babe, because if it weren't for you killing Horsehair, that animal would have definitely come back to finish me off as soon as he realized that bomb didn't go off here....so we're even," Amber replied softly in return.

"True, he would have killed us both as 'loose ends'....heenh, still can't believe all this shit that happened over the past four years of my life, wow," Shaya sighed matter-of-factly.

"You survived babe....we both did....count your blessings," Amber said with a snicker.

" A veteran Porn Starlet and a Feminist Attorney," Shaya giggled back then leaned into Amber for another kiss, their hands on one another again in familiar contact, a sight clearly seen by the young man who struggled down and up across the small ravine between his home and Amber Duffek's, getting a much better view of the two naked ladies kissing up at the big bay-window as the storm raged on. Soaked to the gills but surprisingly happy, Damien Wolfson stopped at the big Holly bush bordering the backyard there on the other property, looking up at them as rain streamed down from head to feet, none of it bothering him as he gawked up at the incredible bare bodies of his neighbors this afternoon.

"Mmmhh…as much as I'd love to hang out with you here all day, I do have to meet a prospective client in town here for dinner at four…forgive me?" Amber cooed gingerly.

"Mmmmh-okay," Shaya said then wolfed down the rest of her expensive champagne.

"Feel free to stick around if you like Shaya, no rush for you to get back up north…you may even play with my husband some more if you'd like…," Amber spoke next with a wink then a kiss to Shaya's lips as her right hand caressed Shaya's plump n' perky breasts again.

"Heenh, okay I might," Shaya said with a sly smile as Amber turned to walk back across the living room to go get dressed for her meeting at 4pm. Shaya enjoyed watching Amber walk around naked like that, the woman possessing a body so fit and trim it looks better nude than clothed! Shaya turned back to the window and stared out at the storm outside, hands on her ass cheeks as she stood there in pensive thought. She had come "full circle" in a way, and all that she had been through was really of no fault of her own except for the choices she had made in men and "career". She was also surprised at how she felt about killing a man, killing Duncan, a man who had been her lover but threatened her life in a very real way, so she didn't feel bad about it at all! Though some remorse crept into her psyche about poor Woody, sent back to prison for parole violation and charged with the murder of a "homeless man" Shaya reportedly hired to do work around her new mansion. She would be in the news again once Woody's trial began but that was no problem considering what Amber told her. The Feds and local NY Police are supposedly satisfied with the end-game regarding the "Faster

Murders" and those shadowy co-conspirators of her late husband's were happy now that "Horsehair" was in a grave and not carrying out a "war" on his own!

Shaya turned from the window slowly and put her empty glass down, hearing thunder boom overhead, the forecast for today promising rain and thunder till 9pm. She thought about going out back and getting in the hot-tub for a hot soak but decided to wait until it stopped thundering and lightning outside. After all she had survived, getting struck by lightning while in a hot tub cabana would be the irony she didn't want etched on her tombstone! Might as well live a long, old-ass life from here on out! she mused to herself.

Amber was in the shower just a few minutes before she got out, dried off, did her hair and got dressed in a "business-casual" dress that would go well with her rain-parka. Her husband always joked about how FAST she gets ready to go somewhere, not the stereotypical woman who is late for a date! Amber kissed him goodbye and was out the door as soon as she kissed Shaya farewell too, venturing out into the rainfall for her dinner-meeting at 4pm.

Shaya looked over at Amber's husband Kenny in the bed as she re-entered the bedroom, smiling at him as he sat up and stretched, smiling back at the naked brunette crossing the room now, going over to the master bedroom's side-door which led outside to the hot tub.

"What's up Shaya?" he asked her causally as she opened the door there to look outside.

"Hmmmh….I might go jump in the hottub once it stops lightning out, plus there's something else," she said back to the handsome devil sitting on the end of the bed now.

"Something else?" he chimed boyishly as he stood up and stretched, yawning out loud.

"Yeah…something commonly known as a 'peeping tom'," Shaya snickered back at him.

"Haanh-haah, peepers….yeah, this house is known for them, the prior owner was a bit of a nudist from what I hear and Amber is no better, so there are sure to be a few wandering eyes in this neighborhood," Kenny chuckled in reply, stepping over toward Shaya at the door.

He touched a hand to her smooth back and dropped the hand to her bare ass as she stood there staring out the storm door at the back yard and hot tub cabana, thinking.

"Hmmph, funny how the naked body entices strangers to do silly things," she giggled.

"Yep, like all of your porn film fans hunh…a legion of guys and gals out there who adore you because you got naked and performed sex acts on films they purchased," he added.

"Yeah, those people," Shaya sighed as she thought about the man she sent the necklace to, the necklace bearing the man-made killer-virus sealed within it's hard resin "tube" dangling on the silver chain. She didn't want to just throw it away, for it could come up at the landfill and infect from there. No, given by her to one of her loyal fans assured it's safety at least for awhile. Knowing how "devoted" some fans of adult films tend to be, she assumed that necklace and the virus it contains within will remain a "treasured souvenir" from the young man's all-time favorite Porn Starlet! She then saw what she was looking for outside in the rain, out back skulking through the wooded portion of the property separating the house here from the ones on the parallel street. There he was…her "peeping tom"!

"I'm gonna hit the shower….join me if you'd like," Kenny said as he walked back across the bedroom toward the bathroom on the other side, Shaya watching him walk away from her.

Shaya then looked back at the male-sized figure lurking in the bushes out back, taking that he had not seen her there at that extra rear door, moving down toward the courtyard and patio deck around back. She suddenly felt the urge to try and "taunt" this guy lurking around out there and so she left the bedroom, hurried down the hallway and through the dining room to the stairwell, descending into the darkly-kept basement "den" where she would surely catch the "peeper" red-handed as he tries to get closer to the rear of the house, obviously enamored with whom he saw standing naked up in the living room earlier!

That was where Shaya spotted him down in the small ravine between the houses, when Amber turned to go get dressed. Now she wanted to tease the hell out of such a perv!

Down in the dark basement den, Shaya walked to the sliding-glass door totally unafraid.

Damien Wolfson was taking a chance, he knew that, but next to committing suicide like he had intended to do earlier, trespassing was no big deal. He wanted to see more of those two naked woman in the window, but now they were gone from the bay window and he was trespassing on the property of a woman his father calls a "shark" when speaking of her skills as an Attorney. Which would his father prefer he wondered, hanging in his bedroom dead or arrested for trespassing on a neighbor during a thunderstorm?

Running up to the house as close as he could go, some of the rainfall softened in it's deluge as he huddled on the cement patio in front of a brick barbecue pit and grill. Damien looked to his left and saw a sliding-glass door and a light on further inside which made him want to go peer through the sliding-glass door for a look-see but he hesitated to do that just yet.

Shaya saw him clearly as she peeked around the corner to look out the glass door, seeing her "peeper" to be a young White guy with eyeglasses, probably in his late teens she guessed and dripping-wet from the rain, clad in what was once a clean white shirt and slacks. She unlocked the door and slowly slid it open, getting the young man's stunned attention as she stepped to the threshold of the doorway there at the lower patio, totally-naked but not getting wet from the rain inches away from her, facing the stunned "peeper" defiantly.

"Get a good look perv....see something you like....wanna get arrested?!" Shaya spoke up with hands on her bare hips as she faced Damien Wolfson like an Amazon, not threatened by him whatsoever, judging him to not be one of those "attacker" types....just a Voyeur!

"Uhhh...no ma'am....no, I live next door...and I uhhh...well, you caught me....," Damien responded in the nervous truth, hands up in a defeated "surrender" gesture as he stood.

"Damn right I caught you, and if my lover had seen you, you'd be hurting big time....he's an Ex-Green Beret and he'd rip your balls off if he caught you here spying on me," Shaya lied to the frightened-yet-respectful young man standing in the rain there on the cement patio.

Wouldn't be the first time she lied to a man about having a kick-ass boyfriend nearby, it was as tall-tale that saved a lot of unwanted advances from weaker men!

"I'm sorry....I'm so sorry ma'am....really, please don't call the police on me," Damien said as he stood there eyeing her through winced eyes as the rain pelted him ferociously, stunned by the woman standing there totally nude so casually after catching him spying on her.

"I know you're sorry....and I should call the Police on you, it's a crime to peek in on a lady when she's indoors and out of the public eye," she continued in her best "shame on you" tone of voice, watching the young man standing there in the rain like a wounded duck.

"Yes ma'am....yes ma'am...and I'm sorry," Damien said again and meaning it.

"What's your name peeper?" Shaya asked him in a chuckle at his expression of fear.

"Damien....Damien Wolfson, I live next door," he told her honestly, hoping his parents don't find out about this embarrassing excursion of his. Shaya appreciated the honesty.

"Well okay Damien...I'm not gonna call the cops on you, now come on inside out of the storm and I'll get you a towel to dry off," Shaya said in a nicer tone now, gesturing for him to follow her inside the basement den there. He couldn't believe the sudden "niceness" but the rain was about to make him sick the longer he stood in it, so he cautiously followed the naked woman through the sliding-glass door and inside the air-conditioned interior.

"Wait right there Damien," Shaya said pointing to the spot where he stopped upon entry, his eyes on her as she walked across the darkly-atuned basement den, past a pool table and into another room. He just realized that he got what he came over here for: SEEING THAT NAKED CHICK UP-CLOSE! Standing there dripping-wet, Damien waited for her to re-appear, hoping like hell her "Ex-Green Beret" boyfriend doesn't appear instead to rip his balls off for looking at his naked sweetheart! Shaya walked back out with a long towel in hand, smiling as she approached him, tossing it to him when she was about 3 feet away.

"Hope you're happy now Damien....heenh-heeh....came all the way over here just to see me naked, are you pleased?" Shaya chimed as she stepped back to the pool table, leaning back against it on her bare ass as she faced the young man in a more genteel manner.

"Uhh....yes ma'am.....yes ma'am," Damien said as he quickly dried his head and hair then his arms with the towel she tossed at him, looking at her pensively as he stood still.

"Actually, I don't really blame you, Amber and I were standing upstairs at the window and practically invited someone to peek at us," Shaya said in humor, winking at Damien.

"She's a lawyer right?" he asked nervously, wondering about the relationship there.

"Yes, and a damn good one too, she sues people for a living and if she had caught you peeping on us, you'd be sued for everything you've got plus everything you'd ever have for the next twenty years, heenh-heh," Shaya quipped in jovial humor, though her young visitor was not amused by the revelation, hoping that lawyer wasn't coming down those stairs!

"Don't worry big guy, she'll never know about you peeping on us today," Shaya told him.

"Thank you ma'am...thanks a lot," Damien said with a dozen nods of his head now.

"Oh you're welcome Damien from next door.....heenh, you have a girlfriend?" Shaya chimed impishly, wanting to goad this nervous young intruder a little bit more.

"Uhh...no ma'am, I don't," he answered her truthfully, feeling ashamed by the admission.

"Really, well you're young....just be mindful not to get your balls cut off for sniffing around someone else's lady...work hard and stay out of jail, you could have a woman who looks like I do, all to yourself…one day," Shaya said softly to Damien as he placed the towel down.

"Yes ma'am," he replied respectfully, nodding again as he stepped more into the light shining from the other side of the pool table, the lamp she turned on when she came down.

He was a respectful guy but a normal one she thought, an erection noticeable in his soaking-wet pants, and she smiled sweetly at him as he stood there not knowing she noticed such.

Shaya always enjoyed that "power" she wielded over straight men like this young guy.

"Is your boyfriend home?" he asked out of nervousness, looking around where he stood.

"Yes, but don't worry….as long as I don't scream, he'll stay upstairs," she answered softly.

"Cool…I'd never hurt you ma'am," Damien said with hands up in surrender again.

"I know…and please, call me Shaya," she said with a wink and a kiss blown his way.

"You're beautiful Shaya, and I apologize for peeking at you like I did, I shouldn't have," Damien said in a more relaxed manner this time, eyes down in sincerity of his statement.

"Thanks Damien, apology accepted…..it's okay to appreciate a woman and her body, one day you'll find a good woman and put that hard-on of yours to good use," Shaya said with a casual point of a finger toward the front of his pants, making Damien blush beet-red!

He turned askew in reaction to her spotting the raging erection in his rain-soaked pants, but could tell she wasn't offended at all. Why would she be? Talking to him naked like she is???

And to think he was going to kill himself just 30 minutes ago!! Damien stood there corrected in the stupidity of his most recent plan, standing here in a stranger's home eyeballing her while she was naked which was what he wanted to do when he came over here in the first place, he got what he wanted by taking a chance……no chances at all when you're dead!

She walked over closer to him now, her eyes fixed on his as he stood still in less-nervous stance, eyes going to her big bouncy breasts as she stopped there right in front of him.

"Shaya?" came the voice of Amber's husband at the top of the stairs all of a sudden.

She looked at Damien with an "oh shit!" expression to denote the "danger" he was in and the young man bolted for the sliding door, fleeing back out into the storm in mere seconds, gone from her sight in a flat-out run for his life, and she laughed in spite of herself.

"I'm down here Kenny," Shaya called back to the man who didn't know what was going on.

Damien Wolfson never ran so hard in retreat, even from bullies back in high school, fleeing through that courtyard and the holly bushes down the small ravine gulley between his home and the naked women's house, hurrying back to the back door of his home where he collapsed once he was inside of it. He was out of breath but thrilled in the same sensation, his mind afire with the images of that well-built female who talked to him like she did.

"Shaya," he said to himself as he caught his breath seated on the floor by the back door.

Now, the entire idea of killing himself was almost unthinkable, untenable, and unlikely!

Now, he was going to launch himself into manhood, into a life bigger then what he had here at home with his elitist parents, now he was going to do exactly what he wanted to do….

"Mom, Dad, I'm leaving at the end of the month for that Photography school I've been wanting to attend….it's settled," Damien spoke abruptly as he walked through the kitchen where his middle-aged parents were sitting at the dinner table, his words not surprising them as much as the fact their only son was dripping-wet!

"Damien…..what on earth…?" his father spoke up hesitantly in reaction as his dripping-wet son marched up the stairs now toward his bedroom on the top floor of their home here.

"It's final Dad....I'm not going to Law School, I'm going to take Photography....and try to get hired by Playboy Magazine as one of their Photographers," Damien retorted as he made it to the top of the stairs, leaving his parents down in the kitchen shocked by the revelation.

From that moment on, Damien Wolfson was a changed young man, and his life would never be the droll, meaningless existence he had almost killed himself over today, for he had just discovered his life moments before he could have ended it! Now, thanks to that beautiful, naked woman named Shaya next door, Damien Wolfson was going to live like he had not yet imagined he could live....from that moment forward, the sunlight would be a little bit brighter, the breakfast he'll have the next morning tasting better than ever before, and the people around him seen in a whole new light.....

Next door, Shaya Gold thought about getting dressed and leaving for New York anyway, despite the ongoing storm and the distance from here to there. She amused herself with what she did with that male "peeping tom" who took off out into the rain like a coyote when Kenny called down to her from upstairs minutes ago, the poor guy actually thinking Shaya's "Ex-Green Beret boyfriend" was really going to rip his balls off if he found him there!

She walked back upstairs and to the living room after checking to see where Amber's husband was right now (taking a hot shower in the hallway bathroom). She kept thinking that perhaps she might end up "clipped" by some assassin hired by shadowy government people wanting to eliminate all ties to Kelsh, Horsehair, and those missing millions of $$ but like Amber told her, it was not worth the worry since events tend to unfold in chaotic and unpredictable ways, no one can even try to predict their own future, bright or gloomy!

Amber still had a small collection of X-rated videos of the past, most of which were filmed and produced by Faster Productions so she popped one in the DVD player over the big TV.

Sitting naked on the sofa with the storm still raging outside, Shaya Gold relaxed with the sole intention of watching one of her past adult features starring herself as well as Jonny Faster and FM Dexter. The opening scene was of her kneeling between the two well-hung studs and performing fellatio on both of them as they stood flanking her, with silly music playing in the background. The camera zoomed in on her face as she orally-indulged both men then down at her jiggling boobs as she knelt between the two male porn stars.

"That's it baby....show'em how it's done," Shaya said at the video sex scene of hers, once again realizing that sex was her only real "career" and her undeniable "power" over men....

Chicago, Illinois. July 5th: The package came in the mail without a return address but as soon as Rufus Seastone opened it, he knew who it was from and accepted it as a gift he had not expected, least of all from her! Shaya Gold had sent him a personal gift, a short hand-written note saying how much she appreciated his loyalty as a Fan of her Adult Film work all these years and she wanted to give him something special. It was a necklace unlike any other he'd seen in any store, a silver chain with a bluish resin "stone" hanging on it by a sealed clasp. The note said that the color of the tube-like "stone" reminded her of his last name:

"Seastone" and so she got it especially for him.

Rufus was wearing it ever since he took it from it's package earlier, though it would make for a bit of a bulge under any shirt, he decided to wear it as often as he could in honor of the gift his favorite Porn Starlet had bestowed upon him without him ever even asking for anything in return for his loyalty. His buddies would call him crazy but he didn't care because Shaya Gold had finally recognized him as her #1 Fan and like she said in the letter:

"Rufus Seastone my #1 Fan, you'll always be in my heart".

Love Always~ Shaya Gold.

He wasn't gullible like his buddies tried to tell him, Rufus just adored a female "celebrity" from afar like so many other men do, only his was an X-rated Film Star and she had finally shown him a gesture of appreciation! Sitting here on his sofa in his solitary apartment, Rufus held the strange memento around his neck in reflection of how many times he had watched Shaya Gold on his TV screen, how many times he wanted to be one of those long-horned guys cast with her in those films. Being in love with a stranger wasn't abnormal like his mother had once told him, sometimes strangers were the only ones who really showed him any personal gratitude or appreciation unlike most of his buddies from college or his older brothers. Shaya Gold was a stranger to him, technically-speaking, but he was all the more admiring of her now that she had sent him a unique gift.

"Thanks Shaya baby, thanks a lot....I'll never forget this, you're my girl," Rufus said softly as he picked up his remote control and engaged his TV set, a DVD already in the player.

The screen came alive with the image of an X-rated sex scene (in-progress) showing his favorite Starlet Shaya Gold with Jonny Faster hiding his big salami inside her, the two of them going-at-it "doggie style" on a picnic table out in the woods somewhere. He loved it, vicarious sex performed by strangers for his viewing inside the comfort of his own home.

"Give it to her Jonny Faster....give it to her ma white brotha!" Rufus quipped jokingly to the TV as he watched the outdoor sex scene from the X-rated film entitled: "Grab n' Go".

"What I would have given to have been that dude just for a few days...I would have boned Shaya for hours!" Rufus chuckled to himself as he took a sip of his beer with one hand, the other hand touching the resin-like "stone" around his neck now, his mind vicariously drifting off into daydreaming as he often did. His teachers back in school used to tell his mother that he "daydreamed" all the time in class....now he was daydreaming about his favorite Porn Star again, unaware that within the sealed resin "stone" around his neck right now was the last sample of the one of the deadliest man-made viruses ever conceived.

He had no clue whatsoever as to the composition of the gift Shaya Gold sent him, nor the assumption of hers that of all her Porn Fans out there, Rufus Seastone was one who'd keep the strange gift as a cherished memento from his favorite Porn Starlet and therefore the deadly virus sealed within was safely, anonymously...."in good hands".

Hudson County, New Jersey. (same evening): Bruno was a happy man despite being indicted by the Feds on a bullshit "racketeering" charge which he is confident he'll beat, and the fact he had to clip two of his men last night for snitching to the cops regarding his immediate whereabouts. Bruno was always happiest right here inside his subterranean "den" deep within and below his house here in Jersey, because here within his windowless "bunker" as his ex-wife called it, Bruno could just relax and enjoy safe solitude from all the cops, back-stabbers, rivals, and smiling cheats he has to walk amongst everywhere else.

It is also here in his underground "den" where he keeps some of his most prized and rare, personal possessions, not trusting them to be kept anywhere else.

His gold bars, his heirloom stuff from his father, rare coins worth $100,000 and two of his "trophies" mounted on one wall for only him to see whenever he comes down here to relax.

One was the severed hand of his brother Freddy who betrayed their father when he was the Don and so had to be clipped the old fashioned way (chopped up into nothing) but Bruno had the goons save his brother's right hand, the one Freddy shook hands with when the fool gave Bruno his word that he was not dropping dimes to anyone. The hand was kept in a jar of formaldehyde on a shelf next to the shelves of rare hard-bound books he collected.

The next human "trophy" was mounted on one wall all by itself in perfect taxidermy done by the one man Bruno could pay to do such a grisly thing to a human body portion.

It was the ASS of the late Detective Justine Cheeks, stuffed-and-mounted in smooth taxidermy on his wall down here, well-preserved using a special material to preserve it's sheen and shape, the woman's bare ass mounted perfectly to appear as if a white woman with a great physique was sticking her bare ass through the wall!

"Ahhh....hunh-huh-hunh...what a fitting end for Justine Cheeks," the Italian Mobster named Bruno said to himself in humor as he walked over to his wall-mounted trophy, touching a hand to the smooth buttocks he had collected from the body of the rogue cop immediately after lopping off her pretty head with his machete a week ago.

"Gambling is one bitch of a bad habit isn't it babydoll?" he chuckled as he ran a hand over the smooth, mounted asscheeks on his wall, enjoying the trophy and what it said about his iron will when it came to collecting debts owed him by gambling junkies. Justine Cheeks ended up with her head severed and tossed into the Atlantic Ocean, the rest of her grinded into cube-steak except for her hind quarters here on a wall.

"Hunh-hah, I should have Amber Duffek's ass mounted right next to Justine's....hunh, if I was to add to my collection here I'd have that ass as well as her pretty head mounted as trophies," Bruno said to himself in a chuckle, enjoying the macabre act of taking human "trophies" much like the infamous Marcano Mafia Don "The Sicilian" used to do. It was the ultimate relish to have something taken from one's enemies, a war-trophy from the "war" that is life! Life is war, let no one say otherwise! Bruno told himself with a grin as he stared up at the woman's ass mounted on his wall. He knew he wasn't the only one who had such things "collected" from late human beings....Attorney Amber Duffek supposedly has the balls of her "first love" preserved in a jar of formaldehyde, so Bruno is not the only collector of human trophies. He turned from the late Justine Cheeks' ass mounted on a wall and walked over to his leather recliner here in his underground "den", picking up the glass of Cognac he had brought down here with him minutes ago, thinking about the others who are into gambling debts with him lately and how he was going to collect what they all now owe.

New Rochelle, NY. (Night of July 5th): He didn't know whether he was going to kill the woman or ravish her like he had a year ago down in Virginia. All that Mered Aladdin knew now was that he was going to see Shaya Gold here at the "Faster Mansion" she had recently purchased for herself, the place where he had been filmed performing sex for X-rated movies years ago, his second secret "career" next to murder-for-profit! Getting up to the mansion without anyone noticing wasn't a problem for someone like him, but the place appeared to be without its semi-famous resident, no vehicles parked in the driveway.

Still, he had to make sure, or the trip here was for nothing, so he cautiously approached the rear of the infamous mansion as the sun set and darkness gave him the cover he desired.

The wind promised a storm which would be yet another "concealment" for him since most people do not stay out in rainfall long enough to really notice strangers lurking about!

Mered Aladdin wanted Shaya Gold here tonight, and he decided he'd wait for her if he has to, guessing she may have just driven to a store or somewhere close-by and would return.

Stepping around to the backyard as darkness rolled over the fat-cat neighborhood, he made his way up to the wooden patio deck to peer inside where he remembered a sliding-glass door being located. Mered was clad in black t-shirt and jeans, his dark hair and lean build a bonus for any prowler, getting up close to peer inside the infamous mansion on a hill here in New Rochelle. Not surprisingly, there was someone inside the mansion tonight even though she did not appear to be Shaya Gold....unless Shaya had recently morphed into a cute petite blonde white woman with perky tits and ass now strolling through the huge living room totally naked except for a ball cap on her pretty blonde head.

"Hnnnnhh.....Shelly......Shelly James?" the Turk asked himself as the wind picked up all around him, his left hand touching his bushy moustache as he stared through the glass door.

He had to guess the naked blonde bouncing through the mansion's interior at the moment was none-other-than the bubbly blonde bimbo he performed with in the X-rated film titled

"Turkish Poker" back in 2005 before the Company collapsed and it all went into the shitter.

The naked blonde headed for the stairs and started trotting up the stairwell for the upper floors when Mered reached the sliding glass door's handle. Finding the door unlocked was a surprise but he considered it to be a stroke of luck rather than an oddity. Illegally entering the private domicile, the Turk watched as the shapely blonde with the ass of a cheerleader bounced her way up the carpeted steps, convincing him that she had to be Shelly James who might now live here with Shaya he mused as he quietly, cautiously entered the mansion.

Rushing to the bottom of the stairs and looking up to see the bare female ass turn right onto the second floor of the big house, where the main bedrooms were located! He started up the steps without making a sound, wanting this to be a surprise. Shelly and he had not parted on bad tidings back then so why would she be frightened of him now? Mered was not above rape but he hoped it didn't come down to that since he sort of liked Shelly back when he performed with her, for she was a sweet little cupcake to feast upon! Once he reached the top of the stairs at the second floor, he turned to face down that hallway and found the lovely blonde cupcake staring back at him from the other end of the hall, not surprised at all.

Mered froze where he stood, trying to make out her face due to the shadows of the hallway, but he thought the well-shaped naked blonde to be the former Porn Starlet Shelly James.

"Hey there handsome....about time you showed up," the woman spoke sleazy to him, a voice not one he remembered to be Shelly's and his "fight or flight" instinct rang a bell.

"Not very gentlemanly to keep a woman waiting!" the blonde snapped next as she raised her right hand and squeezed off two rounds from the silencer-equipped Glock-19 pistol gripped in her fist, both round smacking into his upper chest, one striking inches above the heart.

The naked blonde cupcake walked down the hallway toward her wounded prey, her silenced weapon down at her right thigh, something Mered failed to see when he came to the top of the steps here at the second floor, a naked chick who looked a lot like Shelly James armed with a silenced 9mm handgun! Felt as if his entire torso had been lit on fire, he tried to raise back up into a sitting position but he knew he was done for, his vision slipping into a more two-dimensional view now as he lay there mortally wounded with a beautifully bare blonde walking up to him, leveling her weapon at him.

"Mered Aladdin….I'm making this quick for ya…call it 'professional courtesy'," the blonde said as she now stood over him with her weapon out in one hand aiming for his face now.

"Wait….wait….why?" he managed to speak despite the pain of the bullets in him now.

"Besides making money using your dick in porno films, you were like me….a free-lance assassin, and about two years ago you eliminated a man for a British mobster to whom the idiot had stolen money from…only along with the target you clipped the man's wife and two small children in the car bomb you set…..I am the end-result of that brutality on your part, because innocent children murdered during a hit is just…plain…unnecessary," spoke the pretty blonde with the icy blue eyes, then she squeezed off a final round from her Glock-19 which punched through Mered's skull, exiting out the back of his skull into the floorboard.

"Hmmmph….what an asshole," she said in a chuckle as she turned to walk back down the stairs, the entire mansion now rigged to catch fire and be consumed as soon as she keys a remote device that'll trigger the incendiary charges she set in here earlier. Hanging around this infamous mansion in New Rochelle for the past 2 days and nights was cozy but a little dangerous for a woman such as Rani Kovetts, hired to kill another assassin-for-hire by the family of two of his collateral victims. She had tracked the Turk to New Rochelle and having studied his background extensively as any contract-killer normally would, she denoted that he would likely pay a visit to the "Faster Mansion" here in town. Sneaking into the place was easy because it had no alarm system to speak of and hanging around with little to no clothes on only made the place appear all the more realistic because it was once the home and filming location of the Porn Legend Jonny Faster who was now a missing person. Rani Kovetts staked the place out in wait for Mered Aladdin by injecting herself inside and hoped he would show up exactly how he did, by surprise. The foolish Turk did what was expected and she shot him dead where he stood, thinking she was one of the porn starlets that used to frequent this darkly-attuned household years ago. She knew she could easily pass as some "bimbo blonde porno slut" hanging around here as long as the rightful owner of the mansion didn't come home, which did not happen! Rani Kovetts' preferred method of execution was her exotic poisons but she did not want to get close enough to Mered Aladdin to poison him, so she gunned him down like the dog he was here inside the infamous "Faster Mansion". Her job was done and a cool $500,000 deposited in her off-shore account and now the only thing left to do was get rid of the evidence by incinerating the entire damn mansion from the top-down. Rani Kovetts walked down to the living room where her black jumpsuit lay in wait and the flip-switch detonator that would ignite the incendiary devices she placed at key points within the mansion. In no hurry to get out now that it was night time and therefore easier for her to retreat unseen by curious eyes, she paused to pour herself a shot of tequila at the in-home custom bar counter there.

"Shame really....nice place that Pornographer had here, but.... business is business," Rani Kovetts spoke to herself as she looked around the swank living room, then wolfed down her shot of tequila before pulling on her black jumpsuit to make her escape, clutching the detonator in her left hand, smiling sleazy as she flipped it's tiny switch.

Long Island, NY. Midnight: Reynaldo Piazzi was once again surprised by his lady friend's uncanny ability to enter his luxurious Long Island Condominium here without triggering his alarm system and without breaking a lock in any way. Then again, having a "mysterious" mistress was exciting as well as pleasurable, so he allowed such a breech of personal security.

Leading a secret "double-life" was just as exciting as cheating on his wife of 10 years with such as woman as Rani, and he never even asked her what her last name was even though he'd been meeting with her like this for a year now. Reynaldo Piazzi walked into his air-conditioned Condo to find the shapely blonde dish named Rani already disrobed and lying naked on the King-sized bed reading a book of some kind as she waited for her lover.

"Good evening....," Rani Kovetts spoke gingerly to the handsome Italian man entering his own condo, removing his tie and cufflinks as he stepped around to the foot of his bed there.

"Hmmph....said the spider to the fly," Reynaldo said in response, smiling at her lovely form.

"Which one of us is the spider?" she chimed next with a sleazy expression on her cute face.

"You are my dear Rani....whatever your last name may be....you are," Reynaldo chuckled.

"Get you clothes off and then talk to me," she sighed with a smirk at him in the lamp light.

She looked back down in her book, a copy of MIGHT IS RIGHT by Ragnar Redbeard, a title her lean Italian lover was not familiar with, nor did he care enough to ask while he was getting out of his clothes at the foot of the bed. He just wanted to make love and fall asleep with her afterward, the mere sensation of that exercise being all he yearned for tonight.

"Oooohh....you are in a good mood after all I see," Rani cooed upon seeing his erection at full-mast as soon as he stripped off his boxer shorts, hurrying into bed with her. Their bare bodies clasped together in passion, Reynaldo began his usual foreplay with her familiar body.

She felt so good to slide into, and Reynaldo gave in to the sensation, thinking of nothing more than getting laid by this incredible woman he knew far too little about. Rani began her own sexual routine with her Italian lover, groaning out in reception of his manhood thrust inside of her now, hugging his pulsing body into hers as intercourse began.

"A....verrreeeey......goooood.......mood!" Reynaldo crooned as he sailed into her flesh, arching upward to drive forward as far as physically possible, surrendering to the moment.

"Oaaah-unnnooaaah....unnoooaaah!!" Rani cried out in delight of the intercourse as her lover continued his onslaught, pumping into her in a vigorous missionary position there on the unmade bed with steady rhythm. The two lovers became one grinding beast of carnal fury as their desire flamed red-hot, pure raw carnality ruling supreme. Reynaldo was giving her his all, and she appreciated it, letting him indulge her as he usually did with full-on fury. Rani soon found herself on top of him after he exploded first, riding on his man meat in easy motion, taking his length up inside of her to continue their intercourse in "cowgirl" format, bouncing happily up and down on the man's stiff dick.

"Rey....nahllll-doh!" she cooed with impish delight, savoring the sensation as she rode on him like many times before, eyes closed and mouth wide open as she moved up and down on his flesh, moaning out in fiendish delight as she got her rocks off the same time as she was now getting rid of a "liability" who lay beneath her bare bucking body.

"Ooaaah-baby, you....allllhhh-waaays....made....... meeeee.......come!" Rani Kovetts moaned in satisfaction of her own orgasm as she bounced wildly on his manhood, then slowed to a stop in conclusion, eyes on the man's sweaty face as he lay there motionless beneath her, eyes closed and a near-grin as his head lay on a pillow. Rani had been screwing a dead man for about the last ten seconds, her poison having done its job faster than usual.

She slipped off him and stood up to stretch, yawning as she looked back at her poisoned lover she regretted having to kill but his continuance on planet earth was a threat to her ever since Reynaldo Piazzi came into contact with the American FBI and INTERPOL over his illegal computer hacking and profitable wire transfers those Agencies had him cold on.

Why was he out of jail tonight? Simple, because he had agreed to become an informant for the Authorities regarding "international organized crime syndicates".

"Idiot," she snickered back at the man she just poisoned during sex, a trick of assassination she was adept at and well-experienced in, something the hacker named Reynaldo never imagined happening to him as he sucked on her tits that had been covered in a thin gel which resembled perfume but shut down the heart after ten minutes once ingested orally.

With her special man-made poisons, Rani Kovetts had made a career as a Contract Killer, though she wasn't making any money off this hit, this one was personal. Poor Reynaldo fucked up and got caught by INTERPOL and the goddamn FBI, so she had to clip him or she'd find herself in handcuffs sitting inside a Federal holding cell soon if she did not!

She stepped over to the Condo bedroom's window, looking out toward NYC and the alluring nighttime skyline it possessed, standing there naked with her hands on hips.

"Hmmmph....maybe I should retire to some tropical island, sit on the beach with pineapple margaritas, Don Diego cigars, and a young man with a big penis," she spoke to herself then laughed it off as she turned around to look over at the late Reynaldo Piazzi, lying there on his back with a slight death-smile across his lifeless face, erection still at full-mast.

"Well now Reynaldo, look at it this way stud....you got shipped in a way most men would prefer to go," she giggled to the corpse on the bed as she picked up her jumpsuit to slip it back over her body for a discreet exit out the service entrance of the Condo building here.

Rani Kovetts left the condo the same way she had entered it, unseen by other eyes and therefore not a suspect in her lover's death, their "relationship" unknown to anyone other than she and Reynaldo for the past year she'd been sleeping with him on occasion. Even if Reynaldo bragged about having a "mistress" to other guys he knew, he didn't have enough info on Rani Kovetts to detail her to anyone else in any compromising manner!

"Now it's on to Washington D.C.," she said to herself as she made it out of the Condo building into a rear alleyway which also bordered a fenced-in basketball court next to it.

Once she was through the unlocked little gate between the condos and the parking lot of the neighboring complex, she realized something she had not prepared for: her car being stolen!

"Shit on me," she sighed as she stopped there in the shadows of the thin tree-line between buildings, her parked car gone from its space where she clearly remembered parking it.

Rani Kovetts was adept at adapting to dire situations, so she simply remained calm and looked around for a solution, not walking out in the open of the street lights just yet.

"That's New York for ya.....hmmmh...," she sighed to herself in lament then noticed another vehicle sitting at the end of the lot off to her left about 20 yards or less and in it was the driver alone. Rani considered that option carefully because to expose her face and descriptives to a civilian meant that person could later finger her for a police inquiry, and she did not see an **easy** way of killing bystanders while trying to get the hell out of New York.

The lone driver sitting in the used Lexus hadn't seen her yet, so she made it so that he would not see her until she made it to the other side of his car there in the dark lot, his attention focused upon "texting" a message to someone and so it was damn easy for her to reach the front passenger door of the used Lexus, open it since it wasn't locked, and climb on inside with her Walther PPK pistol gripped in her right hand to greet the surprised young black man sitting behind the wheel with cell-phone in his hands.

"Don't say a word....start the car and drive...or I re-decorate the interior of this piece of shit Lexus in brain-matter-grey, got it?" Rani Kovetts spoke in convincing stoic firmness.

Reggie Bannicker couldn't believe the bullshit he just slid into tonight! First off, his girlfriend broke it off with him via a text-message and just as he was trying to answer her back and ask the real reason she was ending their relationship (i.e. another dude!) this crazy white chick in a black jumpsuit gets in the car with him and presses a gun to his face demanding that he drive her somewhere she has yet to tell him! If losing his honey to some other nigger wasn't bad enough, to get car-jacked by a smoking-hot white chick was the most screwed up thing he could have imagined happening immediately afterward.

"Be cool Super-Fly and you'll be back at the crack house safe and sound before ya know it, I just need you to drive me somewhere out of New York City area, and I'll let you go," Rani spoke next, breaking the eerie silence between the two of them as he drove out of Long Island and back toward Manhattan for the Interstate. He couldn't believe the racist shit she just said but he didn't argue since she does have a gun leveled at his abdomen region.

"Super-Fly?" he muttered under his breath, keeping cool for a 20-year old from the Bronx.

"Yeah, don't see too many afros like yours g-money....what's ya given name anyway?" Rani Kovetts chimed in casual aplomb, her pistol remaining still in her right hand, pointing.

"Reggie....what's yours?" he replied as he frowned at her remark about his puffy afro hair.

"Off.....Fuck Off," Rani replied in gingerly rancor, smirking at her captive as he drove.

"Well....hmmph.....Miss Off....where we headin?" Reggie responded in kind, frowning.

"Get onto I-Eighty-Three and drive till I say stop," Rani said softly as she relaxed in her seat next to him, eyes on the young man as he piloted his Lexus along the outskirts of NYC into the evening traffic that was as endlessly thick as it usually was this time of New York night.

"And this better not be a stolen car or I'll blow your balls off," Rani said next with a scowl.

"It ain't stolen....it's mine....was my brother's but he died last year," Reggie answered flatly.

"Good, now relax and drive Reggie," she said as she sat back in her seat, gun still on him but her eyes looking ahead at the highway, noticing Reggie cutting eyes at her every few seconds in steaming fury over the fact he was now her captive, "victim" of a car-jacking.

"What's a hottie like you doing out here jackin' niggas?" he asked her in boyish chuckle.

"Heeenh...oh, it's certainly not my primary occupation I assure you, but curveballs are thrown at me sometimes," Rani answered the 20-year old black man driving her.

"You don't say," Reggie chuckled again in sarcasm, eyes glancing at the pretty blonde sitting in his front passenger seat with a handgun on him. He guessed her to be in her late 30's but still smoking-hot, the black jumpsuit she wore still showed her pleasant features enough for him to surmise that she was one of those chicks who'd look better with no clothes on at all!

He hadn't panicked yet, but as soon as the unmistakable blue-and-red lights of a Police car popped into view in his mirrors, Reggie began to feel that awful pull-sensation of real panic!

They hadn't made it outside of the City Limits when the Police Cruiser pulled up directly behind the Lexus with lights flashing indicating for the driver to pull over immediately.

"I'm not speeding….shit, I ain't doing anything wrong….you see me," Reggie spoke up to his armed captor in fear of what she might do now that a cop was pulling them over.

"I know, I know goddammit….be cool and play-the-part Reggie, take the ticket or whatever but if you're wanted for anything that'll mean the cop will check me out too and I'll have to kill both of you right here, or if you try to signal the cop about me, I'll paint this car red with your blood," Rani retorted as she showed him her gun one more time then tucked it under her left thigh for easy-access as Reggie slowly pulled over to the right shoulder of the road.

"Okay, okay….I'm not wanted for anything….I'm a college student…shit," Reggie sighed as he pulled to a halt on the shoulder, the NY State Police cruiser stopping behind him and the uniformed Officer getting out. Rani just sat there in the passenger seat with her best "tee-hee-hee" girly face on for the cop to see her as "harmless" or maybe better.

After asking for the kid's driver's license and registration, the white male cop proceeded to tell the visibly nervous Reggie Bannicker that his Lexus had one brake-light out and that he had better get it fixed or next time it'll mean a citation. Rani smiled sweetly at the cop every time he glanced through the open window at her, and he didn't give Reggie a citation, only a warning. Reggie played it nice and didn't give the cop any lip so the situation was over in just a few minutes, which both he and his lovely female captor was happy about!

"I thought we were toast back there….shit!" Reggie snapped as he drove back onto the highway after the cop let him off with just a warning about his brake light being out in back.

"Why, you handled it well?" Rani snickered at his apprehension as she pulled her gun out.

"Yeah, right....usually a white guy cop pulling over a young black man with a gorgeous white woman in the car with him.....hunh, that usually ends up with the nigger going to jail for some bullshit reason," Reggie told her in a huff as he drove onward through the traffic.

"Naaah, it's two-thousand-nine Reggie...heenh, there's a nigger in the White House for cryin' out loud, ya know?" Rani chimed in sarcastic humor, grinning back at her nervous young driver who just shot her one of those "if only you didn't have that gun" looks.

"Maybe you're right Reggie, it's a mean world out there and there is no real racial solidarity when it comes down to it, but maybe that communist in the White House will throw all his homies a big juicy bone from the white man's table, and you'll be all set," Rani continued because she sensed that she was getting to his silly sensitivities all too easily. He cut eyes at her again without saying a word in rebuttal, and she respected the fact he didn't lose his cool when being insulted like this, even with a gun trained on him.

"What's your story Miss Off, what do you do besides car-jack Reggie Bannicker?" he asked.

"Hmmm....none of your fukkin' business Reggie, but I tell ya what....if you can name nine of the elements of the Periodic Table... .I'll suck your dick right here n' now," Rani chided him with a slinky expression in the streetlights flashing through the moving car.

"Name tha what......nine elements?" he reacted in surprise, wondering if she was serious.

"Don't even know what the Periodic Table is?" she asked girlishly, seeing him shake his head in wonder of both the question and what kind of game she was playing him for now.

"Thought you were a college student Reggie....suppose you got in on the 'affirmative-action' plan and didn't have to really go to class.....heenh, a mind is a terrible thing to waste," Rani continued impishly with the handgun leveled up toward his head now as he turned to give her a far meaner look than he had so far, at a loss for words really considering this was the first time he'd ever been car-jacked and by a giggling female racist to boot!

The two of them rode in silence for miles until I-83 was reached and then Rani pointed to

a certain exit for him to take once they were 50 miles south of the New York State Line.

Driving for almost 2 hours now, Reggie was less nervous and more curious of who the pretty blonde with the gun was because a hot white chick like this usually isn't the kind who car-jacks a man and not the type who'd shoot a dude in cold blood….but he may be wrong!

"Alright Reggie, pull over there at that empty lot," she said as she noticed a familiar-looking address just outside of New York where a closed and abandoned store was located in the dark. Reggie reluctantly complied and slowed his Lexus as he pulled into the dark lot.

"Good, good boy Reggie….," Rani said softly as she raised her Walther handgun again to aim it directly at the young man's face while he brought his car to a halt and shifted to park.

"I'm going to take over from here," she added as she gestured for him to get out of the car.

"You're gonna leave me here?" he asked nervously as he opened his driver's side door now.

"Unh-huh…why….if ya scared….say ya scared," she giggled as she got out on her side.

"No, I ain't scared," Reggie sneered in defiance as he got out of the car, looking across his hood at the blonde with the gun, seeing her in his car's high-beam headlights.

"Heeenh…that's good, because fear of death is worse than the real thing….now take off all of your clothes, but you can leave your sneakers on if you'd like," Rani Kovetts spoke next.

"What?" Reggie snapped in surprise of the demand, wondering what she had planned now.

"You heard me Reggie, get naked….I can't have you pursuing me after I take off and without any clothes on, you're not calling the cops anytime soon…because they'll arrest your black ass for 'indecent exposure' and you know it," Rani explained with casual aplomb as she stepped around to the front of the idling Lexus, pointing her pistol at him in the headlights.

"Word," Reggie sneered as he began to disrobe in front of his own car parked in an old store lot facing an armed white chick who had a very racist sense of humor. Rani leaned against the front corner hood of the car as she watched Reggie strip in the headlights of his own car.

Reggie tossed his clothes at her, all of them landing at her feet, standing there totally naked with his hands on his hips in nervous defiance, worried that he would be arrested for this!

"Good boy Reggie.....heenh...but I've seen bigger," Rani snickered at the sight of him as he stood there facing her naked and semi-erect from the situation of being forced to disrobe.

"What's next bitch, hunh, what's next?" Reggie announced with his arms high in the air as Rani stepped around to the driver's side of the Lexus, sliding in behind the wheel to drive.

"I'm taking your car, and leaving you here, that's what is next," she laughed in response.

Reggie spun around on his sneakers and took off into a flat run across the parking lot away from her, naked from the heels-up but just wanted to get away from his female car-jacker since she couldn't beat the hell out of her like he wanted to do, tears streaming down his face as he ran the hardest he'd ever run in his young life, even on the basketball team!

"Bye-bye Reggie," Rani Kovetts snickered as she held her Walther PPK out in both hands, taking an aimed shot at the fleeing shadow, then another. Two "pops" sounding in the night and both of the bullets struck the fleeing naked black man, dropping him like a rock.

"Thanks for the ride Supa-Fly," Rani giggled as she sped off onto the road leading south into Pennsylvania, leaving her car-jack victim back there in the dark lot to be discovered when the sun comes up. Leaving a naked dead black dude back there would be seen as either a "love-triangle-gone-bad" or a "gang hit" by the Police, she mused as she drove on, deciding to take the Lexus as far as it would go on it's tank of gas then park somewhere and torch it.

Killing was easy for Rani Kovetts, it was the art of leaving the carcass in a way which might lead the late police investigation in a direction **away** from her, that was the hard part!

Having been in the past employ of the Marcano Mob, the Israeli Mossad, and numerous rich people who wanted their enemies discreetly eliminated, the 39-year old Rani Kovetts was one contract-killer who had not only survived over the past 15 years as an Assassin but prospered! One of the reasons she survived in this cut-throat profession was her innate ability to recognize personal "threats" and keep them from affecting her in any way, as in the case of her now-deceased former lover Reynaldo Piazzi back in Long Island. As for the few who cross her path and become liabilities such as Reggie back there, she didn't know them so she didn't have the slightest amount of give-a-shit. Rani Kovetts did enjoy the morons she comes across now and then (like Reggie back there) they humored her a bit even when she had to clip them because they'd seen her face. Now she had a date in Washington D.C. and was going to get there two nights early, so she was ahead of schedule!

"Keep me comin'.....keep me comin' oooohh.....dance till ya can't dance...," she softly sang to herself, citing a song she recalled from the 1990's back when she was in College. She had learned much while attending a renown University, which is why she specialized in poisons, her Master's Degree in Chemistry! Driving the stolen Lexus southbound, she thought about who she knew in the D.C. region and another past lover came to mind......

Washington D.C. July 8th: One of those Soirees in D.C. where power-brokers and wealthy entrepreneurs strutted around with their trophy-wives, trophy-boys, and/or trophy accomplishments for all the other assholes to see and take envy. Shaya Gold knew the scene all too well, so she regretted agreeing to attend this one with Amber Duffek tonight although she did want to meet one particular "eligible bachelor" whom Amber swore would be here, plus the "protocol" of being a former "Washington Wife" of a late

US Senator whose cohorts in some grandiose conspiracy don't think she knows a goddamn thing and so perusing about town so care-free like this is better convincing behavior to the watching shadows than dropping off the radar completely (as Shaya had originally intended to do).

"Does this party bring back any memories for you doll?" the gorgeous Amber Duffek asked her buxom friend up close, then lightly kissed her left cheek after she spoke in her ear.

"Yes, the pomp and circumstance of Washington D.C. is quite unforgettable Amber, from the phony politicos, closeted queers, and money-launderers, I almost feel as if I have come home in a way," Shaya answered in casual tone, eyeballing Amber intently as they stood there at the back of the rented Georgetown residence hosting the party of D.C. Elite.

"Like I told you babe, it's for show…you coming to this soiree shows whoever was working in secret with your late husband Rupert….that you are innocent of knowing anything that would compromise anyone because you haven't vanished from the scene as typically would someone….who knew too much," Amber explained softly.

"Yes, either that's true or I just painted a huge bull's-eye on my ass by coming here," Shaya added with a slinky smirk back at her pretty, well-dressed lawyer and friend.

"Oh there's a bulls-eye on that ass Shaya, all the straight guys here tonight want to get you out of that dress," Amber said gingerly with a finger touching Shaya's left forearm again.

The red, strapless, form-fitting, pull-over dress snug around Shaya's impressive physique caught the eye of everyone here tonight, as it was intended when she chose to wear it.

"Pardon me for not being in the best of moods tonight, being homeless does that to a lady you know?" Shaya chimed back at the shorter and leaner Amber Duffek in a green dress.

"I know, losing the mansion to that mysterious fire….but you do have a nice Hotel Suite," Amber said in return, touching a hand to Shaya's backside for a moment's gesture.

"The fukkin' thing burned to the ground and the Fire Marshal found remains of a man who burned with it, all while I was in Fredericksburg Virginia with you and your husband……it just doesn't make for comforting news to know shit like that happens two years after two of your homes blew up rather 'mysteriously'… shit girlfriend, someone's gunning for me and it's just a matter of time before my ass gets nailed by something other than a big dick," Shaya whispered to Amber as she stepped closer for the younger woman to clearly hear her.

Amber had to grin at that remark, nodding her head in semi-agreement of the "danger" but she didn't feel it was anything directed at either of them, it was just a break-in and the perp got toasted when the mansion caught fire, strange but probably true!

"See that handsome man in white standing over there with that tall Mexican waiter?" Amber asked Shaya in slight change of topics for the moment, pointing a finger toward the men.

"Yeah, the guy that kinda looks like Rupert only more muscular and a bit younger?" Shaya asked in return, wondering what scoop Amber had on the stranger in the white tuxedo.

"That is Herbert Von Rossbach, a millionaire venture-capitalist and benefactor of the American Gun Lobby, too right-wing for my tastes but I know he's recently single and prefers big-breasted brunettes," Amber continued as she held Shaya's left arm in close.

"You brought me here as your 'date'…gonna pimp me to a rich Lobbyist?" Shaya chimed.

"Heeh-heh, yeah….I want to ask him a favor later on," Amber giggled back in response.

"You are a credit to Feminists everywhere Counselor," Shaya snickered in sarcasm.

"See that hot blonde he came here with?" Amber asked as she got serious for a moment.

"Yeah, the one in the diamond-strap dress?" Shaya replied with a nod, looking over at the man Shaya wanted her to meet and the shapely blonde female who accompanied him here.

"Thought you said he prefers brunettes?" Shaya added in more sarcasm for her friend.

"He does, that bitch he's with is a stranger, never seen her before tonight," Amber retorted.

"What about her?" Shaya asked back then took another sip of her Cognac poured earlier.

"She looks a lot like someone else we know, doesn't she?" Amber asked rather impishly.

"Yeah, heenh-heh, she kinda looks like Shelly James," Shaya said in agreement with her.

"Same kind of blonde hair, even wears it like Shelly.....about same height, tits and ass about the same as Shelly's, but she's a little older....close to forty I'd guess, and she looks very delicious," Amber spoke on about the stranger she and Shaya were now watching from afar.

Rani Kovetts was one who always "surveyed" her surroundings, even at upper-class parties of decadence like this one, her "date" Herbert Von Rossbach distracted by his sycophants and flirtations with other guests, her "radar" picking up on the fact she was being eyeballed by two attractive bitches across the room right now, both of them strangers to her but still worth noting at a "V.I.P" gathering like this in Washington D.C. The dark-haired woman with the big tits in the strapless dress that hugged her body like a red glove wasn't taking her eyes off her for some reason, and for another strange reason she looked familiar to Rani!

"Eyes and face are the only real difference, doesn't look forty yet...I'd say late thirties and never had any children, that ass of hers is like Shelly's....ass of a cheerleader," Shaya mused.

"Well they say everyone in the world has a 'twin' out there somewhere, someone who looks just like you, even if you're not related," Amber added then sipped her own alcoholic drink.

"Hmmph....makes me wonder where our little cupcake Shelly James is right now and what or who she is doing?" Shaya chimed with a slinky smile at Amber who laughed in response.

Minutes later: Shaya Gold was never too tired of being the "eye candy" of an event like this, surpassing all the other women present even younger ones with her very-well-shaped physique barely clothed in attire that costs more than what some folks make in two weeks. She actually found it funny how Amber Duffek liked to have a shapely female on her arm for D.C. parties like this one, but she brought her here tonight for the sole purpose of meeting Herbert Von Rossbach, so of course Amber gleefully introduced her to the handsome middle-aged man who had a woman on his arm resembling the former porn starlet "Shelly James", least to Shaya and Amber anyway.

"Shaya Gold, very nice to meet you Mister Von Rossbach," Shaya spoke graciously as she shook the man's right hand meekly with a sweet smile, Amber stepping behind her now.

"Shaya, please call me Herb, and the pleasure's all mine....my associate Sherilyn Marshall," the millionaire spoke in return, smiling as he stared through the buxom brunette before him.

No one calls a lady friend or lover an "associate" so Shaya greeted the blonde politely.

"You're Shaya Gold....former actress and model who recently lost your home up in New York to a fire....I read about it online the other night, sorry for you property loss," Rani Kovetts spoke up gingerly as she shook Shaya's right hand, realizing who the busty brunette was now and found it fortuitous she would run into her here in D.C. like this. Rani Kovetts was used to being called by any one of her many names and pseudonyms, so when the grinning idiot Von Rossbach referred to her as her fake name "Sherilyn Marshall" she kept reminding herself to use that name for the duration this sure-to-be-decadent evening.

"Yes, that's me....insurance company is not happy with me right now, I had my mansion insured for three million dollars," Shaya added with a girlish smirk at the sexy blonde in the diamond-strap dress that was much like hers in the sense it was really too tight for her body!

"Well at least you weren't in the mansion when it caught fire," Rani chimed in casually.

"True....hate to think I'd be a grilled sirloin instead of Amber's date tonight," Shaya said with a slinky glance back at the blonde stranger with the sky-blue eyes staring back at her. Shaya intentionally stepped off talking with the blonde named "Sherilyn" so that Amber would be stranded talking with Herbert Von Rossbach, which is what the conniving bitch wanted anyway. For some reason, Shaya found Von Rossbach's female associate more interesting than the man himself, so they continued their party small-talk, walking away from Amber and the well-dressed millionaire Lobbyist who was just another rich dullard to Shaya.

"I daresay you are the chit-chat of this party Shaya Gold....heenh, between your infamous past, your late Senator husband, and that awesome dress you're barely wearing...," Rani spoke as they walked across the room toward the cash bar for refills on their drinks.

"Of course, being friends with Amber Duffek gets me paraded around like some kind of trophy, but you are quite sexy yaself Sherilyn...I like your dress," Shaya answered gingerly.

"Haanh...yes, and thank you...but you win the 'booby-prize' tonight," Rani said in humor.

"Heenh....yeeaah....so do you know Amber?" Shaya replied in slight change of topics as she stood by the cash bar with the woman who resembled Shelly James a little too much.

"Not at all, just what Herbert told me about her....rich lawyer who specializes in sexual- harassment lawsuits, likes to eat sushi but is married to some famous writer," Rani replied.

'That's her!" Shaya chimed impishly with a wink at the blonde stranger standing there.

"So what's it like being an ex-porno star and still looking good after forty?" Rani asked.

"Hmmph, funny....between you, me, and the wall....it sucks, because I just lost over half my inherited wealth in the tanking stock market and sinking real estate investments, with not much to fall back on except a past career in the adult entertainment business, which is more useless as I get older," Shaya spoke in causal revelation, feeling the need to vent to strangers.

"Money is the first to go," Rani said with a shrug of indifference, but still listening to the buxom woman of mixed racial extraction, sipping her champagne in interest of her story.

"I really should break with all my old friends, make a clean cut from my past associations just to be on the safe side, ya know....start over somewhere else?" Shaya continued as she leaned against a wall as she and the shapely blonde stranger talked on.

"Doesn't hurt....and besides, you'll get insurance money on your mansion I'm sure," Rani said as she sized the woman up as she listened to her, judging her demeanor and mentality.

"Yeah, enough to pay off all my debts....should have listened to my late husband about investing wisely and all that shit...even a million dollars doesn't last forever," Shaya added.

"Hmmmh, neither does property, careers, or men," Rani answered softly with a sly smile.

"Men, they're the least of my worries right now, though whoever the asshole was who got burned to a crisp inside my house while I was out of town last week can rot in hell for getting me in a police jackpot," Shaya continued frankly, letting off steam in chit-chat.

"Ahh, don't worry....the New York newspapers called him an 'unknown intruder' who likely set the fire himself," Rani added knowingly, seeing if Shaya would pick up on the oddity of carrying on a conversation about one's home burning down in New York with a complete stranger who just happens to know what the local New York papers wrote about it when they stood in Washington DC right now? Shaya didn't hone in on that so Rani considered her a less "liable" entity after all, and probably lower in overall IQ than expected.

"Ironic, the Faster Mansion burns down with a stranger inside it....kind of a fitting end to the place really, considering the fact it hosted and made money off strangers wanting to see nudity and sex," Shaya said softly then took another swig of her sweet alcoholic drink.

Rani was not as apprehensive about running into the actual owner of the mansion she torched several nights ago as she was when she had been introduced to her moments ago.

Shaya Gold was a little stupid mixed with defeatism, so Rani decided right then and there she would not have to bump her off tonight as a "loose end". No, this busty brunette was just as she implied she was: a worn-out porn film star from the past who has now lost most of her financial nest-egg because she was not well-schooled in financial responsibility.

Before Shaya knew it, the blonde stranger was gone from sight, as if she had just up and vanished! Not impossible in a crowded party like this, she mused as she stood there sipping her drink and watching the other guests surrounding her now. Shaya had no clue of the fact she had just avoided being discreetly murdered tonight, her naiveté just now saved her ass.

"Shaya darling....I got to speak with Von Rossbach extensively without your assistance, so it's all good...however I was informed of a rather lucrative-sounding exclusive poker game being held here later this evening," Amber spoke to Shaya as she closed in on her suddenly.

"Poker?" Shaya chimed in surprise of what Amber was suggesting to her right now.

"Yes, a rather fortuitous chance to regain some of your lost finances perhaps?" Amber replied with a girlish grin as she touched a hand to Shaya's backside for the moment, and then stepped past her to chat with some of the other party guests. Shaya was good at Poker, though she was not a degenerate gambler, and right now the prospect of playing in a game for money seemed both reckless and prospective, considering the other super-rich guests here at this invitation-only party in Georgetown. Then again, to lose any more of her dwindling finances could mean ruin for her as far as the checkbook goes, but as she often lamented not taking chances on opportunities in her past; she stood there considering a risky endeavor such as high-stakes gambling to regain a portion of her money lost in the 2009 Stock Market fall and subsequent Real Estate crash that was sure to be in the history books.

Amber Duffek left the party without informing Shaya of her departure, and since Shaya came here with Amber tonight, the busty brunette in the form-fitting dress will now have to acquire other means of transportation. It was also Amber's way of nudging her old friend and part-time lover into the exclusive high-stakes Poker game to be held there after the party ends at midnight! Getting her friends into compromising situations was a kinky "hobby" for

Amber, and she guessed that Shaya would be conned into putting up what was left of her dwindling bank account in a Poker game the bitch was sure to wager big and lose bigger....

Driving her BMW back across the river into Virginia, Amber turned her radio up and relaxed to the R+B tune playing now, relishing what she had accomplished tonight without much effort, namely meeting and dealing with Von Rossbach as well as suggesting that Shaya Gold join the high-stakes poker game (which she really shouldn't do!).

That idiot Von Rossbach agreed to retain her as his lawyer in an upcoming court battle over his late ex-wife's estate, which Amber has a stake in as well considering the man's recently-deceased ex-wife was an old College girlfriend of Amber's so she wanted a piece of it herself.

She noticed a tiny warning light come on inside her car's dashboard, then the awful vibration of her car's engine failing as she drove along Rt. 1 south near Alexandria, Virginia.

"Shit......oh shit!" Amber exclaimed in sudden frustration of having her car break down this time of night nowhere near home in Fredericksburg. Pulling to the right onto the shoulder, she slowed to a stop along the dirt and gravel, the looming shadows of trees to her right and traffic whizzing-by on her left. Great goddamn place to break down! she kept thinking.

Once she was parked on the shoulder, she grudgingly got out of her car and decided to walk the ½ mile or so ahead where what she thought to be lights of a Filling Station could be seen and after locking up her BMW, she began the walk along the dirt and gravel shoulder in her high heels, wishing now that she had not left Shaya Gold behind at the party, because she realized what precarious situations like this could mean for a woman like herself all alone on a roadside in the middle of the night!

"I swear, I am going to shoot my mechanic and serve his balls to stray dogs!" Amber spoke to the night air in frustrated angst as she walked toward those lights, cars speeding past her on the highway, no one stopping of course, not for even a stranded female, not at nighttime!

She had her BMW serviced not too long ago and she was pissed off it failed her tonight.

By the time she made it into the outer lights of the Filling Station, her feet ached from the long walk on dirt in her stiletto heels, but she was glad to get off the dark highway roadside.

"Hello....are you open?!" Amber shouted as she walked up to the gas station's storefront, noticing it to be one of those privately-owned stations that kept it's lights on all night but a CLOSED sign dangling on the inside of the door to the storefront interior.

"Double-fucks!" Amber snapped in anger at the realization the station closed an hour ago.

She was not alone there however, a fact which became apparent the moment three male strangers jumped out to surround her from out of nowhere, and by the looks of them she doubted any of the trio was a mechanic who worked here at "Gas-n-Run" Filling Station!

"Hey baaabee....yeeaah....weeez open fer bizz-ah-nezzz," spoke a grinning black guy with gold teeth and clad in a black t-shirt and ripped jeans, the other two men white guys with leather vests jeans and boots, circling her in hawkish maneuvers.

"Lookit what we gots here!" said one of the white guys as the other one laughed childishly.

"Guys....hey, my car broke down, I'm just looking for a tow... really," Amber spoke in her own defense, something she quickly discovered to only egg them on to harass her more.

"You came to the right place for a 'tow-job' sweetcheeks," the gold-toothed black dude chortled as he reached out and grabbed her left arm, pulling her around the corner of the garage there, out of sight from the highway, his two buddies following in laughter.

Amber found herself helpless to resist as the three goons pulled her into the dirty alleyway beside the closed garage, the one with the gold teeth pulling up her blue silk dress as another pushed her against a wooden crate low enough to bend over. She felt her skirt pulled up and panties yanked down as the three men laughed in sadistic glee.

"Well-well-well...isn't dis sweeeet?" the black guy bellowed as he began to undo his own pants to proceed, all three of the would-be rapists focused full-attention on Amber's ass in the shop's rear floodlights thus failing to notice someone else approach from their rear.

Sounded a bit like one of those old-fashioned typewriters, the silencer-equipped handgun going off six times in rapid succession. Amber heard both the sickening "clicks" as well as two of her attackers "yelp" in pain, and then all three men fell to the dirt behind her.

Amber no longer had male hands holding her down, so she reacted by standing up and spinning around, finding three dropped males of the species on the ground around her, motionless and appeared to have been shot, since mister gold-tooth's head had been split open by a bullet. She looked to the front of the gas station where they had grabbed her and saw a familiar-looking woman standing there about 20 feet from her holding a silencer-tipped handgun down by her right side, staring back at her in casual pose.

"Hello again Counselor....seems we meet again," Rani Kovetts spoke to Amber gingerly.

Amber stepped a few paces forward as she straightened her dress and began to absorb what had just happened here. Three men had tried to rape her behind a closed gas station and the hot blonde chick who was Von Rossbach's date at the Georgetown party had arrived just in time to shoot the three would-be-rapists dead using a pistol equipped with a silencer......

"What tha....?" was all Amber Duffek could speak at this moment of stunned realization.

"Don't sweat it babe....I followed you from the party because I want to retain your services not as a legit lawyer but for the other 'off the radar' shit you do, and it just so happens I despise rapists, so the three assholes on the ground there are dead as a freebie," Rani spoke softly as Amber stepped away from the three dead goons to approach the woman.

"Really?" Amber asked as she walked toward the armed blonde who just saved her ass.

"Really, you come highly-recommended as an Attorney who knows the criminal underworld and who snakes through Federal and Police investigations without fail, so I want you to assist me with a project of mine," Rani continued as she gestured to Amber with her pistol.

"Okay.....uhhhm....okay," Amber said meekly with a shrug, unsure of what to say otherwise because the stranger she met briefly tonight had her at a rather pivotal position right now.

"Good...now I'll call for your BMW to be towed, so let me take you home....but first I will have to insist you lose the clothing completely," Rani said next as she pointed to her black Dodge Challenger sitting in the shadows just out of the station's outer lighting.

"Hunh?" Amber replied in nervous wonder about the less-than-subtle demand just now.

"Those three gang members lying dead back there put their grubby DNA all over your dress and panties when they grabbed you like they did, get it off and get in to the trunk of my car over there... .I'll take you home to Fredericksburg Amber Duffek....either trust me or I'll have to blow your sweet ass up with the rest of this gas station," Rani Kovetts added, raising the pistol in her right hand to make her point more than frank.

"Okay...whoever you are....okay, just don't hurt me, I'll help you in return," Amber replied.

"If I wanted to kill you Counselor, I'd have done it back in Georgetown," Rani said softly as she watched Amber Duffek strip right there in front of her as ordered. Amber couldn't believe this shit was happening: almost gang-raped but saved by a female shooter clad in a diamond-encrusted evening dress and heels who is making her strip naked for the ride home or wherever the bitch is going to really take her! Once she was naked except for her heels, Amber started walking across the lit filling station's lot toward the parked Dodge.

Rani was amused watching the well-shaped Amber Duffek walking naked across the cement to her parked Dodge Challenger, doing what she was told out of forced-suggestion and not boo-hooing about it like most chicks would, which Rani had to respect a little!

She had one timer-switch block of C-4 plastic explosive to use on the gas station here, make the whole thing appear to be a "gang war" thing to the cops and fire marshals investigating later. Someone like Rani Kovetts has to be prepared in the ways of "disposal" and so the gas station was set on fire then the C-4 detonated one full minute after Rani drove off down Route 1 in her Dodge Challenger, hauling a naked female attorney in the car's trunk, the gas station they were both just at consumed by fire as the C-4 lit the fuel pumps to cause an even greater inferno which covered Rani's tracks there.... as well as Amber's.

"I don't believe this shit!" Amber snapped to herself as she lay curled up inside the Dodge's trunk as the vehicle drove along the highway heading south as far as she could tell. She felt all the more helpless because the blonde stranger with the gun made her get naked before the trunk but she didn't tie her up at least....which means it's possible this is a ride home.

"This is how I end up, lassoed by a gun-wielding babe who kept me from getting three dicks put to me and god-knows-what-else..... going down the highway at midnight naked in her trunk," Amber chimed to herself, having to silently admit she felt a bit "turned on" by such an adventure, grateful to the shooter who had followed her from the Georgetown party to that gas station. As an Attorney, Amber read the score card in her mind as she listened to the sounds of the highway outside the trunk she lay in. The three dead goons back there might be found in the burned-out husk of the gas station the blonde killer just blew up, but nothing to denote the two women had been there...the fact she left her dress and panties back there to get burned up left no DNA evidence that could link her in any way to the three dead assholes who tried to rape her....the explosion would also take out any security cameras the gas station might have had on at the time.....yes, it all looked good and solid!

"Now what the hell does this woman want from me?" Amber asked herself out loud as she lay there curled up in the hot trunk, sweating as if inside of a sauna right now.

"Off-the-radar stuff hunh....heenh-heh, she's heard too much about my past," she sighed.

"Well…I survived working illicit shit for the Marcano Mob… cleaning up legal puke for New York Pornographers….as well as covering Senator Kelsh and his shady co-conspirators in the Federal Government…..hunh, I can survive this," Amber told herself in re-assurance.

She heard rainfall on the car now, hard rain, so she hoped the trunk didn't leak then hoped the driver of the Challenger doesn't get pulled over because some nosy Virginia cop might want to open the trunk! Of course Amber could always claim she'd been "kidnapped" by the female in the front seat but then again a news story about such a tawdry spectacle of being kidnapped while naked by another woman was not the kind of press Amber Duffek desires.

Wait a damn minute….how does this blonde bitch who looks a lot like Shelly James know where I live in order to drive me home??!! Amber thought in realization, doubting once more the woman would be taking her directly to Beverly Lane in Fredericksburg, then again if the sexy blonde with the silencer-tipped pistol knew her reputation as a lawyer and underworld aficionado, then she probably knew her current home address. Lying there listening to the rainfall on the trunk and the sounds of other traffic on the highway, Amber relaxed her mind from all avenues of panic. If the chick with the pistol wanted to kill her she could have easily popped her back there with those three gang members at the gas station and incinerated her body along with theirs when the station blew up ten minutes ago.

"Hmmmph….what a trip my life is…literally," Amber snickered to herself as she laid her head back, curled up here in the trunk of a 2009 Dodge Challenger heading down Rt. 1.

Georgetown 12:30am: Seven players at the round oak table deep inside the house where the party had been hosted earlier, that party having officially ended at midnight. Seven players here at a game that was not legal but 100% accountable for those involved, seven players who know the stakes and have the wherewithal to ante-up higher than the average bear! Monte Harrelson was the card shark of the crew tonight, and they all knew it but two of the players were new faces….one of whom was named Arturo Brigante, a tall

Mexican from nowhere who wore a $4,000 leisure suit and shined leather boots and the second one "unknown" just stepped into the room, getting the full attention of all players at the table.

She was a big-breasted, raven-haired woman of about 40 standing a shapely 5'8" or so, with a beautiful, youthful face of mixed racial extraction, her attire a single-piece red dress stretching snug from her thighs up over her bulging breasts like a glove pulled over her.

"And who might you be?" asked Monte Harrelson sitting to the left of the big Mexican at the table of players all looking at the body of the dusky-hued lady who just barged in.

"The name's Shaya…and I want to be dealt in," Shaya Gold replied softly in return, smiling as she stopped six feet from the table here in this windowless room, hands on her hips.

"Shaya…what do you have to wager?" asked one of the regulars sitting to Monte's right.

"One-hundred-thousand on my debit card, it can be verified online," she said as she held up a black debit card between two fingers for them to see and consider, hoping it was $ enough.

"Hunh, what makes you think….hell, this is a private game sweets," Monte added with a smirk of sarcasm as he looked around at the facial reactions of the other players. The one at the table staring a hole through Shaya was the Mexican in the Leisure suit, his gaze that of a predator who was eyeing his next "meal". Shaya looked at the Mexican as she raised her right hand toward the top of the sleeve-like dress, pulling it down off her big bare boobs and slipping out of it entirely within two seconds right there in front of the six male strangers.

"I know it's a private game, but I'm upping the ante a bit….you guys won't hold it against me that I'm the one woman in your Poker game?" Shaya chimed softly as she stepped up to the table totally naked except for her stiletto-heels and dangling loop-earrings, taking a seat on the one spare stool in the room, all eyes on her physique as she became Player #7.

"Not at all….you're in!" the tall Mexican spoke up for the first time with his gravel voice, eyeing her as if a hungry man seeing a juicy steak put in front of him all of a sudden.

"Five Card Stud to start off....four-figure pot," Monte said with a nod at the naked woman.

"Five thousand....," Shaya said as she lay her debit card on the table next to her.

"You better have a hundred grand to lose honey," one of the players to her right said gruffly.

"I do, you can go online and check my account if you must....I'm good," Shaya retorted without looking at the man who made the comment, her gaze once again on the tall Mexican across the table from her staring back with an intensity she thought the man might explode!

"Yes you are good Shaaa-yaah....good all over," the professional gambler named Monte said next as he ogled her plump and perky bare breasts there at the table, that pair of headlights so beautiful to look upon he was nearly distracted from dealing the first hand of cards.

Not only did her bare body impress the six men playing the secret game of high-stales poker but also her brazen courage exemplified by her willingness to get naked in front of six men to play cards with them, the "trust" she showed them just now by stripping in front of them and tossing out a debit card that has $100,000 on it. No woman would do this unless she was damn serious about playing the game and either winning big or losing everything to her opponents. No shame, no fear, no glory but to either win or lose and every man at the table right now respected her for that....and wanted the naked female stranger to join them!

Fredericksburg, Virginia 1:20am: The Dodge Challenger pulled up to the front of 1705 Beverly Lane and stopped right at the brick walkway leading to the front door of the place.

Rani Kovetts popped open the car's trunk to let her naked captive free here at her home, expecting to see the famed Attorney scurry toward the house in an embarrassed rush, but not Amber Duffek.... she calmly stepped to the passenger's side door and opened it to climb into the front bucket seat next to the driver, as casual and calm as most women would not be in a similar situation! Rani turned to face the lawyer she brought home in her trunk and smiled at her brazenness, then again it was one in the morning, so really how many damn neighbors are going to be up and outside to see the woman dropped off minus her attire?

"What is it you want from me bitch.....really?" Amber asked directly without missing a note.

"You're an Attorney who can get shit done Amber Duffek, and to get right to the point, I want you to get a certain name and identifiers off the Federal databases," Rani answered her.

"You want me to help you vanish off the Police and FBI radar?" Amber chimed in retort.

"In a nutshell, yes....and in return I will pay you five million dollars laundered cash," Rani said with a shrug, then winked at Amber's calm facial expression of confidence.

"That I like.....alright, as long as I don't end up with a bullet in the back of my head," Amber snickered as she opened the door to exit the vehicle, eyes on the stranger intently.

"Why would I kill a lawyer who can't afford to be snitching.... all those underworld and political connections of yours would chop your ass into cube-steak before I could?" Rani Kovetts spoke matter-of-factly as the naked woman exited the car in casual motion.

"True dat," Amber snickered back, closing the car door as she looked back at the blonde.

"I'll be in touch real soon Counselor, but for now I'm just a stranger to you," Rani said conclusively then watched the well-formed naked woman turn and begin strolling for the front door of the big brick house here at 1705 Beverly Lane. Amber didn't look back as she heard the Dodge Challenger roar off into the night behind her. She dealt with weird and dangerous strangers all of her career as an Attorney, so this one was no big difference.

She could make someone "vanish" off police files for $5 million cash....no sweat!

Walking up to the front door of the house she now owned after the Mafia heiress Isabel Marcano had it for a couple years, Amber found the door unlocked and went right in, feeling the air-conditioning on her bare skin, light R+B music playing in the background as she had often left it, her husband never turning it off since she left for the Georgetown party earlier.

Not bothering to call out for her husband, the naked Amber sauntered on down the hallway toward the master bedroom, considering a hot shower right now, just a quick one for now.

"Hey-hey," she spoke out as soon as she crossed into the master bedroom, glimpsing her husband over at the computer writing of course, not bothering to inform him that she had narrowly escaped a gang-rape thanks to a female murderer who she now owes a big favor.

"Amber….baby, you leave your dress at the DC party?" the man at the computer asked in response, not turning around but knowing she was butterball naked when she arrived here.

"Uh, yeeeaaahh…..lost it in a bet, had to drive home naked with a friend because my car conked out on me up there," she answered in a half-truth, knowing he won't press the issue.

"Guess I'll have to buy you another one," K.R. Knight said as he spun around on his swivel chair to face his shapely-fit wife standing by the bathroom door with hands on her bare hips.

"A new dress or a new BMW?" she chimed impishly as she stared slinky back at him now, noticing his gym-shorts in front stretched upward like a "tee-pee" as he grinned back at her.

"Depends on how much you want either one," Kenny snickered in slick suggestion.

"I see, well it looks like you caught me at the right moment once again my darling husband, because I would very much like a new BMW, so allow me to perform one of my favorite wifely-duties and earn it," Amber spoke gingerly as she walked toward him like a cat toward its dinner. She flung herself between his athletic legs and yanked the shorts free to afford her indulgence on the raging manhood turgidly awaiting her.

"Aaaannnhh…..Ammm-berrrrrr…..you are sooooo….goood to me," Kenny said in a voice of sheer satisfaction as Amber eagerly began fellatio on him, slurping on his manhood with and expert talent at the oral act. After tonight's events in Northern Virginia,

Amber wanted to throw herself into sexual intercourse and her loyal husband was there to fill the need!

He ran his right hand through her light brown hair, always felt like silk her wavy mane, eyeing his pretty wife as she sucked on his pole without hesitation, a fluid act of carnal delight he adored about the repertoire of sexual favors she often showered him with, for few women truly know how to give oral pleasure to a man....unlike his beloved wife.

"Oaaahh-yeah!" he sighed as rested his hand on her head while she steadily serviced him while kneeling between his bare legs, worshipping his manhood in steady, smooth fellatio.

Suddenly her head arose from its work grinning at the seated man as he stared down.

"Now it's your turn big guy....devour me," Amber said in a hot whisper of pure desire.

Amber's husband gleefully took his turn with head between her legs now as she spread out on the fluffy white rug below them, wrapping his arms around her thighs as he gorged at her sweet spot with all the passion he had for her when they first met like this. Amber knew she was lucky to find herself a husband who knew how to eat her out properly as well as an overall great lay in bed. This man was perhaps the only male of the species she could ever have married; something she was once again convinced of as he orally serviced her so well.

"Ooonnnh....yessshhh....oooohhh-yesssshhh......you hungry man!" she yelped out loud as she lay there squirming on the floor on her back, Kenny's face buried where it belonged.

No man had ever done this as well as Kenny, nor any woman she had ever been with either!

Both of them entranced in their marital sexcapade, neither one heard the sounds of someone entering the house through the front door in an uninvited manner of course. Kenny and Amber hadn't closed the bedroom door though the R+B music playing in the background muffled the clicking sound of the front door being opened by the assassin Rani Kovetts.

"Oooaahh....that's it....ooohh!" Amber yelped in giddy delight as she rose up toward the end of their bed with her husband wrapped around her from behind, his hands exploring.

He engaged her in a standing doggie-style intercourse from behind, slipping his sausage into the sweet roll he'd been eating on a minute ago. He ran his hands up her smooth back as she leaned over the end of their bed, hands out on the bedspread as her husband pumped into her as she enjoyed, servicing his wife in fervent lovemaking while standing behind her.

Rani Kovetts had decided to check this place out for herself and now wore not the expensive evening gown she had on earlier but her form-fitting black jumpsuit with her blonde hair pinned up in a ponytail for easy maneuvering. Unlawful entry was not her usual "crime" but since she was investing a rapport with this female lawyer, she wanted to check the bitch out a little bit more and drive home the fact she doesn't have a choice but to assist her! Walking through the swank living room and dining room, Rani was semi-impressed with the décor but she had seen better interiors in Mobster and Kingpin homes over the years.

Stepping into the kitchen through the swing-door, she opened the fridge to pluck a cold bottle of beer from inside, popping it open to take a swig of the chilled brew. Curious to see what someone like Amber Duffek eats, she opened the pantry door and found something far more intriguing placed on the middle shelf there....a time bomb! Rani kept her cool as she looked over the 8-inch-high device consisting of electronic detonator and timer attached to a brick of C-4 plastic explosive. She was no explosives expert but she knew it was enough C-4 to completely obliterate this house and anyone in it. The electronic timer was counting down to the end which was eight minutes from now....if she had not snooped around this kitchen, the damn thing would have gone off with her inside the house as well as the lawyer! Rani saw a kill-switch on the rear face of the device and knew it to be safe enough to simply turn it off, which she did at 7 minutes 51 seconds remaining on the timer. This bomb was a very professional device meant for easy triggering and easy disarming if necessary but whoever set it here hours ago and turned it on, had not expected the homeowner to find it here in her kitchen's pantry this late at night (before it would have been too late!). Rani palmed the device as she walked out of the kitchen in awe of it, musing about who might have set it here tonight to kill Attorney Amber Duffek, a woman who clearly has very tangible enemies who would love to see her pretty ass blown to smithereens on a hot summer night like this one!

Rani walked to the front foyer by the door from whence she came and heard something denoting Amber was indeed home and not alone down the dark hallway in her bedroom.

It was the distinctive sound of a woman in carnal bliss, obviously being well-served by someone indulging in the pleasures of the flesh, Rani told herself as she walked on down that long dark hallway toward the open bedroom door, disarmed bomb in one hand.

Rani Kovetts peered inside the dimly-lit bedroom to find the naked lovers over at the big canopied bed: The gorgeously-Caucasian Miss Duffek was bent over the end of the bed while a lean and fit white man she didn't recognize was happily drilling her doggie-style from behind where he stood. Rani smiled at the titillating sight of the lovers as she stood in the open doorway watching them for the time being since they hadn't noticed her just yet.

Kenny ran his hands under Amber to squeeze her plump and perky breasts as he hammered her in steady intercourse without fail, and then brought his hands back to squeeze her ass cheeks roughly while pumping his fuel into his wife as she cried out in sudden orgasm.

It was then Amber and her husband both glimpsed the stranger standing in their bedroom doorway with something sinister-looking in her right hand, along with the kittenish smile crossing her alluring face at the moment as she interrupted their intense lovemaking.

"You!" Amber quipped as she looked up toward Rani Kovetts , hands on the bed to rise up straight and face the intruder, her husband slowing in his intercourse as he saw the intruder.

"Hi there.....Attorney Duffek and whoever her stud is...be cool and I won't reset this bomb I found in you pantry a minute ago," Rani spoke gingerly to the startled lovers.

The man pulled out of Amber and stood there facing the intruder with a perplexed look.

"This is my husband....I thought we made a deal earlier, why are you here and what the hell are you saying about the....bomb?" Amber chimed in as she turned around to sit on the corner of the bed facing the armed female intruder who literally saved her ass earlier tonight.

"Well sweet-cheeks, I returned to check you out a bit more, snoop around your home here since we'll be doing business soon enough, and I found this in your pantry, a C-Four kill-switch device that would have gone off a few minutes from now if I hadn't found it and switched it off....someone wants you deceased dear lady and that makes my business proposal with you all the more interesting," the shapely blonde contract-killer said as she stood there in her black jumpsuit holding the time-bomb she had saved Amber and husband from minutes ago. Amber could see the device from where she sat as the same sort of bomb she had allowed to destroy two of her homes in Northern Virginia not along ago in order to further the aims of herself as well as the late Senator Kelsh. The next thing she thought about was that bastard "Horsehair" and the fact he had visited her once again someone, or one of his followers perhaps since Shaya Kelsh supposedly killed him up in New York!!

Silently freaking-out right now, Amber was nearly speechless as she sat there while her husband stood to her left facing the intruder in a calm but defiant manner, naked and semi-erect in the face of death. Rani Kovetts knew right then and there that she had Amber over a barrel in more ways than one and that means she could count her in as an "asset" to use!

"What is it you want?" Amber's naked husband spoke up next after seconds of eerie silence.

"I want your lovely wife to assist me in something for the future....and after tonight, she owes me twice-over for saving her ass....as well as yours," Rani answered him as she stared over at the helplessly mortified Amber Duffek with a coy smirk now. "Right now however, what I want is for the both of you to do me a naked favor," Rani said in softer tone of voice as she placed the deactivated bomb down onto the dresser beside the door and then unzipped her black jumpsuit in front to reveal her well-crafted bare body underneath, slipping out of the jumpsuit in one fluid motion while the married couple looked on in stunned wonder as to what this stranger was demanding of them.

"Watching you guys got me hot……so, either you satisfy me by daybreak or all three of us get blown into the atmosphere," Rani said as she quickly reset that bomb's timer for four and a half hours, when the morning's light would reappear. Rani sensed they would comply and so it would be fun for her to have these two lovers at her carnal disposal for the next few hours. Amber and Kenny looked at one another then at the naked blonde walking toward them in a slinky manner, the look on their faces priceless as Rani approached them.

"Now let's get it on….," Rani snickered as she walked up between the married couple at the canopied bed and touched one hand to Amber's right breast, squeezing it gently, her other hand wrapping around Kenny's spear as he stood ready to fuck the busty blonde stranger who had just saved them from a bomb which she was now blackmailing them with for sex.

Georgetown, 2:30 that morning: Losing in an illegal game of high-stakes Poker was not something to complain about to anyone of Authority, and one does not "welch" on bets laid down in such a Poker game because of the one or two players at such a table would take out their own brand of "cheater's justice" on whoever was stupid enough to cheat or abscond!

Losing $100,000 in an illegal Poker game was something to cry about, but Shaya Gold had not cried in years and didn't even after losing that amount to the other players this morning in Georgetown. Still technically wealthy in the sense she has a million-dollar insurance claim for the burned-down mansion in New Rochelle, she was "broke" until that money came in.

Naked inside of a stranger's bedroom….namely one of the spare bedroom's of the rented house here in Georgetown not far from the house she used to live in with a US Senator, Shaya Gold took stock in the weird feeling of "freedom" she felt right now, not giving a damn about the money she lost at Poker earlier tonight, nor the fact she had been very intentionally left behind by her friend and lawyer Amber Duffek, not even the fact she was single with no family (and financially unstable) at age 42. She now lay on the bed inside this stranger's bedroom, completely naked and awaiting the male winner of the Poker game and subsequent "winner" of her for the rest of tonight and probably beyond if she likes him!

When the door creaked open, the silhouette of a broad-shouldered man appeared and so she rose up on her right side, lying there in provocative "come and get it" posture for her male suitor, the shadows of the doorway masking him just a moment more.

"Oh…migod…..you!" Shaya sighed out loud in shocking realization of who she now faced.

It was Duncan Horsehair, alive and closing the door behind himself as he entered alone.

"Back from the dead once again Shaya….," Horsehair spoke in his gravel voice of disdain, stepping closer toward the bed where the voluptuous beauty sat staring back at him frightened like she had never been before in his presence. Shaya had shot him, convinced he was dead, a man sent back to Prison for the shooting in her place, this cannot be happening!!

"Duncan….you died, the Coroner's report….Woody was sent back to Prison for it, I shot you, omigod….you're alive," Shaya stammered in stunned apprehension of the revelation.

"Shaya darlin'…Coroner's reports can be bought and paid for and the corpse that took my place in the Ambulance that night was compliments of a man your late husband knew and trusted to carry out a plan which has yet to be implemented," Horsehair spoke defiantly as he opened his jacket to reveal a bullet-proof vest under it, denoting he had been wearing one the night Shaya shot him with her .380 caliber pistol. Shaya now realized that she had been effectively "played" once more, brought and left here by Amber Duffek and cornered by a man who seemed impervious to being murdered himself, here in a house still occupied with partying politicians, lobbyists, and corporate millionaires even at this late hour.

"It's all been a big trap hasn't it....I wasn't going to be let-off-the-hook by my late husband's secret friends seeking to take over the government during a so-called 'emergency', hmm?" Shaya spoke up as she stared at the man in black almost smiling back at her for once.

"No, neither of us were going to be let free of the past....but I have always known that no one would kill me except.....me," Horsehair said as he stepped to the end of the bed there, raising his right hand which held a professional detonator, clearly the device to unleash whatever explosive he had planted in this house tonight. Shaya knew this was the end.

"Lots of politicians and power-brokers in this house tonight, plus one loose-end....me," Shaya sighed as she sat up on that bed facing the dark assassin who was once her lover, his returning gaze one of silent torment as his right hand gripped the electronic detonator.

She rose up onto her knees, eyeballing him and bringing her hands to the detonator as well.

"It's okay Duncan....after all we've done....we belong dead," Shaya sighed with a wink at the man then meeting her finger along with his thumb, the detonator switch was pressed.

The End

"TAIL END"

It's entertaining to read about other people and their fun and/or failures, isn't it?

I daresay it's been the most thrilling of all entertainments in a way, to read about, view on a screen, or just having been told and re-told tales of enticing fortunes, misfortunes, and peccadilloes had by others whether fiction or non-fiction. One can even learn something from the lives of others they see in reality as well as on a TV screen or buried in the pages of a book. Throughout history, writers have given their readers thrilling fictions to entertain as well as to get something "off their chest". DH Lawrence and Mary Shelley being among the most notable of past "controversial" authors whose visions of "life lived by others" transposed onto paper, thrilled readers long after they died and inspiring other writers to toss in their own visions of fictional "un-life" for the next generation to read.

I cheerfully acknowledged the works and accomplishments of OTHER writers, directors, actors, actresses, producers, and filmmakers in this book The Naked Diaries because I wanted to give well-deserved credit and reviews to some of the "un-sung" heroes of the entertainment genre devoted to an adult audience here in the Land of the Free and Home of the Brave. Their form of legally-produced entertainment fascinated me from my late teen years to now, being it a uniquely-American entertainment venue also makes me very proud and happy that I live in a Country where consenting adults have the right to create (as well as view)adult-themed stories and films without fear of prison.

My exclusive novella THE STRANGERS here was written as one example of my own personal brand of erotic-story-telling and I hope you enjoyed it!

When a writer creates characters within a story, **sometimes those characters become something** (much like everyone out there has their personal favorite cartoon-character, movie villain, or sports figure). Certain female characters I have used in some of my other stories such as "Shaya Gold" and "Shelly James" in The Midnight Oil, not to mention the busty "Isabel Marcano" in Isabel At Midnight, so if you want to see more of them, order yourself a copy of those books which are still available online.

A Literary Agent once told me that once a storyline gets "dull" to the writer; juice it up with a sex-scene! I couldn't agree more, though I do recognize the pitfall of accidentally turning a novel into a "porno-script" if the writer has too much fun detailing carnality.

To give credit where credit is due in this regard, the best example of a fiction author detailing sexual congress in a storyline has to be the works of novelist Hope Tarr.

Ms. Tarr has a uniquely-mastered style of detailing a lovemaking scene in her novels that really packs-a-punch when read, her vocabulary far better than mine when it comes to "fleshing out" that particular portion of a story! I don't know what it's like to direct a sex-scene for a film but it has to be **more fun to write-it-out** as opposed to dealing with an actor and actress whom are not personally-intimate and trying to get them to look like genuinely intimate lovers for the cameras!

Money and Sex rule the world....we've safely established that as our singular paradigm regardless of what Fundamentalist yahoos might say to the extreme contrary. Procreation aside, humans are the only animal on the earth to have sex as a very real entertainment year-round, not in some limited and really short-lived "mating season".

Yes, the human sex drive is a powerful entity indeed, enough to cause lifelong marital pledges but also rebellion aboard sailing vessels (i.e. Mutiny on the HMS Bounty) and even wholesale slaughter (that "Helen of Troy" thing). It's strong enough to scare some people into bullshit political movements (such as the Feminists) and unstable enough to cause some weaker human elements to indulge in illegal carnal perversity.

I am no Sociologist, but it's an understatement to say that sexual frustration in the general public is really not a good thing! Speaking only on STRAIGHT SEX, perhaps legalizing prostitution (as in the State of Nevada) is something every State should really consider. What the hell am I talking about? Well let's just say perhaps if the Oklahoma City Bomber Timothy McVeigh **got laid**, then he may have not committed that terrorist act.

According to one interview, one of McVeigh's top complaints was his lack of a sex life (he was evidently unpopular with women). Nothing makes a man angrier than when he is denied the company of a woman for an extended period of time. The Prostitution rests!

You might say "I'll never pay for sex!" Well my male reader, you PAY for it in one way, shape, or form whether you like it or not guys, haha. Matter of fact, legalized prostitution (like in the State of Nevada) would be a far cheaper avenue for satisfying the itch than for one to get hooked up with some shameless hussy who sees men as just sperm-donors- with-wallets they can siphon from after they've had a kid and demand child support.

Pride? Come on dude, the only guys I laugh at nowadays are the ones who can't afford to go out for beers because their "baby-momma" has all their cash, not to mention the hen-pecked men whose wives won't let them hang around their single buddies anymore.

Let me also point out that **single-men-over-the-age-of-35** are considered the "niggers" of the twenty-first century (forgive my euphemism here) regardless of race or class simply because we are over-taxed, frowned-upon (even in church), sexually-suspect, blatantly disrespected in entertainment venues, and treated as second-class citizens by married and/or cohabitating folks in general. Yes, I once had a Church Lay-Leader tell me to my face that single men sitting alone in Church are seen by the rest of the congregation as "recovering" from something (such as alcohol or drug abuse) and are thence "avoided" by the others there. I no longer believe in the "Ancient Tales of the Torah" so I don't waste my time or money attending the clucking social hatcheries called Churches, but I had to tell that example because it is a sobering one. Single guys over age 35 are often derided as having something "wrong" with them because they are not married or living with a girlfriend, and if they're too neat and effeminate some women call them queer, but if they're properly macho, then some women consider them to be "players" (whatever the fuck that really means). However, much like anything else that is GOOD in life, having too many other people involved in the fun can indeed ruin it for everyone else eventually.

There are more available women in America than the other way around, but some guys just have to act like they have "dibs" on any and every cute female of any race or creed, whether they're married or otherwise.....assholes just have to flirt, cockblock, and make passes at nearly every skirt that walks by, even if she's with someone at the time. Too many men in the fun-zone ruin it, which is why many of you really (deep-down) hate to go "Clubbing" nowadays, isn't it?

Kill-Joys, Buzz-Kills, Busy-bodies, and Prigs....lowly humans whom take fiendish pleasure in **not** minding their own goddamn business and intentionally curtailing, stifling, hampering, dampening, denying, and/or snitching-on someone else trying to have FUN!

The same sort of jabbering moron intentionally "cockblocks" other men from hooking up with ladies (i.e. a frustrated Mormon or Feminist Radical) usually by subtle means and pesky "interruptions" because those whom are lonely....secretly hate all of the Lovers!

This phenomenon stretches further when it comes to guys seeking legal American Adult Entertainment of either the R-rated or X-rated variety, for the admirers of gorgeous women minus any clothing may find themselves stymied by the Prigs of the EEOC, Buzz-Kills of the "Religious Right", the Busy-bodies of the workplace "Sensitivity" monitors, and those hooded cockblockers who'd like nothing better than to impose tyrannical "Sharia Law" throughout all of the Free World, more especially in the USA!

I like the worthy phrase Hustler Magazine Publisher and 1st Amendment Activist Larry Flynt brought into the debate about adult entertainment: **"The right to be left alone"**.

Imagine what those politically-correct "Hate Crimes" Laws (being considered for legislation as I write these words) would be like for us if amended to include legalese such as "offensive images and photos that degrade women"? Yeah, scary isn't it....

Having worked in the Criminal Justice Field myself, I saw countless examples of poor "stock" in humanity's barnyard, and also came to the conclusion that all men and women are selfish creatures (don't let anyone convince you otherwise) and those other mortal fools whom take upon themselves a "Crusade" are too often seeking something that is missing (or twisted) within themselves and seek to correct or "find" that something by crusading in a "cause" that wages war on something other people legally enjoy! Again, it goes back to how men and women are inherently selfish creatures whom more often than not wish to impose their own "values" upon others by force of law if allowable, even when their own values are **less** than what they are preaching! Take for example the high-and-mighty Christian Evangelist a few years ago who was revealed to have been having homosexual liaisons with a male prostitute (while using the illegal drug crystal-meth!)

The human sex-drive is a powerful thing as we've already noticed, and many of our fellow Earthlings handle theirs in normal ways, others foolish and illegal ways, while many seek satisfaction in denying or stifling the sexual desires of others around them by doing such things as telling the boss about another employee kissing his girlfriend in the company parking lot or how someone danced with someone else at the office Christmas party, etc. Many others go further with their "crusades" to stamp out adult porn and men's magazines, strip-clubs, and even Hollywood films depicting male/female nudity (such as in the Mormon-owned Video stores in Utah "censoring out" scenes of nudity and sex from their inventory of VHS and DVD videos the public rents from them).

The next big censorship-loving "crusaders" to soon hit the streets and courtrooms against adult entertainment of all varieties will be the Liberals and Feminists claiming that such "depictions" of women are harmful and degrading, followed by the growing sector of Islamic "activists" in America whom seek to slowly (and legally) bring as much "Sharia Law" here to the US Legal system as possible. Mark my words, those certifiable assholes are coming to a Legislature nearest you! What is often laughed at as just "PC" may one day be enforceable LAW if we're not mindful to what some people wish to impose upon us. Can't happen here? Just ask the First Grade boy who got suspended for "sexual harassment" just because he kissed a little girl on the cheek.......

"Hard" Adult Entertainment has been with us more prevalently in the past few decades and as I think I've pointed out here, was far more "adults only"(kept from under-age viewing) in the years prior to the Internet coming into play during the mid-1990's.

The Internet "let the genie out of the bottle" and through increasing the "access" to adult entertainment, it actually "ruined" it in the same way one ruins something exclusively good by letting everyone and their baby sister in on the action....so now that minors have all-too-easy access to things they shouldn't be viewing, that ever-lurking monster called Censorship sharpens it's claws for yet another scheme to shut down our personal freedom under the guise of "protecting the children". Yes, all children should have a porn-free life until (if) they choose to view such <u>after</u> they turn age 18, but what has the Internet done besides broaden the market for straight adult-oriented films, images, etc. with more money made yes, but also letting every form of human pervert and butt-pirate out there run rampant preying on internet-users of every age? Pandora's Box comes to mind......

Has the Internet helped or hurt adult-oriented entertainment? Honestly, it's actually a double-edged sword that does both. One side it is easier to make money selling the films and other items, but on the flip it's also opened the door for minors to see and obtain such whereas before, "Adults Only" meant exactly that! Yes it's true, more copies of my own books sell over the Internet than in bookstores, but if I were a Musician, I'd be stark-raving-mad over kids pirating/downloading my hard work (the music) onto their laptop computers and thus not having to buy my CDs! The Internet and its "basement bandidos" have made movies, music, and even porn videos accessible via "pirate" sources as well as sites that allow one to download whatever they desire for a seriously-reduced price tag!

I have to mention that many of the vintage X-rated films of the 80's and early 90's never made it onto DVD and can only be found nowadays online and obtained via download, though I cannot yet recommend that option because I could never bring myself to use my credit card number to download 15-20 minutes of who-knows-what-it-might-actually-be!

Some X-rated films did make it onto DVD....compilation-videos such as **Sex Toy** with Tami Monroe and Cheri Taylor (in their infamous "Diner Threesome" with Ray Victory) and then there is the fabulous spoof **Dirty Sharry** starring the legendary Christy Canyon (in one of her best performances ever) and John Leslie's classic **Oh What A Night!** where porn actress Cheri Taylor learns all about "affirmative-action" from her male co-star Sean Michaels. Then of course there is the infamous porn classic **Nurse Nancy** starring "Sandra Scream" which made headline news in 1991 when Hollywood Actor Paul Reubens of "Pee-Wee Herman" fame was arrested for lewd conduct during a showing of that film at an X-rated theater in Sarasota, Florida. The vintage X-rated films of the late 80's/ early 90's had an appeal all their own, filmed with corny music but naturally-shapely, beautiful women engaging in legal sex acts for an adults-only market. Those films are certainly "mild" in comparison to really smutty amateur porn films flooding the market on the Internet now. Being someone who is practical about the matter, I admit that sometimes I look back to those "good ol' days" (before the Internet) and seriously think that X-rated entertainment was much better-off....twenty years ago!

The R-rated "Erotic-Thriller" films of the 1990's suffered the same vanishing fate as far as being marketed onto DVD after 1999, and the Internet has allowed fans of the genre to obtain copies of those films to this day, and for those still in possession of a VCR, the used-VHS copies of 90's Erotic-Thriller films are still abundant even in online auctions.

One may also find copies of the R-rated/Un-rated 90's "Erotic-Thriller" films such as **Color of Night**, **Sins of Desire**, **Illicit Dreams**, and **Victim of Desire** at some of the "mom n' pop" Video-Rental stores that have been in business for the past decade or so.

I hereby wish you luck in your quest to find some of the "unsung" entertainment of yesteryear before there was the Internet, **before** there amateur-filmmakers and "reality shows" helped sour adult-oriented entertainment, and like I've been saying...**back in the day** when adults-only meant precisely that, and the adult playground was safe from the innocent eyes of under-age Americans not old enough to comprehend nor be responsible.

Bare Naked Ladies have an appeal all their own, whether it be sexy female images, live female performance (like in a Strip-Club) or in the written word (erotic stories) the fact that sex attracts and entertains is now undeniable. And for all the recent bru-ha-ha about "sensitivity" toward the obese and less-than-attractive people in American society, sex still sells the whole damn ball of wax and **no one** (even in this sadly "politically-correct" climate nowadays) enjoys the sight of a homely or less-than-sexy person.

Why do you think major Beauty Pageants have a "swimsuit" portion of the show?

To exhibit the female contestant's physical attributes! (BTW: Miss California 2009 Carrie Prejean looked delicious in her white string-bikini during the Miss USA Pageant).

Adult Beauty Pageants are not just displays of vanity but formal contests of beauty and sexual attractiveness in the form of an entertaining show watched by millions each year.

Some could say "fashion" shows may be under the same banner except for what I'd have to say about the god-awful attire forced on the often-way-too-skinny female fashion models in recent years (BTW: most of the American fashion industry is run by gay men).

Let me tell you a secret: most gay men hate heterosexual women, which is probably why the homosexual bosses in the so-called "Fashion" world dress up all of those rail-thin models in such horrific clothing for all of the female shop-a-holics out there to see.

Sex Appeal is instinctual for anyone below the age of 70. Anyone who makes an effort to "look good" does so for the benefit of other people looking upon them favorably. From the woman who goes to the gym and gets a make-over to the woman who buys low-cut dresses and expensive perfumes, it's to attract the opposite sex or to at least look good in her travels. Same goes for a man only in different ways. Tell me a woman doesn't squeeze into tight slacks or a mini-skirt and intentionally racks up her cleavage just for the hell of it! So why do certain blushing denizens get all bent out of shape with adult-themed movies, strip-clubs, and men's magazines being available? For the most part, it's insecurity around reminders that they too are sexual animals!

Long before naked adult human images were drawn, photographed, and published, there was the **written word detailing sexual escapades**, examples of such dating back to pre-Biblical centuries and even in the Christian Bible and Hebrew Torah such as the mention of the "Sin of Onan"(Mr. Onan pulled-out of his female mate to purposely avoid impregnating her). The Story of "Samson and Delilah" is a tale of seduction/betrayal and Shakespeare's epic "Romeo and Juliet" tale is one of sexual love and youthful frustration over not being able to unleash sexual desire, and Shakespeare showed other characters conspiring to keep the lovers apart.....which is art-imitating-life to this very day as scores of other people you and I both know take great pleasure in trying to keep lovers apart and deny a straight man his happiness in regards to normal, consenting sex. Whether it be other men around you, your so-called "buddies", homosexuals who hang around women and "shield" them from straight men, or even Priests and Pastors~(whose job it is to keep us from indulging our natural instincts) someone else occasionally gets in the way of nature taking it's course, oftentimes those curiously aforementioned "weaker" men!

Again, nothing makes a man angrier than when he is denied the company of a woman for an extended period of time! Although he was a communist heathen, Jean-Paul Sartre said it best when he profoundly remarked "Hell is other people!"

Doesn't over-exposure of sex and nudity in entertainment ruin the delights of it in real life? Hell no, unless you're truly neurotic and put the cart before the horse. I daresay that for one to have the best sex of his/her life, one should both imagine what he or she personally desires and watch (or read) sexual congress portrayed in R-rated, Unrated, or even Straight-X-rated films to see what it's all about before finally jumping into the bed with the opposite sex ☺. Would you get behind the wheel of a motor vehicle without at least first consulting a manual (or taking a class) on how to drive????

Sexual Fantasy snakes through the human mortal brain as naturally as one's random, everyday thoughts do, so what better (and safer) way to vicariously enjoy sexual fantasies (as well as find new ones) than by viewing adult-themed films, reading men's magazines such as Playboy®, watching exotic dancers at a nightclub, or even reading a sexually-charged fiction story? Living vicariously is something we all do in one form or another, quietly wishing we were someone else, somewhere else, and yes, screwing someone else!

Just never forget the catch-22 about bringing too many (other people) into your fun-zone, because it is a proven fact that too-big-of-a-crowd ruins your fun before you know it....

We see other people enticingly portrayed in magazines, on film, and even written about, and we often wish we had a life like those people have....even the fictional characters.

Yes, it's true that sexual love bonds a man and a woman for the inevitable offspring to come later on, but entertainment depicting sex and nudity is by no means an antithesis.

Marriage between a man and a woman is a necessary aspect of civilization and yes, married couples often "spice up" their loving sex-lives with adult-oriented entertainment!

Jesus Christ did warn against the perils of Adultery, and it's still a simple solution for those who just have to chase skirts all over the place getting it on with various women other than one love-of-your-life, just STAY SINGLE if that's what you want to do! ☺

What some of us would give to be a Secret Agent getting laid in Buckingham Palace or paired with that shapely sweetheart in that R-rated action flick, or perhaps being the real athlete whose wife posed nude in a magazine recently? Imagining things to be different for us (as individuals) is what helps keep us sane and keeps us working for the one day when it's a better life, or when life actually "imitates art" and the dream comes true...

"And when we get behind closed doors, then she lets her hair hang down,

and she makes me glad, that I'm a man....Oh no one knows what goes on

behind closed doors". **-Charlie Rich "Behind Closed Doors" 1973 (Songwriter: Kenny O'Dell)**

Naked Truisms

A whiskey glass and a woman's ass have been the downfall of many a foolish man!

Even the ugliest, gelatinous, female dog needs a good hard bone now and then.....

Ever wonder why women who are in favor of keeping abortion legal are ones most guys wouldn't want to sleep with anyway?

Only a woman can see a man as "just a friend". The man views her as a potential sex-buddy (some day....just maybe...some day)

When she said "Let's just be friends" I calmly replied: "If I wanted to make friends, I'd go to summer camp".

I once knew a Stripper who complained about her boyfriend being "as small as a cigarette". Later that night, she switched to my brand of cigar.....

All a good-looking woman has to do for male companionship is wink at a guy.

Men have to work (like in everything else) to get a woman's interest.

Size matters. Boobs big enough to risk a black eye.

Legalized Prostitution would cure many of America's ailments...the frustrated and lonely would have a safer outlet, getting laid would be cheaper in the long run, adultery wouldn't be so risky, and the taxes collected from the brothels could pay off the national debt in one year's time!

Those who get it love it and those who don't hate those who do.

So it hasn't changed after all these years....the lonely hate the lovers!

Women are destined to pose nude after all; most of their clothing is designed for quick and easy removal.

Only a certifiable Jackass gets married on a Golf Course.

Many women dream about their "soul mate". Catch is...he just got hit by a Bus!

The only officially-recognized Religion today that does not preach against sexual desire is.....The Church of Satan.

The Naked Book and Video Shelf

More highly-recommended (and available) reading and viewing!!

"Bullets, Bombs and Babes"

~The Films of Andy Sidaris
Hardcover book published by Heavy Metal Magazine.

"The Naked Truth About A Pin-Up Model"

by Devin Devasquez
Persona Publishing July 2009

"Hef's Little Black Book"

by Hugh Hefner and Bill Zehme
Diane Publishing 2004
Also available for Amazon Kindle on Amazon.com!)

Young Lady Chatterley 2

(1985) Directed by Alan Roberts. Castaway Pictures (DVD)
Starring Sybil Danning, Harlee McBride, and Adam West.

Sorceress

(1995) Directed by Jim Wynorski. Image Entertainment. (VHS)
Starring Linda Blair, Julie Strain, and Edward Albert.

ACKNOWLEDGEMENTS

Front Cover Photo by Photographer Dennis Berry.
(All Rights Reserved).

Front Cover Model: Kristie Walker.
Back Cover Photo Property of the Author Ken Knight
(All Rights Reserved)

Movie Poster/Videotape images used in Fair-Use tradition
to describe the film being reviewed herein for historical purpose.

Still-shots from the films PICASSO TRIGGER and
HARD HUNTED re-printed with permission from
Producer Arlene Sidaris.

Interview of Arlene Sidaris conducted in Fall of 2008.

Also by Ken Knight……

THE MIDNIGHT OIL

They are all here….Jonny Faster, Shaya Gold, Shelly James, and the Mafia Heiress who wants the big stud's secret with or without his manhood intact!

His name is Jonny Faster and he employs a secretive cast of Porn Stars whom all work "upstanding" careers by day then moonlight as Adult Film Performers at night. From the New York Cop who can't get a date in his private life but "hammers away" at his new part-time job, to the young Catholic Nun whose alter-ego has now become an adult film icon and a secret double-life she cannot hide from the Church for much longer, and the U.S. Air Force Officer who risks court-martial to perform sex on film, every one of them have a secret to keep and some may do anything to keep the lid on as they take their clothes off! When a snooping Tabloid Reporter arrives to take down the "secret" Porn Stars of Faster Productions, someone will discover the hard way how selfish people will do nearly anything to cover their own interests, even commit murder!

But it is not just the "upstanding" daytime lives of Jonny Faster's secret cast that is in jeopardy, but a hidden recipe for immortality and a Mafia Heiress who wants it (along with the well-endowed Jonny Faster) all to herself…..no matter the cost paid by others!

THE MIDNIGHT SHOW

Late Night Cable TV "Guy-Flicks" of the 80's

Are you old enough to remember staying up late back in the 1980's and watching Cable TV and/or videotapes in your parents' VCR?

If so, return to the late nights of yesteryear where the movies were ripe with Ninjas, Secret-Agents, unstoppable Cyborgs, and sexy, scantily-clad women with writer Ken Knight as he reviews some of the best "guy-flicks" one dared to watch back in the late night 80's. He also interviews some of the Stars of those late night movies such as Silvana Gallardo (Death Wish II) Sybil Danning (Malibu Express) and Playboy Magazine's Miss May 1984: Patty Duffek!

Reviews, Interviews, unfiltered commentary, and two exclusive short-stories from the 1980's era sure to make you think back to the days of big hair, parachute pants, and all-too-gratuitous nudity!

All Author's Royalties from the sale of this book donated to Make-A-Wish® charity.

Available online at Authorhouse.com and Amazon.com

Coming Soon by Ken Knight…

DIRGE

What was supposed to be a scientific breakthrough…..

No one outside of closed government doors and the shapely CEO of a major International Corporation has one damn clue as to how previously-deceased persons have now inexplicably "come back to life".

Of all the "doomsday" scenarios discussed and planned for in the United States, a technological experiment of immortal proportions resulting in the return of the dead to wage war on the living was never taken seriously outside of Hollywood B-movies and trashy horror novels.

Between the tragic death of one unpopular young man, a secret scientific experiment in nanotechnology to repair human tissue, and the cover-up to conceal the escaped "test-subject" from the general public, a disastrous chain-of-events heralds either a golden opportunity or the end of all things.

Every "Zombie Apocalypse" has to begin somewhere!

The Dead wage war on
The Living….SUMMER

About The Author

Born in 1970, Ken Knight grew up in rural Stafford County Virginia and began writing fiction as a "hobby" shortly after an 8th grade English assignment sparked his interest.

Kenny served in the US Army and worked in the Criminal Justice Field, his experiences there lending him plenty of ideas and scenarios to later apply in his torrid fantasy stories.

After years of writing out stories in spiral notebooks just for fun, he submitted his first horror novel CRYPTX for publishing in 1999 and has since published adult-oriented suspense novels such as ISABEL AT MIDNIGHT and THE MIDNIGHT OIL as well as his treatise on late-night Cable TV movies of the 1980's, THE MIDNIGHT SHOW.

Far from being out of fresh and original story-ideas, Kenny has more tales to be told in the years-to-come!

He may be reached at: chapt19@yahoo.com
as well as on **Facebook**.

Breinigsville, PA USA
22 December 2009
229685BV00001B/50/P

9 781449 036041